BY WALTER JON WILLIAMS

NOVELS:

Ambassador of Progress
Angel Station
Aristoi
Elegy for Angels and Dogs
Hardwired
Knight Moves
Voice of the Whirlwind
Days of Atonement
Metropolitan*
City on Fire*

DIVERTIMENT I:

The Crown Jewels
House of Shards
Rock of Ages

COLLECTION:

Facets

*Published by HarperPrism

CITY ON FIRE

Walter Jon Williams

HarperPrism
A Division of HarperCollinsPublishers

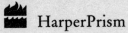

HarperPrism
A Division of HarperCollins*Publishers*
10 East 53rd Street, New York, N.Y. 10022-5299

This is a work of fiction. The characters, incidents, and dialogues are products of the author's imagination and are not to be construed as real. Any resemblance to actual events or persons, living or dead, is entirely coincidental.

ISBN 0-06-105442-9

HarperCollins®, ®, and HarperPrism®
are trademarks of HarperCollins*Publishers,* Inc.

Cover illustration © 1997 by Tim White
Cover background illustration © 1997 by Phil Heffernan

A hardcover edition of this book was published
in 1997 by HarperPrism.

First paperback printing: January 1998

Printed in the United States of America

Visit HarperPrism on the World Wide Web at
http://www.harperprism.com

❖ 10 9 8 7 6 5 4 3 2 1

For KATHY HEDGES

~~~~~~

With special thanks to Christopher Schelling,
for his support in a crisis; and also to the
Very Small Array, Sally Gwylan,
Gene Bostwick, Pat McGraw, Pati Nagle,
and Sage Walker, without whose relentless
good advice this would have been
a very different book.

~~~~~~

CITY ON FIRE

～～～～～～～

ONE

The car shoots through the InterMet tunnel, flying beneath the world-city as if propelled by the breath of a god. Drowsing on the car as it flies beneath the world, Aiah dreams of the Burning Man.

He stands tall above the neighboring buildings, a figure of fire. A whirlwind surrounds him, a spiral blur of tortured air, flying debris, swirling ash. Holocausts leap into being at his approach; buildings explode into flame merely at his passage. A torrent of fire flies from his fingertips, turning to cinders everything it touches.

Unwilling, unable to help herself, knowing somehow it is a duty, Aiah approaches the Burning Man. A scream comes from the hollow throat, a cry mixed of terror and rage, and Aiah realizes that the giant figure is a woman.

As she comes a little closer, Aiah looks full into the face of the raging figure and sees that the Burning Woman is herself.

She wakes with a start and finds herself in motion, in the pneuma car that hisses along beneath the world. Sweat plasters her collar to her neck. She swabs her throat with a handkerchief and again closes her eyes. Fire pulses on the insides of her eyelids.

The arrow-straight tunnel of the pneuma is surrounded by

the eternal weight of the city . . . brick and stone, steel and iron and alloy, concrete and glass, rising from bedrock and stretching toward the Shield far above. The mass of it all is beyond comprehension. So is the power it creates.

All that is human is a generator—every building, every foundation, every conduit or sewer or elevated trackline. All the world-city, every frame and stone of it, produces and stores plasm, the foundation of geomantic power.

Power which, for a moment or two of brilliant comprehension, Aiah had held in her mind. She had possessed its possibilities, its glories. Felt it change her. Felt herself change the world. Felt its fires scorch her nerves.

Those certainties are gone now, replaced by confusion, hesitation, danger. If she can get the power back, she thinks, even for a moment, all will become clear.

If.

If.

If she can somehow get the power back.

MARTIAL LAW STILL IN FORCE

SURVIVING KEREMATHS DENOUNCE
COUP FROM EXILE

By the time she gets to Caraqui, Aiah has almost talked herself out of it. Foolish, she's decided, to leave her place in Jaspeer, foolish to run, foolish to think that the new government in Caraqui would give her a place. No Barkazils here—she will be even more a foreigner here than in Jaspeer. And Constantine will not give her anything—he did not love her—he had only used her for what she could give him, the keys to power, and could not possibly have any further interest in her.

But the police had been after her, the Plasm Authority creepers, and sooner or later they would have found something that would put her in prison. It was time to leave Jaspeer. In her mind she had already leaped a hundred borders—crossing them physically was almost an afterthought.

And once exiled, once that leap has been taken, where else is there to go?

Caraqui. Where the New City, consigned to ashes years ago, might undergo an unscheduled rebirth.

Caraqui. Where her future waits.

Assuming, of course, it waits anywhere.

LORDS OF THE NEW CITY BREAKS RECORDS

THIRD SMASH WEEKEND FOR BIO-CHROMO

Gravity tugs at Aiah's inner ear as the InterMet brakes, drops out of the system, comes with a hum of electromagnets to a stop at the platform. A banner splashed with red letters hangs against a bright mosaic on the back of the platform.

Welcome to Free Caraq . . . The last letters are obscured by the banner's dangling upper corner, come loose and fallen across the message.

And that's it. There is no one on the platform, just the message on the banner.

Somehow Aiah had expected more.

Pneumatics hiss as the car's doors swing open. The other two occupants disembark. Aiah rises, takes her bag from the overhead rack, and carries it out onto the platform. The bag is light—she had left all her belongings behind as she fled, and only bought a few things in Gunalaht on her way. There is only one heavy thing in her bag, a book, red plastic leatherette binding with gilt letters. Her legacy to her new home.

As she walks past the mosaic she realizes that it's political, a noble-looking man wearing a kind of uniform and gazing off into the far distance. *My father made the political revolution,* it promises. *I will make the economic revolution.*

Covered now by the banner of the *real* revolution.

She doesn't know precisely who the figure on the mosaic is supposed to be, but she knows it has to be one of the Keremaths, the family that had ruled Caraqui for generations. The promise of economic revolution had been a lie—during their years of power the Keremaths ruled by kleptocracy, a government by gangsters bent on looting their own economy, their own people.

They were mostly dead now, the Keremaths. Constantine's revolution had killed them, and it had been Aiah who had, against every law, given Constantine the plasm necessary to accomplish their destruction.

It is a matter of more than casual interest to discover how grateful Constantine will prove. Especially as she now has nothing to offer him, and gratitude is all she can expect.

The book in Aiah's bag bangs against her hip as she walks down a short corridor lined with adverts—familiar posters for the new Lynxoid Brothers chromoplay, the Inter-Metropolitan Lottery, Gulman Shoes ("Meet for the Street"), all alongside more exotic promotions for Sea Mage Motor Craft and the New Theory Hydrogen Company. Then suddenly she's out of the tunnel and into the main body of the station, and her heart leaps as she sees armored soldiers with their guns out, sets of goggled eyes gazing at her. Mercenaries, she thinks, because half of them have the black skins of the veteran Cheloki exiles who have been following Constantine for years.

The masked eyes pass over Aiah without pause. They're not interested in arrivals. They're clustered around the departure platforms.

They're interested in people trying to escape.

There are counters for customs officials to interview arriving passengers, but no one is there: perhaps they haven't shown up for work. Outside Aiah finds herself on a promenade overlooking a canal. A pair of ascetics, bearded and grimy, sit on beds of nails before their begging bowls. One of them brandishes a handmade poster about the "Uniting of the Altogether." The canal water is bright green with algae. There is salt in the air and bobbing rubbish in the water. Caraqui, except for a strip of mainland here and there and some islands, is built across its sea on huge, ancient concrete pontoons, all linked together by bridges, cables, and anchors.

From atop the worn promenade rail allegorical bronze

statues, weathered, pitted, and green, gaze down at Aiah from ruined, pop-eyed faces. She is uncomfortable under their gaze, but isn't certain where to go from here.

She looks up as shining silver-blue letters track across the gray sky: *There is no need for alarm. All fighting is over. The curfew has ended. The revolutionary government encourages citizens to go about their normal business.*

An elderly female lottery seller, going about her normal business, shuffles toward Aiah on bare, swollen feet. She was probably selling tickets at the height of the fighting. Aiah buys one.

For luck, she thinks.

There's a sign pointing down some steps, with the legend *Water Taxis.* She follows it.

The taxi is a small outboard with a tattered red plastic awning, driven by a weathered man of middle years. The hand that reaches for her bag is missing the first two fingers. A handwritten sign next to the meter says, *We take foreign currency.*

Aiah has read a guide to Caraqui on the *Wire,* and knows the name of a hotel near the government center. She had tried to call to make reservations but the lines were down.

"Hotel Ladaq," she says.

He helps her into the boat with his clawed hand. "Can't do that, miss," the driver says. "Hotel Ladaq's full of soldiers."

"Do you know another hotel in the area?"

"All full of soldiers, miss."

"Get me as close to Government Harbor as you can."

He starts the meter. "Right away, miss."

But it doesn't happen right away. The driver casts off, but then he can't start the outboard, and as the wind pushes the water taxi broadside down the canal he has to take the cover off the motor and tinker with it, and then try to start it again, then tinker some more. Several taxis leave from the station in the meantime, and Aiah's taxi rocks in their wake.

The meter, Aiah notices, is still running. She points this out to the driver, but he affects to be too busy with the engine to notice.

He tries to start the engine and fails. Aiah points out the

meter is still running, but the driver starts kicking the motor and screaming.

It's a chonah, Aiah thinks. The driver's a confidence rigger and there probably isn't anything really wrong with the engine.

If she were home she'd know what to do. But the fact she's a stranger in this place makes her hesitate.

Finally Aiah steps forward and turns off the cab's meter. The driver is stern.

"Can't do that, lady. It's government regulation. Only the driver can touch the meter."

He steps forward to turn it on again. She keeps her hand over the button. "Start the engine first," she says. "Then you can start the meter."

The driver shrugs. With showy, large gestures, he tinkers with the engine again. Puts the cover on. Starts it without so much as a cough.

Aiah is entertained. She's a Barkazil, one of the Cunning People. Her ancestors have rigged chonahs for thousands of years. This sort of thing is in her blood.

The pontoons and barges are old in this district, layered with barnacles beneath the waterline. The buildings on the pontoons are old as well, and as layered, new structures barnacled atop the old, until the form and shape and function of the original building has been completely obscured.

When she arrives at her hotel, she tries to calculate exchange rates, and gives the driver what she thinks is the correct amount in Gunalaht dalders. She knows, from the driver's sudden bright grin, that she's overpaid. Suddenly he's pressing a plastic business card into her hand.

"My name is Callaq, miss! Please call at any time! I will show you the sights, the Aerial Palace, the place where all the battles were fought, anything!"

"Maybe."

"Please call! I'll take you anywhere!"

"Thank you, Callaq."

She carries her bag up corroded marble steps slippery with sea slime. Beggars hold out cupped hands on the stairs. From the top she turns to look back at this strange metropolis, sees the taxi churning away, an old moored tugboat that probably hasn't moved in years and is flying a string of laundry, a flock of scabrous waterfowl staring at her with agate eyes.

And then, in the air above the canal, there forms a pattern, lines and colors interlinking, the pattern flowing like water. . . . It bursts so swiftly in the sky, like a flower opening in time-lapse photography, that she can only catch a fragment of the wholeness, a curve, a maze, a wonderment. Aiah stares openmouthed.

"The Dreaming Sisters," says a strange male voice.

The colors fade, leaving an imprint on Aiah's vision, which glows for a few seconds like the afterburn of a photographer's flash.

She turns to see who was speaking, her tongue poised to ask more questions; but it's a businessman, sallow and sleek, and from the glint of his eye she can tell he'd like nothing more than a frolic with a strange woman, so she merely nods, then takes her bag indoors.

NEW GOVERNMENT CALLS FOR EXILES TO RETURN

"WE NEED YOUR SKILLS TO REBUILD CARAQUI," SAYS TRIUMVIR DRUMBETH

The hotel is an ancient place that has seen better days. Prostitutes cruise the lobby, either shockingly young or shockingly aged. Ribbed plastic sheeting protects old, broken tiles that were once bright with abstract designs dating from the old Geoform movement. Aiah's room has a lovely plastered ceiling with a life-size figure of the immortal Khomak brandishing his assault rifle overhead and riding that fabulous animal, the sea horse . . . but from the sea horse hangs a wire, and on the end of the wire is a naked bulb. The bed has a cheap steel frame and the bedsprings squeak. There is no other furniture. Over the sink hangs a sign: *Hot Water Available 05:00–07:00.*

It's 10:31, according to Aiah's watch. She guesses she's missed her bath for the day.

There is a communications jack but no telephone. Aiah finds she can rent one by the hour and does so. It's an unusual piece, with a pair of heavy brass earphones and a trumpet-shaped mouthpiece braced up in front of her face by a butter-smooth brass prop in the shape of a human arm.

Constantine, she knows, is Minister of Resources in the new government. She calls the ministry in Government Harbor, but all they will do is take a message, so she phones the Aerial Palace and asks to be connected to his suite. She can't even get anyone who will promise to take a message to him.

"Not unless you're on the list," she's told.

"Can I speak to Mr. Khoriak, then?"

"Who's he?"

"He's a member of Constantine's suite." One of his guards.

"I'll see."

Aiah waits for ten minutes, hoping that Khoriak wasn't killed in the fighting.

"This is Khoriak."

Relief pours through Aiah, relieving tension she hadn't realized she'd possessed.

"Khoriak, this is Aiah. Aiah from Jaspeer. You remember?"

"Of course."

Of course. Idiot. It had only been a few days since she'd seen him.

"I'm in Caraqui. Hotel Oceanic. I would like to see the Metropolitan Constantine, but I can't seem to reach him."

"I'll tell him."

Half an hour later, she's on Constantine's private launch. Fast work. She's been in Caraqui less than two hours.

TRIUMVIR PARQ CALLS FOR
DAY OF PRAYER

DALAVANS TO FAST ON FRIDAY

The launch seems to have been liberated from the Keremaths or their supporters: the hull is a shiny black polymer

composite with silver trim—not chrome but actual silver,
kept bright by the endless polishing of the crew, or perhaps
through some hermetic process.

There is a deep whine as the boat accelerates, hydrogen
burning through its turbines. It clearly has a lot of power to
spare.

The captain is a black-skinned Cheloki, a newcomer. He
drives the boat well but doesn't know the territory: he constantly refers to the map pinned to the chart table next to the
wheel. There is a soldier who places a fine white wine and a
basket of sandwiches atop the table on the fantail. He is
clearly uncomfortable in the role of servant—less than a week
ago he was probably in combat—but he's gracious enough, all
things considered. Aiah realizes she hasn't eaten since second
shift yesterday, and she tries not to bolt the sandwiches.

The sleek motorcraft arrows neatly through the green
water. The pontoons that loom on either side are painted
with fading slogans and the images of dead Keremaths. *Our
family is* your *family*—the slogan arches above dead, flaking
faces. Aiah finds herself looking for dolphins—she had met
one once, and spoken with him, and she knows they inhabit
these waters. But no pale dolphins break the surface of the
water.

Aiah is startled to see a large tram car float overhead
along a set of cables. The green car, with its rounded, aero-
dynamic corners, is big as a bus, and obviously serves the
same purpose.

Practical, Aiah thinks. It avoids congestion on the
bridges, or building expensive tunnels underwater for
pneuma and trackline transport.

Images of the Blue Titan and the Lynxoid Brothers
brighten the sky, a plasm advert for the new chromoplay. . . .

The buildings grow nicer as the boat approaches the
Aerial Palace: expensive apartments, tinted glass and jutting
balconies with fancy gingerbread scrollwork on the rails, and
broad-shouldered office buildings crouching on their pontoons like animals ready to spring. Buildings don't reach as
high here as in Jaspeer, because it would make the pontoons
top-heavy.

And then the boat passes through a battlefield, and the

contrast is shocking: a series of squat blackened buildings, roofs fallen in, piles of rubble spilled in the street. Barges rock silently at the quayside, filled with slick plastic body bags. Priests with surgical gauze over their lower faces process the dead as they are brought from the rubble.

Come to mourn! a sound truck cries. *Come to mourn the dead!*

The Burning Man had appeared here, a firestorm of plasm in human shape. He had been fighting for Constantine, trying to stop a government counterattack; but the mage had been inexperienced and everything had gone out of control.

Twenty-five *thousand* dead. Including the mage. Several thousand soldiers. The rest civilians.

Aiah, in the coup's headquarters, had watched it happen, had tried to stop it . . . too late.

Her fault. She had provided the plasm.

Come to mourn the dead!

There are people hanging, she sees, from the ruined buildings. Hanging in what look like sacks, feet sticking out the bottom, the sacks swinging free on lines secured to broken rooftops. They are not dead people, not casualties—they have hung themselves there since the burning.

Mad people? Mourners? Aiah cannot tell—they are all too far away.

Blowing soot brings tears to Aiah's eyes. She dabs at them with her sleeve.

Then fantastic architecture of the Aerial Palace appears on the horizon, all swoops and spirals like the path of a falcon traced through the air. Shieldlight shimmers off the arabesques of the building's collection web, bronze patterns set into the building's exterior and designed to absorb and defuse any plasm attack, defense and ornament in one. The burnished bronze adds lovely bright accents to the building's design, but its defense aspect failed drastically—the building is scarred, pocked by machine guns and punctured by rockets. Plastic sheeting is tacked up over shattered windows. The Keremaths lived here, and they died here, too. When the assault teams fought their way up the stairways they found only corpses.

Jewels appear in the air behind the Palace. An advertisement for diamonds.

Surprise moves through Aiah as she sees people hanging here as well, dangling from sacks set into niches in the building. When she comes close, however, she sees they are not real people, but statues.

A mystery. When she finds an opportunity she will ask.

The colossal structure is built on a raft made of several pontoons, and the motor launch drives between two pontoons into a narrow, watery alley lit with bright sodium floods both above and below the water. Aiah looks down into the milky water for dolphins and finds none.

The motor launch pulls into a slip alongside other, equally flamboyant craft. The soldier/steward jumps onto the floating pier and holds out a hand.

"This way, miss."

There are soldiers patrolling up and down the quay in dark gray uniforms and helmets—Constantine's Cheloki again. Constantine isn't trusting the local troops that had actually captured the place: they'd changed sides once, and could again.

There are probably telepresent mages scoping the place as well. It would be the safe thing to do.

The door leading into the pontoon, Aiah sees, is an airlock, but it doesn't look as if the heavy steel portal has been shut in a long time. Inside is a gold-rimmed desk where Aiah is checked in and given a badge.

"Someone is coming down to escort you," Aiah is told.

The someone appears a moment later, and she recognizes him and smiles. He doesn't smile back: he looks as if she's a problem he doesn't want.

"Mr. Martinus," she says.

"Miss Aiah."

He is a huge man, one of Constantine's bodyguards, not only trained for war but bred for it. His genes are twisted to produce a massive, muscled body and catlike reflexes. His face looks like a helmet, eyes sunk beneath protective plates of bone. Heavy slabs of callus ridge his knuckles.

"Welcome to Caraqui," he says.

"Thank you, sir."

Martinus escorts Aiah into the elevator and presses the lever. There is a smell of burning that lodges in the back of

Aiah's throat, a souvenir of the fighting. The elevator doesn't go straight up, but swoops as it rises to match the building's architecture: the Aerial Palace, for all its extravagance, is a generator of plasm, built to distill the essence of mage-power. Its alloy structure is a maze of careful, intricate alignments, intended to take advantage of geomantic relationships that increase plasm generation.

The elevator doors open. The deep wine-red carpet is plush and the walls are paneled with dark wood—genuine wood!—broken with diagonal stripes of brightly patterned tile and solid gold wall fixtures in the shape of birds in flight. A percentage of the latter seem to have been torn from the walls by looters.

The corridor is blocked at regular intervals by sliding glass doors set into polished bronze frames. The doors open automatically on approach, though Aiah sees that they can be locked if necessary. Crosshatched bronze wire winks from inside the glass. It is part of the building's defense system: the huge Palace is divided into sealed compartments to prevent a single attacking mage from raging through the whole building.

Martinus opens a paneled door and ushers her in.

"Wait here, please."

Aiah steps into the room. "How long will I have to wait?"

"I don't know."

Martinus closes the door. Aiah looks about her. More wood paneling, gold-framed mirrors, two huge oval windows miraculously undamaged by war. The room is intended for meetings: there's a huge kidney-shaped table—more wood!—and metal-and-leather chairs, gold frames with luxurious brown calfskin cushions. Even the ashtrays, laid out two-by-two down the length of the table, are solid gold.

The burning scent is here as well, like embers smouldering in the back of the throat, and it won't go away.

Outside, a peregrine dives past the windows, a swift dark streak against the opalescence of the Shield. Aiah steps to one of the windows and looks out, hoping to find the falcon against the backdrop of the city. She doesn't see it—perhaps it's already sitting on a ledge somewhere, eating the pigeon it's just caught.

The room projects out from the Palace and gives Aiah an exemplary view of the world-city, the buildings and towers and water-lanes that go on forever, unbroken to the flat ocean horizon. One of the green aerial tramcars floats in midair between two distant towers. *I am on the water*, she thinks, having to remind herself of the fact. . . .

The sky blossoms with a giant plasm-image, the stern face of the actor Kherzaki hovering over the Caraqui, his expression commanding. An advertisement for the chromoplay *Lords of the New City*, based on Constantine's early life and career. Fire-petals unfold beside the image, become words burning in air.

See it now . . . , the sky commands.

An advert, Aiah wonders, or a command from the ruling triumvirate? Should it be *See it now . . . or else?*

The door opens behind her, and she gives a start and spins, a brief giddy disorientation eddying through her inner ear . . . and as the whirling stops the false, burning mage in the sky is replaced with the real Constantine, a far more dangerous commodity. He looks almost respectable in modest white lace, black pipestem pants, and a black velvet jacket, and Aiah knows right away that her having come here is a mistake. Her heart sinks.

He doesn't love her. They had been lovers, yes, but that was an accident, the chance result of a combination of unreproducible circumstances, a particular time, a particular place, a particular urgency. . . . If he gives her anything it will be because of some horrid sense of obligation, not because he wants her here, or has any real use for her.

"Miss Aiah," he says, and approaches. The voice is baritone, a rumble that vibrates to her toes. Aiah remembers—remembers in her nerves, remembers deep in her bones—the way he moves, the sense of power held barely but firmly, consciously, in check, strength mixed oddly with delicacy.

"We find ourselves in the Owl Wing," Constantine says. Irony glints in his voice as he steps around the big table. "Those windows"—gesturing—"are supposed to be the eyes of an owl."

Aiah is tall, but Constantine is taller, broad-shouldered, with powerful arms and a barrel chest. His skin is blue-black, and his hair is oiled and braided and worn over the left shoulder, tipped with the silver ornament of the School of Radritha. He is over sixty years of age, but plasm rejuvenation treatments have kept his body young and at the peak of health. His face is a bit fleshy, a suggestion of indulgence that serves to make him more interesting than otherwise, and his booted feet glide over the thick carpet without a sound.

The deep voice rolls on, imitating the clipped delivery of a tour guide. "We also have the Raptor Wing," he says, "the Swan Wing, with its luxury apartments, and the Crane Wing. . . ." His eyes never leave hers, his intent mind almost visible behind them, clearly considering subjects more vital than a verbal tour of the palace.

The voice trails off as he comes within arm's reach. There is a touch of caution in his fierce glance, a sense again of something withheld. A decision, perhaps. Or judgment. Or both.

"May I ask why you are here?" he says.

Aiah's heart is a trip-hammer in her throat. Mistake, she thinks, mistake.

"To work, I suppose," she says.

He smiles, and Aiah concludes it's the right answer. A sudden wave of relief makes her dizzy.

He opens his arms and folds her in them. His scent swirls through her senses, and she realizes how much she's missed it.

Absurd to care so much, she thinks. Constantine is a great figure, a part of something huge, much bigger than even he—he does not belong even to himself, let alone to her.

Aiah tells herself this, and sternly.

But her lecture has nothing to do with her longings. Her longings are self-contained, and happy within themselves.

Through the embrace Aiah can feel Constantine's weight shifting slightly, a sign of restlessness. He is not a notably patient man. She releases him, steps back.

Still he watches her, fierce intelligence afire within the gold-flecked brown eyes. "The police?" he says. "Were they after you?"

"Yes," she says, then, "No. Maybe." She shrugs. "They knew I was a part of it somehow, but I don't know if they could prove it. They had me under surveillance."

"You got away without trouble?"

"I got away." She hesitates. "I had some help. I think. It was easier than I expected."

"What of your young man? Gil?"

She straightens her shoulders, steels herself against the threat of sorrow.

"Over," she says.

"And your job at the Plasm Authority?"

"I wired them and told them I was taking time off." She shrugs. "I don't know why I didn't resign outright."

There is amusement in his glance. "You are cautious, Miss Aiah. Wise of you, not to quit until you discover if you have a new job waiting."

She looks at him. "And do I?"

"I think I have one that will suit your talents." He puts his hands in his jacket pockets and begins to prowl around the table, his restless movement an accompaniment to the uneasy movement of his thought.

"You know that the last government was worse than bad," he says. "They were corrupt beyond . . . beyond *reason*." He waves a big hand. "Even granted that they were thieves, that they wanted only enrichment and perquisites . . . the scope of larceny that they permitted, *against their own metropolis,* was *irrational.* The amount of plasm stolen is staggering. It constituted a vast plundering of their own power, a threat to the security of their own state of which they seemed unaware. Well." He plants a fist on the table and looks at Aiah with a defiant glare. "Well, *I* am not so blind, not so unaware. The theft of this most singular public resource must stop. But what force do I have to enforce any new edicts—or even the old ones?"

He shrugs, adjusts the position of one of the gold ashtrays, begins to pace again. "My soldiers are not suitable to police work. The local authorities are as corrupt as their former masters, and it is hopeless to expect anything from them until years of reform have done their work. For this purpose I must build my own police force, my own power base. But the New City movement here is limited to a few intellectuals, a few discussion groups—I have no cadre, no organized group of followers ready to step into place. And . . ." He

looks up at Aiah, eyes challenging hers, and she feels ice
water flood her spine.

"You," he says. "You will build this force for me. You
have found plasm thieves in the past, and in my service you
were a plasm thief. I wish you to find these thieves and
return their power to the service of the state."

Aiah blinks at him across the table. She doesn't know
whether to laugh or simply to be appalled by the suggestion.

"Metropolitan?" she asks. "Are you sure it's me you
want?"

Cold amusement enters his glance. "Of course," he says.
"Why not?"

"I'm a foreigner, for one thing."

"That's an advantage. It means you're not part of the corrupt structure here in Caraqui."

"I've never done police work."

"You will have people, qualified people, to do the work
for you. But I want you in *charge.* I need someone I can trust
heading the department."

"I'm twenty-five years old!" she says. "I've never run anything like this in my life."

He gives her a sharp look. "You have worked within a government department concerned with plasm regulation. You
know where it went right, went wrong. You studied administration at university." He assesses her with his gold-flecked
eyes, then nods. "And I have faith in your abilities, even if you
do not. You have never disappointed me, Miss Aiah."

"I wouldn't know where to start looking for plasm
thieves."

Constantine bares his teeth. "Start looking in my office.
My waiting room is full of people offering me bribes." He
smiles. "I will give you a list."

"I—"

"And the Specials—the old political police—their records
should be valuable. The instant the fighting was over, Sorya
led a flying squad to their headquarters to seize their files.
The records belong to us now, and . . ." Constantine gives a
feral smile. "They're *very* useful."

Aiah's spirit sinks at the thought of Sorya, Constantine's
lover—or rather, his *official* lover.

"Would I have to work with Sorya?" she says. "Because . . ." Words fail her. "Well, I don't think she likes me."

A touch of cold disdain twists Constantine's mouth. "It is in *both* your interests," he says, "to cooperate on this project."

"Yes," patiently, "I'm sure."

Constantine's restless prowling has brought him around the table again, standing next to Aiah. He picks up one of the gold ashtrays, holds it in both hands. "The government will announce an amnesty for plasm thieves," Constantine says. "A month or so. It will take at least that long for you and your team to set up operations, consolidate your files, make a few preliminary investigations. And after that—" He smiles down at her, suddenly warm. "You have always exceeded my expectations, Miss Aiah. I have no reason to believe this will be different."

Aiah sighs. "Yes," she says. "If that's what you want."

"Gangsters, Miss Aiah," Constantine reminds. "What in Jaspeer you called the Operation. Here they are the Silver Hand, and they are a threat to us and to the New City, and they must be destroyed. Destroyed completely. And it is best to do it as soon as possible, before the Handmen make . . ." He frowns. "Inroads. Inroads into the new structure."

Aiah thinks of the Operation, the street captains with their stony, inhuman eyes and their utter, perfectly human greed. Their dominance was difficult to avoid; they had injured her family, and her hatred for them had burned long.

Damn Constantine for reminding her.

"I'll do it, if that's what you want," Aiah says, "but only if you want it *really done.*"

His brown eyes challenge hers. "I said *destroyed.* Did I not?"

She nods. Fists clench at her sides, nails digging into palms. "Yes," she says. "I can do that."

He looks down at the gold ashtray in his hands, and her gaze follows his. His massive hands and powerful wrists have twisted the ashtray, turned it into a half-spiral of yellow metal, all without visible effort. He holds it up and smiles.

"Too malleable," he comments. "I find myself disliking the useless ostentation in this place more and more."

Aiah looks at him. "I will bear that in mind, Metropolitan."

A knowing smile dances about his lips. His arm flies out, and the ashtray gives a little metallic keen as it skids across the tabletop. It strikes another ashtray with a clang and knocks it to the carpet before coming to a halt, spinning lazily on the polished wood.

"I will find you an office," Constantine says. He takes her arm, guides her to the door. "We can postpone discussions of salary, and so forth, for the moment. Budgets," he smiles, "are in flux. But I will assign you an apartment here in the Palace. I want you close by."

His hand is very warm on her arm. Close by, she thinks, yes.

"Congratulations on your revolution, Metropolitan," she says.

Constantine opens the door. "We have had only a change in administration," he says. "The *revolution* is yet to come."

"Congratulations, anyway."

"Thank you," he says, and smiles as she passes through the door.

LIFE EXTENSION

WHAT'S WRONG WITH LIVING FOREVER?

REASONABLE TERMS—PRIVACY ASSURED

Constantine leaves Aiah to underlings who don't quite know what to do with her. But by the end of first shift Aiah has an office in Owl Wing. It has a receptionist's office (sans receptionist), a rather nicely finished metal desk complete with bullet holes, and a communications array that doesn't work. An Evo-Matic computer sits in the corner, brass with fins, but it requires a three-prong commo socket and the office isn't wired for them. The plastic sheeting tacked up over the window booms with every gust of wind.

The carpet is nice, though. Gray, with black patterns that look like geomantic foci.

From this office she will direct a team that as yet does not exist, that has no history, no personnel, no records, no budget; but which nevertheless is charged with a task of awesome complexity and importance.

Gathering plasm. The most important element of power, because it can do anything.

Mass transformed is *energy*—the most fundamental difference is not one of matter, but of perspective. And mass, in the right configurations, can *create* energy.

That's plasm.

And the science of configuring mass so as to produce plasm is geomancy.

And because plasm exists in a kind of resonance with the human will, it can be used to create realities—create almost anything the human mind can conceive. Cure disease, alter genes, destroy life, halt or reverse aging, creep into the human mind to burn every neuron or, more subtly, to turn one emotion into another, to create love or hate where neither existed before. Plasm can knock tall buildings down, move objects from one place to another, build precious metals from base matter. Or create base matter from nothing at all.

In Constantine's system of thought, plasm is the most real thing in the world. Because it can make anything else real, or it can take something that exists and uncreate it.

Making something real from nothing would now seem to be Aiah's job.

Create a police force.

What kind of magecraft is necessary for that? Absurd.

Aiah tries, sketching idly on paper, to make plans. It's usually easy enough to find out who the big thieves are, but discovering where they keep the goods is another matter.

You have always exceeded my expectations.

After a few hours, she wants to spit the words back in Constantine's face.

She throws down her pen, stands, paces the carpet while the plastic rattles in the wind.

Welcome to Free Caraq—she thinks. Why is it up to her to fill in the missing letters?

And then Sorya is standing in the door, and Aiah's heart leaps.

"Hello, missy." Sorya walks into the room and holds out Aiah's bag. "This was brought from your hotel."

"Thank you." Aiah takes the offering. The cinders in the back of her throat make her cough.

Deliberately, Sorya's green eyes rove the room. There is a languid smile on her lips. She is balanced like a dancer, hips cocked forward, blond-streaked hair framing her face. She usually clothes her panther body in brilliant colors, apricot or green silk, the coiled muscle and curve of breast and hip garbed brightly as a flower . . . but at the moment she wears a green uniform with no insignia, a faded military greatcoat with brass buttons thrown over her shoulders, a peaked cap set with deliberate nonchalance on the side of her head. Not a flower, but something else.

A mage, a potent one. A warrior, a general. Powerful and intent on growing more so.

"We paid you well for your services in Jaspeer," she says. "I was under the impression we had said good-bye."

"The cops were after me."

"That was careless of you." She arches an eyebrow.

Sorya turns, walks to the door, pauses deliberately, and looks at Aiah over her shoulder. "Let me take you to your suite in the Crane Wing."

Aiah clears her throat, finds her voice. "Don't you have a more important job to do?"

Sorya gives a lilting laugh. "I am providing orientation to a valued colleague. Please come."

Aiah follows. Sorya leads Aiah down a corridor with a shallow outward curve, a design feature presumably intended to enhance plasm creation.

"I've been appointed head of the Intelligence Section," Sorya says.

"Drumbeth's old job?"

"Colonel Drumbeth was *military* intelligence. I'm civilian, under the Ministry of State."

Aiah feels a tightness in her chest. "Head of the Specials, then." The old political police, infamous for their torture and brutality.

"We are going to be renamed the Force of the Interior, I believe." Sorya throws the words carelessly over her shoulder.

"The commanders of the Specials will be debriefed—they are valuable only for their information, and once that is extracted, I expect they will be tried and shot." She flashes a cold smile over her shoulder. "Their crimes were real enough, and the population expects no less."

Sorya comes to an elevator, presses a button. The elevator door is polished copper, and Aiah can see her distorted reflection looming over Sorya's shoulder—tall skinny body, brown skin, corkscrew hair pulled back in a practical knot. A gangling, hovering, uncertain form, quite the opposite of Sorya, with her perfect body, her exotic dress, her dancer's poise and ruthless assurance.

"Your principal duty will consist of intelligence gathering," Sorya says. "I trust you will share any intelligence with my department."

Aiah gropes for an answer. "I will if my minister consents," she says.

Her minister is Constantine, or so she presumes. Let him take the heat, one way or another.

The elevator doors scroll open, revealing an interior of mirrors and velvet plush. Aiah and Sorya step inside. The elevator control handle is brass and wrought in the shape of an eagle's claw closed about a glittering crystal egg. Sorya sets the handle to the desired floor and the elevator begins to move. Then she leans one shoulder against the mirrored wall as she regards Aiah from beneath the brim of her cap.

"You have put yourself in a dangerous position," she says.

A cold river floods Aiah's spine. The elevator, moving unevenly along its shaft, causes little flutters in Aiah's inner ear.

"Are *you* a danger to me, madame?" she asks.

Sorya's mouth lights with a cold, cynical little smile. "Why should I concern myself with your destruction? I have repeatedly told you that I have never borne you any animosity—whether you care to believe this is scarcely my concern. Besides"—she gives a lazy shrug—"I reserve my power for dealings with the great and for enhancing my own scope of action—it would be a contemptibly small exercise to destroy you, and I have no inclination to think myself either small or contemptible. Give me credit for pride at least, Miss Aiah."

There is a delicate chiming chord that hangs in the air for a moment. The elevator comes to a stop and the doors open. Sorya reaches out a hand, twists the brass knob that locks the doors open, and turns to Aiah again. Her brows are lightly furrowed, as if she were contemplating a minor problem.

"I mean only that Constantine's friends, speaking generally, do not live long. Those who do not have their own share of greatness do not survive for long in the company of the great."

Aiah steels herself, holds Sorya's gaze. The elevator seems very small. "You have told me this before," she says.

"And you had the sense to follow my advice," Sorya says. "You took our money and went your way. But now . . ." She shrugs again. "You are in the line of fire. Do not claim you were not warned."

"Line of fire?" Aiah says. "The fighting is over."

Sorya slits her eyes. "The fighting is *never* over," she says. "All truces are temporary. All wars are the same war, with occasional pauses for readjustment. War and politics are different facets of the same phenomenon, which is the conflict of *human will,* the will for power, for greatness, for enlarged scope. . . . The rest, the medium through which one will challenges another—war or peace, law or politics—that is mere mechanics." Her green eyes glitter. "Learn *that* if you wish to survive."

Aiah takes a breath, clears her throat against the smell of cinders. "Do you think there will be a war?"

"There will be conflict. I cannot say what form it will take." She cocks her head, her look going abstract with thought. "Consider: Constantine knows what he wants, but this new government does not—not surprising, with all the factions it represents—the triumvirate is divided and does not speak with one voice, or act with one will. There is a Keremath party still, though there are precious few Keremaths left to lead it. The Caraqui army is being supplemented by mercenaries long loyal to Constantine. That is opportunity . . . for *someone.*"

"You think Constantine will take power himself?"

"Only if he must. Only if the triumvirate fails. Constantine is a foreigner and cannot hope to seize a metropolis that is not his own, not unless . . ." Sorya shows white teeth in a smile. "Unless the metropolis *asks,* from lack of any other palatable alternative." Her eyes flicker to Aiah. "So build your department, find your plasm. It will increase Constantine's power . . . and opportunity."

Thoughts scurry from place to place in Aiah's mind, alarmed but with no place to run. Sorya seems amused. With an unconcerned roll of her shoulders, she pushes herself from her leaning posture against the elevator wall and steps into the hall outside. Aiah follows. The wood paneling here is beautifully, intricately carved with patterns of fruit and flowers. They pass through two sets of the bronze-strapped airlock doors, which open automatically at their approach and close behind them.

"We're in Crane Wing now," Sorya says. "Some of the junior Keremaths lived here, with their dependents and loyalists. All chucked out now, or sent to the Shield." Her hand dips into one of the greatcoat pockets, comes out with a key on a silver chain. She puts it in a door, pushes the door open.

"Your suite," she says. "Have a pleasant sleep shift."

"Thank you," Aiah says. Sorya drops the key in her hand, tips her cap mockingly, as if in imitation of a uniformed doorman, and strides away.

Aiah stands for a moment looking into the dark room, then reaches in to find a light switch. Her fingers touch cool metal. She turns the knob and the lights come on.

The room glows, all polished woods and gleaming metal and soft, sumptuous fabric. Aiah steps in and her feet sink into deep carpet. The room is three times the size of the apartment in Jaspeer she shared with Gil. Wonderment tingles in her nerves. This place is *hers?* Hers alone?

She puts her bag down and closes the door behind her: it moves in silence on brass hinges, with a push of the finger. Aiah explores the suite in wonder—the gleaming kitchen, the luxurious lounge, the bar with its shining crystal decanters. There is food in the refrigerator, stores in the cabinets, fruit trees blossoming on the terrace. Her fingertips brush over the smooth, polished surface of wood tables, and she wonders if she will ever get used to so much wood around her.

There had been a revolution, a complete readjustment of power; but it had not touched this room.

There are plasm connections everywhere, as available as electric power outlets. Aiah checks the communications array, the headset with its priceless ivory earpieces and gleaming silver keys, and finds it doesn't work.

Not everything, she reflects, can be perfect. She opens the door into the bedroom—

—and smothers a scream with her fist.

She slams the door and staggers away on a wave of nausea. The room swims around her, and she sinks into a chair. Soft leather receives her.

The suite's previous occupant had died in bed, and he had not died well.

Clearly magecraft had killed him. The sheets and mattress were crusted in dried blood, and there were sprays of red on the walls, floor, even the ceiling. The body had been removed, but the mess had not.

Sorya, Aiah thinks. Sorya chose this room for her.

All truces are temporary. The words echo in her mind.

Aiah jumps up from the chair, walks to the door, puts her hand on its bronze handle. And then wonders where she's going to go.

Beneath a lovely carving of grapes, outside in the hall, Aiah finally catches a few hours' rest, sleeping on the carpet with her jacket for a pillow.

TWO

"Hello, little bird."

Aiah looks up and sees Charduq the Hermit gazing down at her. He has been there all her life, on his pillar at the Barkazi Savings Institute, with rain and Shieldlight falling alike on his head, and the wind blowing his long beard up in his eyes.

"Hello, old crow," says Aiah.

Charduq smooths his beard with a gnarled hand. "A little bird should have more respect for the older birds of this world," Charduq says.

Aiah is only eleven years old, but she knows better than to let some mangy holy man get the better of her. "If the old crow wants more respect," she says, "he should fly down off his perch and get some for himself."

The hermit giggles. "The little bird's claws are sharp," he observes. "And she has got herself some new feathers. What is that uniform?"

"For my new school." Aiah's new skirt, vest, and blouse are all too large, to allow room for growth, and the long sleeves of the blouse are rolled up to her elbows. She is not proud of her appearance, swathed in acres of cloth, and wishes Charduq had not mentioned it.

"What new school? I haven't seen that uniform."

"Miss Turmak got me a scholarship. I have to take the trackline to Redstone District." She holds up her plastic trackline pass.

"The little bird flies far." Charduq raises his eyebrows. "Miss Turmak is a longnose, ne?" he says. "It's a longnose education they'll give you in Redstone."

Aiah shrugs. "It's a longnose education they have in the state school, too. It's just not as *good* an education."

"But if you don't go to school in Old Shorings, you'll be away from the Children of Karlo."

Aiah has heard this argument before, mostly from her own family. "You'll forget who you are," they tell her. "You'll grow up a longnose and lose all your cunning."

She looks around the bustle of Old Shorings—the crazy old buildings propped up by metal scaffolds, the street stalls and liquor stores, the jobless young men lounging on street corners and the Operation bagman making his collections— and wonders what is so great about this place that she should have to stay here for the rest of her life.

"I'll still live here," she tells Charduq. "How can I forget who I live with?"

Charduq smiles down at her benignly. "The little bird will not forget her nest." He cocks his head. "You're an Old Oelphil family, aren't you?"

Charduq, Aiah figures, is the sort who would care about this kind of silly superstition. The Old Oelphil families are supposed to be the guardians of the Barkazil people, reincarnating from generation to generation rather than continuing on to paradise.

They seem not to have done the Barkazil much good the last few generations, though, Aiah muses. Where were the Oelphil, she wonders, at the Battle of the Plastic Factory?

"I'm supposed to be Oelphil on my mother's side," Aiah says. "I don't know about my dad."

"I remember your father," Charduq says. "He looked Oelphil to me."

Charduq has been on his pillar so long that he knows practically everybody in Old Shorings. And he's a relentless gossip as well, always happy to retail the latest scandals.

"When you're in Redstone," Charduq says, "you remember that you're one of our people's guardians. You learn that longnose education now, but remember that it's for our benefit, so we can grow in our cunning."

"I'll remember," Aiah promises, becoming restless. "I need to catch the trackline now."

She opens her satchel and drops her lunch into Charduq's plastic collection bucket—she knows that once she is in her new school she will be too excited to eat—and Charduq hauls the bucket to his perch with his rope. "You're generous, little bird," he says. "A blessing on you, and a curse on your enemies."

"Thank you." Politely.

Her thoughts are already on the trackline, away from Old Shorings, toward her new life.

> *Item #1:* Get commo array fixed.
> *Item #2:* Arrange for cleaning re living quarters.
> New mattresses, new linen.
> *Item #3:* New office furniture.
> *Item #4:* Resign from Plasm Authority.
> *Item #5:* Gil?
> *Item #6:* Family?

Items 1 through 3 are the easy tasks, though they take almost until midbreak. Item 4 proves more difficult than she expected—she had been raised on the dole, in apartments provided by the Jaspeeri government in a shambles of a district called Old Shorings. Aiah's grandparents were refugees from the war that had destroyed the Metropolis of Barkazi, and Aiah had been raised among a people that had lost almost everything: family, tradition, culture, security, hope.

The Plasm Control Authority had been a route out of Old Shorings and all that it represented. Despite its sloth and ineptitude and pointlessness, the civil service provided security, which was of prime importance to a Barkazil girl who had no stability in her young life.

Resigning from the Authority was saying farewell to all the security she had ever known. And in exchange for a job in what is perhaps the least secure civil service in the world—the last inhabitant of this office had probably been pitched out of his job at the point of a bayonet.

But of course it is foolish to think she can ever go back to the Scope of Jaspeer. Not with the police after her for what the statutes quaintly called "crimes against the public interest," in this case stealing millions of dalders' worth of plasm and giving it to a political adventurer who promptly used it to overthrow a friendly government.

She sends the wiregram and feels a moment of loss as a part of her former life falls away.

Item #5. Item #6. Her lover, her family.

Two more parts of her former life. By now she doesn't want to contemplate losing either.

Aiah looks at her watch. 11:41. Almost midbreak, and she suddenly realizes she's very hungry.

She hasn't eaten since yesterday's sandwiches.

She stands, stretches, wonders where in this giant place she can get something to eat. Aiah walks through her empty receptionist's office into the hallway, and her nerves give a little jump as she sees Constantine bearing down on her at his usual earth-devouring pace—elemental energy, balanced and directed and walking on two long legs.

His black velvet suit, trimmed with lace, makes him look like a pirate at a bankers' convention. He carries a black leather briefcase with a combination lock.

A smile breaks across his face. "Miss Aiah," he says. "Are you comfortable in your new quarters?"

Aiah's answering smile freezes to her face. "As soon as they scrape the former occupant off the walls, yes."

Constantine looks surprised.

"My apologies. No doubt a mistake was made in all the confusion."

"No doubt." Aiah's tone is meant to indicate that there is a story here if Constantine wants to hear it.

There is an awkward pause. Apparently it is not the time for stories.

"Are you engaged?" he asks finally.

Aiah suppresses a bitter laugh. "Not until I have a budget and personnel, no."

Tigerish pleasure glows in his eyes. "I am now in a position to give you both. I have just come from a meeting of the cabinet, and your department is approved. You will be pleased to know you are the Director of the Plasm Enforcement Division. Gentri, the Minister of Public Security, objected loudly to your endowment, because you're in competition with the plasm squads of the police, and therefore in a position to make him look bad—but the rest understand the necessity." He bows, absurdly formal, and holds out the briefcase. "Your commission, madame. And some documents for your files. The lock combination is on a plastic flimsy inside. Read, memorize, destroy."

"Sounds serious." She takes the briefcase and finds it heavy.

"Names, biographies, public information, informers' reports pulled out of the Specials' files by Sorya. The Plasm Enforcement Division's first cases."

Aiah's nerves tingle as she feels the weight of the briefcase on the end of her arm.

My commission, she thinks. I have just joined an army, and these are my marching orders.

"Do you have time for a meeting?" Constantine asks.

"I seem to have little else on my schedule." *Except a meal,* her stomach reminds her.

Constantine cocks his head and looks at her, intent eyes narrowing. "You lack your usual energy, Miss Aiah. Have you eaten? Shall we have our meeting in the dining suite?"

Aiah rocks back on her heels with relief. "Yes. Absolutely."

"You skip too many meals."

"If I knew where to *get* a meal around here, that might change."

A smile dances across his face, and he makes another elaborate stage bow. "I shall direct you. If you would follow me?"

Aiah returns the courtesy. "I would be pleased to do so."

"This way, then. The Kestrel Room has a lovely view, and a private room where we may talk."

CENSORS SENT HOME

CENSORSHIP OF NEWS ENDS IN CARAQUI

210 MILLION DINARS SAVED BY
GOVERNMENT ACTION

Toying with a salad and sipping at a glass of wine, Constantine watches with amusement as Aiah eats. The Keremaths' kitchen staff are undergoing a screening—no one wants some legitimist partisan poisoning half the new government in one swoop—so tne cooking is being done by military personnel, Constantine's mercenaries. What the food lacks in subtlety and flavor is made up for in quantity, and the vat shrimp with vegetables served on noodles is more than acceptable.

The Kestrel Room—rooms, in truth—is another example of Keremath extravagance. Wood is everywhere—parquetry floors, parquetry walls, carved, beamed ceilings. And the huge outcurving windows of transparent plastic offer a spectacular view of the city.

"I obtained for you a personal plasm allowance," Constantine says.

Aiah looks up sharply from her plate, suddenly greedy for more than food. "How much?" she asks.

Amusement kindles in Constantine's eyes. "A quarter of a kilomehr."

Aiah is impressed. "Per year? That's good."

"Per month. Commencing immediately."

She stares at him. His smile broadens, turns a little predatory, sharp teeth flashing. "Being a part of the power structure has its benefits, does it not?"

"I am beginning to see that it does." She gives the matter some thought. "Is the cabinet so obliging to every department head?"

"Our job, yours and mine, is the management of plasm. Other departments will not require these allocations." Constantine shrugs his big shoulders back into his chair and gives a catlike smile. "Oh, it was a splendid meeting, on the whole. Drumbeth backed all my proposals, including your department, and Drumbeth has the loyalty of the army, so the others in the triumvirate have to tread warily when he makes his wishes known." He toys with his fork, twirling it on the linen tablecloth. "There were some conditions. Allies that want their rewards."

"Who, in this case?"

"Adaveth. You remember him?"

Distaste tingles its way along Aiah's nerves. "The twisted man."

"The Minister of Waterways," Constantine says. "He will appoint your second-in-command, though I will have a veto if the individual is entirely inappropriate."

Ten percent of humanity, Aiah knew, had twisted genes. Most genetic alterations were for small things, hardly noticeable—boosted immune systems or outright immunity to certain diseases, cosmetic changes, genetic tweaks relating to the strength of the body or the power of the intellect. But Adaveth and his kindred were different: small, hairless, goggle-eyed. Probably intended to be semiaquatic. It gave Aiah the shivers just being around anyone that inhuman.

"Will he be twisted?" she asks.

Constantine gives her a sharp glance. "I would not be surprised. That is Adaveth's constituency." He pauses, toying again with his fork. "Many of the twisted here were *created,* by the old Avian oligarchy, for certain tasks. Positions in the civil service are traditionally reserved for them, and many of these have to do with servicing and maintaining plasm connections. Possibly because the workers are twisted, the jobs are low-status, low-pay. But I think they know more about how Caraqui is wired together than anyone, and if Adaveth chooses well your assistant should be invaluable."

"I understand the rationale," Aiah says. But, she thinks, she reserves the right not to like it.

"I desire to make use of every opportunity," Constantine says. "Every untapped resource, every talent, all the ability that has been wasted or suppressed." His intent eyes burn Aiah's nerves. "That is why I make use of *you,* Miss Aiah. Your gifts were unappreciated in your previous life."

Aiah holds his glance by an act of will. "I would like to think so, Metropolitan."

Constantine smiles, his gaze shifting to the window. "You should learn to call me Minister. I haven't been a Metropolitan in a very long time."

"I'll try to remember."

"It's an overrated title." He scowls, and suddenly his chair is too small to contain him—he rises and paces the room. "When I was Metropolitan of Cheloki I felt little better than a slave," he says. "Flung this way and that by circumstance, forced to respond to every shift in the situation. All responsibility was mine, but there was precious little I could do to alter anything—even to aid my own cause."

Aiah puts down her fork. "My impression," she says, "is that you were magnificent."

He makes a growling sound deep in his throat. "Well." Dismissively. "I'm a good actor. I *played* a Metropolitan well, and that's what people saw. But it was far different from what I'd expected when I first set my mind on power."

He marches back and forth across the room and flings out phrases with tossing motions of his arms. Passion burns behind his eyes, a world-eating force that Aiah can feel in the tingle of her nerves, the prickle of her nape hair.

We are not small people. Sorya had told her that once, and she was right.

"I knew precisely what I wished to do with Cheloki," Constantine says. "I knew that my ideas would prove correct. I thought that once I achieved position I could snap my fingers and cause miracles to happen, that I could change everything. . . . But no, that did not happen."

She sees frustration in his glance, thwarted rage. His shoulders have slumped, drawn inward, less in defeat than as if he were sheltering from an attack.

"You had a civil war to cope with," she says.

"If I'd been wise enough," bitterly, "there would have been no civil war. If I'd managed it all a bit better . . ." Constantine's big hands throw the notion behind him as he makes a contemptuous growl. "*If, if* . . . The truth is, I was helpless. Every reform in Cheloki was perceived as a threat by our neighbors. But . . ." He looks through the outcurved window, hands propped on his hips, and scowls at the world. "In Caraqui we are safer, I think. I can manage things better now, and all the knowledge cost me was the destruction of the Metropolis of Cheloki, the deaths of hundreds of thousands, and the knowledge that all the responsibility was mine. . . ."

Aiah pushes away her cooling noodles, stands, approaches Constantine from behind. She puts her arms around him, presses her cheek to his shoulder. "It wasn't all your fault," she says. "You had to fight gangsters and your own family and Cheloki's neighbors. Even so you did well. You lasted for years against all of them, and you inspired millions." Her tone softens. "You inspired *me*."

"You weren't *there*," he grudges, but his tone is softer.

Constantine's warmth steals into her frame. She can feel his anger soften. "Much better to be a mere government minister," he says. "I will be responsible only for my own department, and even if I have my way in larger issues, success or failure will be up to someone else."

For all that he finds this thought comforting, Aiah cannot quite believe that Constantine will find himself this detached when anything important is at stake.

"Everything must be in place as soon as possible," Constantine says. His voice is low, thoughtful, and perhaps he is talking as much to himself as to Aiah. "We have a new government, and many more actions are possible under martial law than otherwise . . . but they must be the *right* actions, not abuses or pointless pursuit of revenge, and martial law must soon enough be lifted, and by *then*, we must all be ready."

He turns, puts his arms around her waist, and looks at her levelly. "You must have your department prepared by then. I can guarantee you independence as long as I am minister; but no appointment lasts forever, and after I'm gone—well, you must be in place, with an independent, efficient, and incorruptible force. Once you have that, once you have proved your worth, they will have a much harder time dislodging you."

Aiah's head swims. "I understand."

"Do you need anything right now? Anything at all?"

"I need to see as much of the apparatus as possible. Control stations, broadcast antennae, receivers, connections, capacitors."

"I will arrange to give you a tour."

"Of course."

He kisses her—a moment's softness brushing her lips—and then Constantine is already in motion, his body moving toward the door, mind focused on another item of his agenda. He reaches the door and turns.

"I will send you an engineer, Miss Aiah. Within the hour." He reaches for the door, then hesitates and breaks into a smile. "Apologies for my haste," he says. "By all means finish your luncheon, and order as many desserts as you like."

"Thank you," Aiah says, his taste still tingling on her lips, and then he is gone.

She returns to her meal, and wonders how dangerous it is that, after all this, she is still so very hungry.

TRAM SCANDAL REVEALED!

KEREMATHS RAKED IN MILLIONS!

CONTRACTOR HELD FOR QUESTIONING

Constantine sends a Captain Delruss, who is plainly annoyed at having been drawn away from his other duty. Delruss is stocky and gray-haired, a native of the Timocracy of Garshab, where the military profession is an honored and highly profitable tradition among its fierce mountaineers. He is a military engineer with a specialty in plasm control systems—and probably a mage of sorts—and though he has had only a few days to acquaint himself with the systems of the Aerial Palace, he has learned them well indeed. If Delruss performs his new assignment grudgingly he performs it efficiently enough, and becomes visibly happier when he finds out that Aiah knows her business.

The tour starts in the heart of the Palace, deep underwater in the largest of the giant barges that support the extravagant structure overhead. This is clearly the center of Caraqui's power: the concrete pontoon is armored with slabs of steel, segmented into watertight compartments, laced with a defensive bronze web intended to absorb plasm attack.

There is one compartment after another filled with giant plasm accumulators and capacitors—each four times Aiah's height, layers of gleaming black ceramic and polished brass and copper that tower into the darkness overhead. Above them are the huge contact arms poised to drop and connect the accumulators to Caraqui's plasm network, the all-embracing web that can draw all the power of the city into this one place.

The control room is as vast as everything else, one bank after another of controls, levers, switches, glowing dials. In one corner is an icon to Tangid, the two-faced god of power, with a few candles burning in front of it, and in another corner is another icon to a figure Aiah doesn't recognize, with no candles at all. Looming overhead, video monitors show unblinking views of the outside of the building, of the entrance areas, of Government Harbor several radii away, and of other points deemed important to Caraqui's security.

Mages, some civilian and some not, sit before consoles, eyes closed, bodies swaying as power pours through them. Captain Delruss's comrades, the uniformed personnel operating the system, seem dwarfed by the enormity of it all.

"During the fighting all this could have given us a lot of trouble," Delruss says, "but afterward we discovered there were very few calls for plasm made during the coup."

"Why was that?" Aiah asks, gazing up at glowing monitor screens. She can't imagine anyone *forgetting* to use the colossal power of this place.

"There was sabotage of the communications system and of the plasm delivery network," Delruss says. "But nothing that couldn't have been overcome by competent people in the control room. What really won the coup for our side was that the enemy leadership was completely decapitated. There was no one left alive with the authority to make big plasm calls."

Aiah's mouth goes dry as she remembers the splashes of red-brown on her bedroom walls. "Do you know how our side managed it?" she asks.

Delruss has clearly been giving this issue a lot of thought. "Very good intelligence, for one thing. It looked as if we knew where almost every last one of the enemy leaders were, and were able to target them. And there were probably holes in the security screen here that our side had discovered, so mages could slip an attack through. . . ." Delruss frowns, shakes his head. "But what sort of attack was used, miss, I can't say. There are a large number of possibilities. But it was done very well, however it was done."

Aiah remembers a moment of choking terror in a deep underground tunnel, the appearance of a thing that seemed made of purest black and silver, the chill waves of ice that flooded her nerves. . . .

Ice man. Hanged man. *The damned* . . . an evil thing, whatever label you chose to give it. Its personal name was Taikoen, for that was its name when it was a man—a hero, Taikoen the Great, the leader who saved Atavir from the Slaver Mages. Now debased, beyond humanity, a creature that Constantine could summon out of the depths of the plasm well, a thing deadly to everything that lived. . . .

The enemy leadership was completely decapitated. Perhaps literally. And Aiah has the feeling she knows how it was done. A large part of it, anyway.

From the deep underwater plasma fortress, Delruss takes Aiah to the highest point of the Aerial Palace, where the huge bronze transmission horns are set in clusters like the outgrowths of a strange, intricate forest of gleaming metal. The horns are ornamented with ornate baroque swirls and scallops and, at each end, the sculptured figure of a hawk about to take flight. A cold wind buffets Aiah as she gazes out at the city—pontoons, buildings, roof gardens, long gray-green canals packed with ship and barge traffic—an endless procession stretching all the way to the distant volcanoes of the Metropolis of Barchab. Several of the aerial tramcars are visible in the distance, dancing on invisible wires. The volcanoes, Aiah realizes, are the only object in sight that, on account of altitude and danger of eruption, were not inhabited by the swarms of humanity that otherwise covered the globe.

She looks in the other direction, toward the North Pole only three or four hundred radii away. She sees giant buildings

looming up out of the sea, one group twenty or so radii away
and another dimly visible in the distance behind a cluster of
spires. The Shield glows on their gleaming windows and burnished metal. Jagged transmission horns top almost every
building.

"Lorkhin Island, and Little Lorkhin," Delruss says.
"Extinct volcanoes. They build tall here, when they can find
bedrock." He peers out into the distance. "The whole
metropolis is ringed by tall buildings where the sea turns
shallow. It's called the Crown of Caraqui."

Here on the Palace roof, some of the transmission horns
have been blown from their moorings, and others damaged.
Engineers are rigging a big tripod of steel beams to hoist the
damaged horns in place while repairs are made.

"We tried to take these out at the start, miss," Delruss
says. "We used helicopters with special munitions, but we
had only limited success. If these transmission horns had
been able to broadcast power to where it was needed, we'd
have had a much harder time."

"But there was no one to give the orders."

"Correct, miss."

The cold wind knifes through Aiah's bones. Somewhere
below a ship's siren whoops three times, like an unan-
swered call for help. Aiah steps toward the edge, her feet
crunching on glass from a rooftop arboretum blown open
in the fighting, its rare trees and shrubs already withering
in the cold.

Above, between her and the Shield, plasm lines trace
across the sky: The Situation Has Returned To Normal.
Everything Is Safe. The New Government Asks That All Citizens Return to Work.

"*Are* we safe?" she asks.

"Against what?"

"An attack."

Delruss shrugs. "A lot of the collection web has holes
blown in it. We've got telepresent mages patrolling the
perimeter, but they can't see everything. Twenty percent of
the transmission horns are off-line, and a lot of the sabotage
inflicted during the coup hasn't been repaired yet . . . well,
not exactly *not repaired.*"

He sighs, prepares his long story. "Certain of the sabotage was performed by groups with particular interests, in anticipation of particular rewards. They are making certain they get these rewards before repairing the damage they made."

"I see," Aiah says. She believes she now understands how she's getting one of the twisted as her deputy. "So it's lucky there's no fighting going on right now."

"Yes, miss."

Aiah steps to the parapet and brushes wind-whipped hair from her eyes. She looks down, sees a statue in a niche below her, hanging from bronze straps. It's the first time she's seen one of these up close, and she sees that it's three times human size, and that the upturned face is set into an expression of agony—eyes staring, lips drawn back in pain. Cold fingers brush her spine as she looks into the featureless metal eyes.

"What *are* these?" she asks. "They're all over the building."

Delruss looks over the parapet and gazes unmoved into the agonized face. He's probably seen much worse in his time.

"Martyrs," he said. "The Avians used to hang political and religious criminals from buildings to die of exposure."

Aiah is appalled. "Hanging off the *Palace?*" she asks.

"Not the Palace, but other buildings, yes. Originally there were other statues in these niches—gods, immortals, and Avians—but when the Avians fell, they put *these* here instead. And a lot of the local Dalavites hang themselves off buildings as a kind of ordeal, to commune with the spirits of their martyrs."

He looks at her, a trace of a smile touching his lips. "There were some tourist brochures in an office downstairs. I read them."

"I don't suppose your brochure mentioned the Dreaming Sisters?"

"Sorry, no. That's new to me."

The sky shapes into an advertisement for the new Lynxoid Brothers chromoplay, the Lynxoids and the Blue Titan performing a violent dance across the sky. Aiah is freezing, and she's seen enough for today.

From the roof they descend into the structure, and Aiah

inspects some of the local conduits, the electric switches that divert plasm from one place to another, the meters that record consumption for purposes of billing.

She thanks Delruss and returns to her office to see if anyone has called—no message lights on the commo array—and finds that her new office furniture has been delivered. Since there seems little to do, she returns to her living quarters.

The suite smells of fresh paint. The carpet has been cleaned, and a brand-new mattress waits on the bed, still in a clear plastic wrapper.

It occurs to her that the situation is so fluid that she can only discover the limits of her authority by giving orders and seeing who obeys them. That she could so easily get service for her room and office argues for the fact that at least some people are inclined to do what she says.

Get the office window repaired tomorrow, she thinks.

She should make a list of everything she needs. Office supplies, access to the computers, scheduled use of the transmission horns, maybe access to secure files, if she can figure out where the secure files *are*. . . .

Ask for it *all*, she thinks. Maybe she'll get it.

She finds a piece of paper and begins to make lists.

THE WHOLE WORLD IS TALKING ABOUT

LORDS OF THE NEW CITY

MORE THAN JUST A CHROMOPLAY

A bar. Middle of service shift, after the stores have started to close. The place is a glittering profusion of mirrors, brass ornaments, crystal chandeliers, black sculpted furniture made of a shiny composite. It's crowded and noisy, with a good cross-section of the local inhabitants—most of whom seem to possess both youth and dinars—but no twisted, which Aiah is relieved to discover.

During the course of this shift's explorations she's found that about half the inhabitants of Caraqui feature the stocky build and copper skin that registers as "normal" here, but the rest are every conceivable variety of build and skin tone, a wide enough variety that Aiah, with her brown skin and eyes and black hair, doesn't feel as out of place as she would on a normal street home in Jaspeer.

Aiah sits in a corner surrounded by packages and waits her turn in the restaurant section.

"A gentleman is buying drinks for the house," the waitress says. "What would you like?"

The waitress tugs at the hem of her red velvet vest while Aiah considers. The number of customers leads Aiah to conclude that whoever is buying could afford another round of what she's drinking.

"Markhand white. Two-Cross," she says, and taps her crystal glass. Not without a twinge of guilt.

Before she'd met Constantine she hadn't ever realized that wine could be good, or that food could be delicious *as a normal thing,* without special effort. When Aiah was growing up, assembling a good meal was akin to a treasure hunt: good vegetables traded for, or plucked from roof gardens; favors exchanged for a good grain-fed chicken or squab or, on special occasion, a goat; fruit acquired through a process of barter too complex to be apprehended by the outsider.

But for Constantine good food is simply part of the background—he can afford the best: fruit and vegetables grown in select arboretums, animals and fowl fattened on food that otherwise would have been given to people, wine grown in rooftop vineyards, fermentation and acids balanced by magecraft.

Being around Constantine had left Aiah with expensive tastes, tastes at variance with the thrifty habits of a lifetime, but then Constantine had also left Aiah with money in a bank account in Gunalaht.

She has spent a lot of money this service shift, almost a month's wages at her old job in Jaspeer. She'd realized that she needed new clothing—she'd fled Jaspeer with only the clothes on her back, and bought only a few items in Gunalaht on her way to Caraqui—and so she'd crossed one of the graceful arched bridges leading from the Palace on a shopping expedition.

It was an expensive part of the city. When she handed

over her checktube in order to pay, it required a certain effort of will.

But at least she will be able to dress as befits her station, whatever that turns out to be.

The waitress brings Aiah the complimentary glass of wine and takes her empty glass. "Another round!" someone shouts. The voice is loud and male, and followed by cheers.

"Another round?" the waitress asks.

"Not yet."

Aiah sips the wine, and a tingling taste of apples and ambrosia explodes across her palate. A young couple—both in subdued lace and velvet, the man in black, the woman in violet—struggle through the crowd and dump a pair of heavy briefcases under the bench next to Aiah's table.

"I can't believe they let him go," the man says. "After all the people he disappeared."

"He probably knows something," the woman says. "Something about Drumbeth or Parq or someone else in the new government."

"That wouldn't surprise me."

The woman smiles thinly. "Are you growing cynical about our new government already?"

"I am a good citizen," the man says, "and will be pleased to support the revolution if it will support me to a promotion."

"Plenty more where that came from!" roars the man buying drinks. More cheers. He comes into sight, dancing clumsily in hobnailed military boots. He's wearing a uniform that Aiah doesn't recognize, but she gathers from its ostentation that he ranks high. The tunic is unbuttoned, revealing a broad stomach and a shirt stained with wine, and he hasn't shaved in days. He waves a bottle of wine in one hand and a checktube in the other.

"Let's dance!" he bellows, and makes a bearlike pirouette. The couple next to Aiah watch with clear distaste.

Aiah half-raises her glass to her lips. The officer staggers, recovers, looks up at Aiah with pale blue eyes. . . .

The hair on Aiah's neck rises. Ice floods her veins. The blue eyes stare back at her in a terrifying moment of mutual recognition.

The man staggers again, recovers, then turns abruptly and

heads for the door. The crowd gives a good-natured groan of disappointment as he stalks out. He wanted to be anonymous, and Aiah has somehow spoiled his fun.

Aiah feels beads of sweat dotting her scalp. Her heart throbs in her throat.

Ice man. Hanged man. The damned.

Taikoen, Constantine's creature.

Aiah could tell the couple seated next to her that the officer, whoever he is, hasn't been set free. He's *gone,* obliterated, and soon his body will follow.

The hanged man is a creature of plasm, trapped in the pulse of fundamental energy, and so hostile to life, to matter, that he's cut off from it, from the comforts of humanity or the distractions of the flesh . . . he can't escape the single elemental fact of his own existence.

Not without the help of a first-rate mage.

Constantine had put the hanged man in the officer's body, had sent him lurching out into Shieldlight to seek his pleasures. Thus was the creature rewarded for helping to overthrow the Keremaths.

The hanged man, in the long run poisonous to life, would wear out the officer's body within a matter of days. The man would be found dead, and the new government would not be blamed. And Taikoen would slip back into the plasm mains, into the heart of the power that gave him life, and wait for his next victim.

Aiah looks down at the wineglass she's half-raised. Her hand is trembling and the wine splashes over her hand and wrist. She firmly places the glass back on her table.

She wants to leave the bar and flee back to the Palace, but for all she knows the hanged man is still outside, and she doesn't want to encounter him.

Best wait for her meal, she decides.

She wonders if it will taste like anything but ashes.

SNAP! THE WORLD DRINK

LIFE IS BETTER WITH A *SNAP!* IN YOUR FINGERS

It's almost sleep shift before Aiah gets back to the Palace. Her room, clean and smelling of paint, awaits her, antiseptic as a room in a hotel.

The walls are bare in the bedroom—all mirrors, pictures, and ornaments have been taken down while the paint dries. Aiah begins to put them back up, but several are chromographs of people—the former occupant, or his family or friends—and Aiah puts these in a closet designed as a pocket garden, with buckets of loam and grow lights but with nothing planted, presumably because the former occupant could afford to buy vegetables instead of growing them.

She goes to her bag, takes out her icon of Karlo, and puts it on the wall.

With its lacy frame of cheap tin, the icon looks incongruous on the wall of the luxury suite, but Aiah finds it comforting. Karlo is *her* immortal, the hero of the Barkazils—the great first leader of the Cunning People, who man who refused the Ascendancy because it was not granted to all, and was thus condemned to remain with his people when the Malakas, the Ascended, built the Shield as a barrier between themselves and the planet's teeming billions. . . .

Aiah walks toward the terrace doors. Bronze wire in a diamond pattern is sandwiched between the glass plates of the doors, part of the building's defense system, and she gazes through the gleaming diamonds at the Shield, the world's opalescent shell, which provides light and heat but which is also the wall of a prison, at once the world's savior and warder.

Karlo had tried to prevent the Shield from going up and failed, and that was both his tragedy and the world's. And in the thousands of years since nothing, fundamentally, had changed: the sky was barred, no human had Ascended, and all was pointless, or folly.

Until Constantine. With him, perhaps, the world could change—Aiah could see in him the blend of ideas, desire, vision, talent, ambition, brilliance, and world-reaching passion that offered the possibility of change. *If the New City comes into being,* he told her once, *then any sacrifice*—any-thing—*is justified.*

He saw no hope elsewhere. He desired liberation, for

others as well as for himself, liberation from the archaic systems that had ruled the world since before Karlo's day, and—an ambition expressed only in his powerful whisper—ultimately liberation from the tyranny of the Shield.

Aiah thinks of Taikoen, the hanged man, reeling through the floating districts of Caraqui in the body that Constantine gave him, and she tastes the bile that rises in her throat.

What could justify Taikoen? she wonders.

Steel firms her thoughts. *She* could justify him, she thinks. If she is true to her new life, if her department can do what it was designed to do, if she can break the hold the Handmen have on the people and liberate the stolen plasm for Constantine to use to build the New City. . . .

Only then, she thinks, is a monster like Taikoen justified.

So, she decides, she had better get busy and make it all work.

ATTACK OF THE HANGED MAN BANNED IN LIRI-DOMEI

ALDEMAR'S THRILLER CLAIMED "TOO VIOLENT"

Aiah gets only a few hours' sleep, since she's up late making lists and plans. Constantine has authorized her to hire a staff of 120 people, of whom a third can be mages, "preferably with specialties in telepresence and police work." During raids on plasm dens, she is authorized to call on the military.

Forty mages, not to mention soldiers.

She puts aside any doubts concerning whether she can organize and command forty mages, all with more experience than she, and concentrates instead on making lists of what she'll need.

Aiah looks with a start at the clock, and discovers it's 03:00. She looks for a window crank and can't find one, then discovers that the windows polarize against the Shieldlight with the press of a button.

Luxury. Right. She keeps forgetting.

She's too keyed up to get much rest, and when the alarm chimes at 07:00 she comes awake perfect in the knowledge that she's going to spend the day thick-witted and dragging herself from one task to the next.

During a search for coffee she comes across a plasm tap in the kitchen, and only a few seconds later thinks to wonder what in the immortals' name they could have used a kitchen plasm tap *for.*

Personal plasm allowance. Constantine had wangled her one.

If there's a tap in the kitchen, there will be taps elsewhere.

Aiah sets the coffee brewing and looks for taps, finding three in the main room alone. A search through drawers discovers a wire, a jack, and a copper transference grip, an "orthopedic" design custom-shaped for a hand somewhat smaller than Aiah's.

A dose of the goods, she thinks, is better than coffee any day.

She moves an armchair near the tap, puts the t-grip in the seat, and jacks the wire into a tap. With a flick of her thumb she can connect herself to the plasm well, the huge system that creates, moves, and stores plasm within the Metropolis of Caraqui. All the vast apparatus she had seen yesterday—the accumulators and capacitors and control boards, the transmission horns and receivers, the bundles of cable and taps and substations—all of it exists, Aiah realizes, only so that she, and people like her, can do just what she intends to do right now.

Aiah reaches into the collar of her sleepshirt and pulls out the plasm focus she wears on a chain around her neck. She had bought it just a few weeks ago, at the start of her adventure with Constantine, from an elderly man who earned a precarious living selling junk and trinkets from a desk made of a battered door. He had sold it to her as a "lucky charm," a cheap bit of popular magic alleged, through its connection with genuine magework, to have virtues even without plasm. The token is in the form of the Trigram, and like all plasm foci its scrolling lines are meant to give a pattern to the flow of plasm through Aiah's mind, a kind of safety device to prevent plasm from taking any unexpected turns.

She sits in the chair, looks at the focus in her palm, tries to relax, let the Trigram center her mind. And then Aiah bends to pick up the t-grip and thumbs the button that switches on the plasm connection. Her nerves come awake with a snarl. Her mind, comes alive with a cold neon glow.

It has been far, far too long since she's had a chance to touch this reality.

The Trigram burns in her backbrain. Power sings in her ears.

The first thing Aiah does is send the Trigram through her body, flushing out fatigue toxins, filling every cell with energy. Then she simply sits back in her chair and closes her eyes and lets plasm fill her senses, awareness expanding like ripples in a pond. . . .

She can sense the plasm network around her, the Palace delivery system, conduits and branches, that laces the building like a network of veins, arteries, and capillaries. Sense the vast well of plasm beneath, the fiery lake of raw power that floods out into the city . . .

Hypersensitive, hyperacute, her senses encompass physical reality as well. The texture of the walls impresses itself on her mind, the nubbly surface of a throw pillow, the coolness of the lacy tin frame on the icon of Karlo. The carbon-steel frame of the building, all gentle plasm-generating curves, glows in her perceptions like bones in a fluoroscope. And two people passing in the corridor outside flare in her mind like passing torches. Other, more distant people glimmer at the outside of her awareness.

But there is a curious constraint to her physical sensation. It is as if she is in a box of which her suite is only a component. Focusing her concentration, Aiah expands her senses, gently probes outward . . . no result. She frowns, draws more energy from the plasm tap, pushes her sensorium outward. The only result is the alarming sensation of power flowing away, bleeding out of her, as if her plasm is spiraling down a drain.

Her heart thrashes in her chest. Frightened, she draws her senses inward and tries to understand what has just happened to her.

And then she remembers the diamond-shaped crosshatching in all the window glass, the shining bronze wire.

Aiah realizes she has run up against the Palace's collection web, the network of bronze designed to intercept any plasm attack, deprive it of will, break it into bits, and feed it into the Palace's own plasm system. As long as she was willing to be a passive receiver of outward sensation, the plasm merely amplifying her senses, she was able to enjoy her enhanced sensation; but once she tried to expand her awareness outside the bronze barriers, it absorbed all the plasm she was directing outward.

She hopes she hasn't wasted too much of her precious plasm allowance. If she wants to use telepresence techniques to carry her outside the Palace, she realizes, she'll have to schedule time on one of the Palace's transmission horns.

Aiah allows her passive senses to expand again, swelling to the limit of the artificial constraints imposed by the building's design. The Palace, she remembers, is compartmentalized, like a deep-sea vessel divided by watertight bulkheads. A breach in one component of the building's defense will not necessarily endanger the rest. Her own particular compartment seems to encompass her suite, the two suites adjacent, corresponding suites across the hall, and the same units one floor down—twelve suites in all.

Her sensorium—the plasm-generated extension of her senses—is already in place. Aiah concentrates and builds an anima, a telepresent plasm body, a focus for the sensorium that she can move from place to place, and then she floats the anima out into the hallway outside.

A door opens in the suite to the anima-Aiah's right—just past the bronze barrier—and a man steps out. He is a military officer, middle-aged, uniformed, with a briefcase in one hand. He frowns intently, as if his face had been trained to that expression by long years of practice. Straight-backed, he marches down the corridor, passing right through Aiah's invisible anima. Aiah feels an illusory tingle in her insubstantial nerves.

The man marches on. Aiah drifts slowly down the corridor, tries to listen to what her sensorium is telling her. Only three of the twelve suites within her compartment of the Palace seem to have anyone in them at present, flares of warmth and life floating in Aiah's perceptions. She takes a deep breath, exhales, lets the Palace speak to her, whisper in her ectomorphic ear . . . and then her breath is taken away by a surge of sexual desire that sets her nerves alight.

It originates on the floor below hers. Two people are tangled together in a moment of passion so intense that, once Aiah has opened herself to it, it floods her senses. Her mouth goes dry. For a moment she hesitates, indecisive, uncertain whether she should permit herself to pursue this path, and then she floats downward, passing through floor and wall, and finds the two lovers on their bed.

They are both soldiers, both young men. Uniforms and weapons are stacked neatly on chairs, ready to be donned at the end of their interlude. A bundle of keys sits on a table. Aiah doubts that either one of them is authorized to be here.

The ferocity and certainty of their passion sends a pang through Aiah's nerves. Her heart is racing. She finds herself wanting to join them, to fling herself onto the bed in a sweaty knot of limbs and furious delight.

Voyeurism, she knows, is one of the privileges of the mage. No one, unless they're hiding in a room sheathed with bronze, is immune to this kind of observation. She has never known if she has ever been seen in any of her own private moments. The odds are against it—she can't conceive of anyone with access to that much plasm ever being that interested in her—but there's no way of knowing for certain.

Watching the soldiers, she realizes, is only making her conscious of her own loneliness. . . .

Aiah draws herself away from the scene, dissolves her anima, allows her sensorium to fade into her own natural perceptions. She thumbs the switch on the t-grip and the plasm ebbs from her awareness, leaving her alone in her silent room, aware of the rapid throb of her heart, the warmth and arousal that flush her tissues, the fiery pangs of lust that burn in her groin.

She closes her eyes. An image of the two soldiers seems seared onto her retinas. Loneliness clamps cold fingers on her throat.

She dips a hand between her legs and, in a few urgent moments, relieves herself of her burden of desire.

Aiah draws her legs up into the chair, hugs her knees, lets her breath and heartbeat return to normal. The scent of brewing coffee floats past her nostrils. She has a whole day ahead of her, a long list of things to do.

She wishes she had someone to talk to.

THREE

Aiah is well into her list of requisitions, and the rest—access to certain files, the precise methods by which she will recruit her talent—is not entirely up to her. She is trying to reach Constantine to schedule a meeting, but he's persistently unavailable.

There is a knock on her receptionist's door, and there is no receptionist to answer. She rises from her desk, anticipating workers come to fix her window, and instead her skin crawls at the sight of a pair of the twisted, small figures with black goggle eyes and moist salamander flesh.

"I am Adaveth," one says. "Do you remember me?"

"Yes, Minister, of course," she says. She steels herself and shakes Adaveth's smooth gray hand. Her nostrils twitch for expected odor, but she can detect nothing.

"This is Ethemark," Adaveth continues. "He has been appointed your deputy."

"Pleased to meet you," Aiah lies, and clasps the offered hand.

"Honored, miss," Ethemark says. The voice is surprisingly deep for such a small figure. He is dressed in subdued white lace and black velvet—velvet is worn a great deal here, Aiah has noticed, much more than in Jaspeer.

"Ethemark has a degree in plasm engineering," Adaveth

says. "He is also a mage with specialties in telepresence and tele-engineering."

And therefore, Aiah reads behind his bland, expressionless face, *is much more qualified for your job than you are.*

"I'm sure he will be very useful, Minister," Aiah says.

"During the revolution," Adaveth adds, "Ethemark coordinated several sabotage teams."

"I ran the plasm house in Jaspeer," Aiah says, the defense rising to her lips without her quite intending it. Her claim is not precisely true, but she feels she ought to add a qualification or two to her side of the ledger.

"Ah," Adaveth says. Transparent nictitating membranes partially deploy over his big eyes, giving him a sly look. "In that case, I am sure you will have much to say to one another concerning your service during the coup. I will leave you to your work."

"Thank you for taking the time from your schedule, Minister," Aiah says.

"You are very welcome. We have great hopes for your department, Miss Aiah."

Adaveth leaves in the ensuing silence. Aiah turns to her deputy and looks at him. He gazes up at her with his huge eyes—all iris and pupil, no whites—and gives a little meaningless nod. Aiah wonders if he will ever have anything to say.

At least he doesn't smell bad.

"Truth to tell," Aiah says, "the two of us constitute the entire department right now. I'm keeping the whole of the department files in my briefcase. I have requisitioned rooms and equipment, but I can't be sure I'll get them."

"I expected as much," Ethemark says, the deep voice rolling out of the tiny frame. "The cabinet was pleased to create this department, but each minister will want his own constituency served."

Aiah considers this. "May I expect other deputies to arrive in the next few days?"

"Not if Constantine and Adaveth can keep them out, no." Ethemark's head cocks to one side. "I don't suppose we might sit down? I've been on my feet a lot in the last few weeks—they are webbed, and these shoes are new."

"My office," Aiah says reluctantly. "I would offer to show

you yours, but I don't know where it is, or shall be. Perhaps you should just find one on this floor and take it."

"Perhaps I shall." Agreeably.

"Would you like some coffee? I brought a flask."

"Thank you, no."

They sit. The broken window's plastic sheeting rustles as they talk.

"From my own point of view," Ethemark says, "I am concerned with any potential threat of interference from Triumur Parq."

Parq, Aiah knows, is a priest who had betrayed both sides in the rebellion, playing his own duplicitous game, but managed to end up in the ruling triumvirate anyway.

"Do you think he is likely to interfere?" Aiah asks.

"When the Keremaths took power from the Avians," Ethemark says, "it was in alliance with those of the Dalavan faith, who the Avians had subjected to continuous persecution."

"Dalavans?" Aiah says. "They are not Dalavites? Or are they two different branches of the same—?"

A smile tugs at the corners of Ethemark's lips. "The followers of the prophet Dalavos consider the term *Dalavite* pejorative. The reason involves their rather complex history, and I will spare you the details unless you are truly interested."

"Thank you," Aiah says. "I'm glad you told me this before I met Parq. But I've made you digress—do go on."

"The prophet Dalavos preached continually against those with twisted genes, claiming that they—*we*—are a spiritual evil polluted by our altered genetics." He clasps his hands together, the knuckles turning white. His voice maintains its objective tone, but the gesture informs Aiah of his feelings with perfect eloquence. "His target was the Avian aristocracy, of course, but the rest of the twisted fall almost by accident within the scope of this condemnation."

Aiah watches Ethemark's hands, the furious, trembling pressure they exert on one another.

"I would not find it congenial," Ethemark says, "if Parq were able to control personnel in this department, or indeed in any other. The Dalavan prejudice against the twisted would be exerted to the full."

"If Parq ever controls hiring to that extent," Aiah says, "I would leave. I am not willing to offer my services to a theocracy."

Ethemark's huge deep eyes gaze at Aiah. Regret touches his voice. "You are lucky in having someplace to go, Miss Aiah."

For a moment there is silence. Aiah's nerves tingle with the force of this rebuke.

"You are very frank, Mr. Ethemark."

Nictitating membranes half-shutter Ethemark's eyes, and Aiah feels another eerie shiver up her nerves at this inhuman gesture.

"I answer frankness with frankness," he says. "You were open in regard to our department's deficiencies, and I in regard to what the future might bring us." He sighs, his short child's legs swinging below the chair, and uncouples his hands.

"To tell the truth," he says, "we both owe our jobs to our loyalties. You are loyal to Constantine and I to Adaveth—or perhaps to the purpose each of our patrons represents—and therefore we have no present cause for conflict, as our two patrons are in alliance."

Aiah raises an eyebrow. "No *present* cause?"

Ethemark presses his gray palms together and cocks his large head at a strangely birdlike angle. "I understand that you spent yesterday studying the plasm system within the Palace."

"You are changing the subject, Mr. Ethemark." *And Adaveth has some good spies,* she thinks.

"I hope to return to the subject by way of illustration, but in order to make my point I would like to take you outside the Palace. May I?"

"Now?" Dubiously.

"If you are not otherwise engaged. I gather you are not."

Aiah hides her amusement. Ethemark is trying to rig a chonah for her.

It will take more than this little gray-skinned homunculus to catch one of the Cunning People.

At this point there is a knock on the outer office door, and Aiah rises to discover the workers come to replace her window.

At least she can successfully give orders to the maintenance staff. This was more than she ever achieved in her old job at the Plasm Authority in Jaspeer.

She turns to Ethemark and resigns herself to spending more time with him. "Very well," she says. "I hope we will not have to go too far."

THE BLUE TITAN THREATENS . . .

BUT THE LYNXOID BROTHERS ARE READY!

NEW CHROMOPLAY AT THEATERS NOW!

It isn't far—forty minutes by aerial tram from the station nearest the Palace—but in terms of a difference in character, for sheer existential antithesis, a hundred hours would not be far enough.

Aiah leaves the department files, still in their briefcase, at one of the palace guard stations. A change of clothing is necessary: Ethemark advises waterproof boots, overalls, a waterproof hat. Aiah buys them en route. Dressed like a sewer worker, she enjoys her first ride on an aerial tram. It flies much faster than she'd expected, and when the high winds catch its slab sides the tram bobs alarmingly on its cable. Below, boats leave silver tracks in gray, watery canyons. The white granite towers of Lorkhin Island loom close, then are left behind.

Once they leave the tram station, they find a water taxi, but the taxi will take them only so far, and drops them off on a steel-mesh quay scarred with rust and graffiti. Aiah looks uneasily around her at a decaying, abandoned factory structure and ramshackle brick tenements.

"You are safe," Ethemark says. "These people know me."

Weathered Keremath faces gaze at Aiah from the pontoon opposite. *Our family is* your *family*.

The white towers of Lorkhin Island are still visible on the near horizon. Ethemark hails and hires a boatman who happens to pass the quay. The boatman is twisted—a huge creature, broad and powerful, a walking slab designed for a hard life of manual labor. His family lives on the boat with him, beneath a tarpaulin roof: an old grandmother—a white-haired, wrinkled slab, still powerful as a truck—and a number of children. Their deformities, the boundless terrain of bone and muscle, become more pronounced as they grow older—the youngest is almost human in appearance, the oldest a near-copy of her father. The hull is some kind of foam which, when scarred or torn, can be repaired simply by adding more foam. The boat's engine is a noisy old two-cycle outboard that runs off the same hydrogen tank as the single-burner stove, and also powers a dim light stuck up on a short mast forward.

Ethemark nods toward their hosts. "These people are among the more common of the altered," he remarks conversationally. "They're commonly called 'stonefaces.'" Nictitating membranes shade his eyes. "*My* kind," he adds, "are 'embryos.'"

"Are these terms, ah, insulting?" Aiah asks. "Would I use them in polite company?"

"It depends on how you use them," Ethemark says.

Aiah nods. There are Jaspeeri words for the Barkazil that can vary the same way in their meanings.

Aiah feels a chill of apprehension as the boat slips away from the warmth of Shieldlight, into the darkness beneath a pair of lumbering concrete pontoons: the buildings above the pontoons are crumbling brick tenements, bad enough in themselves, and who knows what lives underneath?

The boat moves slowly onward. Aiah's eyes adjust to the darkness. Ethemark stands by the little mast forward and signals to Aiah. "Will you join me?"

Reluctantly Aiah makes her way forward in the last of the light, stands, and holds the mast for balance. A webwork of lights glows ahead, dim yellow dots that resolve, as Aiah nears, into bulbs strung on long strands. Somewhere there is the unmuffled cough of a generator, heard even over the racket of the boat's two-cycle engine.

Slowly the dimensions of a floating city emerge, a city

built in the shadow of the larger, Shieldlit floating city above. On the fringes are boats packed together, seemingly at random, and farther in are rafts, barges, a listing old tug . . . everything strung together by planks, rope or cable bridges, scaffolding, ladders, a structure of arcane complexity. . . . Cooking smells float in the thick air, along with the odor of fecal matter, of ooze and rich salt ocean. And, dimly seen in the light of the strung bulbs, the twisted: hulking shapes like the boatman, moving massively in the darkness like moving walls; lithe small forms like Ethemark that scamper over the scaffolding; and other, rarer figures, fantastic things in nightmare shapes, things with horns and claws, with extra limbs or no limbs, with serpent scales or green-glowing lamp eyes that turn to follow Aiah as the boat moves deeper into the darkness.

"There are hundreds of these places," Ethemark says, his voice a deep counterpoint to the high-pitched bang of the engine. "Perhaps thousands. No one has ever counted them. No one knows how many people live in them, but there must be many millions. They are called half-worlds, and those who live in them are accounted half-human."

There is a splash ahead in the water, and Aiah's heart leaps. Whatever it was has disappeared, leaving a ring of oily ripples. She puts a hand to her throat, looks at Ethemark.

"Plasm is generated here, isn't it?"

The strung bulbs glow yellow in Ethemark's saucerlike pupils. "Of course. The plasm-generating matter in the boats and rafts is insignificant, but some plasm is generated in resonance with the larger structures of the city around us, and additional plasm is . . . acquired from one place or another."

"And what is done with it?"

"The people here own it. They use it for their own purposes. The boss decides."

Aiah scowls. "Who picks the boss?"

"They are self-appointed, most of them. One might consider them a type of gangster, though gangsters of a lower order. The Silver Hand lives on the population as a predator lives on prey: the bosses of the half-worlds live among their people in a kind of symbiosis. The bosses cannot afford too great a tyranny—people could always leave—and besides, in the end, the rafts are dangerous places, and a tyrannous boss would not survive them."

Aiah finds this assonance unconvincing. In her experience, a minor gangster is only a major gangster who hasn't got the breaks. She hates them all.

A huge barge looms to starboard, sides streaked with rust. Aiah looks up to see a horned head gazing at her with glittering eyes, and her heart skips a beat before she realizes it's a goat in a pen, kept for milk or meat. Elsewhere on the barge a large video set, its oval screen set high, burns its images downward for an audience of twisted children. Poppet the Puppet sings a song about the alphabet, her image gleaming off the restless goggle eyes and corded muscle of her audience.

Aiah remembers watching Poppet during her own childhood. The juxtaposition of the familiar and the strange sends an eerie shiver up her spine.

"This place is called Aground," Ethemark says, "because as the sea has receded the pontoons around us have settled on the bottom. I was born here."

The lights of his childhood home glimmer in Ethemark's big saucer eyes.

"Why is the sea receding?"

"People have found other things to do with the water."

A stench floats toward the boat. Aiah shrinks from it. "The conditions. . . ," she begins, appalled. She had grown up poor in Jaspeer, but has never seen anything like this.

"Infant mortality is very high," Ethemark says. "Sanitary conditions are not very good, though they're better than one might expect, and everywhere there is poverty and neglect. The twisted often have special medical needs, and there is no medicine here in any case. Educational opportunities," dryly, "tend to be limited."

Aiah looks at him. It is the first hint of irony she has seen in him.

"I was the son of the boss," he says, "so I got out. I was lucky." He stands on tiptoe, points. "My cousin is the new boss, and lives there. We will visit him."

Aiah's courage quails at the thought. Ethemark's large eyes turn to her.

"This place is illegal, of course. All the half-worlds are, but certain people are paid off, and others don't care or find the people who live here useful . . . and besides there is a need for places like this, so they exist. But any of these people could be driven out of here at any time, and all these homes dispersed or destroyed by any official inclined to do so. The population has no rights in the matter."

He looks up at Aiah, and urgency enters his voice. "I said that your patron and mine have no *present* cause to disagree. I bring you to this place to show you where my loyalties truly lie. If anyone strikes at these people, tries to cut them off from what little they have, then I will owe your people no loyalty. Do you understand?"

Aiah shrinks from a cold drizzle that falls from some invisible drain high overhead. The boss's house, covered in scaffolds and with red lights dangling overhead, floats nearer.

"What of the bosses?" she asks. "These little gangsters you talk about, one of whom is your cousin. Are your loyalties to them?"

Ethemark's thin lips draw back from his teeth, giving him a strange urgency. "Miss Aiah," he says, "at this moment in time, the bosses are *necessary*. If these people were no longer driven to live here, the bosses would no longer exist. They would disappear of their own accord."

Aiah lacks Ethemark's optimism. She has never known gangsters to vanish of their own free will.

The boatman cuts the engine and the boat drifts up to a half-submerged landing. One of the children lashes the boat to an upright. From somewhere comes the surprising smell of coffee.

"This way."

Ethemark reveals an unexpected agility as he springs from the boat, touches one boot to the half-submerged platform, then leaps to the rungs of a ladder that seems to be bolted together from bits of old pipe. Aiah is less graceful, and while Ethemark scurries up the ladder Aiah soaks her boots to the ankle as the platform sinks beneath her weight.

"Ethemark!" It's a juvenile voice, but the sound comes from a mountainous shadow, dimly seen in the faint light on a catwalk above Aiah's head.

"Hello, Craftig," Ethemark says. "How's the family?"

Craftig's answer is expansive, enthusiastic, and full of digressions. Aiah climbs the improvised ladder to a narrow overhead catwalk that runs across several of the moored vessels. The half-world of Aground spreads out below her on either side like some strange half-lit blight spreading across the water. She can see grotesque faces flickering in the reflected light of gas stoves. The generator thuds at her ears, and the smell of fecal matter is overwhelming.

"Hi, lady," the boy says.

Aiah's attention snaps back to the two twisted. "Hello, Craftig," she says.

Craftig, not having got his growth, is about a head shorter than Aiah, but he is built on such a massive scale that he must outweigh her by at least a factor of three.

"This is Miss Aiah," Ethemark says. "She's my boss."

"Nice to meet you," Craftig says.

"We need to see Sergeant Lamarath," Ethemark says.

"Great! This way!"

Craftig turns and scurries back along the catwalk. He has a bad limp—one knee folds under him at every step—but that doesn't seem to slow him down. Now that Aiah is closer, she can see that something's gone very wrong with his twisted genetics. Bone masses seem to have grown abnormally, and gray lumps of bone protrude through the skin in some places. Aiah's stomach turns over, and she clenches her teeth and marches herself deeper into Aground.

Ethemark and Aiah follow the boy down the platform, then along a swaying bridge made of scavenged cable. Below, Aiah can see faces turned up to watch her. She can't tell whether they are curious or hostile, but the sea of glittering eyes gives her the shivers anyway.

"I apologize for the smell," Ethemark says. "We have an agreement with the dolphins to keep the water clean. They provided us with the generator, and we power it with methane made from human waste. That way Aground gets electricity, the water doesn't get fouled, and we can sell the residue for fertilizer, which is used to pay the people for bringing in their night soil."

Aiah places her feet carefully on the swaying bridge. She's

incredulous at the thought that *this* water is considered clean. And the implications of Ethemark's statement seize her attention.

"The dolphins? Do you—do the people here—deal with them on a regular basis?"

"Naturally. We have a number of issues in common—we are both exiles from the world above, and neither of us were high on the old government's list of priorities. The dolphins have an interest in sanitation because they are susceptible to a wide range of human diseases, so they've made similar deals with most of the other half-worlds. I've heard it said that they are not a separate species at all, but humans adapted for an aquatic environment. Twisted genetics, just like ours."

He turns, his unblinking eyes gazing at Aiah like spheres of polished black glass. "The dolphins turned against the Kere-maths because of the water situation. Did you know that?"

Aiah shakes her head. The bridge sways uneasily beneath her feet, and droplets of condensation spatter on her hat.

"The Keremaths allowed their waste disposal systems to deteriorate. Thousands of tons of waste were being dumped untreated into the water every day. The repair went out for bids, but there was the usual fiddling over the contracts, and the dumping went on for *twelve years.*" Fury sharpens Ethemark's deep tones. "Once the fighting was over, Constantine sent in some military engineers to the waste plants, and they fixed the problem in two days. *Two days!*"

"Hey, Ethemark!" Craftig's voice calls through the darkness. "Did you forget the way? It's over here!"

Ethemark turns abruptly and steps off the swaying bridge onto another platform. Aiah follows, placing her feet carefully. The only route down is a ladder, then a pair of planks spanning the gap from one craft to another.

At the end of the journey is a barge with a building constructed on its rusting deck plates. It's an assemblage of parts thrown together almost randomly: the superstructure of some other vessel; a picture window out of a streetfront display; a large trailer, wheels removed. The whole thing is decorated with long strands of decorative red lights, giving it a misplaced holiday air.

Aiah feels her spine stiffen as she nears the building: there are some stonefaces waiting here, scarred visages atop huge, muscular bodies, obvious bodyguards. An assortment of people sit waiting: a mother with children overflowing her lap, an elderly woman holding a scabrous-looking chicken in a cage, a young gray-skinned embryo reading a book in the darkness with his large goggle eyes. Petitioners, Aiah assumes, here to ask the big man for favors.

Craftig speaks to one of the guards, and then Ethemark, and the guards look at Aiah before one of them disappears into the structure. Aiah stands for a long, uncomfortable moment, hating every second of this gangster ritual, and then the guard returns and gestures for Ethemark and Aiah to enter.

"See you later, Miss Aiah!" Craftig calls.

Aiah stops, turns to the boy, forces a smile onto her face. "Nice to meet you, Craftig. Thanks for showing us the way."

The building is tidy inside, one small, whitewashed room after another. The boss meets Aiah in a comfortable office that features a battered metal desk, gunmetal file cabinets, and the strong smell of cigar smoke. Brass-rimmed portholes look out into the darkness, and the interior lights are dim: the big-eyed twisted probably have no problem seeing, but Aiah finds herself squinting. There are no straight lines in the architecture, or angles, but rounded corners and a barrel ceiling. It's not a feature of nautical design, but defense: the room's been wrapped in bronze mesh in a crude attempt to defend against plasm attack, then plastered and painted. Bits of the plaster have flaked off to reveal the mesh beneath.

High on one wall, something coiled hangs from a projection. At first, in the dim light, Aiah thinks it's a canvas fire hose, and then she realizes it's alive. A huge snake, or a monster created by plasm, kept as a pet. She shivers.

"Miss Aiah," Ethemark says, "this is my cousin, Sergeant Lamarath."

"How do you do," Aiah says, and offers her hand. *Pleased to meet you,* under the circumstances, would be a hopeless misrepresentation.

Lamarath takes her hand in his moist, nicotine-stained grip.

"The 'Sergeant' isn't official," he says. "It's just something that goes with the job." His voice is husky with smoking.

He's one of the small, gray-skinned, large-eyed twisted—as of course he would be, being a cousin of Ethemark's—and is dressed casually in high-clipped boots and a pair of tan overalls. His expression, like all expressions here, is unreadable. Aiah realizes that if she has very many of these people in her department, she's going to have a hard time telling them apart.

Lamarath picks up a small cigar from an overflowing ashtray and props it in the corner of his mouth. "Please sit down."

"Thank you."

The chairs are metal, with—incongruously bright—plastic-covered cushions. She sits.

"Congratulations on your appointment," Lamarath says. "You must be very excited."

"At the moment," sitting, "I'm very overwhelmed."

"Would you like something to eat? Drink?"

The journey has left her without an appetite. And gangster hospitality is something she could do without.

"No," she says. "Thank you."

He sits, inhales smoke, blows it out, then leans forward and props his elbows on his desk. "What do you think of our little community?"

"I think it could use some light," Aiah says.

Nictitating membranes eclipse a third of the Sergeant's eyes. "Has Ethemark told you of my proposition?"

Aiah looks at her deputy. "No. He hasn't."

"Simply this," Lamarath says. "I want my people to be left alone until things change outside."

So this visit is, perhaps inevitably, official. Aiah straightens her back, puts her feet flat on the floor, clasps her hands in her lap. The proper civil servant, ready to bargain.

"Change how?" she asks.

Lamarath jabs his cigar into the ashtray. "My people need a lot of things."

"Housing, obviously. Medical care."

Aiah looks at Ethemark, who shifts uneasily in his seat. "That isn't our department," she points out. "We're strictly plasm hunters."

"That plasm is all we've got," Lamarath says. "That and the strength of our bodies. The plasm we steal doesn't amount to much, and if we sometimes tap some electricity or fresh water, or steal some phone or video service, or even motor off with some equipment left lying around on the quays, well, that doesn't add up to a great deal."

"But the half-worlds are vulnerable," Ethemark points out.

"Yes." Lamarath's husky voice grates with anger. "If your superiors demand some cheap victories, the half-worlds are where you can find them on short notice. The cops can bust up ten half-worlds per day for *weeks,* and it will all look very good on video—*'Dockyard thieves arrested. Underworld plasm theft ring broken up. Fifty suspects taken into custody. Vagrants dispersed from illegal, unsanitary settlement.'*—We know how this sort of thing works, you see."

"It's happened often enough," Ethemark says. "The cops get enough complaints from their superiors, they'll come after the easy targets instead of the real thieves. The real thieves can afford better payoffs."

"If you disperse the people here," Lamarath says, "there's no housing for them, so they'll have to find another half-world; and in the meantime you've taken everything they own and deprived them of protection. Our plasm is all that keeps the Silver Hand off our necks, not to mention the fact that we use it for doctoring and so on." He turns and looks up at the huge snake hanging on the wall. "Right, Doc?"

The snake slowly raises its head. "Absolutely," it says.

Cold terror floods Aiah's veins. It isn't a snake, it's some kind of twisted human being—the thing's bald head is that of an old man, with wizened features, deep brown skin, and glittering, yellow eyes. Writhing feathery tentacles circle the creature's neck.

"This is Doctor Romus," Lamarath adds. "He's my advisor."

"The title, like that of Sergeant, goes with the job," Romus says, then adds, "Pleased to meet you." His voice is high-pitched, with odd, reedlike overtones.

"Hello," Aiah manages. Her nails dig into her thighs, a reminder not to run screaming from the room.

"I would have greeted you earlier," Romus says, "but I

was engaged in a little act of telepresence." He turns to Lamarath. "The Mokhrath Canal house is still active."

Lamarath nods. "Thank you, Doctor."

"My pleasure."

Dr. Romus isn't hanging from a hook, Aiah realizes, it's a plasm connection. He's a mage, and he's been on a mission.

Lamarath opens a drawer, pulls out a folder, and pushes it across the desk.

"The twisted get around, you know," he says. "People make a point of not seeing us, or think we're too stupid to understand; or they employ us for things that aren't strictly legal."

Aiah finds a reply bubbling from her lips. "My people, too," she says. The Jaspeeris had never known quite what to do with the Barkazils. Her teachers at school, and her superiors at the Authority, had always been faintly surprised whenever she said something intelligent.

Lamarath gives her a curious look at this remark. He nudges the folder toward Aiah again. "This is for you. A list of twelve plasm houses in this district. Most of them Silver Hand, some not."

Aiah restrains the impulse to take the folder, clasps her hands in her lap again. "Please understand," she says. "I'm not in a position to really dictate policy."

Lamarath frowns at her. "*Influence* policy," he says. "That's all I ask."

Aiah takes a breath. "All I can assure you," she says carefully, "is that any minor—I do mean *minor*—plasm thefts in the half-worlds will not be given a high priority by my department."

"I will speak to my . . . counterparts in other half-worlds," Lamarath says. "I hope to be able to provide you with more information along these lines."

She looks at him—her heart bangs in her throat, and it's difficult to steady her gaze into the huge dark eyes—and she takes good care with her words. "I will be grateful for any information. But understand that I will make no bargains with anyone concerning any plasm thefts brought to my attention. I can't set policy. All I can say is that, from the limited knowledge I have of the subject, the half-worlds will not be a high priority."

Lamarath holds her eyes for a long moment—behind her own composed expression, Aiah thinks wildly of assassination, of how no one knows she is here and how she could so easily be disposed of—and then gives a brief nod and reaches for another cigar.

"That will have to do, then," he says.

"Nice to have met you," says Dr. Romus.

Aiah's mind swims as she follows Ethemark out of the barge. The boy Craftig waits outside, playing on the deck plates with toy figures of the Lynxoid Brothers, and cheerfully leads them aloft and back to the landing, then calls "Long live the revolution!" as the boat begins its journey to the open air.

Outside the day has became overcast, a skein of gray cloud over the Shield, and Aiah shivers in the faint light. She considers the bargain she has just made—for it was a bargain, deny it though she would—and wonders if she is a fool. She can't even tell if she's just been bribed. If she has become the hireling of some minor gangster, and betrayed everything she holds dear, all through ignorance, or fear for her life, or through some hopeless flaw in herself.

Whatever decisions she makes, correct or not, corrupt or not, she knows she will pay for them sooner or later. She only hopes the payment is something that she can bear.

---

*A STATUTE AGAINST THE WILL OF GOD
IS NO LAW.*

A THOUGHT-MESSAGE FROM HIS PERFECTION,
THE PROPHET OF AJAS

Item #5: Gil?
Item #6: Family?

There's yesterday's list, its final two items still a weight on her conscience. Aiah still can't bring herself to contact Gil, but she decides she can talk to someone else back in Jaspeer and at least let them know she's well.

She looks at a wall clock: 20:04, halfway through third shift. People at home are probably still awake. Aiah goes to the communications array set into the wall near her bed, dons the headset—a nice lightweight model, with gold accents on the earpieces and the mouthpiece, a far cry from the heavy black plastic rig she's accustomed to—and then presses the bright silver keys to connect her to her grandmother Galaiah back in Jaspeer.

"Hello?"

"Nana?" Aiah says. "This is Aiah."

"It's Aiah!" the woman bellows to someone else in the room. Aiah winces at her grandmother's volume. There's a sudden expectant babble of voices in the background, but then Galaiah hushes them.

"Where are you?" she demands. "Are you all right?"

Aiah turns down the headset volume. Her grandmother is a bit deaf and has a tendency to shout.

"I'm fine, Nana. I'm in Caraqui, and I have a new job."

"You've got a good job?" Galaiah shouts. A refugee from the Barkazi Wars, she has a fine grasp of the essentials.

"A very important job. I'm going to be running a government department."

"She's running a government department in Caraqui!" Galaiah relays the information to her listeners.

"Who's there?" Aiah asks.

"Landro and his family."

Landro is Aiah's cousin. He had been a plasm diver once, searching through forgotten tunnels and sealed-off basements in search of plasm he could sell. Caught, he'd done his term in Chonmas Prison, and now works in a hardware store.

"Have you talked to your mother?" Galaiah asks.

"Not yet."

"You should call her."

"I will." Reluctantly. Aiah's mother is an indefatigable dramatist, and Aiah dreads the inevitable reaction: breast-beating, weeping, *how could you do this to me?* She can predict every word of the call.

"Those Authority creepers are still looking for you," Galaiah says.

"Let them look." She smiles: she'd got clean away, money in the bank and a new future.

"Esmon's witch Khorsa told everybody how she helped you get away."

"Did she tell the creepers?"

"Of course not," scornfully. "She said she didn't know anything!"

It occurs to Aiah that perhaps they have already told the creepers more than they ought to have.

"Perhaps we shouldn't talk about this on the phone. . . ."

"Hm?" Galaiah thinks about it for a moment. "Fine, then," she says, and changes the subject. "There's a lot of news about Caraqui on the video. They say Constantine's in charge and that he's going to change everything."

"That's . . . not really true, Nana. Constantine is only a minister in the government. But yes, we hope things are going to change."

"That Constantine, he's another of your *passus,* isn't he?" she asks, using the Barkazil word for dupe or victim. She chortles. "That's a lovely chonah you've rigged."

"Constantine isn't my *passu.*"

"Either he is your *passu,* or you are his."

Aiah can't find the strength to dispute this simple logic.

Besides, her grandmother might well be right.

"Your longnose lover is back in Jaspeer," Galaiah adds. "He's been calling the family and trying to find you."

Sadness catches at Aiah's throat. "Gil?"

"You haven't called him, either, hanh?" Galaiah is gleeful—she'd never approved of Aiah taking up with a Jaspeeri. She holds the traditional Barkazil opinion that the rest of humanity is only useful as prey for the artful, devious, and highly superior Cunning People.

It's precisely that attitude—that the Barkazil are a magical species above the laws that govern lesser beings—that led to the self-destruction of the Metropolis of Barkazi, and therefore to Galaiah's journey as a refugee to Jaspeer. Aiah has always refrained from pointing this out to her grandmother. "I didn't know Gil was back from Gerad," Aiah says, perfectly aware of the inadequacy of her excuse.

There's a buzz on the commo array and a flashing green light, the signal that someone else is trying to call. "Excuse me, Nana," Aiah says. "I'm getting another call. Hold on a moment."

She pushes the hold button, then turns the dial that switches the solenoids in the commo array. There's a click and electric buzz, and then Aiah answers.

"You left messages for me." It's Constantine's baritone, and Aiah's warm blood sings in her ears at the sound of it.

"I couldn't get back to you earlier," he says. "What did you require?"

Aiah tries to organize her thoughts. "I needed to talk to you . . . ," she begins, and then begins to look frantically for her list.

"You're in your suite? May I come see you?" The voice takes on a lazy, self-satisfied tone. "I would like to relate my latest triumphs. I am pleased to report that it has been a very good day."

"Yes. Of course."

"I'm just a few corridors away. I'll see you in a couple of minutes."

He presses the disconnect button, and Aiah jumps for the switch to connect herself to Galaiah.

No time to bathe and change. Damn it.

"Nana? That was business. I've got to go."

"Give me your phone number!"

"Yes." She gives it.

"I got a question!" the old lady says.

"Yes. Quickly."

"Can you get jobs for some of your family?"

The question stops her dead. "I don't know," she says.

"Most of us have never had a good job."

"Let me think. I'll call you again. Okay?"

"Call your mother!"

The imperious command rings out just as Aiah presses the disconnect button. She brushes her hair, checks herself in the mirror, wishes again there was time for at least a shower. She puts on the priceless ivory necklace that Constantine bestowed upon her, then anoints herself with the

Cedralla perfume Constantine gave to her their last time together, before he flew off to Caraqui and the coup.

Memories, scent and sensation, worn about her body like little charms. She can only hope the tiny magics will do the job.

When she opens the door to his knock, Constantine rolls into the room like the irresistible tide. He's no longer wearing the proper velvet suit of the minister, but clothing meant for ease and comfort: a blousy black shirt, a jacket of soft black suede imprinted with a design of geomantic foci, suede boots, no lace. The clothing suits him better than the confining garb of the politician, provides him a physical scope to match the ranging of his mind.

"The cabinet meets daily," he says, "and all the news is good."

"Would you like to tell me the details over a bottle of wine?"

"And food, if you've got it." He prowls to the kitchen, opens the refrigerator, gazes inside.

Aiah scurries after. "I can throw something together, if you like."

He turns, his massive hands close on her shoulders, and he propels her firmly to a chair next to the dining room table. His scent eddies along her nerves.

"Sit," he says. "I'll cook."

"You don't know where—"

"Yes I do. All these suites are built alike."

Aiah surrenders—the fact of his touch, this near-embrace, make surrender all too easy—and allows herself to sit. She has been in the kitchen so little she has no real notion it's hers. She cocks her head and regards him from this new angle. "I didn't know you could cook, Minister."

An amused glow warms his brown eyes. "I didn't say I could cook *well*. But I have absorbed at least a few principles of cooking which I hope, in this case, will prove universal."

He takes off his jacket, opens the pantry door, gazes in thoughtfully. Plucks things from the shelf and finds a saucepan. He cocks an eye at her.

"I take it all this dates from the previous administration?"

Aiah shrugs. "Who has time to shop?"

"I wish you would remember to eat from time to time." His big body prowls the confined kitchen with perfect assurance. He surveys his finds, then reaches for a knife.

"Our main course will have to come out of cans. And the vegetables are far from fresh, but I will try to make do."

"There are few sights as attractive," Aiah observes, "as that of a man cooking."

"Wait till you see how dinner turns out before you judge how attractive I am."

He sets water boiling, opens cans, and finds a bottle of wine on the built-in rack. "Do you know," he says, looking in drawers for a tool to remove the bottle cap, "that thirty percent of the population of Caraqui are on the government payroll?"

"The drawer on your left, Minister. We have that many civil servants?"

"Civil servants plus the dole, yes. Besides a civil service so bloated that it defies comprehension—the Keremaths wanted *everyone* on their payroll—the government owns a surprising number of commercial firms. All the communications companies save for the broadcast station controlled by the Dalavans, the Worldwide News Service, the video networks, construction and shipping firms. Factories. Fisheries. Office buildings. Even restaurants! And if you add the firms that the Keremaths owned personally, the total is even higher." He gives a knowing smile as he opens the wine bottle and pours. "They arranged things with a certain criminal inevitability," he says. "I find the pattern familiar—my own family in Cheloki were no better. There was a law that all streets had to be paved with a certain grade of concrete, but the only company offering such a grade was owned by the Keremaths. And another special type of nonporous concrete was required for the pontoons that underlie all the buildings, and again the Keremaths' company was the only company that offered it. To prevent dependence on foreign energy sources, only domestically produced hydrogen is permitted in the metropolis, but the New Theory Hydrogen Company, the only one in Caraqui, was owned by the Keremaths. . . ." A laugh rumbles deep in his barrel chest. "The only New

Theory, so far as I can tell, was that the Keremaths got *everything*." He touches glasses. "To your health."

"To yours." The amber wine tastes of smoke and walnuts.

"Have you seen the news? How one scandal after another is being revealed?"

"I have been a little busy, and haven't watched the news."

"It is the function of a new government to discredit the old, and fortunately in our case we have but to tell the truth." He tilts his head back, savoring the wine. "Within a few months the scandals will multiply, and the Keremaths will be so discredited that no one will want them back."

Constantine returns to the kitchen, and gives a cynical smile. "Last shift the cabinet reacted to these continuing scandalous revelations, and have annexed the Keremaths' companies, personal property, and bank accounts."

"And thus the state acquires that many more civil servants. Was that one of the triumphs you mentioned?"

Constantine smiles coldly. His bright steel knife slices onions as if they were Keremath livers. "No. Acquiring the companies was not a difficult decision—we could hardly leave them under the Keremaths' ownership, after all. It was in deciding the companies' ultimate fate wherein my brilliant political talents were fully deployed."

"You wanted to sell the companies," Aiah says. "And others wished to keep them."

Constantine gives an impatient smile. "It is a source of astonishment to me that such things are even matters for debate," he says. "The state should be an instrument of evolution, not a bank, a stock exchange, or a nursery for inefficient enterprises. But—" He shrugs. "Not all the cabinet members are soldiers or idealists. Some have political instincts that are quite sound, in their fashion. And the possibility of employing the New Theory Hydrogen Company and the other concerns as a source for patronage was, I suspect, a temptation to more than one."

"And the triumvirate?"

"Parq was anxious to stuff the companies with his retainers. Colonel Drumbeth was of a mind with me. And Hilthi—an interesting man, Hilthi—seemed to have no interest whatever in the economic issues, but rather a care for the

companies' moral health." He laughs. Chopped onions fly
from his fingers and fall hissing into the pan. "An unusual
attitude for a journalist, don't you think?"

"I know nothing of Hilthi."

"A noble man, truly. The greatest enemy the Keremaths
had—" His eyes turn to Aiah, glittering. "Until myself," he
adds. Steam rises as he throws noodles into the boiling water
and stirs things in the pan. His voice turns reflective. "In a
tyranny, a single dissenting individual can sometimes engage
in a dialogue with the entire government. Hilthi was raised in
Caraqui and found the Keremaths repulsive and denounced
them. Was sent to prison, came out, and denounced them
again, after having sensibly put a border or two between
himself and the Specials. He made it his life's work to expose
the Keremaths for what they were. He meticulously gathered
facts, published them, made brilliant propaganda. It is a
monument to his skill that the Keremaths referred to dissidents as 'Hilthists.'"

He laughs, a low rumble. "He was invited into the triumvirate to offer a certain moral tone to what otherwise
might have been seen only as a tawdry adventure in military
government." He gives Aiah another sly, sideways glance.
"Certainly he provides a tone that *I* lack." He sighs. "But the
fellow knows nothing about government. He desires only
that we practice virtue. He doesn't care whether the companies are sold or not, only that any Keremath loyalists in their
hierarchy be punished."

"Is that so bad?"

"The crime of which most stand accused is making the
money for the Keremaths. There are far worse crimes in
Caraqui for us to concern ourselves with. I was able to edge
him along to the position that any serious crimes on the part
of any of the managers would be dealt with, but that running
a company was not necessarily a crime."

"Very good."

"So Hilthi was brought around. Parq was outnumbered.
The army was bought off—it will be doubled in size to two
divisions, an unnecessary expense, but it gives the officer
class new commands and new promotions and may serve to
keep them quiet. And, after a little political magic"—he

sprinkles things into the saucepan—"decisions were made. The companies will be sold. We anticipate no difficulty with that—they were all remarkably profitable, after all. The profits will help to finance reorganization in various other state enterprises, which will also be sold as soon as they can be made efficient. I convinced them, you see, that it had to be done now, while martial law was still in force, because a popular government would not be able to shrink in size with the proper ruthlessness. So the enlarged army will hold the metropolis together while structural changes take place, and then—we hope—they will march back to the barracks before they are all possessed of the delusion that they can actually run a modern state."

The smoky wine murmurs in Aiah's veins. "But they run Caraqui now, don't they?"

"They have some notion they might be in charge, yes. But running a metropolis requires the ability to count above a hundred, which generally speaking the officer class of Caraqui does not possess. Here." He passes her a plate.

Noodles, and on them onions, smoked pigeon, and shredded black olives in a light sauce. Tossed salad. The amber wine.

Surprisingly delicious. The onions, pigeon, and olives are three stark flavors that should not blend, but somehow they do, and the wine goes beautifully with it all.

"I'm very impressed, Metro—Minister," Aiah says.

Constantine gives his rumbling laugh. "Metro-minister is a title in which I could rejoice." He brings his own plate to the table. "You may consider this dish a metaphor for politics." He points to his plate with the tip of a knife. "Onions, olives, smoked fowl. Drumbeth, Parq, Hilthi. Diverse people, diverse interests, diverse tastes. Brought into union with a little skill on the part of your deponent."

She raises her glass, offers him a salute. "Congratulations."

"Thank you." He tastes his creation, raises his eyebrows in pleasant surprise. "Better than I thought, in truth."

"Let's hope it's an omen."

"Let's." He sips the wine, takes a few more bites. Looks up from his plate. "And how are you getting on with Ethemark?"

"It was—" She takes a breath. "An interesting day."

"Tell me."

She tells him. They finish their meal and take the wine bottle to the couch. "So what have I done?" she asks. "Have I sold the department to some little gangster in return for a handful of names?"

He considers this. "You judge yourself overharshly," he says. "You have made no promises to this man, none at all. What you have done is make a policy decision—the first of a great many—to the effect that you will concentrate your efforts on one area of your mandate and not another." His frown changes to a catlike smile. "It is a decision I support fully, by the way. The half-worlds are potentially a great resource. We should not waste them, or their people."

Relief eases the tension that clings between Aiah's shoulder blades. "But what about Ethemark? His loyalties are clearly with the half-worlds, and not with us."

"That will require tactful handling, if and when the difference becomes important. But you need not worry over the loyalties of most of your people—I've decided that everyone will require deep plasm scans, to discover where their loyalties really lie."

Aiah looks at him in surprise. "Who's going to do the scanning?"

"The Force of the Interior. Sorya's department. It's the sort of thing they're good at."

Alarm jangles along Aiah's nerves. "I don't want Sorya in my brain!" she cries. Involuntarily she lifts a hand protectively to guard her head.

Constantine reaches out, takes her hand in his, gently lowers it to her lap. "Not you," he says. "Nor Ethemark, nor any other political appointee I am forced to accept. But everyone else, yes. You need an absolutely straight department, even if we have to hire every single one of them from outside Caraqui, and plasm scans are the only way to make certain."

She clasps Constantine's big hand in her smaller ones, looks at him. A shiver of memory raises the hairs on her nape. "I saw Taikoen yesterday, Metropolitan."

He looks startled, then masters himself and nods. "Yes. He is . . . making use . . . of an officer of the Specials. A killer, a torturer. He broke hundreds in his dungeons, and murdered many." His lip curls in disdain. "Such people are best disposed of with the trash. If anyone deserves Taikoen, it is he."

Aiah finds her lower lip shivering and wills it to stop. "Who knows about him? It."

Constantine's eyes gaze somberly into hers. "You. Martinus, my bodyguard. Myself. Sorya may suspect, though I have not told her. And lastly that torturer, who though his body lives is already dead."

A shudder runs through her. "He recognized me. I was terrified."

· "He will not harm you." Constantine puts his arms around her, cradles her against his massive chest. "Making use of Taikoen is the worst thing I have ever done. It is the worst thing I can ever *conceive*." His hand caresses her jawline, turns her face up to his. There is a smouldering anger in his eyes, in the twisting muscles of his jaw. "Taikoen weighs on me," Constantine says. "He is necessary, but . . ." There is a flicker in his pensive eyes, echo of a chill thought that passes through his mind. "I hope I judged this aright. The balance of rights and wrongs, the hope of a better outcome."

Aiah smiles wanly. "It isn't all as easy as cooking, is it?"

He nods in answer. There is a kind of painful hopelessness in his eyes. "Taikoen is a trap, I know. He is too powerful a weapon to ignore, but the very knowledge of him is . . . corrupting. I hope that someday I may be strong enough to do without him." He takes a deep breath. "And he is, sometimes, still the Taikoen who fought the Slaver Mages. Even in his current form he is not without his share of greatness. And he is . . ." Constantine searches for a word. "He is *impaired*, and, for all his power, diminished. . . . He has lost his humanity, and he wants it again, and he can't find it."

He straightens, visibly summons himself, and gives Aiah a sharp glance. "You know that I worshipped Taikoen once, as part of a . . ." He licks his lips. "A cult. My cousin Heromë was priest."

"You told me this," Aiah says.

"It isn't a part of my life that fills me with pride. I was debased and desperate, and I sought company as debased as

I . . . and there was Heromë, in charge of my grandfather's prisons, feeding prisoners to this *thing,* and playing at worshipping it. But strangely, it was seeing Taikoen so degraded that brought back my own pride—I had no great opinion of myself, princeling of a bandit regime, but I knew that I was better than *this.* And when I came to know him, I managed to remind him of his own greatness, and managed to instill in him a memory of his own pride. . . ." An image of that pride broods in Constantine's eyes, along with bright defiance.

"And that," he says, "was the end of Heromë and his worshippers—Taikoen engulfed them all. It was my first strike against my family, for all they never knew it." He looks down at Aiah, his glance uneasy. "And Taikoen has followed me ever since. And I have made use of him from time to time, and paid the price."

She reaches up a hand, touches his cheek. He looks down at her, a kind of need plain on his face. "I hope I may have your understanding in this," he says. "And better, your compassion."

Aiah kisses him, driving her lips up into his. The only comfort she can offer, she thinks, is the comfort of her body. For a moment Constantine absorbs the kiss, inhales it as if it's a consolation, an absolution, and then the kiss awakens in him a tigerish spirit, a fierceness, and his answering kiss is like a kiss of fire.

He carries her bodily to the bedroom, then lays her on the bed and takes off his clothes. She presses the button that polarizes the windows, and in the resulting shadow she looks at the half-light gleaming off his huge shoulders, his massive arms, the powerful muscles of his thighs and buttocks. . . .

Either he is your passu, *or you are his.* Her grandmother's voice floats through her mind, and she puts the treacherous thought away.

Aiah welcomes Constantine into the circle of her arms, the circle of her legs. Outside the circle all is dubious, in flux, but the weight of Constantine's body on hers assures her of her own certainty in the world, of her own consequence, at least until all identity, all thought, is obliterated by climatic fire.

They lie together only a short while before Constantine

has to leave. "A meeting," he sighs, "*cocktails*. Would you believe it? But he is the Polar League's ambassador, and we need League funds if we are to accomplish anything at all."

She touches his shoulder, her fingers following the sheen of light on his black skin. "I wish you would stay."

He bends over her, kisses her gravely on the forehead. "I cannot treat you as you deserve," he says. "And for that, as much as anything else, I require your understanding."

"Sorya—," she begins, then cuts short at his frown.

"Don't ask me to choose between you," he says. "It is not simple. Sorya is what she is, and for a variety of reasons, I need her—her mind and skills more than anything."

"I was not asking for a choice," Aiah says. "I was wondering if she would kill me. She and I had . . . a side-agreement . . . concerning you. I may have violated it by coming here. And she has already sent me a message."

All truces are temporary, Sorya said.

Constantine's brows knit. Aiah can see muscles working on the side of his neck, as if he is chewing the news over before he makes his calm answer.

"If she harms you," he says (his eyes are stone, cold as the breath of Taikoen), "then it will be the end of her."

"I hope you will tell *her* that."

"I will see that she knows."

He kisses her forehead again, sealing the promise, then rises and begins to dress.

Aiah lies still for a moment, her nerves humming with the strangeness, the peculiar uncanny intensity, of this life-and-death bargain, and then she remembers she has carried something with her to give to him. She rises from the bed, looks for a moment for a dressing gown before remembering she hasn't as yet acquired one, and then goes to her baggage to find her treasure.

She approaches him naked, the book offered on her upturned palms. "Yes?" he says, and cocks an eye at the gift.

"I brought this for you. You can judge it better than I can—but I think it will help our work."

He picks up the book, looks at the gold lettering on the red plastic binding. "*Proceedings of the Research Division of the Jaspeeri Plasm Authority.* Volume Fourteen, no less." He sighs. "An attractive title. You don't want me to start at the beginning?"

"The first thirteen volumes are all formulae and proofs," Aiah says. "I don't understand them. This volume has the recommendations, and they involve a way to increase plasm by about twenty percent through use of something called 'fractionate intervals.'"

Constantine looks skeptical.

"The Authority spent eight years producing the data," Aiah says, "but then the Research Division got flushed. I think the decision was political, but I don't know the details. The man in charge was Rohder—he's brilliant, a real wizard, but I don't think he's very practical. Now he's in charge of a whole suite of empty offices back in the Plasm Authority Building."

Constantine frowns, runs his thumb along the spine. "I will give it my attention when I can," he says.

Aiah puts her arms around him and holds him close, hoping to carry some last imprint of Constantine on her flesh. He kisses her—and for a moment she feels him softening, as if he might throw off his clothes and join her on the bed again, but the moment passes, and he says good-bye and returns to the Polar League's ambassador and his duty.

Aiah decides she might as well follow his example, and begins to make a list for the next day.

FOUR

~~~~~~~~~

In the end, Aiah's heart fails her where Gil is concerned. She writes him a letter and sends it surface mail instead of using a wiregram or making a phone call. Her written explanations and excuses are awkward, unconvincing even to herself. She knows that he will have a hard time paying for the apartment they'd shared, and so she wires him ten thousand dalders out of her account in Gunalaht.

Conscience money. And sure proof to the Jaspeeri authorities of her profitable, and to them criminal, activities.

She and Ethemark march through the Owl Wing, putting plastic slips on the doors of empty offices that announce they are now part of the Plasm Enforcement Division. She then informs the Palace Property Department, in charge of room allocations, that the offices are now theirs. Theirs, by right of conquest and the fact that no one, in the confusion, disputes them.

The interviewing and hiring begins. Drumbeth announces publicly that plasm thieves have a thirty-day amnesty in which to inform the authorities of their illegal plasm taps, meters, and connections. Public response is tepid, but the deadline provides Aiah with a firm date by which she has to be ready.

She promises herself that the first arrests will be made at

24:01 on the day following the deadline. One minute after the amnesty ends.

During the next two weeks, Constantine visits her twice more in her suite, spending his rare moments of spare time in her company. She is working double shifts, but his schedule is worse. Depending on the state of his elusive progress through the complexities of coalition politics, his moods swing between booming elation and fretful anxiety. But when he touches her, when he kisses her or moves with her in bed, his mood shifts: he is entirely *there,* intent eyes holding her as if she were pinned in the radiance of searchlights, a kind of scrutiny that would be frightening if it weren't for the fact that, apparently, he approves of what he sees.

Daily Aiah feeds on plasm-energy to keep away the bone-weariness that, in normal circumstance, her responsibilities and schedule should inflict upon her. But the plasm also makes her fearless, gives her a sense of invincibility. She is bolder than she would be otherwise.

The taste of power sings through her nerves all day, an echo of the world's ultimate chorus, of its strangely pliant reality.

She is willing certain things into being. Time will tell if she is successful.

SECOND TITANIC MONTH

LORDS OF THE NEW CITY

SEE IT NOW!

Aiah soars out over the city. Plasm sings a song of triumph in her ectoplasmic ears. In the distance, ringing the metropolis on all sides, she can see the city's crown, the point at which it becomes possible to build on bedrock, and where thousands of tall buildings loom over the flat aspect of the sea.

A vast, invisible technical array makes possible this flight. Underneath it all is the well of plasm that interlaces Caraqui, that underlies it like its very own sea, that flows in mains and is collected in capacitors and powers the aspirations of a thousand mages.

Beneath the Aerial Palace is one collection point, the huge room sheathed in steel and bronze, holding its collected plasm in towers of gleaming brass and black ceramic. Governing this power, beneath the watchful eyes of the icon of Two-Faced Tangid, are the technicians in the control room, watching their dials, consulting their schedules, throwing worn butter-smooth brass levers that lower contacts into the receptacles atop the accumulators, that start the flood of plasm along its predestined route. And from there the plasm floods upward, like water under high pressure, along circuits and conduits to the roof, where it pours along the scalloped transmission horn set at 044 degrees true, and from there leaps into the sky.

Aiah sits in her office, the t-grip in her hand now wired into the circuit. Her mind molds the plasm to her will, controls her flight over the dome of the city. Her sensorium—the complex of senses with which she has endowed herself—sights for landmarks, finds them, corrects her flight. She brings her awareness from her plasm-sensorium into her body, laying a mundane reality onto the hyperreal sensations of plasm.

She looks at her office clock. She has a few minutes before she has to keep her appointment.

She will stay, then, in flight a moment more.

Aiah expands her sensorium, concentrating on the city's distant crown and the places that lie beyond. The Sea of Caraqui is wide, and Caraqui covers much more area than the average metropolis, though its population densities are lower. The long borders have given Caraqui a large number of neighbors, most of whom cannot be delighted with the new government popping up among them.

Aiah has done her homework, laboring away on one of the terminals of the Worldwide News Service. Worldwide was the Keremaths' wire and data service, and its background reports showed the signs of their policy and their censors, but Aiah was able to read between the lines of censorship, the shifting boundaries of what could be said and not-said, and has now gained an idea of what lies beyond Caraqui's crown.

Behind Aiah, to the south, is Barchab, with its prominent twin volcanoes. Barchab is a kind of oligarchy, reasonably prosperous, with an economy based on mining the mineral resources of its volcanic plateau. The government features a dozen major parties, each representing a coalition of moneyed interests, all vying for control of a weak legislature. Governmental influence is limited, and the wealthy arrange things among themselves.

Aiah does not believe that Barchab will look on the new government of Caraqui with any great delight.

Southeast and east is Koroneia, where a conservative oligarchic government called the Committee of Sixty has displaced a well-meaning military junta, the Metropolitan Social Revolutionary Council, whose staggering ineptitude reached its climax when its own military declined to fight in its defense. The Committee of Sixty, which took power with Keremath support, has ruled for three years now, and has not yet succeeded in defining its objectives, let alone managing a coherent policy.

Ahead, to the northeast, is Lanbola. Though the constitution is that of a federal republic, the Popular Democratic Party has managed to win every election for the last sixty-seven years through methods ranging from bribery and extortion to a low-level terror campaign waged against its rivals. Lanbola's attitude toward Caraqui's new government may be summarized by the fact that, since the coup, it has banned the chromoplay *Lords of the New City* and has given refuge to some of the surviving Keremaths.

Northward Caraqui shares a short border with Charna, a state that sprawls north to the Pole. The military seized power in Charna fifty years ago and haven't given it up, despite occasional brief periods of fighting among cabals of officers. Charna had got along perfectly well with the Keremaths.

Northwest is Nesca, a smallish metropolis that rejoices in a functioning parliamentary democracy. Its government seems inexplicably hostile to Caraqui's new rulers, and has issued a number of statements condemning the violence with which the triumvirate established itself.

West is the horror of Sabaya, which has been dominated

for the last seventy-five years by Field Marshal the Serene Lord Dr. Iromaq, Doctor of Philosophy, Doctor of Magical Arts, Savior of the Nation, etc., etc., a man from whom even the Keremaths recoiled. Sabaya's ghastly regime, inept, cash-poor, and brutal, is a byword for poverty, terror, and oppression. Whatever goes on behind its closed borders goes on largely unobserved, as if within some all-encompassing shroud of darkness.

These are the neighbors among which Caraqui's new government now stands. Uneasy, hostile, or unstable, friendly for the most part with the Keremaths, none are likely to welcome an unruly set of newcomers like Caraqui's triumvirate, let alone an ominous foreign presence like Constantine.

And then, below her hovering anima, a miracle blossoms: color expands in midair from a central point like water bursting from a main, like a kaleidoscope gone mad . . . but soon concrete images begin to form—faces, images, fancies—one turning into another like the products of dream. A man on skates. A tree that blossoms in seconds and produces red fruit, which falls of its own accord into the laps of a circle of smiling children. A tall building, granite and glass, which begins to contort, to shimmy in a kind of dance. Disembodied hands and eyes, a burning egg, a burning key, a wine bottle made of stone . . .

The Dreaming Sisters are at play in the sky.

Aiah looks for a sourceline for the cloud of images but can't see one. The vision begins to move westward, toward ominous Sabaya, skipping through the air like a plate skimming the sea. Aiah watches in delight until it vanishes in the distance.

She will have to find out more about the Dreaming Sisters someday.

But now her concerns are more mundane. She orients herself over her target, then drops into a district of cheap flats, warehouses, and illegal factories where the children of Caraqui toil at unforgiving machines for double shifts every day.

The half-world of Aground lies somewhere hereabouts, hidden beneath the streets. On these shallow mudflats, many of the buildings have conventional architecture, with foundations reaching to bedrock; and others, centuries old, are on concrete pontoons that moored themselves in mud long ago.

Aiah is looking for one of the latter. It isn't hard to find, a sprawling, crumbling warren of brown-brick tenements so ancient that the only thing keeping them upright are the rusting iron braces and props added to the structure. Once there, Aiah has to be more circumspect, on the chance that the people she is looking for might also be on the lookout for her.

She carries her sensorium in an anima, a plasm body that she hasn't bothered to will into the shape of an actual human body: it's a diffuse cloud of plasm she has configured to remain sensitive to its environment. Carefully she drops the anima beneath street level, where the huge grounded pontoons loom on either side and the dark brackish sea slops over the mudflats below. There is little light here, but plasm can be configured to see in the dark. Aiah moves between the pontoon walls until she comes to a mark, scored lightly into the crumbling concrete, that she has left earlier.

At this point she reconfigures her anima, confining it to a narrow pipette of plasm that should be difficult to detect, and then rises through the midst of the tenement, through iron beams and brick arches and worn plastic flooring, through uninspiring sights of people cooking or doing laundry or watching video, past children playing or sleeping or fighting with each other, until she reaches the hallway outside the Silver Hand plasm house she has been observing for the last week.

The hallway's flaking paint is scarred with decades' worth of graffiti. The crumbling plastic flooring, a cheap imitation of an old Geoform design, has worn clear through in spots, and has been overlaid with ribbed plastic mats—probably not for the convenience or safety of the tenants, but for the benefit of the Silver Hand, who moved truckloads of plasm batteries through this hallway.

Aiah ghosts along at floor height, looking for the mage she's relieving. She wills her sensorium to become sensitive to plasm, and finds a little flare from a not-quite-concealed sourceline in the hallway, near the baseboard. She ghosts up to the flare, wills a little extrusion of her own plasm to touch the sourceline.

—This is Aiah, she pulses. Anything doing?

She senses a flare of surprise from the other ghost. He is one of Aiah's new hires, a newly graduated mage from Liri-Domei, a little inexperienced but learning quickly.

—The deliveries went out before midbreak, he broadcasts. The Ferret's inside filling batteries. The Slug is there with him.

—The Mole?

—Been and gone.

The code names date from an earlier phase of the observation, when Aiah and her unit were ignorant of the names of the Handmen they were observing. But the codes were more descriptive than the Handmen's actual names, and remain in force.

—I'll relieve you, then, Aiah sends.

—Nothing much happening. Good luck.

The other mage fades. Aiah slides through the wall and extrudes a minute part of her plasm-body to the other side.

The Silver Hand is very confident here. A plasm house should be sheathed in bronze or at least bronze mesh, like Lamarath's office in Aground, to prevent anyone like Aiah from peering inside. But the Silver Hand isn't worried about the forces of the law, or apparently anyone else. They operate openly. Thousands of people must know about this place.

The Silver Hand will learn caution in time. But Aiah intends to gather as much information as possible while they are still careless, and then strike. If she had more time, and more people, she could fashion a single powerful attack that would prove lethal to all of them; but as it is, with the knowledge she possesses and the weapons she has been given, she will do her best to make the blow a heavy one.

Aiah opens her plasm-senses, sees the two Silver Hand men inside their place of business. Each is of a type. Gangsters, Aiah suspects, are the same everywhere. The young are exuberant and dress in exaggerations of fashionable styles—the Ferret wears yards of lace and a plush velvet jacket, purple with brass studs in decorative patterns. His hair is permed and dressed in shining ringlets. He wears a heavy Stoka watch on one wrist, and suede boots with heels.

Older Handmen carry themselves with a different style.

The Slug's suit is more conservative, his face masklike, his ruthlessness complete. In the younger ones you can still see traces of humanity; in the older ones, never, nothing but the inhuman glimmer in their calculating eyes. Back in Jaspeer they all had military ranks: captains, colonels, generals. Here they have a family structure and call themselves cousins, brothers, and uncles. All the same.

The Ferret wrestles heavy plasm batteries to and from his illegal tap. It's a struggle for him because he's a slender man, and sweat drips from his forehead to splash on the scarred soft rubber flooring installed to muffle the thuds of the heavy work.

The other, the Slug, is obese and in authority. He is in charge of the cash, which is kept in a drawer of his desk. He has his feet propped atop the desk while he watches the younger man work, and gestures largely with both hands as he talks on a telephone headset.

The Ferret wrestles the last battery into place, puts the tap on it, and stops to light a cigaret. The Slug, talking to a girl-friend, drones on without cease.

Plasm stolen by the Silver Hand is usually not consumed by the gangsters themselves. They sell it, at inflated prices, to customers who have no choice but to pay their extortionate fees. But a certain percentage of the plasm is used within their own operation: to locate cargoes worth hijacking, to intimidate and murder, to provide life-extension treatments for their leaders. If necessary, to kill each other, though there hasn't been a war among the Silver Hand in twenty years, and being a Handman is as safe as—probably safer than—banking.

Aiah watches the pair for two hours. Junior Handmen or independent affiliates—"brothers" or "nephews" in Hand-man jargon—turn up every so often to drop off empty plasm batteries and bags of cash and pick up newly charged batter-ies. Sometimes they stay around and gossip for a while before leaving. It's all routine.

Aiah approves of the Silver Hand's having a routine day. They're much more likely to relax their security and give their operations away.

Except when there are visitors, the Slug stays on the

phone the whole time, alternating business and romantic interests. Aiah keeps careful tabs on when each call is made, and the subject matter of the conversation, and plans to requisition a copy of the phone records in order to discover to whom the Slug's been talking. Eventually the Slug takes his headphones off and goes off to a midbreak rendezvous with one of his girlfriends. Now that the phone is free, the Ferret fastidiously cleans the earphones and the mouthpiece with his handkerchief, then makes a few calls of his own.

Until there's a visitor. He's a stranger, an older man with gray hair and the unnaturally healthy flesh of someone on life extension. He is thin and dapper, a mixture of characteristics—youthful stride, hatchet face, a grizzled mustache. He hammers angrily on the door, and is annoyed when he finds the Slug is gone.

"He didn't know you were coming," the Ferret apologizes.

"I told that stupid whore of his," the thin man says, showing yellow teeth.

"Which one?" the Ferret asks, but the stranger is unamused.

"I need access to the tap, third shift. My boys are hijacking a barge down at the Navy Yard."

The Ferret is interested. "I used to pick stuff from the Yard sometimes, when I was nephew with Daddy Cathobert's crew. But we'd have to take care of Commodore Grophadh first."

The stranger scowls. "Grophadh's gone—got his ass retired after the coup. But his lad Armaki's still there, and I make sure he's taken care of."

(Aiah, back in her office, carefully detaches a fragment of her consciousness from her anima and scrawls notes to herself across a pad of paper. *Grophadh. Armaki.* People who got paid off when the Navy Yard got looted. And a theft in the Navy Yard early tomorrow—she would have to put experienced observers in place.)

The thin man marches off to rouse the Slug from his girlfriend's bed. Aiah continues her surveillance for another hour, then turns the business over to one of her mages and writes a formal report of what she's overheard, which goes into a file in the secure room. There, she looks through books of known Handmen the department had got from the central police headquarters—armed with one of Constantine's warrants, she and some assistants had just marched in and *taken* them, much to the cops' chagrin—and in one of the books she finds the gray stranger. His name is Gurfith, and his rank within the Silver Hand is given as "underuncle," which puts him fairly high in the hierarchy, working directly under one of the powerful uncles, the equivalent of a street colonel back in Jaspeer. For him to be involved personally in a hijacking means that whatever is being taken has a greater than average value.

The plasm house where she's made these observations is one of those given her by Sergeant Lamarath. Every single one of them has proved genuine. Lamarath is holding by his agreement.

And now that word of her arrangement with Lamarath is leaking out into other half-worlds, more tips are coming in through Ethemark, arriving faster than the department's limited resources can process them. She is beginning to realize that the half-worlds are some of the best intelligence sources she'll ever have.

She looks at the file, then closes it and returns it to the shelves. Aiah will probably have to let the hijacking take place. She doesn't know anyone in the police structure or the Navy she can alert, not without a chance of it getting back to Under-uncle Gurfith.

Unless, she thinks, some of Constantine's mercenaries decide to hold some unscheduled maneuvers in the area of the Navy Yard.

She'll have to think about that.

TWELVE YEARS OF MISMANAGEMENT

WASTE DISPOSAL SCANDAL
"CRIME OF A LIFETIME"

Constantine's level eyes gaze out over the tips of his tented fingers; he looks somberly out the oval windows of his

Owl Wing office while Aiah sits before him and makes her report. "We're trying to set up a proper operations center," she says, "but because the technicians and engineers spend most of their time repairing damage, the job isn't getting done, and so we're doing our mage ops from our offices. It's inefficient and any surveillance requiring more than one mage is difficult to coordinate."

Constantine continues to direct his gaze out the window—it is as if his mind were worrying over another problem entirely—but his answer shows he had been paying attention. "Will you have your ops room completed by the time you commence active operations?"

"That is hard to say."

He turns to Aiah and places his hands on the surface of his desk. It is a beautiful piece of furniture, ebony, inlaid with gilt and mother-of-pearl.

"Let me know when the deadline approaches, and if necessary I will assign more people to you. The repairs to the Palace are crucial to the physical safety of the government and its workers, and should take precedence."

There is a gentle knock at the door, followed by the appearance of Constantine's secretary, a Cheloki named Drusus. "President Drumbeth wishes to see you, sir," he says, and Drumbeth is in the room before Aiah and Constantine have more than half-risen from their chairs.

The president of the triumvirate is a small man, but he is made taller by erect military posture and bushy gray hair. Though he resigned from his colonelcy after the coup, he wears his blue suit as if it were a uniform. The coup that overthrew the Keremaths was his creation, and he had been intelligent enough to make Constantine a part of it, and of the government he formed afterward.

He shakes Constantine's hand briskly. "I was passing by your office," he says, "and thought I would take the opportunity to speak with you."

Drumbeth's impassive copper face and slit eyes are impossible to read, and Aiah concludes that his unresponsive face must have served him well in his previous post as director of military intelligence.

Constantine introduces Aiah. "Miss Aiah was giving a

report on her progress in establishing her department," he says.

"I would be interested to hear it," says Drumbeth. He takes a chair without being invited, and nods at Aiah. "Please continue, miss."

Aiah is near the end of her presentation, but for the triumvir's benefit she begins again from the start. His narrow eyes watch her impassively as she speaks. Occasionally he interrupts to ask a pertinent question.

"Very good, Miss Aiah," he concludes. "You seem to have done well for someone"—his slit eyes flicker for a moment—"for someone so young."

Aiah is conscious of heat rising to her face. "Thank you, sir."

Drumbeth turns to Constantine, then seems to remember something. "Ah—it occurs to me to ask you," he says, "about some prisoners you have ordered released from our jails."

Constantine gives him an expectant look. "Prisoners?"

"A commissioner of the Special Police—Anacheth. One of his subordinates, Commander Coapli, and a general of the former regime's army, Brandig. The worst kind of men the old regime had to offer, torturers and killers. After you interviewed them, you ordered them all released from the Metropolitan Prison."

A cold finger touches Aiah's spine. These are Taikoen's victims, the men Constantine was feeding to his creature.

"Ah," Constantine says. "I recall now. I released them after I received their medical reports. They were all in the last stages of a fatal illness, and it seemed needless cruelty to keep them confined. In fact, I believe Anacheth and Coapli have already died."

Drumbeth nods. "So I have been told. It was Coapli's death, reported on the news, that made me wonder how he had come to be released from prison."

"I hoped," Constantine says, "to be able to set a better example of humanity than our predecessors."

"That was good of you, I suppose." Drumbeth's tone implies indifference to the fate of Anacheth and his minions.

"Also," Constantine adds, "I did not want it said that we secretly murdered them while they were in custody."

Drumbeth nods agreement, but as he nods he continues to speak. "But nevertheless you are Minister of Resources, not Security, and you aren't among those authorized to order the discharge of prisoners."

"I apologize if I exceeded my authority," Constantine says. "Since my Cheloki had arrested these people in the first place, and in view of the great challenges facing Gentri and the safety ministry, I thought it was easier simply to order them released myself."

"That will no longer be necessary," Drumbeth says. His voice is firm: Aiah sees an officer here, used to command. "Gentri now has a firm enough command of his department. If there are people whom you wish to have released on humanitarian grounds, call my attention to them, and after a review I will order their discharge."

"You are busy enough. I would not want to trouble you with these minor matters."

"Then don't." Drumbeth's voice remains indifferent. "But if criminals are to be released, I wish it to be with my knowledge, or with Gentri's."

Constantine nods gracefully. "As you wish, Triumvir."

Drumbeth tilts his head. "By the way—I wonder if you have seen the early news reports?"

Constantine looks at him with grave curiosity. "I have not had the opportunity."

"There are stories in several media of a decision made at yesterday's cabinet meeting concerning the fate of the Qerwan Arms Company. The reports are unanimous in indicating the government's decision to sell. In fact, my office has already been contacted by firms wishing to tender a bid."

Constantine nods. His usual dramatic tones and extravagant gestures are suppressed: he sits upright at the table, and speaks in a lowered tone. "Such eagerness would indicate that the sale of the company, complete with its current set of government contracts, should provide the government an excellent source of revenue."

"That may be true," Drumbeth says. "But the fact remains that, contrary to the news reports, the government has not as yet decided the fate of the company, and may not decide to part with a resource so vital to its security."

"Guns and ammunition," Constantine says, "are available in quantity, and for rather better prices, in many other places."

"So you said yesterday," Drumbeth says. "It isn't my intention to renew the debate, but instead to note my concern at reports of the inner workings of our cabinet now appearing in news reports." A glint, steely in Shieldlight, appears in Drumbeth's narrow eyes. "It would seem that someone is attempting to manipulate the situation through selected leaks to the media."

A ghost of a shrug rolls through Constantine's shoulders. He continues to hold his gestures to a minimum, and Aiah wonders if he is afraid he might give himself away with one of them. "It is to be expected, I suppose," he says. "If they are to have wider participation in government, as we seem to agree they should, the public must be educated in such matters."

"*Educated,*" Drumbeth says. "Not *manipulated.* Forcing the government's hand this way will not be tolerated, and if I can discover the offender he may find that some of his most cherished projects—" His slitted eyes glance for a deliberate moment in Aiah's direction. "His most cherished projects," he continues, "will be vetoed, or given to someone else."

"I've been a neglectful host," Constantine says. "May I offer you coffee? Tea? A glass of brandy perhaps?"

"Some other time," Drumbeth says, rising. "I have a full shift ahead of me."

"*Damn* the man!" Constantine cries after Drumbeth leaves. He hammers a heavy fist into his palm. "He is—" The words jam in his throat, and instead he waves the fist at the door. "This is unsupportable! Dressing me down in front of a subordinate!"

Aiah shrinks from the storm of anger. "I wouldn't call it *dressing down* . . . ," she says.

Constantine is not consoled. "How *dare* he check me!" he roars. "After everything I have done! After I set him in power!" He paces behind his desk, marching back and forth as fury sparks from his eyes. "An *arms company!*" he says. "Badly managed, fat with overpaid Keremath sycophants, their product inferior and overpriced . . ." He laughs. "And *this* shambles is so vital to the security of Caraqui? Our ex-

colonel Drumbeth of all people should know how common
arms companies are, how easy their product is to come by—"

"What are you going to do about Taikoen?" Aiah interrupts.

Constantine stops dead, looks at her with the anger still
blazing from his eyes, but the rage is gone from his voice,
and his tone is thoughtful. "Taikoen?" he says. "He has General Brandig now—he's an old man, in bad condition, but
still should last him another day or two. I will not owe him
another for two weeks or so. . . ." He straightens, fingers his
chin in thought. "I must look at your files," he says. "Taikoen
can feed on the Silver Hand for months . . . may even do us
some good."

Aiah swallows. She has observed the Handmen closely
and hates them all, but she wouldn't wish Taikoen on any of
them, can't imagine desiring that the cold, vicious intelligence of that deadly monster should dwell in the heart of the
worst imaginable villain.

"I don't want anyone going through my files in that way,"
she says. "Not to give people to . . . that creature."

"Miss Aiah." A dangerous growl. "It is *necessary*."

"*No!*" Aiah cries. "It is *mad* to feed that thing!"

In less than a moment Constantine has crossed the room
to stand before her, his big hands crushing her shoulders,
fiery eyes burning into hers. She shrinks back, afraid of
sudden violence, but Constantine's voice is low, without
anger. "Without Taikoen we would not have Caraqui," he
says. "Feeding him is the price we pay for the good we are
able to do now. And if I should break the agreement I have
with him . . ." His tongue licks dry lips, and there is a
haunted look in his eyes. "My life would not be worth a
half-dinar."

A shadow of Constantine's fear shivers through Aiah,
and she locks her arms around him, holding him close,
pressing her cheek to his velvet shoulder. "There must be
another way. Destroy him. It is possible to kill a hanged
man, isn't it?"

"Do you think we live in a chromoplay?" Scorn burns in
his eyes. "We find the monster, then kill it with a magic dagger, or by using an obscure geomantic focus found in some

old book?" There is a moment's hesitation before Constantine says, "Taikoen may yet be useful. I will choose the people carefully. There will be no accidents, and I will make his subjects the most deserving imaginable."

His big hands caress her, but nevertheless a chill runs up her spine. She has become a *part* of this now, a part of the apparatus that feeds people to Taikoen.

She is a party to this atrocity. But that's what she *must* be, if that is what it takes to preserve her lover, and to create the New City.

"I don't want to know when it happens," she says. "I don't want to know who, and when, and why it is being done."

Constantine gives a bitter laugh. "I would not burden you with that. Taikoen is my poison alone. You will never see him or hear of him after this." His arms tighten around her, threaten to drive the wind from her body. "Taikoen is the greatest burden I bear, the greatest evil I know. Yet I *must* deal with him. And though it is unjust of me even to ask, I find I need to share this burden a little—I wish your understanding and support. I *need* you to believe that what I am doing is right."

Aiah's mind whirls. She has never seen Constantine like this, never seen him in a situation where he did not possess absolute confidence and mastery. He needs her support, her trust. What can she do but give it?

He is, she realizes, almost as isolated in this country as she. For all his talents, when Constantine faces Taikoen, he faces the creature alone.

"Yes," she says numbly, "of course. I understand."

She will do what she can.

TRIUMVIR HILTHI SPEAKS

"THE MORAL WEALTH OF THE NATION"

THIRD SHIFT TODAY!

"If some of the family want to apply," Aiah says, "I can give them some jobs. But I need particular skills."

"*Skills?*" Aiah's grandmother sounds suspicious, as if Aiah is speaking a foreign language. "What kind of skills?"

"The department is hiring only two kinds of staff: mages and clerical. And a few supervisors who will *also* be mages and clerks."

"Your brother Stonn needs a job."

"Stonn has a criminal record," Aiah says. "He'd never pass the security check."

Galaiah is unperturbed. "You're in charge, ne? *Fix* the security check. Stonn needs to get out of Jaspeer, away from friends who get him in trouble."

Galaiah is an optimist where Stonn's character is concerned. He is a petty criminal, with a petty criminal's mind: impulsive, feckless, unpredictable, short-tempered. He would be a disaster as a member of the PED.

"Nana," Aiah says. "I can't fix the security check. It's not done in my department—we contract it out to the political police."

Sorya's Force of the Interior. The last thing Aiah wants is for Sorya to get access to the minds of her relatives.

"It's a bad day when you won't give your brother a job!" Galaiah says. "You got to help out your family!"

Aiah changes tack. "Let me tell you what the department pays," Aiah says. "I've checked on Worldwide News and put the figures in Jaspeeri dalders."

Galaiah listens to the figures, and when Aiah finishes there is a dubious silence on the other end of the line. "That's not much," she says. "Your niece Qismah is getting more on the dole."

"That's because she's got kids," Aiah says. Raised on the dole herself, she absorbed the intricacies of its regulations with her mother's milk.

"But no," she goes on, "we can't pay much. If the department does a good job, I'll get a bigger budget."

"How about your longnose lover?" Galaiah asks. "Can he get one of your kin a job?"

"Constantine's not a longnose, he's a Cheloki." Aiah can't quite resist the correction.

The old lady is firm. "If he's not one of the Cunning People, then he's a longnose."

"Clerks and mages," Aiah says. "That's what I can hire. Without criminal records, without knowledge of crime. Because anything shady would come out in the plasm scans, and then they'd use it against me, ne?"

"Got no mages in the family," Galaiah says, thinking out loud. "Well, there's Esmon's Khorsa."

"Khorsa I would hire." She is a witch, engaged to Aiah's cousin Esmon. She had also helped Aiah on her flight from Jaspeer.

"I think she probably makes more money at the Wisdom Fortune Temple."

"Probably," Aiah agrees.

"And clerks," Galaiah says. "You need clerks."

"Tell everyone," Aiah says, "what I need. But I can't promise I'll hire anyone."

"If someone wants to try for one of these jobs," Galaiah says, "can you send them some money for the trip?"

Aiah sighs. "Yes," she says. "I'll do that."

And hopes, as she ends the call, that she isn't subsidizing her family's vacations.

QERWAN ARMS TO RECEIVE NEW MANAGEMENT

POLITICAL APPOINTEES SACKED!

Anstine, Aiah's newly hired receptionist, makes his way out of Aiah's office, and then the door fills with Constantine. Observing office protocol, he very properly closes the door behind him before he folds her in his arms and kisses her.

"Can you stay long?" she asks.

His head gives a brief shake. "I came only to warn you," he says.

"Yes?"

"You are to receive a visit tomorrow, 13:00 or thereabouts. The triumvirate, plus any cabinet ministers who feel an interest. They want to see what you've accomplished."

Alarm sings through Aiah's veins. "But we've barely *started*. . . . They're not going to see anything."

He slips from her embrace, moves to stand by the window. "That's as may be," he says, "but they already have plans for you."

"What plans?" Promptly. "And who?"

"Colonel Drumbeth is considering placing a military officer in your department to advise on matters that cross into his department. I suspect it's to make certain that the military gets its share of what you find."

Aiah bites back annoyance. She has no inclination to be the military's personal plasm diver.

"Can't you head him off?" she asks.

Constantine shrugs. Below, Shieldlight winks silver off glass, glows green off rooftop gardens. "I can argue against it, to be sure, but—as we have observed—I can't stop Drumbeth from doing anything he really desires to do. He and the military are in *charge,* after all. But . . ." He makes a little sideways gesture with his hand, indicating room for maneuver. "We may have to do a little trading. It may be best to accept Drumbeth's officer in exchange for keeping out Parq's priest."

"Priest?" The notion seems too absurd for Aiah to even take alarm.

Constantine flashes his teeth as he speaks. "The Keremaths took power with the backing of the Dalavans, remember. The Keremaths gave the Dalavans special privileges afterward, and various sumptuary and moral laws were passed obliging the population to conform to rigorous Dalavan standards of conduct and morality."

Pigeons bob about on the window ledge, red button eyes all without a hint of life. "I can't say I've observed any stringent moral codes in force since I've been here," Aiah observes.

"The laws, as with all Keremath laws, have been loosely enforced, or not enforced at all. But now that Parq is a third of the government, he wishes to enforce the laws that give his faith its special privileges. He wants to create a Dalavan police force to enforce the moral strictures, and he wishes to put an ombudsman in every department to make certain that department guidelines are not in conflict with the Dalavan faith."

"Great Senko!"

He looks at her sidelong, irony curling his lips. "I would avoid any promiscuous mention of the immortals when Parq is around," he says.

"Drumbeth and Hilthi won't permit this, will they?"

"I assume not. Hilthi is a moralist, but he's not a Dalavan moralist. And Drumbeth no more wants one of Parq's spies in every office than we do." He frowns, and his fingers tap lightly on the window glass in thought. "Parq may have brought up the issue only in hope of heading off the activist wing of his own party, which has denounced his personal version of the faith as halfhearted, indulgent, and temporizing—which is true—and which has denounced Parq himself as tyrannous, corrupt, and venal—which is also true."

"Perhaps Parq has made the demand only to trade them for something else he really wants," Aiah says.

Constantine looks at her, approving eyes gleaming in reflected Shieldlight. "I see you have learned somewhat of politics since you have been in Caraqui."

"I have a good teacher."

He gives a low, immodest laugh, then turns back to the window. An airship lies on the far horizon, Shieldlight flashing silver off its skin, off its propeller disks. Behind it, the sky suddenly flashes with the profile of Gargelius Enchuk, plasm hype for his new recording.

"We shall see what Parq truly wants in time," Constantine says. "It may be that he has no true plan at all other than to seek advantage wherever he can find it. But we must give him a victory sooner or later, or he may realize that he is better off in opposition. And as he is the spiritual leader of rather more than a third of our population, we cannot afford to have him oppose us."

Aiah's thoughts churn uneasily. "What can you give such a man that will content him?"

"He is so corrupt that he may settle for money, or an hour of video time every week to preach to the citizens, or a beautiful woman. We shall see."

Aiah turns, puts her arms around Constantine's waist. "And what will content *you?*" she asks.

Constantine affects to give this his consideration. "Dominion of the habited world," he says, "and the ordering of it; the piercing of the Shield and the discovering of the glories that lie beyond; the captaincy of the great outflowing of humanity into the worlds there discovered, or built entire if there are none to be found; the creation of the nations into which humanity settles; the assurance that all patterns and powers are in order . . . and then, perhaps, I may retire and write my memoirs."

There is a languid smile on Constantine's face as he speaks, and irony puts an edge on his voice; but there is a chill glow in his eyes as he speaks the words, and Aiah feels an answering shiver along her spine as she realizes that he is at least partially sincere.

And then he laughs, a sudden surprising boom that shatters her awestruck mood, and his arms cinch her below her ribs; he picks her up and she is flying, spinning in circles, her feet sweeping papers from her desk. . . .

He sets her down lightly, kisses her before she can catch her breath. "Perhaps I will forfeit it all," he said, "for a few hours in your company, after our business is concluded today."

"I wouldn't want you to give up so much."

He laughs again, spins round on his heel, thrusts out an arm at the scene beyond the window, the long cluttered view of the city built out over its sea. "Foolish to speak of ordering the world," he says, "when I am confined to the role of a minor minister in a chronically misruled and impoverished metropolis. . . ." He laughs again. "You would not believe the absurdities to which I am subjected. Yesterday's cabinet meeting spent hours discussing a problem having to do with capital spending. It was a thousand radii beyond trivial, with no remedy besides, and it occupied a full day."

"I believe you volunteered for the job," Aiah reminds.

He gives her a sly look. "Miss Aiah, I believe you will keep me honest."

She walks up to him and straightens a fold in his lapel. "We must both learn to be good subordinates."

He gives a dry little laugh. "I will do what I can."

"Will I see you third shift?"

"Ah. 21:00, perhaps?"

"And no cocktail parties later? No receptions? Cabinet

meetings? Duty calls on the dolphins? Visits from the winner of the Junior New City League's essay contest?"

"I believe not." He gives a lazy smile. "But I will have to consult my calendar in regard to that last point."

She stands on tiptoe and kisses his cheek. "Till later, then."

His brows rise in mock offense. "Such a slight good-bye? I would have a better memory of you than that."

His arms coil around her again—the pigeons on the window ledge see the swift movement and fly in panic—and Aiah laughs as Constantine bends her over backward, like a swooning girl in a chromoplay, and dines for a long moment on her arched throat.

1.5 MILLION FOR CHARITY!

ALLEGED GANGSTER GIVES
TO CHILDREN'S HOSPITAL

HOSPITAL HEAD RECEIVES
"GREAT-UNCLE" RATHMEN

21:00. Aiah's veins tingle with the plasm she's just fed herself to keep weariness at bay. Constantine is on time, with a bottle of fine brandy and a crystal bowl of fruit plundered from one of the Keremaths' rooftop arboretums.

Aiah feasts greedily on grapes, red-skinned and with a cool taste, their tiny seeds sweet like crystal-sugar, as if the fruit were stuffed with candy. Constantine pours brandy, swirls it in the glass, and sniffs it delicately, nostrils high, like a haughty bronze figure standing on some ancient wall gazing down at some conquered city. It is made, Aiah knows, from actual grapes, grown in actual gardens, not in vats with chemicals and hermetics.

"You have done admirably with your department," Constantine says. "Two weeks, and it is actually functioning."

"Not well," Aiah grudges. She sighs, looks at her brandy, then puts the glass down. "When I worked for the Plasm

Authority in Jaspeer I discovered that no one there ever talked
to anyone else—our suggestions and complaints were trans-
mitted off into the void, and were never acted on or even
acknowledged, and orders came down from the hundred-
fiftieth floor as if from beyond the Shield, with no consultation, no notion of how things actually stood, no concept of
how to make it work."

"Institutionalized dysfunction," Constantine says.

"Oh yes. And institutionalized frustration as well. So now
I am trying to set up the PED in order to facilitate lines of
communication, to make certain that everyone has access to
authority when needed. . . ." She sighs again and picks up
her brandy glass. "But that authority is *me,* and that means I
am consulted on everything. I have never worked so hard in
my life, and still the department only lurches along."

"It will dance and skip, given time."

"The Ascended willing," Aiah says, conceding somewhat
to superstition as she sketches the Sign of the Ascended in
the air with her brandy glass.

"But you have a department," Constantine says, "and you
have not gone mad, or had a fit of the vapors, or checked
yourself into the hospital for a long course of sedation."

"Give me time," Aiah says, and smiles into her glass as
she takes a sip.

"You deal well with Ethemark?"

She shrugs, feels a little insect-twitch of distaste crawl
cross her face. "As I must. He is gifted, even if he isn't my
choice."

"But you have hired other twisted people."

"They're applying in swarms!" Aiah says. "Ethemark or
his kin must have put the word out. I'm hiring only the most
qualified."

"As you should." He cocks his head, regards her. "But you
don't like them?"

She sighs, puts down her glass. "Is it bad of me to wish the
twisted people well, but not to wish them in my vicinity?"

He purses his lips as he chooses words. "*Bad,* I will not
say. Inconsistent, perhaps?"

Aiah sighs and throws up her hands. "Then I am inconsistent. But it is what I feel."

"You are honest with *yourself,* at least. You do not lie to yourself about your feelings. But despite your distaste you hire them, if you think they're qualified, and that is admirable of you."

She looks at him. "They never make you uneasy? Or even afraid?" She thinks of Dr. Romus, the snake-mage, and represses a shudder.

Constantine considers this for a moment. "I must admit," he says finally, "that I find myself comfortable amid all manner of unlikely people."

Aiah reaches for her brandy. "That is your gift. It isn't mine."

"People born with money and position, I find, often possess this talent. I was raised a prince, and even considering that I was a prince of pirates, still it makes for a level of security in dealing with others."

"And I'm a poor kid raised on the dole," Aiah says. "But I don't see what that has to do with consistency, or the lack of it. The rich seem to be as inconsistent as anyone else."

He smiles. "Conceded absolutely," he says. "But we were speaking of security, not hypocrisy. The Barkazil were refugees in Jaspeer, poor, confined to low-status jobs. Perhaps they competed with the twisted for work or for living quarters."

"So far as I can tell," Aiah mumbles into her drink, "we competed with poor longnose Jaspeeris, who hated us. I hardly ever saw a twisted person when I was growing up."

"A theory only." Constantine shrugs, and then his eyes turn to her. She sees in them a glow as mellow as that in the brandy that swirls in his glass. "Since you put such store in communication between members of the department," he says, "let me communicate to you what I perceive in your PED. I am utterly gratified that you came to Caraqui. I was right to choose you for this work. You confirm my judgment every day, and I thank you."

Heat rises in Aiah's cheeks. She touches her glass to his, the crystal chime singing in the air for a long moment before she drinks. Constantine's lips, tasted next, are afire with brandy.

Desire has its way. Neither is in a hurry, and both in a

mood to prolong this banquet of pleasure as long as possible:
there are hors d'oeuvres on the sofa, soups and salads sam-
pled on the bed, and then the main course, served with a full
range of tangy condiments.

Aiah pushes Constantine onto his back and captures him
between her legs, gazing down at his supine body, the broad
cords of muscle that cross his massive shoulders and barrel
chest. Her breath hisses between her teeth as she rides him.
He regards her with a lazy, catlike smile, indolent eyes half-
closed. His big hands set her skin afire where he touches her.
She bends to lick his scent from him, covering his chest with
a waterfall of her dark hair.

"I adore you utterly, Miss Aiah," he says, baritone voice a
resonant murmur in her ear, like the deep bedrock far below
whispering a secret to her; and the words set her plasm-
charged nerves alight, firing her flesh, melting her groin, and
suddenly she finds herself peaking, the climax coming all
unexpected, and from the words alone. . . .

Breathless, she grabs fistfuls of his pectorals and pushes
herself upright, arching her back, looking down at him
through the skein of her hair.

That was fun, she thinks. And fortunately, she adds to
herself, there are plenty more where that one came from.

She has yet to purchase any sleepwear, so afterward she pulls
an undershirt over her head so that she and Constantine
won't stick together. He smiles at the sight.

"I should buy you some dainties," he says, "satins and
lace." He smiles. "I need recreation, a break from my official
worries. It will be good for me to exercise my imagination in
this regard."

"You gave me that lovely negligee of gold silk," Aiah
recalls, "but I had to leave it behind in Jaspeer."

"I will replace it with a better," Constantine says. He
throws his arms over his head and brings his body to full
stretch, arching on the bed as he brings slumbering muscle
awake. "What now?" he says. "Shall I fetch the brandy bottle, and we toast each other till end of sleep shift?"

"I had in mind a more literary pursuit."

She reaches to the bedside table, takes Volume Fourteen of the *Proceedings,* then returns to the bed and depolarizes the window to let in a little illumination.

Constantine screws up his eyes against the light. "You've trapped me, by the immortals," he murmurs. "Trapped, deprived of my strength, and no hope but to attend."

"Exactly," Aiah says, "it was an ambush all along." She joins him on the bed and props the heavy volume on her sternum. "Now listen, and I promise you will not be bored."

He bolsters his head on his arm. Aiah turns pages, tries to find the choicest place to start. *"We therefore recommend the complete reformation of human infrastructure along the following lines,"* she begins, and hears Constantine puff disbelief.

"Give the fellow credit for ambition."

"You'll be giving him credit for more in a moment."

She reads on, spicing abstruse comments about building codes and social foundations with her own footnotes. Rohder's Research Division had uncovered what they called "fractionate intervals," a distance at which plasm generation could be multiplied that was smaller than the smallest accepted unit, the radius. The results, all things being perfect, would be at most a 20 percent increase in the generation of plasm. . . .

"Let me see that," Constantine says, and reaches over her to pluck the book from her hands.

Aiah watches Constantine's constant scowl as he reads, snorts, flips to another page, reads again. At the point where he reads three consecutive pages, she snatches the book from his hands and throws it over her shoulder to the floor. He looks at her in surprise.

"Why did you do that?"

"What do you think?" she asks.

He frowns critically. "Badly written," he says, "the worst of scholastic- and specialist-prose, never to the point, fogged with obscurities and solipsisms. And the matter, these fractionate intervals, is either the greatest delusion in the world, or—"

"Or Rohder is a genius," Aiah says, "though maybe not in

writing reports." She looks at him. "Remember that I told you no one in the Authority ever talked to anyone else? They had a way of augmenting plasm, but they never realized it."

"If all this is true, then you may have saved the revolution, and perhaps the world." He reaches across her. "Give me that book again."

Aiah puts a hand on his shoulder and firmly pushes him back to the mattress. "If I have just saved the world," she says, "don't I deserve to have your undivided attention for the next few hours?"

Constantine's look softens. One hand enfolds her shoulder, the massive instrument, made for smashing bricks or bending iron, now gentle as the warmth in his eyes.

"Very well," he says. "You shall have it."

Aiah can sense, in the taste of his lips, the tangy flavor of possibility. *You may have saved the revolution. . . .* She is, then, more than the mistress of a powerful man promoted above her abilities: she has seen something no one else has, and will now arrange to bring it before the world.

It is as if the future has her name written on it. She wonders if this is how Constantine feels all the time, if he looks on the future as something he *owns,* has nestled in the palm of one of his giant hands.

Maybe so. But for now, Aiah is content with her triumph, and with her place in things to come.

FIVE

"Here is our secure room, for our sensitive files."

The triumvirate and their entourage look into the bronze-lined room with polite disinterest. They have seen secure rooms before, and this one is no different. The bronze sheathing and the bronze-barred door are designed to keep plasm out, and there is a guard and a pass system that allows only authorized people inside.

The shelves are mostly empty. Drumbeth looks at them with a military eye.

"How soon do you anticipate being able to commence operations?" he asks.

"We've already commenced," Aiah says. "Though our operations at present are directed at gathering intelligence."

"You would seem not to have gathered *much*," says Gentri, observing the empty shelves. He is the Minister of Public Security, head among other things of the police, and no friend to the Plasm Enforcement Division. He is a balding man in wine-colored velvet, and he looks about with obvious disdain as he strokes his graying mustache with his right index finger.

"It's early days," Aiah says. "We're not up to strength yet."

"I meant *active* operations," says Drumbeth.

She looks down at him—he is half a head shorter than she.

"That's a policy decision," Aiah says. "We can start arresting people right away, of course, but there are still some weeks to go in the amnesty, and I'd rather keep gathering information for the present."

She's making a deliberate hedge. The triumvirate are traveling with a large entourage, and she doesn't know how many of them might be conduits to the Silver Hand.

"Can you give me a date?" Drumbeth presses.

Aiah clenches her teeth. "I'd . . . rather not, sir. May I show you our ops room? It is just down the hall."

Hilthi gives her an accusing look. He is another triumvir, the former journalist whose opposition to the Keremaths became a byword. A tall man with tilted, supercilious eyes, he jots in a notebook with a golden pen as he speaks.

"You are not prepared to arrest these criminals? The problem of stolen plasm is vast and requires immediate remedy." He frowns at her. "Totalitarian governments always find their chief allies within the criminal classes. Though the last government is gone, their allies still remain, causing untold suffering among the population."

It is as if Hilthi were caught between his old profession of journalist, interrogating guilty members of a wicked government, and his new occupation, a politician who makes speeches.

"We can arrest a few now," Aiah says. "Or *many* later. No official policy has yet been formulated concerning which of these options we consider desirable." She casts a glance at Constantine. He has been in the back of the crowd, looming over the triumvirate with an imperturbable expression on his face, and till now content to let her do the talking.

"I'm afraid that's my fault, gentlemen," he says. "I wanted better information on the dimension of the problem before taking action. The amnesty is still in place, after all, and we have *all* been on the job only a few weeks."

Hilthi scowls and writes on his pad.

"May I point out," Gentri says, "that Public Security *has* a policy in place, and that our plasm squads arrest criminals almost daily? Was it not Mr. Hilthi"—he gives a slight bow to his superior—"who issued the directive about eliminating redundancy whenever possible?" He looks at Aiah. "I do not doubt the enthusiasm of these, ah, *amateurs,* but I very much doubt if they will give you anything like satisfactory results."

Aiah feels Gentri's sting lodge in her heart. It would hurt less, she knew, if she weren't, in fact, such a complete novice at everything she's done.

She looks at Gentri levelly. "Give us six months," she says, "and we shall see whose record is better."

"A bold challenge," Gentri says, "but my personnel outnumbers yours by tens of thousands. You don't have a chance."

Aiah's response is ready on her tongue—*in your pants,* perhaps, or *call the neighbors,* or some other expression from her old neighborhood—but though the words are ready, she manages to bottle them up at the last second. Perhaps Drumbeth senses her struggle, because he chooses this moment to speak.

"Perhaps," he says, "we will observe an exhibition of the values of competition. Now shall we go on to the ops rooms?"

The ops rooms, one large and one small, are still a shambles: video monitors with their copper cables hanging, plasm connections with hardware yet to be installed, plastic flooring still in huge rolls in the corner. But Aiah finds herself growing enthusiastic as she explains what it will look like when it's finished, how supervisors will use the monitors to coordinate the actions of mages and military police.

"This is all very well, and you speak with enthusiasm and charm," says Parq, whose title is not only triumvir but Holy. "The material functions of the room—its mighty purpose and dread, impersonal power—are impressive indeed. But I sense a certain moral uncertainty at work here. Perhaps the young lady stands in need of guidance." He approaches Aiah and takes her hand.

Aiah cannot conceive of a more perfect image of a spiritual leader—Parq is tall and dignified and handsome, with solemn brown eyes in a long, copper-skinned face. His curling gray beard is long and silky and perfumed, and his soft, satin baritone projects a perfect sincerity. He wears gray robes, beautifully ornamented with silver lace, and a soft mushroom-shaped hat.

If Aiah didn't know he was a corrupt tyrant who had only been elevated to his position because he was willing to collaborate with the Keremaths, she might well have fallen under his spell.

At close range, Parq gazes into Aiah's eyes with utter concern. "Wouldn't your task be made easier," he asks, "if you had a spiritual guide in your division, one to give you insight into the complex decisions with which you will be faced almost daily?"

Aiah restrains the impulse to yank her hand back from his satin grip.

"I'm sure that's not for me to say, sir," she says.

Parq presses on, taking a soft step nearer Aiah so that she can feel the warmth of his breath on her cheek. She suppresses the urge to claw his face to ribbons. "You would find such guidance to be of use, I'm certain," he says, his soft voice like that of a suitor whispering into the ear of his beloved. "You are a stranger here, and so is Minister Constantine, and a wise advisor familiar with the local conditions would be worth everything to you. . . ."

"That's a decision that will have to be made at a higher level than mine, I'm afraid," Aiah says, and slides her hand from his grasp.

"Perhaps," Constantine says, secret amusement glittering in his eyes, "you gentlemen would care to observe a few of our mages conducting a surveillance. . . ."

GRADE B EARTHQUAKE IN DOLIMARQ

75,000 DEAD

TRIUMVIRATE EXPRESSES SYMPATHY FOR VICTIMS

"A delicate escape from Parq," Constantine says, "but nicely done. I could tell that you wanted to strike him, and on behalf of the Ministry of Resources I would like to commend you on your restraint."

The tour over, Constantine and Aiah take refuge in his office.

Weariness and relief beat down on Aiah's shoulders. She can't tell if she's done well or ill, but she is thankful that she will not have to deal with any more triumvirs today. She collapses into a chair, feels leather and hydraulics receive her.

"I wish I felt I could have spoken to them more frankly," she says. "I would like to tell them I'd make a hundred arrests the very day the amnesty ends."

He looks at her, fingers thoughtfully touching his chin. Behind him, visible through the huge oval window, plasm adverts glow in air. "Can you make a hundred arrests? Will you?"

"You said you wanted them *destroyed*. I can't do that, I suppose, but I'll do what I can. If, of course, you'll give me the soldiers to do it. And warrants."

"Naturally I shall. Geymard's troops will get bored if they do nothing but guard the Palace."

She glances up at him. "I have learned something from you and Geymard and Drumbeth," she says. "A tactic I wish to employ."

"Yes?"

"*Decapitation is best.* I want to slice the head of the Silver Hand clean off in one stroke."

"There are more Handmen than there were Keremaths," Constantine observes. "And more heads."

"With their leaders gone, I hope the rest will fight over the spoils. And perhaps even inform on each other, to weaken their rivals."

Constantine nods. "A policy that promises well. Though you should not count on them to inform—it is the one thing, the one guild rule, that is ruthlessly enforced."

"I would like to publicize a telephone number that informants can call. With rewards, perhaps. But that means hiring more clerical staff and coming up with reward money."

Constantine gives this notion a moment's thought. "Wait until after your first arrests. If they are successful, I will have more leverage with the triumvirate."

"If you think that's best."

Constantine looks down at his ebony-and-gilt desk. He

opens a drawer, reaches inside, takes out Aiah's copy of *Proceedings,* and pushes it across the desk toward her.

"I have ordered the entire set from the Jaspeeri Plasm Authority," he says, and his grin broadens. "I wonder what they will make of it? Double-express delivery, and addressed to me personally, a man to whom the Authority police would very much like to talk."

She takes the heavy book from his desk and holds it in her lap. "I imagine they will take your money and send the books."

"I imagine they will." His head cocks to one side, and he regards her from beneath half-closed eyes. "How well did you know this Rohder?"

"Not well, though I worked for him at one point. Catching plasm thieves, because the Authority had given him no other job." She smiles. "And because he needed a hobby."

"Would he come to work for us, do you think?"

"I will call him, if you like."

"An interview first. At his convenience. I will send an aerocar for him."

"He has almost three hundred years' seniority at the Authority. It's a lot to give up."

"Well." Constantine shrugs. "We will see how badly he needs a hobby."

Aiah smiles. "I will make the call."

There is a knock on the doorframe, and Sorya walks in. She wears a silk dress the color of apricots and a belt of linked gold geomantic foci low on her hips, and carries a file folder.

Aiah's nerves cry an alarm, but Sorya ignores her. She walks past Aiah's chair with her languid panther stride, drops the folder on Constantine's desk, then pulls out a chair and sits uninvited.

"The interrogations have gone well," she says. "I have uncovered a few dozen foreign accounts where these Keremath men, these little losers, have been keeping their millions."

Constantine gazes at Sorya with a hooded expression, lips turned up in a smile. A cruel little predatory glimmer dwells in his eyes, a twin to the gleam Aiah can see in Sorya's glance.

"The question is how to retrieve this money," Sorya says,

and draws her legs up into the chair, coiling herself in the soft leather as if it were Constantine's lap. "We can go through the courts, and, on convincing them that these Keremath men are guilty of theft, and that the money was corruptly gained, we may in the end retrieve it, *or . . .*" She smiles. "Or we may mount an operation. I have their chops. An agent with the right passwords and the right chop can gain the money in a half-shift's work."

"I will review the files."

"In my judgment a few of these sums are worth the risk. I have already had my people in the banks here in Caraqui, torn out deposit boxes with crowbars, and found bonds and jewels enough to run the Force of the Interior for a week."

"Ah." He deliberately examines a dangling jewel about her neck. Rubies and brilliants, glittering amid a nested serpent design, wink Shieldlight back at him.

"*That* is very fine," Constantine remarks, "and new, I believe."

Sorya gives her lilting laugh. "A souvenir only," she says. "I will return it to the state when I tire of it. But I think I will wear it to Justice Gathmark's reception this sleep shift, and let him wonder where he has seen it before, and around whose pretty neck, and wonder as well what has happened to that old crony of his, for whom he did so many favors."

They laugh at this conceit. A leaden weight sits on Aiah's heart as she watches these companions at their clever play.

She pushes her chair back and stands.

"I'll leave you to your work, Minister," she says.

Sorya laughs again and looks at Aiah from beneath a soft wave of her blonde-streaked hair. "I was sorry to miss the tour last shift," she says. "I hear good things of your department."

And I hear nothing good of yours. Aiah burns to say it, but instead says "Thank you," and makes her way out.

She hears Sorya's laugh again as she closes the door behind her, and she remembers Constantine's words: *A personal power base in your department may not be a bad thing.*

Indeed, she concludes, not a bad thing at all.

WHY LIVE WITH BLEMISHED SKIN . . .
WHEN YOU CAN BE PERFECT?

REASONABLE RATES—INQUIRE NOW!

Another plasm house confirmed.

Another tip from the half-worlds proven accurate.

Aiah throws the switch and feels the transphysical world fade, sees the smaller of the two operations rooms come back into focus. The room is a shambles, gear piled everywhere and cables taped to the floor, with only a few plasm stations operational. Even though it's early first shift, every station is being used by mages on surveillance. Aiah's own shift ended at 24:00, but she stayed for another hour in order to make notes on a conversation the Handmen were having concerning a hijacking they'd pulled off in Barchab. The Barchabi police would probably be interested to know the names of the Barchabi accomplices.

It takes half an hour for Aiah to write her notes into a form suitable for transcription, next shift, by one of the department's clerical aides; and then she tucks the file under her arm and makes her way out of the room.

The secure room is down a short hall. She'll put the file there till work shift, then head to her apartment to take a shower and get some sleep. If, that is, the blazing plasm she's been feeding into her nerves over the last hours will permit her even to close her eyes. . . .

Aiah nods to the guard and says hello to the clerk, a little goggle-eyed embryo woman, who's on duty and bent over her desk, keeping the index up to date. Aiah gives her the file number so that she can log it in. Then she steps to the door of the secure room itself, puts her hand on the cool bronze bar, and prepares to punch the day's code into the twelve-key pad. No, the *next* day's code, because it's after change of shift. . . .

She looks up and feels her heart turn over. Constantine is in the secure room, sitting at a metal desk, head bent as he copies something from a file. There is a cold light in his lowered eyes, and his upper lip is curled, as if in distaste for the task he has set himself.

Constantine, normally so aware of his surroundings, hasn't even glanced up at her approach.

She steps silently back from the barred door and puts the file on the desk of the clerk. "I don't want to disturb the minister," she says. "Could you file this for me after he leaves?"

The big eyes lift to hers. "Certainly."

Aiah walks away. *I don't want to know when it happens,* she had told Constantine. *I don't want to know who, or when, or why it is being done.*

He is choosing Taikoen's victims, Aiah knows. Going through the files to find the most deserving of the Handmen. She probably won't know which.

Until Taikoen is done with each, when Aiah will tell the clerk to retire his file.

GOVERNMENT DECIDES TO
SELL ARMS COMPANY

QERWAN EMPLOYEES PROTEST DECISION

Aiah, telepresent, watches the old man snore. He lives in a fashionable district, in an expensive apartment building that presents to its canal a long, sinuous, reflective ribbon of black glass. The ownership of the building seems obscure, and is being looked into. The man himself seems untroubled by the ambiguity. From the corner, an icon of the prophet Dalavos regards this domestic scene with approval. A little glittering jewel of drool hangs in the corner of his mouth as he sleeps, next to his third wife, beneath an expensive Sycar comforter.

It is 02:00, early first shift, and the amnesty on plasm thieves expired two hours earlier, at 24:00. The opalescent Shield is bright overhead, undimmed by cloud, but most of the world is in bed, and few see the purposeful powerboats or the shrouded military convoys leaving the Palace district. The old man has polarized his windows, and his room is dark.

The man in the bed is Great-Uncle Rathmen, the head of Caraqui's Silver Hand, and he is 111 years old, a thin, precise man fond of handmade boots and sentimental tokaph music. Like Costantine, he has kept aging at bay with regular plasm-rejuvenation treatments. Except that his are illegal, performed with bootleg plasm; one of Aiah's observers even saw one of the procedures being performed out of an illegal plasm tap in the man's apartment. The tap appeared to have been in place for a long time, and may have been designed into the building when it was built.

To live longer than a century is unusual in a Handman. It speaks less of his skill than of how comfortably the Silver Hand lives in Caraqui, that none of his underlings has seen any profit in removing him.

He has taken precautions, however: there is a crosshatching of bronze mesh in the glass windows, and other bronze grids in the wall paneling, beneath the floor tile, and hidden behind the ceiling. But he's remodeled since he moved in, and some of the bronze mesh wasn't properly reinstalled: one of Aiah's surveillance teams found a way to sneak a sourceline in. And so Aiah, sensorium configured so as to see in the dark, plays plasm angel and hovers over Rathmen's bed.

Back in the Palace's big ops room, she feels her assistant touch her arm. She lets her telepresent sensations fade, nods, and hears a voice in her ear. "The soldiers are in the building." She nods her comprehension.

Aiah returns her awareness to her anima, and the command center fades from her perceptions.

In a few minutes there's a crash as the door goes down—with martial law there's no particular reason to knock—and Great-Uncle Rathmen comes awake with a start. To him it must mean the crash he's waited for the last eighty years, the sound that marks his assassination and the end of his reign.

"Police!" the soldiers shout. "Police!"

But it's what Great-Uncle's assassins would say, whether they were police or not. Looking many decades less than a hundred years old, he throws back the Sycar comforter and vaults over his drowsy wife to the closet at the other side of the bed. There he slides open the door and fumbles for a panel built into the back of the wall.

Tension jolts through Aiah at the sight. She hadn't known the panel was there, nor what is on the other side of it. She'd expected him to jump for the plasm circuit set into the wall near his desk.

Number three wife is awake. *"What should I do?"* she screams. *"What should I do?"*

"Call Gemming!" Rathmen says, but all his wife does is shriek her question over and over.

Call Gemming, Aiah writes automatically, scrawling blindly in loopy handwriting on a pad balanced on her chair arm. Something else for the files. But her nerves are screaming, and she has no confidence that the writing, at the end of the episode, will even be coherent.

At least as agitated as Aiah, Great-Uncle Rathmen is having a hard time with his secret panel. His hands are shaking so hard that he can't seem to work the mechanism. The soldiers are stomping down the hall, crying "Police!" The beams of their torches jitter into the room.

Rathmen finally tears away the panel by main strength. He reaches inside, and Aiah sees, with her plasm-enhanced vision, the tube of a weapon propped in the interior.

Aiah's act is instinctual, like a parent swatting from her child's hands the bottle of rat poison. She forms an ectoplasmic hand faster than thought and slaps Great-Uncle Rathmen with it, knocking him away from the closet. There's a strange unreality to it all—if she'd hit him with a real hand there would be feedback, her hand would sting and register the impact, but the hastily formed plasm hand isn't configured to register sense impressions, and when Aiah sees Great-Uncle Rathmen flying across the room it seems as unreal as an image in a chromoplay.

With more deliberation, Aiah plants the insubstantial hand on his chest and pins him to the ground like an insect until the soldiers, a half-second later, storm into the room—weaponed, in full battle armor, faceplates lowered to guard against explosion or plasm blast. They are followed by a cameraman with a huge spotlight, providing a feed to the ops center. At this intimidating sight the third wife screams and cowers.

The officer flicks on the lights and everyone blinks. The

woman on the bed even stops screaming. Aiah stifles a giggle—she's the only one who sees how silly everyone looks. The captain marches up to Great-Uncle Rathmen, compares him with a chromograph he's carrying in his file, and informs the Great-Uncle he's under arrest.

Aiah dissolves her ectomorphic hand and the officer handcuffs his prisoner. The old Handman accepts this stolidly—reassured, apparently, that he won't be assassinated, at least not yet.

Aiah concentrates on expanding her anima, configuring it into a recognizable human shape. The last time she did this, back in Jaspeer, she failed to provide the anima any clothing and delighted the witnesses more than she'd intended, but in this case she mentally sculpts a more abstract image—female-shaped, yes, but without any detail, like a weathered statue, or a smooth metal abstract. She wills the image to fluoresce, and the soldiers blink again as the room is flooded with golden light. Aiah looks at her reflection in the mirrored closet doors—a glorious figure of shimmering gold—and spares a few seconds to admire her handiwork.

Some of the soldiers shift nervously, take a firmer grip on their weapons. They can't be sure whether this apparition is friendly or otherwise.

"Can you hear me?" Aiah says, and some of the soldiers clap hands over ears. She tries to speak more softly, and raises a fluorescent hand to point into the closet.

"There is a weapon in there. He was trying to get to it when I prevented him."

"Thank you, ma'am," the officer says.

She allows her image to fade as the officer peers cautiously into the closet. He reaches in with a gloved hand and pulls out the weapon, a short metal barrel with a functional black plastic grip and a metal stock telescoped to its shortest configuration. There's a wire that runs from the gun into the hidden closet compartment.

"Shotgun," the captain says. "Semiautomatic. Wired to a plasm circuit. I'm wearing insulated gloves, otherwise I'd be getting a dose of the goods right now." He holds it up. "Felk, get a picture of this. And I'll need an evidence bag."

The weapon is a nasty one, enabling Great-Uncle Rathmen

to smite his enemies with shot and plasm at once. It's at least a dozen ways illegal, and mere possession of such a thing is enough to guarantee Rathmen a stretch in prison.

Triumph burns in Aiah's mind. Her anima follows the soldiers as they seal the rooms, then march their prisoners to their waiting boats. Then Aiah thumbs off her t-grip, and the distant quay fades from her mind, is replaced by the busy ops center.

With some help from Geymard's mercenaries, the big ops room was finished by the deadline. Though some of the flooring isn't yet in place, plasm and electric connections still snake over the floor, and the room smells strongly of paint, the place is at least functional. Banks of monitors glow down on the proceedings, and mages sway in their chairs, their eyes closed as they concentrate on telepresent sensations.

She looks down at the form propped on her chair arm, checks the wall clock, and logs the time she finished her part of the operation.

"Very nicely done, Miss Aiah." Constantine's voice rumbles in her ear. She gives a start, then turns to see him standing behind her chair.

"Thank you, Minister," she says. She stands, stretches. Plasm's fierce glow fires her cramped muscles.

Constantine's eyes flicker along the rows of video monitors, pausing at each for a brief moment, then going on to the next. There is a pleased, ruthless little smile on his face.

"Your operations are going well. A few of your teams have got lost in crowded tenements, but your telepresent mages seem to have put them all back on the right track."

"Colonel Geymard's staff were a great help."

"They will need the practice. Most of their operations for the foreseeable future consist of arrests. I have persuaded the government to import two more battalions of military police." He folds his arms, looks at her seriously. "How much thought have you given to what happens to your prisoners after their arrest?

She looks at him. "Trial, conviction, imprisonment. But that isn't my department's problem, is it? We just gather evidence, make arrests, present the evidence to the prosecutors."

"Yes, but interrogations of these people would be invaluable, both to your department and to others. The information could lead to many further arrests."

"True." She hadn't considered interrogations, in part because her informers' information has been so good, in part because she doubted the Handmen would talk, and more conclusively because she hadn't the time or personnel.

"We can conduct interrogations, of course," she says. "We have their dossiers, we have a good idea what questions to ask."

"But you don't have trained interrogation specialists. Other departments do."

"The police, you mean?"

"Yes, after their fashion . . ." He nods patiently. "Amateurish, and reluctant to deal with Handmen at all. One could have Colonel Geymard's people do it, but they don't know which questions to ask, and they're not familiar with local conditions in any case." As he gazes down at her his expression hardens, grows commanding. "It was the Force of the Interior, of course, that I meant."

Distaste curls Aiah's lip. "Sorya's political police."

"Yes." He cocks his head and considers, weighing his thoughts. "I wish them to no longer *be* political police—I plan that soon there will be no more political prisoners, not once the remaining Keremaths and collaborators are dealt with. I wish the F.I. to become merely national police, with a mandate to deal with espionage and crimes against the state. And as the Silver Hand is the greatest organized force that threatens us at present, I wish to direct some of Sorya's specialists against them."

A protest bursts from Aiah's lips. "There was torture in the Specials' prisons," she says. "Those people were—"

A fierce light burns in Constantine's eyes. "The torturers are gone," he says firmly. "Or in prison themselves. Torture is a pointless and stupid exercise—there are more sanitary methods, and far more effective."

"Plasm scans." Grimly.

"Everyone in your department has already had one. You have had one yourself, when I first met you. Are they so inhumane?"

Aiah struggles to form another protest. She couldn't remember her own scan—Constantine had gone into her head on a ruthless probe of plasm in order to discover if she was a police informer, but if he had found anything else he had kept it to himself.

"I want it understood," Aiah says, "that civilized methods will be observed."

"Of course. There is no conceivable reason to behave otherwise." Warmth kindles in his eyes as he looks at her. "This concern does you credit."

She looks away. "I still don't like it."

"I will arrange the protocols with Sorya's office, so they will have access to the prisoners and you will have copies of all the interrogations."

"Yes. Of course."

Some of Aiah's people raise a cheer: someone has made a particularly stylish arrest. Constantine looks up at the monitors. "Arrests in future may not be so peaceful, not once surprise is lost," he says, and turns to Aiah again.

The monitors' reflection kindles a cold flickering in his eyes. "The government passed a new decree last shift, making it a capital crime to belong to a criminal organization."

Aiah's heart gives a lurch. She looks at Constantine in surprise. "Which means what? Some of these people will be executed?"

Constantine makes a dismissive, growling sound. "*All* of them, if I have anything to say about it. Great-Uncle Rath men particularly—he was one of the first in my office with his bribes, only a few days after the coup. Smiled, brought me a new jacket of expensive goatskin lined with silk and, for all I know, a fortune in jewels in the pockets . . . offered me the locations of a couple of his plasm houses under the amnesty program, said it was an oversight. I turned down the jacket, but sent ministry crews to wire the plasm into the circuit—didn't keep it for myself, as he probably expected." He straightens, lips curling in distaste. "A plausible, bloody-handed bastard. It never occurred to him that I *wouldn't* accept his payoffs. He had probably never met a civil servant who wasn't on the take."

Aiah turns to the monitors, sees the jumpy camera feed,

half-dressed sleepy-eyed handcuffed men, pompadours hanging in their eyes, being marched onto trucks or into boats.

All condemned, she thinks. She shivers at the thought that she is watching men who soon will die.

"I wish there was another way," she says.

"Mercy is a privilege of the powerful," Constantine says. "Our power is uncertain, and theirs is great, and we cannot afford to show them any lenience. If our situation were improved, if we were secure in our power, perhaps then a degree of forbearance would be possible." He shakes his head. "Besides, the only way to defeat the Handmen is to enlist the population, and these executions are the only way to show the people that the Hand is vulnerable now." A cold laugh rumbles from his throat. "And for what it's worth, each of the Handmen will have his fair trial—all your evidence will be considered by the military courts in the next week, and then sentences carried out."

"They are all guilty," Aiah says. "We know that." And therefore will all die, because of her. After Sorya's specialists rummage through their brains for useful information.

He raises a hand to touch her shoulder. She wants comfort, wants to rest her cheek against his rough knuckles, but is too conscious of the presence of the people surrounding them.

"Save sympathy for their victims," he says, voice low in her ear.

"I will." She looks at the video images again, looks for familiar images—the Slug, the Ferret. The images are all those of strangers. Strangers soon to die.

A cold wind seems to blow through her bones. She turns to Constantine again.

"These Handmen," she says, "they're like your family, aren't they? You were raised with people like this. And . . ." Her tongue stumbles on the words. "You destroyed them."

Constantine's face is a mask. The reversed video images of condemned men float through his eyes.

"My family deserved what happened to them," he says, "and so, Miss Aiah, do *these*."

With that, he turns and prowls away.

Somewhere, audio feed from one of her teams, there comes the sound of cheering.

CRIME LORD PROTESTS INNOCENCE

"GOVERNMENT ILL-ADVISED,"
SAYS ATTORNEY.

CRACKDOWN ON GANGSTERS CONTINUES
UNDER MARTIAL LAW

"Well," Ethemark says, "the suspect just *exploded*. He was under arrest; our soldiers had him handcuffed and were marching him out of the room—and then . . ." His mouth twists with distaste. "We had a camera on him at the time. You can watch the video, if you like, but unless you want to see your lunch again I wouldn't recommend it."

It is an inquiry on the PED's only complete disaster: suspect dead while under arrest, the dead man's wife and children witnesses to everything, everyone involved under suspension pending the outcome of the investigation.

Aiah looks down the table at the three members of the commission she'd appointed when the incident occurred. "The plasm angels saw nothing?"

"Three mages were telepresent in the room," says Kelban, one of her team supervisors. "They maintain they had configured their sensoriums so as to be aware of plasm, and they saw nothing . . . not till after it was over."

"They saw something then," Ethemark says. "They were all aware of a powerful . . . presence. It hovered over the body for a moment, then disappeared. No one saw a source-line. And they all say . . ." He hesitates. "They were all *terrified*. Not just the mages, but the soldiers, too. The soldiers couldn't even see it, whatever it was, but they could somehow feel it, and it spooked them."

"If you ask me," Kelban says, "a man exploding right in front of them is enough to scare any number of soldiers."

Aiah's mouth goes dry. *Taikoen,* she thinks, or another creature like him. Constantine had put him in the Handman's body, and when the soldiers came, Taikoen had seen no point in staying.

"Do we have any conclusions?" she ventures.

"I think it's down to the inexperience of our personnel," says Kelban. "They got careless, or overexcited, and weren't paying proper attention. The suspect was killed by some enemy, or by other Handmen who were afraid he would turn informer."

"I have another theory," Ethemark ventures, "though I admit it's very tenuous."

Aiah looks at him warily. She must protect Constantine, she thinks, and discourage even the notion of a hanged man.

"Go on," she says.

"It may be some kind of time bomb," Ethemark says, to Aiah's relief. "A plasm bomb planted inside him, with the instruction to kill him if he were ever arrested."

"That kind of time bomb would be very difficult," Kelban says. "And time bombs have a temporal limit—you can't confine plasm in a human body for more than a few hours. And who would have done such a thing . . . to *him?* And why? He was only a cousin."

"He might have done it to *himself,*" Ethemark says. "We know he had access to plasm. And some Handmen are simply crazy."

"Well," Aiah says, "if the Silver Hand possesses a mage capable of such a difficult piece of work, then we shall discover it soon enough. The next time . . ."

Kelban finishes her sentence. "The next time one of our suspects blows up."

And then he laughs and shakes his head.

Aiah does not find herself amused. She has a suspicion that more than one Handman is going to die this way.

"Finish your report," Aiah says, "and have it on my desk tomorrow."

GARGELIUS ENCHUK ON TOUR

NEW RECORDING BREAKS RECORDS

"NEW CITY WORLD" TOPS CHARTS

A week later, the first sheaf of typed interrogation transcripts arrives on Aiah's desk. An eerie sensation creeps up her spine as she reads them.

All of them are in the first person. There are no questions included, as if the Handmen were dictating lengthy confessions rather than responding to interrogators. The typed pages are all in the same format.

My name is such-and-such. . . . On such-and-such a date I committed the following crime. . . . This was at the instigation of so-and-so, and assisting me were the following accomplices. . . . I am aware of plasm houses at the following locations. . . .

The last information, she decides, she can check. She does, and her mages discover it is all perfectly accurate.

The transcripts keep arriving, a new bundle every few days.

Military courts move briskly through the long line of cases.

Eventually soldiers draw lots, and the losers are assigned to the firing squads.

SIX

The balcony rail of the Falcon Tower is a huge bronze likeness of a peregrine, gazing fiercely over the Palace and the city below, wings outspread to shelter those who stand on the balcony. Constantine, standing behind the peregrine with no less fierce an expression, looks as if he is riding the falcon's back, aimed like an arrow at the city. A brisk wind rattles the air around him and he clearly rejoices in it, in its cold perfect vigor.

"Governing," he murmurs. "All contradictions, all paradox."

The city spreads out below him: green sea, rooftop gardens, glittering mirrorglass. In the distance, the spikes of Lorkhin Island sit on the horizon like a strange, alien crown.

"Plasm makes everything more intense," he says. "It fills the world's political history with turbulence even as it opens realms of political possibility. Plasm is transformative in this as in everything else."

He gives his cynical demon grin. "How many of our histories—hah! our legends, our chromoplays and operas—how many concern a leader, a Metropolitan or king or general, who is destroyed by some bright spark who gets lucky with a plasm strike? And then this spark becomes the new leader—absolute power leaving a greater vacuum than other sorts—

and our young hero gathers dominion until he has it all, is able to wave a transphysical hand and give foundation to his dreams, and perhaps he achieves wisdom as well as glory . . . ah, but then, death at the hands of some other political entrepreneur."

"That tale describes you, except for the ending," Aiah says. "You survived."

He looks at her, raises a thoughtful eyebrow. "In a sense, I did not. The man that I was did *not* survive. All that sustained him died—friends, family, nation, ideals. I had to make a new self afterward." His look turns inward. "I am wiser now, but it is the kind of wisdom that turns a man bitter. I do not know if I am better for having achieved it."

He looks down at the city again. The blustery wind paws at the lace at his throat. He throws out a hand, encompassing the world below, and then closes a fist, takes possession. Irony tugs at his lips. "To be the *one man* is dangerous. When I was Metropolitan of Cheloki, when the whole state rested on my shoulders—what happened to my dreams then? I wanted to change the foundations of everything, but it was all I could do to keep my head safely on my neck. But to *give up* power—that is dangerous, too, because to surrender power is to surrender the ability to create change. . . ."

He nods, looks out to the southwest, to the distant metropolis where Aiah was born. "That is the solution of the Scope of Jaspeer, to divide the power sufficiently that no one strike can threaten the survival of the state. The assembly, the senate, the powerful intendants, the premier, the president, the council of ministers . . ." He shakes his head. "But with division of power comes division of responsibility. No one in Jaspeer possesses real power, and no one is really responsible for anything, least of all positive change—a certain discrete flow in the negative direction is permitted, a calcification of the public arteries. . . . But while the decay slowly sets in, it is the boast of Jaspeer that nothing has changed there in hundreds of years." Amusement sparkles in his eyes, and he gives a low laugh. "Perhaps not *boast,* perhaps rather a self-satisfied little moan, *we are as our grandfathers were, and want nothing more.*"

Aiah's laugh echoes Constantine's own. She worked in

the Jaspeeri government for years, and her impression of her superiors is no more positive than Constantine's.

"And so the cycles continue," Constantine says. "Despots follow despots, bureaucrats follow bureaucrats, each condemned to do the job of his predecessor, sometimes a little better, usually only a little worse. When the decay gets too pronounced there's revolution or war, but then a new despot or faction takes control and begins the game all over again. Can it be changed, I wonder, without bringing it all down?"

"You've changed it," Aiah says. "You've got rid of the Keremaths and replaced them with something better."

"I've done as well as could be expected," Constantine says. He looks pensive; this self-deprecating mood is not a natural one for him. "One person can change little," he muses, "but a person's *idea* . . . an idea tested, perfected, demonstrated, *shown to be true* . . . that is real power. Ideas—the good ones, anyway—can be immortal."

His hard raptor eyes gaze down at the city, looking at it as an opponent, a thing to be subdued and brought to heel. "This Caraqui is the testing ground," he says. "Here, with a little luck, things can be made to happen. Here, the ideas may meet their proof. But the place is poor, desperately poor, the workforce has little education and few skills, and I have little time. . . ." He frowns.

"There is a recipe for creating wealth," he says. "It is simple enough. Reduce tariffs, reduce state spending, reduce controls on borrowing and lending. Protect the value of the currency while allowing free exchange, permit the citizens free access to foreign currencies. Permit the citizens to keep any wealth they earn—no confiscations or extortions, such as were practiced under the Keremaths—and tax with a light hand, with a tax code renowned for its evenhandedness and a revenue bureau renowned for its incorruptibility. . . ."

He laughs. "Incorruptibility in Caraqui! But it is necessary: one must be *seen* to do all this, because it works only when it can be seen that you can be trusted, and to build full trust requires at least a generation. There are plenty of other places to put money where one *can* get a good return, and an investor wants guarantees. . . .

"And in the meantime, to make certain the wealth is not so

completely concentrated at the top, one encourages trade unions, one promotes safety standards and discourages child labor . . . but that is all one *can* do at this point, for there is no money yet, nothing for good universal education, nothing for housing, and that places the most vulnerable portion of our population in jeopardy, isolated, hopeless, confined to slums or in half-worlds, subject to extortion by the Silver Hand. . . ."

He looks at Aiah. "That is where *you* come in. You must show the people that the Silver Hand is vulnerable, that they *can* be broken. It is a way of building trust in the new regime, a way just like all the other methods, only more visible. And like the other ways, it will take a generation or more. Building a nation is slow work, one has to think in long spans of time; but that works against instinct, because in politics one always reaches for a *solution,* and the only realistic solution in Caraqui is that if you do this now, your grandchildren may be happy."

Aiah steps forward, touches his arm. "I think you may be underestimating the strength of your argument."

He looks at her, a glow in his eyes, and puts his hand over hers. "Possibly I am. But still, the problem is wealth, and how to get it. And that is why your Mr. Rohder is important. He can increase the wealth of the nation, and in a short space of time; and then the problem becomes one of *conserving* the wealth, keeping the government from pissing it all into the canals. . . ."

Constantine laughs, and Aiah laughs with him. And then he shakes his head. "And it is not up to me. I am but a voice in the government. I must persuade, and I must persuade for the next thirty years."

"You're doing pretty well so far."

He shrugs. "I have the PED, yes. I have given it to you, because I can trust you to carry on with it."

The keys on Aiah's office commo unit are stainless steel, ranked in a gleaming, efficient array. Here in her bedroom the commo keys are silver, and set amid a polished fruitwood setting, a design of interlocking sigmas that climb into a third dimension through clever use of trompe l'oeil.

Aiah wonders if living amid this type of ornate luxury is changing her, even if the luxury is not precisely hers.

She remembers Rohder's extension number perfectly well, and punches the number onto the silver keys of her commo array. Through her gold-and-ivory headset she hears the clatter of relays, and then the ringing signal.

"Da. Rohder." The voice is breathy, distracted, cigaret-harsh. Aiah finds herself smiling at the familiar sound.

"Mr. Rohder? This is Aiah."

There is a moment's silence. "I am surprised to hear from you," Rohder finally says.

"Why is that?"

Aiah hears the sound of Rohder pulling on a cigaret, then the exhalation. "The Authority police seem to think you are a criminal," he says. "They have questioned me repeatedly. Perhaps I am under suspicion myself."

"They would be pretty foolish to think that."

"You embarrassed them." There is a little pause. "And you embarrassed me."

A pang of conscience burns in Aiah's throat. "I'm sorry if that's the case," she says. "I hunted plasm thieves for you. And I found them, too."

"Yes, you did. Which makes your other behavior even more surprising."

Time, Aiah thinks, to change the subject. She is tired of dwelling on her sins.

"Perhaps I can make it up to you," she says. "I head the Plasm Enforcement Division now, in Caraqui."

Rohder takes a meditative draw on his cigaret. "Caraqui, yes. People are being shot there, I believe, by foreign mercenaries. I have seen it on video."

Aiah winces. The executions of the first few Handmen were widely publicized, to demonstrate to the population that the Silver Hand was no longer immune to justice.

But the publicity didn't stop at the borders. Now all most people knew about Caraqui was that Constantine's government was employing firing squads.

"I—it wasn't my idea to shoot them," she says. "They *are* gangsters, of course."

"Were," Rohder corrects. "And if you ever engage in the

sort of activities in Caraqui in which you seem to have engaged here in Jaspeer, you could be shot, too."

Aiah feels herself harden at the implied accusation. "You don't know *what* I did in Jaspeer, Mr. Rohder."

"True." After a moment's thought.

"The fact that I helped you take down some Operation plasm houses should show you what side I'm on."

"Perhaps."

"Since my department started its work just a few weeks ago, we've put the hammer on ninety-one plasm houses in Caraqui and arrested over three hundred people, many of them high-level Operation types. There are another sixty-odd plasm houses we'll move on in the next few weeks, once investigations are completed. I wonder, Mr. Rohder—how many plasm houses has the Jaspeeri Plasm Authority taken down since I left?"

There is a long silence, filled only by the meditative drawing on a cigaret.

"Perhaps you have a point, Miss Aiah," he says.

Aiah plunges ahead. "My boss, the Minister of Resources Constantine, has read your books. *Proceedings,* I mean. All fourteen volumes. And he thinks they, and you, are brilliant, and wants to meet you."

There is another silence, then, "He must be a fast reader."

"He would like to arrange a personal meeting to discuss your work. You would be picked up by aerocar, taken to Caraqui, lodged in the Aerial Palace for the duration of your stay, and returned by aerocar. Your fee would come to two thousand Jaspeeri dalders."

"That is remarkably attractive."

Aiah smiles. "Constantine makes attractive offers to those whose work impresses him. Is there a time when the visit will be most convenient?"

There is a hint of humor in Rohder's reply. "Well, I seem to have little occupying my attention at present. Though I suppose it would be best if I came to Caraqui on a weekend, just for appearances. And also for appearances' sake I will decline the fee, lest someone conclude that I am being paid for . . . well, past services rendered, and not a lecture."

"Perhaps I could arrange for the aerocar to fetch you this Friday? Service shift, after work hours?"

Arrangements are made. A glow of triumph warms Aiah's heart.

Things are progressing.

She hangs her headset on the hook, leans back on the pillows she's propped up on her bed, and considers what to do next. Perhaps she could go down to the operations center and see how the shift's activities are advancing. Several arrests have been scheduled for midway through sleep shift.

But no. Ethemark is in charge this shift. Aiah would just be in the way.

She wonders if there's anything on video worth watching.

The truth is, outside of her work and the few hours each week she spends with Constantine, she has no life in Caraqui. What she has seen of the metropolis does not attract her, and though she's grown familiar with parts of the city through telepresent surveillance work, most of her physical knowledge of Caraqui is confined to the carpeted, paneled labyrinth of the Aerial Palace.

It occurs to her that she could use a few friends. Perhaps she should try to recruit a few.

There is an urgent knock on the door, and then the door chime, the soft tone repeating itself over and over again as Aiah's visitor leans on it.

There is no reason for anyone to behave this way. If there's a situation in the department, someone can call. It's certainly faster than running all the way over from the Owl Wing.

Aiah puts her eye to the peephole. She doesn't see anyone.

Reflexes honed in her old neighborhood remind her not to open the door.

"Who's there?" she calls.

"Ethemark."

Ethemark, too short to be visible through the peephole. Aiah opens the door, sees herself reflected in her deputy's goggle eyes.

A cold hand touches Aiah's neck at the expression on Ethemark's face.

"What's happened?"

"Great-Uncle Rathmen. He's gone."

"Gone? How?"

"Teleported out of his cell, apparently. Right out of the secure unit."

Cold anger clenches Aiah's fists. "Somebody's been paid off."

"Very likely. I've got a boat waiting at the northwest water gate."

So that's why he'd come in person: Aiah's apartment was on his way to the northwest gate.

"Let me get a jacket," Aiah says.

TRIUMVIR PARQ ADDRESSES THE FAITHFUL

"DALAVOS, HIS PROPHECIES, AND YOU"

THIRD SHIFT ON CHANNEL 17

The prison dates from the period of the Avians, who liked their official buildings to aspire to a certain magnificence. Shieldlight gleams from its white stone walls and winks off the baroque bronze traceries, functional and ornamental at once, designed to ward off attack. It is as if the building were designed to deny the horrors that went on inside.

As with the Palace, evidence of the Avians is all over the building, stylized reliefs of wings over every entrance, the wing tips curled outward as if to embrace the prisoners as they approach. Transmission horns in the shape of hawks or eagles, statues of raptors in niches, and even the bronze collection web is an abstract design of interlocking wings.

Aiah hasn't had a reason to be here before. As the boat approaches the prison's water gate, she looks up at the outcurving wings above her and shivers as the shadow comes between her and the light.

Inside, the place is strangely hygienic and functional, like a hospital, or a modern abattoir. Unstained bright colors, polished metal, bright fluorescent light. The Keremaths had remained true to the Avians' spirit and kept their dungeons tidy.

The special secure wing is deep in the heart of the building and smells of disinfectant and despair. The triumvir Hilthi had paid for his journalistic dedication with a few years here, and so had many others released by the coup. Now the place was filled with Keremath supporters and gangsters.

Great-Uncle Rathmen had been tried by a military court and condemned to death within a week of his capture. He had been kept alive only because his interrogations were producing valuable information. Because he knew so much, the plasm scanners wanted to be very thorough with him, and the interrogations were many and painstaking. His file in Aiah's secure room was growing thicker every week, long lists of contacts, payoffs, funds hidden in banks or basements.

To reach through the secure area, Aiah has to pass through two airlocks, sets of double doors screened with bronze mesh, intended to prevent even the smallest probe of plasm from slipping through. No expense or effort was spared to keep the prisoners out of the reach of any mage who might have wished to liberate them.

No expense was spared, that is, except on the guards. They are paid poorly, as are all civil servants here, and Aiah finds that Rathmen has almost certainly been paying them commissions. His cell is filled with homey touches: a piece of colored paper taped over the recessed light to moderate the harsh electric bulb, a thick carpet with a Sycar design, Sycar wall hangings, photographs of Rathmen's family propped on a little table, cigarette butts in an ashtray. Even a box of sweets and a half-eaten pigeon pie.

Pillows—thick, soft, pleasant-looking pillows—are stuffed under the blanket to give the illusion of a sleeping prisoner.

Anger steams through Aiah's veins. She turns to the officer on watch, a big, balding man with a nervous gleam of sweat on his forehead.

"Have any of the other prisoners been allowed personal items?"

He shakes his head. "Not to my knowledge."

She decides to find out for herself and walks up to several cells at random. Just a few glimpses through peepholes show that a great many of them contain nonregulation items: colorful blankets, wall hangings, lamps, videos, even small refrigerators. Many are large enough to contain hidden plasm batteries.

Aiah turns to Ethemark. "Kelban is off this shift. Call him—I want him to create a plasm hound here and see if he can trace where Rathmen went."

Little creases form at the inner edges of Ethemark's eyes. His expressions are very subtle, but Aiah is slowly learning them. This is his uncertain look.

"Miss, if Rathmen was teleported out of here, there won't be a trail for a hound to follow."

"*If* he was teleported. He might have walked out, possibly with a bit of plasm-glamour to disguise him, and in that case I want to know where he went."

Understanding crosses Ethemark's face. "Right away," he says.

The watch officer clears his throat. "Beg pardon, miss, but there's a problem."

Aiah glares at him. "Yes?"

"There are no plasm outlets down here—we don't want the prisoners ever getting ahold of the goods. So if you want to create a hound here, you'll have to bring plasm in on a wire, or open enough doors so that a plasm sourceline can be sent into the area." He adopts a pained expression. "I wouldn't recommend that. Not if there's a teleportation mage who's already found a way in once."

Aiah sees his point. "Mr. Ethemark, did you hear that?" she calls.

Ethemark turns on his way to the phone. "Yes, Miss Aiah."

"Have Kelban bring a long wire."

"I'll do that."

Aiah turns back to the officer. "I want a list of everyone who's been on watch within the last twenty-four hours. And the names of whoever carried out Rathmen's interrogations."

"I—" The officer looks up, and his eyes go wide for a moment. Aiah turns, and there is Sorya walking through the door. She is dressed casually—baggy slacks and a rollneck sweater and scuffed suede boots, with her worn green military greatcoat thrown over her shoulders. On her, this unlikely ensemble looks superb.

Two bodyguards are with her, Cheloki, big men with black skins and twisted genes, facial features sunk into bony armored plates, knuckles the size of walnuts.

But Sorya doesn't need bodyguards to make her dangerous. She carries the glamour of authority with her, and it is evident in every step she takes, in the cold fluorescent gleam of her eyes.

She walks past Aiah to stand before the officer, hands propped on her hips, the greatcoat flared out behind her like a cloak. "I have put guards on the doors," she says. "No one will leave till this is resolved. I will need the names of everyone who has been in this area within the last twenty-four hours, because the ones who aren't here are all about to be got out of bed. I have other people on the way . . . specialists."

The word *specialist* seems to make the officer even more nervous.

"We are under the Ministry of Justice," the officer ventures. "The ministry may wish to make its own investigation."

Aiah and Sorya ignore this.

"The gentleman was already getting that information for me," Aiah says.

Sorya doesn't spare Aiah a glance. "That is well," she says. "You can leave now, Miss Aiah. I'll assume responsibility for the investigation."

Aiah feels her mouth go dry. She stands erect at Sorya's shoulder and wills the other woman to face her.

"He was my prisoner," she says. "My own investigation is far from complete. I would like to—" She stumbles, corrects herself. "I *will* stay."

Sorya turns her head, eyes Aiah for a long moment. Then she gives a shrug inside her greatcoat. "As you like," she says. She stands close to Aiah, and lowers her voice. "Since you are here, I may as well tell you now: there are two Handmen whom I wish released. They have agreed to serve as informers. Can you contrive to lose the paperwork on them, or free them in some other plausible way?"

Resentment stiffens Aiah's spine. "I will . . . consider it. If I may share the intelligence."

"I will pass it to you." Her lips turn up in a cold smile. "A personal favor. In exchange for this little kindness to me."

The next hours are long indeed.

GOVERNMENT TO SELL WORLDWIDE NEWS SERVICE

INTERFACT AND THE *WIRE* CONSIDERED LIKELY BUYERS

By work shift the next day Great-Uncle Rathmen has surfaced in Gunalaht—"perched like a vulture over his bank accounts," as Constantine remarks. Constantine is on his way to a cabinet meeting and Aiah walks along beside him, moving fast to keep up with his long strides.

"I've received Sorya's report," he says, "concerning the duty officer who sabotaged the airlock mechanism and propped the doors open to allow a thread of plasm to enter. And the other guards on watch obeyed his orders to keep the doors open, even though they must have known how dangerous it was."

"Timing was crucial," Aiah says. "You can't leave a plasm sourceline just sitting there in a prison for hours. This must have been prearranged, and in detail."

"By Rathmen's lawyer, we presume, as well as the duty officer." A wry smile touches Constantine's lips. "The duty officer cannot be found, and is presumably either at the bottom of the Sea of Caraqui or sitting next to Rathmen atop a new bank account in Gunalaht. And the lawyer, we are told, is 'unavailable'—a good idea, since under martial law we could confine him to Rathmen's old cell and search his mind for evidence of guilt." He gives a sigh. "And no one will believe this was not by prearrangement of the government. No one."

Aiah looks at him. "Was it?"

He stops dead in the corridor, and a thoughtful frown creases his brow. "Who?" he wonders. "Who would do such a thing?"

"I've been thinking about that. Rathmen's interrogations were almost complete. We have enough to blackmail him into cooperation fifty times over. Free, he could be of use passing information on to, say, one of our intelligence organizations."

She does not want to mention Sorya by name, but she found it odd that Sorya should personally want to control the investigation into what after all was merely a prison breakout.

Constantine considers this for a moment, calculation visible behind his eyes. "I do not find your theory entirely persuasive," he says, "but I will explore the possibilities. And I think . . ." He pauses for a moment. "Rathmen is condemned to death," he says finally. His expression turns hard. "Perhaps the sentence should be carried out regardless of his current location. It would do much to correct any erroneous impressions this escape may have created."

Aiah thinks about this. "Dangerous," she says.

"Taikoen," Constantine says. The single word, spoken softly in Constantine's resonant voice, seems to vibrate in the air for a long time. Aiah feels a palp of cold horror touch her neck.

"No," she says instantly; and then, because she has to justify this instinct, says "No" again. "Too dangerous," she adds. "It would be remarked. We don't want Taikoen known, or even rumored."

He gives her an equivocal look. "I would not in any case order such an extraordinary sanction on my own authority. . . . Drumbeth, at least, will have to concur, though I will not tell him the means." He smiles. "I am a *good* minister," he says, "a *good* subordinate." The smile turns rueful. "A *good* dog. I will have my allotted biscuit, and nothing more."

Amusement tickles Aiah's backbrain.

Constantine probably repeats these words, like a prayer, every day.

THIRD RECORD-BREAKING MONTH!

LORDS OF THE NEW CITY

TIME TO SEE IT AGAIN.

"We in Caraqui are uniquely suited to test your theories," Constantine says. "May I light your cigaret?"

"Don't bother," Rohder says, and lights his new cigaret off the old.

Constantine is all charm, all attention. His manner suggests that Rohder is the most important, most fascinating thing in the world.

Rohder seems oblivious. A splendid meal has been laid on in the Kestrel Room, not a single thing grown in a vat, and Rohder eats a few bites and pushes it away. Fine wines and brandies are rolled out, and Rohder asks for coffee. By way of showing his familiarity with Rohder's achievements, Constantine offers endless compliments on *Proceedings* and Rohder's other work—a solid record of scholarship stretching back centuries—and Rohder shrugs it off.

Constantine puts his lighter back in his pocket, calculation glowing in his eyes. He hasn't given up yet.

Aiah sits between them at the table, nibbling her food and watching this contest of champions. She knows Constantine's charm—she has had this intensity turned on her, and knows how difficult it is to resist.

Indeed, she reflects, she had *not* resisted it.

Her onetime boss sits in his cloud of smoke, oblivious not only to Constantine's attentions but to the glorious view from the outcurving windows. Rohder's gray suit manages somehow to be both expensive and ill-fitting. His lace is dotted with ash and cigaret burns. His three-hundred-year-old skin, though crisscrossed with a network of fine lines, is pink and ruddy with health, and he peers vaguely at the world from watery blue eyes.

"Caraqui's infrastructure," Constantine continues, "is suited to constant experimentation with plasm-generating distance relationships. Over eighty-five percent of the metropolis is built over water, on big barges or pontoons. This has formerly been considered a disadvantage as regards plasm generation, because we can't build as tall as other districts. Less mass, less plasm."

"I noticed from the aerocar that the buildings seemed small," Rohder says.

"The barges are strung together with cables, or with

bridges that, generally speaking, are to one extent or another engineered with a certain degree of flexibility in their spans."

A light snaps on in Rohder's eyes as if someone has just thrown a switch. For the first time he seems aware, his mind focused on his environment.

"You can alter the relationships between the barges?" he asks.

Aiah recognizes the hint of a smile that touches, feather-light, the corner of Constantine's mouth. The smile that says, at last, at last, he has found his way.

"Yes," Constantine purrs. "Absolutely. Imagine what you could do in Jaspeer if you could move entire city blocks around to find the proper geomantic relationships. Well," and the smile rises full, white incisors gleaming, "well, here it is possible."

Rohder's look is intent. "What is my part in all this? Can't you do this yourself?"

"I am Minister of Resources," Constantine says, "which in our local political cant means plasm. Resources I have, but not all those I would wish, and my greatest need is for minds. Minds such as yours do not come along every day."

"I do not think," Rohder says, "that quite answers my question."

"I will create a new department within Miss Aiah's division," Constantine says. "I think I have enough credit with the triumvirate to be able to do that, particularly when I explain how, and to what degree, our nation may be enriched by such an action. You will be the head of it, though unless you have some strange, unfulfilled desire to be involved with personnel matters, funding, and so on, I will make an effort to find some sympathetic deputy, agreeable to you, to take that business off your hands." He leans forward and looks close into Rohder's eyes, searching for understanding.

"I want you to devote yourself to working your theories out in practice. I will provide you with all necessary support, with aerial surveys and as much computer time as you deem necessary."

Rohder draws on his cigaret as he absorbs this, and lets the cigaret dance in the corner of his mouth as he replies.

"And what do you plan to do with this plasm if I can generate it for you?"

"Ah . . ." A laugh rolls out of Constantine's massive chest. "That is the critical question, isn't it?" He leans even closer, lowers his voice in intimacy. "If it's made available to other departments, then it will simply be diverted into fulfilling the other ministers' agendas. I wish to preserve any plasm generated by your theories for other work—other *transformational* work."

Rohder absorbs the word *transformational* with a little frown. "What sort of work do you have in mind?"

"Have you read my book *Freedom and the New City?*"

"Sorry. No."

"Are you familiar with Havilak's Freestanding Hermetic Transformations?"

"Yes." Rohder nods. "Improving the plasm-generating efficiency of structures that already exist by altering their internal structures through magework. It's an old idea, far older than Havilak."

"Of course." Conceded with a smile. "That part of my work is just a popularization."

"But even after the hermetic transformations, all you get is more plasm. What do you plan to do with the surplus?"

"Plasm is wealth," Constantine says, and then shrugs. "What does one do with wealth? Spend it, if you're a fool— and most governments are foolish in the long run. Invest it, if you're conservative, in such a way as to live off the dividends and never disturb the principal. But if you're *very* wise, and possess a certain daring in your spirit, you use it to generate more and more wealth. The very *existence* of such a stockpile of wealth is transformational, especially in a place like Caraqui, which is so poor."

Rohder leans back and contemplates Constantine from amid a cloud of cigaret smoke.

"You have a habit of not fully answering my questions," he says. "Assuming all this comes to pass, and assuming you manage to keep your job, you will have an enormous reservoir of plasm, and *you* will be in charge of it—so what do you intend to do with it?"

Constantine holds out his hands, smiling gently. "Truly, I

am not trying to be evasive," he says. "The fact is that all actions have unforeseen consequences. It will be decades before this pool of plasm even exists, and in that time Caraqui will, I hope, have changed for the better. I can answer your question only in the most general terms."

Rohder regards him from unblinking blue eyes.

"Very well," Constantine says. "I will speak generally, then—I would use this fund to accomplish what the political transformation, by that time, had not. Sell plasm to provide education and housing and medicine for our population generally, clean and replenish this abused sea on which we sit, perform other work of . . ." He smiles. "Of an exploratory nature. Transformation is very difficult in our world—it takes tremendous resources to build anything new, because one must disrupt the life of the metropolis by settling everything and everyone that is displaced, and tear down the old thing and build the new. But with plasm—with *enough* plasm—all things can be done. And the geography of Caraqui makes it easy—slide an old barge out, a new barge in, and the disruption to life and the economy is all the less." His face turns stern, like one of the Palace's bronze eagles sniffing the wind. "I confess that my ambition is such that I will not leave the world in the same condition as I found it. Reading your *Proceedings,* I sensed a similar scale of thought. Will you not join me in uniting our dreams and bringing them to reality?"

"I will give it consideration," Rohder says, and reaches in his pocket for another cigaret.

Constantine produces an envelope and slides it across the table. "This is my offer. I hope you will do me the courtesy to consider it."

Rohder picks up the envelope and looks at it as if he does not know what it is. Then he crumples it absently, and puts the ball of paper in his pocket with one hand while he lights the cigaret with the other.

Constantine watches this, the gold-flecked eyes glittering with amusement. "If you have finished your meal," he says, "perhaps you would like a tour of the city on my boat? You may see these barges for yourself, observe how you can transform our entire world with a few engineers, some cranes, and a handful of workmen. . . ."

CRIME LORD DENOUNCES "NEW CITY TYRANNY"

Aiah says good-bye to Rohder and then watches as the man shambles to the waiting aerocar. Wind flutters Aiah's chin-lace. Constantine leans close, speaks over the whine of turbines. "I hope I may be optimistic."

"I hope so, too."

She had enjoyed watching the two operate, Constantine seductive and manipulative, Rohder alternating intense interest with total, blank-eyed opacity. Aiah had found herself wondering if Rohder's detachment, his total withdrawal from the world, was a strategy. A way of not acknowledging the things he didn't want to deal with.

How would the Cunning People rate this? she wonders. Who is the *passu,* and who the *pascol?*

Turbines whine as they rotate in their pods. Suddenly there is the presence of plasm, crackling in the air like ozone, and Aiah's nape hairs stand erect as the aerocar springs from the Palace's pad and jets toward the Shield. The aerocar is a wink of silver in the distance before its trajectory begins to arc toward Jaspeer.

"Now," she says, "we will find out how bored he truly is."

Constantine looks at her. "Bored?"

"If he is bored enough in Jaspeer—if he is fed up enough with the pointlessness of his life there—he will come." Her eyes follow the aerocar on its way across the world. "He only chased criminals with me because he was bored," she says.

Constantine's eyes narrow as he absorbs this. "I wish you had told me. It would have made it easier to deal with him."

"I only realized it just now."

"Ah." There is an amused glint in his eye, and he puts an arm around her. His laugh comes low in her ear. "That is your gift, I think, to drive away the boredom of old men. Where was I before I met you? Stewing in my penthouse, occupying myself with trivialities—writing my memoirs over and over in my head, as old men do when there is nothing else to occupy them. And then"—he laughs again, a rumble she feels in her toes—"and then here was Miss Aiah, in the expensive new suit she'd bought just to impress me, with her plans to sell me a treasure trove of plasm she'd just happened to acquire, in hopes I would use it to make her rich and myself the master of the world. . . ."

He pushes back the corkscrew ringlets of her hair and kisses her neck. "Thank you," he murmurs as his arms go around her, "for giving me all this."

She presses her body to his, hesitant because they are in public, an open landing pad with a dozen people standing by. But his lips find hers, and she shudders with sudden desire, all thought of the onlookers gone.

"Do you have an appointment now?" he asks.

"A thousand."

"Cancel them."

She smiles. "Yes, Minister." With a sudden sweep of his arms he picks her up bodily—she laughs from the thrill of it, her gawky legs dangling—and carries her through the long public corridors of the Aerial Palace, past a hundred staring faces, and does not set her down until he reaches his suite, where he carries her into the bedroom and places her, delicately as if she were a piece of fine porcelain, upon the rose satin spread.

SEVEN

Perhaps Aiah should be grateful for the fact that Constantine cannot resist a gesture. After he carries her off through the corridors, things change.

It is hard to say exactly how. People react to Aiah differently—she catches a speculative look here, overhears an expression there, and sometimes she observes mere puzzlement, as if people are trying to understand just where she fits in, or what it is that Constantine sees in her.

She can't blame them. It is not as if she has not speculated along these lines herself.

On occasion she finds the difference an unpleasant one. People condescend to her, assuming that she is merely Constantine's plaything and knows nothing, or they try to use her as a conduit to reach him. Sometimes she has to administer a sharp correction.

Constantine himself is almost a daily presence: there are meetings, working lunches, reports commissioned and given. He drives and exhorts, setting an example of furious activity; he works on fifty things at once, somehow balancing them all, keeping them all filed within his capacious mind.

And yet, in their private moments together, he is somehow able to forget all business. He has learned from somewhere—the School of Radritha?—the art of relaxation. In her company he is happy to linger over a meal, or speculate about the implications of Rohder's theories, or spin absurd theories about sorcery, society, or life beyond the Shield.

Every so often, sleep shift, she finds Constantine in the secure room, or discovers, looking at the log, that he was there the previous shift. Then she knows to avoid him, for when his thoughts are on Taikoen he is abrupt, uncivil, and distracted, and Aiah doesn't know how to help, how to resolve the forces that are driving him.

Daily the mercenary teams continue their work, the anonymous powerboats slipping out at odd hours, returning with cargoes of Handmen for the prisons. The Silver Hand grows smarter and begins to fortify their plasm houses with bronze mesh and massive armored doors, but it doesn't help them—the locations were betrayed before the Handmen ever began taking precautions, and thoroughly scouted in the days since. Arrests continue.

Fear of the firing squads makes the Handmen desperate, and when the storming parties arrive they try to defend themselves with the plasm available to them—but Constantine's mercenaries, and their supporting mages, are professional enough to evade these hasty attacks.

Interrogation reports continue to arrive on Aiah's desk, along with the occasional request to release Handmen for use as informers.

The soldiers continue drawing lots to discover who will make up the firing squads. Aiah finds grim satisfaction in hearing that the Handmen's insurance companies have long since canceled their policies.

Six weeks after his escape, Aiah sees a video report of a failed assassination attempt on Great-Uncle Rathmen. The three shooters, Silver Hand types, are all dead. Two of the names are familiar: Aiah's group had arrested them, and Sorya had asked them to be released as informers.

Deniability has been maintained—no one could connect the Caraqui government to this action. Pity, however, that Sorya had not chosen better instruments.

Aiah takes some comfort, though, in the fact that Constantine has not made use of Taikoen. Though she finds evidence of the creature's activities elsewhere.

I committed the crime with Luking, but he died. He got the Party Disease, and I hope he didn't give it to me.

There it is in one of her prisoners' transcripts, a strange remark in the course of the narrative. The interrogator apparently found this avenue worth pursuing, but the interrogator's questions are never provided, and the narrative simply continues.

The Party Disease must be new. It's where you just go mad trying to have fun. You drink and pop pills and chase women and go to the clubs, you do it nonstop till you're dead. Luking died of it, and I know three other people who died.

Apparently the interrogator found this too bizarre to be worthy of any further questioning, because the narrative then returns to more conventional paths, a list of crimes and accomplices and where the accomplices might be found.

The Party Disease. Enough Handmen had died of it for them to start talking.

Aiah pushes the matter out of her mind. She doesn't want to know where Taikoen has left his footprints.

And then, after her department has been in existence for three months, Aiah is asked to make a report to the cabinet.

TRAMCAR SCANDAL WIDENS

EX–KEREMATH MINISTER BROUGHT IN
FOR QUESTIONING

She hates talking before an audience.

Aiah marshals her statistics, her facts, her anecdotes. She memorizes the faces and biographies of cabinet members. Charts and handouts are prepared. She barely sleeps the shift before her presentation, and she takes a jolt of plasm beforehand, burns off the fatigue toxins and gives herself a dose of courage, a fervid high that sings through her veins. She hopes it will last the day.

Constantine fetches her from her office, along with Ethemark and two assistants to carry the charts. The polished-copper elevator doors open, and Aiah's heart leaps as, inside the mirror-and-red-plush birdcage, she sees a twisted man, a cripple—no, not a twisted man; a dolphin—a dolphin sitting in a kind of mobile couch on wheels, pushed by a pair of human assistants. The couch is beautifully constructed, a polished frame of brass, and the cushions are upholstered with a colorful pattern of bright orchids.

"Most precious and gemlike greetings to you, illuminous Prince Aranax," Constantine says.

Aiah has met Aranax once before, when she and Constantine slipped into Caraqui on a scouting mission. Since then Aranax had been named Minister of Oceanautics, a reward for dolphin cooperation in the coup.

Aranax's beaklike face is fixed in a permanent grin, and his voice is a strange nasal drone. His skin is pinkish-white and covered with scars and open sores. He wears a streamlined vest with many pockets. There is a strange scent in the air, a mineral-laden salt-sea tang.

"Salutations to the godlike and immortal Constantine," Aranax says. The first consonant of Constantine's name is pronounced as an inhaled click.

The elevator doors threaten to close, and one of Aranax's human assistants jumps to turn the brass knob that locks them open.

"Desolate though I shall be without your presence," Constantine says, "I would not trouble your wisdom nor interrupt your sagacious meditations. Melancholy though I shall be in my desperate isolation, I shall with hope and fortitude await another elevator."

Aranax snorts through the nostrils atop his bald head. "Truly would I chide myself for inconveniencing such a glorious one as the ever-brilliant Constantine. I hope you will condescend to share this conveyance with me, you and your perfect assistant, the sublime Miss Aiah."

Constantine and Aiah step into the elevator, their knees up against Aranax's couch, and Aranax's assistant turns the knob to allow the doors to close, then sets to the top floor the eagle-claw control lever. There is no room for Ethemark or the others, and they will have to catch up later.

Aiah, her heart throbbing as she tries to frame a properly formal response to Aranax's invitation, casts a longing glance over her shoulder as the polished-copper doors close behind her.

"Your illumination gives me great honor," she manages, "in remembering our brief acquaintance." *All-too-brief,* she thinks, the more extravagant the adjective the better, but too late to say it.

"Who would not remember even the briefest acquaintance with the exalted Miss Aiah?" Aranax replies effortlessly. "Warrior mage, and conqueror of the Silver Hand?"

Aiah blinks. "Your illumination does me far too much credit," she says.

The flowery language is customary among dolphins, as are the old-fashioned titles, echoes out of some ancient romance. A human prince—assuming you could even find such a thing in the post-Metropolitan world—would be a rare thing indeed, but all dolphins seem to be titled: somehow they manage a society with all nobility and no commoners.

With Aranax in it, the elevator has become a glittering miniature palace, complete with ministers, functionaries, and royalty on his divan. Aiah wonders if all dolphins sat in such state once, before the wars that subdued them, and before human civilization expanded over the Sea of Caraqui and the world's other bodies of water.

The passengers swoop upward along the slight arcs dictated by the Palace's geomantic relationships. Constantine and Aranax engage in an ornate conversation about monetary supply and the Bank of Caraqui, and between them the elaborate language and abstruse subject matter combine to make the discussion completely unintelligible.

Being a high official, Aiah thinks, means having these sort of conversations *all the time.*

The elevator doors open into a circular room, and the party makes its way past deferent guards up stairs to the glittering Crystal Dome, where the cabinet meets. The dome is set atop the Palace like an insect eye gazing out at the sky, a sparkling webwork of bronze and crystal that slowly rotates above the world-city, providing the cabinet with spectacular views of the metropolis they govern. The long table, the chairs, and the tables are marvels of gleaming cantilevered tubes and faceted jewel surfaces. How it all survived the fighting is a mystery to Aiah.

Drumbeth sits at the head of the long crystal table, first among the triumvirate's equals, looking down the table with his slitlike, impassive eyes. Before him, on the surface of the table, is set a small pyramid of crystal a hand high, apparently cast with the table surface in one huge piece. Hilthi and Parq flank Drumbeth, Parq in full clerical dress, with his soft gray mushroom-shaped hat atop his handsome head, and each has his own group of functionaries in support.

Constantine sits in the next tier of officials, with the uniformed War Minister, Colonel Radeen, across from him. Aiah sits among other subordinates behind Constantine, perched on the white leather sling of one of the tube chairs. Sorya, in silken green and orange, sits behind Belckon, the elderly, white-haired Minister of State, a dignified individual who might well have been chosen simply because he *looked* so much like a soothing, accomplished diplomat. Conspicuous among the eleven other ministers are Aranax on his couch, the little twisted embryo Adaveth, and another with twisted genes, rocklike Myhorn, a massive creature who Aiah knows is female only through once having heard her speak. The large number of assistants makes the big crystal room seem close.

Drumbeth picks up a small hammer—it is clear crystal, with a silver handle—and raps once on a side of the crystal pyramid before him. The glass table sings, a clear bell-like sound that hangs in the air, its hovering presence almost physical; and Aiah hears answering chimes, bits of the Crystal Dome resonating to the song of the long table, then answering each other, and Aiah feels her long bones answer as well, a tremor deep in her limbs. . . .

Everyone falls silent.

"Let us begin," Drumbeth says, and after the song of the Crystal Dome his mild voice seems harsh.

CRIME BOSS MEETS WITH GOVERNMENT IN EXILE

KEREMATHS AND GREAT-UNCLE RATHMEN SEEN IN CONFERENCE

There are lengthy reports on other subjects first. When she finally has a chance to speak, Aiah finds her audience polite and reasonably attentive. Some—Constantine, Drumbeth, Sorya, and Hilthi—even seem interested. Hilthi, the former journalist, gazes down through crescent-shaped reading glasses as he jots into an open notebook with his gold pen. Gentri, the Minister of Public Security, seems far *too* interested—his own police plasm squads are suffering by comparison.

"In conclusion," Aiah finishes, "the figures amount to this: we have brought almost three thousand Handmen and associates to justice. The Plasm Control Board, as a result of our actions thus far, will be able to sell no less than thirty-five thousand monthly megamehrs of plasm to the public. That is enough plasm to lift the Aerial Palace and sail it to Mount Chukhmarkh—" A few eyes lift to gaze at the distant volcano, which peaks blue on the horizon. "Or," she says, "put another way, the Plasm Enforcement Division, in less than three months, has just added another four hundred and eleven million dinars to the treasury for this year alone."

Around the table, Aiah sees chins lifting, a little abstract look entering the eyes. *Yes,* she thinks. *Money.* Think about it.

"With every day we continue our work," she adds, "that figure increases."

Constantine begins a round of polite applause. Aiah nods, relieved to have the formal part over with, and asks for questions.

Drumbeth folds his arms and frowns. Behind him, visible through the dome, a pair of eagles spire high on the Palace thermals.

"How badly has the Silver Hand been damaged?" he asks.

"In one sense," Aiah says, "not at all."

Drumbeth's frown deepens. Gentri permits a smile to ghost across his face.

"There are an estimated two hundred thousand Handmen in Caraqui," Aiah says, "along with perhaps a half a million known associates who work alongside them without necessarily being formal members of the organization. Of this total, we've arrested not quite three thousand, an insignificant number compared with the total."

"Seven hundred thousand," Drumbeth mutters. "That's an army."

"However," Aiah says, "we have arrested much of their leadership, or driven them into exile or underground. We've probably confiscated a much larger percentage of their plasm than we've arrested of their membership—we have seriously damaged their business, and we've made it a much more dangerous business to be a part of. Without plasm, their power is much reduced."

"And ours," Constantine says, "becomes greater." He clears his throat, as clear a call for attention as Drumbeth's rap with the crystal hammer. "I have said," he says, "that so much plasm in the hands of criminals is a danger to the state, and Miss Aiah's division was created in response to that danger. There are seven hundred thousand of them—that's five times the size of our army and our hired soldiers together—and who knows how much plasm they can summon among them."

"Enough to get their chief out of prison," Hilthi mutters, "or was money used instead?"

A huge plasm advert, flashing overhead, gives Hilthi's face a greenish cast.

"The young lady's work is commendable," Parq says, "especially in one so young," and proudly strokes his silky beard as if he was himself to be commended for saying such a thing.

Drumbeth's eyes turn toward Aiah. *"Reinforce success,"* he says. "That is an army maxim. What can we do, Miss Aiah, to reinforce yours?"

Gentri permits himself a cynical little sneer. "Money, I expect, and more personnel," he says.

Aiah's temper flares, quickened by plasm-energy, but she bites down on her anger and any intemperate reply. *"Time,"* Aiah says, "most of all. We are all new to our job, and we are improving day to day. But yes—money and personnel will help us, of course. As will better salaries—though our people are proving to be extraordinarily dedicated, very few are experienced in this sort of work. We can't afford to hire the people who are, so we hire others and hope to train them."

"As the Plasm Enforcement Division is one of the few branches of government actually earning wealth for the state," Constantine suggests, "I think any increase in its budget would be money well spent."

Gentri leans forward and passes a hand over his balding head, smoothing into place strands of hair that are no longer there. "Perhaps I should point out once more," he says, "that the plasm squads of the police *already* have a mandate to find plasm thieves. Though I compliment my colleague Aiah on her accomplishments, nevertheless I feel constrained to remark that my own ministry contains all the expertise and specialists necessary for this job. Not only that, but my department has sufficient personnel to arrest people without the necessity of calling out foreign mercenaries to break down doors and arrest citizens in their beds."

Plasm snarls in her nerves and Aiah begins to reply, but Constantine looks up at her and gives a little flicker of his eye, and her reply dries up on her tongue. She settles for a glare at Constantine instead, and he smiles in answer and turns to his colleagues.

"Our respected colleague makes a telling point." Hilthi nods, and looks down at the notebook he's opened on the table. "I have viewed foreign newscasts, and they show little of our government but pictures of soldiers hauling citizens off to be shot. They make it look as if we've unleashed the military on our people."

"The soldiers are a convenience," Constantine says. "It is the fault of no one here, but it is a fact that the Silver Hand and their associates have made inroads into our political and police structure. If we used local forces, I fear our quarry would be alerted, and would escape ahead of time. Our soldiers—military police, most of them, brought into the country after the coup to keep order, and not assault troops or anything *dangerous*—have not been corrupted. Perhaps it would look better on video," he smiles, "if we were simply to equip them with different uniforms and make their soldierly aspect less obvious."

"May I make another point with regard to the government's use of mercenaries?" says Colonel Radeen, the War Minister. He is a dark-haired, dapper man in a tailored uniform. He had commanded the Second Brigade when it stormed the Aerial Palace during the coup, and was rewarded with leadership of the armed forces. He holds a lit cigaret between his thumb and two fingers, like a pointer, and for the present keeps it aimed at the Shield.

"The Keremaths degraded the regular armed forces," Radeen says, "and used the mercenary Metropolitan Guard to keep themselves secure. This did army morale no good, of course, and eventually contributed to the disaffection that led to the Keremaths' overthrow.

"But now . . ." Radeen shakes his head. "I fear that we are slipping into the same situation. Army troops—my own brigade, in fact—captured the Palace, but it isn't my brigade that guards the Palace *now*. . . . The security of the government is now in the hands of a mercenary unit—and furthermore, a mercenary outfit that has a long record of service *with a single member of the cabinet*." His hand tips his cigaret, slightly, in Constantine's direction.

"I do not question my colleague's loyalty to the triumvirate," Radeen adds, again with a tip toward Constantine, "or that of the soldiers in question. But I do question appearances, and it concerns me how the morale of the army will be affected."

"I should think," Hilthi says, looking up from his notebook, "that our regard for the army should be apparent in our decision to double its size and to promote large numbers of officers. Did that not have a beneficial effect on morale?"

"Naturally," Radeen says. "The officers were much gratified at the signs that the previous policy of neglect was being reversed."

"Good," Hilthi says. "I'm happy to hear that our budgetary excess had *some* good effect. Because if spending all that money didn't work, we could reduce the army to its original size."

Radeen reacts to this with a thin smile, as if he's decided to treat Hilthi's remark as a joke.

Drumbeth turns to Radeen. "We are satisfied with the performance both of the regular army and our hired troops," he says. "While the armed forces are rebuilding, the security of the government is best guaranteed by a highly trained, professional unit such as that commanded by Colonel Geymard."

Radeen decides, Aiah concludes, upon a tactical readjustment. "I spoke to appearances only," he says. "The appearance of Geymard's men is not good; nor is the appearance of mercenaries battering down the doors of our citizens."

"We do not intend for this situation to last indefinitely," Hilthi says. He looks to the other triumvirs for agreement. "After the state of emergency is over, and Caraqui returns to normal, we anticipate that the use of mercenaries will be scaled back."

"There is no reason," says Gentri, "not to scale them back *now.* My plasm squads—"

Constantine looks at Gentri, a little smile curling his lips, eyes alight with the anticipated sparring to come. "May I inquire of my esteemed colleague how many Handmen his plasm squads have of late arrested?" he asks. "And how much plasm has been returned to the state?"

Gentri strokes his little mustache. The rotating Crystal Dome has placed the tall gray spires of Lorkhin Island behind him, so that it looks as if his bald head has suddenly sprouted winged granite buildings. "Until recently," he says, "the Silver Hand was given a degree of political protection by the Keremaths. My squads cannot be held accountable—"

"I mean only since the Hand's protection was abolished," Constantine says, "I wonder if my colleague can provide me with statistics concerning—"

"Our record-keeping doesn't distinguish between arrests of Handmen and others," Gentri says. "Allow me to reassure my colleague that my police place Handmen under arrest all the time. Nearly every day, I should imagine."

"Can my colleague give me any *names?*" Constantine asks. "Any specific charges? Anything?"

"Our record-keeping—" Obstinately.

"I ask only," Constantine says, "because most of our Enforcement Division's records of the Handmen originally came from your police files. Miss Aiah's units and your own, on the day the amnesty ended, had much the same information about the Silver Hand. But she seems to have been much more effective against the Silver Hand, even though she had to create her organization from scratch."

"I dispute that!" Gentri snaps.

"Ah. Well." Constantine gives a languid smile and draws from his jacket a piece of paper. "Fortunately I have some estimates," he says, and opens the paper. He looks up at the other ministers. "You see," he says, "when Mr. Gentri's police raid an illegal plasm house, they have to call on workers from the Ministry of Resources—from *my* ministry—to wire the illegal plasm source into the system and to install meters to regulate it. And since the meters are read regularly, I have access to excellent data concerning just how much plasm my colleague's experts have returned to the state. In fact," his catlike smile widening, "I had all these meters read just yesterday, to make certain my statistics are up to date."

Gentri licks his lips. "I have not seen these data," he says. "How do I know—"

Constantine's reply is smooth. "You may send your own people to read the meters, and correct me if I am in error." He looks at the piece of paper. "Like my colleague," he says, "I do not have the total number of Handmen arrested by the police for plasm theft—but I *do* have the total number of those whose meters my workers were called upon to install or adjust, and a cross-check with Enforcement Division computers records the total number of correspondences as . . ." He smiles, flashing white teeth. "Three. Three Handmen arrested by the plasm squads in the seven weeks since the end of the amnesty. Returning to the state a total of one hundred fifty kilomehrs monthly, or about nineteen million dinars per year. Roughly one-tenth what Miss Aiah has accomplished with far fewer resources."

Gentri gives Constantine a stony look. "I am certain there have been more arrests than three," he says.

Constantine shrugs. "Double the number, if you like. Triple it. There remains"—a laconic smile dances on his lips—"something of a contrast."

"Our mandate is broader than containing the Silver Hand. We don't just arrest Handmen—our concerns are far more wide-ranging than that." Gentri takes a breath. "For instance," he says, "just today we have begun a new campaign against a long-standing source of plasm theft: the illegal settlements called half-worlds."

Aiah starts as Ethemark clamps a webbed hand on her thigh. *"The half-worlds,"* he whispers. *"Did I not warn you?"*

Gentri opens a folder and glances at a paper inside. "Since my colleague is so fond of statistics, let me furnish him some. First shift today my police entered two illegal settlements, those called Hog Sty and Dark Eighteen by their inhabitants. We arrested eight major plasm thieves, and dispersed over six thousand illegal settlers. At least a score of wanted fugitives were found among their number and a warehouseful of stolen property was recovered, along with thirty or more vessels believed to have been stolen." He smiles and folds his arms triumphantly, like a conqueror. "I think we may say the operations were a success. Many more are planned."

Ethemark's fingers dig into Aiah's thigh as he whispers fiercely to Constantine, *"Do something!"*

Constantine glances over his shoulder at Ethemark, frowns lightly with a shake of the head, then turns back to Gentri.

"I congratulate my colleague on his successful and well-planned operations," he says. "May I ask him how much plasm will be recovered?"

"It's too early to say. Several illegal taps were discovered."

"I asked because the Plasm Enforcement Division had of course considered raiding the half-worlds, but concluded that it wasn't cost-effective at the present time."

"I disagree." Gentri's response is instantaneous.

A new voice speaks up. "With all humility and deference to my esteemed colleague the glorious Gentri," says Prince Aranax, "who spreads his wisdom over our gathering like a god spreading a refreshing shower over the land, I myself, humble slave of fortune though I am, must in the most submissive fashion beg to disagree with the position he has so wisely maintained before this august gathering."

The others watch Aranax with a mixture of anticipation and impatience. Aiah wonders how long he can string these sentiments out.

"The half-worlds," Aranax says, "degraded though they may be in the eyes of Caraqui, nevertheless share the watery realm with my own lowly and miserable race. Such brilliantly planned and executed operations as envisaged by the ever-sagacious Gentri are bound to cause a disruption among my own unworthy kind, and I must implore and entreat my colleagues to spare my wretched and undeserving people the confusion necessarily caused thereby."

"I agree with my esteemed colleague the minister and Prince Aranax," says Adaveth, the gray-skinned embryo. "The half-worlds are the last refuge of the poor and desperate. Any police actions directed against them would cause great hardship."

"And they would gain the state little but instability," adds the giant Myhorn in her strangely feminine voice. "As Constantine has said, they are hardly cost-effective."

Hilthi, scribbling in his notebook, gives a sharp glance over his spectacles at Constantine. "What do you mean, colleague?" he asks.

Constantine makes an equivocal gesture with one big hand. "Most of the half-worlds steal small amounts of plasm, true. They also steal fresh water and electricity, once again in insignificant amounts. And other things."

"But all together," Gentri says, "the amount is far from insignificant."

"No doubt." Constantine brushes the objection aside. "Still, no one lives in the half-worlds from choice. These communities exist because there is nowhere else that will have them."

"Or because the police are looking for them," Gentri says.

"Conceded. But my colleague speaks of dispersing six thousand inhabitants. May I ask where he expects these people to go?"

Gentri's tone clenches his teeth. "The settlements," he says, "were *illegal.* Where the inhabitants go is not our concern, provided they find a legal residence."

"Where do the inhabitants have to go but other half-worlds? And once those are cleaned out, they will have no place to go but the streets, where they cannot help but create disturbances, and even a riot or two." He turns to Hilthi. "How will the video broadcasts regard that? It is one thing to turn military police loose on the likes of the Silver Hand—it is regrettable, but most viewers will concede its necessity, given their threat to the state and a certain . . . *reluctance* . . . on the part of the proper authorities—but to set swarms of police loose on the most defenseless of our citizens, those on whose behalf we hope to create the revolution, to deprive them of shelter and set them out on the streets—"

"I object to these provocative descriptions!" Gentri shouts. "*Swarms* of police! *Defenseless* citizens! *Reluctant* authorities! My colleague is attempting to turn a perfectly legal police action into some grotesque act of brutality!"

There is an amused glint in Constantine's eye. "*I* did not turn it so."

Gentri looks at the others around the table. "Colleagues! This is outrageous!"

Constantine holds up a hand, forefinger tucked away with the thumb, remaining three fingers extended. "*Three* arrests of Handmen. *That* is outrageous."

The room buzzes with the sound of everyone talking at once. Voices are raised. Finally Drumbeth picks up the crystal hammer and brings it down. The Crystal Dome rings with harmony, and—for the moment anyway—the babble of discord dies away.

Drumbeth looks at Gentri. "I had hoped for better results against the Handmen," he says.

"Mr. President," Gentri says, "they are a large and difficult target."

"Miss Aiah has not found them so difficult." Drumbeth frowns. "After the Keremaths, the Hand is the chief target of our administration. They are the chief threat to the security of our metropolis. When may we expect you to move decisively against them?"

Gentri licks his lips. Plasm adverts, red, yellow, green, bloom behind his head like fireworks. "Intelligence must be gathered, targets chosen, plans made. . . ."

The commanding light that glitters in Drumbeth's eyes is like the hard gleam off a diamond facet. He sits erect and motionless in his chair, and his presence seems to inflate: despite Drumbeth's small body he suddenly seems to *mass* far more than Gentri, and to tower over him like the stoneface Myhorn.

"My understanding," Drumbeth says, "is that you *have*

gathered intelligence, that the police have *years* of intelligence."

Gentri shifts uncomfortably in his seat, rearranges his thinning locks with a distracted hand. "We are in a process of review. To determine its accuracy."

"And when may we expect to have the review completed?"

Gentri raises his hands helplessly. "I—have no estimate. I did not understand that any of these issues would be raised at this meeting."

Constantine leans forward and speaks. His speech has turned silky; he is generous now that he has made his point.

"I sympathize with my colleague's dilemma. He is new to his position, and he is not responsible for the fact that he has inherited a police force renowned for its corruption. I have a few of the same problems with some of the organizations under my ministerial control. One understands the situation, but one doesn't want to admit the system's failures among one's peers."

Gentri is in no mood to be appeased, and scowls as he makes his reply. "Steps are being taken to rectify this situation. I have made full reports to my colleagues on my efforts."

Constantine continues soothing, his deep voice evoking odd little harmonies from the crystal surroundings, individual panes and plates ringing with his voice. "May I offer my colleague the technique that has produced such admirable results in the Plasm Enforcement Division? That each employee be subjected to a plasm scan in order to determine that he is not beholden to the Silver Hand or any other extralegal agency?"

Gentri glares at Constantine. Behind him, plasm letters hang burning in the sky. "The effects on police morale would be incalculable."

Constantine's laughter rumbles out, and somewhere a crystal pane hums in sympathy. "I should *hope* so."

Gentri looks at the head of the table. "Am I to understand that the half-worlds now possess the same sort of political immunity formerly enjoyed by the Silver Hand and various Keremath enterprises? What possible use could such protection be for us—what is gained?"

Drumbeth frowns, thinks for a long moment. "I am concerned principally with returning plasm resources to the state. If there are plasm thieves, or other criminals, within the half-worlds, let them be arrested, by all means."

Hilthi looks up again from his notebooks. "But deporting whole populations . . . ," he says.

"I think not," says Drumbeth. He looks at Gentri, and his voice turns commanding. "And we desire action against the Handmen. Names, charges, facts, totals of plasm and other stolen materials returned. All this, and soon."

Gentri visibly bites down his resentment, and nods. "Very well, sir," he says. "Soon."

Soon. Aiah thinks she tastes an odd flavor in that word, as if Gentri is offering another promise entirely, something quite different from what Drumbeth has in mind.

But no one else seems to hear what Aiah hears, and suddenly there is a blaze of light overhead. Several in the cabinet start, afraid this might be some kind of attack, but there is no danger, it is only a plasm display—an *illegal* plasm display, because no displays are permitted over the Palace in the event they might be used to disguise an assault. But all faces turn upward in any case. . . . A dolphin spins through space; a cat wearing white gloves and a vest makes a commanding gesture with a stick; a woman in tall boots contemplates some kind of net she is holding in her hand, a window which allows a glimpse of an unnaturally green plain, as if someone had sown the surface of a large roof entirely in grass and placed on it a few black-and-white cows. Each image leaping into being, moving, dissolving into another, all too fast for the mind to follow.

"What is *that?*" Constantine breathes in wonder.

"The Dreaming Sisters," Aiah says.

"And who are *they?*" Constantine says.

Aiah doesn't have an answer, and it is Ethemark—gazing upward, the images reflected in his huge eyes—who supplies the reply.

"They are a religious order," he says.

"They must be a rich religious order," Constantine says, "to afford so much plasm."

"No doubt," says Ethemark.

And then the image fades, leaving in Aiah's heart a burning droplet of wonder, even as the cabinet meeting drones on.

CHARNA COMPLAINS TO CARAQUI GOVERNMENT

"CARAQUI IS EXPORTING GANGSTERS TO ITS NEIGHBORS"

CARAQUI OFFERS TO SHARE POLICE INTELLIGENCE, WELCOMES EXTRADITION

COMPROMISE CALLED "INSUFFICIENT"

"A division within our ranks," Constantine observes, "and not the first. There are those who wish true change, a revisualization of our world, and those who simply want the same old Caraqui with a new set of faces at the top." He shrugs lazily, massive shoulders straining the seams of his velvet jacket. "Perhaps it is not Gentri's fault. He is a product of the system here, and his imagination simply may not be sufficiently flexible to see that there is another way."

The meeting is over, and Constantine's air of satisfaction fills the mirror-and-gilt elevator as it swoops and slides its way down its curving shaft. He smiles; he gestures expansively.

Tiny Ethemark, in his shadow, is not so pleased. "But what of the half-worlds?" he says. "Gentri's still allowed to send his police in."

Constantine doesn't look at him directly, but instead gazes at the twisted man's distorted reflection in the polished-bronze door. "Those who steal plasm must take their chances, no?" he says. "And if the amounts the half-worlds are stealing are trivial, as you have always maintained, there will be little reason to go in at all. And in any case, the majority of the people will not be thrown out, and that is what we want most."

"What I *want*," Ethemark says forcefully, "is for the half-worlds to be let *alone*."

Constantine gives Ethemark's reflection a sharp look, a

steely edge glinting through the velvet tone of his voice. "That was naive. I intend to let *nothing* alone—to allow nothing to remain unchanged at all."

Their reflections are sliced open as the polished doors part. "Miss Aiah," Constantine says, "a word with you."

Ethemark makes his way down the corridor to his office, giving Aiah and Constantine a look over his shoulder as he retreats. The look on the smooth gray face, as always, is unreadable.

Constantine leans close, puts a warm hand on Aiah's shoulder. "I have heard from your Mr. Rohder," he says. "He says he will leave his position in Jaspeer and join us."

Warm pleasure dances in Aiah's veins. "I'm *very* happy." She finds her lips twitching with the urge to kiss him, but it is a public corridor, and since he carried her away from the aerocar pad there have been no more demonstrations of affection in public.

There is a hidden glow in Constantine's eyes, and Aiah senses that the thought of a stolen kiss has not eluded him either. But then the glow turns cold, the expression grim.

"Gentri," he says, and before finishing lets the name hang for a moment in the air, "troubles me."

Aiah hears a confirmation humming through her nerves, a sense that her intuition was not entirely misplaced.

"Yes," she says. "There was something . . . not quite right there."

"His performance was a little too fervid, I think. As if he was not defending merely his plasm squads—which is understandable, and after all his job—but perhaps himself as well."

Aiah nods. "I see what you mean."

Constantine straightens, a contemplative frown touching his face. "He was a prosecuting judge before the coup, and reckoned honest, as such people go. There was no reason to think him connected to anyone . . . untoward." He nods to himself as if reaching a decision, then looks down at her. "I wish you to start a file. A discreet little file that most eyes will never see—none but yours, mine, perhaps Ethemark's."

Aiah considers this request. "Isn't Sorya the person to ask for that sort of thing?"

"I have *seen* her file. There is little of any interest in it."

"I'm not very qualified for this."

He shrugs. "Do what you can. There may, after all, be nothing to find." He takes her arm. "Come. I would like to review the day's projects."

She falls into step alongside him. "Three big arrests planned for first shift tomorrow. And a number of known associates for dessert."

"Ah." He smiles. "Progress made, then. And more to tell the cabinet, when next they meet."

"Sir! Miss Aiah!"

It's Ethemark, coming back on the run. "Bombings, sir! Alaphen Plaza, by Government Harbor—and the Exchange! Hundreds of people hurt!"

Constantine stops walking, his head held high, nostrils flared, as if to scent the wind. He nods. "Well," he says, "*someone* makes a counterattack."

"Who?" Aiah feels panic thrashing in her chest. "The Hand?"

"Someone . . . *weak.* Only the weak use terror." He tilts his head, licks his lips as if to taste something. "Great-Uncle Rathmen, perhaps, letting us know he is displeased with the late assassination attempt. We shall see what news the investigation brings."

The two bombings kill a handful and injure many, though fortunately there are not so many casualties as first believed. Sorya's service is using plasm hounds within the hour, and though the bombers have taken precautions to clean themselves of any trace, the procedure was flawed in one case, and one of the killers is tracked south to Barchab, and there positively identified: a Handman. Barchab is quietly asked to arrest the individual and hand him over, and video reports of the stunned survivors staggering among the overturned carts and blasted barrows of the open-air Alaphen market prompt the Barchab government, not known for its efficiency, to act quickly for once.

Members of the government begin to walk about with guards, and their families move into the Aerial Palace. Hilthi protests—he wants to live among the people—but though he will not leave his apartment, at least he is persuaded to keep a guard about him.

Two days later, with the bomber still in Barchabi hands, a far worse catastrophe. Constantine and Aiah view it from his launch, the gleaming black-and-silver turbine-powered machine he had confiscated from the Keremaths.

Cold rain drizzles down as Aiah looks at the overturned apartment building. One of its two support pontoons had been bashed in, and the entire building, with upward of four thousand people inside, had capsized in minutes. The huge concrete pontoons are built with watertight compartments below the waterline and had capsized in minutes. The pontoons are built with massive redundancy, and such sudden and catastrophic failure should not be possible.

Not without help, anyway.

The apartment building, brick on a steel frame, had collapsed when it was overturned, though its watery grave is shallow and the intact pontoon is still visible, barnacle-encrusted flank exposed to the air like some strange leviathan floating dead on the water. Boats sit on the slack green water around the structure, picking up debris and the dead, and barges with huge cranes stand ready. But most of the rescue work is invisible: telepresent mages at nearby plasm substations scouring the rubble for signs of anyone trapped in an air pocket, and other mages with the rare and difficult skill of teleportation stand by to pop any survivors to the nearest hospital.

Constantine watches grimly, the collar of his windbreaker turned up as the rain falls in a soft mist on his bare head. Disposed about the boat are his guards, all twisted Cheloki with bony faces like armored black visors, and led by Martinus. They have followed Constantine all these years, from the Cheloki Wars on, and they have never failed him.

Constantine had not used so many guards until recently. Aiah assumes that telepresent mages are on guard as well. This business, she reflects, has made Constantine wary.

"It will be the Hand sending a message," he says. Drops of rain course down his face, and he blinks them from his lashes as he speaks. "Who else has the plasm to waste? Sorya taught them not to use bombs."

Aiah huddles beneath her jacket hood as rain patters on it, a steady percussion near her ears. "What can we do?"

Constantine tilts his head back, as if to consult with the low clouds. He opens his mouth and lets the rain refresh him. Then he looks at Aiah, and a dangerous light burns in his eyes.

"I want you to give me a list," Constantine says. "Ten Handmen we have not arrested. Not necessarily the highest-ranking, but the *worst,* and all married—with large families, preferably. I want their addresses and the names of their close kin. I want them by the beginning of work shift tomorrow."

Aiah's mouth goes dry. Her hand, holding her rain hood closed beneath her chin, begins to tremble. "Yes, Metropolitan," she says.

He does not correct her use of his old title. Instead he looks at the rubble of the building. His tone turns meditative. "And another list, I think. Every Handman in your files. Names, pictures, current addresses." He looks at her sharply. "But *that* for later. The list of ten, first of all. I would send Great-Uncle Rathmen an answer to his message."

INTERFACT PURCHASES WORLDWIDE NEWS, DATAFILES

THE *WIRE* PROTESTS BIDDING PROTOCOLS

There are three bombings in the next wave. Three Handmen are killed, along with their families. Three Handmen from the list of ten that Aiah had prepared. The explosions are carefully controlled, and there are no other casualties.

After this, the bombings cease entirely.

Aiah concludes that Constantine's message has been received.

She does not watch the video for days, in order to avoid any pictures of dead children, but she finds, regardless, the dead haunting her dreams, a sad and silent procession, gazing at her with drowned, frozen, reproachful eyes.

EIGHT

~~~~~~~~

Weeks pass.

The Plasm Enforcement Division hones its moves, gathers more data, makes more arrests against increasingly powerless, increasingly desperate opposition. Mercenaries, now dressed in more politically acceptable Shield-gray uniforms instead of full combat gear, continue to storm the bastions of the Silver Hand.

Even the police begin to do their bit, rounding up Handmen on one charge or another. Not major figures, scarcely anyone ranked above brother, but every arrest helps.

The firing squads continue in their work, though the executions are no longer publicized, and terse press releases—providing just names and the crimes of which the Handmen were convicted—are given out instead. It is not work of which anyone is particularly proud.

Aiah hears more and more reports of Handmen and their associates who have decided to leave Caraqui and seek a life elsewhere. The knowledge gives her nothing but satisfaction.

Other Handmen turn up with growing frequency in byways and canals, all dead by violence. Aiah follows these cases in hopes that they may turn out to be a sign that the Hand has turned on itself, is warring over the remains of its power in the absence of its leadership, but the available evidence suggests this is not so. The members of the Hand are too terrified of the government to spend time fighting each other. These bodies are the result of private vengeance, citizens no longer afraid of the Handmen and considering themselves free to act without fear.

Aiah supposes that she can't approve. But neither, she decides, can she much blame the citizens for turning on their persecutors.

She spends a certain amount of time compiling a dossier on Gentri. There is little to discover beyond what is in the public record. She spends some time surveilling him through telepresence, but it's impossible to monitor him when he's at work in the heavily shielded Palace, and otherwise his life seems unexceptional—he works long hours, returns to his family on his off shifts, and if he spends time skulking with Handmen and Keremaths it's when she's not looking. She doesn't feel comfortable peering in at him this way, and is wary of the consequences should she be discovered.

This is Sorya's sort of work, anyway.

Rohder arrives in Caraqui, and there is a party to welcome him, but afterward Aiah sees him only rarely, at weekly meetings in which he reports to her and Constantine. He spends his time closeted with engineers and plasm theorists from the university.

Eventually Aiah and her entire division hit the wall. Everyone is exhausted, arrests fall off, mistakes are made that result in the wrong doors being bashed in, the wrong people arrested, military police wandering down the wrong corridors, the wrong canals. Aiah prevails upon Constantine to declare a ten-day amnesty in which people are encouraged to report to the government any stolen plasm they may possess without fear of retaliation, and during which she and her department can catch up on their sleep.

Unlike the first amnesty, this one produces results. Aiah has the impression that people are relieved to give their stolen plasm back. "Apparently the guilty knowledge of all that plasm has been weighing heavily upon the thieves' consciences," Constantine remarks. Then a devil's smile dances along his lips, and he adds: "That or the weekly lists of the defunct."

It is the fifth day of the amnesty, and Aiah is beginning to regain an interest in things other than surveillance, arrests, and stolen moments with Constantine. Early second shift she'd actually phoned her mother—voluntarily!—and spent an hour talking with her.

"There's some dirty hermit saying *things* about you," her mother reports.

"I'm not interested," Aiah says. "I want to talk about Henley."

Henley is Aiah's sister, and Aiah has a plan for her. Ten years ago Henley had been crippled by an Operation street lieutenant who had broken her hands—just for the fun of it—and afterward arthritis set in, and Henley's budding career as a graphic artist had come to an end.

"I want to buy her some plasm treatments," Aiah says. "Straighten the bones, erase the arthritis. I can afford it now."

Arrangements are discussed, and Aiah hangs up with an unusual feeling of righteousness. Then the com com unit chimes, with Constantine calling to invite her to a picnic of sorts.

"Rohder has finished his calculations and has called in some engineers, and is going to be shifting some buildings about. Would you like to attend? Food and drink will be available on my launch should you desire refreshment."

Refreshment, Aiah suspects, means choice wines and ten or twelve courses: that is Constantine's style.

The day is blustery, with deep gray clouds scudding low and threatening possible rain, so Aiah wears a blue wool suit with red piping, a red scarf to add extra color, and boots with modest heels, and clips her hair back so it won't blow in the wind. She takes a hooded windbreaker along in case it rains, and shieldglasses in the event the clouds clear.

Constantine meets her at the water gate and smiles as he hands her into his boat. He is dressed casually, cords and a leather jacket—much more the rogue than the minister, and the more attractive for it.

"You look lovely, Miss Aiah. Would you care for a glass?"

The wine bottle is already uncorked and waits in a silver bucket. Constantine pours her a glass, hands it to her with a flourish, and then takes the helm of the launch himself. The turbines purr under his command as the black composite prow rises and cuts the water. His big hands handle the wheel with a fine delicacy, fingertips transmitting the boat's vibration up his arms. He handles the boat with supreme skill: the liquid in Aiah's wineglass trembles only slightly as he accelerates onto the Khola Canal and cuts a neat path through the traffic.

Martinus the bodyguard is on board, his black, bone-plated face expressionless as he looks out for any possible attackers. Two other guards also keep a silent watch, and a guard boat follows, with a half-dozen others on board. Telepresent mages are probably on hand as well.

Aiah looks at the guards and considers how one is never allowed to forget power, either its reality or its consequences.

Another power launch whips past on an opposite course, providing a blast of wind and the sight of laughing, copper-skinned young men; Constantine's boat vaults up the other boat's wake, finds itself airborne for a moment as the sound of the turbines climbs to a shriek, then slaps to a landing in a fine burst of spray. Constantine laughs as wipers scrape salt-water from the windscreen.

Aiah looks at Constantine's joy and wonders how it is possible for him to experience such pleasure, surrounded as he is by guards and constant care. It is astonishing, she muses, how he is able to live so thoroughly in the moment, as vital as the plasm that keeps him young.

Office buildings loom up on either side, granite and steel and glass reflecting the scowling clouds overhead, tall as any-one dares to build atop the Sea of Caraqui. One of them has a tower constructed as a giant golden glass lotus, and in it a beacon that gives the glass a fine amber glow. Rohder is con-ducting his experiments in a business district because, manipulating these giant buildings in accordance with his theories of geomancy, he expects to gain results more con-clusive than if he uses less mass.

"The Lotus District," Constantine remarks.

The launch passes beneath a glittering gold bridge, all white enamel and gilt gingerbread, each upright topped with the brushy golden image of a lotus; and then the dark cranes are seen ahead, with hawsers drooping low over the canal.

Weathered Keremaths smile from the side of one of the pontoons: *Our family is your family.* Constantine slows, cuts the power, and the launch settles onto its bow wave as it drifts up to a rusty floating jetty. Crewmen throw hawsers, which are made fast; Constantine leaps from the boat to the jetty, then helps Aiah out of the boat and onto the mesh-steel surface. The jetty rocks under their weight.

The guard boat doesn't come to a mooring, just waits in the canal with its engines idling, and in the relative silence Aiah can hear the ominous throb of helicopters echoing off the tall buildings, and looks up to find them, with no success—all she can find is a shaggy hermit hanging in a canvas sling fifteen stories up. He sways in the wind. Aiah glances at Constantine to see him gazing up as well, a thoughtful frown on his upturned face.

"Army on maneuvers," he says. "Civilians wouldn't fly that many copters at once." He looks down, shrugs. "Readiness is best, I suppose. Though Radeen has complained of insufficient funds for fuel."

They climb the battered steel stair to the road surface above. A woman with a video camera records their arrival: a ministry employee, Aiah notes, not media. A man stands next to her with a boxy microphone on a telescoping stick. It's for history, then, not for broadcast—if the experiment doesn't work, then no embarrassed explanations will have to be offered, and the recordings will probably be quietly tossed down some Palace oubliette.

Rohder, in a red windbreaker and an orange hard hat, stands near another of the gilt-lotus bridges, conferring with a group of helmeted engineers. Others call obscure orders into boxy handheld radios made of heavy black plastic. Constantine is content to let them do their business uninterrupted. He raises his collar against the blustery wind, then turns to Aiah.

"How do we fare with the amnesty?"

"Enough people have turned themselves in to keep ministry teams busy for the next three weeks, repairing and installing meters," Aiah says. "It is difficult to say how much plasm reserves will be increased, but I suspect the amount will be considerable."

Constantine is amused. "That will be a nice tidbit to drop at the next cabinet meeting." He sidles closer, gives her a covert look. "I have not seen any information on our friend Gentri."

Exasperation plucks at her nerves. "Nothing, Minister," she says. "He works long hours, he seems to be faithful to his wife, his record is clean. His name has not come up in any interrogation. And I have little time to pursue any investigation, not when I have a department to run and the investigation is so private I can have no help."

"There have been complaints lodged. That where the Silver Hand is absent or ineffective, the police have been filling the vacuum. Extortion, strong-arm work for loan sharks or local bosses . . . Perhaps only fear of the Hand was keeping the police out of the crime business."

Aiah shrugs. "Gentri may not be a part of it—probably is not, unless we can find money going to him. Unless it's got to do with plasm, it's not our mandate anyway."

"Perhaps you could find someone close to Gentri who, for a consideration, might be persuaded to make reports. . . ."

She looks at him, annoyance tautening her vocal cords. "I'm not a spy!" she says. "I'm not suited for this, and I have other work!"

He frowns, draws a little away from her. "As you wish," in tones both cold and silky.

Anxiety hums through Aiah. She wants to follow him, offer him further explanations, further excuses, an apology. But then her moment of distress is followed by another of stubborn anger, and she decides, *The hell with it. What else could I tell him?*

Constantine, eyes narrowed, seems to detect her defiance, and he walks off to confer with Rohder, leaving Aiah alone. The helicopter throbbings seem a little farther off and disappear into the background noise of traffic. Wind sluices between the tall buildings, and Aiah shivers in her wool jacket.

The group of engineers around Rohder breaks up. Curved antennas bob as people shout commands into their radios. Police stop traffic on the bridges and police boats move into position to block the canal, because if one of the cables breaks it could whip into a boat and kill somebody. Aiah moves back, stands at the entrance of the tower-topped building, a cool alcove of polished copper engraved with the district's lotus design.

What else could I have told him? Aiah demands of herself.

A fine spray dots the walkway in front of her alcove. The hermit pissing into the wind.

Hydrogen engines cough into life, and their barking roar echoes off the buildings. Winches roll; the huge cables straighten, then grow taut. Engineers peer at the bridges as the structures begin to creak—they are built to expand and contract as needed, at least within limits, but nothing has moved these structures in the centuries since the buildings were erected, and though everything has been cleaned and greased there is nevertheless anxiety that the bridges may not behave. Other engineers peer into bulky brass viewfinders set atop portable tripods: they are determining the distance between the buildings.

The wind moans around the cables, a baritone hum that rises occasionally to a shriek. Nothing anchors these buildings on their pontoons, nothing but the hugeness of their own inert mass and the mass of the other structures to which they are moored. Although the winches are slowly drawing in cable, it's impossible to estimate by eye whether the buildings are moving closer or not. Elsewhere, out of sight, other cables are being slacked as these are drawn in.

The men at the viewfinders shout into their radios, and the winches grind to a stop; there is the sound of banging from the bridges, and then Rohder is waving his arms and the engines rumble to a stop. The sound of helicopters beats surprisingly loud in the sky.

Aiah walks out of the alcove and looks up—no copters, but letters flaming red against the dull gray clouds: *The Provisional Government orders the public to behave in an orderly manner.*

Provisional? Ridiculous. And what has there been but calm? Who is wasting government plasm on this?

Above, the hermit twists in the wind. Below, Constantine is amid a clump of engineers, but he's clearly visible, a head taller than any of them. His presence seems expanded by a wide grin. In the crowd, Rohder is distinguished only by the puffs of his cigaret smoke that are whipped away by the wind. The camera circles the group of men, patiently waiting for a revelation. Aiah approaches, reaches the fringes of the group, then hesitates. She really isn't a part of this.

Rohder is shouting into a handheld radio, pink face flushing. *"What did you say? Say again!"* Its curved antenna dances with every word. Constantine, grin broadening, reaches for the radio, takes it, turns a little plastic knob, and hands it back. "That should work," he says.

Rohder shouts again. When he gets his answer, he looks up at Constantine and speaks in a soft voice. "Six percent." Aiah can barely hear him.

Constantine tilts his head back, and his laugh booms out above the sound of helicopters. He is playing, Aiah knows, to the camera, but his joy must be genuine enough. "Congratulations," he says.

Rohder frowns. "We'll do better next time. These buildings are two or three hundred years old, and the plans are lost. Our mass estimates were approximations."

"Six percent is very good!" Projecting his voice to the man with the microphone.

That frown again. "I had hoped for better." In a mumble that the soundman almost certainly did not catch. Apparently Rohder is not interested in securing his place in history.

Rohder has people monitoring the plasm outflow from the two buildings in order to get instant readings on any increase. The data is preliminary, since it might be skewed by any plasm use in the buildings, and only averages over the next several weeks will produce a final figure.

Still. Six percent. Worth millions a year, and all it took was some winches and cable.

Aiah approaches Rohder, who is now holding the heavy black radio in his hand and looking at it with a puzzled expression. "Here," Constantine says, and switches it off for him.

"Congratulations," Aiah says. "Are you glad you came to Caraqui?"

Cigaret ash drops onto Rohder's windbreaker as he speaks. "I suppose. Too early to tell."

"Mr. Rohder," Constantine says formally, "I authorize you to proceed with further work."

"Thank you," Rohder says. "I can start tomorrow, if I can get the cooperation of the police."

"Very good. I will speak to Mr. Gentri on your behalf." He glances over his shoulder at where his boat is moored to the jetty. "Would you care to join me aboard my boat? I can offer you some wine and other refreshment."

"In a moment. I need to, ah, deal with a few things. Send people home, and so forth." He looks at the radio again, then—having learned where the switch is—turns it on. Little yellow dials begin to glow.

Constantine turns and heads for his boat. The camera follows him with the obsessiveness of a jealous lover. A seraphic smile graces Constantine's face, as if all the problems in his world had just been solved. Behind, traffic begins to flow once more across the bridge.

He approaches Aiah and a cloud crosses his face, suggesting the recollection of a minor problem he'd forgotten about, and then the smile brightens again and he takes Aiah's arm.

"Never mind . . . that individual we mentioned," he says. "He is not worth—"

Then with utter suddenness and purest design, as if he had intended this all along, his powerful arms clasp her shoulders and fling her along the pavement. She is too bewildered even to cry out. Falling, she sees Constantine throwing himself in another direction, the camera still following him, the bright windbreakers of the engineers whirling like a pinwheel, the hermit swaying overhead in his sack. Aiah hits the ground and feels pavement bite her knees, her hands, her cheek. There is the sudden shock of a blast and then a breath of hot wind. Flying fragments cut Aiah's flesh. Tears are startled into her eyes.

There is a crackling in the air above, flashes so bright they penetrate Aiah's closed lids. The overwhelming sensation of plasm lifts hairs on her neck. Somewhere police sirens are crying out. Aiah rolls over, sees Constantine rise from amid a cloud of dust or smoke, then sprint, with astonishing speed for such a big man, toward his launch. Guards circle, the black outlines of evil little guns in their hands, guns with curled magazines.

Unsteadily, Aiah rises to her feet. Coughing sends a bolt of pain through her chest. *"Help!"* someone screams. *"She's hurt!"* Part of the pavement where she and Constantine had been walking is shattered, as if struck with a giant hammer. The woman with the camera, Aiah sees, is sprawled on her back, arms outflung, flesh blackened: it is her soundman who is calling. Some distance away, the engineers in their colorful jackets are scattering like a flock of frightened birds.

Aiah's only impulse is to follow Constantine. She gains her feet, sways, staggers after the darting, leather-clad figure. A police car rockets around the corner, lights flashing, siren calling out. Bangs and flashes continue overhead; she hears windows shatter. The sensation of plasm is so strong Aiah can almost taste it. There is a shocking rattle of gunfire, rapid percussion striking hard at Aiah's ears, and the window of the police car turns opaque; the car slews sideways and, tires shot out, seems to slump. The gunfire goes on, striking sparks from the car's flank. *No!* Aiah wants to shout, *they're on our side!*

Constantine reaches the top of the metal stair that leads to the jetty and flings himself down it. His chief guard Martinus follows, wicked little gun held high in one big paw. Other guards pelt after. More police sirens cry. Aiah follows in the press, finds herself at the top of the stair, grabs the rail for balance. Blood from her abraded hands streaks the rusty stair rail as she runs down as fast as she can, aware that guards are clumping up behind her. Turbines whine as the guard boat chews water, heading for the broader canal beyond the lotus-bridge. The guards on board have guns out—larger, longer guns, as purposeful and evil as the small ones. The floating jetty bobs and bangs under racing feet. The two guards pass Aiah as they run.

The lines are cast off and the turbines are ready, the boat drifting away from the jetty. Constantine is standing in the cabin hatch, turned briefly to scan behind him. The boat comes up fast as Aiah runs for it. Constantine's eyes widen and his mouth opens.

"Aiah! No!"

Too late. She leaps as the boat's turbines throttle up. Her boots hit the deck and then shoot out from under her as the boat flies forward. She falls onto a black plastic chair bolted to the deck and feels the chair arm bite her ribs. She scrambles up, sees boiling foam under the stern counter, a bottle of wine spilling its contents as it rolls on the deck, shattered windows in the buildings, and the hermit, half his flesh burned away, swinging lifeless in his harness, dangling limbs and blackened hair. . . .

Aiah quickly looks the other way. Constantine has disappeared into the cabin in search of the emergency plasm batteries she knows are kept charged belowdecks. The guard boat plows on ahead. And then, lights flashing, a police boat, one of those that had been blocking traffic, turns into the canal. Fire crackles from the guard boat, a sudden drumming of rifles; and to Aiah's amazement the water police are shooting back, a cluster of men on the foredeck carrying weapons and wearing helmets. There is a snapping sound, like firecrackers going off next to Aiah's ear, and she realizes that it's *bullets,* bullets snapping the sound barrier just over her head. It occurs to her that she should take cover, hide somewhere, but there's nowhere to *go,* she's on a *boat.* . . .

And then Aiah feels sudden heat on her face as the police boat explodes, first a yellow blast like a sunburst, then a beautiful blue cloud going up like a blooming flower, the hydrogen fuel flaming as it rises. The rattling gunfire shoots only one way now, the helmeted figures on the police boat falling to the deck or jumping into the water.

Dead Keremaths smile from the pontoon. *Our family is* your *family.*

Aiah jumps as a hand touches her shoulder. "Go into the cabin, miss," a guard tells her, and Aiah sees it's blond Khoriak, the first person she'd contacted when she'd come to Caraqui.

"Thank you," she says, and gives Khoriak an apologetic grin for being in the way—all she needed was direction, really—then makes her way down the hatch.

There are three people slumped on couches in the cabin, Constantine and Martinus and a guard Aiah doesn't know. Each of them has a copper transference grip in his hand and has his eyes closed—they're telepresent now, guarding the boat. Blood trickles down Constantine's face from cuts on his scalp. His clothing is scarred and covered with dust.

Ahead, through glass windows, she can see the guard boat ram the police launch—it's not an offensive move, it's just intended to shove the police boat back into the broader canal and out of the way. The explosions overhead have ceased: whatever mage was attacking has given up, or had his sourceline cut off.

Aiah finds a place on one of the couches and sits. Soft black leather sighs beneath her, luxury inappropriate to the setting. There is a lot of food here, chafing dishes and elegant glass bowls sculpted with vines and bright red berries.

A celebratory feast, interrupted . . .

The sinking police boat is pushed into the wider canal. Constantine's launch sways as it turns into the larger channel and accelerates. His eyes slit open, plasm power glimmering in the whites as he gazes at Aiah. "I did not want you to join us," he says. "You would have been safer if you'd stayed behind."

"I want to help," she says. "What's happening?"

"Countercoup. More than that I don't know." Constantine's voice is strangely calm. "You will be of use," he says, "if we can reach the Palace." His eyes close.

The boat's bow lifts as it accelerates. Aiah can feel waves beating at the hull beneath her feet. Then the boat cuts power, turns, crashes into something, grinds as it bounces off, and accelerates. The light fades away.

They are diving into a dark passage between a pair of pontoons. Evading pursuit.

Who is chasing us? Aiah wonders.

She will know soon enough, she thinks.

CIVIL WAR IN CARAQUI?

FIRING HEARD FROM DIRECTION OF PALACE

The Provisional Government orders the public to behave in an orderly manner.

The words float in the sky above the Aerial Palace, and oddly enough, despite the battle that is going on, even the participants seem to be following orders. An orderly queue of helicopters floats in the air near the Palace, each waiting its turn to attack. The lead helicopter methodically fires rockets and cannon into the Raptor Wing—there is a hiss, a flat slapping boom that echoes off nearby buildings, a flash of fire and smoke—and then, once ammunition is gone, it heads back to the aerodrome to rearm, after which it will presumably take its place at the end of the queue.

Even the columns of smoke, rising here and there about the city, are dispersed by the wind in an orderly manner.

The Raptor Wing, headquarters of the largest and most powerful government departments, is pockmarked with shell and rocket holes, and several areas seem to be on fire. The Owl Wing has suffered as well. Aiah thinks of her people working inside when the coup started, and her fists clench in anger.

"I think it is safe to say that the Aerial Brigade has declared for the Provisional Government," Constantine observes. He frowns, but does not seem overly troubled. "That means the aerodrome will be in enemy hands, and that means they can fly in reinforcements whenever they like. If they *have* reinforcements, of course. We shall see."

The boats wait in the darkness near the Palace, under cover of overhanging pontoons that support government office buildings. Constantine sits with his legs hanging over the edge of the bow and watches the fight with interest. He would like to get into the Palace, but would prefer not to be killed while doing so, either by attackers or by defenders who fail to recognize him.

Aiah stands near him, feeling useless. She paces back and forth, kicking at the spent cartridge casings that litter the deck and dabbing at her cut face with her ruined scarf. Adrenaline surges through her, little bodily earthquakes readying her for flight or combat; but nothing is going on, and the surges leave her only with jitters and sweats.

There are roadblocks set up on the bridges leading into the Palace, but it is not clear whose roadblocks they are— people in uniforms and carrying weapons all look remarkably similar, whichever side they are on. Whoever they are, they watch the aerial bombardment with every appearance of indifference, as if they too were obeying the Provisional Government's orders to behave in an orderly manner.

"They're all waiting to see what happens," Constantine says. "If enough people line up on one side or another, the other will surrender, and then they won't have to fight."

He has decided not to contact the Palace by radio, because it might alert the rebels to his location. So he has sent Khoriak off into one of the local office buildings to make a phone call.

The phones are safe. The Avians, in their political wisdom, long ago demonstrated their concern for secure communications by installing the main telephone switches for the whole capital district in the lower depths of the Aerial Palace.

Something happens. There is a flashing in the air near the lead helicopter, and reports. Aiah's heart leaps into her throat as she turns to watch. The helicopter begins firing all its rockets rapidly, as if in a hurry to leave . . . and then another helicopter, two places behind in the queue, suddenly gives off a series of loud bangs. It is shedding rotors, as if an invisible hand has stuck itself into the whirling rotor blades—a hand, Aiah knows, of plasm. Fragments of blades fly out over the city, each one death for anyone they strike, and then the copter pitches down, its whirling tail rotor giving a corkscrew motion to its fall. There is a crash as it drops into an apartment building, then a number of explosions as munitions and fuel begin to detonate.

The lead helicopter slews off to the side, making good its escape. The next helicopter in the queue fires off all its weaponry at once, without moving any closer: rockets hiss through the air, some striking the Palace, others hitting somewhere in the city. Then suddenly all the helicopters are firing and the air is full of snarling, random death, the rockets like a nest of angry snakes striking at anyone within reach. Aiah's nerves leap with each explosion.

The helicopters flee in disorder; six, eight, twelve of them. "I think we can say their degree of commitment to the counter-revolution is limited," Constantine observes with a smile. A distant crash rings out from one of the helicopters, and it begins belching smoke and losing altitude. A wave of anxiety pours through Aiah as she sees it drop: they are enemies, but she doesn't want them to die.

The helicopter trails smoke over the horizon. Aiah can't tell whether it has crashed or not.

Constantine rises to his feet, brushes dirt from his trousers. "This would seem to be an opportunity," he says. "If Khoriak doesn't return soon, he may have to make his way back alone." He tilts his head up as if listening to an invisible speaker. "Ah. Yes. Here he comes."

He *is* listening to an invisible speaker, Aiah realizes. Telepathy. She wonders how long Constantine has been receiving information this way.

Khoriak arrives, coming down a rusted iron ladder from a passageway above. "All set," he said. "Use the southwest gate. They're expecting us."

"Sorya's cleared the helicopters out," Constantine says. "We can expect no trouble."

Sorya, Aiah thinks. That's who's been talking to him.

Unexpectedly, the knowledge makes her feel safe.

NINE

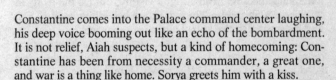

Constantine comes into the Palace command center laughing, his deep voice booming out like an echo of the bombardment. It is not relief, Aiah suspects, but a kind of homecoming: Constantine has been from necessity a commander, a great one, and war is a thing like home. Sorya greets him with a kiss.

"It is Radeen behind this," she says. "The Second Brigade is with him—his old command—they are on their way to Government Harbor. The First Brigade and Marines are in their barracks, I am told—not that the First Brigade matters in any case, since it has not recovered from its mauling in *our* coup. And there is word of police roadblocks going up here and there, so Gentri or someone high in his ministry is also a part of it."

"Radeen the Minister of War," Constantine says. "Trying to do what Drumbeth has done. And Gentri . . ." He utters the shadow of a sigh. "Gentri, well, too late."

Guilt stabs Aiah to the heart. If she had investigated Gentri properly, if she had simply done what Constantine had asked, then perhaps all this would not be happening. . . .

Her head swims, and she gropes her way to a chair and collapses into it. The others in the room pay her no heed, a fact for which she is deeply grateful.

The white glow of video monitors burns down on everyone,

outlining cheekbone and brow, casting eyes into shadow.
Sorya glides to a chair, sits in it, flicks a bit of fluff off her uniform tunic.

"I had a little advance warning," she says. "They have
done a more than competent job of keeping their plans
secret—better than we did in our time, truly, but then their
conspiracy is smaller. I managed to keep the assassins off
your neck, but not Drumbeth's."

Constantine glances sharply at her. "He's dead?"

"Yes. Killed in that ceremony reopening the bridge over
Martyrs' Canal . . . was standing with all his aides in the middle of the span when a mage attacked with a power blast. . . .
They're all dead." She shrugs. "I could save one of you, not
both. It was not plasm I lacked, but personnel. We didn't
have enough mages on duty." A superior, amused light glitters in Sorya's eyes. "Forgive me for concluding you were the
indispensable one." Her tongue visibly fondles the irony in
this phrase. She tosses her hair, gives her lilting laugh. "You
may have me indicted if you wish."

Constantine's brooding eyes gaze up at a blank video
monitor. "Drumbeth dead. That is ill news. He could carry a
good many soldiers and officers with him."

"Pfah." Disdainfully. "Soldiers and officers are readily
bought . . . here and elsewhere."

The voices are swallowed by the vast silence. They are
deep in the Aerial Palace, in a cavernous command center
tucked amid the giant brass-and-black-ceramic plasm accumulators and capacitors, the conduits of command nestled in
perfect union with the font of military and magical power.
The room is paneled in dark wood and lit by fluorescents set
in long, scalloped brass chandeliers. On three walls are
paintings of scenes from the military history of Caraqui, such
as it is. Oval video monitors are mounted high on all sides,
mostly set to outside views of the Palace, dull views of
bridges and roadblocks, here and there a pockmarked wall
or a wisp of smoke.

A map of the metropolis and its environs, three times
Aiah's height, occupies one wall. The map is painted on
translucent plastic and is divided into sectors, with colored
lightbulbs behind each sector to show whether it is held by

friendly or enemy forces. Friendly is blue, neutral is white, and the enemy shows as a pale pink stain, blotches of a bad complexion.

Most of the city is white, there being no information one way or another. But the only blue light on the map is the Aerial Palace, and there is more pink than blue.

The Avians built the map decades ago, precautions against a war that never happened. It has waited unused till now.

Tables and chairs are set up in front of the display. Elaborately styled telephone headsets, white ceramic with gold wire and gold ear- and mouthpieces, are placed at intervals along the table. A silver vase filled with red carnations sits on one of the tables. In the back of the room are two carved wooden doors, set in brass frames, that lead to a communications center. A side door leads down a short passage directly to the plasm control room, with its glowing dials and its icon to Two-Faced Tangid.

Constantine paces as he thinks, hands locked behind his back, eyes shifting from the map to the video monitors to Sorya. Aiah watches in silence. Everything is collapsing into war and ruin, and it is all her fault.

There are two dozen people in the command center, though several of them, like Aiah, seem to have no particular job to do. Half of them are in uniforms, and the rest are civilians, mostly clerks. Sorya is perfectly at home in her tailored green uniform, and sits with one polished boot thrown up on a table while jotting in a notepad on her lap. Constantine stands in front of the city map, his eyes brooding on the symbols, gauging times, distances, forces.

"What of the cabinet?" Constantine asks.

"You and the Minister for Economic Development seem to be the entire cabinet at this point," Sorya says. "He was in his office when things started—Faltheg is a banker and of limited use in this crisis, but I have him in the communications center trying to rally people to us. He has tried to contact the other ministers, but I suspect they are under arrest, in hiding, or with Colonel Radeen."

"Hilthi? Parq?"

"The aide I sent to call Hilthi said there was no answer at

his residence. I have not sent anyone to go in person. The young gentleman who phoned Parq could only get a secretary, but was told there had been shooting in the Grand Temple, so I suspect the comforts of religion are to be denied us." She laughs and tosses her head. "It was you and Drumbeth they were afraid of. You and he they wasted plasm over. They knew who could stop them, and who could not. They knew the journalist had no army, and that Parq's Dalavan Guard is a collection of pensioners in splendid uniforms."

"We've lost the aerodrome. And Government Harbor will be gone soon."

My fault, Aiah thinks dully.

Constantine looks up at the map. "How about Broadcast Plaza?"

"The guards report no disturbances."

"We have how many people there—half a company?"

"A little less than that."

"They should be reinforced. If we have radio and video, then we have a way to inform the people that resistance is possible."

Sorya gives a cynical laugh. "How many guns do the people have?"

"*People,* I remind, make up the army. Perhaps they do not know what their commanders are about, and would refuse if they knew."

"Ah." Sorya shows teeth. "Yes."

"Miss Sorya." It is one of her aides, a smart young man in one of her green uniforms. "I have a call from Hilthi. Shall I switch it to your phone?"

"Put it on the speakers." She takes one of the headsets from its hook, sweeps her long hair back, settles the gold earpieces on her ears, and speaks into the conical golden mouthpiece.

"Mr. Hilthi," she says. "This is Sorya. Do you know what is going on?"

"They tried to kill me!" Electronic distortion mars Hilthi's voice as it booms from overhead speakers. The voice mingles excitement and anger with sheer resentment at the assassins' effrontery. Constantine winces, motions to turn down the volume.

"Are you safe now?" Sorya asks.

"I suppose so. We're at . . . another place. The police came to my home to arrest me, but I told them no and . . . there was violence." A tremor shakes Hilthi's voice. "My bodyguards killed all the police, and moved me to a safer location."

My fault, Aiah thinks. Gentri's men. If she had only done as Constantine had asked . . .

Constantine gestures at Sorya for the headset, and she passes it to him. He doesn't bother donning it, just holds the mouthpiece to his lips.

"This is Constantine. I'm very pleased you are safe, Triumvir."

A howl of feedback whines from the speakers. Constantine claps his hand over the mouthpiece and the sound ceases.

"What is going on?" Hilthi asked.

"Radeen is trying to overthrow the government. He has one brigade of the army and at least some of the police. Drumbeth is dead, but I am in command here in the Palace."

"Radeen." There is a thoughtful pause. "What can I do?"

"Are you near Broadcast Plaza? That would seem to be your natural place in an affair like this. If you could get on video and issue a proclamation . . ."

Hilthi leaps on the chance. "Yes! But we've seen roadblocks everywhere."

"I will send soldiers to escort you, Triumvir, but I need to know where to send them."

There is a moment of silence. "How can I be certain you are not behind this?"

Constantine laughs, teeth flashing in amusement. "Sir—don't you think I'm more competent at this sort of thing than Radeen? If I wished you harm, believe me when I say that you would be harmed."

There is silence.

"Besides," Constantine says, "you are the only member of the triumvirate known to be alive. I am willing to place myself under your orders and do as you command."

Sorya scowls at this willing subordination, but it seems to bring Hilthi around. "Very well," he says. "I will go to Broadcast Plaza."

He gives his address, and Constantine makes note of it. "I will send soldiers as soon as I can," he says. "In the meantime, be of good cheer—I believe their strike has miscarried." He returns the headset to its hook. "Where is Colonel Geymard?" he asks.

One of the Cheloki soldiers answers. "Out inspecting our positions. I expect him back any moment."

The steward pours coffee into a fine gold-rimmed porcelain cup with geometric Keldun designs. The coffee's scent sends a bittersweet tang through Aiah, a familiar perfume rising amid the sour scent of the day's disasters. Her stomach growls and Aiah remembers that she hasn't eaten today: the banquet aboard the boat had all gone to waste.

And then she remembers her department, and another sick sensation of guilt flashes through her . . . at least eighty of her people would be on duty this shift, working in the Owl Wing as the rebel helicopters swung closer. She should have checked with them as soon as she arrived.

She drops her coffee cup into the saucer, splashing warm droplets on the tabletop in her haste, and reaches for one of the headsets. She settles the earphones around her ears and flicks the gold-plated switch that opens the line; rapidly she punches the number for her department on the twelve-key pad.

The ringing signal sings in her ears for some time, and then there is a click, the answering words "Enforcement Division" spoken in a whispering voice that suggests the speaker is afraid enemies might be lurking just around the corner.

"Ethemark," Aiah says. "This is Aiah."

"It's Miss Aiah!" Said to a third party. Then, to Aiah, "Miss Aiah, what's happening?"

"An attempted military coup. Is everyone all right?"

"First thing we knew of it, a helicopter fired a rocket right into the clerical office. Marberta and Grundlen were killed, and some others were injured by debris."

"Great Senko." Aiah sighs. Marberta and Grundlen were clerks, an older woman with children to support and a young twisted man just out of school, working to earn money toward a college degree. Aiah had hired them both personally.

There is no reason in the world why either of them had to die.

"I sent everyone else down to the shelters," Ethemark says, "but since the explosion triggered the sprinkler system, Heorka and I stayed behind to try to save the paperwork and files. We've been hiding in the secure room; it seemed the safest place. And the sprinkers turned off in a few minutes—I think they lost pressure, with all the fires in the building."

"There doesn't seem to be anything happening right now," Aiah says. "You should probably go back to the secure room. Maybe I'll join you in a while." She looks up at the uniforms clumping beneath the big illuminated map. "There doesn't seem to be anything happening here."

"Miss Aiah, who is behind this?"

"Radeen, apparently. And probably Gentri."

"Radeen." Ethemark's tone turns bitter. "I doubt he is staging this for the benefit of the twisted."

"I doubt it," she says, a sensation of weariness ghosting through her. Agendas, she thinks; everyone has an agenda.

But at least Ethemark's is where she can see it.

Unlike Radeen's.

"Miss Aiah, we want to *fight*." Ethemark's sudden volume makes Aiah wince: she twists the volume knob on the headset.

"I'm a mage," Ethemark continues, "and so are many people here. I'm sure we will all be willing, the entire department, to do our part."

"You're not a military mage," Aiah says. "And neither am I."

"There are some things we can do, even if we're untrained! We're telepresence specialists, most of us . . . we can scout the enemy if nothing else."

True, Aiah thinks, and clouds lift a little from her heart. "We might be able to free military mages for more important work."

"Exactly!"

"I will tell Constantine," Aiah says. "In the meantime, go back to the secure room and keep safe."

"May I send Heorka to the shelters to find our mages?"

"Yes. Go ahead. Find out how many are willing to assist us, and then call in a report to me in the military command center."

"Very good, miss."

Feeling less hopeless now that she has something to offer, Aiah hangs the headset on its hook and looks up. Constantine is in conference with Colonel Geymard, the Garshabi professional whose mercenary soldiers have fought on Constantine's behalf ever since the Cheloki Wars. Geymard is an erect, crop-haired man in battle dress, with a lined, weathered face and cold ice-blue eyes. It was his brigade that dropped from the sky to confront the Metropolitan Guard of the Keremaths, and now his unit, reinforced, defends the Aerial Palace.

". . . and mortars in place," he says. "I'm setting men on the rooftops around the Palace—the Palace overlooks the roofs, so they'll be of limited use to the enemy, but when the enemy comes for us we'll be able to set up a kill zone."

"I need you to send a detachment to rescue Triumvir Hilthi. Armored vehicles, I think—drive through some of those police roadblocks, liberate the streets around the Palace so that more of our folk can join us. And then you need to take the triumvir to Broadcast Plaza so that he can make his appeal to the people."

"If you will give me his location, I will arrange it."

Constantine and Geymard make the necessary plans while Aiah sips coffee, and then Geymard leaves to give the orders. Aiah stands up, says "Minister," but Constantine waves her back to her seat.

"In a moment, if you please. I have business more urgent."

He takes a headset and tries to contact the Marine Brigade. Whoever answers puts him on hold, and Aiah can see Constantine trying to control his impatience, lips pressed to a thin line, free hand clenching and unclenching in his trousers pocket. Eventually he picks up another headset. "Put me through to somewhere else in the Marine Brigade. Try—" He tilts his head to one side as he thinks. "Try the gunboat maintenance pool." A grin spreads wide as someone answers.

"Sergeant Krang?" he repeats. "I am pleased to be able to speak with you. This is Constantine, the Minister of Resources." His grin broadens and amusement lights his eyes, another of those lightning shifts of mood, from truculence to pleasure, that take Aiah's breath away. "I am very well, thank you for asking. How are you?" Another pause, and Constantine's eyes glow with delight. His grin beckons everyone in the room to share in his relish of this conversation.

"I am sorry about the sciatica," he says, "and I hope the new treatments will be effective. The reason I call is to discover if you have been attacked. Some part of the Second Brigade has been trying to overthrow the government that you Marines helped us install a few months ago."

The light in his eyes turns somber as he listens to the answer, and his grin fades. Aiah's rising hope falls. "I see," Constantine says. "Is there anyone to argue the other case? Anyone who speaks for the government?"

Another long pause. Constantine begins to fidget, his thick fingers idly spinning a gold-plated pen on the polished tabletop, watching it bob as it whirls in silence. . . . "And the troops are not inclined? That is good." He frowns. "Is there anyone I can send to you? Obvertag. Very good . . . Will you do me the favor of remaining on this line, Sergeant Krang? I thank you."

He looks up, gestures at an aide as he covers the mouthpiece. "Get me Colonel Obvertag. He is deputy advisor to—"

"Dead," Sorya says.

Constantine looks at her, brows lifted. "Yes?"

"We tried to contact him early in the game," Sorya says. "He was valuable—brought the Marines to us before, after the Keremaths forced him to retire for the crime of being an efficient officer. But his . . . *widow* . . ." A little smile flashes catlike teeth. "His widow said some officers visited him earlier today, in hopes he would join them, and when he refused them there was a scuffle, and he was killed. A bungle, apparently—they hadn't meant to harm him, but when he began to call them avaricious incompetents and greedy fools, they defended their honor and professionalism by filling him full of lead."

"You did not tell me this before?"

She looks at him with a degree of patience. "It has been a complex day, Constantine. A few things, now and again, may escape my memory." She rises, tugs her tunic into place. "I will go to Plasm Control. We should organize a counterattack soon, just to see how good these rebels are."

Constantine uncovers the mouthpiece. "I regret to inform you that the rebels have killed Colonel Obvertag. Shot him down in his own apartment, in front of his wife. You may confirm this simply by calling her. Will you share this news with your comrades?" Pause. There is a glow of triumph in his eyes.

"Thank you, Sergeant Krang. Please leave this line open and return to it when you have confirmed Obvertag's assassination to your satisfaction. I hope I may use you as a conduit to the other Marines." He flicks the switch that places the sergeant on hold, glances over the line of uniforms in the room.

"That may swing things our way—if the Marine Brigade loved anyone, it was Obvertag. His last service to us might have been the foolish fashion in which he died." He glances up at the map, reflected coordinates glittering in his eyes, and then turns to his assembled staff.

"Several of the Marines' officers, including their brigadier, ordered them to embark and head for Government Harbor," he tells them, "but the soldiers have the scent of them and do not like it, and have so far refused. But neither will they declare for us, and I must find someone to bring them over. Do we have someone here willing to make the journey? Preferably a Marine, or someone else who will know their people?"

The uniforms glance at each other. A youngish man, bull-necked and bespectacled, steps forward. "I've served with the Marines. Gunboats and bellyachers, both."

"Your name, Captain?"

"Arviro, Minister."

Constantine nods. "Very good, Captain Arviro. May I

ask—I realize this is a delicate question, but—when you served with the Marines . . . did they *like* you? I understand that one may be a fine officer, taut and meticulous, and nevertheless not have the soldiers in love with you, so if you answer in the negative I will not hold it against you."

The captain considers this question. "My platoon gave me a party when I married, so I suppose they liked me well enough. There are always discipline problems, even in a good unit, but I don't think I gave them cause to hate me."

Constantine straightens and looks down at the officer, his voice like an incantation, magic to work his will on the world. "I will give you a boat, then," he says, "and an escort. I would have you go to the Marine compound, talk to the soldiers, and bring them back to the government. Arrest any rebel officers—if they resist, you may shoot them—then report to me."

The captain nods, very serious, oblivious to any notion of high drama. "Very good, sir."

"In the absence of any loyal senior officers," Constantine says, "you may consider yourself the commander of the Marine Brigade. But you will have to win the brigade to you, and that will not be easy." He looks at Arviro with steady eyes. "It is not given to many officers to earn their command this way."

The captain blinks behind his spectacles. "Yes, Minister. I'll do what I can."

"I will write an order confirming your authority, and then arrange for an escort with Geymard when he returns."

The captain hesitates for a moment, then speaks. "Beg pardon, Minister, but Marines will *not* be gratified to see me escorted to them by foreign mercenaries. If I could arrange for an escort of Marines . . . ?"

Constantine is surprised. "Are there Marines in the building?"

"There's an honor guard at the Ministry of War. It's only a squad, but they have combat gear available. Besides, if we're seriously opposed, we'll be killed no matter what our force, and if there's only light opposition or none, the squad and the boat's crew should suffice."

Constantine nods. "Very well. Let me write out your orders, and then I will leave you to your work."

As he bends over a sheet of paper and picks up his golden pen, one of Sorya's aides approaches to murmur in Constantine's ear. Understanding glimmers in his eyes, and as he presents the captain with his orders, urgency underlies his voice.

"I have received word that planes are landing at the aerodrome and discharging troops. So your first task, on taking command of the Marines, is to move to the aerodrome and retake it."

The captain nods. "Very good, sir."

Arviro leaves and Constantine looks after him, a thoughtful frown on his face. He turns, looks at the others, and murmurs, "Well, between Sergeant Krang, Captain Arviro, and the late Colonel Obvertag, we may be able to throw a fistful of diamond dust in our enemies' gears." He looks up. "How many combat mages do we have available? We may be able to create some mischief among these troop transports as they land."

Aiah glances up sharply—perhaps this is the time she should mention her mages in the shelters.

"More are reporting, sir." Another aide. "Perhaps a dozen, though not all are trained."

"And sufficient plasm for them?" He turns and glances at Aiah, sitting alert in her chair. "Miss Aiah, I believe I need you now."

Aiah puts down her coffee—she has almost emptied the cup, she sees, all without realizing she had been drinking—and rises. "Yes, Minister?" But Constantine is already in motion, his broad back to her, and she has to trot to keep up.

Words fly to her lips, the words she's been wanting to speak this last hour. "Minister," she says, "I'm sorry about Gentri. You were right and—"

He dismisses her apology with a wave of one big hand as he dives into the tunnel that leads to Plasm Control. The passage is claustrophobic despite the cheerful brass fixtures and vermilion carpet: Aiah can sense the huge plasm reservoirs on either side, the vast weight of the concrete and armor, holding back the infinite patient power of the sea. . . .

"It is not your fault that Gentri was clever," Constantine

says. "I suspected something, and Sorya could not find an answer, and I asked you to help . . . I had not the right to expect you to find a thing when the experts could not."

"But *this* . . ." *I am to blame,* she wants to say, but her tongue trips on the words.

Constantine booms out the door at the end of the tunnel, and the vast space that is Plasm Control swims into giddy perspective. People sit intent before banks of glowing dials and brass levers. The icon to Two-Faced Tangid glowers down at them with red electric eyes.

Poised like a dancer with one foot turned out, Sorya stands leaning against a console, intent in conversation with Captain Delruss, the stocky engineer who had given Aiah her first tour of the palace. Constantine and Aiah approach.

"These reinforcements landing at the aerodrome," Constantine begins. "Our friends in the Timocracy did not warn us that these people were mobilizing?"

Sorya looks disturbed. "I have heard nothing."

Delruss—born and raised in the Timocracy of Garshab—speaks in a soft voice. "We are very good at operational security. Possibly the destination was kept secret until the units were actually in flight. So unless someone very high up was sympathetic to the current government here, or had a friend here he wished to warn, it isn't surprising you were caught off guard."

"Who is paying for them?" Sorya wonders. "I do not think that Radeen or Gentri have that kind of money, and the soldiers of the Timocracy do not move without ready coin." Her eyes narrow. "I suspect our neighbors. Lanbola does not love us, nor does Charna. Barchab wants the Keremaths back, but their government is so disorganized I doubt they could keep something like this secret."

"We shall find out in time," Constantine says. "But until then we need to deal with the soldiers themselves. Sorya, I think we need to make their landing considerably less pleasant."

Pleasure glitters in Sorya's green eyes. "May I have free use of the available mages?"

"So long as security here is not imperiled, yes. At the very least, try to crater the runways."

Sorya gives an elaborate, ironic bow. "Your servant, sir."

As Sorya glides away, Constantine turns to Delruss. "How much plasm can we call on? Can we afford to go on the offensive?"

"We've ordered all the plasm stations in the city to cease non-emergency use and to prepare to send us any stored plasm beyond that required for station defense, but three have not responded. We have thrown emergency switches to take them off the well, but these did not answer properly and have probably been sabotaged. Four other plasm stations reported that police tried to talk their way past security, but were turned away by the military police guards without violence."

"So the other stations probably made the mistake of letting the police inside?"

"Very possibly." Delruss looks apologetic. "There was no alert, of course. No reason to suspect them."

Constantine's eyes light with calculation. "Three stations," he muses. "And of course the Second Brigade's own headquarters plasm. That isn't enough to breach our defenses, but it can raise a lot of mischief and will probably be supplemented with plasm purchased abroad. If our enemies can afford foreign troops, they can certainly afford foreign plasm. But—" He smiles. "They tried to take seven plasm stations and got only three. They attempted to bring all the army with them and got only a single brigade of infantry and the Aerial Brigade, which seems to be somewhat less than enthusiastic. At least one of the triumvirs is still at large, and their attempt to murder me was foiled by Sorya." He puts a large, warm hand on Aiah's shoulder. "And they have not had Miss Aiah to provide a well of plasm vast beyond reckoning, as we did in our own strike. And that is where *they* are at a disadvantage." At his words, Aiah feels a welling of pleasure that wars with the despair in her heart.

"Minister," she says. "My department has mages in the building. Not trained for military work, but—"

"How many?" Constantine's response is immediate.

"A dozen or so. I should be getting a report very soon."

He nods briskly. "We will see if we can put them to use." He leans closer to Aiah and speaks in a low rumble. "In the meantime, I need you to organize some ministry employees—form teams—and get out into the city. Find the plasm connections to those three stations, and cut them. Destroy them, so that they cannot be repaired with any ease."

Aiah's heart gives a lurch. "I—" She hesitates. She will need maps, she thinks, equipment for manipulating plasm connections. Boats. How many teams? And Constantine wanted the plasm connections destroyed—how? Demolitions? No—not unless Constantine can give her people who know how to use them.

Acetylene torches, she thinks. Close the switches and weld them shut.

Constantine's eyes, cold and commanding, glitter down at her.

"Yes, Minister," she says.

He nods. "Very good. You may draw what you need from our ministry supplies here in the Palace. Take food from the cafeterias—you may be gone for some time."

Aiah's head whirls. "Yes."

He looks at her gravely, and to her immense surprise sketches the Sign of Karlo over her forehead with his thumb.

"At once, Miss Aiah," he says, his voice surprisingly gentle, and turns away.

CHELOKI RECOGNIZES CARAQUI REBELS

DENOUNCES "CONSTANTINE'S ILLEGITIMIST METHODS"

Marine engines rumble in the darkness beneath the city. The combined reek of floating garbage and floating humanity is clenched in the back of Aiah's throat like a fist.

The boat's spotlights carve a misty tunnel in the darkness. Rusting hulls, strange scaffoldwork, misshapen bodies, and dully glittering eyes loom on either side. The boat is passing through one of the uncharted half-worlds, a far more primitive place than Aground, a randomly assembled collection of human and nautical rubbish. Edged by the spotlights, perceived only in fragments, the rusting barges and silent, unresponsive people have a nightmarish jigsaw quality, eerie fragments assembled at random in some huge, unguessable formation.

It had taken several hours for Aiah to assemble her teams—to find them in the shelters, to persuade them to volunteer, to locate the necessary equipment, and to plan the operation on ministry maps laid out over the tables in the Operations Room. And all the while the situation outside was changing, the balance of power shifting as more elements entered the volatile situation. . . .

Sorya's team of mages failed to significantly damage the mercenary units landing at the aerodrome—they were well guarded by their own mages—but she succeeded in cratering the runways to prevent further reinforcements. The incoming mercenaries were forced to divert their flights to neighboring Lanbola, where it is presumed they will be interned. Hilthi was plucked from his hideout by Geymard's troops and delivered to Caraqui's broadcast center, where radio and video began to air his appeals to the population. And to everyone's surprise the third member of the triumvirate, Parq, phoned in from his office in the Grand Temple. He had survived a brawl between his guards and police sent to arrest him, and several people had been killed. He had thought the plot aimed against himself alone—perhaps initiated by a band of religious dissidents—and had only belatedly discovered the extent of the countercoup.

He was declaring for the government, he said, and was mobilizing his Dalavan Guard and would soon be making a broadcast on his own Temple-owned communications channels.

Constantine seemed pleasantly surprised by this. In view of Parq's history of treachery, he clearly had anticipated a great deal of bargaining before the triumvir chose one side or another; but apparently the assassination attempt had frightened him—"He cannot be encouraged by the thought that our opponents find him dispensable," as Constantine remarked—and Parq was now firmly in the government camp, even if his Dalavan Guard was a lightly armed joke.

Following this news came another strike by the Aerial

Brigade—much more timid this time: the helicopters darted from the aerodrome, fired their rockets at extreme range in the general direction of the Palace, then raced back to safety. The rockets rained down everywhere but the Palace, setting fires in the surrounding district, and Geymard's military mages and antiaircraft weapons managed to bring two of the helicopters down in spite of their caution.

Aiah had packed her teams into their four official ministry powerboats and waited for the all-clear. It was all, she suspected, her fault. Now she had a chance to repair some of the damage, and the only way to be certain of success was to do the job personally. A mage's place, she realized, is probably in the Palace, but unless she was in the field with her teams, she could not make sure the job would be done right.

But it was an ominous sight, as the day eased into its third shift, that greeted Aiah as her motorboat slid from the government marina—low gray clouds obscuring the Shield, a cold wind shouldering its way between the buildings, columns of black smoke rising from the city on fire. The sky was empty of plasm adverts—all plasm had been diverted to other purposes—and there were no people to be seen other than soldiers huddling behind barricades. There was a strange silence in the air—none of the usual noises, the hiss of motor traffic or the roar of boats. Even the sound of helicopters, so prominent earlier in the day, was gone. There was a sense of wariness, of hidden eyes looking down at Aiah's boats from darkened windows. It is as if her little flotilla is the only thing moving in the whole city, the only thing alive, the only target. . . .

As if the metropolis was waiting to discover who would be its master.

Motoring out of sight in the half-submerged world beneath the city's structures is like cruising down a huge flooded sewer, the hulking barnacle-encrusted concrete pontoons looming huge on either side, overhead a distant, shadowy roof or the narrow slit of Shieldlight permitted by overhanging buildings. Here the turnings are largely unmapped, and navigation is largely by instinct and by compass. Uncharted half-worlds filled with equally uncharted humanity block the channels and impede progress.

Now something large and black runs along a half-world gangway on Aiah's left, then disappears into a darker piece of shadow. Aiah's heart leaps, and her eyes strain into the gloom. Nothing moves. Whatever—whoever—it was remains hidden.

Ahead, a bright patch of Shieldlight transects the channel. Aiah gnaws her lip, looks hopelessly at the map pinned to the table in front of her, then takes one of the boat's spotlights and trains it on the side of the pontoon near the splash of light. Every pontoon is required to have identification numbers painted on each end, and there are also supposed to be hanging metal signs giving the names of the various nautical lanes and channels; but the usual Caraqui slackness has been applied to the regulations, the signs have been scavenged for their metal, and what inspector would ever visit the underworlds anyway?

Aiah motions with her hand and the boat slows while she scans the pontoon, and then the pontoon opposite. Narrowing her eyes, she can faintly make out the flaked, weathered paint, centuries old, only visible because there is no real weathering down here. Each numeral is twice her height, and the pattern is only visible at all because it's so huge. 4536N: a coordinate. She returns to her map, squints down at it, looks at the boat's compass, then back at the map.

"Left," she says, hoping she's worked the compass deviation correctly—this close to the Pole, the deviation is enormous—and that the new course will take them all west, to their target at Fresh Water Bay.

The turn takes the flotilla into a narrow alleyway overshadowed by tenements of brown brick. The place actually has a name: Coel's Channel. The sky is a long, narrow slit directly overhead, dark cloud skimming low overhead. Far above, laundry strung on lines floats gray in Shieldlight. Arrangements of guy wires and planks, sometimes at dizzying heights, connect the buildings over the little canal. A female hermit, long gray hair shrouding her face, hangs like the laundry from a wire in what looks like an old flour sack.

One of the boat's crew has been listening to the radio, earphones pressed to his head, turning knobs as he stares fixedly at yellow glowing dials. He looks up with a start.

"Listen to this," he says, and turns another knob, and an official-sounding voice comes from the buzzing metal grid of the speaker.

"—al Government of Caraqui," it says, "was formed in order to unite those patriotic citizens determined to free our metropolis from the pernicious foreign ideas of the ex-Metropolitan Constantine and his gang of outland mercenaries."

"Who *is* this?" growls Davath—large, twisted, a stoneface with features like pitted concrete. The answer to his question is obvious enough.

The enemy has finally declared himself publicly.

"I will now surrender the microphone to our president, Kerehorn."

"Kere*horn?*" asks Prestley. "Which Keremath's that?"

"Kerethan's son," Aedavath says.

"No, Kerethan's son was Keredeen, and they both got killed."

"Kerethan's *other* son." Stubbornly.

"No, he's dead, too."

"Hush."

Kerehorn's voice is reedy and uncertain. "Greetings, fellow citizens. The day of liberation is nigh."

"Nigh?" someone offers. "Who *wrote* this?"

The speech is a vitriolic personal attack on Constantine, along with his "gang of foreigners and oppressors." Other major figures in the government, Drumbeth and Parq and Hilthi, are not even mentioned. But Kerehorn is not much of a speaker, and the whole speech falls flat, interrupted every so often by the rustle of paper as he tries to find his place in his prepared text.

Aiah looks at the others as they all listen: their faces show skepticism, amused contempt, grim humor. They've lived under the rule of the Keremaths, and she hasn't: they know better than she how to take this. Apparently their respect for Kerehorn, or any of his family, is limited.

"We pledge ourselves to the restoration of the ancient liberties and traditions of the Caraqui people," Kerehorn says, and cynical laughter floats from one team member to the next.

"Why does he even bother to justify it?" someone says.

Cold certainty suddenly floods Aiah's mind: *Kerehorn is not the real leader*. This unprepossessing a character could never have organized something as dangerous as the countercoup. He is a figurehead, intended to provide a degree of legitimacy for the coup's genuine leaders. But whose figurehead is he? Radeen's?

Perhaps Radeen is using the Keremaths' money to wedge himself into power. Perhaps they are both pawns of someone else. Or perhaps there is no real leader, only a group of people, each with different reasons for wanting to destroy the current government. . . .

Coel's Channel comes to an end up ahead, and the waters of a wide canal open out, its water bright green with algae and home to a flock of pelicans preening themselves in the unusual stillness. The boat's helmsman throttles back. Aiah looks at the map again.

Ideally she wants to go straight on, but looking ahead she can see nothing but the gray slab wall of a pontoon on the far side of the canal. Obviously they will have to traverse the open canal for at least a while before turning west again.

The helmsman reverses the engines briefly to bring the boat to a complete stop, its prow barely jutting out beyond Coel's Channel. Another crewman airily steps out onto the foredeck and peers left and right past the high concrete walls on either side. Aiah can tell from the sudden stiffening of his spine that he sees trouble. He returns to the cockpit, and Aiah's mouth goes dry as she sees his grim expression.

"There's a bridge to starboard, right in our path," he says. "I can see a police roadblock on it, several cars, maybe a dozen cops."

"Armed?" Aiah asks.

An unreadable expression passes across the crewman's face. "Of course."

An idiot question: Aiah doesn't know what she's going to do, what she *can* do, and is just playing for time. She delays further by going onto the foredeck herself, moving far less surefootedly than the boat's crewman; she peers gingerly around the corner, heart pounding, and sees the bridge a few stades away. Suspension wires curve in a graceful arc, and the iron uprights are covered with an untarnishable black ceramic impressed with the oval cameo profiles of long-dead Caraquis. Square in the middle of the span is the roadblock: cars drawn across the span with their lights flashing in silence, uniformed men standing with long weapons in their hands. Should they choose to fire down into boats passing beneath them, they could cause a massacre. But getting around them will require an endless amount of backtracking, with little assurance of not encountering another roadblock somewhere else along the way.

"Long live the Provisional Government!" The chorused words ring out from the radio. Aiah gnaws her lip and tries to figure out what to do.

Pelicans drift in the canal ahead, mocking her with eerie pebble eyes.

"We now take you live to Government Harbor," the announcer says, "where officers and men of the Caraqui Army will swear allegiance to President Kerehorn and the new government."

There is a pause, a howl of feedback—apparently people in Government Harbor are listening to the broadcast with their speakers turned up—and then a commanding voice, speaking a bit too far from the microphone.

"This is War Minister Radeen!" he says, and immediately afterward, as the techs sense his distance from the mike, his volume cranks up a bit. He has a tendency to shout every phrase and then stop, breaking every sentence up into little exclamations. "I have before me the officers! And the soldiers! Of the Army of Caraqui! Soldiers—!" The volume goes up again as the proclaiming starts. "I will now lead you! In the oath of allegiance to your new government!" He takes a breath. *"I, a soldier of Caraqui . . ."*

"I," a great chorus roars, *"a soldier of Caraqui . . ."*

Aiah is struck by the idea of Radeen, far before the issue is decided, actually lining up the soldiers of the Second Brigade—or a large number of them, anyway—in Government Harbor square in order to swear an oath that, judging by the Second Brigade's adherence to past oaths, isn't worth a brass hundredth. . . .

"Here in the sight of the gods and immortals . . . ," Radeen continues.

Government Harbor is a symbol—it's the official seat of government, with the Popular Assembly and offices for most of the government departments—but it has no real military value. True civil and military power is concentrated in the vastness of the Aerial Palace. During the coup of Drumbeth and Constantine, Government Harbor had been seized, but the Marines then pushed on to aid in the storming of the Palace. Now Radeen seems content with the seizure of deserted office buildings and the mouthing of empty oaths.

Aiah has no military background, but in the past months she has seen real soldiers at work, and if she were in charge of the Second Brigade her soldiers would already be hammering at the doors of the Palace.

She snarls. These people do not *deserve* to win.

"I swear allegiance to the Provisional Government, representing the people of Caraqui . . ."

And then over the radio comes a whistle and an explosion, and then another and another, and then shouts and screams. There is the crackling sound of rolling thunder, and Aiah remembers plasm heat on her face as she recognizes the sound of telepresent mages doing invisible combat. More cries and explosions buffet the microphone. She pictures neat parade formations dissolving in blood and chaos. Perhaps this is the ordinary soldiers' first clue that they are not unopposed.

Government Harbor, she concludes, is entirely within the range of the mortars that Geymard had readied on the Palace roofs, and Radeen's mages can't keep out every round.

She looks back over the boat's crew and sees their grins—twisted Davath throws back his head and laughs, cold amusement bubbling from his vast trunk—and then quite suddenly she knows what she will do.

"Turn on the flashers," she says. "Lean on the horn. Everyone put on your hard hat, and stay in plain sight." A strange, daring humor courses through her, and she gives a reckless smile. "When we see the police, everyone wave!"

The crew looks at her in surprise, then obeys. She puts on the official red hard hat that marks her as a member of the ministry's Plasm Bureau. The emergency lights flash on, tracking yellow and red across the narrow concrete walls of

Coel's Channel. The helmsman leans on the air horn, and the blast startles the flock of pelicans into sudden flight. He throws the throttles all the way forward, and the boat's stern digs into the murky canal water and leaps forward on a sudden boil of white foam. . . .

Wind blows Aiah's hair back as she sees the bridge sway into view. Police in black shiny helmets look down at the small convoy of motorboats driving a flock of frantic birds before it. Aiah senses their eyes on her and feels a defiant blast of fire in her heart, burning as fierce as if it were plasm. A grin drags her lips back from her teeth, and she raises a hand to wave at her fellow civil servants on the bridge above.

There is a moment of hesitation. Then black gloves lift and wave in answer. Some of the gloves carry weapons, but the barrels are pointing at the Shield.

The bridge passes, a black shadow like the wings of death, and then the boats are past. The police have not been instructed to impede emergency vehicles.

The helmsman gives Aiah a hollow graveyard laugh, and there is a hot glow of reckless terror in his eyewhites as he turns to Aiah. "Go west again?" he says.

Aiah shakes her head. "Stay in the main channels. Faster that way." The helmsman laughs again, defying his own fear.

"Aye aye, miss," he says.

The carnage on the radio ceases as switches are finally thrown in Kerehorn's headquarters. Someone puts on music, something with a lot of violins.

Aiah's teams pass half a dozen police roadblocks on the way to Fresh Water Bay, but the police never do anything but wave.

TEN

~~~~~~~~

They are deep in the bowels of a concrete barge long as a Jaspeeri city block, in a place walled off by bulkheads and watertight steel doors. Somewhere a pump is thudding, there's a constant loud humming noise from the generators in the next compartment, and the electric cable that services the light fixtures is tacked to the ceiling with metal staples. The oversized lightbulbs, with little nipples on the tips, are in metal cages.

—Carcel's team is not quite in place. Took a wrong turn.

Ethemark's disembodied mental voice, ringing in Aiah's head, is different from his real voice, pitched a little higher, and with little resonance.

—Tell the others to stand by, Aiah sends.

And then, to Davath and Prestley, "Not just yet."

When Aiah's little convoy got to Fresh Water Bay, she called the Aerial Palace on a portable handset she plugged into a communications junction. Constantine, who had not felt he could spare any mages to escort them during their trip, had then assigned each of Aiah's four teams a telepresent minder.

Accompanied by their invisible guardians, the teams split up and surrounded their target plasm station. They were going to try cutting all its plasm supply at once, at each of the four plasm mains leading to the structure.

—The station will be attacked once you cut it off from the net, Ethemark says. Constantine is sending two companies of Garshabis. Once the station's plasm reserves are drained, the soldiers can move in.

—Are the soldiers on their way now?

—Yes. They should be there in fifteen minutes or so, depending on how well they deal with roadblocks on the way. Thus far the police have always scattered when challenged by our soldiers.

—What else is happening?

—The Marines have come over to us. They shot their traitorous officers and are moving on the aerodrome under the command of Captain Arviro.

The satisfaction in Ethemark's voice is apparent even in this tenuous telepathic communication.

—Radeen's lost then, Aiah judges. The balance has swung against him.

—So Constantine believes. The Second Brigade at Government Harbor has made no moves other than to direct a few mortar rounds our way, and the Aerial Brigade has not budged from the aerodrome—wait a moment, please.

There is a pause.

—Carcel says he is in place, Ethemark finally reports.

—Let's begin then.

Plasm is like water, flowing through every available conduit until it reaches a kind of equivalence. But some structures are capable of containing more plasm than others: plasm accumulators, capacitors, and batteries are constructed so as to fill with plasm, and draw in even more from the surrounding grid. The mains carrying plasm from the structures where it is generated to the plasm stations are composed of woven bundles of cable made of an alloy designed to carry a perfect flood of plasm along its length.

There are four main cables going into the plasm station in Fresh Water Bay, one for each cardinal direction; and they must all be cut at once, for otherwise the plasm would reroute itself, like water pouring through a system of pipes, into the uncut cable. Probably the single cable would not be capable of carrying as much plasm as the four, but it is a supposition that Aiah would not care to test.

Aiah looks at Davath and Prestley. "Let's get started."

The cable is thick at this juncture, thick as three Davaths coiled together. The junction, where other cables from other structures merge with this one, features an electric-powered rotor that can take any of the cables off the line, including—because all cables must at times receive maintenance—the main cable that brings all the plasm in the district to the plasm station.

Prestley has stripped the cover from the electric junction box and disabled the communications line that allows the plasm station to control it. "Ready," he says.

Aiah nods at him. "Go."

A loud rattle hammers at Aiah's ears as the rotator shifts to the neutral position. The plasm station is now cut off.

—Mission accomplished, Aiah sends to Ethemark.

—Good. Get out of there fast.

—Fast. Right.

The truth is, they must stay around a while.

Davath strikes a light on an oxy-acetylene torch as Prestley uses both hands to draw by its handles the heavy black plastic-encased fuse from the junction box—"I'll throw this in the canal later," he says—and then takes a hammer to the manual controls. Bits of plastic and wire fly around the room as he batters the box into ruin. Aiah's heart hammers—in Fresh Water Bay Station they've *got* to know what's happened—but Davath calmly bends to apply his torch to the plasm junction, welding it into the neutral position.

If there are combat mages in the plasm station, Aiah thinks, we could be dead any second.

Sweat drips from her brow. The room, with its steel-and-concrete walls surrounding the welding torch, suddenly seems close and hot.

—Our mages have launched their attack, Ethemark says. The soldiers are accelerating and should be at the station soon.

Plasm stations are notoriously designed with insurrection or war in mind. They are heavily armored, and covered with a bronze collection web designed to absorb plasm attacks, disperse them over the web, and then draw the plasm into the station's own stores. The chief way to attack such a station is to throw heavy things at it—usually armor-piercing shells, but in a pinch big rocks will do—until the defenses are breached and telepresent mages can enter on a raging wave of plasm to sweep away opposition.

Aiah counts the drops of sweat that fall from her chin onto the scarred steel floor. *Thirty-one, thirty-two* . . . At last Davath finishes his work. He stands, pulls his goggles down around his thick neck. "Done. Let's go."

They leave the tiny compartment on a run. "One last thing," Prestley says. "Turn on your torches." He goes to the generator room next door and throws a switch—the cage-enclosed lights die with a whimper.

Aiah leads the other two upward at a run, taking the gridded metal steps two at a time. Slamming and locking a steel door behind them, they emerge into a corridor filled with anxious civilians. Poor people live here, in lightless compartments below the waterline, with wealthier residents in the airy flats above.

"What's going on?" people ask. "What's happening?"

"Listen to Hilthi on the radio," Aiah gasps, breath almost gone. "Do what he says."

They jog up another stair, then turn onto a gangway that leads to an outside door. Plastic flooring booms under their feet. Shieldlight gleams through the door.

They burst out onto another gangway, this one webbed by chain-link. Their boat awaits, moored to a pier at the bottom, engines idling. As the crewmen see the party running, the engines roar into life.

There is a concussion, a flat slap that strikes painfully at the ears. An explosion at the plasm station.

Aiah leaps into the boat, throws herself gasping into a padded chair. "Go," she says.

Another explosion shocks the air, and the boat throttles up, standing on its wake as it races away.

TRIUMVIR HILTHI CALLS FOR POPULAR UPRISING!

"DESTROY THE REBELS WHO WOULD ENSLAVE YOU!"

Aiah's four teams rendezvous at a Dalavan temple—Constantine's people had given them the address. The place is a strange blocky building, the façade a structure made up entirely of pillars, pillars built around and next to and on top of each other, like a double handful of pencils. They are bright red or yellow, and each is topped with a little bell-shaped dome. Gateways are cut through the pillars, their curving arches carved with a wild variety of threatening monsters, all painted in lifelike colors. Ascetics hang from the building in sacks, and some, it appears, have been dead for some time—dead in a holy cause, they are allowed to hang there until they rot, inspiration for the faithful.

The temple priests provide them with a hot meal and an office in which Aiah can spread out maps and plan the assault on Xurcal Station. On the wall, an oval screen shows Triumvir Parq speaking on the Dalavans' video link. Parq has donned the ebony-and-gold Mask of Awe worn when speaking as the official head of the Dalavan faith, and his magnificent voice booms from the mask in a tireless call to strife and battle. Where formerly Aiah had heard only the silky tones of the politician and born seducer, now she hears the ringing voice of a commander calling on his troops. She is struck with admiration for his verbal skill at the same time as she is chilled by its effect.

"I declare the rebels to be the enemies of the Supreme One Dalavos and his people!" he cries. "Their secret purpose, a conspiracy plotted in the very pits of Hell, is to destroy both our state and our faith. The wickedness of the Avians was as nothing compared with the evil of these rebels, for the Avians were deformed in body and spirit while these appear as normal men, even if their souls are twisted."

He takes a breath. Eyes glitter, red and silver, from the depths of the mask. "All those faithful to Dalavos and his teachings must resist them to the utmost of their power," he proclaims. "Ambush their patrols! Shoot them down from hiding! Steal their plasm!" His fists clench, pounding the air like hammers as they beat time to his thoughts. "I declare, as the supreme leader of the faithful, that those who, having heard my word, continue the obstinate fight for the rebel cause are condemned as traitors to Heaven. *Never* shall they be accepted in our temples! *Never* shall they be seen among us! *Never* shall they share our food or taste our drink! *Never* shall they take the least shelter from us! I *curse* them!"

Aiah shivers, tries to focus on her map. Parq's voice drops and he speaks rhythmically as he begins an incantation. The camera closes in on his face, on the eyes like embers lying in the mask, the lips of flesh writhing behind the frozen lips of ebony.

"Curst be their hearts, for their hearts are filled with evil. Curst be their minds, for their minds are the dwelling place of rebellion. Curst be their feet, for their feet bear them on the road to Hell. Curst be their throats, for the words in their throats are the wicked lies of demons and the undead. . . ."

Aiah is having a hard time concentrating on her maps.

"I don't suppose," she ventures, "it might be possible to lower the volume?"

Surely before he gets to the *spleen,* she thinks, but she doesn't know how devout any in her party might be, and she dares not say it aloud.

Davath approaches the video and snaps it off. The picture vanishes, shrinks down to a little white eye in the center of the oval screen, and then this disappears as well.

Parq's resonant voice can still be heard from speakers elsewhere in the building, but his words are indistinct. Aiah looks down at her map, points with a pencil.

"We'll take Gernan Canal to Bannaltir," she says. "That's where we'll split up. Hoyl and Parasqof will turn east."

The telephone gives a loud electric buzz. Aiah picks up the headset, presses one earpiece to her ear.

"This is Aiah."

"Congratulations, my lady. Fresh Water Bay Station has fallen, and the battle was brief."

Constantine's resonant voice and apparent cheerful mood bring a ghostly smile to her lips. She settles the headset into place and adjusts the mouthpiece on its flexible mount.

"Thank you, Minister," she says, and she sees the others exchange glances, knowing now who is on the other end of the line.

"My people have done an exceptional job," she adds.

"Xurcal will not be as easy. The rebels have learned from

their mistakes, it appears. Our mages tell us that police are guarding the cables near the station, and that there are roving patrols elsewhere."

"Can you give me locations?"

"I will give you such information as I have," Constantine says, and does so. Aiah jots it down with her pencil. "The situation is fluid, of course," he adds. "I should be very careful."

"Can you give me more crews?" Aiah asks. "It would be safer for us all in the long run."

"I will see what I can do."

"What else is happening?"

"The admirable Captain Arviro and his Marines will be pitching into the aerodrome very shortly. We are husbanding our plasm in aid of that fight. We have cleared the area around the Palace of police roadblocks, which is allowing our mages to come in from the city and join us. Radeen and his brigade at Government Harbor are not moving. I received a number of reports that a great many of the roadblocks dissolved once the police found out what they were in aid of, and that many of the cops simply went home. I have *other* reports of police gangs marauding and looting shops, however, so apparently some are not beyond using the situation to their advantage."

"If there's a fight about to start, we'd better drop the shoe on Xurcal soon."

"Whenever you can." Constantine lowers his voice, and at the intimate sound, like the touch of bedroom silk in the darkness, Aiah feels a yearning eddy along her nerves. "But be careful, Miss Aiah. I would not lose you for Xurcal or all the plasm stations in the world."

Aiah's heart fills her throat for a moment; when she can find words she says, "I don't plan to do anything foolish."

"I wish you had been less scrupulous, and not gone out with your people. I would have talked you out of it had I known what you intended."

"What else could I do? I couldn't stand it sitting in the Palace giving orders and wondering if my people would . . ." The word *die* withers on her tongue as she looks up at her crew and sees their patient eyes. "Run into trouble," she finishes, lamely.

"Yes," he says, "waiting in the Palace is *my* lot, and I

know its frustrations. I would rather be with you, on your little boat, than here in perfect safety."

Aiah licks dry lips. "I wish you were here, too."

Her fellows exchange glances again. It is not often they hear a comrade exchange intimacies with one of the Powers.

Constantine's voice turns weary. "Each in our spheres, we move according to our degree. At least certain political choices are now made easier."

"I wouldn't know."

"I will try to get you more crews. Would Ethemark know how to raise more people?"

"Yes."

"I will have him call you."

"Good."

There is a moment's hesitation. "We are going to have a battle any moment, so I cannot speak for long."

"I understand."

"Please understand that when I said I wanted you here, that was for *my* peace of mind only. But it is the Aiah who puts herself in danger for her people that has my devotion, and even for peace of mind I would not have you other than who you are. . . ."

Aiah's nerves sing at these words, flame and sorrow together. "Thank you," she says.

"I am getting a signal. The war begins anew. Farewell."

"Senko's blessing," she says, but he has already pressed the disconnect button.

She puts the headset on its hook and looks down at the map again. Now that she knows where some of the police are, she realizes that her plan will not work.

And so she makes another.

FIRST STRIKE FAILS

COUP PLOTTERS COUNT ON REINFORCEMENTS

GOVERNMENT CONTINUES APPEALS TO PEOPLE

Dark water surges at Aiah's left hand as she walks along a rust-eaten catwalk of mesh. More water drizzles down from above, flashes of falling silver in the beams of helmet lamps.

They are between two of the giant concrete pontoons. At some point in the distant past iron beams were laid down to connect the pontoons, and a roof built to seal out the light; and on top of this roof a series of office buildings now stands.

In the half-forgotten darkness below, Aiah's people scramble in the Shieldless gloom. Seawater sloshes around their feet as the catwalk sags under their weight. The operation is woefully behind schedule, and this time it is Aiah's party that is late.

At Fresh Water Bay, Aiah's group was able to get adjacent to the station and turn off the plasm mains at the easiest and most convenient place. With police patrolling the plasma mains near Xurcal Station, the sabotage has to be much more dispersed, and more prolonged. Instead of four faucets, thirty have to be turned off, all at a greater distance from the target. Since the plasm reroutes itself, Aiah hopes that the operators at the station may not even notice that their supply is in jeopardy—she supposes they may be receiving less than previously, but with both sides in the fighting making more demands on the city plasm grid, this should not be surprising.

Aiah and her teams have descended, over and over, into the dark wells of the pontoons, into the subbasements of office buildings, into dank sweating steel-walled rooms ankle-deep in seawater. They worked into the sleep shift, and then into the work shift—it has been over a day since Aiah slept. But sleep was surrendered without protest: a battle is raging, and Xurcal may be critical. Either enemy mages are operating there, or it is beaming its power to mages operating elsewhere.

But now Aiah's job is almost over. All but four of the thirty taps have been turned, four taps on the main plasm cables leading to Xurcal. All the branching cables have been shut off. And from this point it should be as simple as it was to turn off Fresh Water Bay.

Four simple operations.

If only Aiah weren't lost.

Her maps are out of date. Where the map showed a cable junction complete with a rotating control, Aiah found only an empty steel room, rusting door swinging on its hinges. The cable was there, but it was covered by armored plates and surrounded by the heavy steel footings of the scavenged rotator box. And so there was nothing to do but to follow the cable onward, toward Xurcal, and hope to find a place where the tap could be turned.

One gloved hand trailing along the pontoon's crumbling concrete wall, Aiah follows the cable and hopes that, if a junction appears, it will be within arm's reach. The cable is above her, fixed to the pontoon wall above her head with iron staples as thick as Davath's arm.

—Ethemark? she sends.

No answer. He has been with the party only intermittently—with the head of the Plasm Enforcement Division wandering around in Caraqui's sweat-walled basements, Ethemark has a lot more distractions in the office than usual.

He might, Aiah thinks charitably, be scouting up ahead.

"Careful," says Davath. "Slippery here."

The catwalk is covered with guano, probably from a bat or bird colony somewhere overhead. The stuff has mixed with seawater to form a slick white clay that slides treacherously beneath Aiah's boots. Aiah steps cautiously in the mess.

Beyond, one of the cables supporting the catwalk has broken or rusted away, and the catwalk sags into the water at a dangerous angle. Aiah is breathless by the time she gets to the other side, and her boots are full of water. She wishes that when she realized the junction had gone astray, she had thought to go back for her boat.

"Here it is, miss!" Davath increases his pace along a sturdier section of catwalk, and Aiah breathlessly follows. Davath's hand torch and helmet lamp play on a junction box and rotator, both of them bolted to the side of the pontoon where another cable joins from the pontoon above.

"Looks like a temporary installation," Davath says, but his torch shows big deposits of rust scarring the ostensibly stainless surface of the rotator box, and it is obvious that the junction has been here for years. Decades, probably.

—Ethemark? Aiah sends again.

Nothing. She scans the wall for a communications box for her portable handset, and doesn't find one.

Wonderful. Now they've found their objective, but they have no way to tell anyone they've reached it.

And they can't just cut the plasm here, because the taps have to be turned all at once, otherwise the mages at Xurcal will know what's happening and take steps to prevent it.

Davath, no sign of frustration crossing his cinder-block face, unshoulders the cutting torch and its heavy gas cylinders, which he's been carrying this long distance. His body is built for carrying burdens, and he shows little sign of weariness.

He places the cylinders gently onto the catwalk. "Whenever you're ready, miss," he says.

"I'm waiting for Ethemark. He's . . . off somewhere."

"Very good, miss."

Prestley reaches into his jumpsuit for a cigaret. He lights it and the three wait in silence, the darkness warm and close around them. Drips of water fall steadily from above, plash into the water nearby.

Aiah's nerves jump at the sound of bolts being thrown, and then yellow light pours out into the darkness as a hatch is thrown open only a few paces away, farther along the plasm line.

"Senko only knows where we are," a voice says, and then a helmeted man steps from the hatch onto the catwalk. He stares at them for a startled instant before raising his boxy black pistol and pointing it straight at Davath.

"Hold it right there!" he says, a thread of panic in his voice.

Aiah can only stare at him, heart hammering in her throat, as another two police follow him out onto the catwalk, weapons drawn. One of them has a submachine gun, a little gleaming wicked thing, held in his two fists.

"Who are you?" the first officer says. "What are you doing here?"

Aiah stares and tries to talk, but finds that something has stolen her breath.

Prestley shrugs and tosses his cigaret butt into the water. "We're Plasm Bureau," he says. "We've got a repair order."

"Down *here? Now?*"

Prestley frowns. "Plasm gotta move, man."

Another police voice chimes in. "Don't you people know what's going on?"

"Hell with that!" says the first. "I don't believe 'em anyway!" His pistol barrel gives a little jerk toward the wall. "Up against it, all of you. Hands up on the concrete."

Aiah mutely obeys, places her palms on the sweaty wall. She can't seem to find her voice at all, or her mind.

She doesn't know what to do. What she *can* do.

"Look at the torch!" the first cop says. "Sabotage!" He kicks the oxy cylinder with a steel-capped toe. "ID, all of you!"

His mates cover Aiah's party with their weapons while the first cop edges out onto the catwalk behind them and begins patting down Davath. He finds the man's ID card, looks at it in the light of his torch. "Plasm Bureau, all right. But I haven't heard the Bureau's on *our* side." He produces a pair of handcuffs. "Put your right hand behind your back," he says.

And then Davath moves. The huge gray body spins out of the line of fire and both hands reach out, seizing the first policeman high and low. The man gives a yelp as Davath's big hand crushes his groin. Holding the first policeman's body by crotch and collar, Davath charges the other two police, using their comrade as a shield.

There is a half-second's hesitation and then guns bark out. Flashes light the huge artificial cavern. Sound hammers Aiah's ears and she throws herself down, falling across Prestley's legs, seawater splashing her as she sprawls on the catwalk. Over the sound of her thudding heart she hears shots, screams, and splashes; and then desperate shrieks for help.

"No! Don't—!" And then a horrid, crunching thud. And another. Screams. More thuds. A strange rushing sound, like an underground river. Hollow-sounding screeches that can come from no human throat.

Aiah dares to raise her eyes, sees Davath's huge form looming against the light of police torches, an upraised gas cylinder in his hands. A desperate scream rings out. Davath brings the cylinder down, and there is a squelching thud, and the scream is cut off. Davath tries to raise the cylinder again, but instead sags against the concrete wall.

Prestley scrambles to his feet, boot-soles kicking Aiah in the face, and rushes past Davath to kneel atop the sprawled policemen. Aiah can hear him panting for breath as he makes a frantic search. One of the police whimpers. The strange rushing sound continues. The air is full of grating chirps. Prestley finds what he's looking for and rises. Aiah can see the outline of a gun against the light of the open hatch. The cop whimpers again.

Don't! But the words never get past Aiah's lips, because her breath is just gone, *gone*. She may never breathe again.

The pistol booms once, twice, thrice. And then Prestley turns to Davath just as the big gray man finally falls, and supports Davath's great weight until he can be lowered to the catwalk.

Aiah blinks eyes dazzled by gunshots. She forces herself to take a breath—the most welcome she's ever tasted—and rises unsteadily to her feet. She has to hold on to the concrete wall for a moment or two because her knees have gone to rubber, and then she edges toward the sprawled bodies.

Davath lies bleeding, half-supported by Prestley. The police fired right through their comrade in order to hit him, but he still had enough strength to knock them down and beat them to a pulp with the acetylene cylinder.

"Senko, Senko, oh hell," Prestley swears. Aiah pats herself, wondering if she's got a handkerchief or something to stop Davath's bleeding. Something black darts through the beam of her helmet light and she looks up to see a river of bats overhead, startled by the gunshots, thousands of gray bodies flashing in the light as they flood past. Their strange chirping grates on Aiah's ears.

She kneels by Davath, presses her hands to the chest wounds. A gunshot has taken off most of his left ear, splashing his face with blood, and another has drilled him through the right hand, but most of the wounds seem to be at the center of body mass. Davath's yellow eyes regard her with a strange tranquillity as she searches the front of his jumpsuit.

Three shots, she thinks, maybe four; it's hard to tell in the dark. One of them whistles ominously with Davath's every breath, and Aiah presses her palm over it to stop the noise. His gray skin is turning milky. "See if the cops have first-aid gear," she says.

The cops do. Just disinfectant and gauze and some patches, but it's better than nothing, and it stops the oozing from Davath's wounds, not to mention the whistling noise.

Davath, beyond speech, takes Aiah's hand and kisses it with chill lips. Tears sting her eyes at the gesture.

She looks at the plasm main running over their heads. If only she had some way to tap the vast store of power, she could make some attempt to repair Davath—but she doesn't have the hardware, or the medical skill.

"What do we do now?" Prestley asks.

"We can't carry him all the way back," Aiah says. "So I'll stay here and you'll have to run back and bring up the boat."

"I don't know how to get here by water."

She looks at him, heat flashing through her. "Find a way, damn it!"

His eyes widen. "Sorry," he says. "But it may take a while."

Regret chases the anger through her mind. "Sorry I shouted," she says. "Ethemark will return soon. I'll have him fetch you here."

"Good."

"Give me the gun. I may need it."

He looks at the gun he's stuck in his waistband, then turns to bring a fresh weapon from one of the dead cops. He puts it in her hand and it's surprisingly heavy, surprisingly awkward, surprisingly *gunlike*. She licks her lips. "How do I work it?"

Prestley's expression is unreadable in the dark. "Hold it like this. Press your thumb here to take the safety off, then press the trigger. You'll have seven shots or so."

"It's that easy?"

"Shooting it, yes. Do you want me to show you how to reload?"

Aiah shakes her head. "No time. Get the boat here now."

She doesn't see herself as a gunfighter anyway.

"Stay with us, man." Prestley gives Davath's shoulder a squeeze, and then scrambles away down the catwalk.

Aiah waits in the dark, her heartbeat marking time.

Davath's massive trunk leans against hers, his head on her shoulder. Wounded, his massive stoneface frame useless, he seems to become more human with every drop of blood that oozes from his body. His hoarse breathing moistens the corner of her neck and shoulder. Her arms are around him, hands clasping the gun. She points the gun at the open hatch, wondering if anyone will miss the three cops, if police reinforcements will arrive.

And then her heart leaps at the sound of a massive crash. The concrete wall next to her seems to leap as well. Rust particles flake down in the beam of her headlamp like falling snow. Another crash follows, then another.

A battle is being fought nearby, perhaps right overhead. She tries to decide whether she should cut Xurcal Station's power or not, and eventually decides that if a battle is being fought, she should cut off as much of the enemy's power as she can.

As gently as she can, she moves Davath so that he leans against the concrete wall, then rises to inspect the plasm junction. She reaches for the control box, moves the rotator to the neutral position, takes the fuse box from the controller, and throws it in the sea. She takes a hammer from Davath's belt and beats the control box into fragments, then waits, the hammer in her hand, as she catches her breath.

She doesn't know how to use the welding torch, so she can't do any more damage. She puts the hammer down, picks up the gun, and sits by Davath again. She puts her arms around him, then waits.

A few minutes later, Davath's death rattle begins. She rests her head on his shoulder. Blood stains her cheek, then tears. A few bats circle hopelessly overhead, looking for safety. Explosions send rust and dust drifting down onto the sprawled humans, living and dead. She brushes it from Davath's face. His skin is clammy and cold.

—Aiah! Vida's mercy! What's happened here!

Primal rage coils around Aiah's heart.

—Ethemark! Where *were* you?

—There's a mage battle going on upstairs. Someone kept cutting my sourceline. I've been *trying* to get back here and—

—Davath's been shot. Prestley's gone back for the boat.

—The police? Are they dead?

—Yes.

—Vida the Compassionate. Her mercy on us.

—Can you get a plasm surgeon here? Aiah asks. We might be able to—

—We don't have enough of them, Aiah. They're all busy and—

—*Try*, will you? Davath saved our lives!

—I'll see what I can do. But you've got to cut plasm to Xurcal.

—I already have. But I couldn't weld the rotator closed; I don't know how.

—It's only important that you cut it. The rebels won't have a chance for repairs anytime soon.

—See if you can find us a plasm doctor. And check if you can find the boat.

—Which first?

—The doctor, I think.

—I'll try. I'll have to go for a while.

—Then *go!*

Ethemark vanishes from Aiah's mind as abruptly as if someone had thrown a switch. The rattle in Davath's throat seems to fill the darkness, crowding out the sound of battle overhead.

The boat finds Aiah before Ethemark returns, but by then Davath has stopped breathing and lies cold in Aiah's arms. She, Prestley, and the boat's crew pick up the huge corpse and wrestle it into the boat. Only then does Aiah notice the boat is damaged, windscreen starred with bullets and gouges scarring the gunwale.

"We can't go back the way we came," the helmsman says. "Police there, and they shot at us."

"Pull out into midchannel," Aiah says. "We'll wait for Ethemark."

But Ethemark does not return. Artillery continues to hammer overhead. Eventually the crew grows too nervous remaining around the plasm junction and try to find a way around the roadblock, moving into mazes of dark watery corridors, barnacle-encrusted steel and concrete, tangles of forgotten barges and half-sunken boats. Every way out seems guarded by police. Eventually they give up and just drift in the darkness, alone with the boat, the body, and their own weariness. Heavy guns continue to pound overhead.

Aiah is drowsing, leaning in despair against the gunwale, when there is a sudden splashing astern. She snaps upright, fumbling for the gun in her lap.

"Is this the magnificent watercraft containing the illuminous Aiah, princess of plasm and all humanity?" A bright, burbling voice.

"Aranax?" Aiah gasps. She lunges out of her seat and looks over the stern, sees the dolphin grinning at her from below.

The dolphin splashes in the water with spatulate fingers. "I do not have the honor of being the magnificent Prince Aranax, sublime and wise, who even now is engaged in combat against the forces of darkness and ignorance. This insignificant being is Arroy Pasha, and the glorious, all-knowing Constantine has sent me to find you and bring your exalted self to safe harbor."

Aiah wants to throw off her hard hat and dance, but she composes herself to reply to the dolphin in his own strain.

"Arroy Pasha," she says, "your wisdom and compassion exceeds that of the immortals. If your sublimity is ready, I humbly beg you to lead our trivial selves away from this battlefield."

"It is my exceptional joy and delight to take some insignificant part in the preservation of your illuminous self," the dolphin says, and then tosses his head and submerges, out-curved feet kicking high as he dives.

The helmsman presses the ignition and the boat's engines growl into life. He turns on the spotlights, and ahead Aiah sees the dolphin's humped back as it breaks the surface in the channel ahead.

"Follow," she says, and they keep the dolphin in the spotlights, through turns and twists and brief spurts across open water, until he has brought them safely to a berth in the Aerial Palace.

ELEVEN

The command center is alive with tension, as if there were an invisible thread of burning plasm connecting everyone in the room. Constantine stands before the map wearing one of the golden-and-ceramic headsets, but when he sees Aiah enter he speaks a few words into the mouthpiece, then strips off the headset and moves—swiftly, with that incredible certitude of movement—to fold her in his arms. Weariness falls on Aiah at that instant, and for a moment her knees threaten to give way.

Constantine absorbs the extra weight, and then she feels him stiffen with tension. The bristle on his chin scratches her cheek—he hasn't shaved. "There's blood on you," he says. "Are you hurt?"

"No. We ran into police. One of my people was killed." She swallows. "He was a hero. Davath."

"Are you hurt at all?"

"Not really, no. Some scrapes." And, of course, the knowledge that one of her people was gunned down while she did nothing but watch.

"Thank you for sending Arroy to get me out," Aiah says. "I don't know what became of Ethemark."

Constantine flakes dried blood from her chin. "It wasn't Ethemark's fault," he says. "We had to cut off plasm to all mages who weren't actually fighting, and in our haste we didn't realize that it would leave you vulnerable. The battle over Xurcal started before we were ready, there was already a fight going on over the aerodrome, and we were exhausting our plasm supplies. All nonessential plasm use had to be cut." Constantine's fingers idly stroke her hair, and Aiah wants to melt into him, fuse with his comforting warmth. . . .

"Sir." An aide. "Hilthi on the line for you."

"The war will not wait," Constantine says. He kisses her forehead. "Get a shower, some rest—there are showers in the room adjacent, and cots in the shelters."

Aiah is sufficiently exhausted that she finds herself in her own apartment, in her own shower, before she realizes that she has put herself in danger in the event the building is shelled or rocketed again. The realization drifts through her mind like a cloud, light and without effect. She is too tired to care, and, wrapped in a towel, collapses onto her bed and is asleep the instant she closes her eyes.

Some hours later she comes screaming awake, every nerve jangling, certain there has been shooting or an explosion. Her eyes gaze into the darkened room in search of an enemy while her heart hammers in her throat. And then the communications array chirps again, and she realizes that it's only the phone. She picks up the headset with shaking hands, and it takes a long time to settle the earpieces over her ears.

"Aiah?" It's her grandmother's voice.

"Nana?" The voice from her past is disorienting: for a moment she thinks she's back in Jaspeer.

Old Galaiah's voice is stern. "We've all left messages! We're frightened to death!"

"I'm sorry," Aiah says. She brushes tangled curls from her eyes and tries to remember if she saw the message light when she returned to her apartment. "I've been . . . out in the fighting. But I'm back, and I'm safe."

"When you hear the all-clear," Galaiah says, "I want you to go out and get food. Get it now, before there's rationing, ne? Bulk food—rice is good, or dried noodles, because vat curd will spoil and you can't trust that the refrigeration will stay on. Otherwise flour, any kind. Condensed or powdered milk—goat's milk is best. And canned vegetables and fruit—don't eat the fruit, you can trade it for other stuff later, because it will become very valuable. People will pay anything for the taste of a peach, you'd be surprised. . . . Hey, are you *listening?*"

"Yes, Nana." Overwhelmed by all the detail.

"Just rice, with a little extra protein from eggs or meat, will last you a month. You can live for months that way if you have to, ne?"

Galaiah's instructions go on, explicit and detailed, and Aiah listens, first in confusion and then in growing understanding, because she remembers Galaiah has gone through this before, *years* of war, when the Metropolis of Barkazi was broken.

Her grandmother, Aiah realizes, is passing on useful skills. It's what she's always done.

"Nana," she says. "This fighting won't go on long. It's not a war, it's a coup, and—"

"That's what *we* thought."

The retort brings Aiah up short. "Yes, Nana," she says.

Her handwriting is out of control—it's like the Adrenaline Monster has her by the wrist—but she writes it all down anyway on the pad she keeps by her bed, then thanks the old lady and asks her to call everyone else in the family and tell them she's all right.

"You do what I tell you," Galaiah says.

"Yes, Nana."

"Do you know about this *hermit?* He's been saying *things* about you."

"Nana, I have to go. I'll call you when it's over."

"You do what I say!"

"Tell everyone I love them. Good-bye."

Aiah presses the disconnect button and puts the headset on its hook. Waves of adrenaline keep shuddering through her. She listens carefully, but can detect no sound of fighting, no aircraft, no shells falling, no rockets.

Her brief rest has only made her aware of how tired she truly is. She brushes hair back from her face and depolarizes the windows, wincing away from bright Shieldlight. The low clouds have broken up to let pillars of light shine down—it's like the gods are using searchlights—and one such light-pillar causes raindrops on the window to glow like diamonds. A short distance away a black cloud releases rain on the city.

Then, in an instant, an image forms across the sky, a huge face scowling down on the city, and Aiah recognizes the image as Parq in his Mask of Awe, even though it is canted at an angle in the sky and is obviously aimed at nearby Government Harbor. Letters surround the face, and Aiah cranes her neck to read them.

The Supreme One has declared the rebellion to be treason against Heaven. For confirmation call any temple or 089-3857-5937.

Smart, Aiah thinks. Any soldier near a telephone can confirm that the message isn't just propaganda. Parq was making it hard for any Dalavan soldier to continue fighting for the rebellion.

There was something to be said for panic after all.

Aiah rises and goes into her front room, reaches for the t-grip she's left plugged into her plasm source, and triggers it.

Nothing. Domestic plasm use has been switched off.

She might be needed, she thinks.

She finds clean clothes and heads for the command center.

THE BUILDING DOES NOT FALL TO THE FIRST BLOW OF THE WRECKING BALL.

A THOUGHT-MESSAGE FROM HIS
PERFECTION, THE PROPHET OF AJAS

Uniformed staff mass quietly beneath the illuminated map, which now displays much more information: large areas of the city glow a friendly blue, and the angry pink areas held by the enemy are reduced to three—the aerodrome, Government Harbor, and Xurcal Station.

"The rebels are holding on there," Ethemark says. "I don't know why. All I know is what I'm overhearing." His goggle eyes narrow. "The map is misleading as far as the aerodrome is concerned. I think we've recaptured it, mostly if not completely, but they haven't changed the map."

Ethemark still sits in the back of the command center, presumably because no one has thought to ask him to leave. He bends wearily over the long table in front of him, chin resting on his folded arms, a cold cup of coffee in front of him. Aiah finds a chair and coffee and sits next to him.

"There's a morgue set up here now," she says. "I've just come from it. Davath is there, and our two others that were killed in the rocket attack."

"Ah."

She rubs her face. Little jitters of adrenaline jump through her nerves, and contrast strangely with the bone-weariness trying to drag her into sleep. "Davath was a hero. He saved our lives. I'd like to contact his family."

"He has a mother still alive, I know. Somewhere in a half-world. I'll have to find out where."

She looks around. Very little seems to be going on.

"Has Constantine asked us for anything?"

"No. We're just—"

And at this point Constantine enters with Sorya. She is still in the smart uniform that looks as if it were pressed three minutes ago, and he is still in his cords and leather jacket. Even if Constantine hasn't had time to rest or change his clothes, his body seems charged with power, and he moves like a monarch surveying his realm. Pleasure glows on Sorya's delicate blonde features, and her cap is tilted at a confident angle. Suddenly, as if a switch has been turned, the room comes alive: the background hum of conversation grows louder; people begin to bustle on errands; others approach Constantine with news and queries. He listens to them, nods, makes brief replies, his lips turned up in a secretive half-smile.

The atmosphere in the room seems lighter. It's as if everyone can sense the tide turning, that all the news from this point on will be good.

Constantine takes one of the ceramic-and-gold headsets, speaks briefly, and gives some orders. He speaks with Sorya and she leaves for Plasm Control, almost skipping. He puts the headset down, sees Aiah waiting in the back of the room, and moves to join her.

"I hope you are refreshed," he says.

"A blast of plasm and I'll be fine."

He considers, head atilt. "In a few hours perhaps. We haven't the plasm to spare at present."

Weariness enfolds Aiah's mind like a swaddling of soft foam. "I understand," she says. She looks up at the map. "Things seem much the same."

"On the contrary." Constantine smiles and perches on the table. "We're about to finish it, I think. You turned the tide at Xurcal Station."

Aiah blinks at the map. "They're still holding it."

"Only because I permit it. It's the anvil on which I am beating the Second Brigade." He laughs, and the deep, familiar rumble lifts Aiah's heart. "While you and your teams were isolating Xurcal, Geymard and I were prepositioning troops to storm the place. Radeen either observed our preparations or realized Xurcal was vulnerable, because he sent a detachment out to reinforce the station. So instead of attacking the *station* I sent Geymard's soldiers against Radeen's *troops,* caught them in marching order, and mauled 'em— vehicles burning on the bridges, soldiers killed or scattered, what was left went running back to Radeen, two motorized companies toasted to cinders, a morale-booster for the rest of the Second Brigade. *That* was the battle you heard over your heads."

"It didn't seem so one-sided from my perspective," Aiah says.

Constantine looks at her, and there is a hint of sadness in his glowing eyes. He reaches out, strokes her cheek with the back of his hand. "It was hard fighting, yes," he says. "I had to commit my own people premature, and it cost us. But afterward I realized I could use Xurcal as bait, and so I declined to take it, even though its plasm was exhausted and many of the police guarding it were deserting. I set Geymard's people about the place in ambush, and sure enough Radeen took the bait. Sent a reinforced battalion to Xurcal, and we sprang the trap and wrecked Radeen's whole force. . . . A few we allowed to escape to Xurcal, so that their

appeals for help may tempt Radeen to send another force to
its doom, but he seems to have learned his lesson, too late
for him. . . ."

He turns to the map, gestures. "Meanwhile, the enthusiastic Captain Arviro has been assaulting the aerodrome with
the entire Marine Brigade. A bit ponderously—no tactical
elegance, and more casualties than I would have liked—but
with great spirit. Radeen's mercenaries were pushed out of
the aerodrome buildings, but they withdrew to other buildings overlooking the runways, and now the two forces are
glowering at each other, neither able to make use of the
'drome—and that is satisfaction enough, for the present.
And so there we are—mercenaries and Marines stalemated
at the aerodrome, Xurcal ours whenever we wish it, and
Radeen still in Government Harbor with a battered force."

"And plasm?"

"The plasm station at military headquarters still works
for them. Xurcal is useless. We doubt that the morale of
Radeen's troops is high—we have reports of desertions. But
they are getting plasm beamed to them from abroad—from
Lanbola principally—and Radeen can keep his tanks topped
up, alas." He shrugs. "I have asked the diplomats to do what
they can, but in the meantime I'm going to finish it."

He points to the map. "Arviro will leave a force to hold
the aerodrome," he says, "but he is disengaging the balance
of the Marines and sailing them to Government Harbor.
Geymard is readying an assault from the direction of the
Palace. And soon—" He holds his hands out, then claps them
together. "Bang, we'll hit Radeen from both sides at once,
and that will finish it."

Aiah looks up at him. "That simple?"

Constantine favors her with a cynical smile. "Nothing is
that simple. Combat is, by its nature, volatile. We can't tell
what Radeen will do, whether he will surrender or try to
fight. But what will happen in the end, yes, is a clap of the
hands and an end to the rebellion, and Caraqui will wake
from this episode as if from a bad dream, and blink and gaze
at the world and wonder how it is that so many things have
changed. Ah . . ." His head tilts up as he observes a newcomer, eyes focused over Aiah's head.

Aiah turns to see Sorya approaching, walking with her confident, catlike stride. Her green eyes turn in Aiah's direction, and she acknowledges Aiah's presence with a close-lipped, superior smile. Then she turns to Constantine and—Aiah has never seen this before—salutes.

"My boss," Sorya says, "the Minister of State Belckon, has lodged protests with the governments of Barchab and Lanbola for supporting the rebels with plasm. Barchab professed ignorance, and has agreed to shut off the plasm supply at once and also to supply us with plasm on request, at their usual rates. The Lanboli situation is more complex—their president is a figurehead only, and their party chairman is visiting another metropolis, and the foreign minister is at a meeting of the Polar League. . . . Mr. Belckon doesn't seem able to find anyone to complain to, other than some clerks."

Constantine considers this, his hooded eyes alight with calculation. "Lanbola is also where the rebels' mercenaries diverted, once we closed our aerodrome."

"And where their Provisional Government is broadcasting from," Sorya adds.

Aiah looks up at Constantine in surprise. This is new to her, but she can tell from Constantine's expression that he's known this for some time.

"The absence of senior officials may not be coincidental," Constantine says. "They may be delaying any response while waiting to see how Radeen fares." He fingers his unshaven jaw and considers. "Please give my compliments to Minister Belckon," Constantine says, "and suggest to him this: perhaps he should hint that if the government of Lanbola should choose to disarm these mercenaries who have so inconvenienced them by landing at their aerodrome, the arms would find a ready buyer in Caraqui—or perhaps the weapons could be added to Lanboli stocks instead. Either way, Lanbola will enrich itself at the expense of the rebels."

Sorya laughs, and bobs Constantine a compliment with a little tug of her chin. "I will suggest it to Mr. Belckon," she says. "In fact, I will suggest as much as I can, in hopes of keeping him sufficiently busy that he fails to realize that he is the senior minister here."

Constantine lifts his eyebrows. "He is senior?"

"State is superior to Resources, yes. Technically he may place himself in command. . . ." Her lip curls, and she gives a disdainful glance at the command center staff. "If anyone will obey his orders, that is."

Constantine gives her a serious look. "I think we should avoid any suggestion that he make the experiment."

Sorya's green eyes glitter from beneath the shiny brim of her cap. "There is an easy way to prevent these little disputes." She glances around the command center, at the people standing ready, waiting for orders, at soldiers bent over maps and pressing headsets to their ears. She leans close to Constantine's ear. "You are in command here," she says. "Declare yourself triumvir. Or better yet, Metropolitan. No one will stop you."

"No." Constantine's response is instant, and Aiah's heart gives a jump at its vehemence. His teeth flash in an angry snarl, and then he visibly exerts command over himself, and repeats himself more calmly, "No." He adds, "I am a foreigner here. I would find no support among the population."

Aiah looks at Constantine, and wonders if this is true.

"Pfah." Sorya snaps her fingers to dispose of this argument. "Drumbeth held office because it was believed he controlled the army—but he was deluded, and now the army's killed him. The loyal half of the army will tear itself to bits subduing the disloyal half. The police are in a state of insurrection—they cannot keep civil order. The only way *anyone* can hold Caraqui now is with mercenaries, both soldiers and military police; and if *you* are the soldiers' paymaster, the metropolis is yours, and the people will sing your praises to the Shield for restoring order and beating down these little matchstick military men who would trample them."

Constantine listens, but resentment still burns in his half-closed eyes. "No," he says. "I will not."

And then Sorya's own anger flares—her spine stiffens as color flames in her face, and Aiah takes an involuntary step back at the savagery of her look, at the memory, *all truces are temporary.* But then Sorya swallows her fury as visibly as Constantine had swallowed his, and after a moment of thought she gives a shrug, and her tinkling laugh rings out.

"As you wish," she says, "but you had best start thinking

about Drumbeth's replacement in the triumvirate, because if
you believe Hilthi and Parq can hold this place together, you
are as deluded in your thinking as Drumbeth and Radeen."
She laughs again, the sound a little shrill, and then draws
herself up and salutes, fingertips touching the brim of her
cap, and with a moment's mocking smile strides away.

Aiah looks at Constantine, at the hidden calculations
flickering through his face. She realizes she has been holding
her breath, and lets it out.

What exactly just happened? What is going on? The
words fly through her mind, and she wants to repeat them to
Constantine, but an aide approaches, and she never has the
chance to speak.

"Sir?" the aide says. "May I interrupt? We have reports of
enemy movement at the aerodrome."

Constantine's reaction is immediate, but there remains an
abstracted look in his glittering eyes that demonstrates his
mind is elsewhere, still appraising this last moment with
Sorya.

"Do we know their axis of movement?" he asks.

"Not yet. But they're requisitioning transport and getting
ready to move out." There is a moment's uncomfortable
pause, and then the aide offers, "Our mages could harass
them as they load up."

Constantine's head snaps suddenly toward the aide—
clearly he has decided to dismiss Sorya from his mind and to
deal with the current problem first. "Our plasm reserves
aren't sufficient," he says. "Wait till they start to move—
they're more vulnerable on the march anyway. And if they
wish to abandon the aerodrome, I am willing to hand each
one of them a pneuma ticket personally, so long as they
leave." He smiles at his own joke.

"But where are they going?" he wonders. "Reinforcing
Radeen at Government Harbor, perhaps. I will tell Arviro to
shift his mobile forces to prevent it." He turns to Aiah and
gives a satisfied smile. "They are showing more initiative
than I expected, but I think this will not change things to any
great degree. If the mercenaries truly expose themselves in a
move of this nature, our mages will tear them apart." He
puts a hand on Aiah's shoulder. "I will speak to you later."

"Good luck, Minister," Aiah says.

He flashes a smile, then heads toward the table and his waiting aides.

"He is very confident," Ethemark says. Aiah's nerves give a little leap—she had forgotten the tiny man at her elbow.

She sits down. The scene between Sorya and Constantine replays itself through her mind. *Declare yourself triumvir. Or better yet, Metropolitan.* And Constantine declined.

"I think he was right," Ethemark says, as if he were reading her mind. "If he took power now, he could keep it only with force."

Aiah's mouth is dry. "I think I'll get some coffee," she says.

Aiah gets her coffee and waits, watching the map, as Arviro slides part of the Marine Brigade into the gap between the aerodrome and Government Harbor and waits for Radeen's mercenaries to walk into his trap. But there are sudden reports that Radeen's Second Brigade is not waiting for reinforcements, but piling into their vehicles. Arviro now stands in danger of being caught between two enemy forces.

Constantine's reaction is fast: he launches Geymard's mercenaries straight at Government Harbor, hoping to pin the Second Brigade before they can move. Geymard's men encounter only a rear guard, but it's a rear guard that's well fortified and takes some digging out. Mages burn plasm as they battle back and forth overhead. Columns of smoke stand above the Popular Assembly.

But the invading mercenaries, when they move, don't head south toward Radeen, but instead race east; and Radeen doesn't head toward the aerodrome, but northeast. Aiah tracks their course on the map, and sees the paths will eventually cross: Radeen should meet his mercenaries just south of Lorkhin Island. And beyond Lorkhin Island is the Metropolis of Lanbola, where Kerehorn waits with the rest of the Provisional Government. Perhaps they are giving up and retreating off the map entirely.

Constantine takes no chances: he hurls everything he's got at Radeen's group, reasoning that though the rebel mercenaries are better fighters, they are useless without Radeen's political direction. The Marines and Geymard's soldiers harry their retreat, and mages hurl thunderbolts at their heads. Radeen's units have been hit hard already in the battle over Xurcal, and their retreat turns into a shambles—wrecked vehicles sending out columns of smoke, troops abandoning arms and vehicles and fleeing into the surrounding buildings, others surrendering the first chance they get.

Popular vengeance now turns the retreat to nightmare. The Caraquis, till now held in check by their fear of rebel arms, fly into a frenzy once they realize the rebels are trying to run. Their rage brought to a boil after listening to speeches by Parq or Hilthi, ordinary people try to build barricades against Radeen, fling brickbats, incendiaries, and filth from rooftops or open fire with weapons long hidden from the authorities. Aiah hears reports of trucks being attacked by mobs, of soldiers who try to surrender but who are instead torn to pieces, and their weapons then seized to use against their comrades.

Half an hour after the retreat begins, the Second Brigade dissolves under the assaults, and its leaders—Radeen, Gentri, and their officers—are only saved by their mercenaries, who send a detachment into the rout to pluck them from the talons of the mob.

There is a pause while Constantine gives out orders to shift the line of attack against the mercenaries, and then suddenly the communications arrays light as new reports come in. There is a hush in the room. "Confirmation!" someone shouts into a mouthpiece. "We need confirmation!"

"Assign a mage to it," Constantine says, his voice a soft rumble audible only in the sudden hushed silence. There is a quality to his words that causes a shiver to run up Aiah's spine.

People wait frozen in place, statues silvered by video light. Then the hushed words, "It's confirmed."

Aiah holds her breath. There is a clicking as gold-filigree control buttons are pushed, click click click.

Pink lights glow on the northeastern corner of the map, then advance toward the heart of the city. Click, click, click, whole districts falling to an unknown enemy. Three plasm stations, Aiah thinks; four. Undefended except by lightly armed military police.

"Ohh, heart of Senko," Ethemark moans.

A final click and Lorkhin Island glows pink. Aiah thinks of the huge buildings there, sentinel towers looking down on the city, towers soon to be ringed with guns. An alien fortress.

"Tell Geymard and Arviro to cease their pursuit and regroup," Constantine says. "We don't want them running headlong into that before they're ready. Mages are to cease action till we get more plasm." He looks at Sorya. "Contact the Timocracy. I think we're going to require two divisions at least, with support elements. And tell Barchab we will need their plasm as soon as possible." He turns to another aide. "I need an estimate of how long it will take to repair the aerodrome. We will need to land heavy troop carriers there."

He looks around the room, at the aides, soldiers, and technicians standing in stunned silence. "You have all done very well," he says. *"This—"* He waves at the map. *"This* is the fault of no one here, but the result of *treachery—"* His voice booms on the word, and he shakes a fist at the map. "Treachery on the part of certain criminals in Lanbola, who will, with their friends, soon be brought to account." There is a strange wild light in his eyes, something fierce and feral. *"That,"* he says, "I can guarantee."

Taikoen, Aiah thinks. A memory of the blood-splashed walls of her apartment flashes before her eyes, and she tastes bile in her throat.

Suddenly Constantine is in motion, marching from the table toward Aiah in the back of the room, the crowd parting before him like the sea. His glance is fixed on the double doors behind Aiah, but he hesitates as he nears her, then steps toward her.

"Do you know how to get ahold of Rohder?" he asks.

Aiah looks at Constantine in surprise. Rohder hasn't crossed her mind since the rebellion began.

"I know where his apartment is," she says. "I don't know whether he ever made it back there. The fighting blew up right around him, and he might be injured or in prison somewhere."

"He was well last I saw him. Call his apartment. We'll

need every drop of plasm we can generate, and I want him back on the project. He can call on unlimited manpower and as much computer time as he needs."

"Yes, Minister."

Constantine gives a frowning look at the door. "As for me, I must call Hilthi and Parq and summon them here. I cannot fill this political vacuum forever, for all that Sorya thinks I can."

"Good luck." She stands, makes the Sign of Karlo over his forehead. His look softens.

"Thank you," he says, and makes his way out.

Aiah turns back to the room, the hushed people going about their work. Sorya stands by the big table, a pair of gold-and-ivory headphones worn over her peaked cap as she tries to reach someone in the Timocracy, and she glances at the map with a complacent look as she puts a cigaret in her mouth and flicks her platinum lighter. As the little flame brightens Aiah hears Sorya's words again, *Declare yourself triumvir. Or better yet, Metropolitan.*

Aiah's hand flies to her mouth in shock.

Declare yourself triumvir. That's what this is about.

Aiah's blood turns chill.

Sorya has *arranged* it all somehow. The countercoup is, in some sense, hers.

Probably she did not conspire with Radeen and Gentri and Great-Uncle Rathmen, no. But she had to have known at least some of their plans. She *allowed* their coup to take place, careful to preserve only those people she needed. She was able to save Constantine from assassination, but not Drumbeth. She and certain loyal people were on hand in the Palace in order to respond.

All truces are temporary. Sorya's principal maxim.

How else could she advance, except in a world of chaos? Who needs a political intelligence department in a time of peace and relaxed tension? But in a time of madness and war, Sorya will become indispensable.

And when Constantine rises, Sorya will follow in his wake. Until, in the end, she no longer needs him, and *then . . .*

Sorya's green eyes flicker across the room, and Aiah looks

abruptly down at the floor so that Sorya won't see the terrible knowledge behind her eyes. . . .

What can she *do?* Aiah wonders. She bites her lip.

In the humming silence, no answer comes.

TWELVE

~~~~~~~~~~

Aiah asks for a meeting with Constantine, but doesn't get one till the next day, and then it turns out to be in a basement room, and with a swarm of other people.

There is a conference room in Constantine's suite of offices, but its huge bay window faces Lorkhin Island and any rocket batteries or artillery that might soon be placed there, and so the meeting is held deep in the Palace, in a lounge intended for maintenance workers. The furniture is cheap plastic and the walls vibrate to the sound of generators and compressors in adjacent rooms. Taped to the bare walls are pinups of seminude women, some faded with age. Aiah even recognizes the Nimbus Twins, frequently seen cavorting on her brothers' walls when she was growing up.

Constantine's department heads sit impatiently in the plastic chairs and glance frequently at their watches. Constantine has called this meeting, and he is late.

There is little conversation. Aiah feels her eyelids droop. Her abbreviated sleep seems a long time ago.

And then the door booms open and Constantine enters. He greets everyone, grins as he inspects the pinups, and then sits on a waiting plastic chair. "I've just come from a meeting of the cabinet," he says. "Minister Faltheg has been appointed triumvir and president in place of the late President Drumbeth."

People glance at each other, brows raised. Few seem to have heard of Faltheg till this moment. Aiah knows at least a little about him—she'd studied the cabinet members before making her presentation to them—but knowing his biography makes her even less certain what might qualify him to become a third of the government.

Constantine sees the puzzled looks. "The former Minister for Economic Development," he explains, "a banker and a worthy man." A devil's grin plucks at his lips. "It was felt that an image of stability and continuity should be projected. No more military people." His grin widens, and he gives his subordinates a confiding wink. "And no *controversial foreigners,* either," he adds. Low laughter sounds through the room.

Besides, Aiah thinks, *Faltheg was in the building.*

"I have been given the War portfolio as well as Resources," Constantine goes on, "along with a brief to run this war, as long as it lasts, and extraordinary powers to mobilize war, economic, and plasm resources. Because I will not be able to give full attention to the Resources post, I am hereby appointing Secretary Jayg to run the department day to day in all matters not relating to the war." He nods to one of his people, who smiles nervously at the news of this two-edged appointment.

Constantine turns his intent gold-flecked eyes on Aiah, and she feels her nerves stammer. She knows that look by now.

"Miss Aiah," he says, "I am going to invest your department with extraordinary powers to increase the government's plasm reserves by any and all means necessary."

Aiah stares at him. She has had her fill of impossible jobs lately. "Sir—"

"Have you contacted Mr. Rohder?" Constantine asks.

"No. I've tried several times, but he's not answered." A wave of guilt floods Aiah's veins, and she gnaws her lip, wondering if she'd brought Rohder to Caraqui only to have him killed.

"Then you must reassemble Rohder's team," Constantine

says, "and recruit more members. I want that work to go forward with all possible speed."

"Sir—" She wants to protest, to announce to everyone here that she's unqualified, already overwhelmed; but Constantine's gaze is on her, and in the end she just says, "What about budgeting and so forth?"

"Bring me a budget," Constantine says, "and I'll sign it."

The answer staggers her. "Yes, sir," she says.

"The cost of all civilian plasm use, with some obvious exceptions such as hospitals, food factories, and established religious institutions, will be increased," Constantine says. "Our meter-reading teams will be sent out into the city, working double shifts until they can read every meter in Caraqui and we can begin billing at the new rate." His eyes light on Aiah again. "Your department will be even more necessary now, because the increased rates will make bootleg plasm all that much more attractive, and more profitable to the Silver Hand."

"You make it seem as if this is going to be a long war," says the newly promoted Jayg. He is a slight man, blond, with spectacles. Young, like so many of Constantine's recruits. He wears a New City badge on his throat lace.

"We must be ready for that possibility," Constantine says. "Lorkhin Island is a strong position—huge buildings with solid foundations, and overlooking the entire city. If our soldiers have to fight our way up each building staircase by staircase, it will take a long time and our casualties will of necessity be high. Much depends on how much plasm we can mobilize in the early days—if we have a significant edge in plasm, we can keep them off-balance and prevent them from fortifying themselves properly." He looks from Jayg to Aiah. "You two bear the most responsibility here. I need results, and fast."

Oh, Aiah thinks, so the war is up to me.

And, her thoughts continue, I have practically no department now. I've got to scrounge clerical workers from shelters and mages from war work.

Bring me a budget and I'll sign it. Now *that* will help.

"The cabinet made a few other decisions that do not directly affect us," Constantine says, and his face assumes a deliberate cast of neutrality. "Since our police force is at worst collaborating with the enemy and at best unable to function, Triumvir Parq will be organizing a citizens' militia based around the various Dalavan temples. These militias will assist such police as remain in keeping civil order. Triumvir Parq will also be greatly expanding the Dalavan Guard, with the intention of producing high-quality combat units."

Aiah looks at the others as they absorb the fact that Parq is now building his own army and police force. She doesn't know everyone well enough to know whether they are Dalavans, but whatever their convictions, nobody seems very pleased.

"The cabinet," Constantine says into the thoughtful stillness, "also decided that the registration of political parties may now begin, with the eventual intention of seating a new Popular Assembly. The only party forbidden to register is the Citizens' Progressive Party of the Keremaths."

Jayg raises a hand. "Isn't that dangerous? Isn't the creation of political parties at a time of civil war likely to simply increase the level of disorder?"

"It is hoped," Constantine says, "that increasing the degree of popular representation will serve to draw large elements of the populace into the political arena, and toward a position of support for the government." He gives a glittering, cynical politician's smile. "In any case, Triumvir Parq is in the process of recruiting his own partisans, and others in the cabinet will not do less." He stands, brushes his knees, affects an air of casual modesty.

"Tomorrow I shall announce the formation of the New City Party of Caraqui. I would find it pleasing if some of you were to join it. But if you are not so inclined, it will in no way affect the conditions of your employment by my administration. And if you decide not to join the New City, I hope you will participate in the process in another way. But for *now*"—a sudden fire lights Constantine's gold-flecked eyes—"we all have much work to do. Unless there are questions . . . ?"

Aiah has a thousand, but voices none of them; and no one else speaks either. After Constantine leaves, as she is gathering up her unused papers she overhears a pair of her colleagues.

"I'm going to be first in line to join this party," one man says.

His friend seems surprised. "I didn't know you were such a radical."

"I'm not. But I plan to keep my job."

A cynical chuckle. "Surely you don't think Constantine will favor only members of his own party." The tone is mocking.

Aiah straightens and turns to them. They see her look and fall silent.

"I really don't think party membership will matter to him," she says.

One of them gives a little snort. "You're his lover. You've got a *different* sort of job security."

Aiah's cheeks burn. Her temper burns as well, flaring like wildfire—and seeing the blaze, the speaker takes a step back and turns pale as he realizes Aiah's potential for revenge.

"You people have lived under the Keremaths too long," Aiah says. "You're not used to politicians who aren't petty little shits."

The room has fallen silent. Jayg adjusts his spectacles and gnaws his lip as he judges whether or not to intervene.

Aiah turns on her heel and marches out before she says something else.

There is a war to win. She'd better win it.

"LANBOLA IS AND HAS ALWAYS BEEN NEUTRAL," INSISTS MINISTER

PROVISIONAL GOVERNMENT CONTINUES MEETING IN LANBOLI OFFICES

"Every plasm house we've found," Aiah says. Gears click over as she presses keys: there is an electric hum, and the heavy barred secure room door swings open.

"I want the complete list," she says. "We're going to have to take all the houses down now, whether we're got our cases against the users properly prepared or not."

She goes to the files and unlocks a bronze-sheathed drawer. The drawer opens silently on smooth steel bearings.

"How are we going to take them?" Ethemark asks. "We've always used soldiers, and now the soldiers are . . . busy with other things."

"We'll hire new ones if we have to," Aiah says.

Bring me a budget and I'll sign it. A company or two, she thinks, could do the job.

Maybe she could wheedle a few troops out of Constantine. Lightly armed military police weren't going to be much use in storming Lorkhin Island anyway.

"Miss?" One of her assistants, rapping lightly on the thick steel-and-bronze door. "I've just got a call from Mr. Rohder."

Aiah's heart eases as she realizes Rohder's alive.

"Is he here?" she asks.

"Not quite," the assistant says. "He's in jail."

CRIME LORD SEEN IN LANBOLA

MEETS WITH KEREHORN

Rohder and his entire crew had been arrested by police who'd turned up too late to assist in the attempt on Constantine's life. After waiting in jail for over a day without being charged, or fed, they'd put all their money together in order to bribe a jailer into letting Rohder make a phone call.

"I can't say, miss," the answering officer says when she calls.

"You can't confirm you're holding these people?" Aiah asks.

"I can't *say.*"

Aiah taps a pencil impatiently on her desk as she strives for clarification. "You can't say because you don't *know,* or because you decline to answer?"

"I . . ." The officer gropes for a response. "I can't say," he says finally.

"We *know* you're holding them," Aiah says. "Please don't try to deny it."

"All right." The officer agrees amiably enough. Aiah restrains the impulse to sigh audibly into the mouthpiece.

"Can you tell me," keeping a grip on her patience, "if any charges have been filed against them?"

"No. We haven't received any instructions."

"Whose instructions do you need?"

"Captain Albreth."

"Is he available? May I speak to him?"

"No. He made the arrest, but he's been out of touch since then."

"I suggest you let them go," Aiah says. "They've committed no crime that you know of, you've held them for over twenty-four hours without a charge being filed, and your Captain Albreth may be dead or in jail himself for all you know."

"Well," the officer says. "I don't know if I have the authority—"

"Let me speak frankly, sir," Aiah says. "The coup against the government has failed. Gentri and Radeen and the others are either dead or in hiding. Their forces have fallen apart. The Palace is now in a position either to reward its friends or punish its enemies. *Now,* sir—which of the two are you?"

"I'll have to talk to some people about this," the officer says.

Aiah decides that the time limit on her patience has expired. "If you are a friend of the administration, you will let these people go," she says. "If you are an enemy, I'll come down with a company of soldiers, and I'll free my friends. And if I have to shoot every policeman in the place to do it, that's what I'll do." She pauses to let this sink in, then adds, "The choice, of course, is yours."

"I . . ." She can feel the officer struggling. "I'll have them released," he finally says.

"I'm happy that reason has prevailed," Aiah says. "Have Mr. Rohder call me when he's set free."

She hangs the headset on its hook and observes Ethemark looking at her meditatively, nictitating membranes half-closed over his eyes. When she returns his gaze, his eyes clear and he turns away.

"You've changed," he says.

"Not just me," she says. "Everything is different now."

A man died in my arms, she thinks. *He died to save me.*

One death, among so many, that she must not allow to be in vain.

NEW CITY PARTY FORMED

CONSTANTINE PROMISES "VICTORY AND LIBERTY"

Finally. Finally. Finally she will see Constantine alone.

He has moved his office to a part of the building facing away from Lorkhin Island, into a place in the luxurious Swan Wing. In the anteroom, bodyguards, soldiers, and messengers loiter on a priceless Kivira carpet and scatter cigaret ash on sofas glittering with gold and silver thread. All the windows have been polarized against both light and observation, but a chandelier, all chiming teardrop crystal, provides light enough.

Aircraft drone overhead. They are bringing in mercenaries from the Timocracy, just as other aircraft are bringing other troops into Lanbola to reinforce the invaders' strong point at Lorkhin Island.

Plasm sings in Aiah's head like a chorus of angels. A few hours ago she was exhausted, both from work and from her inability to get proper rest—during the course of a single shift's sleep, random bursts of adrenaline would bring her awake at least two or three times. Sometimes the chemical alarm occurred in response to something happening—a crash of shellfire or a fire gong—but often as not she was awakened completely at random, as if something in her mind had concluded it was too dangerous to let her sleep for long.

But the plasm circuits in her department have finally been turned on so that she can now surveil target plasm houses, and the first thing Aiah did was to get her t-grip and bathe in the stuff, burning away fatigue toxins, burnishing her mind, filling her nerves and heart with energy.

The world does not seem as bleak as it had a few hours ago.

Aiah sits in the anteroom among the guards and bustle. She has to beg Constantine for military police to take down the plasm houses, and must wait her turn like the other supplicants.

The door opens and a small woman walks in. Heads turn, and there are double takes. Aiah feels surprise at the sight, then confusion as the woman recognizes her, then walks toward her with an outstretched hand.

"Lady," she says.

"Lady" was Aiah's code name during the final stage of Constantine's coup. The other woman's was "Wizard One," but her real name is known to almost everyone in the world, for she is famous.

She is Aldemar, the chromoplay actress, in person a petite figure with delicate wrists and ankles and bobbed dark hair. Across the world, a giant on screens three stories tall, she regularly fights evil in any of a series of third-rate melodramas with titles like *Revenge of the Hanged Man* and *Rise of the Thunderlords*. Her publicity has always maintained that her chromoplays are based on fact, hype that Aiah had never believed until she'd met Wizard One and found her competently directing Constantine's secret plasm house.

Aiah takes Aldemar's hand. "My name is Aiah," she says.

The other woman smiles. "I know. Constantine has spoken of you. May I join you?"

"Of course," Aiah says, and she wonders in what context her name arose in a conversation between those two.

Aldemar smooths her long dark skirt and joins Aiah on the sofa. Aiah sees flashes of jealousy radiate from others in the room and smiles inwardly.

"Have you just arrived?" Aiah asks.

The actress shakes her head. "Oh no. I've been here for two days, directing part of the plasm war."

Aiah looks at her in surprise. In an elegant long skirt and a white lacy blouse, her face a natural-seeming composition of artful cosmetic, Aldemar hardly looks like a general fresh from the wars.

"You got here fast," Aiah says.

"I teleported in as soon as I heard the news. Had to shut down production on the new chromoplay, but I hope the additional publicity will mollify my investors."

Teleportation was one of the surprising skills Aldemar was revealed to possess in the aftermath of the coup. This ability had given Aiah greater respect for Aldemar's skills as a mage than she'd ever had for her chromoplays. Teleportation is difficult and dangerous, and though there are mages who cheerfully accept large fees for teleporting equipment and personnel, few ever dare to teleport themselves.

"What's the new play about?" Aiah asks.

Aldemar's eyes glitter with amusement from beneath her black bangs. "Coincidentally enough, I play an actress who helps an idealistic and charismatic political leader overthrow a corrupt government."

"Is it good?"

Aldemar dismisses the production with a little shake of her head. "It's no *Lords of the New City,* but it will probably make everyone concerned a great deal of money."

They are interrupted by one of the soldiers, who asks for an autograph. Aldemar graciously complies, and this begins a general movement toward the actress, who signs bits of paper or the backs of official requisition forms for a few minutes until Martinus, Constantine's chief bodyguard, steps into the room and calls her name.

Aldemar rises, hands the last autograph to one of her fans, and turns to Aiah. "Let's meet when there's a lull. I'd like to talk to you sometime."

Aiah blinks. "Certainly."

"I'll call your office," Aldemar promises, and gives a little wave as she walks to her interview.

Aiah sits back on the sofa and is aware of a new respect in the eyes of the other supplicants. Strange how exchanging a few casual words with a celebrity should suddenly make her so much more interesting.

She wonders how Aldemar and Constantine happened to meet, and how long-term—and intimate—their relationship is.

Time passes. Aldemar bustles out after a few minutes, waves to Aiah again as she departs, and then a whole group of officers are called into Constantine's presence. After they leave, a number of Constantine's staff exit the inner rooms as well and stand waiting in the anteroom.

He has sent them out for some reason. Even Martinus stands waiting, his impassive armor-plated face showing no emotion.

A slow chill crawls up Aiah's spine. The hairs on the back of her neck rise in shivering terror.

Perhaps it is intuition only, or perhaps there is some tangential connection with the plasm that still warms her blood. But somehow she knows the identity of Constantine's visitor, the meeting so private he had to send even his intimates out of the room.

Taikoen. The hanged man. The damned. The *creature,* once a man, now a disembodied entity living in the drumbeat of plasm.

Cold terror fills the hollow of Aiah's bones. The next minutes seem to last centuries.

Suddenly the terror fades. Aiah looks wide-eyed at the others, wonders if any of them sense the creature's presence.

Apparently not.

The door handle turns, and Constantine appears briefly in the partly open door.

"Aiah," he says briefly, then walks off, leaving the door open. She rises from the sofa and follows, closes the door softly behind her.

Her every nerve is alight, straining for sign of Taikoen. But she senses nothing, and slowly she feels herself relax.

"Is he gone?" she asks.

Light shimmers from mirrored walls. Constantine stands in the center of the priceless carpet surrounded by boxes and stacks of files, the work from his office now stacked atop the glittering luxurious Keremath tables, chairs, and shelves. He seems unsurprised by her question.

"Taikoen?" he says. "Yes." He cocks his head, looks at her. "You are unusually sensitive to his presence."

Aiah hugs herself and shivers. "I wish I weren't."

Concern glows amber in Constantine's eyes, and then he crosses the distance between them and wraps his arms around her. She rests her head on his shoulder and tries to let her anxiety sigh from her lungs like a breath.

"I'm afraid of him," she says.

He strokes her hair. "I will never let him harm you."

The words bubble from her mind, and she can't stop them. "Have you sent him to kill?"

"No. Since he can get through shielding, I have sent him to find certain people. The headquarters of the enemy soldiers, the communications center. So that we can disrupt them later."

"And you will give him his price."

"I will," simply. "It will save lives, many more lives than Taikoen can inhabit in my lifetime."

Aiah presses herself to him, inhaling the familiar, comforting scents of his body, his leather jacket, the scented hair oil. "I wanted to touch you these last few days," she says. "And I couldn't."

"You were braver than I would have believed, than I *wished* to believe." He kisses the top of her head. "I will arrange for some official thanks—a citation, a medal, something trivial but the best the state can do—but you must not take such risks in the future."

They fall silent. Aiah tightens her arms about Constantine, pressing herself as close to him as possible, wanting to annihilate herself, to dissolve into him. For once he shows no sign of impatience, seems content to allow the embrace to go on as long as Aiah wishes. Finally it is she who stands back.

She wants to tell him about Sorya, but she can't find a place to start.

"I can take down almost a hundred plasm houses," she says instead, "but I can't use just my clerks—I need police to do it."

He considers. "I can take some of the military police guard from the Palace," he concludes, "but they're not the units you've worked with before—those are scattered throughout the metropolis, guarding vital installations."

"If you will tell the commanders to get in touch with me . . . ?"

"Yes. Of course."

"Secondly, I have sprung Rohder from jail, and he's either on his way to the Palace or, more likely, has already arrived."

"Excellent. Very fast work." He turns, fingering his chin,

and begins to prowl among the piles of boxes, thinking as he paces. "There is another thing I need you to do."

A weak little laugh bubbles up from Aiah's throat. *"Another?"*

His eyes are on her, intent and commanding as a pair of shotgun barrels. "You need to build your department," he says. "Double it in size, triple it. And you must make it loyal to *you.*"

"Yes." She stands amid the clutter and feels suddenly alone. Objections, perfectly good organizational objections, spring to her mind. "Yes, but—expanding it so quickly, we—"

He glides toward her, his expression so intent it frightens her. He leans close, takes her forearm in one of his big hands, bends toward her ear. "Do you recall the moment when Sorya was urging me to declare myself Metropolitan?"

Fear crawls over Aiah's scalp with clinging spider feet. *He knows,* she thinks. "Of course I remember," she says, "but—"

"I turned it down," he says.

"Yes, and I wondered why. Because she seemed to make sense—but now—" The words come reluctantly from her throat. "Now I realize," she says, "that it was because you knew the coup is hers."

She feels him stiffen, and there is a dangerous edge to his words. "How can you know this? Do you have evidence?"

"No. I just know it, that's all."

"And so do I." His words are meditative. "My dear one," he says, "I wish you had not come to this realization. Because it is very, very dangerous for you."'

"You've got to get rid of her," Aiah says.

He gives a tight-lipped smile and a little shake of the head. "Firstly, I have no proof of any of this, nothing but an insight that whispers to me that I am right. Perhaps evidence more concrete will turn up in time." He takes a breath. "But more significantly, I can't afford to act against her now. She miscalculated, you see—she must have intended that the coup miscarry, and then the perpetrators be disposed of, clearing the field not just of Drumbeth but Radeen and Gentri and everyone else that could possibly stand in the way of my ascension. But elements of the plot must have eluded her—she couldn't have known the full strength of the enemy, or that the government of Lanbola would permit an invasion from their territory, that it would turn into a real war."

He stands back, rubs his chin. "But now that it *is* a war, I cannot afford to fight it without her. Having miscalculated and permitted this conflict to come about, she will do her best to win it. I can trust her to do that."

"But she'll turn it to her advantage."

A calculating gleam enters his eyes. "So shall we all."

"You've got to look out for yourself," Aiah says. "What if she decides that you're standing in her way?"

"That will not be anytime soon. Aside from her department, which no one trusts, she has no base of support here that does not come from me. She wished me to rise so that she could follow in my wake and gain power and adherents." He ponders for a moment. "We will watch," he says. "The war will provide us opportunity to build our own power, and it will also compel her to reveal her tools, her sources, and her methods. We will take note, and use the information when the time comes."

"Get rid of her now!" Aiah cries.

He gives a minute shake of the head. "Unwise."

"And I suppose," Aiah says, "you'll be fucking her in the meantime." For some absurd reason her eyes sting with tears.

Constantine looks at her. Not coldly—not *quite* coldly—but appraisingly, objectively. "This has not bothered you in the past," he observes.

Heat flashes red before Aiah's eyes. "It's *always* bothered me!"

"The details of the arrangement were known to you before you entered it," he points out—then shakes his head, throws up his hands. "But what does that matter? Arrangements can change. . . ."

He considers again, head down and frowning, and then raises a hand and points to the polarized window, the featureless black glass set into the wall. His dark reflection in the window confronts Aiah's. "I am hiding in this building," he says, "because there are enemy forces who would be glad to kill me. I cannot even *look out a window* for fear of some mage flinging a bomb or rocket or plasm blast. And in that world outside, which I dare not look at, there are nightmares forming. *Familiar* nightmares. Because I have been through all of this before."

He licks his lips. A vision of fear seems to haunt his expression as he stares at the black glass, and there is an unfamiliar wildness in his eyes.

"If I misstep," he says, "then Cheloki happens all over again here in Caraqui. Endless war, endless misery, a metropolis turned to wreckage, the destruction of all that I sought to save. I failed once—" Bitterness crosses his features. "Great Senko," he cries, "I can't let the nightmares loose *again!*"

Aiah watches him in astonishment. She has never seen him like this, terror and rage so plain on his face. In battle, even while the assassins' plasm rattled and boomed overhead, he had been cool and detached, ironic phrases falling from his lips as easily as commands. Now he almost seems someone else, a man overwhelmed. . . .

He turns toward her and advances, huge and powerful as a battleship, and then to her utter surprise falls to his knees in front of her, bent over like a supplicant, and takes her hands. "If I am to win this war," he says, "if I am to keep the nightmares out, then *I need my generals!* Sorya is one, and you are another. I can trust her to fight well, if not faithfully, and you—" He kisses her hands. "You I trust absolutely. You are necessary to my success, to all that I hope to accomplish. You must let me arrange things, for now, the way I need them."

Aiah stands in wonder at the massive figure huddled before her. Hot tears splash onto her hands. "Yes, of course," she murmurs. "Of course I will."

He puts his arms around her, pressing his head to her abdomen; she caresses his head, gazing down with a growing sense of astonishment, of a strange rising tenderness at this evidence of his need.

There is a discreet knock on the door.

Constantine disengages himself and rises, a startled look on his face. "Is it 17:00?" he asks. "I'm supposed to make a broadcast."

Aiah looks at her watch. "16:51," she says, "yes."

"Damn." He sighs. "I haven't even worked out what I'm going to say."

"You're good at this," she says. "You'll think of something."

She reaches for him, wanting to touch him again, to feel again that fragile tenderness. He holds her wordlessly for a long moment, then murmurs into her ear that it is time for him to go. She raises her head, feels his lips press hers, and then he is gone, walking away with his usual decisive tread.

She looks at herself in the black mirror of the window, and wonders what thing it is, newborn and vulnerable as a child, she sees there.

"WHAT FOOLS ARE THESE WHO FIGHT HISTORY?"

CONSTANTINE'S BROADCAST RALLIES FREE CARAQUI

Rohder is in her office when she returns, smoking the last of a pack of cigarets; the rest of the pack fill Aiah's ashtray. He is in his shirtsleeves, with circular salty crusts under his arms, but otherwise seems unchanged by his time in jail.

"Thanks for acting so promptly," he says.

"All I needed was to threaten every cop in the station with death," Aiah says.

"You seemed to have engaged their attention."

Aiah glances out the window for a moment—her office doesn't face Lorkhin Island, and it's safe enough to let in light—and then she sits in her chair and glances at the pages placed on her desk: a complete list of every plasm house in the files, a note from Ethemark clipped to the front reporting, "All we need now are some troops."

She looks up, sees Rohder watching her with his mild blue eyes. "Constantine wants you to get your team together and start moving buildings around," she says. "Hire as many people as you need, and Constantine will also make certain you get enough computer time to complete your calculations."

"The calculations are already complete for the district where we made our first attempt," Rohder says. "I can send our team in there tomorrow. But if I'm going to be closing off bridges, stringing up cable, and rerouting traffic, I'm going to need police, or people like police, to handle that for me, and as I understand it the police are not our friends."

Aiah runs her hands through her hair. "Perhaps we could call the Public Maintenance Department."

"I imagine they're going to be busy repairing bridges and public services wrecked by the war, but I will call and see what can be arranged."

Aiah makes a note to herself. "I'll have Constantine call their minister."

"That may help." Dryly. "And the computer time will be useful. I will also need a large number of structural engineers to calculate the amount of mass in each building. Where do you expect we could get them?"

Aiah stares at him blankly. "Structural engineers?" She shakes her head and writes it down. "I will consult," she says. "For the moment, you might as well get a good shift's sleep."

He stands, and then his eyes lift from Aiah to the window behind her. He stares for a moment, mouth dropping open in shock, and Aiah swings her chair around, afraid she will be staring straight at a hovering enemy helicopter, its weapon racks loaded with rockets.

For a terrifying moment she fears it's worse than that, for the horizon seems to roil with images of conflict. Aiah sees arms bearing weapons aloft, faces distorted in terror or rage, rows of sharp teeth, flashes like bursts of gunfire, shattered skulls in rows, all the images mingled together or following in swift succession, the display's chameleon form altering too swiftly for any single impression to remain for long.

"What is *that*?" Rohder demands. His voice trembles.

"The Dreaming Sisters," Aiah says. "They seem to have noticed that we're at war."

THIRTEEN

∿∿∿∿∿∿

An endless round of exhausted labor follows, dreary days that leave Aiah feeling as if she has spent weeks slogging through a mud storm. Any restful sleep is impossible: it seems as if she has only to close her eyes for the Adrenaline Monster to jerk her awake and leave her staring wide-eyed into the darkness, nerves alert to any sign of danger, pulse beating in her ears, sweat moist on her nape. The endless hours and infinite frustrations of work are made possible only by periodic injections of plasm, jolts of fiery energy straight to the heart.

But perhaps the entire government is running on plasm-energy, because things are moving quickly. Due to an unusual spirit of unity among the triumvirs, Rohder's problems are solved with remarkable speed: Parq's fledgling Dalavan Militia performs traffic control duties around Rohder's crews—a task well within the inexperienced militia's capabilities—and his teams of estimators are provided by engineering and architecture students, two entire senior classes of whom are simply conscripted for the duration.

Aiah presents Constantine with a budget, and he signs it without even a glance.

She gives everyone in her department, excepting herself, a raise of 25 percent—a nagging scruple prevents her from raising her own salary. Her deputy Ethemark now earns more than she does. She hopes the raises will do morale some good.

While the Plasm Enforcement Division grows under emergency pressures, the war continues. The northeast horizon glows around the clock as more plasm becomes available to the contending mages. Droning fills the air as reinforcements shuttle through the aerodrome. Shellfire lessens as both sides begin to conserve ammunition for the battle they know is about to take place.

As soon as he has his military units positioned, Constantine launches the Battle of the Corridor, designed not to attack the enemy strongpoint at Lorkhin Island, but instead to cut the Provisionals off from their support in Lanbola.

It fails.

HEAVY FIGHTING IN CARAQUI

ENTIRE DISTRICTS AFLAME

TENS OF THOUSANDS OF REFUGEES

Aiah finds Constantine in his emergency suite, a place he stays when battle threatens, an old storeroom deep in the concrete-and-steel caverns beneath the Palace. It is near the command center and Plasm Control, so that he might appear in either place on short notice, but it is a dismal place, airless and cold, with moisture beading the scarred metal walls. Light comes from battered overhead fluorescents. The furniture is ornate and comfortable, scavenged from state apartments in the Swan Wing, but it is out of place in this tall, narrow, oppressively lit room.

Constantine is sunk into a winged armchair, head bowed over his chest. His jacket is thrown on the bed, and great blooms of sweat darken the fabric beneath his arms. He glances up as Aiah enters. The expression of sullen anger on his face makes her hesitate, and her words dry up on her tongue.

"Betrayed," he says, and lets the word hang in the cold air for a moment; then he throws his head back, runs his hands over his face. "I should have anticipated it," he says. "Lanbola has violated its own neutrality repeatedly to aid the Provisionals, but this . . . this last *outrage!*" His hands clench into massive fists; the cords on his neck threaten to burst his collar. "The Corridor was *won,* it was hard fighting but the Provisionals were *beaten!*" He stands, unable to keep his seat, the anger marching him up and down the narrow metal-walled room.

Aiah bites her lip. She remembers Constantine being in this violent, reckless mood once before, when Drumbeth had checked him over Qerwan Arms. She doesn't know how to curb this kind of rage, not when her every instinct is to leave now, or hide, until it is all over.

"For Lanbola to permit the Provisionals' mercenaries to make such an attack!" he roars. "Upon our flank, and out of their own territory! Such a prodigious violation of all law, all decency, all honor . . . !" He walks up to the metal wall and smashes at it with a gigantic fist.

Aiah holds her breath as the room seems to give a leap. She is waiting for the cry of pain—her brother Stonn broke his hand in just this fashion, enraged over losing a bet on his favorite football team—but Constantine has judged the force of his blow well, and he merely draws back the hand, examines the bruised knuckles, and scowls as if he were angry that something had not shattered.

"These wretched petty treacheries have followed me all my life," he murmurs. "Checked me at every point, hindered every action, fettered every reform, compromised every victory. The gods trifle with me for their debased amusement, and the froward perversity of humanity is without limit. *Enough!*" He makes as if to strike the wall again, thinks better of it, lowers his hand. He looks at Aiah from under his brows.

"What I wish to do seems so very simple," he says. "Must I wade thigh-deep in blood to accomplish it? And is it worth the cost?"

Aiah gropes for words. She had come to offer comfort, not to answer questions. "You didn't start this war," she says.

Constantine gives a low laugh. "Of course I did," he says. "You helped me—you gave me the plasm for Drumbcth's coup, and everything since, all this tragedy, has followed. And so . . ."

He glides toward her, eyes glittering beneath his brow, like a great cat stalking its prey. Aiah feels a thrill of fear run up her neck. He moves close to her; she can smell sour sweat, feel the heat of his body.

"What do you think of your gift now, Miss Aiah, that great well of plasm whose power you gave me?" There is a mocking tone in his voice. "Are you pleased with the result?"

Aiah straightens her spine, looks at him coldly. "I think this is Sorya's reasoning," Aiah says. "She is the one who says that all wars are one war, that there are no truces, that it's all one grand struggle for power, back to Senko's day I suppose. I gave you the plasm, and I will take responsibility for *that*, but this war is not something I created. It is not *mine*. I decline to be answerable for it, and I don't think you should try to make it my fault."

He looks at her for a long moment with that dangerous light still in his eyes, then takes a step back, and then another. He turns away and faces the far wall, head high, as if he were contemplating a view. His voice is a soft, penetrating rumble echoing from the metal walls. "You humble me," he says, "and you are right. I was finding the blame for this failure hard to bear," he says, "and looking for somcone to help me shoulder it."

"I will help you," Aiah says, "but not by taking blame that isn't mine." She licks her lips. "And the blame isn't all yours either. There are still Gentri and Radeen."

"No, there are not." Constantine's voice is cold. "They died, four days ago, as the offensive began, along with all their staff. And I am responsible for that as well, though it is a burden I can bear more lightly than many another."

"Taikoen," Aiah says. In the metal room the name echoes louder than she would have wished.

"Yes," Constantine says. "My greatest weapon. But the purpose for which I used him came to nothing, and the use of such a weapon comes with a cost. . . ." He looks at Aiah over his shoulder, and his face is a mask of self-loathing. "I will be giving him lives, month after month, for *years,* and all for nothing, for *worse* than nothing: a military offensive that killed thousands and ended in stalemate."

He breathes deep, shoulders lifting as he fills his lungs, and then lets the air out. "I must report to the cabinet," he says. "They have given me their trust, their resources. What can I tell them?"

Aiah takes a step toward him. "Tell them that you couldn't anticipate everything. Tell them you had the battle won, but Lanbola intervened. Tell them that you have learned, and that the next battle, you will win."

Constantine listens, his head cocked, and then he turns. The dangerous brilliance is gone from his eyes, replaced by mere exhaustion. "Yes," he says, "I will tell them exactly that. What can I tell them *but* that?" He sighs again. "I will bring you to the meeting, and you can report on Rohder's progress. I may as well season the bad news with a little good."

He walks toward her, wraps his arms around her, holds her against his barrel chest. Aiah closes her eyes, inhales the scent of him, flesh and hair oil and sweat, the scent of a man who has worked for days at a frenzied pitch and now is close to the end of his endurance.

"I need you now, and desperately," he says. There is a kind of mourning in his voice. "I can trust you, and there is no one else, no one to help me stand against the nightmares . . . all the dead of Cheloki who haunt me, and now the dead here, too, in their thousands. . . ."

Aiah presses herself against his weight. The need in his voice frightens her. She must be strong, it seems, even for him, even for the strongest thing she knows. . . .

And then cold terror floods her spine. She can feel her nape hairs spring erect and gooseflesh prickle her arms. Constantine stiffens, suddenly alert, and she hears his heart crash in his chest. There is suddenly a *presence* in the room, a terror, and the lights seem to go dim, as if viewed through a thickening fog.

"Metropolitan," says a voice, "I have done the thing you bade me." The voice is deep and resonant, as if from out of the earth, as if it were calling through rock and magma and clay.

Aiah's knees go weak. Constantine supports her with his

arms, shielding her protectively from the terror, from Taikoen the Great. There is a strange shimmering on the metal walls, swift and indistinct sensations of prismatic color, and Aiah doesn't know if it is something Taikoen is somehow projecting, or his *body*, his *being*, somehow expanding through the room.

"This is not a good time," Constantine says firmly. "We are not alone."

"I have met the lady before," says the creature—ice man, hanged man, the damned—and from around Constantine's shoulder Aiah catches a glimpse of the heart of him, a deep shadow in the room's corner, a shadow strobing with lines of silver and of color, as if plasm itself had taken on both form and evil intent. . . . This place is well shielded, but not against a creature of plasm like Taikoen, who can creep through plasm mains at will, who can appear anywhere that plasm can be found.

"I have come for my reward at the time appointed," Taikoen says. "I have killed as you desired, Metropolitan, and now I desire my delight." His voice turns silky. "I have delayed my reward to do this thing, and I would not delay any longer."

"I can't help you now," Constantine says. "I do not have the means at present. Give me some few hours to prepare, and I will give you what you need."

"Do you think, Metropolitan, that I enjoy killing?" The creature's voice is petulant. "I do your bidding for one thing only—I wish to clothe myself in flesh. I wish the joys and pleasures of matter. I wish to have on my tongue the gladness of a feast, to sense in my mind the delirium of liquor, to feel in my loins the ecstasies of love."

Aiah shivers uncontrollably in the cold that the creature seems to project, and she expects to see her breath blossom out in frost; but she can see sweat standing out on Constantine's forehead as he faces his ally.

"So you shall," Constantine says firmly. "But I must have some time to prepare. I do not have a subject ready for you."

"This is the time appointed," Taikoen insists. "Give me this girl, if you have no other."

Aiah gives a cry, her mind quailing, a shudder quaking through every limb. Constantine holds her upright through main strength.

"I will not," Constantine says. "I will give you someone, and in a short time, but this lady is vital to my purpose, and you cannot have her."

"It is the time appointed," the creature insists.

"Come back in three hours!" Anger snaps in Constantine's voice. "Come to my apartment then. I will have someone for you—but not *now!*"

Taikoen hovers for a moment and seems to swell, as if threatening to engulf them, and then he subsides, seems to slip away like mist, fleeing as if from reality itself.

"As you wish," the creature says finally, and adds, with a touch of disappointment, and perhaps even sorrow, "It *was* the time appointed, Metropolitan."

Then Taikoen is gone, and Aiah can hear nothing but the uncontrollable chattering of her own teeth. Constantine walks her to the winged armchair, lowers her gently into it. She draws up her legs into a fetal posture, still shuddering. Constantine caresses her cheek, her forehead.

"I am sorry," he says. "I had lost track of time; I had forgot he would be seeking me."

"You must get free of him." The words shivering out of her.

Constantine looks at her sorrowfully. "It is not possible." He touches her cheek again. "Besides, he may be useful yet."

She turns her head away, unable to bear his touch. He looks down at her pensively, teeth worrying at his lower lip, and then turns and walks to the door.

"I must find Taikoen a villain to live in," he says. "While I satisfy him, prepare a presentation for the cabinet meeting—as optimistic as you can make it." He looks over his shoulder. "Optimism is in short supply, and therefore valuable. Make what fortune you can."

He walks away on his—on Taikoen's—errand, and leaves Aiah in his armchair with only her terror for company.

LANBOLA CLAIMS NEUTRALITY

NO ATTACKS LAUNCHED FROM LANBOLI
TERRITORY, MINISTER INSISTS

The War Cabinet meets in the Crystal Dome two days later. The delicate glass structure has withdrawn for the duration into an armored vault, lowered on huge hydraulics into the depths of the Palace. Now Aiah knows how the room survived the violence of Constantine's original coup.

Smooth polished steel surrounds the cabinet room, forms a roof overhead. Fresh flowers in cut-crystal vases, placed at intervals along the table, serve only to make the room even more bleak by contrast. The War Cabinet is a reduced version of the entire cabinet, and consists of the three triumvirs as well as Constantine, Sorya, and Belckon, the aged Minister of State, all of whom cluster at the head of the long glass table. The effect is a sense of isolation, a cluster of defeated people, hiding behind slabs of armor in a room designed for three times their number.

Aiah reports that Rohder's teams are making good progress with their untested theories, that she expects they will pay for themselves and much else, and that if the teams were enlarged, the plasm supply would be as well.

Aiah is told to increase Rohder's division as fast as she can, after which Constantine makes his report on the failure at the Corridor. He describes how his soldiers had the Provisionals on the verge of cracking until Lanbola had permitted a force of mercenaries to cross the border and attack his flank, and sent his troops reeling back.

"And then the Provisionals *halted*," Constantine says. "Our units were in disorder—there was some panic—but the enemy didn't press their attack home."

"Could that be because of the disorganization of enemy command?" Hilthi asks.

This being the current euphemism for the mysterious way that Radeen, Gentri, and their entire staff were killed in their headquarters.

"It is clear by now that the Provisionals are taking direction from Lanbola," Constantine says. "Their forces halted when they didn't have to, and that shows us Lanbola's strategy. Lanbola doesn't want the Provisional Government to *win;* Lanbola wants—by squeezing first one side, then the other—to dictate the peace. They can attack our flank at any point, and that makes us vulnerable. And the Provisionals are dependent on them for supplies and political support."

Faltheg, the new president and triumvir, is a spare, balding man with the eyes of someone drowning. He looks hopelessly down the table and murmurs in a voice almost too low to hear, "What is the status of the army now?"

Reports from the military commanders are bleak, Constantine informs him. Since the failure at the Corridor, enemy mages have been unleashed on Caraqui, plasm raging through the disputed no-man's-land between the two forces, setting unquenchable fires, tearing the bottoms out of barges and pontoons, creating a watery, ruined desolation between the contending armies. It is a brand-new atrocity, unknown within living memory. Tens of thousands of refugees, dispossessed of everything they own, flee from twin threats of fire and water, and the world's compassionate statesmen bleat in sympathy but do nothing.

If Constantine is to attack again, his forces will have to make their way across open water or masses of rubble, all within the scope of pre-sited artillery.

Belckon the diplomat reports that he filed a vigorous protest to the Lanbolan government, which simply denied everything—denied the mercenaries, denied the invasion, denied the atrocities, denied its support for the Provisionals—after which Belckon also lodged a protest with the Polar League, which will place the matter on the agenda for its scheduled meeting next month. The World Council has expressed its concern, and is considering sending humanitarian aid, but has otherwise deferred to the Polar League.

Sorya tilts her head back, her eyes narrowing as a satisfied smile plays across her features. Languidly she places one polished boot on the crystal table. Among all the people here, she alone seems satisfied with the situation outside this steel shell.

"They strive for stalemate," she says. "We fight to win. Despite appearances, the advantage still lies with us."

She reports on the enemy army, the makeup of its new leadership and command staff. She also produces some neat figures showing who is paying for the enemy's efforts, Lanbola principally, money siphoned through its Foreign

Ministry and the Ministry of Trade, with more money coming from Nesca and Charna and Adabil, all people who got along well with the Keremaths in their heydey.

Hilthi's gold pen hovers over his pad. "Great-Uncle Rathmen?" he asks.

"He produces a little money now and again, to demonstrate his sincerity," Sorya says. "Why should he pay for his war, when others are so willing?"

"Willing to feed with Rathmen off our corpse," Hilthi mutters.

"All these people—the Lanbolans, the Nescans, and so on—are also pouring money *here,* into free Caraqui. They have each started their own political party and are recruiting as many adherents as they can buy."

"Good," Constantine says.

The others look at him. Constantine smiles back.

"It's so much easier to keep track of foreign agents when they print newspapers and attend conventions," he says. "And at any point we can bring them down, just by revealing they work for a foreign power."

The others nod sagely. The new president and triumvir Faltheg gazes grayly down the long crystal table. Aiah has never seen him actually meet anyone's eyes. "What can we do?" he mutters. "I need recommendations. I need . . ." Dull light gleams off his bald scalp. "I need *something.*"

Sorya gives a superior smile. "Lanbola has signed its own death warrant," she says. "Their own army is insignificant, a couple divisions of ill-trained militia, badly emplaced. Their border with us is largely unguarded except for police—they are confident that their neutrality, which they themselves violate daily, will protect them. *They* may invade *us,* but to them the opposite is unthinkable. Two corps swung round our right flank, with sufficient air and mage support, can take Lanbola in a matter of hours. Not only will it rid us of a vexatious neighbor, but it will cut the Provisionals off from their source of supply and their biggest provider of cash. And it will give our other neighbors a lesson they would do well to heed."

"No," says Hilthi. His voice is loud, echoes harshly from surrounding steel. "Invading another metropolis can only make matters worse. Our other neighbors will learn a lesson indeed, but the wrong one. The only thing the Polar League ever accomplished was demilitarizing the region a couple centuries ago—if we invade and conquer a neighbor, that's the end of stability for the whole region."

Sorya's ambiguous smile does not fade: destabilizing the region is not a problem for her, but rather a solution. "Wars, once begun, generate their own logic," she says. "The opportunity exists *now.* At some point—soon, I imagine—Lanbola will awaken to the fact they are in danger, and act to correct the situation."

"But neutrality . . . ," Faltheg murmurs.

"All neutralities are imaginary," Sorya says. "When a third party to a war chooses neutrality as a policy, in reality the neutrality always favors one side or another. Our neighbors' neutrality in the present conflict favors our enemies—it demonstrates that neighboring states have *already* taken sides against us. We should show our neighbors that such a neutrality is more dangerous for them than they believe."

Sorya's genius, Aiah realizes, consists in doing just what she always says she will do. She wants to enlarge her scope, increase her power. *All neutralities are imaginary. . . . All truces are temporary.* It is all of a piece, a perfectly consistent view of the world.

It's *other* people, she thinks, who see something else in Sorya, who think she is something other than what she has always said she is.

"I agree with Miss Sorya's premises," Hilthi says, "but not her conclusions. Wars *do* have their own logic, and the logic of war is to grow ever larger and more destructive, and for war's energies to engulf entire nations, entire economies. Occupation of Lanbola would create a cascade of events that would soon run outside our control—the entire region could be endangered."

"I support the idea," Parq says. His normally silky voice is forceful, angry. "The Lanbolans have caused enormous harm to our people, and our people demand justice and punishment for the criminals. If our neighbors object, we can point out that *they* initially invaded *us,* albeit by proxy."

"The Polar League can put the Lanbolans' protest on their

agenda for next month," Sorya mocks. Parq laughs, and there is a rumble of amusement from Constantine.

Belckon gazes uneasily at the room from beneath his shock of white hair. "I must say that, diplomatically, this action would create insuperable difficulties for us. Our perpetual difficulty is in convincing our neighbors that our regime has any legitimacy, and if we prove ourselves not only illegitimate but hegemonist, we can expect only hostility from people who were formerly our friends."

"*Have* we any friends?" Sorya wonders aloud.

Belckon looks at her. "Sympathizers, yes."

Faltheg looks in Belckon's direction—not at Belckon directly—and ventures to ask a question. "Our neighbors considered the Keremaths legitimate, but not us?"

Belckon considers his words before answering. "They were *used* to the Keremaths. It is not a characteristic of diplomacy to enjoy change for its own sake."

A deep laugh rolls out of Constantine. "Seize power, and it makes you a bandit," he says. "Hang on for twenty years, and you become a statesman."

A perplexed look crosses Faltheg's face. "What would we *do* with Lanbola?" he mutters.

"Civilize them, of course," says Parq, head of the Dalavan Militia.

"Make them pay." For once Sorya is not smiling. "They supported the countercoup—one understands their motives, I suppose, but once their little adventure was defeated, they didn't quit the field like gentlemen, they started a *war*. And I think the Lanbolans should not cease to pay until every damaged building is rebuilt better than before, every orphan is guaranteed an education, and our treasury has overcome any embarrassment, present or future."

"That's brigandage!" Hilthi says, outraged. Faltheg gives the ceiling an abstracted look—Aiah suspects he may be adding up sums in his head.

"Miss Aiah?" he says, and Aiah starts. His eyes wander in Aiah's general direction. "Our plasm reserves," he says, "are sufficient for this action?"

"We can support a campaign of a few days," Aiah admits with reluctance.

"It is not possible from a military point of view," Constantine says.

Aiah's heart rejoices. The others look at Constantine.

"All our forces are in the line," Constantine says. "We hold exterior lines, and therefore we use more troops to hold the same line than our enemies do. We would have to pull out large numbers of soldiers, and our opponents would of course observe this. Prepositioning two corps for an invasion of Lanbola would not go unnoticed. We will have to build our forces to a greater strength before we can even consider this option."

"Well," Faltheg says flatly, "that's that." He seems relieved.

No disappointment shows on Sorya's face. She removes her boot from the table and reaches a languid hand to one of the crystal vases. She takes a carnation, sniffs it briefly, unbuttons one of the fire-gilt buttons of her uniform tunic, and puts the flower in the buttonhole.

"In that case," she says, "we can hope only for a military stalemate, which is what our enemies most desire. We will have to consider what we will offer to Lanbola, and to the other powers who support the Provisionals. Because we will have to outbid our rivals, and that will be difficult—Kerehorn and his friends may promise that which they do not possess, whereas we must give away that which we have worked so hard to win."

Belckon and Hilthi look down at the table. No one, it seems, has an answer to her argument.

FOURTEEN

∿∿∿∿∿∿∿

While the armies settle into stalemate, terror is unleashed anew in Caraqui. Once again bombs begin detonating in crowded streets, and unknown mages fill entire districts with fear. Huge tenements are burned down, unshielded pumping stations or utility mains are destroyed, bridges are smashed or burnt. Much of the sabotage seems to come from within the city itself, and a new phrase enters the vocabulary, floating through the populace on the winds of war. *Silver Terror.* Enemy forces throw artillery rounds into the city at random. Hospitals and public buildings fill with refugees, and it is clear that the enemy is trying to make the city ungovernable.

And therefore it is all the more important that Aiah go on with her job, taking down every plasm house she can find, along with the Handmen who have unleashed terror against the people.

———————————

CONSTANTINE DENOUNCES ATROCITIES IN
BRILLIANT SPEECH

SAVAGES LANBOLA REGIME

"THEIR ARMS ARE BLOODY TO THE ELBOW"

LANBOLI GOVERNMENT PROTESTS
"UNDIPLOMATIC USAGE"

It is early second shift, and Aiah plays plasm angel for her military cops. The plasm house she watches has been on her list for some time, but hasn't been surveilled since before the war began. Military police are on their way to bust into the place, but Aiah wants to make certain the Handmen inside aren't going to be delivering any nasty surprises.

The plasm house is in an aging apartment building, once handsome but now failing the test of time, with stained hallway carpet and flaking walls. Although it seems to be producing a large amount of illegal product, Aiah can't be sure from where the plasm house is drawing its plasm—perhaps, she thinks, it's being hijacked from a food factory on a huge pontoon moored alongside. The Handmen have learned a few things about shielding since the PED began its work, and Aiah can't slip her anima into the room, not even on the thinnest pipette of plasm. But there are no lookouts, no signs of anyone prepared to offer resistance, and the door looks as if it will go down easily enough before the assault of her troops.

"Building's in sight." A message from her approaching military cops, whispered into her ear by one of her assistants.

Aiah nods her understanding and concentrates on keeping her anima and sensorium intact.

Sensations from the apartment building wash over her, and her nose wrinkles to the mildewed smell of the stained carpet. She alters her sensorium to lower the intensity of her olfactory sense.

In the apartment building a door bangs open, and back in the Palace Aiah's body gives a start.

A group of people have entered the scene, maybe a dozen. They are all young men, dressed casually but with purpose—they all wear thick-soled black boots laced up to the calf and a red strip of cloth tied around their brows, and many wear plastic jackets made in imitation of leather or vests that rattle with chains and silver studs. They openly carry an assortment of weapons: pistols, shotguns, a rifle. Two carry a crude battering ram, a length of steel with handles welded to it.

Back in the ops room, Aiah shouts, "Armed men in the corridor!" Her body shudders to a surge of adrenaline as if to a rumble of kettledrums.

In the apartment building the leader, a young sturdy man in plastic leathers and a mustache, cocks his pistol and places himself carefully to one side of the door. He booms on it with fist and forearm both, and the door rattles on its hinges.

"Ragdath! Open up!"

The others stand to either side of the door, grinning and readying their weapons.

"Wait! Stop!" Aiah tries to broadcast the words to the group, but in her alarm she fails to focus her mind properly and no one hears her.

"Go," the leader says, a bright white grin on his face, and stands back.

"No!" Aiah tries to tell them.

The sound of all the guns going off together staggers Aiah's senses. The shooters are enjoying themselves, laughing and yipping as they empty their guns through the door and into the apartment. Shotguns blow chunks out of the wall, revealing tattered bronze mesh behind.

Aiah's anima dashes among the group, knocking up gun barrels, slapping down the men with invisible plasm hands. But the realization that there is a mage among them galvanizes the shooters, and Aiah realizes that the only way to stop them will be to kill them all. The door crashes down before the ram, and the shooters swarm into the apartment.

Three Handmen are huddled inside, and two are splashed with blood. Laughing in triumph, the gunmen drag the Handmen out into the corridor, kicking them along with their shiny black boots. Gunpowder stench hangs heavy in the corridor.

The leader looks through a sheaf of papers. "Which one's Ragdath?" he asks.

"The police are hurrying," Aiah is told, an ops-room voice whispering in her ear.

Aiah tries to calm her beating heart. She concentrates, builds her anima into the sleek, featureless golden form she's used before. Power pulses through her, and her anima shimmers into existence in the corridor. The others fall back before the apparition, and she sees sudden fear in their eyes. Guns are hesitantly raised.

Aiah concentrates, lets her anima speak the words.

"I am Aiah, Director of the Plasm Enforcement Division," she says. "I have had this place under surveillance. What are you doing here?"

The leader hands the papers to one of his fellows, shuffles forward, and digs into his jacket pocket for a thin plastic card. "Dalavan Militia," he says. "My name is Raymo. We're here to find Ragdath."

"Here he is!" one of his friends says, and prods a wounded man with the barrel of his shotgun. The man moans in pain.

"I have police on the way here," Aiah says. "We'll need those prisoners."

"You can have the other two," Raymo says. "But Ragdath's on the proscription lists, and he's worth five thousand dinars to us."

"He's on the *what*?"

Raymo turns to his friend, pulls out a sheet of paper. "Here," he says. "Five thousand. Dead or alive."

Aiah looks at the sheet in stunned surprise. The face of Ragdath gazes back at her from the plastic flimsy, a face perfectly familiar from chromographs in her own files.

She realizes that this *is* one of the chromographs from her files.

"Who issued this?" she says.

"The triumvir Parq."

The tromp of Aiah's police is heard in the stairwalls. The Dalavan Militia glance nervously over their shoulders.

"Tell the police the situation is over," Aiah says to her assistant, back in the Palace. "It's the Dalavan Militia."

In the corridor, Aiah asks, "Do you have the rest of the list?"

"Part of it."

As her police step wonderingly into the corridor, Aiah takes the pages in her ectomorphic hands and leafs through them. Many of the names and faces are familiar.

"The whole thing's going to be available on Interfact in the next day or so," the militiaman says. "Anyone can get a copy."

This list is *hers,* she realizes. It was the list of Handmen she gave to Constantine weeks ago, after the first series of bombings.

Five thousand dinars for each name. Dead or alive.

Her list.

CRIME BOSS APPOINTED MINISTER OF PROVISIONAL GOVERNMENT

RATHMEN TAKES TREASURY POST

"Shield above," Constantine says, eyes aflame, "would you have this Silver Terror continue?"

"I gave *you* this list," Aiah says. "Now Parq is using it to kill people."

Constantine gives a snarl. "Then Parq will take the blame, won't he?"

"This list—," Aiah protests. "It's not error-free. We acquired it in the first place from the police, and we know how efficient *they* were. We haven't had a chance to check more than a fraction of it. Much of it is out of date, and people with similar names can be victimized. And the Dalavan Militia look like they were recruited out of the slums— they've all got guns and they're enjoying themselves far too much."

Constantine gives an uneasy glance toward the polarized windows—he is in another suite today, with his files and papers, and moves to a new one each day, carrying his portable ministry, his papers and boxes, with him from place to place.

His leather chair creaks as he leans forward over his desk. "It was *not* my decision," Constantine says. "Parq is triumvir—I *work* for him."

"Couldn't you point out—"

"Aiah." His rumbling voice is cold, and there is a dangerous glint in his eye. "I *supported* the decision."

"I—" Aiah's voice fails. Despair rains down her spine.

"We cannot afford to fight a war against an army and a

war against the terrorists simultaneously," Constantine says. "Five thousand dinars for each Handman—that's cheap, cheaper than hiring mercenaries and mages." He glances to the window again, his face uneasy. "If I had won the Battle of the Corridor . . . ," he growls. "If I had won . . . things would be different."

"Then why—" Aiah's head whirls, and she wants to lean on something for support. "Why are you bothering with my department at all? If you can just offer a bounty for anyone you suspect, why bother with me, with the forms of legality. . . ."

He gazes at her, smouldering resentment in his eyes. "Emergency measures are for times of emergency only. After the war, there must be a structure we can build on. The Dalavan Militia are amateurs—they will do well enough for keeping a rude sort of order, but they aren't investigators, and if they're not kept on a short leash they'll turn as bad as the Silver Hand. So after the war is over, I will be able to argue that the Militia are no longer needed, because the PED is sufficient for peacetime."

Aiah glowers at him. "And will you win that fight?"

"It's too early to say. I have a war to win first." His eyes soften, and he leans forward across his desk. "If you want to keep some of these Handmen from being abused by the Militia, you will have every opportunity simply by arresting them through your department."

Aiah takes a breath. "Yes," she says. "Yes. Very well."

"And then the reward will belong to your people."

Anger simmers in her veins. "Keep the money," she says. "I don't want my people working for rewards."

Constantine looks at her. "I remind you that your military police are mercenaries," he says. "Rewards will keep them loyal. And you can use part of the reward to fund your own department, perhaps give your people a bonus or two."

Aiah reconsiders, backpedals a bit, shifts her ground. "I don't want my people taking heads."

Constantine is curt. "See that they don't, then."

Everything has become my responsibility again, she thinks. Even whether or not the Handmen receive decent treatment.

How does he do it? she wonders.

There is a whir and thump as an artillery shell lands nearby, and then the sound is repeated. Aiah finds herself counting the rounds: there are six guns in an enemy battery, and once six shells have landed, there is a little respite.

Four, five, six. Silence.

Constantine looks up at her. He, too, has been counting. "Is that all?" he asks.

Aiah supposes that it is.

PARQ PROCLAIMS MILITIA "A SUCCESS"

THOUSANDS OF HANDMEN ARRESTED

CRIMES OF TERROR REDUCED!

The amateurs of the Dalavan Militia are as bad as Aiah expects. Lists of the proscribed in hand, they knock down doors, or simply shoot through them; they arrest the wrong people, and sometimes kill them; and it's only a matter of days before the first complaints of extortion are heard.

Enthusiastic citizens make the situation worse. The rewards are available to anyone who brings in one of the proscribed, and Caraqui is full of desperate people, many of them left homeless and rash by the war, willing to risk their own lives by finding a Handman or two and dragging them before a magistrate. Cases of misidentification are legion, and though it's bad enough when the wrong man gets hauled before a magistrate, it's far worse when the victim is dead before he—or anyway his head—appears in court.

And since these enthusiasts charge into the fray without proper intelligence, without support, and usually without mages to cover their backs, the hardened criminals of the Silver Hand are not inclined to go quietly, and they do not always prove to be the victims. By now their plasm houses are shielded and fortified: sometimes plasm attacks leave the attackers dead or injured, and sometimes there are gun battles that put a dozen people in the morgue or in hospital.

Aiah directs her department's efforts toward the most hardened targets she can find, hoping by the efforts of her own professionals to keep the casualties to a minimum. She divides the rewards between her mercenaries and her department's own treasury, with occasional handouts to informants.

And the Silver Terror fades. Scores of Handmen are captured trying to leave Caraqui, and thousands of others join Great-Uncle Rathmen in exile. The number of bomb and plasm attacks declines remarkably.

Progress, Aiah concedes, of a sort.

She does not see Constantine in person, but only as a presence in video or memoranda or news reports. He floats in a circle far above hers: his fight is in the clouds, and hers in the bog below.

She tries not to think of him, not to judge him. The endless worry and activity make it easier.

Her department grows. For once she has her pick of candidates—the war has disrupted enough lives that plenty of qualified people are willing to take a secure government job, even an underpaid one, and even a job in a building that is regularly the subject of enemy attack. Because many of the Handmen are now in hiding, Aiah hires squads of detectives, many former police, people familiar with Caraqui and the ways of the Hand, investigators who can interview witnesses properly and track down the Handmen in their hiding places. She is surprised to discover that many of the ex-police pass their plasm scans: apparently there *were* honest cops out there, trying to do their best but compromised by the corrupt system in which they worked.

She is interviewing a candidate for a clerical position when her receptionist tells her that Constantine is on the line. She finishes making an appointment for the young man's plasm scan, sees him out of the office, then picks up the headset.

"Yes, Minister."

"I'm sorry," he says at once.

"For what?"

"For handing you a thousand impossible tasks. For showing you the worst of my character. For neglecting you for weeks in an unforgivable fashion."

There is a moment's silence.

"Miss Aiah?" Constantine prompts. "What are you thinking?"

Aiah feels a smile tugging at the corners of her mouth. "I'm thinking it's a start."

"I am willing to apologize at greater length, midbreak third shift, if you can clear your schedule."

"I'm supposed to be plasm angel for my troops."

"Get someone else."

She sighs. "I'll try."

"20:00. I will give you dinner. And, if I can beg a favor of you, may I ask you not to dress as you would at the office? I see nothing but suits and uniforms all day, and something soft would be a pleasure."

"I'll make an effort."

"And I will try to make your effort worth your while."

Aiah puts the headset on its hook and scrubs her fingers through her hair. Constantine clearly has a romantic interlude on his mind, and she is not certain if she has any romance left in her.

Not without a month's vacation in some resort, anyway.

She throws the switch on her communications array and tells her receptionist to send in the next candidate.

When he walks in there is a flash of recognition, and Aiah's heart lifts. Perhaps one of her family . . . ? But no: the new candidate is a stranger.

And, she thinks, she knows much about him, even if she's never met him before.

He is Barkazil, almost certainly. Smooth brown skin, brown eyes, curly black hair, a home-district smile. He's dressed Jaspeeri-fashion—shiny gray polymer suit and big swatches of lace dripping from wrists and throat—and he carries himself with a self-confidence almost impudent in someone this young.

He shakes her hand. "Alfeg," he says, then adds, "of the Cunning People," before she can ask.

"Aiah," she says. "The same."

"I know." His white, confiding smile suggests that he and Aiah share a great many secrets.

Guns thunder outside, and Aiah's window, divided for

safety's sake into diamonds by a crosshatching of masking tape, gives a sympathetic rattle.

She sits behind her desk and pulls his file off the stack. Citizen of the Scope of Jaspeer, sure enough. Degrees in chemistry and plasm use from Margai University. Age: twenty-three. Single. Current employer: United Polymer, Arsenide City Complex, Jaspeer. Current salary: 38,000 dalders per annum.

He wants to become one of her mages. Aiah looks up.

"I don't think we can afford you," she says.

"Money isn't of the first importance," Alfeg says. "Do you know the Gar-Chavan Bakeries in Old Shorings?"

"Yes. I grew up in Old Shorings."

"My father is Mr. Chavan. Money is not so much a necessity as a way of keeping score."

"Ah." A rich boy: so that's where he got his self-confidence. "Well, if it's your *only* way of keeping score, you're not going to get a lot of points in Caraqui."

He looks at her with a composed, sincere expression, though there is still a degree of amusement dancing behind his eyes. "I want to do something meaningful before I die," he says. "If that's not a foolish thing to admit."

Perhaps it is, Aiah thinks, in the circles he's used to.

The guns boom again, and again the windows rattle.

"Your search for meaning could get you killed," Aiah points out. "We're fighting a war."

"That makes it more interesting, from my point of view."

"You're not experienced in police work, I take it?"

"No."

"And though you work with plasm, your experience is in chemistry, which would not seem to be of great relevance."

He nods. "But I have considerable experience in telepresence. Dangerous hermetics are always initiated at a distance."

"I see. You haven't ever created or worked with a plasm hound?"

"I'm afraid not." He smiles apologetically. "I never had a reason to track anything."

She frowns, looks at the file again while the guns boom out. *Young, rich person seeks meaning.* And once he's had his little adventure in relevance, he can always return to his social niche.

An option, Aiah reminds herself, not available to herself.

But even so, she finds herself aching to hire him. He is of the Cunning People, and possibly the only Barkazil in all the Metropolis of Caraqui other than herself. The only thing she finds herself missing about Jaspeer is the ability to bathe in her Barkazil identity.

In fact, she thinks, being a Barkazil here might have its advantages. In Old Shorings, she'd have to cope with her family. Here, she does not.

"When can you start work?" she asks.

"Right away. Within the hour, if you like. I can wire my resignation back to United Polymer before they know I'm gone from my desk."

The ease with which he proposes to dispose of an extremely lucrative job seems improbable. And, to someone brought up on legends of Chonah, the immortal so successful at confidence games that she had given her name to a whole species of dubious endeavor, it seems more than a little suspicious.

She puts down the file and regards him. "You're not an agent of the Jaspeeri government, by any chance?"

The question seems to startle him. His eyebrows lift. "No," Alfeg says. "Sorry to disappoint you."

"Or any other government? Or institution? Or criminal enterprise?"

"Immortal Karlo, no!"

There is a bang, a lurch, a rumble. The other side of the Palace, facing Lorkhin Island, has taken a hit from something big.

"You will have to undergo a plasm scan to verify you're telling the truth," Aiah says. "It will be very thorough, and is certain to discover any secret allegiances. Do you have a problem with this?"

He looks uncomfortable for a moment. "I suppose not," he says.

"We look for absolute commitment," Aiah says, "absolute honesty, and absolute discretion."

"I suppose my romantic, futile attachment to the lost

cause of the Holy League of Karlo will prove no impediment?" Alfeg says. "My grandfather fought for them."

The Holy League was one of the many factions that finished off the Metropolis of Barkazi, one of a disheartening, endless list of lost causes from the Barkazi Wars.

Aiah finds a smile tugging at her lips. "My granddad fought for the Holy League as well," she says. "I don't imagine there will be a problem unless you try to resurrect the Holy League here."

Alfeg nods graciously, and playfully sketches the Sign of Karlo in the air. "I was rather hoping *you* would, actually," he says.

A peculiar sensation hums along Aiah's nerves. She looks at him sharply to see if he's joking or not, but she can't be certain.

"I'm here to build the New City," she says, "not to bring back the Metropolis of Barkazi. Which in any case is thousands of radii away."

"Of course."

"If you still want the job, I can slot you into a plasm scan early tomorrow. Second shift, first quarterbreak."

"Yes. I can manage that, though I'll have to wire United Polymer and tell them I need another day off."

"That's up to you. You can make an appointment with my secretary."

He seems a bit puzzled for a moment, as if he had been expecting something more, and then rises and takes Aiah's hand.

"Thank you, Miss Aiah," he says.

"Thank you for applying. I appreciate your coming all this distance." *Even,* she thinks, *if it was in the Rande aerocar your daddy bought you.*

ADAVETH ELECTED HEAD OF
ALTERED PEOPLE'S PARTY

TWISTED UNITE TO SEEK RIGHTS,
ECONOMIC OPPORTUNITY

Buoyed perhaps by the meeting with Alfeg, perhaps by
the thought of having Constantine to herself for at least a
few hours, Aiah almost overdoes it. She arranges for someone to cover her shift, makes an appointment with one of the
Palace hairdressers, gets a manicure while her ringlets are
attended to, and then turns up at Constantine's door
promptly at 20:00, wearing heels and a very short dress of
blazing scarlet that she'd bought during her first day's shopping in Caraqui and never found an occasion to wear. She
also wears the priceless ivory necklace, with its dangling Trigram, that Constantine had given her.

Judging from their smiles and glowing eyes, Constantine's
guards, at least, appreciate her efforts.

She is taken through the layers of security that surround
Constantine's apartment-for-a-day, and finds him lounging
casually on the couch, hands clasped behind his head. He
wears a soft gray chambray shirt with ruffles on the front
and wide sleeves, and his long legs, propped up before him,
are clad in pleated slacks of a darker gray.

Aiah is surprised to find Aldemar here. The petite actress
sits at a desk, eyes closed, with a copper t-grip in her hand, a
little frown on her perfect face.

Constantine bounds to his feet on Aiah's entrance, smile
spreading over his face. "Welcome!" he cries. Takes her
hands, kisses her cheek. "You look lovely!"

"Thank you."

"Did you buy the dress just for me?"

She gives him a sidelong look. "Perhaps," she says, and
then looks toward the actress.

"Aldemar has offered to give us a gift," Constantine says.
"I must say it is an inspired one."

Aiah considers Aldemar's intent concentration on her
magework. "Shall I thank her now," she says, "or is she
busy?"

"Perhaps tomorrow."

Tomorrow? Aiah wonders. Is Aldemar going to be with
them for the rest of the shift?

But then Aldemar's eyes flutter open and after a moment's
vague search focus on Aiah and Constantine. "I've established
the sourceline," she says. "Are the two of you ready?"

Constantine steps close to Aiah, puts an arm around her waist. "At your convenience," he says.

Aldemar gives a knowing smile, then closes her eyes again. She reaches out, her free hand unfolding as if offering something on her palm, and Aiah's skin warms to the touch of plasm, and she opens her mouth in surprise at the sheer *power* she feels surging toward her . . .

And blinks at the sight of another place, a room with plush furniture, a glass table set atop a silver metal spiral, place settings for two, a bottle of golden wine waiting in a silver bucket, candles glittering off the gold rims of fine porcelain and the mirror surfaces of silver chafing dishes. . . .

Aiah gapes in astonishment. Constantine's voice purrs in her ear.

"Aldemar has given us a little vacation. Another place, quite secure, far from Caraqui, far from duty and war."

"Great Senko," Aiah murmurs, and touches the Trigram at her throat.

Constantine steps to the sliding glass balcony door, with its bronze frame and crosshatch of bronze wire, and closes it—that was the pathway, Aiah realizes, that Aldemar used to teleport them into the apartment.

Laughing plasm-warmth tingles in Aiah's bones as her astonishment fades. She bounds forward to the buffet, lifts the lid of a chafing dish at random, sees cutlets of some sort in a brown sauce, with melted cheese; and then she replaces the silver lid and almost dances through the room, runs her fingertips along the plush cushion of a couch, feels the scalloped gilt edge of a mirror, plucks sprigs of jasmine from cloisonné vases to inhale the scent. . . .

Far from duty and war . . . Her heart lifts. She had not been away from the Metropolis of Caraqui for a single hour since her arrival.

She feels drunk with freedom. She turns to look at Constantine, sees the candles glowing gold in his eyes.

"Where are we?" she asks.

"Achanos."

On the other side of the world, eight or ten thousand radii away. A stable, civilized metropolis, filled with prosperous bankers and healthy industries and glowing with economic health.

"No guards?" she asks. "No telephones?"

"There are guards, yes," Constantine concedes, "but they do not know who it is they guard, nor will they disturb us. Aldemar arranged it so that we might seem to be a group of chromoplay producers meeting to arrange financing."

"I'd wish we could stay a month."

He looks at her, and the candlelight dances in his eyes. He takes the sprig of jasmine from her hand and places it behind her ear. "We will try to compress the best parts of that month into the few hours we have."

They do their best, opening with wine, fruit, and little layered pastry curled around bits of spiced squab; then on to dinner, a choice of squab, a noodle dish, beef tenderloin, and the cutlet, all in their appropriate sauces, along with fresh vegetables, long crusty loaves of bread, and fruit.

"Have you heard from your family?" Constantine asks.

"I'm usually out when they call. My grandmother is the most insistent—she calls every so often to urge me to stock up on disaster supplies, and I'd like to be able to oblige her, but this is the first time I've been out of the Palace since I got back from Xurcal Station."

Constantine tilts his head, curious. "Your grandmother survived the Barkazi Wars, yes?"

"Yes. My grandfather fought for the Holy League and ended up a prisoner of the Fastani, and Nana got her whole family out to a refugee center, then to Jaspeer. She raised all the children by herself. She's tough."

"I would like to hear her stories," Constantine says. "I've spent years of my life at war, but I've always been a commander, relatively safe and comfortable. I try to visit the real victims, the refugees and the wounded, but it's usually not safe to go out in public, unsafe not just for me but for the people I'm visiting, and now I share your situation—confined to the Palace—and move from one room to the next."

Aiah remembers Constantine in her little apartment back in Jaspeer, the way he looked with such evident curiosity at the life of an ordinary person, and amusement tugs at her lips.

"And apropos of things Barkazil," Constantine continues, "we have a brigade of Barkazil troops arriving at the aerodrome next week, and I'd be obliged if you will meet them and say a few words of welcome."

Curiosity overcomes Aiah's fear of speaking in public. "Barkazils? From Barkazi?"

"No. The Timocracy is running out of troops to send us, and so I have contracted with an agent in Sayven—another metropolis famous for exporting its soldiers. They are called Karlo's Brigade—and Karlo, I recollect, is the Barkazil immortal."

"Barkazils in Sayven?" Aiah frowns. "That's nowhere near Barkazi. And Karlo's Brigade—I wonder if that means they're Holy League people."

"Do those old factions still exist?"

"In Jaspeer the Holy League and the Fastani have become gangsters in Barkazil neighborhoods—they extort money from businessmen in the name of their old causes—but any actual veterans, unless they could afford life extension, would be ancient by now. They were always sitting in cafés when I was growing up, discussing the bad old days. . . ."

"There are Barkazils on the Provisional Government's side, too. Landro's Escaliers, specialists in urban vertical assault and sniper work, from the Timocracy."

Aiah gives a grimace. "I'm sorry to hear they're on the wrong side. But whoever they are, I've never heard of them."

Constantine shrugs. "I will send you to Karlo's Brigade, and perhaps you can find out."

"I will ask." She considers. "I had a Barkazil apply to me today for a mage's post. Came all the way from Jaspeer."

"Will you give him the job?"

"He's a young man—well, my age, actually. Wealthy family. He's flying the nest in search of, oh, real meaning, or anyway the real something." She shrugs. "I don't know. Perhaps I won't hire him. He's getting scanned tomorrow; I'll wait for the report."

Constantine gives her a meaningful look. "I should think that any Barkazil in your division would be grateful to you for the job. Personal loyalty is not a small consideration, things being what they are."

"He's too rich and good-looking to have loyalties to a bureaucrat like me."

Constantine's laugh barks out. "He's good-looking? You hadn't mentioned that. Send him home!"

Aiah offers him an ambiguous smile. "Well. Perhaps I'll hire him, then. If he makes you nervous, he may have his uses."

Constantine gives a mock scowl. "I think I may learn to dislike this young gentleman."

She takes her wineglass, rises, and walks to the apartment's floor-to-ceiling window. "Do you think it would be unsafe," she says, "if we looked out? You must be tired of blacked-out windows, and so am I."

Constantine follows her, sweeps aside the deep blue drape at one side to look at the window mechanism, and nods. "It's silvered on the outside," he says. "I wish I could say the same for windows in the Palace." He presses buttons, and with a stately electric purr the drapes pull back, revealing the window in its brushed-bronze frame. Aiah looks out through the almost-invisible bronze grid set into the glass, and a sudden singing pleasure makes her smile.

They are high in a granite tower, one of a cluster of white spears pointing at the Shield, each tipped with bright bronze transmission horns and ornamented with extravagant carved arabesques gilded with shining bronze. Shieldlight glows from tall columns of mirrored windows, and far below avenues stretch off into infinity, shadowed by tall brownstone buildings crowned by roof gardens. A bright red aerocar, turbines rotating in their shrouds, descends slowly toward a pad below. Traffic fills the streets even at this late hour, Shieldlight winking from glass and chrome, and the walkways are full of people walking, browsing, shopping.

No gunfire, she thinks; no one hiding from shellfire or rockets. No plasm glow on the horizon to mark where mages are wrestling in midair.

And no water, either. The view is all brick and concrete and stone, like the vistas Aiah had known in Jaspeer.

How many of these people, Aiah wonders, have ever *heard* of Caraqui or its struggles? How many dream of the New City?

Practically none, she imagines. Everything she does, everything she fights for, is less than a dream to the people here, more unreal than the people in a chromo.

Constantine's arms circle her from behind. She tilts her head back against his shoulder.

"I wish I could give you that month here," he says. "Perhaps after the war. It's something you deserve."

She sips wine from her gold-rimmed glass. "After the war you'll just give me another twenty jobs, and I won't have time."

"Am I that demanding a boss?"

A low chuckle invades her throat. "Oh yes, Minister. You are."

"You must learn to delegate, as I do. After all, I trust you with some of the most important tasks."

"And that's precisely why I must do them all myself. If something goes badly wrong, would you accept my explanation that I delegated the job to someone else and he failed?"

He considers this a moment. "I would hope the situation did not arise."

"So would I. That's why I do everything myself."

"And I appreciate your dedication." He kisses her at the juncture of neck and shoulder, and pleasure shimmers along her nerves.

"I think I would like to sit and watch the world for a while," Aiah says.

They drag a sofa to the window, and Aiah reclines against Constantine as she gazes at the city below. She looks at him from the slant of her eye.

"I've talked to you about my family," she says, "but I don't really know anything about yours. Who was *your* grandmother?"

He considers for a moment. "She was the mistress of my grandfather. She lasted a few years, but in the end he lost interest in her, so she had a child in hopes of getting a hold on him."

"Did it work?"

"Of course not. He was a politician who won a rigged election with the help of the military, then betrayed his allies and seized sole power for himself. He would never have let a matter of sentiment get in the way of what he really wanted. But he was decent enough by his lights, acknowledged my father and brought him up well." She turns, takes one of his big hands in both her own, looks up at him.

"Did you know your grandfather?"

"Oh yes. He was a complete political animal, all hunger and corruption, no humanity at all. Tall and thin, lived very modestly—he wanted all the power and wealth in the world, but wouldn't have known how to enjoy it once he got it." A ghost of a smile crosses his face. "Let me tell you a story. After he had been Metropolitan for twelve or fifteen years it seemed everyone had finally had enough of him, and there were strikes and unrest. He could see people maneuvering to replace him and thought it possible he might not win . . . so he gave up!" He laughs. "He announced he would step down and arrange for an orderly succession. He entered into a power-sharing arrangement with the people who wanted to replace him, allowing for the most inept of them to have the most power. They failed miserably, of course—he still had enough power to insure that they would—and their infighting paralyzed the country. So then, with the blessings of the people who had once wanted him gone, he stepped in to 'save' his beloved Cheloki, and ruled absolutely from that point on."

Aiah turns to the view, gazes out at the granite towers, the countless people. "And your grandmother?" she asks.

"Very grand, very beautiful, very mercenary. I do not believe I ever saw her on the arm of any man who wasn't worth fifty million dalders at least. But I didn't know her very well—once she saw that having my father was a tactical error, she lost interest in him and left him to be raised by his father's tutors."

She frowns. "I am almost sorry I asked. They sound like a dreadful bunch."

He smiles at her. "My father was more sympathetic. He was a complete mediocrity, but he tried to do well—he worked very hard at the government departments he was given, but the harder he worked, the worse the departments got. So he settled for being a sportsman—he played polo, if you know what that is."

"I've seen it on video. It's played on horseback."

"It's the most posh sport in the world. Horses cost millions, and my father had the best. You've got to rent huge rooftops for the horses to live on—that alone costs a fortune."

"I've seen horses in zoos."

"Polo was the only thing my father was good at. Polo and women."

Aiah skates fingernails along the rim of her glass. Outside, a plasm advert, an image of a platinum Forlong necklace glittering with diamonds, winds like a ribbon between the granite towers. How long has it been since she's seen a plasm advert? she wonders, one that wasn't a government announcement or propaganda. She never thought she'd miss them. . . .

"Do you know what?" she says. "None of these people sound like *you*. You don't seem like any of your ancestors at all." She turns, looks at him. "So where did *you* come from? *Your* genetics?"

"I would deny my ancestors if I could. I cannot admire a one of them, though perhaps I am more like my grandfather than you suspect." He looks out at the bright city below, face thoughtful. "Possibly I am my mother's child. She was supposed to be brilliant when she was young—beautiful, witty, played half a dozen instruments. She used to give concerts. But by the time my sisters and I grew up she had already . . . withdrawn."

Aiah frowns. "If your father was only good at polo and women, that must have been hard on her."

"The men in my family did not value women. Just bought them, and when they were tired of the first lot, they'd buy more. My father needed an ornament to cheer him at polo matches, and so he got one—and the fact she was very good at music was just a bonus, something else to brag about to his friends."

"Why didn't she leave?"

He tilts his head, considers. "She had a comfortable life. Lots of money, and nobody really cared what she did. She spent a great deal of time with me and my sisters—they were pleasant hours—and she drank, and had dozens of lovers, and over time the music she played got sadder and sadder. Toward the end she became very fond of morphine. Eventually she rode one of my father's ponies right off a building and fell eighteen stories to her death. She was drunk. I was nine years old."

Aiah looks at him in concern. "Suicide?" she asks.

He purses his lips in thought. "Probably not a deliberate one. But there are indirect ways of killing oneself, not with a knife or a gun. One of these is alcohol and morphine together, and that was her choice."

"What about your sisters? How many were there?"

"Five, if you count the two cousins who came to live with us when they were young and were brought up as part of the family. We spent all our time together, were even schooled together, by a tutor."

Aiah thinks of the young Constantine brought up as the adored only son amid this household of women. She sees sadness cross his face. "Two of my sisters are dead now. The others do not speak to me, not after my betrayal of the family."

Who are his family now? she wonders. Martinus, Sorya, herself . . . and Taikoen.

Sadness drifts through Aiah's heart, and she impulsively kisses his cheek. She had not wanted to provoke these memories, this sadness. She puts her arms around his neck and kisses him again. "I forgive you," she says.

He looks at her, intelligence burning in his glance, and his lips twist in a mocking smile. "For everything?" he asks.

She kisses his smile. "Of course."

"For I am using you, lady, and everyone else, and sometimes I confess I no longer know why."

"I forgive you," she repeats, and he smiles again, sadly this time, and returns the kiss with a ferocity that takes her momentarily aback, but then she returns it, nerves answering to his need.

They kiss and caress, and the fiery hunger grows and kindles into flame while the Metropolis of Achanos goes about its life on the other side of the bronze-sheathed window. Eventually they move to the bedroom, and Aiah takes off her red dress, flirting with Constantine as he watches, using little tricks that she's seen on video, pirouettes while halfundraped, showing him glimpses of her body, giving him little pouting kisses over a bared shoulder, flashing him every provoking look in her repertoire. . . . Eventually she turns down the bed and reclines on pearly satin, forearm beneath her head, wearing only the Trigram necklace, and looks at him. Constantine turns and searches in a drawer, smiles, raises his hand with a copper t-grip.

"Oh no," she says.

He looks at her with a predator smile. "It has been too long, lady, since I had the leisure to truly pleasure you. And since through Aldemar's kindness we have this opportunity, I wished to make it as memorable as possible."

Aiah has experienced this once before, the Fifth of the Nine Levels of Harmonious and Refined Balance, and reckons she would just as soon never experience the Sixth through Ninth. The Fifth is intense enough.

"Well," she says, and laughs, "perhaps just this one time. . . ."

Constantine sits on the bed and touches her cheek with his free hand, plasm-warmth tingling along the tracks of his fingers. Aiah looks up into his glittering eyes, sees the power there, the intensity, the plasm coiled in him, all of it focused on *her* . . . and the warmth spreads, touching her nerves, the sensation making her give a nervous gasp.

He kneels over her, hand and lips browsing along her body. The plasm pours over her skin like a sheet of fire, a burning that makes her cry out; she feels his kisses between her breasts, and seizes his head with both hands, pressing him to her heart. Her body shudders at the plasm onslaught, and she drives her legs up around him, heels digging into his back, demanding pleasure. She feels as if her lungs are filled with molten fire, and fire burns in her throat. The fire fills her, and she feels it scorch her bones, consume her organs, blacken her nerves; she can feel her skin split open, molten metal bursting from her, turning the room to flame.

After it is over she lies with Constantine, her lanky body, curled into a fetal shape, fitting spoonlike within the compass-arc of his larger frame, her head resting on his biceps. "Sometime," she gasps, "I am going to do that to *you*."

"I will look forward to it," he says, and kisses her sweat-moist nape.

His arm circles her from behind, and she takes his hand and places it on her breast, feeling herself filling his palm, wanting the intimate touch of him there.

"I'm glad we don't do that every time," she says.

His chuckle comes in her ear. "A pity. We could do it again now."

A startled laugh bolts from her throat. "Vida's mercy!" she says. "Give me time to catch my breath!"

"All right," he says, amiable enough.

She gives him a look over her shoulder. "Are you serious? You must have just burned ten thousand dinars of plasm."

His look is serious. "What I can give you in the next few hours I will give you."

"Who's paying for it?"

"Aldemar and I will settle between the two of us." He kisses her neck again. "You are worth the expense, lady."

Pleasure tweaks the corners of her mouth. "I hope Aldemar agrees," she says, and pillows her head on his arm again.

His body steals closer to hers, stretching flesh against flesh. "Have you caught your breath yet?" he asks.

She laughs. "No," she says.

"A pity. We have only a few hours left."

"*Hours.*" She laughs again, then looks back at him. "Perhaps we could try the *Fourth* level," she says, "if it's less intense."

"It isn't," Constantine says. "It's just intense in a different way."

"Well," she says, "as long as we're *here* . . ."

AN EMPTY SOUL OFTEN SCORNS WISDOM

A THOUGHT-MESSAGE FROM HIS PERFECTION,
THE PROPHET OF AJAS.

Before they leave the apartment they bathe together, fitting their tall bodies with a certain deliberation into a long, oval tub that would have been ample for one. The scented water floats over Aiah like a milder version of the plasm fire that Constantine has called to aid her pleasure. The stress knots in her neck and shoulders, which had already begun to loosen their grip over the last few hours, are dissolved entirely by soap, scent, and Constantine's powerful hands. Aiah dries her hair, then puts on her little red dress while in the other room Constantine calls Aldemar on the phone.

"She is the only person who knows we're here," he says as he hangs up the headset. "If something happened to her, I would be embarrassed to find a way back to Caraqui."

He gives Aldemar a few minutes, and then slides open the patio door to let her plasm sourceline enter. A cool breeze floats in, along with the sound of traffic. He and Aiah fall into one another's arms, Aiah pressing herself to his massive chest, his ruffled shirt against her cheek. She closes her eyes, wanting to prolong the moment, and keeps them shut as the power snarls around her.

"I brought you back to my apartment," Aldemar says as Aiah blinks at the surroundings. She sits on a sofa with her feet up, elegant as possible considering she is dressed in a bathrobe with her hair wrapped in a kind of turban.

Aiah turns to her. "Thank you," she says. "That was wonderful of you."

"These days I seem to be using my talents mostly to move spies and munitions about," she says. "I'm pleased to use my abilities in the service of love. And I would be happy to do so again." She casts a skeptical look at Constantine. "*If* the two of you ever have another free moment."

Constantine bends to kiss Aldemar's hand, then her cheek. "Thank you," he says.

Aldemar looks at Aiah. "We'll have lunch soon, yes?"

"Of course."

Constantine straightens, sighs. A kind of weight seems to settle onto his shoulders, and a distant crash of artillery rattles the windows. "And now," he says, "we must return to our lives." A kind of resentment enters his face. "Our military, militarized lives."

Aiah's heart sinks. She had not wanted a reminder.

Criminals and war and refugees and horror.

The windows rattle again.

Time to go back to work.

POLAR LEAGUE OFFERS MEDIATION

GOVERNMENT CONSIDERS OFFER

Aiah and Constantine hold hands as they walk down the corridors of the Swan Wing. There is a thoughtful look on Constantine's face.

"Karlo's Brigade . . . ," he says, and his voice trails off.

"Yes?" She is mildly surprised at this choice of subject.

"Do you suppose, being Barkazils, that they have a relationship with Landro's Escaliers on the other side?"

"I don't know."

"It occurs to me that we might make use of it somehow. Landro's Escaliers are in the line, holding the Corridor between Lorkhin Island and Lanbola. And if they could be persuaded to switch sides . . ."

"Constantine," Aiah points out, "they're from the *Timocracy!*"

"Yes, I know. Garshab's mercenaries pride themselves on honoring their contracts, and up till now they've been fighting very well for both sides, against people they know and have trained alongside."

"Exactly."

"But there are ways to slip contracts with a clear conscience—that's what small print is *for*—and perhaps we can find Landro's Escaliers an exit."

"Good luck." Skeptically.

"And to that end, I think it is time you became more prominent."

Alarm brings warmth to Aiah's cheeks. "Minister?" she says.

"You have succeeded very well in avoiding celebrity till now. Perhaps it is time people became aware of you."

"No!" Aiah is appalled.

"Celebrity is a weapon," Constantine says. "You should learn to use it."

"I don't want it."

"The likes of Parq will find it much harder to remove you from the PED once you are well-known and appreciated here in Caraqui."

She looks at him. "Why don't we find someone else to be famous?"

Constantine continues as if he had not heard. "We will make you the most prominent Barkazil in the world."

"I don't want it. And besides, it's ridiculous. Who'd be interested in *me?*"

Constantine smiles. "You underestimate the power of modern media, video in particular." His heavy hand pats her shoulder in a gesture meant to be reassuring. "Don't worry," he says with a white smile. "I will handle it all."

That's just what I'm afraid of, Aiah thinks.

FIFTEEN

~~~~~~~

It is the Caraqui Medal of Merit, and Aiah, prominent in her civilian suit, stands amid a line of uniforms to receive it. Constantine, Minister of War, walks affably down the line, pinning medals on chests and chatting with the soldiers.

Aiah's forehead prickles: the video lights are hot. Constantine's plan to expand her fame is gathering speed.

Earlier Aiah's apartment was invaded by a hairdresser, a manicurist, and a cosmetician. Their job is to make her exciting and glamorous for the video cameras. "The planes of your face aren't going to show up on video," the cosmetician tells her.

"I don't *have* any planes in my face." With irritation.

"You will when I'm done with you," the cosmetician says; and now Aiah is to get a new face painted on at the commencement of every work shift. It's an *interesting* face, Aiah has to admit, if not quite hers—the face of an experienced adventuress, ambitious and powerful, and not a young woman madly trying to keep up with her own schedule. It's the face of someone Aiah wouldn't mind *becoming,* if opportunity ever permits.

She also has to admit that she could probably learn to enjoy the pampering.

More video lights glare at her. Constantine arrives, pins

the medal delicately to her lapel, and bends to kiss her cheek. "Congratulations," he says.

She is receiving the medal for her actions at Fresh Water Bay and Xurcal stations on the day of the countercoup. At her insistence, Davath will postumously be given the same decoration.

Constantine hands her the satin-lined case with Davath's medal. Its gold and enamel gleam in the lights of the video cameras.

"This decoration is postumously awarded to your colleague Davath, who died heroically in a skirmish near Xurcal Station on the day the Provisionals attacked," Constantine says.

Aiah clears her throat and takes the decoration from Constantine's hand. "He died to save me and the others in my party," she says. "I will keep it in trust for his family."

If she can ever find them, that is. Their half-world is in occupied Caraqui.

At least she didn't flub her lines.

The cameras linger on her as Constantine passes to the next soldier. Aiah keeps her back straight and tries to think heroic thoughts.

All that comes to her mind is the hope that her family will never see this.

EXPLOSION IN LANBOLA

STOCKPILED MUNITIONS EXPLODE

LANBOLA CLAIMS SABOTAGE, DENIES MUNITIONS MEANT FOR PROVISIONALS

The Crystal Dome, joyless, deep in its armored shaft. Second shift. Constantine reports to the full cabinet. The dolphin Aranax is conspicuous on his couch, next to Randay, the hapless new Minister of Public Security, who is trying to build a new police force from the defeated, demoralized remnants of the old.

Aiah is not here to speak herself, a fact for which she is grateful. Rohdcr will be making a presentation, and Aiah, as his superior, is here to support him. With luck she won't have to talk at all.

Constantine's summary is almost entirely devoted to the war situation: he describes new mercenary units recruited, the amount paid for each, the number of Caraqui recruits sent to the Timocracy for training—for they are trying to rebuild the Caraqui army, cheaper than mercenaries in the long run—and gives an estimate of enemy strength.

The figures, taken together, are staggering. When the Keremaths ruled Caraqui, they did so with a large, inefficient police force, a small but vicious secret police, and an army of under two divisions. Now, just to hold its ground, the new government controls dozens of divisions assembled into corps, and corps gathered into armies, and even the armies are joined to make two "grand armies," each holding different parts of the front.

The original Keremath army would be lost in all of this.

Aiah finds the numbers fantastic. The finances are beyond imagining—so many tens of millions here, so many billions there. But apparently there is wealth to be found, because no one, not even the banker-president Faltheg, seems to think the sums incredible.

Constantine, in midspeech, raises his eyes to Sorya across the table. "My colleague Sorya has sent reports to the effect that the enemy has ceased to recruit new forces, even though their present strength is not sufficient to win the war for them. This may indicate that their financial benefactors have reached their limits. No doubt her report to us will go into greater detail on this matter."

Sorya nods gravely. "Yes, Minister."

Constantine looks over his shoulder at Aiah and Rohder, then turns back to the triumvirate. "I would like Mr. Rohder, who works for the Plasm Enforcement Division as head of the Technical Resources Department, to make a presentation concerning his new techniques for plasm generation."

Rohder stubs out his cigaret with a doleful glance of blue-eyed longing at the ashtray, then stands to make his presentation. Like Constantine's, it is brief and to the point: the altered positions of so many buildings, the massing so many gross tons, so much plasm generated in excess of expectations, worth so many dinars at current rates. The current rates for plasm are high—the war has almost tripled them—and Rohder's profits are much more impressive than they would be in peacetime.

Hilthi, scribbling with his gold pen, raises a hand and waits to be recognized—the lifelong habits of the journalist are hard to break, even though he's now one of those in charge of the meeting. "I'm afraid I'm not familiar with your technical terms," he says. "Could you define these 'fractionate intervals,' these 'resonances'?"

Rohder—casting another longing glance at the ashtray—answers by analogy: the fractionate interval is like a radius, only smaller; the resonance effect is the result of mass placed at fractionate distances and multiples of fractionate distances, the result of which is a modest but definite increase in plasm generation, on the order of 10 percent.

Hilthi looks surprised. "I don't believe I've heard of this technique," he says.

Constantine explains how Rohder's theory is new, but has been thoroughly tested and found sound. Hilthi's eyes widen. "This is revolutionary!" he says. "We can increase plasm generation by how much?"

"Theory suggests as high as eighteen percent," Rohder says, "but we have only rarely achieved twelve."

"Why aren't these techniques known?" Hilthi asks.

Constantine gives a catlike smile. "The history of Mr. Rohder's theory is very complicated—suffice it to say that human society is constructed so as to resist new ideas, and I resisted it myself"—he turns and bows toward Aiah—"until Miss Aiah insisted I look at the matter more closely."

Aiah feels blood rise to her cheeks, but she returns the nod with a professional smile. Constantine turns back to Hilthi and continues.

"May I point out that this increase in plasm is just going into the general plasm supply? I would like to establish a special fund for it—a kind of bank account for the extra plasm Mr. Rohder's techniques create—to assure that for the present the plasm is used for the war effort, and afterward

for tasks of vital national interest, particularly rebuilding."
He looks at the triumvirate, attempting with hooded eyes
and masklike countenance to disguise his particular interest
in this issue. "Shall we call it the Strategic Plasm Reserve?
Shall I put it in the form of a motion?"

The motion passes, and Constantine sips at a glass of
water to hide a smile of triumph. It has always been his concern that this new source of plasm would just be frittered
away, as politicians so often manage to do with almost any
public resource. It has always been his greater object to
establish a huge fund of plasm under his direct control, to
use it for purposes of transformation far beyond that which
the triumvirate would ever think likely, or even desirable.

The war, Aiah thinks, is transforming things in profound
ways. Before the emergency, the Strategic Plasm Reserve
would have been the subject of prolonged debate. Now it is
passed without comment.

Other ministers make presentations. Sorya gives an intelligence briefing concerning the Provisionals' sources of
finance. President Faltheg, who in addition to being triumvir
is still Minister for Economic Development, dons his spectacles to report on changes in the tax code made necessary by
the war—the simplifying, the closing of loopholes and exemp-
tions—and the amounts these measures are expected to raise.

"How long can the war go on?" Hilthi asks.

Faltheg removes his spectacles so that he can better view
his colleagues. "At current spending rates, for at least three
or four years before we run into trouble. Caraqui's economy
is not a complex or sophisticated one—there is no single
industry that is vital, no particular crucial technology.
Despite bruising, despite a fifth of our metropolis either
under occupation or uninhabitable, our economic infrastructure is still intact."

"I have found," Constantine adds, "that war economies
are remarkably resilient, all things considered."

The others—excepting Sorya—look thoughtful, uncertain
whether to consider this good news or not.

The report by the unfortunate Randay, new head of the
police, is little but a sad litany of endless trouble; the others,
understanding, look at him with sympathy.

Hilthi frowns at his notes and without thought puts his gold pen behind one ear. "This is of particular concern," he says. "We desperately need qualified law enforcement in Caraqui. I agreed reluctantly to the proscription lists only on the understanding that they were accurate and contained the names only of hardened criminals, and now I receive reports that this was not the case, that a percentage of those named had no criminal records whatever.

"The Dalavan Militia are a constant presence in our streets, and their reputation is deteriorating—every day I receive protests concerning their brutality, the arbitrary nature of their actions, reports of the Militia extorting funds from businesses, or walking into stores and helping themselves to expensive presents, acting like common gangsters. . . ."

Parq strokes his silky beard and speaks in his deep, reassuring voice. "Teething pains," he says. "Our priests are making every effort to weed out the bad elements, and we are growing more professional by the day."

"The Militia was never meant to be more than a temporary expedient," says Hilthi. "But now it seems as if it will continue its activities indefinitely."

"We have heard the Minister of Public Safety," Parq says. "Our police are in chaos. Imported military police are expensive. Yet it is our duty to keep order. Who can do it but the Militia?"

Hilthi's eyes look down the table for support and alight on Aiah. Panic throbs in her heart at his question. "Miss Aiah," he says, "can't your PED do something in this situation? You have a remarkable record of success."

Aiah bites down on her alarm. *I already have enough impossible jobs,* she thinks. "We were created to handle plasm thefts only," she says, "and that's what we're set up to do."

"But we are in a position to alter your mission," Hilthi says.

"We can't police the entire metropolis," Aiah says. "We're not big enough. We'd have to start from scratch—we'd be in a worse position than Mr. Randay."

"Besides," Constantine adds, "there is the expense. The Dalavan Militia are all volunteers, and serve at no cost to the state. Were we to add a force the size of the Militia to the public payroll in *addition* to the large and expensive force of mercenary soldiers for which the Treasury is now responsible . . ."

"Impossible," says Faltheg the banker. "Besides, the police already *have* a budget."

"I concur," said Constantine.

Hilthi sighs, throws up his hands. "I want these abuses to cease," he says.

Aiah, relief flooding her at this escape, finds herself looking at Constantine, whose head is turned toward the triumvirs at the head of the table. There is a smile of cold satisfaction on Constantine's face, and Aiah wonders why it should be there, what there has been in this matter of the Militia that has pleased him.

She doesn't get a chance to ask, and by the time the meeting is over, she has forgotten to.

VOTE LIBERAL COALITION—

FOR DEMOCRACY AND FREEDOM!

After the meeting Aiah takes a bite of lunch, then returns to her office—and there, as she turns into her receptionist's office, is the feeling again: a lift of the heart, a surge of warmth through the soul. Another visitor from home waits in Aiah's reception area, a blaze of scarlet and gold among soberly dressed job-seekers. Aiah drops her briefcase and folds the short, sturdy woman in her arms.

"How are you?" she says. "How is everyone?"

Khorsa busses her on both cheeks. "Very well. Esmon and I are going to be married next month." Esmon is one of Aiah's many cousins.

"Congratulations! I know you'll be happy."

Aiah looks at the hopefuls waiting for their interviews, all of whom are trying not to look curious, a difficult act because they've probably never seen a Barkazil witch before. Khorsa's long dress is alive with color, and she wears a red turban decorated with gemstones set among geomantic foci.

The hopefuls, Aiah thinks, will just have to wait a little longer for their interviews, and she tells her receptionist to hold all her appointments. Then she fetches her briefcase and shows Khorsa into her office.

"You're the second Barkazil face I've seen this week," Aiah says as she drops into her office chair.

"Well," Khorsa says, a dubious look in her eye, "I may not be the last."

"Are more of the family coming to look for work? I need people with specific skills, you know, and I don't think many of the family would qualify."

"More than that," Khorsa says. "I'm afraid, well, it's a religious thing."

"Oh?"

Khorsa should know religion if anyone does: she and her sister run the Wisdom Fortune Temple back in Aiah's old neighborhood of Old Shorings. The temple is a place where people come for small magics in hopes of healing the sadness and misfortunes that come with being human, and Barkazil, and Jaspeeri, and living in a place like Old Shorings. Khorsa deals with plasm; her sister Dhival goes into trances and talks to spirits.

Aiah had helped them out once, when Esmon was beaten by Operation thugs because Khorsa wouldn't buy their bootleg plasm. Aiah had used twice-stolen plasm to deal with the situation—stolen once from the Jaspeeri authorities, and then again from Constantine—and she'd been terrified every instant.

"What sort of religious thing?" Aiah asks. "Would you like some coffee?"

"No thanks. Do you remember Charduq the Hermit?"

"Charduq? Of course."

Charduq, the fixture of Aiah's girlhood, still—last she knew—on his fluted pillar at the Barkazi Savings Institute. She had waved at him, she remembers, as she fled the city. He was one of the last sights of home.

"I suppose I should start by saying that you've become sort of famous back in Old Shorings," Khorsa begins.

Aiah is startled. "How?"

"Lots of people know what happened. The police

interviewed anyone who had anything to do with you, and you have a large family, and . . . well, they talked."

Alarms clatter through Aiah's mind. "What did they *say?*" she asks carefully.

"Well, nobody really knows anything," Khorsa says, "so they just make things up."

"That's comforting!" The alarm is getting louder.

"But they know you had access to illicit plasm. They know you used plasm to help the temple out when the Operation was after us, and they know you were involved with Constantine's activities. They know the police were interviewing a lot of people about you, and they know that you're here in Caraqui now, in what seems to be a pretty influential position." She gestures with her hands, taking in the Aerial Palace, the Owl Wing, the view through Aiah's windows of the city below, the plasm tap visible on the wall, available whenever Aiah feels the need. . . .

"So they figure you ran the most brilliant chonah of the century," Khorsa says. "Stole a whole well of plasm from the Authority while you were working there, gave it to Constantine's revolution, got yourself rewarded with a place here."

"It wasn't that simple," Aiah says. And it presupposes that Aiah knew all along what she was doing, which she didn't—in her memories of that period she is far from purposeful, but is filled instead with anxiety, indecision, adrenaline, and terror.

"I'm sure it wasn't," Khorsa says. "But it's all meat to the Cunning People, you know that. It's *exactly* the sort of story we all want to hear, how one of *us* fooled the cops, fooled the Authority, fooled the Operation, fooled *everybody,* and got away with it and lived happily ever after. And of course the story of how you fought the Operation on our behalf got all exaggerated, with scores of Operation men lying dead in the street, and they're saying you won the revolution single-handed and that you're Constantine's lover . . ."

Khorsa's brown eyes absorb Aiah's change of expression in this last remark, and she nods, half to herself, and says, "Well, perhaps not *every* story is an exaggeration."

Aiah feels a flush prickling her cheeks. "So I'm a hero in Old Shorings. What's it got to do with Charduq?"

"Quite simply, he's saying that you're the deliverer. That you're an incarnate immortal, or the immortals sent you, and your purpose is to liberate the Barkazil people, and give us our metropolis and our power back. . . ."

"Great Senko!" Aiah sags stunned in her chair.

"And he's saying it to *everybody*," Khorsa says. "Most won't believe him, or won't pay attention, but there are those who will listen. You're going to be seeing a lot of Barkazils in the next weeks."

"Alfeg?" Aiah wonders. "Could Alfeg be one of the people who paid attention to what Charduq was saying?"

"Old Chavan's son?" Khorsa thinks for a moment. "It's a devout family. Chavan is a big supporter of the Kholos Temple and the old Holy Leaguers—wish I had him at *my* services."

"But a rich family like that—even if they are devout, one of them wouldn't listen to some smelly old street sage, would he?"

Khorsa hesitates. "I don't know enough about Alfeg to be able to say. But in my experience, a person will listen to anybody, provided he has the message one wants to hear."

Aiah stares for an endless moment at the wall above Khorsa's head, and then the frustration in her heart boils over. "What am I to *do* with these people?" she demands. "Even with the expansions my department has less than a thousand people. Most of the jobs require specific skills. Any Barkazils throwing up their lives to come to Caraqui are likely to be the ones with nothing to lose. . . . They're just going to end up on the dole here, and the dole in Caraqui is far worse than the dole in Jaspeer."

"Not everyone will be without skills," Khorsa says. "Alfeg isn't." Her calm eyes hold steady on Aiah. "Neither am I," she adds.

Aiah looks at her. "You're here to apply for a job?"

"Yes."

"You have it if you want it. But what about the Wisdom Fortune Temple?"

"We have enough trained assistants to take my place, at least for a while."

Despair wails in Aiah's nerves. "You don't believe

Charduq, too, do you? I can assure you that I'm not an immortal."

Khorsa considers this. "I don't know if it's necessary that you *know*," she says.

Aiah turns away. "I don't like this game," she says.

"The Cunning People need *something*," Khorsa says. "The heart went out of us when the Metropolis of Barkazi was destroyed. Even though that happened three generations ago, we still live like *refugees*. You're a hero to our people— you can change things."

"It's a delusion," Aiah says. "And when nothing comes of it, everyone's going to be hurt."

Khorsa looks at her fixedly. "Is what you—you and Constantine—is what you're trying to accomplish in Caraqui delusional?"

"I hope not." Aiah again turns away from the intent glimmer of expectation in Khorsa's eyes. "If Caraqui fails, however, it won't be *my* fault. But if every hope the Cunning People hold for *me* turns to ashes, whose fault will it be? Who will they blame?"

"Different questions," Khorsa says, "with different answers."

Aiah tastes bitterness on her tongue. "I somehow doubt they will hold Charduq responsible."

Khorsa's voice is soft. "They are coming. I cannot say how many. But they are coming, whether you want them or not."

"Go back to Jaspeer. Tell Charduq to shut up."

"He won't."

Aiah waves a hand. "Then tell him the time isn't ripe! Tell him to wait!" She represses a snarl. "Damn it, if I'm an immortal, he ought to do what I tell him!"

A hint of a smile glimmers across Khorsa's face. "I can tell him that, I think."

She is half the world away from her large and troublesome family, Aiah thinks, and now they pursue her, larger and more troublesome than she ever imagined they could be.

She notices a new folder on her desk, and knows it contains the results of the security scans performed in the prebreak. She grabs the folder, opens it, pages savagely through it until she comes to Alfeg's file.

Clean, she discovers; no police spy, no contacts with the

government of Jaspeer. No one's agent . . . save maybe, in some sense, Charduq's.

Right, Aiah thinks. *You're a rich boy—it's time to spend some of Daddy's money.*

NEW CITY NOW

"You're hired," Aiah says. "Congratulations."

Alfeg looks at her with a questioning expression, eyebrows lifted. "You sound as if you resent the fact you're hiring me," he says.

"There are some services I wish you to perform," Aiah continues, "in addition to those covered by the job."

A frown crosses Alfeg's bemused face. "I'm sorry? There are conditions to my getting the job?"

Aiah places her palms firmly atop Alfeg's file on her desk. "Not officially," she says.

"Ah." He blinks at her for a moment, touches his chin-lace in a self-conscious way, then nods. "What do you wish me to do?"

"Do you know Charduq the Hermit?"

The knowing smile dances across Alfeg's face, a smile that suggests he and Aiah share a secret.

"Yes," he says. "I'm familiar with him."

"He's a lunatic," Aiah says, and watches Alfeg's self-satisfied little smile twitch away. "He's telling stories about me that aren't true, and he's trying to persuade Barkazils to give up their lives and come to Caraqui."

"Ah—he's—," Alfeg stumbles. Aiah holds out a hand.

"Let me finish, please," Aiah says. "Since it seems I can't stop him from talking, and since it would appear that some Barkazils, at least, are coming—and mostly those who have little to lose, I suspect—I want you to establish an organization for their reception. Help find them work, a place to live, that sort of thing."

Alfeg takes a moment to process this. "Will I be receiving any funds for this project?" he asks.

"No," Aiah says. "None but what you can raise yourself."

"I—" He blinks.

"And you'll have to do it in your spare time," Aiah says, "because you'll be starting here right away, and we're all working shifts-and-a-half."

Alfeg clears his throat. "Is this some kind of test?" he asks.
"No."

He stares at Aiah, searching her expression for a clue which Aiah refuses to give. Then, after a long silence, he gives an uncomfortable tug to his collar and turns away. "I'll do it," he says.

"Thank you." Briskly. She hands him a paper. "Your office will be Room 3224, which you'll share with one or two others. You'll be in Ethemark's division—report to him tomorrow at 08:00, start of work shift, for orientation and assignment. Your badge will be waiting at the reception area, northwest gate."

"Yes. Ah." He licks his lips, stands. Aiah rises from behind her desk and shakes his hand.

"And if I hear from any indigent Barkazils," Aiah says, "I'll refer them to you."

His head gives a little jerk.

"Yes," he murmurs, "of course."

WATCH THE LYNXOID BROTHERS . . .

AS THEY FACE THEIR GREATEST MENACE . . .

TYROS THE TERRIBLE

It's an arrest, one like many others. The suspect is a midlevel plasm seller, probably not a Handman but one of their cousins, whose plasm tap is in a secret room in the back of his apartment. He has been having a party for several days, looks like: there are empty bottles and used glasses everywhere, and the acrid tang of cigar smoke fills every room. There are two girls here, obvious professionals despite their youth, and no sign of the plasm seller's wife and children.

Aiah, playing plasm angel, hovers invisibly in the room, along with a pair of her colleagues. They seem redundant: there is no sign of traps or resistance, and the suspect is so drunk he can barely walk.

The military cops cuff his hands behind his back and prop him up while they pat him down. He's wearing only underwear, and looks terrible: pale, unshaven, with deep circles beneath his eyes and patches of sweat on his undershirt, as if forty-eight hours of hangover had caught up with him all at once.

The girls stand naked in the corner, under guard. One modestly crosses her arms over her breasts, the other merely lets a cigaret hang from her lips, drinks from her little bottle of whisky, and watches the soldiers with contempt. They are both licensed prostitutes, each with her official yellow card, and though Aiah suspects at least one card misstates an age, suspicion is not quite enough given the department's wartime urgency, and the two will be released as soon as the apartment is properly secure.

One of the military cops comes out of the bedroom carrying a pair of the suspect's trousers. He and his colleagues try to maneuver the drunken suspect into them, a little comical dance . . . and then the suspect's head explodes.

Aiah stares in shock. The police stagger back, swabbing blood and brains off their faceplates. Red spatters the breasts of the whisky-drinking whore. The suspect drops like a rag doll, leaving a wide streak of blood on the wallpaper behind, and then a cold voice whispers across Aiah's thoughts.

—*You interfere overmuch with my pleasures, lady.*

Ice shivers Aiah's bones. Her teeth chatter. But Taikoen does not speak again—he is gone—and Aiah slowly breathes out, summons her scattered thoughts, and makes visible her anima in the cousin's apartment. She knows what she must do.

"Did anyone see what happened?" she says, and begins the official investigation that she hopes will never point in the right direction.

Afterward, Aiah's had enough.

She takes off, her anima aimed straight up, rising fast as a bullet away from all this, from death and squalor and endless grinding duty. The city fades, a flat plain of brown and gray and green spread like a lily pad over its level sea. Get enough height, she thinks, and you'd never see the war. She tunes her senses to the air, feels its cool, burning touch as if it were her physical body climbing like a rocket, as if she were feeling the burning wind on her cheeks. She penetrates a layer of scattered white cloud and watches it fall away beneath her, become part of the increasingly abstract landscape below, a new bright element added to its jigsaw.

The Shield alone stands above her, barring her ascent—luminescent source of light and life for the world; impenetrable, energy-devouring barrier to the tens of billions crowded on the curved surface below—and as she gazes up at it, a cold anger settles into her. *This* is what has created her world, this barrier put by the Ascended in the path of humanity, allegedly as a punishment for sins that have only grown more obscure in the ages since. It is carefully sited, this Shield: a little higher, Aiah's teachers told her in school, and objects could be put into an elliptical path that would circle the globe without falling—more evidence, if any were needed, that the Ascended Ones didn't want anything or anyone sharing their realm.

The Shield's pearly luminescence brightens, grows hot, becomes blazing white. Its power roars in Aiah's transphysical ears, and she knows it for an enemy. Matter that touches the Shield is annihilated, transformed into bursts of X rays. Plasm, the most powerful terrestrial force, vanishes as if it never were, anima-probes dissolving on contact, giving no information to the mages below and leaving them with nothing but bills for the plasm wasted. Nothing can touch the Shield and survive.

The sensation of wind is long gone—atmosphere is thin up here. Anger drives Aiah ever upward. *Kill me, then,* Aiah thinks at the Shield. *Annihilate me and prove what a bastard you are.*

The blazing whiteness of the Shield consumes her senses. She can feel its heat, its enmity. She knows it is near, and prepares for the touch of annihilation. . . .

And then she is through it to someplace else, a place both

of darkness and blazing light. To her astonishment she sees the Shield curving away beneath her, a perfect white sphere, its snarling energies intact.

Her staggered senses perceive mostly blackness—an emptiness so vast, so infinite, that she finds her own reactions, her very being, contrasted into insignificance. And there are *structures,* spidery things of silvery metal, each flying in the absolute silence of the void, rolling up toward the Pole. . . . Without scale she can't tell how large they are, but she suspects they are *huge,* each capable of containing a metropolis, despite their appearance of fragility. . . . *One,* she counts, *two,* three, four, six, ten; *many.*

A spherical incandescence burns in the sky, white and angry as the Shield, a perfect sphere of raging light. It fixes the silvery surfaces of the flying structures in its glare, limning their surfaces with merciless precision, and it reflects as well off another spherical body, a green little marble with wisps of white cloud and strange, unnaturally brilliant splashes of blue. Part of it, a black unlit crescent, is in shadow.

One, Aiah thinks in staggered wonder, is the long-lost Sun, and the other the Moon.

And then another dimension infuses Aiah's perceptions, as if a transparent sheet had been laid over the void, a sheet painted with another layer of actuality. The Sun, she sees, is also a *person,* a man who dances within the sphere of eternal flame. He wears a full sleek beard with the tip curled up, and a red conical hat with its peak pointed forward; there is a glowing sphere in one hand, and a silver rod in the other. He moves, stepping precisely but without hurry, an enigmatic smile on his lips, through a dance with no beginning and no end.

There is another dancer, Aiah sees, who is the Moon, a woman with gray skin—not mere pallor, but actually *gray,* gray as slate. Her black hair falls free in ringlets, and she wears a red flounced skirt and jeweled toe-rings on her bare feet. She, too, is dancing; Aiah suspects it is the same dance as the man in the Sun, the man who *is* the Sun—but if so, her long dark eyes never seek those of the dancing man, though her lips bear the same equivocal smile.

Aiah's perceptions seem to shift again, and all the structures are gone, and with them the brilliant spheres, and even the Shield with the world below it; Aiah sees only dancers, some of them not even remotely human, stepping across the sky in an unhurried progression, a dance to the rhythm of eternity, to a music that has lasted for an age. . . .

And then there is a snap, a sizzle, a flare in Aiah's mind that fills her vision with molten silver and her ears with white noise; and she finds herself, breathless, in her chair in the op center, the t-grip in her hand, and looks down at the controls that show her broadcast horn still pulsing power, firing plasm straight at the Shield, where, presumably, it is being consumed.

She switches it off.

The Shield had briefly opened, she thinks, a tiny hole, and by chance she had flown through it, giving her a glimpse of what lies beyond; and then it had cruelly shut behind her, snapping off her plasm tether, returning her to her own world, to the war that is Caraqui.

SIXTEEN

∿∿∿∿∿∿

The Adrenaline Monster rips Aiah from sleep—she sits up in bed, sucks in air, every sense straining for sign of danger. Her thoughts automatically perform a checklist: no explosions, no shellfire, no alarms.

No danger. The Adrenaline Monster is just keeping in practice.

She gasps for breath, her heart a trip-hammer beating against her ribs. A face with an ambiguous smile floats briefly before her eyes, a remnant of her dream, the Man who is the Sun.

She falls to the mattress, takes the pillow, crushes it to her chest. She tries to calm herself, to recapture the dream, her journey beyond the Shield, the Sun's self-contemplative smile.

What is she to do? she thinks. Who can she tell?

Come to anyone babbling about the Ascended, she thinks, and she'll get locked up. Or even worse, *taken seriously* . . .

Chosen. Charduq the Hermit insists that she is the redeemer of Barkazi, and even though he's obviously been on his pillar far too long, there are people desperate enough to believe him.

And now she has apparently made the only visit beyond the Shield in millennia. And the terror of it is not what she saw there, but the thought that perhaps she was *meant* to see it. That the Ascended . . . or Someone . . . wanted her there, and that she has been chosen among all humanity to do . . . *something*.

And that doesn't make sense, because she doesn't know what she is intended to do, if anything. Any prophet she's ever heard of *knew* what his visions meant—how to interpret them and how to act on what he knew. Aiah knows nothing: she saw things and people in the sky, and that's all. If this is meant to have something to do with Barkazi, the connection eludes her.

But even if she doesn't understand it, still the experience is *hers*. She doesn't dare permit others to interpret it. Charduq would happily conclude that the gods, angels, and immortals all desire that she go forthwith and liberate Barkazi; and Constantine—well, Constantine would put it on video to subvert Landro's Escaliers, or something.

So she doesn't dare tell anyone. It must remain her secret until she can work out both what it means, and what it means for *her*.

A detonation slaps her awake. She was unaware that she'd even closed her eyes, that she'd lulled the Adrenaline Monster into letting her drift toward sleep, but now she's awake again, counting the explosions as shellfire rains down somewhere close.

Four, five, six. She wipes sweat from the hollow of her throat.

Another series of shells begins to land, and she realizes she will get no more sleep this shift.

She rises from the bed, runs her fingers through her hair.

It is another day, and it begins early.

KEREHORN SPEAKS TO PROVISIONAL CONGRESS

RECALLS "ERA OF STABILITY"

"THIEVES AND GANGSTERS," RETORTS TRIUMVIR HILTHI

The report on the dead cousin lies before Aiah and Ethemark in the meeting room. The mercenary captain who led the raid is there, and so is Kelban, who'd served on the commission when they had last had a catastrophe of this kind.

"I was there myself," Aiah says, "with an anima configured to be sensitive to plasm. I saw nothing. No obvious attack."

—You interfere overmuch with my pleasures, lady. Hearing that rumbling in your bones, a terrifying chill voice that whispers in your head, that is not *seeing*.

"It was Exploding Head Disease," Kelban mutters. "It's like the Party Sickness. It's going around."

He has been most thorough in his investigation. The mages involved in this case were different from those of the prior case, so there was no single secret assassin working within the PED. Each of the mages involved was interviewed, and background checks performed to make certain none was involved with the dead gangster or could have any reason to want him dead.

"Do we give everyone involved plasm scans?" Kelban says. "I'd hate to—there are potential dangers involved—but if we want to clear our own people of any suspicion, it's the only way to do it."

Ethemark and Aiah look at each other. She reads assent in him, considers the matter, finally shakes her head.

"No," she says. "I have to trust our people. It was a mage from the Hand who outwitted us, some enemy of the suspect perhaps, or possibly some elaborate form of suicide."

"Remember the time-bomb theory I mentioned before?" Ethemark says. "That somehow they managed to place in themselves a plasm device designed to kill if they are ever apprehended? Perhaps we should take it more seriously."

"Perhaps we should." Aiah is content enough that they should chase up this wrong alley.

"One of the witnesses had another idea," the mercenary lieutenant offers. "I didn't put it in the report because, well, it was just too wild."

A warning tone sounds along Aiah's spine. But Kelban turns to the lieutenant and says, "Which witness?"

"One of the whores. The older one. She said that she'd met the suspect before, when he was using another body, and that she'd probably meet him again."

Kelban gives an incredulous laugh. "He jumps around from body to body? Had she just seen *Bride of the Slaver Mage* or something?"

The lieutenant gives an embarrassed smile. "Maybe. But she said that she'd met him twice before, in different, uh, incarnations. All gangsters. He called her agency, I guess. Once he took her to Gunalaht for a weekend. She said that his personality was, ah, repellent in a very distinctive way, so that she recognized him from one incarnation to the next, but that he paid very well and always provided plenty of liquor and food. And she also said she'd heard that at least one of his former incarnations had died, of that Party Sickness we keep hearing about."

"The girl probably has so many repellent customers they all just seem alike," Aiah says.

Kelban grins. "She thinks he's a ghost?"

The lieutenant shrugs. "Something unnatural, anyway. Something that can jump from one body to another and kill it when he's done. An ice man, maybe. Or even a Slaver Mage."

There is a moment's silence. Slaver Mages are a serious matter.

And the idea of an ice man, or hanged man, is not one Aiah wants anyone ever to mention again.

Aiah closes the file before her. "I don't believe in ice men," she says. "I'm not sure if I believe in modern Slaver Mages, either, but if there's a Slaver working among the gangsters, it's *their* problem. I propose to accept the report as written unless we have some more *real* evidence before us."

There is silence.

The report is accepted, and goes into the files. Aiah thanks Kelban on behalf of the department, then adjourns the meeting.

She goes to her office and sags into her chair.

Perhaps, she thinks, she should find some way of telling Taikoen that he should vary his women a little more.

PARQ ENDORSES PLATFORM OF
SPIRITUAL RENEWAL PARTY

The Barkazil troops, flown with their equipment from Sayven into neutral Barchab, come across the border into Caraqui in their own armored vehicles, the column protected by a swarm of telepresent military mages alert for any sign of trouble. The bivouac is already prepared, a parking garage appropriated by the government, concrete walls and floors now covered with bronze mesh to keep out enemy mages. No incidents occur—perhaps security measures have worked for a change.

Aiah is sent as official government greeter, and she takes Khorsa and Alfeg, the only two Barkazils she knows of within three thousand radii. She wears her medal pinned to her lapel, in hopes it might establish another degree of commonship. The War Ministry provides a full set of commissary specialists with a buffet meal for an entire brigade, and also a camera and soundman to record the event for posterity. Aiah also brings an amplifier, some speakers, and a platform to speak from, so when the first armored car rolls into the empty concrete parking bay, it is to the familiar sound of Arno's "Barkazi Monday."

Aiah has never been much of an Arno fan, but he's the entertainer all Barkazils recognize—even in the oddly distorted version caused by the government music player's ill-tuned tweaking of the celluloid etching belt—and so Aiah stands between the speakers, waving and smiling as the vehicles roar past and the soldiers, most of them sitting casually on the hatches, recognize the music and break into smiles and laughter.

The soldiers are mostly young, with a few older hands among them, and most of them show at least some Barkazil ancestry: the smooth brown skin, the brown eyes, the thick curls, or some diluted variation of these. But the three generations since the Barkazi Wars have left their mark, and there are many signs of the pale, light-eyed Sayvenese mixed with the Barkazil, mostly visible in cast of feature: longer heads, sturdier bodies, lantern jaws.

The armored cars and personnel carriers are not burning hydrogen, but a less dangerous, less explosive, hermetically created hydrocarbon fuel, and the stuff doesn't burn cleanly: the garage fills with fumes and Aiah, half-deafened by the speakers on either side, tries not to shrink from the stench.

Khorsa is wearing her full witch regalia—red dress, starched petticoats, and gem-encrusted geomantic foci gleaming on her turban—and the soldiers recognize the costume, flashing magic finger-signs at her as they roar past. Many of them have good-luck foci worn as charms on caps or helmets, and weapons strapped with cult fetishes are waved benignly in Khorsa's direction. The vehicles each bear a discreet yellow Holy League badge somewhere on the armor. Alfeg's dress is more conservative—he's still wearing his Jaspeeri wardrobe, with its heavy lace—and he smiles and waves with the assurance of a young politician shaking hands at a factory gate.

"I have done as you asked," he says in an aside, voice barely audible over the booming music. "I'm trying to find employment for Barkazils. You may have a pair of mages applying for work later this week."

"Mages?" Aiah raises her eyebrows. "You happened to find a pair of Barkazil mages wandering around Caraqui looking for a job?"

He waves as vehicles roll past. "They're people I went to school with. I happened to know they were looking for opportunities, so I called them and let them know we had vacancies."

"Well." She considers. "It isn't exactly what I asked you to do, but as long as these newcomers are qualified, I could use the hires." And then she smiles. "They can help you find work for others."

Alfeg gives a little wince.

The last of the vehicles enters and the bronze-mesh gate rolls shut behind it. The soldiers gather around the speakers, and Aiah is awed by their sheer numbers. Millions of Barkazils live in Jaspeer, mostly in little ethnic enclaves like Old Shorings where Aiah grew up, but she has never

seen so many of the Cunning People in one place. Karlo's
Brigade has nine thousand soldiers, and although there
isn't room for all of them here, they're crowded shoulder
to shoulder as far as Aiah can see. She finds herself grinning down at them, lifted by the sheer joy of their presence.

Just then the Caraqui music player gives a final wrench to
the celluloid etching belt, and the belt disintegrates, along
with the instrumental on Arno's version of "Happy as a
Metropolitan," the distinctive sound of the three-string
Barkazi fiddle turning into a nerve-shivering screech. The
soldiers give a good-natured laugh as Aiah slaps at the
machine's chrome on-off lever. The sound, echoing from
thousands of throats, threatens to float her from the stage.

She reaches for a microphone and tries to ignore the
gleaming lenses of the camera that whirs at her from below
the platform.

"On behalf of the government and the Barkazil community of Caraqui," she says, "I'd like to welcome you all to our
metropolis." There is a modest cheer and some applause, and
Aiah finds herself grinning—these are *her* people, she thinks,
and there are *thousands* of them, and even though she
doesn't know a single person here, she hasn't realized how
much she's missed them until now.

Her usual terror of speaking in front of an audience has
flown away. She feels at home.

"My name is Aiah," she says, "and I'm director of the
Plasm Enforcement Division of the Ministry of Resources,
which"—she grins—"makes me a plasm cop. These are two
of my mages, Khorsa and Alfeg. We'll do our best to make
sure that your mages have all the plasm they need to keep
you safe and help you do your jobs."

There is a more enthusiastic cheer at this. Keeping their
military mages supplied with plasm is a task dear to the
hearts of the brigade.

Now that the wind wafting through the bronze mesh is
dispersing the engine fumes, Aiah can scent cooking smells
wafting toward them from the buffet. "I mentioned a
moment ago that the Barkazil community welcomes you.
This was easy for me to say, because"—she glances at her

two companions—"we three up to this point seem to constitute the entire Barkazil community of Caraqui." There is a rumble of laughter from her audience, a few wild cheers.

"But *now*," she says, looking out over the huge sea of faces, "I see there are *thousands* of us!"

A roar goes up, a sound loud enough to carry Aiah back to the Shield. She looks out at the surging storm of humanity and feels as if she could spread her arms and fly out over their heads, supported only by their goodwill.

"I'd like you all to know," she continues, "that we'll do what we can to make you feel at home, and to keep you well fed and supplied. If you're not being provided with something you need and you can't get it anywhere else, please have your commanders—your *commanders*—call me or my associates. We might have an idea who to talk to."

Aiah hopes this won't actually happen. Her knowledge of the intricacies of War Ministry bureaucracy is nil.

"I won't keep you from your meal," she finishes. "We welcome you to Caraqui—now go enjoy your dinner!"

She sketches the Sign of Karlo in the air, and there is the biggest cheer of the day. Aiah's heart leaps for the sky. The War Ministry's cameraman lowers his chromocamera and gives her a wink. Most of the soldiers stream off to their meal, and Aiah steps down from her platform to meet their commander, Brigadier Ceison. He is a thin, tall, stooped man with a bushy mustache, and he politely invites Aiah to dine with him as soon as he has his headquarters and staff sufficiently organized. He introduces Aiah to the brigade's mage-major, a burly uniformed woman named Aratha whose short brown curls and light green eyes demonstrate mixed Barkazil-Sayvenese ancestry. She is pure soldier and all business, and she looks dubiously at Khorsa, with her bright colors and folk-magic jewelry.

"I need to get my people on patrol," she says, "so they can help defend our position and familiarize themselves with Caraqui. And for that I need to get some workers up here to give me access to plasm."

"That hasn't happened yet?" Aiah says. "I'll talk to the ministry and find out what happened."

"Thank you. There's usually problems of this nature at the

start, and knowing someone to call in the right ministry is always a bonus."

Well, Aiah thinks, I asked for this.

Duty calls, but Aiah finds herself reluctant to leave, so she wanders through the huge concrete space, talking to the soldiers. She gets asked out about twenty times, and groped twice, in a perfectly friendly, inquiring way; but she slaps the hands aside with a grin and declines all invitations.

"They *are* from the Holy League," Alfeg declares after obligations finally drag them away. "After peace was imposed, the last of the Holy Leaguers withdrew to Sayven with their entire army. They became mercenaries. These are their children or grandchildren."

They are sharing the backseat of the big armored automobile that the ministry has loaned them for this occasion. Aiah peers out at the city through thick plates of bulletproof plastic and sees no sign of war at all, nothing but people heading places on their business.

"The Barkazi Wars ended two generations ago," she says. "And these are still soldiers?"

"Sayven exports a *lot* of soldiers. But it's not the national industry, as it is in the Timocracy, so we don't hear about it as much."

If her grandfather hadn't been captured, Aiah thinks, she might have grown up in Sayven, in a military family. She wonders if her life would have taken her into the army, if she would have found herself a military mage serving alongside Aratha.

"Does the Holy League still matter to them?"

"Oh yes." Blithely. "They're convinced we'll prevail, given time, and that Barkazi will be returned to us—to the Cunning People."

Aiah smiles. Alfeg hadn't been lying when he accused himself of a sentimental attachment to his grandfather's cause.

"Well," she says, "I hope it happens."

And then she catches Khorsa's sidelong look, Khorsa who has come here—possibly—because she thinks Aiah will somehow bring all the exiles home and restore Barkazi, and Aiah feels her jaw tighten.

I do not want you to need me this way! she thinks in sudden fury, but she swallows it, and makes herself concentrate on business—PED business—until the armored car rolls across the gilded bridge to the Palace.

FOOD FACTORY DESTROYED IN LOTUS DISTRICT

GOVERNMENT BLAMES SILVER TERROR

What waits in her office is not calculated to improve her temper: a Dalavan priest, young and burly, wearing the gray robes and soft mushroom hat of his order.

"I am the Excellent Togthan," he says with a gracious bow, and presents Aiah with an envelope embossed with an ornate red wax seal.

"The triumvir and Holy, Parq, has kindly written this letter of introduction."

Togthan's voice, like Parq's, is soft, and his expression gracious. It puts Aiah on her guard at once.

Aiah opens the letter and frowns at it. *This will introduce Togthan, an Excellent of the Red Slipper Order*—Aiah casts a surreptitious glance at Togthan's footwear and discovers he is wearing black wing tips—*who is, by my authority, appointed Advisor to the Plasm Enforcement Division. You are requested to provide him with an office and total access to any information he may require, including complete details on the scope and nature of all relevant PED activities.*

Anger knots Aiah's stomach, but she tries to keep her face immobile as she glances at Togthan over the letter. "Advisor?" she says. "What kind of advisor?"

"Advisor on spiritual matters," Togthan says with another bow, "and of course on political direction. Triumvir Parq wants to see all government departments unified behind the triumvirate."

"I see," Aiah says. She wants to crumple the letter and fling it in Togthan's face, but instead says, "I wish I had known you were coming. I would have had your office ready."

"It was decided at the cabinet meeting just after shift change. Since the PED has become such an important part of government, I am one of the first advisors assigned."

"Yes." She glances around her receptionist's office, looking for a way to escape. "Please take a seat for a few minutes, and I'll try to arrange an office for you. Please have some coffee. There's a meeting after quarterbreak, and I'll introduce you to the department and division heads."

"Thank you, Miss Aiah." Togthan swirls his robes as he sits, a compliant smile on his face.

"What the hell is this?" Aiah demands as soon as she can get Constantine on the telephone. "Who is Togthan? What is Parq's spy doing in my department?"

The unusual lack of emphasis in Constantine's deep voice signals that he is choosing his words carefully. "The triumvirate honored Parq's request for political supervision of all government departments—especially Resources and the War Ministry."

"Those are *your* portfolios! This is aimed at you."

"If the triumvirate is nervous about an outsider heading two departments crucial to the survival of the regime—one who is furthermore the head of a political party that may run in opposition to their own—I cannot entirely blame them. Try to work with Togthan if you can."

"The triumvirate?" Aiah asks. "All three of them? All three of them voted to put Parq's spies into your departments?"

"Hilthi was against it. But Parq can be persuasive, and Faltheg voted with him, after some hesitation."

"What am I going to do with this man?" Aiah cries. "He's going to be creeping around and—"

"You will work with him," Constantine says. There is a steely edge to his voice. "Our government has concluded that he is necessary, and he will be far less of a danger to you if he is *indulged.* The best possible thing is for you to become his greatest friend in all the world."

Aiah snarls silently into the mouthpiece and wishes she could tell some of her military police to chuck Mr. the Excellent Togthan off the roof into a canal.

"Right," she says. "I'll see what I can do."

Constantine's next question is artfully designed to prevent her from thinking of another protest. "Did things go well with Karlo's Brigade?"

Aiah is still mentally enjoying Togthan's arc into the canal, but follows Constantine's shift well enough to answer.

"Oh yes. They seemed happy to see us. Their mage-major was complaining, though, that she hadn't got access to plasm as yet."

"I will make certain appropriate action is taken."

"Thank you."

Aiah presses the disconnect button, then calls her department heads to tell them that the Excellent Togthan will be joining the department, and that they are all to treat him with the utmost consideration.

"It's because your boss sold us out," Ethemark says. Rage in the little man's deep voice keeps throwing his voice into squeaky upper registers. "He spoke in favor of Parq's proposal at today's cabinet meeting."

"Constantine?" Aiah asks. "Is that who you're talking about?"

"Yes. Your damned Constantine. It was bad enough when he supported the Dalavan Militia. But now because of Constantine, Parq's spies will be in every branch of government. . . ."

Aiah struggles with bewilderment, tries to formulate a response. "Are you sure?" she manages. "Who is your informant?"

"Minister Adaveth," Ethemark says. "And Minister Myhorn also. They were both astounded by Constantine's attitude."

"There must," Aiah says, "must be a *reason*. . . ."

"Constantine is allying himself with Parq. He and the Dalavans together can dominate Caraqui—neither of the other two triumvirs has a following. Adaveth and Myhorn are both considering whether or not to resign."

"*No.*" Aiah's response is instant. "There is—" Her mind stammers, and she tries to work out what is happening. "There has to be something else happening here. If Adaveth and Myhorn resigned, it would be giving Parq exactly what he wants."

There is a grudging silence.

"This has to be some kind of stratagem," Aiah says, and hopes she is right. "Give it time."

"I have no choice but to 'give it time.' We of the twisted have been compelled to cultivate patience for many centuries now. 'Giving it time,'" he snarls, "is what we know best."

"Can we meet outside of the office?" Aiah says. "In my apartment, say? We can attempt to work out some strategies to limit Togthan's influence."

"Hm." There is a brief silence, then, "Very well. Let's do that."

Aiah does some rearranging and gives Togthan an office with Alfeg. Put her *own* spy, she thinks, next to Parq's spy. Then she calls Togthan in to see her.

"I apologize for the delay," she says. "The war and our expansion has caused a good deal of disarray."

Togthan seats himself in the offered chair with a graceful swirl of his gray robes. His voice is smooth and unhurried. "I understand," he says, and sips delicately from his cup of coffee.

"Because of the shortage of office space," Aiah says, "I'm afraid you're going to have to share an office with one of our mages." Togthan frowns—the first hint of disapproval he has allowed himself, so Aiah hastens to add, "But he will often be in the Operations Room or otherwise working through telepresence, and I hope he won't be too much of a bother."

"Well . . . ," Togthan says, "I suppose that if it will assist with the war effort, I daresay I can manage the inconvenience."

If I can put up with *you,* Aiah thinks, you can put up with Alfeg.

"I observe," Togthan says, "simply in walking through the corridors on my way here, that there are many of the polluted flesh working in this department."

"I'm sorry?" Aiah says.

Togthan flashes an apologetic smile. "Beg pardon," he says, "I introduced a Dalavan term. I refer of course to those who have been genetically altered."

"Oh. I see." Aiah hesitates, chooses words carefully. "When our department began we were underfunded, and had to hire those who we could. The, ah, altered were often the most available, because they were denied opportunity elsewhere."

Togthan smiles and sips his coffee. "That is no longer the case, surely? Your pay is more attractive now, I have heard, and there are many more looking for work on account of the disruptions caused by the war."

"Our policy has always been to hire the most qualified."

"Miss Aiah, I'm sure no one desires that you hire the incompetent or deficient." Togthan's smile is all reason. "But there is much popular prejudice against the polluted flesh in Caraqui. I know that they are not to blame for their condition—our Dalavan faith is just in that regard—but nevertheless if there were *too many* of the twisted seen in this department, it might bias the people against you. Whereas if the population of your department more accurately reflected the composition of the population of the metropolis, I think you would find in the people a greater reservoir of goodwill toward your efforts."

Aiah recalls Constantine's wish that she become Togthan's best friend, and compels herself to grace her clenched teeth with a smile. "I'll give your wishes my best consideration," she says.

Togthan sips his coffee again, his confiding smile an answer to hers. "I'm gratified that we understand one another," he says.

Oh yes, Aiah thinks, *I understand, all right.*

TRIUMVIR HILTHI DECLINES TO ORGANIZE POLITICAL PARTY

WISHES TO REMAIN ABOVE POLITICS

"WILL ENDORSE IDEAS, NOT CANDIDATES"

The Kestrel Room faces the guns of Lorkhin Island and is closed on that account; and so Aiah's luncheon with Aldemar takes place at Dragonfly, a restaurant on the other side of the Palace, with a view of the distant blue volcanoes of Barchab. Dragonfly is smaller than the Kestrel Room, without its intimate alcoves and private rooms, and without its luxurious wood paneling; but it is a brighter place, its white plaster walls featuring strips of dark glossy polymer. It looks out over Caraqui with multifaceted, insectlike eyes, each reflecting a slightly different Caraqui, a slightly different plane. Along the walls and between the tables are fish tanks filled with scaled, rainbow-colored exotica, few of which Aiah imagines are actually to be found swimming in Caraqui's sea below.

The actress wears a russet-colored rollneck, gray pleated slacks with nubbles and a subdued russet stripe, tasteful gold jewelry, suede boots with high heels. Her skin is flawless—the result more of genetics and lavish care, Aiah suspects, than plasm rejuvenation treatments, though beneath carefully applied cosmetic Aiah can see evidence for the latter, a kind of eerie, ambiguous glow notable more for its absence of character than anything else. Aiah finds herself envying Aldemar her epidermis far more than her celebrity.

Aiah orders fried noodles with prawns, vegetables, and chiles. Aldemar asks for half a grapefruit.

"You eat worse than I do," Aiah says in surprise.

Aldemar's answer is matter-of-fact. "It's my *job*."

"I guess you're paid well enough for it."

A smile tweaks its way onto Aldemar's features. "Yes. Otherwise I'd never eat another damn grapefruit as long as I live."

"What has become of the chromoplay you were working on? The one you abandoned to come here?"

Aldemar blinks. "Ah." A dissatisfied look crosses her face. "Shut down for six weeks, a deadline soon to be extended. They have very cleverly shot every scene that can be managed without me. There are wrangles over money—I expect I shall have to part with some—but it's not a very good chromo anyway, and letting it age in the bottle will not do it harm, and may do some good. And since in the chromo we get as far as staging a revolution, I suppose I can claim that I'm here researching a sequel."

"Why are you making this chromoplay," Aiah asks, "if it isn't very good?"

Aiah is relieved that Aldemar doesn't seem offended by the question. "To begin with," she says quite seriously, "good scripts are rare, and for the most part they go to other people. Those few that I *have* been involved with have all gone wrong somewhere—bad direction, bad editing, actors who didn't understand their roles, or who demanded inane rewrites to make their parts larger or more sympathetic . . . well—" A dismissive shrug. "I have not been lucky that way.

"And while I am waiting for something good to turn up, I must remain bankable—I must remain popular enough for investors to wish to invest in my 'plays. And it may surprise you to learn that the most popular chromoplay, worldwide, is the sort in which people like me fly and fight and war against evil. The genre transcends problems of ethnicity, dialect, metropolitan allegiance—everyone understands them, and everyone buys a ticket."

"Is it what you intended when you chose to be an actress?"

Aldemar blows out her cheeks, looks abstract, a bit melancholy. "Perhaps that is why I've become interested in politics."

"Are you a believer in the New City?"

"I used to be, but I've grown more modest over the years." The actress tilts her head, props her jaw on one hand. "I support those who are straight against those who are corrupt, those with dreams against those who have none. The details—the precise content of those dreams—no longer interest me, provided they are not absolutely vicious. I've heard it claimed that political visionaries have caused more destruction and havoc and death than those leaders with less ambition—true, perhaps; I have seen no statistics—but I wonder about those lesser figures, those managers who say, *I have no ideals, no dreams, all I want to do is make things run a little more efficiently.*" She shrugs. "What reason is that for us to give them anything? *I am mediocre, I have never had an idea to which you could object, give me your trust.* They appeal only to exhaustion. It is an emptiness of soul into which rot is guaranteed to enter. Phah."

Amusement tugs at Aiah's lips. "But what you do is something more than *support,* ne?" she says. "You're teleporting guns and spies and whatnot behind enemy lines. That doesn't seem very much like disinterested idealism to me."

Aldemar shrugs again. "Understand that I look at the world through a kind of aesthete's eyeglass. Certain classes of people are offensive in a purely artistic sense—and that includes the Keremaths. Drooling, savage idiots, barely able to button their trousers unassisted, and running a metropolis! And this Provisional Government—gangsters, military renegadoes, thieves, and the Keremaths again, all propped up by the Foreign Ministry of Lanbola for no other reason than it gives them something to *do,* something to *meddle in.* Great Senko—I would teleport them all to the Moon if I could."

The mention of the Moon sends a memory on a spiral course through Aiah's thoughts, a slate-gray woman a-dance in the sky.

Aldemar continues, unaware of Aiah's distraction. "Constantine deserves a chance to fix this place. If anyone can do it, he can."

"So your loyalty is to Constantine? Not to the government?"

Beneath her black bangs, Aldemar's eyes glimmer as they look into Aiah's. "Miss Aiah, I do not *know* the government." She shifts her gaze, looks moodily out one of the Dragonfly's faceted windows. "Bad policy, perhaps, to support individuals this way—to expect a single person to change the course of a metropolis, a world—but ultimately who else is there? You either trust the person to do it or you don't."

Their luncheon arrives. Aldemar looks at her grapefruit, with its scalloped edges and the sprig of mint laid on top, sitting on fine china rimmed with gold and painted with delicate figures of plum blossoms, and says, "At least it's presented well." She picks up a silver-topped shaker and sprinkles left-handed sugar on the fruit.

"How long have you known Constantine?" Aiah prompts.

The last thing Aiah wants is to talk about herself. Aldemar obliges her.

"Thirty years," she says. "I was in school in Kukash, studying to be a mage with the intention of going into advertising. Constantine was there to get an advanced degree. We were lovers for, oh, two years or so."

Blood surges into Aiah's cheeks, catching her by surprise. Aldemar perceives it and narrows her brows.

"Are you jealous?" she says.

"It depends."

"I see." An amused smile dances across her face, and Aiah notes an echo of Constantine's own amusement there, his own delight in irony. "One may judge the relationship by its outcome," she says. "I became an actress, and Constantine a monk. He abandoned his degree and went to the School of Radritha. I finished my degree but never made use of it, went to Chemra, and began working in video." Her smile turns contemplative. "Constantine is very good at finding the chrysalis within his friends. I had no more notion of being an actress than becoming a mechanic. But he turned me inside out and found an ambition that wouldn't go away." She looks at Aiah once again. "I imagine he has done much the same to you."

"He's certainly doing his best," Aiah says, uncertain whether it is her ambition or Constantine's that she serves. She glances down at her meal and discovers that she has forgotten to taste it; she picks up a fork and wraps a noodle about its prongs, then looks up.

"I have a hard time picturing what Constantine was like when he was young. He was . . . what, thirty when you met?"

"Just under thirty, I think. And I was just under twenty." She smiles at the memory. "He was in headlong flight from his destiny—trying for a degree in the philosophy of plasm, forsooth, before bolting for the monastery and impractical religion." Her bright eyes turn to Aiah again. "Are you still jealous?"

"Probably not," Aiah decides.

"He and I enjoy each other's company now, but we are both very different people than we were. Not that I wouldn't bed him if he asked nicely"—a wry look crosses her face—"but I don't think he's interested in old ladies like me."

"You look younger than I do."

"Kind"—a brisk nod—"but untrue. I am practiced at *seeming,* but by now, inwardly at least, I'm afraid I am become a very constant and unalterable sort of person. In the future I will change slightly, if at all. But Constantine has always been intrigued by transformation—in politics, in plasm, in bed—and your transformation from what you *were* to what you *are* to what you *shall be* . . . well, that is what delights him in you."

This analysis sends tiny cold blades scraping along Aiah's nerves, and she wonders how often Constantine discusses her with Aldemar—or with others.

Amusement dances in the actress's eyes, and breaks Aiah's alarm. "Besides," Aldemar says, "you're an attractive couple. I can't help but want the best for you."

Aiah wants to ask Aldemar about more practical matters, about why Constantine is allying himself with Parq; but at that moment the maitre d' sits a pair of Dalavan priests at the next table, and Aiah applies herself to her noodles.

Damn it.

After luncheon, Aiah steps to the insect-eye windows and gazes out at the city, at the teeming composition, repeated endlessly in faceted glass, of gray and green that has become her life and burden. Above it roils a flat gray cloud, scudding toward the Palace with surprising speed; and with a start Aiah realizes that the cloud is not a cloud at all, but a plasm projection, a fantasy of images, teeth and heads and eyes and vehicles, all vanishing and disappearing too fast for Aiah to follow, though a few of the icons seem to stick in Aiah's retina: Crassus the actor, an old airship of the Parbund class, a spotted dog with its forefeet propped on a child's tricycle . . .

Aiah stares as shock rolls through her. For there, repeated sixfold by the panes of Dragonfly glass, she recognizes an image, a long-eyed profile of a gray-skinned woman, her hair done in ringlets and an equivocal smile on her lips.

The Woman who is the Moon.

The image vanishes, folding into something else; and in a moment, the entire plasm display is gone.

She must visit the Dreaming Sisters, Aiah thinks, and soon.

SEVENTEEN

~~~~~~~~~~

Aiah wants to cringe as she watches herself on video. "On behalf of the government and the Barkazil community of Caraqui," the woman on-screen bellows, "I'd like to welcome you all to our metropolis!"

Senko. Is her voice really that harsh?

Tumultuous cheers follow, far more impressive than the cheers at the actual event. The sound has been dubbed in after the fact.

The chromo is called *The Mystery of Aiah.* In it, a journalist named Stacie—a woman whom Aiah has never met—attempts to solve the mystery of Aiah's character and personality.

"There's no mystery about me!" Aiah protests when she sees the direction the chromoplay is taking.

"There is *now,*" Constantine says, a purposeful light in his eyes.

Aiah sits on a sofa between Constantine and Aldemar, her hands clutching theirs. The two veteran performers are amused as she shrinks away from the journalist's attempts to "solve" her.

The reporter interviews various figures from Aiah's life in Jaspeer, including Charduq the Hermit, still on his pillar, who cheerfully proclaims her the redeemer of the

Barkazi, a claim that Khorsa's sister Dhival, in full sorceress getup, is all too happy to confirm—she has talked, she says, to spirits on the matter, and they confirm Charduq's assessment. Old chromographs from Aiah's school career are displayed, and some of her teachers from the prep school to which she'd won a scholarship are interviewed, teachers willing to testify as to her brilliance. Aiah remembers the praise during her girlhood as being far less fulsome.

"Aiah's family declined to be interviewed," the narrator reports, managing to imply they fear Aiah's disapproval and vengeance. Aiah is relieved beyond words . . . the very thought of her mother babbling away on video is terrifying, and Senko only knows what she would say. But if the family actually had been approached—which Aiah is inclined to doubt, as she has heard nothing from them—they had closed ranks against the outsider.

Aiah had broken Jaspeeri laws, and her family knew it. No indictments had ever been filed, but there was no sense in giving the prosecutors information.

The section on her life in Caraqui is a hash of suggestion and demented fantasy. Aiah can't even take it seriously enough to shrink from the image presented. There are hints of her great influence in the councils of power. "Aiah has single-handedly broken the gangsters' control of the Caraqui economy and their hold on the people," the chromo intones, and follows with jittery camera shots of police actions and of disheveled Handmen being led off to justice. Images of Karlo's Brigade are mixed with suggestions that they are soldiers loyal not to the regime but, personally, to Aiah. There are pictures of Barkazil neighborhoods, which Aiah recognizes from Jaspeer, but they are ingeniously mixed with images from Caraqui to suggest that a large Barkazil community is in place here, and that Aiah is their unquestioned leader. Supposed Barkazil immigrants, allegedly drawn to Caraqui by Aiah's personal magnetism, are shown being welcomed by Caraqui officials.

"She is our commander," Alfeg says. He looks quite natural and comfortable on camera. "She fights for her people, her nation. We are here to serve her." Two of the department's total of four Barkazils, looking far less comfortable than Alfeg, sit in the background and nod stiff agreement.

"Aiah has transformed this metropolis," Khorsa confirms. She has forgone her witch dress and appears in the conservative gray suit of the professional mage and member of the PED, albeit with one of her glittering jeweled foci pinned neatly to her lapel.

"I can't think of another person," she says, "who could have so totally destroyed such a huge, malevolent, and emplaced organization as the Silver Hand."

"I haven't destroyed it," Aiah points out, but Aldemar hushes her.

There is a short diversion from the chromo's relentless pursuit of its subject while the narrator embarks on a brief biography of Great-Uncle Rathmen and points out that his money is financing the current insurrection.

And then Khorsa is back, smiling brightly. "Of *course* Aiah is Constantine's lover," she says.

"*No!*" Aiah cries in horror.

Constantine glances at her sidelong, and a smile touches his lips. "If I can put up with this," he says, "you can."

Aiah watches with increasing dread as the chromo plunges into her relationship with Constantine. That few of the details are correct doesn't make it any less horrifying.

"He was besotted by her the first time he saw her," reports a talking head, alleged to belong to one of Constantine's friends. "She's his secret general—his good luck."

"What is the *point* of this?" Aiah demands.

"It will make you *interesting*," Constantine says. "Few will care about some shadowy figure in the Caraqui government, but revealed as my lover you will become the focus of millions."

Aiah sinks hopelessly into her seat. "I don't suppose there is any point in protesting," she says.

"Well," Aldemar offers, "it's *true*. The gist, anyway. You are lovers, after all. And you *do* chase criminals, and you *are* a Barkazil." She gives a tight-lipped little smile. "It's much more true than most of *my* publicity."

Aiah looks at Constantine. "What does Sorya say about this?"

Constantine's answer is matter-of-fact. "Sorya is the head

of the secret service. She doesn't *want* publicity. Whereas publicity, the more sensational the better, is exactly what is required for *you.*"

The chromoplay drags on to its conclusion, and Aldemar gives a satisfied smile.

"Satisfied with the edit?" she says. "Other than the few rough spots?"

"Very well satisfied, thank you," Constantine says.

"I told you Umarath would get the job done."

Aldemar releases the second spool on the big commercial etching belt, picks up the red plastic belt, then puts it in its battered metal case.

"Who is this reporter?" Aiah asks.

"She's not a reporter, she's an actress," Aldemar says. "Stacie used to be on *Metro Squad*—ever watch that? She phoned in her performance from Chemra."

"So she didn't actually interview any of these people?"

"Oh no. There wasn't time. We had three units shooting picture, and Umarath put the whole thing together in the editing room."

"It's so . . . intrusive," Aiah says. "And horrid. And all the facts are wrong, too."

Constantine cocks an eyebrow at her. "Would you rather it told the truth? You must have broken a hundred laws working for me in Jaspeer."

"That's not what I meant. It's showing me as a celebrity's favorite fuck."

"Oh no." Aldemar shakes her head at this, and her reply is perfectly serious. "We would have been taking that tack if we'd mentioned you were Constantine's lover *first*. But the image we chose for you is that of the secret mastermind operating behind events. The sex is a validation of your status. It's not that you're important because you're Constantine's lover, it's that being Constantine's lover confirms the fact that you're important."

"This is too sophisticated for me." Aiah shakes her head. "Politics is so . . ." She gropes for the right word. "So solipsistic." She looks at Aldemar. "And so is show business. It can create a reality that has nothing to do with anything real."

A touch of sympathy enters Aldemar's tone. "If you do not like the resulting image, you may alter it in time—give an interview, release a statement, commission another documentary, whatever you like." The sympathy fades. "But let the video do its work first. For the moment, communicate with the public only through the press assistant we will provide for you." She smiles. "In time you may find that you like what this does for you. It will open a lot of doors."

"But will I want to walk through them?" Aiah asks. Aldemar only shrugs.

"I think the video will do quite well for us," Constantine says. "It plays right to the mind-set created by the other side's propaganda—which, much to the annoyance of our government, has always maintained that I am the real power in Caraqui, and the triumvirate my puppets. This chromo is aimed straight at a target which I think it is almost certain to hit."

Aiah looks at him darkly. "Landro's Escaliers," she says.

Constantine's expression is satisfied. "Indeed."

SPIRITUAL RENEWAL PARTY

FOR VICTORY, FOR MORALITY,
AND FOR THE HOLY, PARQ

Aiah's computer terminal hums, and grinds, and wafts a scent of ozone; and then its oval screen displays the message SCAN NEGATIVE. INITIATE NEW SCAN?

The Dreaming Sisters are not to be found anywhere in the ministry's plasm records, or anyway not as such—it's not that there's no record of them, but that they probably have some other, more official name used in the files. The Arch-Revered Order of Transcendental Plasm Suckers, or something . . .

Aiah shuts off her terminal, hearing that little disappointed whine of the gears cycling down, and then sets her receptionist, Anstine, to work on it. That, after all, is what he is for.

Half a shift later the file appears on Aiah's desk. Society of the Simple, 100 Cold Canal. A modest name; a forbidding address.

Aiah opens the file, sees the totals, and frowns.

The huge aerial displays that Aiah has seen since her arrival in Caraqui used enough plasm to cost tens of thousands of dinars. Yet the Society's bills are modest, a few hundred dinars each month.

Which leaves open two possibilities: either their building is so big that it generates all the plasm they need . . . or they're stealing the stuff.

She presses the intercom button on her commo array and speaks a moment with Anstine, asking him if he's *sure*. . . . Oh yes, Aiah is assured, the Society of the Simple is every so often the subject of news and video reports—those big aerial displays attract public attention; all Anstine had to do was call up the information on the Interface.

Aiah puts the headset over her ears and makes some more calls. A boat, a pilot, some bodyguards, and an inspection team.

"Tell the camera crew they may not come."

If they're plasm thieves, she'll arrest the lot of them, whether they spend their days talking to the gods or not.

Parq's spy, floating about her department, has not made her charitable toward the idea of religion.

If they're not thieves, then maybe they're something much more interesting.

LORDS OF THE NEW CITY

MORE RELEVANT THAN EVER!

Travel has become less pleasurable in the days since Aiah became famous. Since Constantine wants to keep her constantly in the news, camera crews follow her everywhere, and—as most of her travel consists of walking from her apartment to her job at the start of the day, and then taking the reverse path ten or twelve or sixteen hours later—the ministry, through her press spokesman, exerts itself to find newsworthy things for her to *do*.

When she accepted Brigadier Ceison's polite invitation to dine with him and his staff, the video cameras followed along, and the next day stories appeared in all the media concerning Aiah's important meeting with Barkazil military leaders. When Alfeg's embryonic relief organization turned up a few indigent Barkazils in neighboring districts and persuaded them to move to Caraqui in search of employment, Aiah appeared on video handing them their dole cards. When Khorsa's sister Dhival, imported for the occasion from the Wisdom Fortune Temple in Jaspeer, conducted for any interested members of Karlo's Brigade "a traditional Barkazil religious service"—there of course existing in reality no such thing, religion in Barkazi being as chaotic as it was in most places on the globe—Aiah was on hand to clap her hands to the beat of the drums and nod approvingly as spirits of the air and the afterlife communicated their wishes through Dhival.

The routine business of her life is suddenly invested with the kind of portentous and highly artificial significance that only comes with heavy media exposure. Her appearances at cabinet meetings become "vital reports on the critical war situation." Her briefings of PED personnel and military cops prior to raids on plasm houses are now considered "transmitting vital instructions to highly trained strike teams." And any of her meetings with Constantine—often on thoroughly routine subjects—are now "a discreet rendezvous conducted in the citadel of supreme power."

At least she can kiss him in public now, a fact of which she takes intermittent advantage.

Grooming takes up an ever-larger slice of her life. Every day begins with the ritual visit of the hairdresser, manicurist, and cosmetician. She finds herself fretting over the work she's missing.

"It's your *job* to look interesting," Aldemar tells her. "This *is* work."

With the increased media exposure comes increased exposure to danger. She is given security briefings, cameras are set up outside her apartment, and she is forbidden to travel outside the Palace without bodyguards. The guards come from a pool available to all government employees above a certain grade—she has no regular guards, as Constantine does—but now she has to become accustomed to looking at the world through a screen of broad, besuited male backs.

Aiah checks out a boat from the vehicle pool, and after the guards declare it safe from bomb or hidden assassin, she ducks down into the cabin and lets the helmsman take the boat out of the immediate vicinity of the Palace, at which point her guards allow her to come out into the air.

It is best, Aiah has been told, to assume that all traffic entering or leaving the Palace is being monitored by someone hostile to the government. Aside from the likelihood that there are observation posts in the tall buildings surrounding the Palace, Aiah knows from personal experience that mages working surveillance can be very unobtrusive indeed.

But any enemy surveillance is limited. Anyone watching will grow tired and bored and soon be overwhelmed by the task. Hundreds of wheeled vehicles and watercraft enter or leave the Palace every day. If nothing intriguing is seen in the boat in the first few moments of its journey, it is unlikely that any observer will maintain interest, and will instead go look at something else.

After the boat has traveled a radius from the Palace, Aiah is allowed out of the shielded cabin. As hydrogen turbines whine, the boat speeds over bright green water through a residential district of elegant flats. The buildings, about three hundred years old, have sinuous fronts, silver-bright metal alternating with long rows of window glass, and each building is topped with a crystal-roofed arboretum; and Aiah's heart gives a leap as she realizes she's out of the Palace again, in a speeding boat, on a bright Shieldlit day, on an errand all her own and none that belongs to the war.

Elections slogans are everywhere. *Vote New City . . . Dalavan Party for Peace, Virtue, and Victory . . . Mariath for the Assembly . . . New City NOW.*

Then she notices other graffiti unconnected with the elections, painted on the slab sides of the pontoons that support the apartment buildings—could gangs be marking their turf even here?; but as she looks closely she sees that the graffiti consists of repetitions of geomantic foci, particularly the White Horse and the Quadromark, one believed to be a warding sign and the other a sign to attract good luck.

The people here are trying to keep the war away. *Drop the shells somewhere else,* the marks are saying. *We've got too much luck to be in danger.*

It's all nonsense, of course, popular magic without foundation in the real world of plasm science. The marks are a sign of how superstition can swarm into the world in times of uncertainty.

But it's happening even in well-off neighborhoods like this one, a sign of how far the war has penetrated.

Suddenly the day seems less bright.

The boat slows and turns into a side canal. The long shining buildings fall behind, and here brown-brick apartments and warehouses crowd up close to the water, overhanging the canal and bridging it in places. The old, rusting bridges are encumbered with structures—shops and even small houses—that hang off them like barnacles. In these narrow watery corridors the turbines rumble loudly. Laundry floats overhead like faded artificial clouds, and swarms of noisy gulls circle. The White Horse and the Quadromark are displayed here as well, on pontoons crowded with other graffiti of a purely local interest.

Aiah sees two groups of Dalavan Militia, neither of them doing anything in particular, just drinking beer and strolling in packs along the quays. Each Militia member, Aiah sees, carries a staggering amount of firepower. An assault rifle over one shoulder, often with a sawtooth bayonet glinting in Shieldlight; a submachine gun under one arm; two or three pistols stuck into waistbands or holsters; knives big as short swords stuck into boots or jammed into cartridge belts.

Aiah can see her guards exchange looks of contempt. No serious soldier, she thinks, needs so many weapons, and no real policeman does either. All the weaponry is just to impress the neighbors, and each other.

Put these people up against the Provisional army and they'd fade into the mist.

The boat passes a stockyard and its adjacent slaughterhouse, pens packed with miniature beeves and sheep with wool the color of industrial grime. The smell is ghastly, but the swarms of gulls are thriving. Animal smells drench the air—wet wool, dung, blood, steam, offal, and a pungent chemical stench that probably has to do with how hides and wool are processed.

Aiah feels her gorge rise and turns away from the sight.

The Society of the Simple is nearby, still within smelling distance. It sits amid the grim old buildings on an ancient rust-streaked pontoon. The squat building is gray granite, with a leaded roof and a central bell-shaped dome of gleaming copper. The granite is overlaid with thousands of carvings woven together into an endless, complex knot that covers the whole building: vine leaves that turn into serpents, faces of pop-eyed demons and monsters leering out of the centers of flower blossoms . . . thorny brambles, ferns, trees with interwoven branches and bearing a dozen different kinds of fruit. Comic, grotesque figures hang out of carved buildings, waving papers or bottles or pigeon legs. Other buildings are ablaze, and little humans leap from the flames to their deaths. Half-hidden by the complex tracings, guns and armored vehicles can be seen. Dead women and babies hang on the bayonets of grinning soldiers, while tall, robed humans with faces of angelic serenity watch unmoved.

Everyone and everything woven together, unable to escape the vines, the brambles, the knots. It's like one of their plasm displays carved into stone.

Aiah examines the exterior carefully as the boat approaches, but sees no figures that resemble those she has seen beyond the Shield.

A pier floats in the water on empty metal drums, and above it a rusting metal stair rises to the Dreaming Sisters' home. A pair of Aiah's guards bound up the stairs to check for sign of ambush, and find none. Aiah follows at a more sedate pace, still studying an intricate pattern of carved quincunxes. . . .

The door, twice Aiah's height, is of thick timbers with a trompe l'oeil relief of polished cast bronze stapled onto it, a relief in the shape of a door, and a young woman, seen from the rear, stepping through it. Superficially, tall and thin and with long hair in ringlets, the woman could be Aiah, or any of ten million other women. Above the relief are graven words, *Entering the Gateway,* in an old-fashioned, round-bellied script that Aiah has only seen in venerable inscriptions like this one.

There seems no doorbell or knocker, so Aiah finds a piece of the design—a border pattern of oak leaves—that curves conveniently in the form of a handhold, and gives the door a firm tug.

Although the door is heavy, it opens smoothly. Inside there is a bare room a half-dozen paces square—gray flags, gray stone walls, a groined arch overhead with a globular electric lamp dangling on an iron chain. Two simple arched doorways on either side lead to corridors. In an arched alcove in the back of the room a young woman lies on a mattress. She wears a simple gray knee-length shift and watches without expression as Aiah's party enters.

Aiah's nerves prickle as she realizes that the woman is wired to a plasm well. Even though there are no visible signs that the dreaming sister is working any magic here, she's broadcasting signals of power perfectly recognizable to anyone who spends her days working with plasm.

Aiah's guards are trained to recognize the signs as well, and fan into the room in case there's any threat of violent sorcery. The three-man inspection team, suspecting nothing, follows Aiah through the door. Aiah approaches the woman, who—reluctantly, it seems—sits up to receive her. A wire trails out of her mouth, her connection to the plasm well. The woman—nun? postulant? Simple Person?—is copper-skinned and black-haired, with the hair kept severely short in a bowl-shaped bob. She's thin and waiflike and looks about sixteen years old. Her feet are bare, and her leg and armpit hair are unshaven.

The dreaming sister removes the plasm connection from her mouth and holds it in her hand. The wire ends in a simple curved piece of copper metal, with a gleaming little copper ball on the end, an appliance like some people use for cleaning their tongues.

"May I help you?" the woman asks.

"My name is Aiah. I work with the ministry." She shows her ID. "We'd like to examine your plasm meter."

"It's behind a door around back. The meter readers normally don't bother us."

Aiah looks over her shoulder at the inspection team, and their leader nods. "We'll find it," he says, and they push back out through the door.

Aiah turns back to the young woman. "Is there someone in charge I may speak to?" she says. "We're here for more than a meter reading."

The woman's disinterested expression does not change. "May I ask what this concerns?"

"You've got a license for a plasm accumulator, and we'd like to see it. And there's also . . . something more complex. Is there someone I can speak to?"

The woman's lips give a little twitch of resignation. "Very well," she says. Her brown eyes glance over each of the bodyguards in turn. Disdain enters her voice. "The gentlemen with the guns can wait here," she says. Aiah sees her guards bristle, and she turns to them and tells them to stay.

If the Dreaming Sisters turn out to be defrauding the government of plasm, she realizes, she'll need more than these few guards to deal with this place. A battalion may be more in order.

The dreaming sister, without looking back, has already drifted down one of the corridors, and Aiah is forced to hurry after her. The corridor follows a series of seemingly random curves, with other corridors intersecting at intervals, and the pathway rises and falls as well. The interior of the building, Aiah realizes, is as much a maze as the carved ornament outside. The dreaming sister walks without once looking back, as if she doesn't care whether Aiah is following or not. Her bare feet don't make a sound. Occasionally one of Aiah's pumps skids out from under her—the flags beneath her feet have been polished slick by generations of bare feet.

The corridor is mostly plain gray stone, lit every so often by hanging globular electric lamps. At intervals there are arched alcoves, each equipped with a mattress, a bolster, and plasm connections. Some of the alcoves are empty, some have women lying in them, each with a copper connector in her mouth, eyes closed or dreamily half-closed. Each has hair cropped short and wears only a gray cotton shift; each looks surprisingly young—Aiah sees no one who looks over twenty. Sometimes the sisters share mattresses, in pairs or threes or more, a pile of dreamy bare limbs and cropped heads. The women strewn atop mattresses might suggest the languid aftermath of a particularly strenuous orgy, but somehow the effect is strangely sexless: even lying in piles the women do not seem particularly aware of one another, of their surroundings, or for that matter of Aiah and her guide walking past them down the corridor. It seems more as if they are all addicted to the same narcotic, the juice of poppies perhaps, and are being stored on shelves until it is time for another dose.

Carvings are also placed at intervals along the corridors, under simple rounded arches of the same style as the alcoves and branching corridors. Each is a carved relief, like the exterior door, and tries to give the impression of looking through a window or doorway; each features a central allegorical figure, a man or woman in characteristic dress, carrying objects peculiar to them: a broom, a rattle, a machine pistol, a lantern. The name of each figure is carved into the arch overhead. *The Apprentice,* Aiah reads. *The Gamester . . . The One Who Stands Outside . . . Death . . . The One Who Drags Down.*

She wonders if in this dreaming cavern she is permitted to speak at all. "How many of you are there?" Aiah asks.

"Two hundred fifty-six," the sister replies. Aiah nods: in geomancy that is a Grand Square, a square of a square.

"How long has this place been here?" Aiah asks.

The sister looks over her shoulder at Aiah. Her eyes are dark and faraway, lost in the world of dreams.

"Ten thousand years," she says, in a voice that suggests, perhaps, that she does not care whether Aiah believes her or not.

Surprise stops Aiah dead in her tracks by one of the alcoves. The dreaming sister lying there has twisted genes, but more than that, she is an Avian, one of the elite class, infamous for their cruelty, who ruled Caraqui before the Keremaths. Her face is thin and delicate, with huge half-lidded golden eyes and a raptor beak that looks as if it might easily bite her plasm connection in half. Her body is dainty and fragile, as if her bones were made of paper, and her hands, two taloned fingers and an opposable thumb, grow from atop the joint of the huge wing, soft brown-gold feathers barred with black, that is folded protectively over most of her body.

"This is an Avian," Aiah says in her surprise. The twisted woman is beautiful, Aiah thinks, but in the same way that a sculpture can be beautiful, or a piece of music. As an artifact, not as something human.

She is glad that the Avian's mind is elsewhere, that her eyes are not fully open to fix Aiah within their golden orbs.

A touch of impatience enters the voice of Aiah's guide. "We accept initiates of all races and conditions," she says.

"It's illegal for her even to be here."

"Is that so?" In a tone of perfect indifference. Aiah's guide turns and begins to walk away, and Aiah follows reluctantly, casting glances over her shoulder at the Avian until the twisted woman is out of sight.

Another figure walks toward them. She is petite and blonde, with creamy skin so pale it seems translucent and a scattering of freckles over her nose and cheeks. She seems younger, if possible, than Aiah's guide.

"You asked for someone in authority?" she says.

Aiah hesitates. "I meant," she says, striving for tact, "someone *older.*"

The girl raises a bare foot and scratches her instep. "I am four hundred fifty-one years old," she says. "My name is Order of Eternity. I am therefore senior to Whore." Her bright blue eyes travel to the other sister. "Who is two hundred and . . . ?" Her voice trails off.

"Two hundred fifty-eight," says the first sister, whose name is apparently Whore. "I celebrated my Grand Square two years ago."

"Of course," says Order of Eternity. "Pardon my lapse." She smiles, balanced like a crane on one foot. "Thank you for bringing our guest. You may return to the door."

"Yes, Sister." Whore turns and walks away, without looking back.

Order of Eternity puts her foot back on the floor and returns her attention to Aiah. She is short and barely comes to Aiah's chin. "I am the most senior of the sisters available. How may I help you?"

If this is a joke, Aiah promises herself, *I am going to have my police take this place apart stone by stone.*

But instead she looks after the receding form of the other sister. "Is her name really Whore?"

"Oh yes." Nodding. "When we enter the order, we take a name either reflecting the outside world, which we wish to overcome, or a name reflecting that toward which, in our new life, we aspire."

"*Was* she a whore on the outside?"

The dreaming sister shrugs. "Possibly. Probably not. It doesn't matter."

Aiah turns to Order of Eternity, looks down at her impossibly young face. "You don't *look* four hundred," she says.

There is a girlish lilt to the dreaming sister's voice. Even her voice box seems not to have matured.

"Our life is healthy and free from stress," she says. "We spend our days in touch with plasm, which is the lifeblood of the world. There is no reason for us to age."

"If you sold your techniques," Aiah says, "you could make millions."

A shrug again. "If we cared for millions," says Order of Eternity, "we would."

A cynical little demon tugs at the corners of Aiah's mouth. "I can't think of many religions that don't care about money."

"Are we a religion?" Order of Eternity cocks her head ingenuously and gives every impression that she has never considered this question before in her life. "I think not," she concludes. "We have no congregation, no worshippers. Though some of us have private devotions, we do not as a group offer obedience or sacrifice to any particular gods or immortals. We live simply, according to the rules of our order, and contemplate that which exists—is that religious?"

"Most people would think so."

"Then they are confusing natural life with religion. It is a comment on how unnatural their life has become. Would you like to walk with me?"

Without waiting for an answer, she begins to stroll down the corridor. Aiah shortens her own long-legged strides to match the other woman's.

Aiah frowns. "You're living on a rusty old barge in the middle of the sea, and you've got electricity and sewer and plasm connections. . . . is that natural? Shouldn't you be living in a cave on a mountaintop somewhere?"

"Simplicity," says Order of Eternity, "is not the same as discomfort. Why recline on a sharp rock when there is a mattress near to hand?"

"Living isolated, in a place like this, hardly seems natural."

"It is natural for *us*. We make no claim for anyone else." Order of Eternity looks up at Aiah and gives a puzzled frown, wrinkling her freckled nose. "What is the purpose of your being here, exactly?"

"I'm from the Ministry of Resources. I'm here to examine your plasm use and check your accumulator."

The sister gives a little nod, as if confirming an inward supposition. They walk past an arch containing a relief, *Entering the Gateway*, similar to that on the front door. The long-haired woman pushing open the door is of stone, not of bronze, but otherwise it is the same figure.

"We do not employ significant amounts of plasm," the sister says, "because we strive not to *use* it. We strive only to live in mutual awareness with plasm, to use it as a vehicle for an apprehension of the fundamental reality of this world."

"You use it to extend your life and youth," Aiah points out.

Order of Eternity nods. "When our bodies are damaged, we strive to repair them."

"When a doctor uses such techniques, his plasm bills are very high."

"When a doctor uses such techniques," says Order of Eternity, "his techniques are intrusive and hasty. He must repair the damage of years, and do it in a matter of hours. We, on the other hand, have years, decades sometimes, to attune our bodies to the ways of health. A doctor cannot afford to spend years working on a single patient, but we can. My name is not chance-chosen—we attempt to live according to the order of eternity, not to the needs of the moment. Years of meditation makes us aware of our bodies and their needs in ways that are uncommon outside these walls. We can become aware of wrongness—illness—years before anyone outside would think to bring the matter to the attention of a doctor. At such times only a small effort is required to correct the problem. Our plasm use is therefore subtle, and our usage small."

Order of Eternity's path takes her through an arch on the right, opposite a relief titled *The Archon,* a man in a long robe holding a multibranched candlestick, or perhaps a stylized tree. . . . Dragging her eyes away, Aiah follows the dreaming sister.

"There are also your aerial displays to consider," she says. "I have seen them, and they are impressive."

A wistful smile crosses the sister's youthful face. "I have not seen the displays in centuries. Not since I came to the Society when I was a girl."

"*Someone* here arranges them."

"We all do, in a way. . . ." Order of Eternity's voice trails away as she searches for words. "These displays . . . they are a glimpse into our meditations, but they are only a side effect. We seek to live in accord with plasm, the greatest creative power in the universe, and sometimes actual creation takes place."

"If I wished to make displays of this sort," Aiah says, "a public relations agency would charge tens of thousands of dinars in plasm fees alone. You can't claim, as with the life extension treatments, that you spend years creating these things, and that the plasm required is therefore small. I *know* how much plasm it costs to light up the sky."

Order of Eternity pauses, again searching for words. Behind her, two women lie in their niche, their eyes closed, dreaming in the soft light. One of them is twisted, her small embryo body looking like a grotesque doll that has been placed by the other's pillow.

"We do not entirely understand the phenomenon," Aiah's guide says. "The displays are not something we create consciously. And yet we live in harmony with plasm, and plasm is a constant of our world—it underlies all matter, all reality, and it reacts to the humans who use it, views the world through their perceptions as if through a lens. It *knows* things of which no human is consciously aware . . . and sometimes it creates things without a human consciously willing it."

A grin spreads across Aiah's face. She has to admit that Order of Eternity had her going for a moment. *Don't try to fool one of the Cunning People,* she thinks. *We'll see who's the* passu *here.*

"You're saying that nobody creates these things? Nobody sticks them up in the sky?"

"Plasm is our life, our breath," the dreaming sister says, "and we live in harmony with its motions and bind to it our souls. Plasm is a higher order of reality—it both creates reality and alters it. It would seem that plasm sometimes reflects our meditations, but it does so without our direction."

"And without running through your meter."

The dreaming sister simply shrugs. "Apparently so. Here is our accumulator."

Aiah follows the sister into a circular room and realizes she is beneath the copper dome. Slits in the dome's base let in Shieldlight, and it glows on a carved screen that holds a small plasm accumulator. The screen is of some kind of dark wood and features intricate carvings similar to those on the building's exterior, a profusion of faces and bodies and floral displays, humans and plants and creatures all laced together, caught in a complex moment of transformation.

There are arched gaps in the screen that allow access to the accumulator, and Aiah steps through one. The accumulator comes only to Aiah's waist, but Aiah can see her reflection in its polished bands of black ceramic and copper.

"You're not the first to wonder about us," says the dreaming sister as Aiah walks a circuit around the accumulator. "Every so often someone from the ministry will come by. She will examine the meter, perhaps subject our building to inspection, and then go away. Nothing is ever found."

"There's a war going on. Plasm is precious."

"Plasm is *always* precious," correcting, "but we have

become aware of the war, yes. The movement of plasm . . . the patterns of use . . . the resonance of violence within our hearts as we dream . . . yes," she nods, "we are aware of the war. The last time we felt such disturbance was eighty-nine years ago, but that war did not last long. We would have to remember two hundred fourteen years for a conflict of similar duration and intensity, and then the fighting was terrible. This building was converted to a hospital, and we sisters were confined to a small part of it."

"What was the war about?" Aiah asks. Her knowledge of Caraqui history doesn't go back that far.

The dreaming sister pauses and gazes at Aiah through the lacework screen. A shaft of light dropping from the dome gleams on her cropped hair.

"Ignorance," she says.

Aiah leaves the screen area and walks to the control panel. It is silver metal and very old, its edges scalloped in a fluid pattern that is dimly familiar to Aiah, perhaps from old college classes on architectural history.

She looks at the dials and switches. The accumulator is topped up with plasm. A heavy black plastic knob sets a rheostat to provide the building with a smallish hourly amount that, divided between two hundred and fifty-six Dreaming Sisters, makes a tiny, truly insignificant dose of plasm for each, an absurdly small amount.

There are other devices on the control panel, clocks and timers, the function of which does not seem immediately apparent. "What are these?" Aiah asks.

"We tend to lose track of time during our meditations. The timer cuts off our plasm so that we will know to take meals, clean the building, have meetings, and so on." She tilts her head like a bird. "All is in order?"

Dials, Aiah thinks, can be rigged to show far less plasm than really exists. To prove it would involve taking apart the mechanism and metering the plasm lines, but Aiah thinks she can demonstrate the sisters are cheating without going to that much effort.

"I see nothing unusual," she says.

Order of Eternity turns and walks through the arch on her silent bare feet.

"There is a political philosophy about plasm," Aiah says, following, "called New City. Do you know of it?"

"No," over her shoulder, "and I do not in any case believe that it is new. I have lived over four hundred years," she says in her young girl's voice, "and I have yet to see a new thing. And of course the world is far older than I, and has spun upon its axis many millions of times since last a new thing stood upon it." The dreaming sister pauses before one of the carved allegories, *The Architect,* a noble-looking man with a protractor and a pair of dividers.

"The Ascended Ones isolated us here," the sister says. "We do not know why, or where they are now, or whether the Shield shall ever fall. We are a limited people, on a limited world, and we are condemned to wait. True freedom is denied us—the most unlimited thing in the world is plasm, and even that cannot penetrate the Shield."

Wrong, Aiah thinks, remembering dancing figures in velvet blackness, but she holds her tongue.

"We are condemned endlessly to repeat ourselves," says Order of Eternity, "in a world of limited choice. Over years, over thousands of years, all things return. That is why we meditate upon these figures," touching *The Architect,* "which we call imagoes. All human possibility, all activity and type and form, are symbolized in these images."

"How many imagoes are there?" Aiah asks, recalling that she has seen duplicates.

"Eighty-one."

Another Grand Square. The Dreaming Sisters are consistent in their numerology.

"This one," the sister says, "*The Architect* . . . a lofty-looking fellow, isn't he? But in our meditations, this imago represents *failure.* Because though an architect will build his dream, and his heart will thrill to the sight of the image that he held in his mind rising floor by floor in the world of the real, nevertheless the world will work its will upon dream. The brilliant new creation will grow old, and crumble, and one day join the architect himself in the dust. And so . . . *failure.*"

"Are all your imagoes failures?" Aiah asks.

"By no means. Some are wise, and have learned to accept the constraints of the world."

Aiah looks at *The Architect* and folds her arms. "No change," she says, "no improvement, nothing new."

"No *permanent* change. No *lasting* improvement."

"Your philosophy sounds very much like despair."

In the dim light the sister's blue eyes are chips of dreaming ice. "Not despair," she says. "*Acceptance.* You will concede a difference?"

"And if the Shield is penetrated?" Aiah asks. "If someone gets outside your world of limitations, into the world of the Ascended—what happens to your philosophy then?"

As Aiah speaks she feels the throbbing acceleration of her heart, feels her feet grow distant, sees her vision contract, narrow to the merest point of photon contact with the dreaming sister. The universe seems to wait for the answer.

"Perhaps nothing will change at all," says Order of Eternity. "Humanity may carry its limitations with it—perhaps the imagoes rule our actions beyond the Shield as they do beneath it. Or perhaps everything will change—who can say?"

I have been beyond the Shield. That is Aiah's next line. But now, the moment come, blood singing in her ears and her mouth dry with terror, she can't say it. It is not as if she brought anything back, nor learned anything while she was there.

It is not as if the Dreaming Sisters claim to know what is beyond the Shield, or have any particular gift in interpreting what Aiah saw there. It is not as if what Aiah saw there resembled the imagoes she has seen here in the sisters' building. It is not as if the Dreaming Sisters do not disclaim any responsibility for the aerial displays, including the gray-skinned dancer that Aiah recognized as the Woman who is the Moon. There seem to be no answers here.

It is not as if the Dreaming Sisters are not, in some way, stealing plasm.

The throbbing tide of blood recedes from Aiah's ears. Her vision clears.

She will postpone the moment.

"Thank you," she says politely. "I think I've seen everything I need, for the moment."

Order of Eternity turns and pads away without a further

word. Aiah follows. Tremors flutter through her. She feels as if she's just fought a battle.

It is not clear to her whether she's won or lost.

Imagoes float past on either side. Women lie in their dimly lit alcoves, limbs splayed as if their dreams had caught them unawares and dropped them in their tracks. The flagstone path winds up, down, curves left and right.

Aiah stops dead as an image strikes her like a thunderbolt. Her mind reels. *"What . . . ?"* she can only gasp.

Order of Eternity stops, hesitates, returns. "This imago? It is *The Shadow*."

Aiah has already read the inscription. "I know this person," she says.

Sorya stares at her, carved in stone. She wears a high-collared gown that floats off her figure into the background, softening the outlines of her form, making it indistinct. In one hand is a dagger.

Aiah raises a hand, hesitates, touches the cold stone face. Sorya's lips seem to curl in contempt at Aiah's confusion.

Order of Eternity studies the portrait, head cocked. *"The Shadow* is she-who-follows, she who pursues the great so closely that she is invisible in their shadow."

"Until she strikes," Aiah says. A chill shivers down her spine.

"Just so."

Aiah's hand drifts along the line of Sorya's chin. Dry rough stone, nothing more. No dust to indicate recent polishing, no cracks or weathering to testify to age. No tingle of plasm to indicate that magic was at work, or that a plasm-glamour has been placed on this image.

"How old is this carving?" Aiah asks.

The dreaming sister narrows her eyes as she looks at the stone figure. "This was not the face it bore when last I saw it," she says. "The figure is no more than three or four days old."

Aiah turns to her in surprise. "Someone carved a new face?" she asks.

"Oh no." Order of Eternity shakes her head. "The figures . . . *change* . . . from time to time. Like the aerial displays, it is another consequence of our meditations, not willed by us.

Say rather that the plasm itself, perceiving an imago active in the world, makes the alteration of its own accord."

Aiah strives to wrap her mind around this idea. "So Sorya—the original of this figure—Sorya has become an imago?"

"You misunderstand." The dreaming sister turns on Aiah the cold gaze of her indifferent blue eyes. "Sorya—if that is this lady's name—has *always* been an imago, one or another of the eighty-one. So have I. So have you. Not always the *same* imago, because our nature is not immutable, nor does our role in life remain constant. If Sorya's face has appeared here, it is because she, and the imago of which she is an image, has become important, or powerful, or somehow key to a critical situation."

They're tricking me, Aiah thinks. This is some kind of manipulation; they found out I'm frightened of Sorya and changed the statue while this woman kept me busy—*they're in my head!* Panic flashes through her. *They're manipulating my thoughts!*

But Order of Eternity's aloof blue gaze is calm—hardly friendly, but not menacing either—and Aiah's panic fades. She's familiar enough with plasm that if she were being attacked, she'd know it.

They are manipulating her, yes. But they didn't need to get into her head to do it; all that was necessary was that they had seen *The Mystery of Aiah* on video.

Aiah looks at Sorya's statue again, gives a remote nod. "Interesting," she says. "I'm surprised, after all these years, you do not more clearly understand the phenomenon."

"It is not our *goal* to understand phenomena," says the dreaming sister. "We strive to live simply and in consonance with plasm. That is all."

Aiah follows Order of Eternity to the entrance. Whore is drowsing on her mattress, and Aiah's bodyguards, and the inspection team, are clearly showing their impatience. Aiah thanks Order of Eternity for her time, then pushes her way out the heavy door.

She turns to the leader of the inspection team. "Anything?" she asks.

"The meter's fine. No sign of tampering."

"Tomorrow I want you to come back and put monitors on every plasm cable leading to this pontoon. Have a mage make certain there aren't any hidden plasm cables under the surface of the water."

The man nods. "Yes, miss."

And then one of the other members of the team gives a gasp—"Look, miss!"—and Aiah's gaze follows his pointing finger to the front door, to the huge cast bronze of *Entering the Gateway.*

A shiver of fear runs down Aiah's back.

The figure on the door has changed. Where formerly the woman entering the door was facing forward, with the back of her head to the viewer, now she has turned her head to face over her right shoulder.

There is a sweet, knowing smile on her lips.

And the face is Aiah's.

EIGHTEEN

〰〰〰〰

"I observe," says the Excellent Togthan, "that you have hired two more genetically altered mages."

"Have you seen their qualifications?" Aiah asks.

"Impressive, surely," Togthan shrugs, "but hardly unique. There were other mages fully as qualified."

"I hired them as well," Aiah points out.

"But still, in view of our understanding that the personnel of the PED would reflect the composition of our metropolitan population . . ." Togthan lets his words trail off while he sips his coffee, and then places the cup in its saucer with a delicate porcelain chime.

Aiah tastes at her own coffee while composing her answer. Togthan has been a presence in her office for three weeks. He has done little on his own other than announce a daily prayer meeting at the start of second shift—a few people attend, Aiah is told. Togthan appears at most of the important meetings, and he has asked to see the applications of all the new hires; but he has, till this moment, offered no comment on the way the department is being run.

Togthan's lack of activity had not made Aiah any easier with his presence. She had dreaded the moment that she knew would come.

And now Togthan sits in her office, sipping coffee and directly challenging her decisions. Politely and smoothly, but then one can afford to be polite if one is in a position of strength. One of the triumvirs is behind him, and Aiah cannot be certain of her own support.

"My impression is that we *are* better reflecting the composition of Caraqui," Aiah says. "Aside from some clerical staff, these are the only two of the twisted that have been hired."

"I would not desire the population to grow offended by this department," Togthan says. "There is much prejudice against the polluted flesh."

"I am sure," unblinking, "that the wisdom of the people's spiritual leaders is capable of mitigating any prejudice on the part of the ignorant."

"It is the wish of the triumvir and Holy, Parq, that the hiring of the polluted flesh cease entirely."

Aiah sips her coffee again and frowns. "The triumvir's requests shall of course be respected," she says. "But in order that there be no more misunderstandings, I wonder if he will put his wishes in writing?"

Togthan tilts his head and favors Aiah with a reproving stare. "On this issue you may consider my words to be those of the Holy. Written communication is scarcely necessary."

So this is how it's done, Aiah thinks.

Up till now she's only been on the other end of this issue. Back in Jaspeer it was scarcely necessary that anyone actually compose directives that Barkazils not get good housing outside their own neighborhoods, or good jobs practically anywhere. She'd never known how these things were decided . . . and now here she is, one of a pair of privileged people nodding in their civil way, sipping coffee out of fine porcelain, and deciding the fate of people whom they may never meet.

"Very well," Aiah says. "I understand." And she thinks, *Time to talk to Ethemark.*

TRIUMVIR FALTHEG JOINS LIBERAL
COALITION, ENDORSES PARTY GOALS

Ethemark's huge eyes darken as Aiah relates the substance of her conversation with Togthan, and he exchanges uneasy glances with Adaveth, the twisted Minister of Education.

"I would resign," Aiah offers, "but I can't think what good it would do. I would be replaced with someone friendly to Parq."

Little folds appear in specific locations around the small man's eyes—expressions of concern, Aiah has learned, and thought—and then he looks up at her. "He has not asked you to dismiss any of us?"

"No. I *would* resign in that case, and as publicly as I could."

Ethemark's coffee sits untouched by his elbow. They are meeting in Aiah's apartment, where Aiah can control security, and where they are well away from the eyes of Parq's spy.

"And," Ethemark continues, "he hasn't put his own people forward?"

"No, and I can't think why."

"I can think of two reasons," says Adaveth. "First, talented Parq loyalists may be spread a bit thin at the moment. He's organizing both the Dalavan Militia and the Dalavan Guard of regular soldiers. Both units require mages as well as other talent."

"And the second reason?" Ethemark asks. Adaveth's looks grow foreboding.

Aiah answers for him. "Parq may already have his spies in place."

The three look at each other. "Watch," Ethemark says. "Wait. What else can we do?"

"Win the war," Aiah says. "Because then Parq will no longer be so necessary."

ALTERED PEOPLE'S PARTY COMPLAINS OF PERSECUTION

ATTACKS OF DALAVAN MILITIA ON TWISTED CITIZENS DOCUMENTED

TRIUMVIR HILTHI RECEIVES REPORT

The claws of the Adrenaline Monster pluck Aiah from sleep, and she wakes, eyes staring and a cry on her lips, to discover herself stretched across Constantine's barrel chest. She has thrown an arm over him and one of her legs is coiled about his thigh. Though her ears are alert to the sound of shellfire or alarm, she hears only the languorous throb of his heart, regular as a clock.

"You fell asleep," he says, voice soft in the silent room.

Not for long, she thinks.

There is an ache in her throat where her frantic heart seems to have lodged.

They are in Constantine's suite-of-the-day, enjoying one of their rare, scattered hours, pleasure snatched from the heart of duty and war. The room is dark, with the windows entirely polarized, and the only light filters from a single lamp in the next room. The Palace and the world outside are silent, and the rhythm of Constantine's pulse is the loudest sound in the room.

Strange, Aiah thinks, that thanks to *The Mystery of Aiah* there are thousands of people who think she is living in some kind of continuous carnal delirium with Constantine, whereas the sad fact is that she hardly ever sees him in the flesh, and even then it is often only to exchange a few words and perhaps a kiss in passing.

Now, thanks to both of them wrenching their schedules out of shape, they actually have a few hours together. Aiah tells herself that she should be grateful.

"You are thinking," Constantine says. He folds his arms behind his head and looks down at her over the foreshortened planes of his face.

"Oh yes."

"Not about work, I hope."

"Not exactly," she says, and she tells him. He laughs, a deep rumbling earthquake that seems to propagate more through the bone and muscle of his chest than through the air. His big arms unfold and encompass her, holding her like a child against his big body.

"Come war's end," he says, "we shall try to exceed your viewers' most sybaritic fantasies."

"And when will that be?" she says, half-rhetorically, but he considers the question and replies.

"The Polar League has sent a representative," he says, "a man named Licinias—by repute a good man, but I don't know what he can hope to accomplish here. There will be a cease-fire, and we will get some favorable propaganda out of it, but unless he can persuade the Provisionals to leave, or neighboring powers to stop supporting them, the war will go on. I will be using the cease-fire to prepare for a new offensive."

She looks up at him. "Is a new offensive possible? Will it succeed?"

"*Yes,*" judiciously, "and *very possibly.* The new Caraqui army—built almost from scratch after the coup, and trained in the Timocracy—has completed its basic training. They are inexperienced, but perfectly capable of holding sections of the line. We will use the cease-fire to put these new units into the front line, then pull back our more experienced mercenaries into a reserve. It is they who will form spearheads for the actual offensive."

Things are coming to a head, Aiah thinks. "When?" she asks.

"The cease-fire will begin in two days. Licinias will begin consultations with the Provisionals in Lanbola, and then he will fly to present their position to us. We will prolong the talks for at least a week, because it will take that long to put our new soldiers into the line."

"And then?"

"Things will happen fast."

"Has—" Aiah has difficulty forming the words. "Has Taikoen a part to play?"

She can feel a grim mood settle like a shroud on Constantine's thoughts. "No," he says. "We used him in our original coup, and in the battle for the Corridor. We cannot use him a third time, not without making it obvious that we have something of his nature working for us." He sighs deeply. "Besides, the Provisionals have taken warning from what happened to their predecessors. Their headquarters and communications staffs have been dispersed to many different locations, to make a decapitation strike that much less likely."

"But their government is still vulnerable. Kerehorn and Great-Uncle Rathmen."

"We wish them both to stay alive," Constantine says. "Kerehorn because he is ineffective, and puts the worst face possible on their movement—and Rathmen for much the same reason. Plus"—his tone darkens—"he is one of the people we could contact . . . if we need to end the war."

If we need to surrender, Aiah thinks with a shiver. That's what Constantine means.

There is a dull, resentful glimmer in Constantine's eyes. "No, I will not use Taikoen again. His exactions have reached their limit—I will not give him more."

"I am glad for that."

There is silence for a moment as Constantine idly strokes Aiah's hair.

"Will we invade Lanbola?" she asks. *All neutralities are imaginary,* she thinks, remembering Sorya's words.

"If nothing else works." Simply.

Aiah closes her eyes, feels weariness and sadness steal into her, into her heart, into her very bones. "And one of the things that may work is *The Mystery of Aiah.*"

"It is proving a very popular video," Constantine says. His voice is cheerful; he is pleased with the success of his idea. "The Provisional soldiers spend days cooped up in fortified buildings with nothing to do but polish their weapons—it is too dangerous to venture out—and so they watch video. And the only video available to them is *that which we send them*—the old Keremath video monopoly assures that they have nothing else to watch. And so the enemy are assured of a constant diet of our propaganda, some of which we know must be affecting them. We *know* that Landro's Escaliers have seen you on video. And we have distributed the video in the Timocracy, so that the Escaliers' families can see it. We hope they will be able to suggest to the Escaliers that they may be on the wrong side."

Aiah sighs. "I want it to be worthwhile," she says. "If I must donate my privacy to this war, and masquerade as the savior of Barkazi, I hope at least some of it comes to *something.*"

Constantine widens his eyes in mock surprise. "You *haven't* been chosen by the gods to save Barkazi?"

She glares at him. "That isn't funny. I wish I didn't have to spend so much time thinking about religion. I'm supposed to be a cop, damn it."

His look turns curious. "Have all the recent war deaths turned your mind to thoughts of the eternal?"

"Most of it's politics. Khorsa and Dhival and that old madman Charduq want me to wave a magic wand and save Barkazi—and you're supporting them, because you want to use this nonsense to corrupt Landro's Escaliers. Parq and the Dalavans are building their own police force and army, and you don't act to stop them; and Parq's spy is conducting a religious persecution in my department, and you support *that*. . . ."

Constantine is nettled by this accusation. "Parq is *necessary*. His acts are distasteful and so is he, but he is *necessary*."

"So you assure me."

"The war must be won," Constantine insists. "Parq is the spiritual leader of two-fifths of the population. If he can inspire them to support the government, then it is good for everyone, including the people Parq aspires to persecute." He pauses. "When one is a politician, one must deal with many unpleasant people, and sometimes one must hold one's nose and do unpleasant things. But one must keep one's true end in view. And my ultimate goal has nothing to do with Parq."

"I've been ordered not to hire any more twisted. Togthan said he was speaking for Parq."

Constantine's glance is sharp. "Your feelings about the twisted would seem to have changed since I first met you."

There is a moment's pause. "I never knew any before." Then she adds, "And I wouldn't like Parq's interference in my department even if I *didn't* want the twisted in it."

Constantine lets his head fall back against the pillow. "Bend with the wind," he says. "It will not always blow from this particular quarter."

"Well," mumbling into his chest-curls, "the Dreaming Sisters tell me it all doesn't matter anyway."

"The Dreaming Sisters?" Constantine's head rises from

the pillow again; he looks at her over his cheekbones. "When have you met the Dreaming Sisters?"

"Last week."

"And why?"

"Because I got curious about them, and when I looked into their records, I discovered that the plasm they *must* have expended in order to create those displays of theirs hadn't been metered."

"They're plasm thieves?" The possibility seems to delight him. "Are they really?"

"They have to be, although we haven't found proof. But I interviewed one of their members, who said she was four hundred years old, and who told me that the best course in life was acceptance, because there was nothing new and no improvement would last—that, and to stick a kind of plasm-pacifier in my mouth and experience fundamental reality without actually *doing* anything with it."

"And accept their raids on the plasm supply as well." Constantine grins and drops his head to the pillow again. "Philosophically, then, they are not unlike my former colleagues in the School of Radritha. They, too, urged withdrawal from the world—because they were afraid, I think. Afraid of power, afraid of what it would do to them when they acquired it." He booms out a laugh. "What does it *matter* if there is nothing new beneath the Shield? There can be new *combinations* . . . surely their imagination will extend to *that*? And even if one's accomplishments fade away, hey, it is something to have *accomplished*. What does one say—'I saw a chance of doing good, but I did not do it, because it has been done before, and because in any case in a thousand years it will not matter'? Ha! What a pathetic argument for inaction!"

"I am not certain that is quite what they were saying," Aiah ventures. "But in any case, they were very good. I was impressed by their presentation. They . . . really worked on me."

"But they weren't good enough to actually *fool* one of the Cunning People?" Constantine says.

"No . . ." Aiah hesitates, and the Woman who is the Moon dances stately in her thoughts. "Except in the one thing that made me go there in the first place."

"Which was?"

She hesitates—it was *her* journey, she thinks, and she has not puzzled out what it could possibly mean, and besides he may think her mad. . . . But then, she concludes, if anyone is going to believe her it will be Constantine. And with *The Mystery of Aiah* already made, the chances of his using it in one of his publicity campaigns is lessened.

Besides, she doesn't want to be alone with this anymore.

"Which was," she says wearily, "what I saw when I accidentally traveled past the Shield."

Through her flesh and muscle and bone, through her body, which are so in contact with Constantine that he could hardly move a muscle or formulate an intention without her becoming immediately aware of it . . . suddenly she feels his body *flare,* as if his entire organism, every cell and nerve, has suddenly become very, very interested.

"You did what?" he asks.

And she tells him.

FOR RADICAL SOLUTIONS . . .
VOTE *RADICAL!*

At the end of her story he is pacing back and forth, lamplight from the next room shining gold off his massive ebon body, while she reclines on the bed, head propped on one hand. "You don't think I'm crazy?" she says.

He glances at her briefly, and then his eyes dismiss the idea.

"No," he says. "Though I am not entirely convinced that the shock of encountering the Shield may not have caused you in some way to hallucinate, or that you may not have been practiced upon."

"Practiced upon?"

Even in the darkness Aiah can see the gravity of his expression. "There were other mages in the ops room, other plasm outlets. One of them may have used plasm against you—perhaps just mischievously—and directed this vision into your mind."

Alarm sings in Aiah's heart. "Isn't that dangerous?"

He frowns. "Potentially. You should arrange an appointment with a neurologist to see if there has been any damage."

"*Damage?*" Aiah bolts upright. Constantine stops, smiles, blankets her shoulder with a reassuring hand.

"Precautionary only," smiling. "If you'd been rendered an idiot surely one of us would have noticed."

Aiah, not comforted, rests her chin on her knee.

"We should also discover the exact hour and minute of your discovery," Constantine says.

"I have the logs. It's all on record."

"Good." Constantine's laugh rumbles out. "And you say that the aperture closed behind your anima as you continued upward?"

"Yes."

He begins to pace again. "I wonder if it opens at intervals, and if so what those intervals might be. How big the aperture is. And if it opens only here, or elsewhere. I wonder if we might mount some very sensitive detectors on the roof of the Palace . . . If the aperture is small—you had no sense of its size?—if the aperture is small, the detectors would have to be *very* sensitive. . . . If the Shield is vulnerable, then, when the aperture opens . . ."

Desperation rises in Aiah. She reaches out and snatches one of his big hands. "*Stop,*" she cries. "I need to talk."

At once he is all attention, the kinetic body still, his formidable concentration directed entirely at her.

"Of course," he says.

"This has all come to *me*," she says. "So far as we know, I'm the only person to penetrate the Shield in thousands of years. I need to know what it *means.*"

Understanding lights his eyes. "Ah," he says. His voice is soft. "I must confess, dearest Miss Aiah, that I do not know what it means either—but if it is any comfort, I plan to get to the bottom of it one way or another."

"Because," she continues, "if I saw these things, perhaps I was *meant* to see them, and then Charduq the Hermit and his followers are right, and I am in fact destined to . . ." Bleak despair flutters in her heart. "To I don't know what."

He sits beside her, his hand still clasped in hers, and his

other arm steals around her waist. She leans against the warm solidity of his body, rests her head on his shoulder, closes her eyes. "I don't know anything," she says. "I saw people and things in the sky, and that's *all*. None of them spoke to me. None of them ever made a sign they knew I was there, or cared. None of them—"

Hot tears spill from her eyes. A sob catches at the back of her throat. Constantine strokes her hair, murmurs unheard consolation into her ear.

"They may not know us, or care about us," he says finally, "but in time we shall *make* them." She feels determination, or perhaps anger, harden in him, turn his muscles to stone. "All these intrigues, these wars . . . they are the university of our race, and after our graduation we will Ascend and demand what is ours." His gentle hand pushes her ringlets from her face, and he kisses her damp eyes. At close range, his gold-flecked eyes gaze soberly at hers.

"You give me a most peculiar sense of hope, Miss Aiah," he says. "If what you have told me is true, then your Dreaming Sisters are wrong, because everything will change. I will *make* it change."

His arms circle her and he holds her close. Aiah closes her eyes, accepting the warmth of his body and the comfort of his scent, but she feels a tremor shiver for a moment in her spine at the knowledge that her shoulders are too thin to bear the weight of *everything*, everything changing. . . .

Within a few days, discreet detectors, each in its own sandbagged bulwark, appear on the Palace roof, all aimed at the Shield overhead. Their purpose is secret: it is assumed they have to do with war work.

The report of the neurologist is negative: she detects no sign that Aiah's mind was ever interfered with. This does not rule out interference by someone highly skilled, but at least it eases Aiah's anxiety.

The doctor also tells Aiah she would benefit greatly from a week or two away from her job, in a carefree resort in, say, Gunalaht or Achanos.

And then Aiah laughs, and the doctor laughs with her.

WARRING FACTIONS ACCEPT MEDIATION

POLAR LEAGUE ENVOY TO ARRIVE

The envoy Licinias has a halo of wavy white hair that contrasts with his copper skin and gives him the impressive air of a patrician. He is tall, and a straight-spined military bearing makes him look taller.

Acute brown eyes look at the video cameras set up in corners of the room. "Do we absolutely need the video?" he says. "People who are being recorded tend to speak in platitudes, or to make speeches for their constituencies, and I would prefer to proceed without all that."

The triumvirs look at each other, at Constantine. It is Constantine who gives the order. "Turn them off," he says, then adds with a smile, "I can make the speeches later."

The steel-lined Crystal Dome, with or without fresh-cut flowers in its vases, had been thought too depressing for the reception of the Polar League's envoy, and so it will be held in the Swan Wing, in one of the Keremaths' extravagant ballrooms: there are pink-veined marble pillars holding up a fan-vaulted ceiling, niches with bronze statues of gods and immortals, a floor of cream and strawberry tiles. . . . In the midst is set a massive table of marble supported by an ornate frame of polished bronze. Tackles on a steel tripod had been needed to move the thing into position.

The government of Caraqui sits on one side of the long table, the triumvirate in the middle, flanked by Constantine and Belckon and their various aides and supporters. Aiah is present, she suspects, largely so that video cameras can record her entrance and exit, more evidence for her audience that she is important, that cities are set atremble at her very word. But Constantine has, perhaps, another reason. "Might as well learn how this works," he tells her, with a smile.

The Minister of State Belckon, Aiah observes, has not

found it necessary to bring Sorya. But Aiah does not doubt that Sorya will find out what happens sooner rather than later.

Licinias, for his part, brings only a pair of assistants, though his air of composed authority seems to weigh the table subtly to his side. . . . It is an interesting effect, and Aiah wonders how he does it.

There are formalities first: the government thanks Licinias and the Polar League for their interest in Caraqui's problems; Licinias thanks the government for receiving him, and expresses the hope he may contribute to a settlement. He then offers to read a position statement from the Provisional Government.

"It is kind of you to deliver it," Constantine replies—he speaks in advance of the triumvirs, but since the three leaders show no surprise, Aiah concludes this is by prearrangement.

"But sir," Constantine continues, "I wonder if you would first enlighten us concerning two points: first, whether the so-called Provisional Government is willing to recognize *this* government as the legitimate government of Caraqui; and second, their timetable for evacuating their forces from our territory."

Licinias listens with apparent courtesy—if he is surprised, he hides it well—and then says, "The Provisional Government's statement addresses neither of these points."

Constantine shrugs, his lip curling. "Then I fear that these proceedings are a waste of our time and yours," he says.

Licinias indicates the papers before him. "Shall I read you the Provisional Government's statement?"

Constantine scowls—Aiah wonders whether this, too, is prearranged—and then Faltheg raises a hand. "Proceed, Mr. Licinias."

It is, as Constantine predicted, a waste of time. The Provisionals' statement is little more than a demand for surrender. The triumvirate rejects it unanimously, then produces a statement of their own position, prepared ahead of time, in which they promise amnesty for all the Provisional leaders but two—Kerehorn and Great-Uncle Rathmen are both named—if their forces are evacuated and disbanded at once.

"You do not give me much maneuvering room," Licinias says as he glances at the terms.

"We cannot tolerate a hostile force occupying a part of our metropolis," Constantine says. "Any settlement must be aimed at removing that force."

Licinias permits himself a delicate shrug. "I will inform the Provisionals of your conditions," he says. "But I'm afraid an impasse may be created, and that will throw the matter before a general League council . . . on which, I am afraid, your opponents may command more votes than you."

"If the Polar League does not support the right of a metropolis to remain free of invasion," Constantine asks rhetorically, "what good can anyone expect from them?"

"The Provisionals maintain that their force in fact represents the legitimate government," Licinias offers, "and that your government is usurping their authority."

"We are preparing, even in the midst of war, to hold an election that will confirm our legitimacy," Constantine says. "What do the Provisionals offer?"

Licinias hands the paper to one of his assistants, who puts it in a dispatch case. "We shall see," he says.

After which the meeting is brought to an end, a luncheon buffet is wheeled in, and the delegates mingle for a while. Aiah, holding a plate of vegetables and munching a stick of celery, finds herself near Licinias, and the envoy bows formally to her.

"You are Miss Aiah?" he says. "I believe I recognize you from video."

Aiah offers him her hand. "I hope you don't believe everything you saw," she says.

He shakes her hand with a dry, papery palm. "I am refreshed to hear that *you* do not believe it," he says. "But I am inclined to wonder"—he looks thoughtful—"why your government has seen fit to place you in such prominence, and in such a sensational fashion."

Aiah smiles. "I am sometimes inclined to wonder that myself."

Licinias gives a dry laugh. "I have often found the actions of governments inexplicable," he says, "but I confess it is refreshing to find such a prominently situated member of the government in question agreeing with me."

"I'm not prominent," Aiah says. "I'm just on video."

Licinias gazes at her with wise brown eyes tucked up under winged white brows. "There is, you will discover, very little difference between the two."

Aiah does not find this thought comforting. Later, as she leaves the meeting with Constantine, and bodyguards fall into step before and behind, he takes her arm and says, "I observed that you spoke to Licinias."

"Yes. We were both reflecting on the puzzling nature of my fame." She looks up at Constantine. "Tell me about Licinias."

"He's from Conpurna. He was a jurist, a specialist in intermetropolitan law. He was Conpurnan ambassador to the Polar League and the World Council and served on the Polar High Court, and after he failed at electoral office back home he began to devote himself to the thankless cause of making peace, which suggests that he is either a towering egoist or a genuinely good person." He pauses, faintly surprised at his own judgment. "One *does* meet a good person from time to time, I find," he adds.

"I liked him."

Constantine raises an eyebrow. "Is it your preference for older men I hear speaking?"

Aiah feigns indignation. "I don't prefer *older* men. I like *interesting* men."

"Luckily for me"—Constantine grins—"I am both."

Since they are in the Swan Wing, he takes her to his current lodgings—marble-sheathed walls, plush carpet, and ornamental, scalloped wings of silvery alloy all deployed to disguise the plasm-generating Palace structure that runs inconveniently through the huge rooms. He has not spent much time here since the war began, preferring for safety's sake to sleep in the empty suites he chose at random for his mobile office, and the rooms have an unused smell to them.

Guards take up position outside the door, and others ghost through the rooms to make sure no ambush has been laid. Constantine closes the door and leans close.

"I wished to speak with you privately," he says. "We are beginning to receive indications that our propaganda is having some effect."

"Yes?" She should be delighted, she thinks, but there is a focused urgency in Constantine's tone that makes her uneasy.

"The Provisionals' contract with Landro's Escaliers expires in ten days. Normally there is an automatic extension—the Provisionals would pay another bonus, and the Escaliers would remain with their army—but now a possibility exists that the Escaliers may be persuaded to change sides."

"Is that what their agents in the Timocracy are telling you?"

Constantine gives a brief shake of the head. "We would never deal with their agents on a matter like this—the agents make their living negotiating for *reliable* mercenaries; they would turn us down flat. We have approached the Escaliers directly, in occupied territory, and they have shown interest—and furthermore, we believe that their interest is genuine."

Dread oozes through Aiah's nerves. She shivers. "And what does this have to do with me?"

As she utters the words she feels she already knows the answer.

Constantine hesitates before he speaks, and Aiah senses the calculation in his mind. "They wish to see you, directly. To negotiate with you, receive their guarantees from you."

"From my video persona, you mean. Or from Charduq's Aiah, blessed of the gods and redeemer of Barkazi." Bitterness flavors her words. "What happens when they meet the real me?"

He takes her shoulders, speaks close enough so that his words puff her cheek with warmth. "You underestimate yourself. You are intelligent and experienced, and your mission will receive the best support I can arrange."

"And where is this mission? Lanbola, Nesca, Garshab—where?"

He hesitates. "Let me tell you first what is at stake."

She looks at him. The Adrenaline Monster plucks at her nerves. "No. Tell me where I am expected to go."

Another moment of hesitation. He licks his lips and says, "Occupied Caraqui. Their officers cannot move freely, and they want negotiations in their area, where they can control security."

Anger flares in her. "Where *they* can control security!" she mocks. "Where is *my* security? Great Senko, I need bodyguards even in *friendly* territory!"

She turns away and walks blindly into the vast room, heels clicking on polished pink granite. Constantine follows, his voice low and urgent. "If we cannot subvert the Escaliers, then we will have to try a direct assault across the security zone the Provisionals have created, and we will lose tens of thousands just crossing the zone, before we can even properly engage them. Or we can attempt Sorya's right hook into Lanbola, and destabilize the entire region."

He catches her, takes her shoulders again. She tries to shrug him off, fails, permits him in the end to wrap his arms around her stiff, resisting frame.

"You have created this," she says. "You created this video image of me deliberately, and now they *want* this thing."

Constantine's low tones sound in her ear. "I did not anticipate they would demand to speak to you directly. I would not have put you at risk in this way."

"Of course you would have." Coarse laughter bubbles from her throat. "*One must keep one's true end in view*—how many times have I heard you say it? And your goal is not love or peace but victory for the New City, and so . . ." She waves a hand. "It is a game, and you move a piece, and the piece is me. And even if you lose the piece, your position is stronger. And that is the way it's always been for me, here in your game."

There is a moment's pause, and then she hears Constantine's sigh, and feels the tension in him fade, the strength ease in the arms that circle her. "If you wish it," he says, "I will tell them no, and we will try to work out something else."

She laughs again. A bitter taste stripes her tongue. "You know me better than that," she says. "You know I won't want thousands of deaths on my conscience. Of course I'll go." She turns, looks up into his face, his guarded face.

A crackling fire, anger and resentment, burns in her heart.

"You say you want me to have my own power base," she says. "Very well, I'll have it. If I bring Landro's Escaliers over, I want them—I want them here with me, and I want command of them, *real* command, whatever other purely paper arrangements might be made. I want Karlo's Brigade as well. I want to be involved in any decision involving their deployment. I want Alfeg's organization to get official backing and money, and any Barkazils he brings over to work or to fight for us—I'll want command of them, too."

Constantine considers this, eyes narrowed, fleshy face impassive. "Anything else?" he asks.

"I would ask for your fidelity, for something like marriage and maybe even children someday, but—" She gulps for breath. "You'd probably rather give me an army."

He nods, as if confirming an observation he has made to himself. He bends and gives her cheek a kiss—not the kiss of a lover but, perhaps, the paternal benediction of a father.

"You have changed much since I first met you," he says.

"For the better, Metropolitan?" she asks. "Or otherwise?"

There is a kind of sadness in his eyes. "Those sorts of judgments are beside the point. The change happened, and it has made you stronger."

Constantine straightens, drops his arms, and walks away from her, lost apparently in his own thoughts. Aiah calls after him.

"Do I get what I want, Metropolitan?"

He hesitates, looks at her over his shoulder with a kind of surprise. "Of course," he says. "I thought it went without saying."

NINETEEN

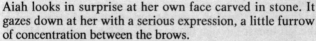

Aiah looks in surprise at her own face carved in stone. It gazes down at her with a serious expression, a little furrow of concentration between the brows.

The carving is called *The Apprentice,* and shows a woman at a kind of crude bench covered with equipment—retorts, burners, the sort of gear that might naively be assumed to inhabit laboratories. The figure looks down into a book for a recipe as she uncertainly holds a beaker in either hand.

Last time Aiah was here, the figure had another face.

"It changed two or three days ago," says Inaction, the dreaming sister who guides Aiah through the winding corridors. "I recognized the face when I saw it."

"You didn't think to call me?"

The sister looks at her. "We meditate upon the imagoes. We do not *phone* them."

Aiah looks at her, feels amusement tugging at her lips. "Have you ever *met* one before?" she asks.

The sister's dark-eyed gaze is guileless. She looks about twenty, with flawless, silken brown skin that excites Aiah's envy.

"In our meditations," she answers, "we strive to meet them all."

Aiah turns again to the image of herself. She had returned to the Dreaming Sisters' retreat without quite knowing why, understanding only that she was due to go into Provisional territory within a few days and might never again have the chance to wander through the ancient maze that is the Society of the Simple.

The department's monitors had failed to discover any sign that plasm was moving into the building in large qualities. But she hadn't seen any of the Dreaming Sisters' plasm displays since her last visit, so perhaps they were avoiding attracting any attention to themselves.

Aiah's image looks back at her, frowning in concentration. It occurs to Aiah to wonder how Inaction recognized her face. She and Inaction haven't met before; Aiah's last guide through the Dreaming Sisters' stone mazework called herself Order of Eternity.

"How did you recognize me?" she asks. "We've never met."

Inaction frowns in thought and scratches herself under the left breast through the coarse gray fabric of her shift. "I don't know," she says. "Perhaps I saw you in our meditations."

The Dreaming Sisters, Aiah has learned, specialize in answers that imply a great deal but don't actually seem to mean anything. Aiah shrugs, steps back from the stonework imago, looks at it again. "Tell me its meaning."

"*The Apprentice* follows upon the imago *Entering the Gateway,* which denotes she who has come to an apprehension of her own ignorance, and who therefore seeks knowledge. *The Apprentice* is she who strives to apprehend nature through the medium of a difficult art. The Apprentice strives at this stage not for meaning but for proficiency—full understanding is not implied, but may come at a later stage. There are associational meanings regarding youth, energy, enthusiasm, duty, joy in learning. There is also a great question, unresolved in this image."

Inaction's words don't come as a set speech, aren't rattled off: her voice is a bit dreamy, her dark eyes focused on something a thousand stades away. It is almost trancelike, a reflection of her own dream state.

"And the question?" Aiah asks.

"The Apprentice is a transitional figure, in movement from one place to another, from the gateway to the world beyond. The question involves the imago's destination—will she surpass her teachers and achieve mastery, or will she find herself with no singular gift, her talent and art lost amid the great clutter of the world. Satisfaction or frustration—the imago promises one or the other, but does not resolve the matter within itself."

Aiah frowns, looking at herself in the improbable act of balancing a pair of beakers. "There are other carvings of this figure, yes?" she says.

"Oh yes. The imagoes are repeated throughout our building."

"Is my face on all of them?"

Inaction looks blank. "I don't know."

"May we look? I'm curious."

"If you like."

Aiah follows Inaction down the stone corridor. Sorya appears as *The Shadow* no less than three times, and Aiah recognizes no one else but herself. No Constantine, she thinks in surprise. Her own face is repeated a half-dozen times, and she feels as if she has entered a hall of mirrors improbably constructed of stone.

For once Aiah catches Inaction in an expression of surprise. "Perhaps," the dreaming sister says, "you have become important."

PEACE TALKS CONTINUE; PROGRESS UNCERTAIN

PROVISIONALS DENOUNCE GOVERNMENT'S "UNREALISTIC CONDITIONS"

The oval screen of Rohder's computer is framed in a polished copper case chased with ornamental scallops and speed lines designed to make the viewer think that the screen, or at least data, is zooming from place to place with mighty efficiency. The ornament fails to convince anyone familiar with the ways of computers. The chief efficiency of the speed lines and ornamentation is to attract Rohder's floating cigaret ash.

Rohder, Aiah, and Constantine sit before the screen and watch crude images, gold on gray, blink and shimmer as Rohder's model of his work slowly moves pictured pontoons and barge outlines into new, ideal configurations. The computer is in the midst of a ponderous, labored dialogue with another, larger computer elsewhere in the Palace, for which it relies on data: Aiah thinks of prisoners laboriously transmitting messages from one cell to the next by beating on pipes. Gears hum, needles click back and forth on the computer's yellow dials. Then there is silence as the final image lumbers up on screen, and the dials drop to the neutral position.

Rohder taps the screen with a nicotine-stained finger. "I've got about as far as I can with the current crews," he says. "I started at a central location and moved outward, but as I expanded, the area to be covered increased geometrically, and in order to continue the work effectively at the current rate, I've got to increase my workforce by an order of magnitude."

Constantine considers this, then nods. "It will pay for itself," he says. "Send me a budget and I'll sign it."

Rohder nods and lights a new cigaret off the old. Aiah briefly considers taking advantage of Constantine's generous mood to ask for an increase elsewhere in the PED, but she decides that this expansion will cause enough administrative headaches for the present.

One of the few benefits of Caraqui's state of war is that many of the necessary government expansions and contractions have been accomplished without the usual amount of paperwork. But Aiah knows the paperwork will catch up sooner or later, and then there will be nothing but paper, pay slips, requisitions, and signatures for weeks and months, and possibly ever.

Constantine turns his eyes from the computer and asks the question that has brought him here. "How many days of full-out offensive can you give me?"

"Can you give me an approximate time frame? When do you intend to begin?"

There is a flicker in Constantine's eyes as he considers how much of his schedule he is willing to entrust to Rohder, or even to speak aloud.

"Before your new crews can make a difference," he says.

Rohder nods, looks at Aiah. "The figures won't change that much, then."

Aiah answers Constantine's question. "Three days of full consumption using domestic resources only," she says. "If our neighbors fulfill their commitments, we will be able to extend the offensive for another day, possibly two."

Constantine nods. "Well," he says. "We must hope to make a breakthrough early. A soldier cannot advance without a mage clearing the enemy ahead of him, and he can only hold an area if enemy mages are kept off his neck."

"We've had some unanticipated side effects," Rohder says. "Do you have a minute?"

"Of course."

Rohder taps keys, the screen flickers and the computer makes a grinding noise as it gets up to speed, and then the crude images are replaced with columns of figures, gold on gray.

"There would seem to be a synergistic effect to the multiplication of plasm through the fractionate interval theory," he says. The rest of the department has taken to referring to fractionate interval theory as FIT, but Rohder prefers the older, more elaborate term.

"This"—he taps figures again with his knuckle—"this is the predicted increase of plasm, by district, in line with theory . . . and *this*," tapping again, "the initial increase. It is less than predicted, because the methods we used to move structures were less than ideal, and our estimates of the composition of the structures themselves were in most cases approximations. But now—note this *third* set of figures. These are *very* recent, based on meter readings conducted within the last two weeks."

Constantine looks into the screen, columns of numbers reflected in his eyes. "Some are larger," he says.

"In some cases," Rohder says, "larger than theory predicts.

There must be another mechanism working here, something we have not previously observed. Since fractionate interval theory has never been tested on such a large scale before, some unanticipated results are to be expected, but *this* . . ." He taps the screen again. "This is different. Two weeks ago, some new effect was introduced."

"Maybe it's cumulative," Aiah suggests. "You get a certain amount of mass into this configuration and then the effect multiplies."

Rohder draws on his cigaret, lets the smoke drift slowly past his lips while he continues to contemplate the figures. "Could be," he says. "We're basing this only on meter readings, and the meters are not really designed to produce the more sensitive data we need to understand the phenomenon. However, I think I can promise you considerably more plasm for your Strategic Plasm Reserve than you anticipated."

Reflected columns of gold figures glitter in Constantine's eyes. "May we keep this information between us?" he says. "I see no reason to inform the government when all these figures are so preliminary."

Rohder shrugs. "You're the boss. But allow me to point out that if this phenomenon continues, and if you can postpone your offensive for a few months, I'll be able to keep it going for a lot longer. Perhaps as much as a week."

Constantine gives a minute shake of his head. "Not possible. There are time-dependent considerations."

Aiah looks at the screen and feels a fist gently tighten on her throat. Those considerations have to do with the six days left on the Escaliers' contract.

But Constantine is absorbed by another thought entirely. "After the war, I want to dedicate the Plasm Reserve to work with Havilak's Freestanding Hermetic Transformations . . . and possibly even more."

"Atmospheric generation?" Rohder's watery blue eyes gaze thoughtfully at Constantine.

"Yes."

"You'll need some highly trained people."

"You're talking about building things out of *air?*" Aiah asks.

Constantine nods. "Hermetics transforms one thing into another, base matter into food, say, or plastic. Why not a freestanding, plasm-generating structure assembled—reassembled really—out of thin air?" He shrugs. "It's not a new idea. . . . There are mages who specialize in such transformations, in places inaccessible or dangerous for people. Reactor cores, say."

Rohder puffs as he muses on the notion. "Those mages are too specialized for what you have in mind. You'll need to create teams of specialists from scratch."

Constantine gives a shrug. "One thing a war leaves is rubble, and rubble would seem to be the perfect experimental medium. If things go wrong in training, we create only more rubble. It seems a safe enough experiment, well worth the risk."

"If you say so," Aiah says. "But it seems horribly complex."

"Mathematics is complex," Constantine says, "but it begins with one plus one."

Aiah turns to the golden figures shimmering in Rohder's computer display, and feels unease roll through her mind. "Some unanticipated results are to be expected," she says, quoting Rohder; and the others nod. Constantine's eyes are agleam.

"One plus one," he says, "and then you keep going," and he laughs, happy in the world of the unanticipated.

PROVISIONALS ACCUSE GOVERNMENT OF BREAKING TRUCE

"SIMPLE REDEPLOYMENTS," SAYS GOVERNMENT SPOKESMAN

After the meeting, as they walk toward Aiah's office, Constantine observes, "I understand you have paid two visits to Karlo's Brigade and General Ceison."

"Yes." She glances up at him. "They are my army—my power base, as you would call it—and I want to know them better."

"How well have you succeeded?"

"Somewhat. I have asked a great many naive questions and, one Cunning Person to another, General Ceison and Mage-Major Aratha have answered them without condescending too very much."

He looks down at her, and the calculation in his glance belies the humor in his tone. "I hope you will let the government borrow your army for this offensive."

Aiah answers the glance and not the voice. "Perhaps I will, if they are not simply to be thrown away. Ceison told me of your plans for the Dalavan Guard, hurled in a diversionary attack against the Island."

"May we not speak so loudly when it comes to these matters?" Constantine cautions. He lifts one brow in thought. "I wonder where your friends heard that story. Surely not from any official briefing."

Aiah smiles and keeps her voice low. "We private armies keep track of one another. I understand that Parq is very happy with his army's prominent role in the offensive, but then Parq is very vain and not a general."

"Whereas you are."

"Whereas," she corrects, "I hope to be, and I listen to those who are. My first lesson concerned the difference between an offensive and a suicide."

Constantine sighs. "Assaulting Lorkhin Island is a job best suited to fanatics who do not measure the odds. And Parq has raised a unit of fanatics who will be very useful as long as the war lasts, and very inconvenient afterward. If they join their faith's long line of martyrs, both they and I will have reason to be satisfied."

Aiah tries to view this slaughter from the point of view of one of the Cunning People. A true daughter of Karlo and Chonah would have no qualms at two enemies massacring each other.

Looking through the twin organic lenses of a human being, however, Aiah finds the idea of the carnage more than a little horrifying.

But ultimately the Dalavan Guard is Parq's worry, not hers. "As long as my army is not added to the martyrs' list," she says, "there will be plenty of satisfaction to go around."

"Your army consists of motorized troops who will be used to exploit any breakthrough. They will capitalize on any victory won at the cost of others." Sharply. "I hope that will satisfy you."

"Yes, I think so."

She wonders about another private army, Sorya's Force of the Interior, a more nebulous organization than the Dalavan Guard, and far less inclined to self-immolation.

"I hope you will enjoy your army for the time being," Constantine says. "You may not have it for long."

She looks at him. "Yes? And this means?"

"Your mission to the occupied zone may be canceled." He looks petulant. "We can't seem to find a safe place for the meeting. For security's sake it has to be within the area the Escaliers control. It can't be in any of the buildings they actually occupy, because we can't trust every single member of their brigade—it only takes one to inform. We had a safe apartment set up, but then Great-Uncle Rathmen moved a detachment of his tax collectors into the building—the Silver Hand is collecting the Provisionals' taxes for them!" He shakes his head in disbelief, then mutters, "At least that means the Provisionals will never have any money."

Relief dances along Aiah's veins. She will not have to enter enemy territory after all—she can quietly vacate her unearned position as Queen of Barkazi and go back to chasing gangsters down Caraqui's brackish back alleys.

But Aiah finds that the initial sensation of relief is followed by an unanticipated sense of loss. She had been, in some way, *ready* for the thing—for the negotiations, the tense bargaining under threat of capture and death, ultimate barter for ultimate stakes. . . . Aiah the Cunning had almost been looking forward to it.

"We're checking out other places for the meeting," Constantine continues, "but the buildings not occupied by soldiers are filled with refugees, and that's not a secure situation, either."

They have reached Aiah's office. She puts her hand on the doorjamb, sees Ethemark quietly waiting to see her, a file in his hand. "And the Sorya option?" she asks. The end run through Lanbola.

"Still undecided."

Her eyes stray to Ethemark. "Have you considered the half-worlds for the meeting?" she asks, and in the hesitation that precedes Constantine's reply, she knows the answer.

Aiah the Cunning, deep in Aiah's mind, gives a cry of triumph.

"May I intrude on your meeting with Ethemark?" Constantine asks. "Strange how, under the pressure of duty, I seem to have forgotten one of my significant constituencies."

PEACE TALKS DEADLOCK

ENVOY LICINIAS TO "MAKE FINAL EFFORT"

The envoy Licinias moves through his final meeting with grace, concealing any disappointment he may feel. Perhaps he is not disappointed after all, Aiah thinks; perhaps he is too wise ever to have expected results. He has been through all this before.

"In view of the government's inability to make further concessions," Licinias says, "I must regrettably declare the negotiations at an impasse."

Faltheg, speaking for the triumvirate, gravely thanks Licinias for his attempts at creating a settlement, and then goes on to offer his thanks to the Polar League for supporting his mission.

The government, indeed, had made few concessions. They had offered to postpone the elections for a further six weeks, and to allow the Provisionals to participate: but Kerehorn and his advisors, coldly looking at the numbers of votes they could expect from their remaining loyalists, rejected the terms, and instead demanded a place on the triumvirate and six seats on the cabinet. The government's masterful, scornful reply, delivered by Constantine, is broadcast not only within Caraqui but throughout the world, in most places simply for its entertainment value.

"We are willing, in any case, to continue the cease-fire," Faltheg continues.

Licinias takes formal note of this, then rises from the table. There will be a dinner afterward in his honor, with toasts and speeches by notables, but in the meantime there is to be a cocktail party. Aiah drifts through it, chatting to people she barely knows about things that within minutes she can barely remember—her mind is focused on Landro's Escaliers—and then she finds herself near Licinias. He bows to her in his courtly way, and she approaches him.

"I'm sorry that your mission wasn't successful," she says.

Gentle regret informs Licinias's tone. "It was not entirely unexpected. I anticipate another round of meetings, after the usual sad experience tarnishes the gleaming optimism of the participants."

"You think the war will go on, then?"

"Experience suggests that most wars end in stalemate. Every building in our world is a fortress, and our world holds very little but buildings. It is too expensive in terms of both money and lives to capture them all."

He glances over Aiah's shoulder, and she turns her head to follow his gaze, directed at Constantine. "The Cheloki Wars stalemated repeatedly," Licinias says, "despite your friend's great military skill. He had the grace to negotiate an exile for himself, when it became obvious that his enemies would never give in."

I can't let the nightmares loose again! Aiah remembers Constantine raving and weeping in the privacy of his office, the tears splashing on her hand, her own terror at seeing the wild fear unleashed in him. . . .

She summons confidence. "I think that he may have learned a few things in the years since."

Licinias gives a cold nod. "I hope that is the case." There is a moment of silence, and then he looks at her with a kind of calculating glance that Aiah finds reminiscent of Constantine. "I have been giving thought to the subject of our last conversation," he begins.

"I'm flattered that you remember," Aiah says.

"It is difficult to forget. You remain singularly prominent on video, Miss Aiah."

She smiles. "I don't watch much video, I'm afraid."

"Still, your prominence remains a fact. And then, in combination with this fact, I consider another fact—that the government is clearly preparing an offensive with both its mercenaries and its rebuilt army. And I further consider that when the military situation threatens stalemate, a natural reaction is to attempt subversion of the other side's forces. And then lastly, when I consider the peculiar mix of troops on both sides, a reason for your sudden prominence begins to suggest itself. . . ."

A cold fist closes on Aiah's insides. She tries to keep her smile stuck to her face. "I wonder, Mr. Licinias," she asks, "if you have shared this insight with anyone?"

Mild brown eyes gaze levelly from his lined copper face. "It is not my job to share insights with people at random. I am a listener, rather, and a conveyor of other people's messages."

She considers this—her smile is aching—and says, "That is not quite an answer, Mr. Licinias."

"True." He pauses for a thoughtful moment, then speaks. "Let us consider, therefore, what the future implies. If the war drags on, certain things, hitherto obscure, shall become more apparent. The Provisionals have sponsors whose naked interest becomes more and more obvious the longer the war continues. The more obvious their interest, the more their prestige becomes involved, and the more difficult it is to negotiate a retreat from their support of the Provisionals. Any attempt to resolve peace becomes multisided, counting all the Provisionals' sponsors, and I assure you that it's hard enough to stop a war when only two sides are involved. The more complex the matter, the more work for me, and in all probability the less desirable the outcome. . . ." He gives another courtly bow. "And so I wish your video appearances all the success they so clearly deserve."

She returns his bow. "Thank you, sir."

He drifts away, an enigmatic smile on his lips, and Aiah stands for a moment watching him. A thrill sings along her nerves at the thought of playing this game at such a high level; though another, more anxious, level of her mind is carefully replaying the conversation to make certain it meant what she thinks it did.

She looks over her shoulder for Constantine, possibly to enlist his aid as interpreter, but finds he is talking to Sorya. Though she hadn't appeared at any of the negotiations, she is nevertheless present, like some carrion bird, at their demise. She is dressed in her green uniform, polished boots light as slippers on her feet. She tosses her head with a swirl of blonde-streaked hair, and Aiah hears her tinkling laugh. Aiah scowls.

"Excuse me, miss." She starts and discovers two men maneuvering a video camera into position. She makes way for it.

The negotiations weren't shown on video, but their termination will be. If Licinias's theory holds, there should be a great many long and uninteresting speeches.

Licinias is right. Aiah drowses through the lengthy platitudes, her mind elsewhere, in the faraway ruined landscape where Landro's Escaliers, her distant kinsmen, hold ajar the gate to Constantine's victory.

PROVISIONALS DENOUNCE DIRECTOR OF PED

"AIAH IS CONSTANTINE'S ASSASSIN," SAYS KEREHORN

"MURDER CLIQUE" CONDEMNED

After the speeches are over, Aiah walks to the offices of the PED—they are on her way, and she might as well check on the next shift's operations. When she goes to fetch a file she finds Constantine in the secure room, a stack of files on the desk in front of him. His skin is drawn taut over his face, and there is a haunted look in his eyes, as if he is gazing into an agony from which there is no escape.

Aiah's mouth goes dry as she sees him, but his attention snaps to her as soon as she steps within his sight, and there is no way to withdraw . . . so she presses the day's code into the pad, opens the barred gate, enters, closes it behind her.

Constantine does not speak, but watches her as she walks to the file drawer she wants, unlocks it, slides open the bronze-fronted door on its silent bearings, and finds the folder she needs. She takes the file, closes the drawer, and makes her way out. Her nape hair crawls beneath his steady gaze.

There was hatred in the twist of his lip, she saw. Hatred and contempt. Though whether for her, or himself, or the world itself she cannot tell.

FEARS OF RENEWED FIGHTING

BOTH SIDES STOCKPILE MUNITIONS

Constantine embraces her, a fierce hug that drives the breath from her lungs. Then Aldemar, the copper transference grip already in her hand, gives her a gentler embrace. The briefest sensation of plasm tingles on Aiah's skin. Aldemar seats herself, closes her eyes, focuses.

Constantine's eyes burn into hers. "Come back," he says, voice low, an earthquake rumble in Aiah's bones. Aldemar tilts her head back, stiffens, throws out an arm. A surge of plasm startles Aiah, and she takes in a breath . . .

And expels it in another place. Warm, humid darkness surrounds her, strangely strung with holiday lights. The air smells of decay, brackish water, fecal matter. A generator's hum is oppressively loud in the enclosed space.

A little gray man approaches, strung lights glowing in his huge eyes. He takes a cigar out of his mouth and speaks in a rasping voice. "I'm Sergeant Lamarath," he says. "Remember me? Welcome back to Aground."

TWENTY

~~~~~~~~

Many of the twisted in Aground, Aiah observes, are carrying guns—part of the payment, she suspects, for the risk Lamarath is taking here. The ominous half-human figures, shadows coiled around oiled weapons, are visible here and there as she takes a brief tour around the floating half-world.

Constantine has sent loyal Cheloki soldiers, Statius and Cornelius, to secure the place ahead of time, though they admit there isn't much to be done. "If we're attacked by the Escaliers or anyone else," Statius says, "this place won't hold out two minutes. Mages could set it alight or just smash it to pieces. And if anyone gets a heavy weapon down here and starts pumping shells into this junkyard, it'll come apart."

Aldemar is standing by, Aiah knows, to teleport her away in case things go wrong, but the problem is how to let Aldemar know when it's necessary. The protocols of the negotiation state that neither side is to send mages into the area, and that any signs of telepresence are to be taken as hostile. Statius and Cornelius have been provided with a radio, but it hasn't been tested—they daren't broadcast for fear the Provisionals would pick up the signal.

There is, as it happens, a telephone. The Agrounders have hijacked some phone lines, and Aiah, because a call to unoccupied Caraqui would almost certainly not go through, has been given a number in Gunalaht she can call if an emergency threatens.

Aiah appreciates all the effort on her behalf, but suspects that in a genuine emergency none of them would be worth a half-dinar.

Aiah is again taken on a tour of Lamarath's arcane headquarters, marine superstructure mated with surface vehicles and stray bits of portable housing, then strung with red holiday lights. The meetings themselves will be conducted where Aiah first met Lamarath, in his shielded office with its locked metal cabinets and massive desk. Aiah's nerves chill at the sight of the serpentine Dr. Romus still hanging from his hook. Romus smiles at Aiah from his brown homunculus face, his wreath of tentacles waving hello; Aiah stammers through a greeting.

"You'll be staying in the next room." Statius opens an oval hatch to reveal a small room set up with a bed and a bedside stand. Bronze mesh is tacked to the walls, floor, and ceiling, reinforcing whatever shielding may already be present under the plaster. "This here," opening another hatch from the office, "leads to a shielded back passage," more bronze mesh, "which leads to an exterior hatch."

The hatch is scaled to Lamarath's size, and Aiah and her guards have to bend low to exit into the darkness outside. "We've clamped a pipe here," Cornelius says, revealing a vertical pipe whose lower end disappears into the black water below. "We've put a tank of air and a regulator down there, about three paces down," Cornelius says, then looks up in sudden uncertainty. "We were told you know how to use them, yes?"

Aiah bites her lip. "I've been underwater once or twice," she says. And hadn't enjoyed herself.

"There's a mask tied down there, a buoyancy harness, and a pair of fins," Cornelius adds. "If you need to hide, you'll have air enough for two hours if you don't go any deeper and don't expend any air swimming around."

"I'll freeze," Aiah says.

"Well"—Cornelius shrugs—"it's for emergencies only. If things really deteriorate, it's better to risk hypothermia than to get shot."

"Hi, Miss Aiah!" says a cheerful voice. "Do you remember me?"

Statius gives a little start, and curses under his breath: he hadn't seen the boy sitting, a shadow in a deeper shadow, on the rusting deck plates.

Aiah's own nerves are in little better shape. "Hello, Craftig," she manages.

The boy stands, massive frame lurching upward, and Statius mutters something again and takes a step back. "The Sergeant said you were coming back," Craftig says. "Are you going to be staying long?"

Aiah considers this. "I'm just here to do some business," she says. "When it's over, I'll go."

"If you get bored," the boy says, "we can play checkers. I'm good at checkers."

"I'll let you know if I have some time," Aiah says, and then adds, remembering her last visit, "How's the family?"

Craftig tells her at length, not caring that she hasn't met a single one of his kin. A few minutes into the narrative, Aiah hears Statius discreetly clear his throat.

"Sorry about your uncle," Aiah says, interrupting the chronology in midflow. "I'd like to stay and chat, but I have an important meeting coming up."

"With those Escalier guys?" Craftig says. "See you later, hey? Have a nice time while you're here."

Aiah hears Cornelius sigh. "So much for security."

Aiah turns to him. "Better finish this in a hurry, then."

The delegation from the Escaliers are due in an hour or so. Aiah changes from the coveralls she'd worn during her tour into a gray wool suit, combs her hair, fluffs her lace. She puts on the priceless ivory necklace she'd received from Constantine, with its dangling Trigram. She wishes the room included a mirror so that she could make certain of the effect, then decides that a mirror would only make her insecure and she was better off without it.

Instead of a mirror, she'd like a plasm connection. A jolt of artificial confidence is just what she needs right now.

She steps into Lamarath's office and reviews her files on Brigadier Holson and Colonel Galagas, the two officers she'll be speaking with.

Landro's Escaliers were formed out of elements of the Fastani army when Barkazi fell. Now, fifty years later, they seem not to be as attached to the Fastani cause as Karlo's Brigade are to the Holy League; otherwise, looking down the road, there might be trouble between the two. Landro, the original brigadier, was killed in fighting in Morveg thirty years ago, though the brigade retains his name, out of both sentiment and convention.

Holson, the current commander, was actually born in Barkazi, in the Jabzi Sector, the part of Barkazi first invaded by a neighbor intent on restoring order and civilizing, or recivilizing, the natives. Aiah thinks it is probably significant that, though Holson received a military education in Jabzi, he hadn't joined its army or those of any of the other occupying powers. He had wanted to serve in a Barkazil force, and that was what he did, traveling thousands of radii to do it.

Galagas was the fifth generation of his family to follow the military life. Aiah's dossier was uncertain as to whether his grandfather had fought with the Fastani out of conviction or because it was the Fastani who happened to command most of the Barkazi army at the start of the civil wars.

But Galagas, also, had not joined any regular army, and had instead stayed with this band of Barkazil mercenaries.

That, Aiah thought, was important. Holson and Galagas, both talented officers, preferred serving with ethnic Barkazil mercenaries than with a regular army that would probably pay better and offer better security. Both were married to ethnic Barkazil women. Being Barkazil was important to them.

They thought of themselves as Barkazil before they thought of themselves as Jabzil or Garshabis or whatever. And that, Aiah thought, was the key.

They were willing to follow Aiah the Queen of Barkazi, or at least to *think* about following her.

It wasn't just that they were exploring their options. If they wanted to involve themselves in a bidding war between the factions, they could do it openly, negotiate through their agents in Garshab.

No, it was *treachery* they were meditating—the deliberate betrayal of their current employers. The mercenaries supposedly had a professional code that prevented such things. They were betraying not only their employers but their profession.

They were meeting with her because they *wanted* to. They were *already* convinced they wanted to switch sides—otherwise they wouldn't be here at all.

What Aiah should strive to do was, in essence, passive—she should not change their minds, but rather allow their preconceptions to model her behavior. She had to be whatever they wanted her to be, whether it was the Sorceress-Queen of Barkazi or the Dreaming Sisters' Apprentice or a superheroine out of one of Aldemar's films.

"I don't suppose I will be allowed to remain," says a voice in Aiah's ear. She jumps, puts a hand to her heart.

"Sorry I startled you," apologizes Dr. Romus in his eerie, reedlike voice. His wizened brown face looks more amused than apologetic.

"I forgot you were here."

"Yes," more amusement, "that happens more often than you'd think. I thought I should remind you I was here before your guests arrive."

"Thank you." Aiah tries to calm her flailing heart. "I suppose you shouldn't stay. Thank you for understanding."

Dr. Romus uncoils his forebody—thick as Constantine's leg—and drops a loop to the floor, followed by the rest of him. He keeps his head raised, at Aiah's level, as he progresses toward the hatch. His feathery tentacles are busy around the lock for a moment, and then, smiling, he opens the door and makes his way out.

"Bye now," Romus says. "See you later."

Aiah tries to focus on the dossier, but her concentration fails. In a few minutes, Cornelius comes in to tell her the delegates' boat has been sighted—two green and one white light, as agreed. "Do you want to wait here?" he asks.

Aiah shakes her head. "I should meet them." She closes the dossier, opens a drawer of Lamarath's desk, sees a pair of large cockroaches scuttle from the light. . . . She closes the door and decides she may as well leave the dossier on the desk.

Outside, in the red glow of the strands of lights, Aiah

waits on the rusting deck plates. There is a creak from the cables that support the swinging bridge that leads from the mooring. Aiah strains into the darkness, sees several shadows crossing the bridge, the first preceded by a tiny cherry-red glow. This proves to be a cigar clenched in the teeth of Sergeant Lamarath, who guides two men in uniform: Holson and Galagas.

Aiah waits for the group to get off the bridge, then steps forward and holds out her hand. If they have come this far, taken this risk, she will at least walk across the deck to greet them.

"General Holson. Colonel Galagas. Thank you for agreeing to meet me."

Holson is a big, broad man with a powerful neck and shoulders; his hair is cropped so severely that the rugged contours of his skull, reflecting red light, are plainly visible. His hand is large, his palm dry; as he clasps Aiah's hand he looks at her with intent, unwinking eyes.

Galagas is smaller, with a mustache. He is formally correct: he tucks his cap under one arm and bows slightly over Aiah's hand as he takes it. Somehow he avoids clicking his heels.

Formality covering nervousness? Aiah wonders. Perhaps he doesn't even want to be here.

"Would you follow me, gentlemen?" Aiah says. "I'll take us to a place where we can talk."

Holson nods. Aiah turns to Lamarath. "Thank you, Sergeant," she says. Lamarath grins and waves his cigar.

"No problem, miss."

Holson gazes uneasily over the floating half-world as he follows Aiah toward the hatch. "How many people live in these places?"

"Millions, if you count them all."

Holson looks unhappy. "And here they are, in our security zone. I had no idea these places existed. These people are a danger."

Aiah pauses, one hand on the open hatch, and looks at Holson. She doesn't want to inadvertently cause some kind of horrid persecution of those who live in the half-worlds.

"These people are a danger only if you destroy their

homes," Aiah says. "Then they *will* be in your security zone, and you won't want them there."

She lets Holson chew that over for a few seconds, then enters the hatch and leads the delegates to Lamarath's office. She offers them drinks, coffee flask, and snacks from a table made ready for them.

Galagas pours coffee for his superior. "Sorry I don't have any Barkazi Black," Aiah says. "I have a cousin who works at the factory, but his last shipment was delayed by the war."

This is not true—the cousin exists; the shipment does not—but Aiah wants through this genial lie to establish some kind of connection here, invoke the tribal longings of her audience. . . .

Galagas hands coffee to Holson. "What's his name?" he asks.

"Endreio. Endreio the Younger, actually."

Galagas pours coffee for himself. "I have a cousin there myself. Franko. And my grandfather was a director there, before the war."

The factory was a strong point for the Fastani during the fighting, Aiah knows. The Battle of the Coffee Factory was one of the early bloodbaths.

Galagas sips his drink. "My grandfather said the coffee never tasted the same after they rebuilt the factory."

"My grandmother says the same thing." Which, it happens, is true.

Holson looks at her and runs a hand over his cropped head. "Is all your family from Old Oelph?" This being the district with the coffee factory, now part of the Metropolis of Garkhaz.

"My maternal line is Oelphil. My father's *might* be, it's hard to say. . . ." She looks at Holson. "Your name was originally Old Oelphil, ne? There was Holson the Praefect back in Karlo's time. . . ."

"He is supposed to be an ancestor." Holson looks a little skeptical as he says this, probably so that Aiah won't think he's boasting by claiming descent from one of the Old Oelphil families, those who, according to the legend, had agreed to be reincarnated over and over again as protectors of the Barkazil people.

Of course, the records from the time of Senko and Karlo have not survived, and anyone can claim descent from anyone else.

"Would you like to sit down?" Aiah invites.

She sits behind Lamarath's desk. Squares her shoulders, folds her hands on top of the desk.

Holson and Galagas sit. Galagas sits bolt upright, plainly uncomfortable, but Holson's bold gaze challenges Aiah.

"And you look different than on video," he says.

"The light here," she says, gesturing at the fluorescents, "is less flattering."

"You're younger than I expected."

Aiah allows herself what she hopes is an enigmatic smile. "I've come a long way," she says.

"And where do you plan to go?"

"Farther. Barkazi, if things work out."

Skepticism narrows Holson's eyes. "And what will you do in Barkazi?"

He is pushing, she thinks. She suspects he will not respect her unless she pushes back.

"What I do," she says, "depends on what kind of support I can acquire in the meantime. Right now there are only two Barkazil military units in the world, and they are fighting on opposite sides of a war that has nothing to do with Barkazi. I like to solve my problems one at a time, and that's the problem I'd like to start with."

"You want Barkazil military units?" Holson says. "For what? Any attempt to liberate Barkazi with two brigades is naive."

Aiah looks at Holson and hopes the surprise she feels shows on her face. "Did I say I wanted to invade Barkazi? I'm not interested in bloodbaths. But see, now . . ."

She leans forward, narrowing the distance between them. "If we can join forces," she says, "then my government will be very grateful, both to me and you. Their gratitude has already extended to settling Barkazil refugees here, to establishing a Barkazil community. And if we wished to try to alter the situation in Barkazi, the government here would help us. Whereas . . ." Aiah looks at Holson for a moment, and then at Galagas. "Well, you know your employers best. What sort of gratitude would you expect from *them?* You'd be lucky if you got a bonus on your way back to the Timocracy."

Galagas nibbles at his mustache with white lower incisors. "If we switch sides in the middle of a campaign," he says, "we *can't* go back to the Timocracy. We have all sworn to obey the Timocratic Code. They wouldn't have a unit that didn't meet with their commitments."

Holson's big forefinger jabs at Aiah. "Your government had better be damned grateful, is what we're saying," he says. "Because if we join you, we're going to have to stay in Caraqui permanently, and bring our families here."

Aiah looks at Holson's forefinger just long enough to make it clear she's not intimidated by the gesture, and then she leans back in her chair.

"I am confident my government's gratitude will extend that far," Aiah says.

"You're certain of this?"

A doubt raises its hand, like an uncertain student in a classroom. Aiah ignores it. "I can confirm it very quickly if you wish."

"A bonus on signing?"

"I am authorized to offer three thousand dinars per soldier, five thousand for each field grade officer, and for *senior* officers," nodding at the two present, "ten thousand."

This is actually half of what she's been authorized, but there's no reason to tip her hand at this point.

"Standard rates of pay afterward?"

"Whatever you're earning now."

"Moving bonuses for our families?"

She hesitates. "Yes. I can get that. Say a thousand dinars per person?" She can take it out of the savings on the signing bonuses.

"How long a contract?"

"A year, extendable by mutual agreement."

There is a pause. The two men look at each other. Galagas gives a little shake of his head. Holson turns back to Aiah, a frown on his face.

"We're giving up our livelihoods," Holson says, "and only for a year's employment? We want more."

"Five years guaranteed," Galagas says.

"Five years, extendable. Or maybe . . ." Holson frowns at the floor for a moment. "Maybe commissions in the Caraqui army. It's not entirely out of line—you've got a lot of mercenaries even in your regular army now, because native officers are so inexperienced."

"With a guarantee," Galagas adds, "that our soldiers will be able to continue serving with one another for five years. We stay together as a unit, not to be broken up, for five years."

Aiah thinks for a moment, but she daren't hesitate for too long. There's momentum building here, and she doesn't want to slow it down.

"I can get you the five-year guarantee," she says, and hopes it's true. "For the regular army commissions I'd have to speak to the War Minister, but I think they'd be happy to have officers of your experience on board."

Might as well ladle on some flattery while she can.

"And then?" Holson asks.

Aiah smiles at him. "Sorry, General?"

"Barkazi. What about Barkazi?"

Aiah hesitates. "If this works, we'll be united. We'll have a power base in Caraqui, a government that will support us." She forces a smile. "The rest depends on how cunning the Cunning People actually are, don't you think? Whatever excuse the occupying forces had for annexing the Barkazi Sectors, the reason is long gone. If we stand united, here and there, surely there isn't anything we can't accomplish."

Holson sits stone-faced, and Galagas gnaws his mustache again, but Aiah senses that she has somehow won. She's said the right thing; she's raised some strange, unreal hope in them.

And oddly enough, she feels hope glowing within herself. Before this situation, she'd never given thought to Barkazi— she'd never been there, and her family's stories, all of horror and war, never gave her the slightest inclination to visit. But now she finds herself wondering if Barkazi would feel different beneath her feet than any other metropolis, if she would, on arrival, somehow sense that Barkazi was *home*.

She could hardly feel more displaced than she does now, sitting behind the desk of a minor, aquatic gangster, in a dark, foul-smelling watery cavern inhabited by twisted people with altered genes, negotiating with potential turncoats on behalf of a government that is not, when all is said and done, her own. . . .

"Those recruiting bonuses," Galagas says, crossing one knee over the other, "they seem a bit low to me. Considering what we'd be expected to do."

Inwardly, Aiah smiles. Love of negotiation must be planted somewhere in Barkazil genetics.

"I think they're fair," she says, "though I suppose there's a *little* room for negotiation."

NEW CITY *NOW!*

Constantine's presence tingles around her. Aiah bathes in it for a moment, fantasizes that she can taste him on her tongue. . . . She raises a hand to touch the ivory necklace he'd given her, a tactile remembrance.

—I think it went well, she sends.

—Any problems?

—They want the sun and the moon, but I have made them settle only for the moon.

She senses Constantine's amusement. After she had agreed with Galagas and Holson to meet again tomorrow, and seen them back across the bridge to their boat, she had called the number in Gunalaht and told them that she would be available for contact every hour, on the hour.

—They want a five-year contract with Caraqui, Aiah sends. They say they can't go back to the Timocracy after violating their Code.

—Five years? I suppose we shall still need mercenaries after that time.

—They suggest, as an alternative, that they could be made a part of the regular army establishment. But they want their unit to stay together for five years.

There is a moment's hesitation. Through the plasm link, Aiah can sense the movement of Constantine's thought.

—Yes, he sends. I can give them that. They are a good unit.

The Treasury was spending tens of billions on this war.

Aiah knows that Constantine is not likely to quibble over payments and guarantees to the people who could actually bring an end to the fighting.

—And there is something else that *I* want, Minister.

—Ye-es? Constantine's answer is wary.

—I want the same arrangement for Karlo's Brigade, if Ceison wants it. If we are going to reward one unit for changing sides, we should also reward the unit that stays loyal.

—*Many* units have stayed loyal besides Karlo's Brigade. Do we make them all such promises?

—Very well. I will modify my request. Let Karlo's Brigade have the same contract as Geymard's men.

There was a powerful silence. Geymard's Cheloki had been with Constantine since the beginning. They were his bodyguard, his spearhead, the steel foundation of his military power.

When Constantine's reply comes, she can sense amusement beneath the concession.

—Five years does not seem so bad, when things are taken all together.

—Thank you, Minister.

Aiah might as well turn humble, she figures. She has pushed her luck as far as it will go.

Constantine's reply is swift.

—Is there any *good* news? he sends.

Laughter bubbles from Aiah's throat.

—I have saved you money. The Escaliers are likely to accept a smaller signing bonus than we planned.

—Thank you, my child. Though the Treasury will *not* be pleased with the five-year contracts.

—Ending the war will save them money, and they will thank you.

Aiah can almost see Constantine's rueful smile.

—The Treasury *never* thanks me, he sends.

—Galagas and Holson will be back tomorrow, 08:00. Once they are presented with the terms, we can work out the details of exactly how they are to slip out of their agreement.

Traced in the air before Aiah's eyes comes the reply, lines of gold flame that form the Sign of Karlo.

—Blessings upon you, Miss Aiah.

—Thank you, Minister.

Constantine's presence fades, and Aiah is alone, listening only to the faint slap of water against the hull of Lamarath's barge. She returns to her quarters. Lamarath and Dr. Romus are gone, and Statius and Cornelius, on guard and in any case unsettled by the strangeness of the half-world, are no company.

Aiah paces back and forth, fretting. She would like to rest, but she knows the Adrenaline Monster would snatch her from sleep if she closed her eyes.

"See if Craftig is outside," she finally tells Cornelius. "We might as well play some checkers."

"ELECTIONS WILL CONTINUE AS SCHEDULED,"

INSISTS GOVERNMENT SPOKESMAN

The next day Holson and Galagas are forty minutes late. "Sorry," Holson says after their arrival. "We couldn't get away—" He looks uncharacteristically vague. "A meeting, with members of the Provisional command."

Aiah wonders if Holson is rash enough to be involved in a bidding war with the Provisionals—but no, she thinks, that would be suicidal. It's bad enough they're contemplating treachery against one side; treachery against both would be fatal. She tells the officers that the War Ministry has given official approval to their agreement.

"Now all that is required," Holson says, "is to honorably extract us from our commitments to the Provisionals."

"Do you have a copy of the agreement? We do not."

According to the agreement, Landro's Escaliers are irrevocably committed to continue with the Provisionals for another three days, after which, if there is mutual agreement, the contract may be extended. If no agreement is reached, the Escaliers will continue in service for another ten days, time enough for them to be evacuated back to the Timocracy and replaced in the line by another unit.

"How are the Provisionals on the warranties clause?" Aiah asks. "They've paid you on time?"

"Yes."

Aiah skims the contract. "Have they arranged for sufficient supply, food, fuel, medical support, and—ah—other classes of logistical support as specified in Attached Agreement C?"

"The brigade whorehouse," Galagas clarifies.

In the last months Aiah has become used to the ways of mercenary units, and is not surprised. She looks at Galagas.

"Has logistical support been, ah, sufficient in terms of the contract?"

Aiah wonders if a mercenary contract has ever been broken because prostitutes were not provided in sufficient number.

"Given the exigencies of war," Holson says, "the government's support has been adequate."

"That's not what I asked," Aiah says. "I asked if the Provisionals' logistical support has been sufficient in terms of the contract. Anything ever delivered late? Or delivered to the wrong people? Or the wrong stuff delivered to the wrong people?"

Given what Aiah knows of the military life, she would be amazed if this were not the case.

Holson and Galagas look at each other. Holson fingers his chin and shifts his weight uncomfortably in his chair. "Arrangements have not been perfect," he says, "but I mislike breaking an agreement on these conditions, all so common in war. It could set an unfortunate precedent—any unit, on any side, would be justified in breaking its contract if this clause were strictly invoked."

"Well," Aiah says, turning pages, "we will keep that option in reserve."

Unfortunately the contract is very straightforward and plainspoken, with few ambiguous clauses worthy of exploitation, and most of these involving situations that do not apply here. Maybe, Aiah thinks, it will have to be the whores after all.

"Can we arrange for the *Provisionals* to break the contract somehow?" Aiah asks.

They look at her. "In three days?" Holson asks. "How?"

"I keep coming back to the warranties clause," Aiah says. "Can you arrange for some supplies to go astray? Suppose your food gets delivered to the wrong place . . ."

They consider this for a few minutes. Ideas are put forward, then rejected as too complex. Aiah scans the contract again.

"The *signing bonus!*" Aiah says finally. "What if *that* doesn't get to you?"

Galagas seems relieved. "Well," he says, "*finally.*"

It takes them only a few minutes to work out a plan, Aiah collaborating with the other two as if they had known each other for years, so smoothly that she wonders if there's something, after all, to this business of the Cunning People having a special gift for duplicity.

Holson, they decide, will drag out negotiations with the Provisionals till practically the last minute. In the meantime, he will establish a new bank account in Garshab in order to receive the money. But the account number to which the Provisionals will be told to wire the signing bonus will be subtly different from the *real* number, a digit or two off.

When the deadline for payment passes without the bonus, Landro's Escaliers will be free, legally and (it is hoped) morally, to sign another contract with someone else.

"We should have the contract with you in place beforehand," Holson says. "That way we can take immediate action—holding a bridgehead, say—in accordance with the wishes of our new commanders."

Aiah is surprised. "You can sign a contract before the old one has expired?"

"It will be provisional only. Full of thus-and-so's, stipulating that in the event we are free of any other obligations before a certain date, we will consider ourselves yours to command. And we will give you an account number in Garshab"—he nods, with a significant smile—"a *real* account number, into which your government can place its good-faith deposit, perhaps one-tenth of the signing bonus?"

"I think this might be arranged." He has anticipated, she

notes, her objection to giving them their entire bonus, in case they re-sign with the Provisionals after all and dupe her government of all its dinars.

"We will return early third shift," Holson says, "and bring the contracts with us. We can't specify an exact hour—our other commitments are pressing."

"I will wait, sir. I thank you both."

Galagas—no longer so stiff and uncomfortable—reaches into a pocket and produces a silver flask. "I wonder, Miss Aiah, if you would join us in some kill-the-baby? It is from Barkazi."

Aiah smiles. Kill-the-baby is a phrase her grandmother has used. "I would be honored, Colonel."

Galagas raises the flask. "To success, and Barkazi."

There is a strange light in his eyes. Aiah wonders at the man's strange faith in her, in his belief that she is somehow destined to change the shape of things far away. It is beyond a mere credulity, and well into some mystical realm of faith she can't herself understand.

He drinks and passes the flask to Aiah, who echoes the toast and takes a swig. It is brandy, harsh and fiery and absent of refinement, without doubt the worst stuff she has ever tasted. This baby is *dead,* she thinks. Eyes streaming, she passes the flask to Holson.

If this is what the homeland tastes like, she thinks, I am not going.

She sees her guests out, and as they say farewell Holson surprises her by embracing her, kissing her on both cheeks.

"I know we will accomplish great things," he says.

Aiah manages through her surprise to retain her air of confidence. "I have no doubt," she says, and then accepts Galagas's somewhat more reserved embrace.

As Aiah watches the two officers make their way across the swaying bridge, she feels a kind of wonder that it has all worked out exactly as Constantine had, weeks ago, anticipated. He has maneuvered all of them, somehow, into this position, and will doubtless get his victory.

But what *then?* Aiah wonders. Aiah and the Escaliers have been maneuvered into this position, true, but the position is an artificial one. Aiah is not the redeemer of Barkazi—except on video, and in the mind of a deranged hermit back in Jaspeer—and the Escaliers are not an army of liberation. She doesn't know how she can ever meet these people's expectations.

We will accomplish great things.

She fears she is going to be a terrible disappointment to everyone who believes in her.

Aiah returns to Lamarath's office to organize her notes and finds Lamarath there, along with one of his hulking guards. One of the locked metal cabinets has been opened, and Aiah sees inside it a video camera, set to gaze at the room through a spyhole. Lamarath has opened the camera and is removing the video cartridge.

Aiah looks at the camera in shock. "The meetings were recorded?"

Lamarath looks at her over his shoulder. "You didn't know?" He seems surprised.

"No. I didn't." Anger blazes up in her. "I should have been told!" she says. "If they'd found out—"

If they'd found out, Aiah thinks, she'd have been killed.

Lamarath opens a briefcase and drops the cartridge into it. "A dolphin will carry it beneath the front to our friends," he says. He pats the case. "Insurance," he adds, "to make sure our mercenary friends won't betray us."

And insurance, Aiah knows, in case they'd failed to make an agreement at all. If the negotiations had failed, Constantine could have threatened to release the video to the Provisionals, which Holson and Galagas would have realized meant the end of them.

Displaced anger and fear rattle in the hollow of Aiah's chest. Constantine, she thinks, is willing to sacrifice her here, if it means a greater chance to win his war.

She feels a tremor in her knees.

One must keep one's true end in view. His end is victory, and Aiah herself—her life, her happiness—ranks somewhat lower on his scale of priorities.

Aiah walks unsteadily to Lamarath's chair and lowers herself into it.

"Insurance," she repeats, and thinks, Who is insuring me?

TIMES CHANGE, BUT OBEDIENCE IS ETERNAL.

A THOUGHT-MESSAGE FROM HIS PERFECTION,
THE PROPHET OF AJAS

—I am very pleased with this, Constantine sends. His tone, silky and satisfied, rolls through Aiah's mind.

—I expect the Escaliers will keep their agreements, Aiah replies. Which means that those recordings made by Lamarath can be destroyed. . . . I would like, in fact, to see them destroyed personally.

Their mental contact is sufficient for Aiah to receive Constantine's jolt of surprise, along with his reaction, chosen from an array of possible responses. He rejects a lie, first thing of all.

—It was to protect you, he ventures. If they had attempted treachery . . .

—The recordings could not have been produced until it was too late. You have put me in danger with this.

—Very little. It was all carefully calculated. . . .

Wordless fury rages through Aiah's mind. She can feel Constantine recoil.

—Apologies, he responds quickly. It was a bad decision, and shall not—

—It will not have the *opportunity* to happen again. I shall guard my own back in future, and not let you do it.

For a moment she senses thoughts rolling in his mind, their exact nature beyond her reach, imponderable.

—That is wise, he judges.

In answer she just radiates anger at him. Constantine absorbs this, and she senses, strangely, his approval.

—You are growing, Miss Aiah, and that is good.

He breaks contact, and leaves her with a reluctant sense of surprise tingling in her bones.

WANTED HANDMAN FOUND DEAD

"CAROUSED TO DEATH" IN NEIGHBORHOOD BAR

Head down, arms folded over the dangling Trigram on her ivory necklace, Aiah paces along the deck, thoroughly in the grip of the Adrenaline Monster. It is third shift, the two officers could arrive at any time, and she is too nervous to wait in Lamarath's stuffy office. It is dinnertime, and the twisted families are settling in for the sleep shift that will begin at 24:00. Cooking smells join the miasma over the dark half-world, mingled with the odor of sea, garbage, and feces. Video screens light the darkness here and there, blue video light glowing on twisted faces, reflecting off dark water. Judging by the laughter rolling up from barges here and there, most are tuned to the weekly episode of *Folks Next Door.* Aiah wonders what these people make of the video they watch, the constant display of goods, wealth, and security they have never possessed.

No one, she thinks, will ever make a weekly comedy about life in the half-worlds.

And then something blows up.

Right in the middle of the half-world, fifty paces away, a bright flash followed by a hot wind that presses on Aiah's face, that blows her hair back and ruffles the lace at her throat and wrists. In the roofed space of the half-world the sound is deafening. Aiah claps her hands over her ears, but this does not shut out the screams and cries for help or the sudden startled pounding of her own stammering heart.

She stands on the iron deck and stares into the darkness, but there is a huge bright bloom on her retinas that dazzles her, keeps her from seeing any of the explosion's aftereffects. Suddenly there is a firm hand on her elbow, and she jumps.

"Miss, you should take shelter." Statius's voice. "It's probably just an accident, there are all these pressurized hydrogen tanks here and open burners, but we should—"

Another explosion rips through the darkness. The pressure wave punches Aiah in the solar plexus and tears a cry from her throat. Statius wastes no more words; his hands close on her shoulders and he half-carries her toward the hatch.

A third explosion, on the other side of the barge from the first two, turns the darkness bright. Actinic light etches the ramshackle structures, the hunched bodies of the twisted people, bent over their meals and only now beginning to react. Aiah can hear metal fragments whistling through the air. There is a terrible stench, the smell of the explosive chemicals themselves. And then Aiah hears sirens, a terrifying wailing that echoes dizzyingly from the concrete and iron that surrounds them, and the sound of a machine gun, thud-thud-thud, and sees tracer rounds flying overhead in a regular stream. . . .

Statius throws her inside the hatch and slams the door shut behind them. Cornelius is there, machine pistol ready in his hand. He licks his lips. "What's happening?"

Statius answers as he propels Aiah through the neat, whitewashed rooms of Lamarath's headquarters. "Some kind of attack. Mage throwing mines or shells, I think."

"Who's doing it?"

"No idea."

The oval hatch to Lamarath's office looms ahead. It is shut. Statius throws himself onto the central wheel and heaves the hatch open as another explosion shifts the deck beneath their feet. Aiah stumbles through the hatchway, pain shooting through her leg as she catches a shin on the lintel.

"Hold the hatch, please," says an odd, reedy voice. Dr. Romus, the snake-mage, swims over the lintel with powerful, swift pulses of his body—for all the weight of his thick trunk, he is *fast*—he shoots across the room and lunges up the wall to the hook, the plasm connection, where he usually hangs, and coils himself around it.

"I will protect you as best I can," he says.

"That's *our* job," Statius says, crossing the room toward Romus. Behind him Cornelius slams the hatch to, spinning the wheel and dogging the hatch closed.

Dr. Romus's eyes are closed as he concentrates on the plasm world. "I am used to this connection," he says. "I am used to working with the little plasm available—*you'd* use it up in a minute or two."

Statius reaches for the plasm hook, grips it firmly. The barge lurches to a near-explosion. Plaster drifts from the ceiling like pollen. "I deflected that one," Romus says. "It would have killed us all. Please—let me do my job."

Statius looks uncertain for a moment, then takes his hand away. Cornelius is by the communications array, jiggling the headset hook. He shrugs. "Line's cut," he says. "I'll have to radio for an evacuation." He picks up the portable radio in its padded black plastic case and slings the strap over one shoulder. Statius joins him, gripping his gun. Cornelius looks back at Romus.

"Can you give me cover?" he asks.

Romus speaks without opening his eyes. "I'll do what I can. There's not much plasm here."

The two guards open the hatch that leads to the back passage, hop over the sill, and slam the hatch shut behind them. A nearby explosion shifts the barge under Aiah's feet, and soft white plaster rains down from the ceiling.

Aiah feels warm blood dripping down her scraped shin. She looks down at herself, at the neat suit, white lace, pumps, torn hose. This is the most ridiculous outfit she can imagine for a battle. She turns to Romus.

"Can I help?" she asks. "Can I do *anything*?"

Romus just gives a brief shake of his head. The sound of battle outside has increased, weapons rattling like a continuous storm of hail. Aiah decides she might as well get out of her absurd clothing, and yanks open the door to her private room. She kicks off her pumps, grabs the jumpsuit she arrived in, and pulls it on over the clothes she's already wearing. There's an unpleasant baggy lump in her crotch where the skirt has wadded up, but she feels a greater readiness now that she's no longer dressed for a business meeting, and no longer so conspicuous.

She closes the jumpsuit up to the collar, over the ivory necklace, then pulls on a pair of boots and slams down the metal clips—she has to hit them with her fist because her fingers are trembling too hard to work them properly. Explosive compression waves slap the barge, rain plaster down.

"Miss? *Miss?*" Romus's voice. Aiah jumps into the other room, sees Romus's fierce yellow eyes staring at her.

"Yes?" Aiah says.

"Your guards want me to tell you this: Statius is broadcasting the pickup signal, but he hasn't got an answer. That doesn't mean they're not hearing it at the Palace, it just means the receiver isn't placed well enough to catch any reply."

Aiah nods her understanding. Adrenaline is making her teeth chatter, causing sweat to pop out on her forehead. There's nothing she can *do.*

Romus continues, voice rapid. "There are mages attacking, and I'm running the plasm batteries low fending them off. Soon this shielding is going to be breached. Your guards say that you need to get into the water and start breathing off that apparatus and wait for pickup."

Aiah gives another frantic nod. "Yes," she says. "I understand."

"*Now,* miss."

She nods again, then realizes that, despite her intentions, her feet are somehow not moving toward the water. She makes them move and runs to the hatch, tears it open, steps through into the low corridor behind.

"*Close it,* miss."

"Ah. Right." Aiah stops, reverses herself in the narrow space, pulls the hatch shut. Then she runs along the corridor, tries the hatch leading outside, and finds it won't open. She slams her shoulder into it; pain jolts her body, and she realizes the door is locked. She claws at the bolt, throws the door open, and then there is the flash of an explosion that lights the hallway from the outside, and all the electric lights die. The mad sound of sirens fills the air, monsters calling their kin. Tracer bullets flash by in the dark, making snapping sounds like a whip, and glowing off every surface is the rolling red glare of fires. Aiah huddles in the doorway as terror scrapes her nerves, hands clenched on the doorjamb, with no intention of ever letting go.

I'm sorry, she thinks, *I can't go in that water.*

Then an explosion rocks the barge and Aiah finds herself pitching forward. The lurch unlocks her hands, lets her tumble through the doorway. Deck plates bite her palms. Bullets snap overhead. The pipe clamped to the side of the barge reflects silver-red fires, and Aiah can see it plainly. She crawls madly for the pipe, clutches it, pulls herself to it. The water below flares with reflected fire. Aiah takes a breath, kicks her legs, and tumbles off the barge.

The freezing water stops her heart for a long, shocking second. The taste of salt floods her mouth. She flails out for the pipe, finds it, pulls herself down its length. She can hear, louder even than the explosions, the whine of high-pitched screws.

Aiah finds the apparatus hanging there, fumbles in the darkness for a length of hose. . . . She finds it, reaches frantically along it, finds the second-stage regulator and mouth-piece at its end. She jams the rubber mouthpiece in her mouth, blows out to clear the regulator, inhales . . . nothing.

Nothing. No air. Terror fills her lungs instead. *She's going to drown!* She flails for the surface, all frantic panic motion, and somehow manages to rise instead of sink. She breaks the surface, splashing, mouth gasping in air. Sirens and battle sounds fill her ears. Fire boils up all around her. In the confined space beneath the platform overhead, the air is filling with smoke. Aiah coughs, sees the pipe nearby, clutches at it. Thoughts whirlpool in her mind.

It's a catastrophe. The mission's gone, she'll be killed or captured, *and there's no air in the tank.* This last treachery, the thoroughness of the way fate has betrayed her, leaves her numb.

A concussion passes through her like a wave, blows the air from her lungs. She looks up at the slablike side of the barge and wonders how she'll get back aboard. If she stays in the water she'll freeze or drown.

The valve. The thought comes to her head unbidden.

The air tank, she realizes, has plenty of air. But its valve was turned off so that the air wouldn't drain away through any minor leak in the connections. All she has to do is turn the valve on and she's got at least an hour of air.

Falling debris splashes water near her. Aiah drags in air, fills her lungs, then shuts her eyes and plunges underwater again. She finds the diving gear, gropes for the valve handle atop the tank, and gives it a yank. Then she reaches for the regulator hose, finds it, pulls on it hand over hand until she finds the regulator. Her teeth clamp down on the mouthpiece and she blows out, clearing the regulator, then inhales. . . .

Air. Sweet air. She feels a moment of indescribable bliss as the dry pressurized air touches her palate.

Aiah floats in the frigid, buoyant darkness. High-speed screws sing in her ears. Detonations slap at the water.

Red light seeps down, touches her eyelids. She opens her eyes, looks up at flame. The barge is on fire and has become very bright. She wonders if Dr. Romus is trapped inside, if Statius and Cornelius will manage an escape. She looks around her, sees the diving gear hanging on a hook. Had Cornelius said there was a mask here?

Aiah reaches out and finds the mask, pushes floating hair back from her face, and puts the mask over her face. She tries to remember her brief lessons months ago, then presses the mask hard to her forehead and exhales through her nose. The water in the mask bubbles away and suddenly she can see quite clearly.

The water is very bright, almost as bright as day. The barge is a huge shadow above her, and she can sense other shadows nearby.

There is a splash, a rush of bubbles. It is one of the half-world's inhabitants, a little goggle-eyed man. He swims with apparent ease beneath the surface, his big eyes like a pair of headlamps. He swims past her strongly, a line of little bubbles trailing from his mouth, and his eyes roll toward her. He watches her expressionlessly as he swims past, his adaptation to the aquatic environment much greater than hers, then kicks on into the darkness.

A line of bullets rips the water over her head. Aiah watches the bullets hit the water in a fury of bubbles, then lose their momentum and spiral harmlessly past her. The fighting, she thinks, is getting very close.

There is another splash overhead, another figure striking the water in a burst of bubbles. It is one of the stonefaces, mouth open, eyes agape. He drifts downward in a cruciform shape, arms wide as if to embrace the water. A thread of blood trails from his mouth.

Dead, Aiah thinks, and then, *Davath!*

She bottles up a scream at the bottom of her throat. She flails as she drags on the buoyancy harness, fighting the tangle of straps. A whole family of goggle-eyed twisted swim by, mom and pop and two curious children. The lead weights in the harness pockets try to drag her to the bottom, so she inflates the air pockets in the harness until her buoyancy neutralizes. Then she kicks off her boots and puts on her fins.

As she handles these routine tasks, her breath returns to normal, her heartbeat slows. But then the barge gives a huge lurch. The pipe kicks up and hits her in the face. An explosion batters at her ears. A surge of bubbles blinds her, and suddenly the pipe is tilting up, bringing her close to the surface.

Fear makes her relinquish the pipe and drop back into the sheltering sea. The barge has been holed, she realizes, and it is filling with water and rolling away from her as it does so.

It's going to sink, and she needs to get away before it drags her down. She backpedals, kicking away from the barge. Bullets rip up the water above her head and she pulls the release valve on the buoyancy harness, allowing herself to sink deeper into the water. . . . She tries to orient herself, tries to think which way is *out*. There is a horrid metallic rending sound from the barge, some internal bulkhead caving in.

Another twisted man swims by, big eyes bulging. He must know a safe place, she thinks, and decides to follow him.

She kicks out and has no trouble keeping up with him. The cold is making her shiver. Her body wants to curl up to conserve heat and she has to make an effort to keep her legs kicking.

It's a hideous failure, she thinks. Statius and Cornelius are probably dead, the half-world is being destroyed, hundreds of people are going to die.

And the war will go on.

An uncontrollable shudder runs through her frame.

And I, Aiah thinks, am going to die of cold, and very soon.

Then she feels plasm prickling her skin, warm like a blanket, and she is sprawling, amid a gurgling, splashing lake of seawater, on Aldemar's carpet. . . .

Powerful arms pick her up, strip the mask from her face, the regulator, begin unclipping the harness.

"A hot bath," Constantine says. "Draw it. Now."

He kisses her cold lips. Aiah looks at him from heavy-lidded eyes.

The diving gear tumbles to the floor, lead weights thudding.

Constantine picks her up and carries her to warmth, to life.

TWENTY-ONE

Aiah lies in the scented bath and tries to let the warm water ease the cold in her bones, the numb and numbing sense of dread and sadness and hopeless failure. She stares at the ceiling, at a bright pattern of blue and yellow Avernach tiles; and her eye keeps following the pattern, up and left and down and then to the right across three tiles, then beginning again, the pattern repeating over and over and over without escaping the inevitability of its own design.

Her eyes keep following the pattern. She dares not close them. If she allows her eyes to close, all she can see is a shimmering surface, like water, aglow with angry fire.

And then all the guns around the Palace open fire at once, a rolling thunder that rattles the window for a half-minute at a time, deep concussions that drive up through her spine, releasing memories of explosions in the half-world, the flashes of blinding light, the acrid scent of used munitions. The dead man, arms splayed, drifting toward her on a red tether.

The war is on again.

There is a knock on the door, and without waiting for an answer Aldemar walks in. She kicks aside Aiah's ruined, soggy clothing, then sits on a little gilt-legged stool and dangles her hands off her knees. The expression below the dark bangs is grave.

"I was unable to bring back the two guards who went out with you," she says. "It doesn't mean they're not all right, it just means that I couldn't find them in all that mess."

Aiah sighs and tilts her head back, despair like a bitter drop on her tongue. Gunfire concussions thud in her ears.

"It wasn't your fault," Aldemar says. "The mission was betrayed somehow—probably on the other end."

Aiah tries to say something and fails. Words do not seem adequate to the appalling scope of the tragedy.

"Those two had followed Constantine from the beginning," Aldemar says. "For twenty years, beginning in Cheloki. He chose to risk them in this, because he thought it was important. He wanted the best to protect you."

"They did," Aiah says. Her tongue is thick, and a pain deep in her throat makes it hard to speak. "They kept me alive." They, she thinks, and Dr. Romus.

Maybe, Aiah thinks absurdly, she will get them medals. Like Davath.

Aldemar leans back on the stool, looks down at her. "I would like to stay with you," she says, "but I can't. Now that fighting has started again, I'll be needed." She begins to stand, hesitates, then sits again. "Stay here as long as you want. I'd offer you my clothes, but they wouldn't fit. I'll try to find someone to fetch some clothes from your apartment."

"Thank you," Aiah says. She sits up in the tub, hair pouring down her back like rain, and looks up at Aldemar. "Thank you for getting me out," she says.

"You're welcome." Aldemar reaches for Aiah's hand, squeezes it briefly, then makes her way out. The window rattles to the sound of guns.

She'd thought she'd done it, she thinks. She'd won, she'd got the Cunning People on her side, had the contract worked out. She would be the hero who'd won the war. Even Barkazi had seemed within reach—She had half-seen the liberated metropolis, the homeland she'd never seen living free under her maternal care. . . .

All dreams, she thought, had come aground in Aground. All gone, all betrayed, in that horrid burst of fire.

WAR RENEWED IN CARAQUI!

GOVERNMENT FORCES ON ATTACK!

One of Aldemar's people, a young bespectacled man, brings her a case of clothes he'd got from her apartment. She receives him wrapped in a towel, and he blushes becomingly.

The contents of the bag makes her smile even through her despair. Aldemar's naive young man seems not to know what women actually wear, and for what occasions, and even in what quantity. He'd emptied out Aiah's lingerie drawer and filled the bag with every item of silk, satin, and lace that Aiah possessed, as if she were off for a romantic weekend in Gunalaht rather than a war. There are also bright flowered skirts, scarves, and lace-ruffled blouses.

Well. At least she can wear some of this as far as her apartment, and then she can change into something more appropriate.

She hesitates for a moment as she leaves, seeing her ivory necklace lying on a tabletop, then decides she may as well leave it here. Aldemar is unlikely to run off with it.

A short while later, more conservatively clothed, she walks into the Palace's command center, the cavernous room beneath the huge illuminated map. The place is full, and half a hundred uniformed communications techs sit with gold-and-ivory headsets clamped to their ears, relaying information back and forth. The overhead rows of video monitors all show views of skylines, smoke, silent flashes.

Here in the shielded silence, the sound of the guns cannot be heard.

Constantine stands near the front of the room, his casual civilian clothes—cords and a shirt open at the neck—a contrast to the uniformed officers standing around him. He spies Aiah the instant she enters, and though he continues speaking casually with his officers one eye remains fixed on Aiah as she walks down the aisle. The officers around Constantine fall silent as she approaches—respectfully, she thinks, while a comrade makes her report. Among them Aiah recognizes the former Captain Arviro of the Marine Brigade, the hero of the countercoup, who is now General Arviro of the Marine Corps.

"Statius and Cornelius weren't brought back," Aiah says.

There is a grim narrowing of Constantine's eyes, then he shakes his head. "I am losing the old ones, one by one," he says. "Statius was with me for thirty years, stood by me in everything I ever attempted."

This is *not,* Aiah wants to say, about *you.*

Constantine's look softens, and he takes her arm. "But he and Cornelius succeeded in their final mission, which was to preserve your life. If I had sent people I did not know as well, we might not have brought you back."

Aiah can feel despair tighten in her chest. "But the whole thing," she says, "was a botch."

He looks at her and shakes his head. "Your part of the mission was a success. That there was a failure somewhere else was not your fault."

She gives a little shudder. It did not feel like a success, not when she was in the water with bullets lighting the air above her.

Constantine gently draws her closer by her arm. "In any case, well, things are not as bad as we might have feared. You succeeded in panicking the Provisionals." He points at one of the video screens, and Aiah's gaze reluctantly follows his hand, sees buildings being battered by shellfire.

"When the Provisional command realized you were on the verge of causing one of their frontline brigades to defect," he says, "they ordered their nearby units to attack Landro's Escaliers. Those gunboats that struck the half-world were among the first units to respond. But their command structure is not very flexible over there—they have dispersed their communications and headquarters units so that they are not, once again, all attacked at the same time—and the first attacks were uncoordinated and easily repelled by a unit as specialized in this sort of fighting as the Escaliers. The Provisionals still have not managed a proper assault, but when they started the shooting they *did* push the Escaliers over to *us.* We have a bridgehead into enemy territory; we now need only to funnel our troops over in sufficient quantity—"

Uncertain hope catches in Aiah's throat. "Do you mean it worked? The mission wasn't . . . ."

"Not a total failure, no. Our forces went on two-hour standby as soon as you crossed to the other side. As soon as we received word of the enemy's movement, we started the clock ticking. The guns are firing already, and as soon as everyone reports ready, we will launch." His lips curl in a wolfish smile. "We have some surprises in store—the Sea of Caraqui provides an unconventional environment for warfare, and we will take advantage of it in ways our enemies will not expect."

Aiah looks up at the screens, at the scenes of violence repeated in one video display after another, Aground multiplied a thousand times. . . . Let it all be for *something,* she thinks.

"May I . . . watch?" she asks. The words just fall out, and Aiah regrets them at once. She does not want to witness the catastrophe of Aground all over again, and multiplied a thousand times.

Amusement glimmers in Constantine's eyes. "Find a perch," he says.

She begins to look for a chair, then hesitates and turns back to Constantine. "Where is Karlo's Brigade?" she asks.

"Mobile reserve, well out of the fighting." He points at a map. "We hope to shift them to exploit any breakthrough. . . ." He bows toward her with mocking courtesy. "*If* you approve, of course."

Aiah clenches her teeth. "Ask me when the time comes," she says tartly, "and I'll let you know."

Aiah finds an unused chair and sits. Suspense gnaws at her insides as she watches the preparatory bombardment, the reports of Provisional units being hammered, of plasm stations hit, ammunition barges blown up by dolphin raiders, of the enemy net, almost all their reserves, being tightened around Landro's Escaliers . . . the enemy response, actions not as certain as the government's, nor as strong, but still finding chinks in the government armor, causing delays as units have to improvise their way around the trouble . . .

invisible mage attacks on both sides, perceived only in an occasional flash, or through a verbal report . . . and then an ominous glow, a towering figure of fire. . . .

The Burning Man walks along the front, his body a raging holocaust. Aiah's heart leaps into her throat. A mage out of control, buildings igniting at his touch . . . and she knows that the Burning Man consumes not only the world around him, but the mage's own body.

The Burning Man withers and dies as someone cuts off the mage's plasm source, but the district he walked through still burns. . . . The battle seems to have slowed down, and despair invades Aiah again, a giddy sense of hopelessness that makes her sway in her chair. . . . When the last unit reports its readiness, and Constantine gives the command to commence the bridging operation, Aiah wants to cry out in relief.

A thousand mortars near the front open fire, dropping smoke into the no-man's-land between the forces, bright swirling splashes of green or purple or red. Government artillery increases its rate of fire, shells dropping right into the enemy front line. And then the soldiers begin to cross the water, thousands of small powerboats moving forward under the cover of smoke. The Dalavan Guard aims at Lorkhin Island, driving straight at the enemy's strongest point, and the Marines cross elsewhere.

Aiah turns from the screens to watch General Arviro of the Marines. He has trained his corps, labored long on their operational plans, and as the powerboats begin to roar he looks up at the screens, chin tilted back, neck muscles taut with tension. He looks as if he is *willing* them across the danger zone.

They cross, most of them. There are too many for the enemy to stop. The boats of the Dalavan Guard drive ashore on Lorkhin, running right up onto the firm ground of the island, and the Guard spill out onto pathways that, it can only be hoped, mages and explosives have already cleared of mines and traps.

Elsewhere, avoiding Lorkhin and its strongholds, the Marines storm across the danger zone. Unlike the Guard, they do not assault the enemy strongpoints—the giant, fortified buildings on their tall pontoons—but instead bypass them, swarming through the dark watery passages beneath the startled, entrenched enemy. Then, grouping in rear areas, the Marines seize communications links, break electricity and plasm connections, and assault the enemy from behind.

At the same time the Army attacks from the front. The Provisionals, when they created the no-man's-land in front of their position, did so by gutting buildings and pontoons, turning them into barges filled with rubble, and by sinking others to create lanes of open water. Instead of building bridges and roads across the danger zone, as the enemy expected, Constantine has simply *built new pontoons,* each more than a stade long, colossal structures shielded from magework by bronze plates and mesh, with highways built not along the tops, but safely through the interior. Seagoing tugs, guarded by telepresent mages, shove these massive structures into position, and military engineers link them together to create long tunnels that stretch toward the enemy.

Aiah goggles at the sight as, on video, she sees these monuments being driven along watery lanes and into position. Shellfire plunges down, fountaining high in the water or hammering the armored roofs of the bridging pontoons. Occasionally a tug is hit and explodes in bright flame, or—listing—is forced back. But still the long bridges, link by link, drive toward an enemy stunned by bombardment, confused and cut off by attacks in their rear.

The first bridge to be completed, because it was unopposed, links government forces with Landro's Escaliers, and government mercenaries roll to the attack in an attempt to expand their bridgehead. Other bridges are, with much greater difficulty, at length fixed in position. Crossings begin, against ferocious opposition.

"Yes, Triumvir." Constantine presses a gold headset to one ear as he replies to Parq's pleas. "We are doing our utmost to get the bridges across to Lorkhin."

He winces, then holds the headphone some distance from his ear. Parq's hysterical voice, released from the cup of Constantine's ear, cries its distress to the room.

The Dalavan Guard have stalled on the Island, cohesion broken, the soldiers huddling in whatever cover they can find. Parq screams for Constantine to rescue them.

"We will reinforce," Constantine reassures. "I guarantee it, Triumvir."

Aiah suspects that the bridges trying to reach Lorkhin may be used more for retreat than for reinforcement.

The Provisional command seems disorganized and slow to respond, but their mercenary troops are all good soldiers, more experienced than the expanded Caraqui army, and the response of the individual units is professional enough. Government casualties mount. Storms of blistering fire are hurled against Landro's Escaliers and the bridgehead. And then—in another part of the line entirely, near the border with Lanbola—a tentative breakthrough occurs. A clear pathway to the enemy rear opens. All enemy reserves are already committed against the Escaliers—there is nothing to stop government forces from slicing into enemy territory and cutting them off from all support—but somehow there is a breakdown on the bridge-tunnel, and reinforcements cannot be got across in any quantity.

"*What ... hideous ... treachery ...*" Constantine's eloquence deserts him as he watches the impediments multiply, one after another. Aiah watches him roar, pump fists into the air, pace manically back and forth. There is a mad desperation in his eyes; he is reliving, Aiah thinks, some nightmare from his past, from Cheloki, some other plan that failed. Engineers work frantically on the bridge. Officers are shouting words like "utmost" and "at all costs."

"Done," someone reports.

"Roll them!" Constantine cries, and communication techs bend over their boards to give the orders.

Constantine sags, fists planted on a table, head bent. The nightmare, for the moment, has been averted. Aiah feels an impulse to walk over and comfort him.

But he thinks of her first. His head comes up, and then he turns to Aiah, straightens, and walks over to her. "I would like your agreement at this point," he says. "Karlo's Brigade has been in reserve all day. I would like to send them across the bridge and have them finish this war once and for all."

"Yes," Aiah says. "Of course." She rises, and blackness invades her vision. She sways from sheer weariness, reaches a hand toward her chair for support. "I want to go to them."

Constantine's hand closes firmly on her shoulder. "Do not, I beg you," he says. "You will contribute nothing to their effort, and your presence will only distract them. After things have settled, perhaps, a visit would be in order."

Her will is not strong enough to resist. "May I speak to General Ceison on the phone?"

"Of course. If he can be found."

He can't: apparently the brigade is already in motion. Aiah sits. Weariness swims through her mind.

"Miss?" Aiah looks up to find a smiling, white-jacketed steward looking down at her. "May I get you a sandwich? A salad? Coffee?"

Aiah wonders how many shifts it has been since she last ate.

"All three," she decides.

The steward smiles. "Right away, miss."

Aiah watches the video while she eats and forgets to taste the food. Some of the images are being fed in from the bridgehead, showing vehicles filled with soldiers rolling out of the bridge-tunnel into newly won territory. And then, directly in front of the camera, someone flashes into existence from out of nothing, popping right onto the roadway. He is small and slight, shaggy-haired, with strange tall ears, and he carries a long glittering blade. He looks about, bewildered, for a second, and then one of the armored vehicles rolls him down.

Aiah stares for a moment at the strange, fated apparition. A teleport gone wrong, she thinks; someone popped a twisted person right into the war, armed only with a *big knife.*

Other, more jittery, images come from the front itself. The door is no longer open—the enemy have used the delay to reorganize their defense—but a strong push should finish them.

And then artillery begins to rain down on the bridgehead. A storm of plasm fire unfolds. Aiah can sense the attack losing momentum.

No! she thinks. Not now.

Constantine stands transfixed below the video images, big

hands flexing helplessly at his sides. The nightmare is enfolding him again.

The vehicles rolling into the bridgehead slow, come to a halt. The bridge-tunnel itself is being hit repeatedly. Aiah watches as the attack's momentum fades.

And then she looks up as Sorya, in her green uniform, comes striding into the command center. She is grim-faced, and flanked by a pair of aides. Without giving Aiah a glance, Sorya walks to Constantine and speaks without hesitation.

"Most of that gunfire directed against the bridgehead," she says, "is not from the Provisional forces—most of their stuff has been suppressed. The firing is from the Lanbolan army, their regular forces. They're firing at us from over the border, trying to seal off our breakthrough."

In the sudden silence, Aiah can see calculations flickering through Constantine. "The rest of their army?"

"Latest report says they're on alert, but in their barracks. But the Lanbolan government has also released its plasm reserves to the Provisionals. . . . They're beaming staggering amounts across the border to the enemy mages. We're going to have to expect much more powerful sorcery to be directed against us."

Constantine absorbs this. Rapid calculation glows in his eyes like a furious heat.

"The next decision is a political one," he says. "I will need to see the triumvirate." He turns to Aiah. "We will need you as well," he says. "Get the latest figures on our plasm expenditure and report to the Crystal Dome at once."

"Sir." It is General Arviro, anguish plain on his face. "My Marines," he says. "They're behind enemy lines. Without a breakthrough to reinforce them . . ."

Constantine nods. "Yes," he says. "I understand. I will raise the issue at the meeting."

BATTLE RAGES ACROSS CARAQUI FRONT

PROVISIONALS HOLDING AGAINST
GOVERNMENT ASSAULT

"It is not an insuperable position," Constantine says. "We are likely still to win—we're in a much better position than we were yesterday, and the Provisionals in much worse. Many of their units have been wrecked. But pressing the war will take time, and casualties on both sides—and among the civilian population—will be formidable."

"Vengeance now!" Parq cries. "Invade Lanbola at once!" His face is gaunt, and his eyes are hollow. He laughs, tugs at his disordered beard. "Why do we bother to discuss this?" he says. "The Dalavan Guard is being wiped out even as we continue this pointless discussion. We must rescue them!"

"General Arviro has asked me to mention the Marines," Constantine says. "They remain behind enemy lines. Many of them are cut off, and they are only lightly armed. Evacuating them will be risky, and we cannot supply them by teleportation forever." He looks at his notes. "Knowing this situation might arise, we have made plans for the invasion of Lanbola. Our mobile reserve alone can accomplish it within a day, should the triumvirate so order. We hope to be able to arrest most of the government as well as the Provisionals."

"I will not support the invasion of another metropolis," Hilthi retorts. "Hegemonism is insupportable at any time, for any reason. This war with the Provisionals is the natural price we pay for our centuries of misrule."

"And the Lanbolan artillery?" President Faltheg speaks hesitantly. "Can't they be said to have opened a war against us? How can we fight this *without* an invasion?" He shakes his head. "We could file another protest . . . I suppose." He looks at Hilthi. "Mr. Hilthi? Do you have a suggestion?"

Hilthi looks troubled, but makes no reply.

Constantine turns to Aiah. "Miss Aiah?"

Aiah testifies as to the availability of plasm. Caraqui's reserves have been cut in half by the first day of the offensive, and the ability of the government to support their assaults is fading.

Faltheg turns to Constantine. "Your recommendations, Minister?"

"I do not offer this advice lightly," Constantine says. "But it seems to me that there would be far less suffering, less damage, if we went into Lanbola and ended the war at its source." He gives an uneasy shrug. "The political problem of what to do with Lanbola," he adds, "may be dealt with afterward."

Aiah looks at her hands. It is the wrong move, she thinks, but she can't explain why. And she has no acceptable alternative.

"Make them pay!" Parq says. "Make them pay for our suffering! Their wealth can make Caraqui a paradise!"

Hilthi sits stiffly in his chair, his eyes locked with Constantine's. "I will not be a part of a hegemonist government," he says. "I will not countenance the looting of another metropolis. If I am outvoted in this, I will resign."

Faltheg's tongue runs round his lips. He sighs heavily. "I must reluctantly agree with Triumvir Parq and Minister Constantine. The Lanbolans' actions are intolerable."

"You will have my resignation before the shift is over," Hilthi says. "I will go into opposition."

Constantine turns to him. "Triumvir, I am sorry about this, and I hope you will reconsider. But may I ask you to delay this action for another day or two? Disarray in the government now will only encourage our enemies."

Hilthi hesitates, then nods. "I will do as the minister suggests."

Aiah turns to Sorya, sees the triumph glittering in her green eyes. This is what she has wanted all along, and Aiah wonders if she has somehow managed it all.

The meeting ends. As they head back to the command center, Constantine takes Aiah's arm. "I would like to use Karlo's Brigade in the assault on Lanbola. They are near the border, ideally placed, and they are not yet committed to the bridgehead."

It is, Aiah thinks, the only way to save Landro's Escaliers and the others in the bridgeheads.

"Yes," she says. "But I want to talk to Ceison personally."

"I will arrange it."

And so, a half hour later, she finds herself talking to Brigadier Ceison, and giving him her personal assent to the invasion, along with her best wishes for its success.

Within another two hours, Karlo's Brigade spearheads the assault into Lanbola, moving deep inland without opposition while assault troops are landed by helicopter on enemy buildings to seize control of the seat of government. Other airborne units engage and capture the Lanbolan artillery.

Within twenty-four hours, its political leadership dispersed or under arrest, the army of Lanbola surrenders without ever having left the vicinity of its barracks.

A day later, the Provisionals have collapsed and the war is over, and Constantine—because there was no one else, no one at all—has taken Hilthi's place in the triumvirate.

TWENTY-TWO

～～～～～～

Sea Mage Motor Craft—Take a Voyage to Victory!

The golden letters burn for a moment in the sky, a garish display, complete with a Marine striking a heroic pose in a motorboat. The sight makes Aiah want to cheer. Not because the Sea Mage company had contributed to the last, triumphant campaign, though they had, but because the plasm advert is there at all.

Peace. The price of plasm has fallen, and the sky is filled with the reassuring fires of commerce.

Another blaze floats up into the sky, happy people dancing with bottles of Snap! in their hands.

"Has the advertising improved in the last months, that you are so entranced?"

Constantine's question turns Aiah away from her terrace window. "I would rather see that ad every minute for the next week," she says, "than have the sky filled with artillery rounds."

Constantine concedes the point. "Yes. I quite agree." He pats the sofa cushion next to him. "Would you join me?"

She does so, leaning back against the warmth of his massive body. His puts an arm around her shoulder.

Outside, the sky blazes with the lights of peace.

On the table before them are the recordings of Aiah's meeting with Holson and Galagas. The plastic casings are broken open, and the cellulose tape cut into coiled shreds by Aiah's scissors. Tomorrow Aiah will throw the fragments out with the rubbish.

It will not be quite as simple to dispose of the memories of how those recordings were made. She is not as easy, leaning against Constantine's strength, as once she had been.

I shall guard my own back in future. Aiah had made that promise in anger; but now, soberly, she was keeping it. Sixteen bodyguards had been put on the payroll at the PED, and were now undergoing training in the Timocracy: in the meantime, when she left the Palace, she was accompanied by soldiers from Karlo's Brigade.

"Are you pleased to find yourself a triumvir?" Aiah asks.

Constantine pauses a moment to consider. "There is less interference in my work," he says, "but the company is not as congenial. In truth, I would prefer to take the place either of Faltheg or Parq, and to leave Hilthi in place." His voice deepens as it grows thoughtful. "In the past it was others who made the compromises, while I resisted and spoke of principle; but now I must compromise my own beliefs, and make certain my people follow my lead. . . ." A kind of self-disgust enters his words. "A particularly nasty compromise has just been made." His arms fold around her, and he murmurs urgently into her ear. "I beg you, do not go outside without guards for the next week or ten days. The city may not be safe."

The warning tingles along Aiah's nerves. She pulls free of his embrace and glances over her shoulder, sees him looking at her somberly. "The war is over," she says. "Why should there be danger now?"

Constantine's gaze is directed toward the terrace window, where the sky blazes with one bright advertisement after another. "The war is over," he says, "but the shape of the peace is uncertain."

"You are a triumvir, one third of the government. Minister of War and of Resources. You can't enforce order in the streets?"

His eyes shift away, and he rubs his jaw with one uneasy hand. "Not when I am opposed from within the government."

"Parq, then," Aiah judges. "Because I can't see Faltheg behind any sort of violence."

Constantine looks at her, eyes narrowing. "I cannot confirm your suppositions. But guard yourself—and if you are given an order, follow it."

"There is no one who can give me an order but you."

Again he looks uneasy. "That is not quite the case," he says.

She will have to talk to Ethemark, she thinks. And if the orders are unacceptable, she can resign.

But what kind of threat, she wonders, is that resignation? Who, besides Constantine, would care? Who, besides herself, would lose? No one gives a damn, she learned long ago, about the high and noble principles of a girl from Old Shorings. She will just be replaced by one of Parq's people, and that would deliver the PED right into the hands of his organization.

Constantine's burning eyes hold her. "Do as your orders bid you," he says. "I will do what I can for you, but it will take time. Remember our time in Achanos, and give me your trust."

She looks at him narrowly, and—she must *decide* this now; it has come to that—she makes up her mind, for the moment, to trust him. It has nothing to do with any sentimental memories of their stolen hours in Achanos, either— very odd of Constantine to mention them—but everything to do with calculation.

He uses her—he has always freely admitted it, a disarming element of his charm—and he loves her, she supposes, insofar as she is useful to him. But what he really loves is something else, power perhaps, or stated even more grandly, his Destiny. *One must keep one's true end in view.* . . . She is not, she concludes, a part of that vision, whatever it is.

But Constantine has given her power. She did not want it particularly, nor had she asked for it—she had not considered it *hers,* had considered herself an extension of Constantine, and her power his on loan.

Now she is not so certain. The PED is hers—she built it, shaped it, hired every single member herself. Constantine wanted it to be loyal to her personally, and it is as loyal as she can make it. Rohder's division of engineers and architecture students, madly making plasm, is hers. The Barkazil mercenary units are hers, at least informally—and she can attempt to make the arrangement more personal, if she desires.

Power. She can learn to use it, to acquire more, to impose her will on the world like an alchemist working with plasm-fired metal.

Or she can quit. Become Constantine's mistress, an appendage of which he would soon grow weary; and then—or now, for that matter—become nothing at all, a private person with a little dirty money put away.

But if she chooses the road of power, she must learn how to use it.

And for that, she reasons, Constantine is necessary. As she once learned the ways of magic from him, so she must now learn the ways of command.

She must learn from him; and in order to do that, she must stay close to Constantine. Closer than she already has been, if possible.

"Very well," she says. "I will do as you wish."

The fiery intensity in his look is banked behind the lids of his eyes. "Thank you," he says. He seems to recollect something, then reaches in his jacket pocket. "Aldemar gave me this for you before she left to finish her chromoplay." He takes out an oblong box and hands it to her. "She said you left it in her room."

She knows what it is before she opens the box. She fastens the ivory necklace around her neck. "Do you know Aldemar's number in Chemra?" she asks. "I would like to wire her my thanks."

"I will give it to you."

His large hand reaches for the necklace, picks up the dangling Trigram, and lets the smooth ivory rest in his palm. He shares with her a smile of remembrance. "This is the best investment I have made," he says. "You have exceeded all expectations."

"I will thank you to remember it," she says.

"You want rewards?" He lifts a brow. "Ask, and I will give it, if I can."

She considers. "I will keep them as IOUs, for now."

"Perhaps you trust overmuch in the generosity of the

powerful, to trust that I will remember, in weeks or months, how much I owe you."

"Had I ever known you petty," Aiah says, "you would already have the list of what I want, each item numbered, on a sheet of paper."

He smiles, lips drawn with a touch of cruelty, then closes his fist on the Trigram and brings it gently toward him, pulling her to him by the priceless collar. They kiss, and Aiah feels the little flutter in her belly that tells her that this is not entirely about power, about abstract desire for knowledge of political strategy.

"We have won a peace," Constantine murmurs. "Our lives are changed, and we may have as much time for one another as we desire. It is a luxury I intend to savor."

"I hope you will," Aiah says, "but I should warn you that my capacity for luxury is very large indeed."

He gives a knowing smile and draws her to him again. "Let us discover," he says, "just how large it is."

POLAR LEAGUE DEMANDS CARAQUI LEAVE LANBOLA

"I had suspected this," says Adaveth. "We knew that Parq would make a move once there was a peace and the triumvirate didn't need us."

The twisted Minister of Waterways' fingers drum angrily on the tabletop. "But none of the *important* things are talked about in the cabinet," he says. "All we discuss is what to do with Lanbola, and that's pointless, because we're going to have to give it back sooner or later. The Polar League is up in arms, wailing about sovereignty—not that they cared about ours, when we were invaded."

"Constantine says—implies, anyway—it will not last," Aiah says. "That eventually he will be able to act to change things."

Adaveth and Ethemark exchange scornful looks. "Constantine is keeping the War and Resources portfolios," Adaveth says. "It was expected he would have to give up at least one now the war is ended. But in exchange for selling the twisted to Parq, he will keep both."

Aiah feels a cold certainty, a draft of ice along her bones, that this is exactly the bargain that has been struck.

It is early service shift, and across the world people are sitting down to supper. Aiah, instead, hosts a meeting of her working group on the problem of Parq and the twisted, and serves soft drinks and krill wafers because she has not had a chance to cook in all the time she's been here.

Ethemark looks at her. "Do you know what Togthan is up to?"

Alfeg still shares an office with the Excellent Togthan, but has had little to report.

"Togthan is spending a lot of time with personnel files," Aiah says.

"Not surprising," says Adaveth.

Ethemark's eyes narrow as he gazes at Aiah. "If we are dismissed," he asks, "you will resign?"

Aiah hesitates. "Perhaps not," she says.

Adaveth and Ethemark exchange another look, and in it Aiah reads their scorn. "Resignation is your only weapon in matters of principle," Adaveth says.

"We had *assumed*," says Ethemark, "you would resign. The people of Aground died for you, and you will not give up your job for them?"

Aiah feels her insides twist. "I have thought about it," she says. "And who would my resignation help? Not you or your people. Not the people in Aground. Who would my resignation harm? Only the department, because Parq would have a hand in the appointment of my successor. Would you like a captain in the Dalavan Militia to have my post?"

They exchange another look, and Aiah knows, heart sinking, that she's lost them. She's become one of those they can no longer trust, another bureaucrat who will not risk her precious position to help them.

How to win them back? she wonders.

And then she wonders whether it is necessary. They are not her natural constituency, nor necessarily Constantine's: they are their own. In the future she should not depend on them—because she is sympathetic to them, it does not

follow automatically that they will wholeheartedly endorse
her. . . .

It is the thought, she realizes, of a politician.

HIGHWAY SCANDAL UNCOVERED IN LANBOLA!

MINISTER POCKETED MILLIONS, SOURCE REPORTS

Aiah watches as her driver—pilot, rather—jacks wires in
and out of sockets to reconfigure the aerocar's computer. He
glances at his checklist, gimbals the turbines, works the control surfaces. Then, after adjusting his headset, he puts a
hand on the yoke and rolls up the throttles. Plasm snarls in
the air. The turbines shriek, the nose pitches up, and the
aerocar leaps for the Shield, punches Aiah back in her seat.

Aiah turns her head and watches Caraqui, flat on its sea,
as it falls away. She has had much the same view while traveling telepresent on a thread of plasm, but the sensation here
has a greater solidity than plasm's hyperreality, a weightiness
that places the journey into the realm of sensation: the tug of
gravity, the scent of fuel, of lubricant and leather seats, and
the cry of the turbines.

The aerocar pitches forward until its flight is level. The
sensation of plasm fades—magic is used only during take-
offs. Yellow dials glow on the car's computer.

Alfeg, in one of the seats behind with Aiah's guards,
clears his throat.

Below, jagged buildings reach high for the aerocar like
taloned fingers, but they fall far short: the car has left flat
Caraqui and its low buildings and entered Lanbolan air-
space. The aerocar glides lower, losing altitude: Aiah
watches needles spin on instrument dials. The turbines sing
at a more urgent pitch: tremors run through the car's frame.
Aiah feels webbing bite her flesh as whining hydraulics
shove dive brakes into place. The aerocar slows, hovers,
descends. For a moment all is fire as the car drops through a
plasm display. The tall buildings rise on either side, and the
car finds a rooftop nest between them.

The turbines cycle down and the aerocar taxies to a stop. Aiah sees her reception committee awaiting her: Ceison and Aratha in the deep blue uniforms of Karlo's Brigade, Galagas in the gray of Landro's Escaliers. Galagas commands the Escaliers these days: Holson was killed in the fighting.

The cockpit rolls open to the right, and the passengers exit to the left. Guards fan out over the landing zone, and Aiah descends more leisurely: General Ceison hands her down the last step.

"Welcome to Lanbola," Ceison says, and gives a salute.

Aiah returns it. She has no military rank, but these troops are hers—in some as-yet-unclarified fashion—and so she might as well perform the appropriate rituals.

As she returns the salute, however, Aiah feels a faint sense of absurdity. She does not quite understand what one does with an army in peacetime. A peacetime army seems something of a contradiction in terms.

She introduces Alfeg to Galagas, then walks briskly across the windswept landing area. "How are things here?" Aiah asks.

"Lanbola is quiet," Ceison judges. "People go to work, do their jobs, get paid. Money still circulates. The stock market is down, but not disastrously so. The army is disarmed but still in its barracks." He shrugs his gangly shoulders. "The Popular Democrats were so authoritarian that once we swept their top echelon off the board, they were easy to replace."

Plasm lights the sky, red-gold words tracking: Pneuma Scandal Widens: Fanger's Name Linked. Details on The *Wire*.

The same tactics, Aiah recognizes, Constantine used in Caraqui. The former rulers would be discredited, along with their chief supporters—"Usually," as Constantine told her, "all that is necessary is to publish the truth." The top people—those few who had been caught—would be hauled back to Caraqui, stuck in prison, and put on trial whenever the political situation demanded it. Any Lanbolans raised into positions of power would be dependent on the new regime, with no local support, and therefore inclined to be loyal. In the meantime, any actual changes introduced would be very gradual—sudden shifts in law or tax structures would make the Lanbolans less inclined to accept the new regime—and rules against plundering and assault against civilians would be strictly enforced.

Galagas sprints ahead to open a battered metal rooftop door, and Aiah enters the military headquarters for the occupation forces, formerly the chief office complex for the Popular Democratic Party, with its bright white stone, gilt ornament, and sense of comfortable permanence, one of the grander buildings in Lanbola's government district.

They move down a stair, then along a corridor flanked by plush offices and into a room with a long cantilever table of glass and polished brass. The paintings on the walls are bright abstracts, splashes of color intended to furnish a tasteful background to the dance of power, but to offer no disturbing comment on its meaning, its intricacies.

Aiah tosses her briefcase down on the desk. "Open your collars, people, and take a seat," she says.

She opens her briefcase, takes out a pair of folders, slides one to Galagas and one to Ceison. "These are copies of the contracts that have been sent to your agents," she says. "Five years, with an option for a lateral move into the Caraqui military at the end of that time. Pension options as discussed. You'll note the signing bonuses are higher than we had previously agreed."

Loyalty is most painlessly bought with someone else's money, as Constantine had remarked when she'd negotiated this point. Occupation of the Lanbolan treasury had liberated a flood of cash from its bunkers. The Lanbolans' cash reserves were paying for their own occupation.

"Thank you," Galagas murmurs, his attention already lost in the maze of print.

Aiah waits for them to finish reading, then turns to Galagas. "The ministry has formally approved your promotion to brigadier and command of the Escaliers." It was mostly an internal matter—mercenaries chose their own leaders—but the contract gave the government right of consultation.

"Thank you, miss," Galagas says.

"I am happy also to announce the formation of the two units into a formal Barkazil Division, to be headed by General Ceison."

Ceison nods, awkwardly pleased, and brushes his mustache with a knuckle.

"Miss Aiah," Galagas says, "I'd like to raise the matter of replacing our losses. That last battle cost us almost half our men, killed or wounded, with particularly heavy losses among junior officers and NCOs. Not all the wounded will be able to return to the ranks. Since we are staying here rather than returning to the Timocracy to recruit, I'd like to send a recruiting party home . . . while the Timocracy will still permit it."

The Timocratic government had announced an investigation of Landro's Escaliers to discover whether deliberate treachery on their part had provoked the Provisionals into attacking them. Galagas, after consulting with Aiah, had decided the simplest option was to deny everything—there were no meetings in Aground, or if there were, then Holson, conveniently dead, had been there on his own. Aiah would keep silent—the Timocracy had no way of compelling her testimony—and the recordings of the meetings had been destroyed. Eventually, it was hoped, the investigation would die.

But the Escaliers' contacts in the Timocracy were keeping a close eye on the investigation. The investigation might at some point reveal just who had betrayed them.

And Aiah wanted very much to know who that was.

"Send your party back, by all means," she says, "and let me know what you hear."

"I'd like to address the problem of recruiting, if I may," Alfeg says. "I have contacts in the Barkazil community both in Jaspeer and in the Barkazi Sectors. Thanks to the *Mystery* chromoplay, there is great interest in Miss Aiah and Caraqui, and I think, General Galagas, I could fill your ranks for you, but I need your permission, ne?"

Galagas raises a brow in surprise. "Do you think you could find so many?"

"Oh, certainly. And if you sent recruiting parties to Jaspeer and wherever in Barkazi they were permitted, the job could be done all that much sooner."

Galagas seems skeptical, but is willing to consider it.

"Your mention of recruiting in the Barkazi Sectors reminds me," Ceison said. "I just heard—*The Mystery of Aiah* has been banned in the Jabzi Sector. And in the rest of Jabzi, for that matter."

Aiah looks at him. "Banned? Me? In Jabzi?"

"Jabzi is particularly insistent that the Barkazil Sectors will never unite again," Ceison says. "They seemed to find the chromo a threat. As a result, thousands of people who never heard of you are now clamoring for bootleg copies of the video."

Amusement tugs at the corners of Aiah's lips. "They aren't very intelligent in Jabzi, are they?"

"No one is likely to mistake them for Cunning People, no."

Aiah glances at her notes and finds the most urgent item on her agenda. The reason she is here, now, instead of paying this visit another time.

"I want to let you know," Aiah says, "that there may be some disorder in the near future. I want you to be ready for it, and I want you ready to move."

Sudden alertness crackles in the soldiers' eyes. Their attention is firmly on her.

"Here?" Ceison asks. "In Lanbola?"

Aiah shakes her head. "In Caraqui."

"Another coup attempt?" Aratha suggests.

"No. I don't think so, though I suppose it may come to that if the government does not . . . react sensibly."

Because if Parq isn't stopped . . . *somehow,* by *someone* . . . he may find himself in power by default.

There is a moment of silence. Ceison gives an uncertain look. "May I have a clarification, please?" he asks. "Does this warning come from you or from the ministry?"

"It didn't come from either one. In fact, you didn't hear it."

Ceison slowly nods, then rubs his long jaw. "I believe I understand," he says.

The notion of a military force in peacetime, Aiah considers, is no longer quite so absurd.

PEACE AND PROGRESS FOREVER

A HOPEFUL WISH FROM SNAP! THE WORLD DRINK

It is a party. Impudent music from Barkazi rocks the dignified walls of the Popular Democrats' former headquarters. A buffet spices the air, a piquant mix of cilantro, garlic, and fierce little Barkazi chiles. White-jacketed military stewards offer chilled glasses of kill-the-baby on silver trays embossed with the symbol of the Popular Democrats, and Aiah finds that the liquor's ferocity grows more agreeable from the second drink onward.

Ceison proves, to Aiah's surprise, a fine dancer. His lean body is unexpectedly adaptable to slippery Barkazil rhythms, the koola and the veitrento. And he pays attention to her, which is nice; she does not have the impression that she and Ceison are a pair of solo acts, but that they are actually dancing together, achieving some level of communication.Not that she dances with Ceison alone. The room is full of soldiers, most of them fit and healthy and happy to find a woman in their arms. The men outnumber the women, and Aiah finds herself pleasantly in demand. Breathless, she sits out for a moment, touches a handkerchief to the sweat on her brow. The dance is a joyous alternative to her activities during the previous shift, first the meeting with the Barkazil Division command and then, because of her insistent, dreaded sense of duty, her visit to its field hospitals. The Escaliers' thousands of casualties were piled up in two hospitals in Lanbola, since the hospitals in Caraqui had long ago been filled, and the medical staffs, though doing their best, were clearly overtaxed. There hadn't even been enough beds, not until thousands were liberated from nearby hotels.

Aiah hated hospitals, and she'd blanched at the scents of disinfectant, polish, old blood, and sickness. She hadn't known what to say to these total strangers whose bodies had been torn apart on her behalf (*your fault*, an inner voice insisted), and entering the first ward, she'd hesitated.

Fortunately Galagas and Aratha talked her through it—they had been through this many times. "Ask their names and where they're from," Aratha said. "Ask what unit they're in. Ask if there's anything you can do for them."

After the first few halting questions, Aiah relaxed, and it

went well enough. Many of the wounded were well into their recovery, were lively and full of complaint against their condition. They were robust young men for the most part, they had volunteered for this unit, and they were not inclined to self-pity. Half of them were lying on big soft hotel beds, mingling absurdity with the tragedy of their wounds.

Her people. It was far less an ordeal than she'd anticipated. She admired the fashion in which, with such limited aid available, they helped each other, changing dressings and administering medication. She understood the tough faces they displayed, their lack of sentimentality, their denial of the pain that so often glittered in their eyes. It was sad, but in its odd way it was home. . . .

For the people in Aground, she thought, there is none of this—no ambulances, no care, no medicine, no homes to receive them at recovery's end. (*Your fault.*) She wondered what she could do for them, and concluded there was nothing. Aground had vanished, its survivors scattered into the darkness beneath the city. . . .

There is a pause as the music fades. A polite warrant officer asks Aiah to dance, and she assents; he takes her hand and leads her onto the dance floor as the music booms out again. Aiah sees newcomers at the door, stiffens, whispers to her escort, "I'm sorry, I will have to postpone our dance, forgive me," and slips away from his hand.

Sorya is dressed in silks, green and orange, and her chin bobs in time to the music. Her guards, attired more soberly, bulk large behind her: two huge twisted men with glittering, suspicious eyes. When she sees Aiah walking toward her, Sorya smiles brightly and advances to meet her. She embraces Aiah, kisses her on both cheeks. Aiah smiles in return, kisses in return—she is a politician now, after all—but wariness tingles up her spine at this unexpected display of sorority.

Sorya takes her arm and begins an unhurried stroll around the perimeter of the room. She gestures with her free hand at the party. "Your young men have done well for you."

"Thank you."

"And you have done well for yourself." Sorya's green eyes regard Aiah with frank interest. "I had not expected that. I may, after all, have to take notice of you."

Aiah tilts her head graciously while, behind her mask of pleasantry, a shiver runs through her soul. "Ought I to fear such notice?" she asks.

Sorya's throat flutters with her lilting laugh, and she speaks into Aiah's ear over the throb of music. "Miss Aiah, our goals are similar: the elevation of Constantine. You, I expect, view him as an alternative to the wretched pettiness and persecutions of other factions; whereas I want his greatness to flourish, and mine with it."

Sorya favors a nearby cluster of officers with a gracious smile, then speaks into Aiah's ear again. "No—I meant that I must take note of your power, which though growing is hardly a threat to mine, and your method, which is unique. The religion racket, for instance . . ." She gives a bemused shake of her head, while annoyance shivers through Aiah's mind. Religion racket, indeed.

"I wish I had thought of that," Sorya continues, "harnessing such a powerful, arcane force as belief. It is a superstitious world, after all." Her laugh lilts again in Aiah's ear. "People need to believe in something, or someone. I shall find a hermit myself, I think, to proclaim me the savior of, oh, something or other, and see how I fare."

"Be careful," Aiah says. "Hermits are inconvenient people."

"*My* hermit won't be," cynically. "And I gather one is expected to enact the odd mystery or perform the occasional miracle, neither of which is beyond possibility, given human credulity and plasm. . . ." She regards the soldiers with a thoughtful expression. "I must say, you have backed yourself into a corner regarding Barkazi. They'll want you to *do* something over there, and what, realistically, can you accomplish?" She gives the matter thought. "Well, the soldiers are still a good idea," she judges. "Look at history. A prophet without an army is bound to fail, whereas prophets with an efficient military can do well. Look at Dalavos, for heaven's sake."

"And look how well Parq is doing," Aiah probes, "with just his rabble militia."

Calculation glimmers in Sorya's eyes. "This is Parq's chance," she says. "Either he must seize all power now, or watch it slip away."

"Which do you think he will do?" Aiah asks.

"He will be Parq," Sorya says. She pauses, takes a slim cigaret out of a platinum case, strikes flame from a matching lighter. She takes a breath of smoke and lets it out with a toss of her head. She smiles.

"I would like to stay, Miss Aiah," Sorya says. "It has been a long time since I danced."

"I hope you have a pleasant time," Aiah says. She pauses, observes her warrant officer waiting discreetly a few paces away, and joins him.

Sorya stays for hours, well into first shift.

She dances, Aiah observes, very well.

JABZI BANS RELIGIOUS "CULTS"

"SUBVERSIVE IDEOLOGY MASQUERADING AS PIETY" NO LONGER TOLERATED

GROUPS WATCH BANNED VIDEO, CONDUCT SERVICES

Aiah returns to Caraqui, bathes, has a few hours' sleep, and reports for work an hour late. As she walks to work through the maze of the Palace, kill-the-baby pokes at the backs of her eyeballs with a sharp pencil.

The Excellent Togthan sits, not in the waiting room, but in her office, and Aiah pauses in the doorway and takes a breath, knowing that the moment has come.

He stands, bows formally, holds out a sealed note. Aiah observes that he is wearing red leather pumps. "From the Holy, Parq," Togthan says. "A change is being made throughout government. The polluted flesh are forbidden to hold a position higher than F-3."

Restricted, then, to manual labor, making repairs, and chauffeuring their betters. Aiah takes the note, breaks the seal, reads it. *Effective immediately,* it says.

If you are given an order, follow it. A memory of Constantine's voice.

"Not only the government will be purified," Togthan says, "but Caraqui at large. The Dalavan Militia will be given a free hand to enforce public order and the sumptuary laws, and to drive the defiled from the sight of the good people of the nation."

Aiah walks around her desk, touches the glass top with her fingertips, and does not sit down.

"There are ninety-eight of the polluted in the department," Togthan continues, and hands her another paper. "Here is a list. I will remain while you call them one by one into the room and dismiss them."

Aiah looks at him, straightens her spine. "I do not think that will be possible," she says. "I will make my own arrangements as regards compliance with this order."

Togthan's chin jerks up. Anger glitters in his eyes. "Miss Aiah," he says, "this is a direct order from—"

"The order," Aiah says, "makes no mention of you whatever, Mr. Togthan. It does not specify that you need to be present anywhere, for any reason. I will comply with the triumvir's wishes, but I see no reason why I need take up your valuable time." Still contemplating the order, she sits down, gazes up at Togthan, and then, dismissively, looks down at the paper again.

"You may leave, Mr. Togthan," she says.

Togthan stands for a moment in silence—Aiah, calmly viewing the paper as her heart hammers in her ears, contemplates calling in some of her guards and having them shatter his knees with heavy sledges—and then Togthan turns and makes his exit.

Aiah looks at the list, opens a drawer for her department directory.

She calls all the victims to a meeting in the conference room at 11:00.

Get it all over with by lunch, she tells herself.

DALAVAN MILITIA CALLED TO TEMPLES

RUMORS CLAIM PURGE OF GOVERNMENT

They know, obviously: Aiah can see it in their eyes as she walks into the room. Goggle-eyed little embryos, massive stoneface slabs, other twisted of a more ambiguous nature, oddly proportioned, odd-eyed. Ethemark sits in front, dwarfed by his high-backed chair, elbow propped on the table as he smokes a cigaret.

Aiah stands at the head of the table, plants her feet apart, clasps her hands behind her back. It is as strong a stance as she can manage, though behind her back the nails of her right hand are digging into the wrist of the left.

"I'm sure you've heard the news," Aiah says. "The Triumvir Parq has signed an order that dismisses genetically altered from the civil service. I have been given this order this prebreak, and told to enforce it."

She pauses, considers her audience. They are waiting, Senko only knows why. If she were one of them, Aiah thinks, she'd want to explode, go mad right here in the Palace, storm through the place destroying everything in her path.

Aiah jerks her chin high, takes a breath. "This is not what I fought for," Aiah says. "This is not why I came here. This is not what any of us wanted from the struggle. *But the struggle isn't over.*" She finds her voice rising. "And when it *is* over . . ." She looks at the roomful of people, tries to make eye contact with as many as possible. "When it *is* over," she continues in a softer voice, "I will see that every single one of you has your job back. Because you have done this department credit, I have never had a complaint with a one of you, and you deserve to be here."

Ethemark's bitter tobacco stings Aiah's sinus. Sadness floods through her, and she finds herself sagging. She leans forward and props her weight on her outstretched arms.

"I advise none of you to travel alone when you leave the building," Aiah says. "And when you go out on the streets, be careful. The Dalavan Militia is going to be out there, and . . ." Sheer futility drags at her words; she has been unable to protect these people, their kindred in Aground, anybody. She straightens, raises a hand, and sketches the Sign of Karlo in the air. "Bless you," she says. "Take good care, and go."

She lowers herself into her chair, trying not to collapse.

The twisted people, murmuring, begin to leave. Ethemark, still in his chair, gazes at her without sympathy.

"Now that you see what it is like," he asks, "are you going to resign over this?"

Aiah looks at him. "I don't know. Would you really prefer that Togthan be in charge of this unit?"

There is a contemptuous curl to Ethemark's lip. He stubs out his cigaret, drops it to the floor, and makes his way out without a word.

Ethemark aside, Aiah finds a surprising degree of sympathy in the twisted as they file past her. Some touch her arm or squeeze her shoulder. "We know it isn't your fault," one says, and the sentiment is echoed by others as they leave.

Aiah finds herself wishing she could agree.

THE PARTY SICKNESS

IS IT REAL? CAN YOU CATCH IT?

FIND OUT THE FACTS AT 18:30 TODAY
ON CHANNEL 14

Aiah doesn't want to be alone after work shift, so she invites Khorsa over for dinner. This involves shopping, something she hasn't done in months, but there's a luxuriously stocked food store in the Palace, and at the moment she finds it comforting to walk the aisles with a cart and examine vegetables.

She makes a Barkazil salad with cucumber and cilantro, cellophane noodles, bits of grilled pork and a mild chile sauce, then prepares crisp beans in butter and garlic and a rice dish with vegetables, chicken, and bits of smoked ham. She chills some beer and wine and brews coffee.

When Khorsa arrives she brings bowls of her own: "roof-chicken"—squab—simmered in spices, coriander, and chiles, and a vinegary salad of sweet onion and assorted legumes.

Aiah calls herself an idiot as she views all the food. She

has been living among the longnoses too long: she should know that a Barkazil never visits empty-handed.

"Maybe we should invite some more people," she says.

Khorsa shrugs. "What's wrong with eating leftovers for a week?"

The meal is splendid, but afterward Aiah makes the mistake of turning on the video, and it is full of Parq's triumph, now called the Campaign of Purification. Adaveth and Myhorn have been dismissed from their cabinet posts. There are pictures of twisted people being turned out of their jobs and the Dalavan Militia driving the twisted off the sidewalks and tearing expensive jewelry off people who violate the never-before-enforced sumptuary laws. There is no indication the jewelry is ever returned. Automobiles deemed too expensive or flashy are scarred or heaved into canals unless their owners are on hand to pay "fines." Organized bands of militia have attacked several half-worlds, driving out their inhabitants, sinking or towing off their dwellings.

They can't live in the half-worlds, Aiah thinks, and they're not allowed on the streets. Where *are* they to live?

Nowhere, of course. They are not to exist.

Aiah thanks Senko that Constantine had disbanded the censorship board, the News Council. The news organizations are at liberty to present alternate points of view, and they do so.

Adaveth and Myhorn speak with anger and regret. Hilthi is prominently featured, eyes burning with a conviction he never seemed to display in meetings of the cabinet. He denounces the purification campaign as inhumane, a betrayal of the revolution, a vile piece of political jobbery and gangsterism. He calls on the people to resist, and his denunciation of the triumvirate is particularly eloquent.

Constantine, Aiah notes, does not comment. He is visiting the army in Lanbola, and has nothing to say about anything happening in Caraqui.

Anger wars with sickness in Aiah's heart. She presses the solid gold button on her media console that turns off the video, and looks dumbly at Khorsa.

"What can we do?" Khorsa says.

"Nothing. We don't have enough power, not really. The

Barkazil Division is only a small fraction of the army, and I don't think they'll go against the government even if I ask them to."

"What of Constantine? He *can't* approve of this. Can't you talk to him?"

Aiah shakes her head. "He's partly responsible, I think. He's made some kind of deal with Parq. He gets to keep the army and Resources, and Parq gets his purification campaign."

"And you and he—?" Khorsa asks. "Between you all is well?"

"I don't know." Aiah rubs her forehead. "He uses me for . . . for his projects. And he gives me things—the department, power, even an army. But he is . . . elusive. And he won't return my calls, won't tell me what he has planned with Parq or . . . or anyone else." She shakes her head. "I don't know what to think."

Concern lights Khorsa's eyes. "I have heard a story about him." She hesitates. "I don't know whether it's true."

"Yes?"

Khorsa licks her lips, looks away. "There is a story that once each week he goes to the prison and interviews prisoners. And he orders some of the prisoners released. And then the prisoners die of the Party Disease."

Despair gnaws at Aiah's heart. She wants to deny the story, but it is so close to the truth that she doubts she'd be able to lie, at least convincingly. All she can say is, "Constantine isn't in charge of the prisons. He doesn't interview prisoners; he can't order releases."

She remembers Drumbeth giving the order. Unless, she thinks, Faltheg and Parq subsequently reversed Drumbeth's policy.

"He's triumvir," Khorsa says. "Can't a triumvir do that?"

"He's only been triumvir for a matter of days. For that story to be true it would have to happen over months." *Has* he, Aiah wonders, been visiting the prisons?

"He's just been triumvir long enough," Aiah says, as sorrow closes a soft hand about her throat, "to set Parq on Caraqui."

She rises from the sofa, crosses to the terrace door. She

looks out at the city, the sky alive with plasm fire, the distant volcanoes of Barchab. Silver cumulus clouds float beneath the opalescent Shield. Aiah crosses her arms and shivers.

"They cut us off, the Ascended," she says. "They put the Shield between us, and denied us the sky. And now Parq wants to build a Shield *below* us, cutting off the twisted people. And it's a tragedy both ways."

"Everything recurs," Khorsa says, her soft voice sounding from over Aiah's shoulder. "That's why the Shield is such a dreadful thing. Because it's cut us off here, and all we can do is dance the same dance over and over."

"I *believed* in him," Aiah says. Tears burn hot in her eyes. "I thought he could change it all—change the dance forever. But now—" She gasps for breath. "I don't even know why I'm here anymore. I don't know—" The words die in her throat.

Khorsa approaches silently from behind, puts her arms around Aiah, rests her head on Aiah's shoulder. "If you are staying only to protect me and the other Barkazils," she says, "you should know that . . . well, we'll get along without the PED. But I think you need to talk to Constantine before you do anything."

"Yes," Aiah mumbles. "I'll do what I can."

She can protest, she thinks, she can explain, but she fears the answer she may receive.

Her eyes drift to the plasm socket near the window, the copper t-grip sitting on the ornate table next to it.

"I'll do what I can," she repeats, and her thoughts whirl in a sudden wind. She has been granted a generous personal plasm allowance for the length of her time here; but the arrangement had been suspended for the length of the war, and her private meter disconnected. Now she is connected to the well again, and the state owes her a large amount of plasm.

Perhaps, she thinks, she ought to make use of it.

Gingerly she probes the idea, like a tongue probing the gap where a tooth once lay, trying to find the hidden source of pain.

Then she looks up at Khorsa. "I know what I can do," she says. "It won't be much, but—if you and I can trust each other absolutely, we can help people directly."

Khorsa's eyes gaze thoughtfully into hers. "I think we have a world of trust between us," she says.

UNREST BRINGS ELECTIONS INTO QUESTION

"BALLOTING WILL COMMENCE AS SCHEDULED," INSISTS FALTHEG

Aiah coasts over the city on a pulse of plasm. She doesn't know where the militia are, or what they intend—there has not been time enough to make plans—but when her anima ghosts over an older, ramshackle neighborhood, one scarred with graffiti and despair, she discovers it isn't hard to find them.

The Campaign for Purification is rolling over an apartment building: armed militia are driving families from their homes. The building circles a brick-floored courtyard with a pair of willows, and beneath the dangling willow branches a pair of goggle-eyed embryos lie in the court covered with bruises from butt strokes. Their children wail around them while their belongings are flung from windows. The trees and the court below are draped with fluttering clothes, and there is a growing pile of broken furniture. Others deemed impure—not all are twisted, so there is some other form of vengeance going on—are huddled in a corner, guarded with rifles by young men wearing the militia's red arm- and headbands. Some of the guards are sorting through the belongings, picking out items of choice.

Aiah's police experience stands her in good stead. There are no more than ten of the militia here, and no sign of a mage backing them.

A moment of concentration is needed for Aiah to form ectomorphic hands, and then she advances on a militiaman and slaps him down. He falls spinning, unconscious before he hits the pavement, rifle clattering on the bricks, but before he is even down Aiah is on the other guards, dealing out nicely judged slaps, each bringing a militiaman to the ground. Sometimes the first blow only stuns, and a second strike is needed, but never more than that.

The impure—the victims of the campaign—stand with wide-eyed surprise. Somehow it never occurs to them to run.

Aiah rises on an arc of invisible plasm to the militia plundering an apartment and slaps them reeling into the walls. She bunches their collars in invisible fists and hauls them out the window, then wafts them—not gently—to a landing.

She lifts rifles, pistols, and knives from holsters, sheaths, and nerveless hands, then piles them near the exit. Cartridge belts are added to the collection.

And then she wills herself to fluoresce, forming the same featureless female image she has used in the past, a blazing gold statue come to life. The huddled group in the courtyard shield their eyes against her brilliance. Aiah gives herself voice.

"Take what possessions you can," she tells the victims, "and run. If you wish a firearm, take one. Otherwise just leave, and seek shelter where you can."

Half of them simply take off, and others pause to snatch a few belongings from the wreckage before leaving. The half-conscious militia groan, rolling on the bricks, hands clutching broken jaws, blood-streaming broken noses. The flaming anima-image keeps them from protesting, even when one of the twisted, a grim-looking stoneface, methodically goes through their pockets and relieves them of all their money, then helps himself to a pair of pistols, an assault rifle, and several bandoliers of ammunition.

He is the only one of the victims who arms himself.

Aiah stands guard over the militia for a few minutes, then allows her anima-image to fade. When one of the militia staggers to his feet, she reaches an invisible hand to his ankle, yanks it, and dumps him to the pavement.

"I'm still here," she booms. "Sit quietly and you won't get hurt."

She picks up the remaining firearms and throws them in the nearest canal. When she returns, the militia are still sitting quietly on the bricks.

She mentally counts out ten minutes—time enough for the refugees to make an escape—and then throws the switch on her t-grip. Her awareness returns to her bedroom.

Exhilaration choruses through her. She bounds from her

bed and almost dances into the front room, where Khorsa is using another t-grip on a similar mission. From Khorsa's exultant expression, she seems to be meeting with similar success.

"Militia roadblock on a bridge," she says when she's finished. "They were extorting money from everyone trying to cross. I threw them in the canal."

Aiah bounds toward her, and they embrace in a moment of joy and triumph.

Then each returns to her t-grip, and for the rest of the shift, and the balance of first shift the next day, they soar on to thwart the militia.

Nothing proves quite as spectacular as her first rescue at the apartment building, but by the time she's finished Aiah is pleased with her record of accomplishment. She breaks up roadblocks, disarms militia bands, shoves militia vehicles into canals. Her golden image shimmers into existence at many of these occasions: she wants the militia to *know* a powerful mage is opposing them.

She tells Khorsa about her golden anima, and Khorsa begins to use the golden form as well.

She is only opposed once, when she finds a purposeful band in four powerboats, heavily armed and obviously up to no good. Aiah's anima dives under the surface of the canal and punches a hole in the bottom of each of the first three boats before she finds her consciousness swiftly dumped into her apartment again. Another mage has cut her sourceline. Quickly she shuts off the plasm before the enemy mage manages to track her to the Palace.

She checks her meter to discover how much plasm she and Khorsa have consumed.

At this rate, she thinks, the fun can't last long.

MILITIA ON RAMPAGE

POPULACE COMPLAINS OF VIOLENCE

HOSPITALS FILLING WITH VICTIMS

The next day is more sobering. The Dalavan Militia numbers in the hundreds of thousands, and Aiah's attacks were but a pinprick. There are hundreds of militia actions going on at once around Caraqui, and none of Aiah's attacks seem to have attracted the attention of the video newswriters, whose works feature nothing but discouraging images of militia depredations.

Once in her office, she tries to call Constantine, but is informed that he's in a meeting. He doesn't return her call, or any of her calls on subsequent days. Nor does she see him, or receive so much as a memo. Unlike President Faltheg, who appears on broadcasts every so often to make a hesitant, unconvincing defense of the government's position, Constantine is rarely mentioned in the news, and seems to be hovering somewhere below the surface of public attention.

And while Constantine leaves Aiah in a vacuum, the situation both in the Palace and the streets grows worse. Togthan informs Aiah that he will be taking Ethemark's place as her second-in-command; and he also presents her with a list of people to be hired in place of those she had been forced to dismiss.

Aiah manages to delay the implementation of this last procedure by insisting on a personal interview with every new hire, so that she knows how to best assign them. It is a depressing task, because they are generally less qualified than the people she'd been forced to dismiss. Many of them seem to have been included on the list solely because they have a close relative in the Dalavan Militia.

Outside the Palace, heavily armed groups of militia prowl the streets and canals. Shops owned by genetically altered people are vandalized or looted, as are pawnbrokers and moneylenders, who, in the terminology of the Campaign of Purification, are now declared "usurers" and "bloodsuckers." Regional offices of the Altered People's Party, the political organization of the twisted, are sacked; and offices belonging to several other parties are vandalized or attacked.

But the twisted swiftly recover from the surprise of the first day's onslaught. Many acquired arms and military skills during the war, and their mages are not entirely without ability, or without plasm. Bloody battles are now waged in the darkness below the city as the inhabitants of the half-worlds try to defend their homes.

Aiah does what she can. She rearranges Khorsa's schedule so that she works third shift and can fly against the militia during work shift, while Aiah is in her office.

Three days into the purification campaign Aiah observes the first graffito sprayed onto the side of a building: *Long Live the Golden Lady!* In the next few days she sees more signs that her anima has inspired hope: *The Golden Lady Rules! All Glory to the Golden Lady!* Five days into the Campaign of Purification, Aiah first hears of the Golden Lady on the news. Two days later, Parq announces a reward for information leading to the Golden Lady's capture.

If only the Golden Lady's plasm weren't running out.

The stockpiled plasm allowance is being consumed fast, and by the end of the first week the Golden Lady is put on a strict ration.

After a few days, the news programs report an increase in sightings of the Golden Lady, and Aiah and Khorsa realize that they are not responsible for some of these appearances. Other people are finding the Golden Lady inspiring, and are using her image in resisting Parq.

While her covert activities are exhilarating, the situation at work sends despair sighing through Aiah's veins. Togthan is running the department in all but name, and once Aiah's plasm allowance runs out, she reasons, there will be very little point to staying, save her desperate, dwindling faith in Constantine, that and her stubbornness, a refusal to admit that it had all been a hideous mistake.

She decides that when she finally runs out of plasm, mere days from now, she will resign.

Perhaps it's just as well, she thinks. It's only a matter of time before the identity of the Golden Lady will be revealed. All it will take is for someone to backtrack her sourceline to the Palace, or for a clerk to go over her plasm records and wonder why she is consuming so much of her allowance all at once.

Ten days into the Campaign of Purification, as she prepares to leave the office at the 16:30 shift change, her receptionist puts through a call from General Ceison in Lanbola.

"Miss Aiah," he says, "something curious has occurred. I wonder if it might be possible to speak privately."

"Yes." It has never been wise to send confidential information through the Palace switchboards, and it is doubly unwise now.

"I will be on the roof of the headquarters building in . . . will 16:50 be too soon?"

"I can manage 16:50."

Aiah finds the compass bearing to the Lanbola headquarters in her directory, calls the plasm control room, and arranges to have plasm delivered to her apartment and the use of a plasm horn set at 040 degrees true. She returns to her rooms, sits near a plasm connection, holds the t-grip in her hand.

Something curious. She presses the trigger.

The plasm sings a song of welcome in her veins. Aiah pauses for a moment to hear magic's song of creation, destruction, and desire, the song of sheer reality running along her nerves. And then she lets herself surge along the Palace's plasm lines and speed from the scalloped bronze horn on the roof.

The horn directs her on course 040, beaming plasm on a bearing to Ceison's headquarters. Aiah pushes her consciousness slowly out along the beam, over the flat surface of Caraqui, the war's great ruined scar that lies across the metropolis, then over the taller cityscape of Lanbola that falls below her as the world curves away. The clouds are low and dark and full of rain, and the plasm beam wants to fire straight through them; with an effort of will Aiah curves the beam, keeping it and her sensorium below cloud cover. Below, clouds and rain have darkened the city sufficiently for it to be illuminated by stormlights.

Rain drifts like a shroud over Lanbola's government district, the proud white buildings erected by the Popular Democrats. Aiah dives like a questing falcon, finds the party headquarters building, and discovers Ceison standing quietly near a sandbagged mortar emplacement, wearing a hooded rain cape and calmly puffing a pipe. Delicate drops of rain cling to his mustache.

Aiah reaches toward Ceison with tenuous mental tendrils. Ceison stiffens, his lean face turning alert. He takes the pipe from his mouth and holds it, hand cupped around the bowl, by his side.

—General? Can you hear me?

—Yes.

Ceison's mental voice sounds much like his speaking voice, reasoned and deliberate, possessing an undemonstrative kind of authority.

—You wished to speak with me?

—Yes, miss.

Ceison ducks farther into his hood as a gust of rain pelts down, frowns as he assembles his thoughts.

—Two days after you visit here, he begins, we had a visit from the War Minister. And he passed on a warning very similar to the one you gave us.

Surprise floats through Aiah at this news.

—Go on, she sends.

—I thought, well, it is good that you and the minister are in accord. But yesterday I received another visit from the War Minister, with very specific instructions, and I thought I should speak with you for . . . for purposes of coordination.

—What were the instructions?

—Karlo's Brigade is to move at 02:00 tomorrow into Caraqui, and occupy certain sites: bridges, plasm stations, and several local headquarters of the Dalavan Militia. The Escaliers are to remain behind to make certain Lanbola remains calm.

Somehow Aiah is not surprised: comprehension falls solidly into place, as if the parts of the puzzle had already been assembled in her mind, and only needed Ceison's words for her to become aware of them.

Parq, she knows now, had been set up for a great fall. Constantine had encouraged him to run wild, to set his mobs loose on the metropolis, to abuse his every authority; and now Constantine would bring him down with the support of every other element in the state.

The only question now, she thinks, is Constantine's ultimate purpose. Is he doing this all on his own, with the intention of setting himself up as Metropolitan, sole commander of Caraqui; or is his goal somehow more modest?

Ceison's mental voice brings Aiah's thoughts back to the present.

—Do you concur in this program, Miss Aiah?

The answer is clear enough. In any struggle of Constantine against Parq, she must support the former, whatever else Constantine's move may imply.

—Yes, Aiah sends. And furthermore I want to be with you when you move. Do you have camera crews on hand?

—Of course.

Cameras naturally accompany any military movement: their feed is used to help military mages orient themselves, project their animas and magic to the places where they are most needed.

Rain beats down steadily. Ceison empties his pipe, shifts it to a pocket.

—I want a camera crew with me at all times. I want us to be able to give the video news *proof* that the Barkazil Division and I are a part of this.

—Yes, miss.

—I will arrange to be here, in person, first shift tomorrow.

—Very good, miss.

—I want you to paint a new name on the side of the vehicle that I am to use. It will be called the Golden Lady. Understood?

Ceison's eyes widen in surprise. The existence of the Golden Lady has not, it appears, entirely escaped his attention.

—I want you to see if you can find an artist, Aiah continues, who can paint a golden lady on the vehicle. Large as you can.

With an act of will she causes her anima to fluoresce, and Ceison shields his eyes against her brightness.

—This is what I want you to paint. Do you understand?

—Yes, miss.

Aiah permits the image to fade. Ceison lowers his hand and blinks his dazzled eyes.

Aiah's ectomorphic sensorium observes Ceison, standing in the pouring rain with water sluicing off his hood and cape.

—Better get inside, she sends. We can't afford to have you down with pneumonia at a time like this.

Ceison smiles.

—Thank you, miss. I will see you first shift.

Aiah touches the off button and feels Lanbola fade from her vision. Plasm sings a song of triumph in her ears.

The Golden Lady will do her part to end the terror, she thinks. And she will be seen to do her part.

COMMERCE COUNCIL PROTESTS CAMPAIGN OF PURIFICATION

"UNREST BAD FOR BUSINESS," SPOKESMAN SAYS

RELAYS COMPLAINTS OF EXTORTION

PARQ DENOUNCES "BANKERS AND BLOODSUCKERS"

Her pilot takes Aiah to Lanbola through a lightning storm, the aerocar flying through great flashing sheets of electric fire that turn everyone in the cabin into pale, glittering-eyed ghosts. Green voltaic flame streams from the car's stubby wings as it descends, and dances like a thing alive along the instrument panel.

The aerocar touches down on the landing pad, and the pilot pulls his headset off. His forehead is beaded with sweat. "I don't want to do *that* ever again," he says.

Aiah looks at him. Her mind was fully occupied during the flight; she had appreciated the spectacle, but her thoughts were elsewhere. "Were we in danger?" she asks.

"I would not have wanted to short out our instruments," the pilot breathes.

"Glad we didn't." Her mind is already on other things.

She steps from the aerocar into pelting rain and blazing video light: the camera crews she'd requested are here to record her arrival. Her guards are prepared for combat, wearing bulky bulletproofs and carrying weapons openly;

and Aiah herself is dressed practically, in boots, pants, and waterproof jacket.

Ceison offers her an umbrella and salutes. "Everything's ready, miss," he says.

"Thank you. Let's get out of the rain."

Armored vehicles jockey for place in the huge nearby garage, filling the air with unburnt hydrocarbons. The carrier *Golden Lady* is decorated impressively, with a fierce, fiery woman, hair ablaze, pointing ahead to victory with a commanding expression on her face. Aiah asks to meet the artist, and compliments him. "Can you paint me another copy of this?" she asks. "Put it on cardboard or something, so I can have it in my apartment? I'll pay you for your work."

The artist is a young man, and blushes easily. "I'd be happy to, miss. And no need for payment."

"Of *course* I'll pay you. It's not your regular job, is it?"

He colors gratefully and Aiah moves on, greeting as many of the soldiers as she can. When Ceison tells her it's time to move, Aiah joins the *Golden Lady,* and the vehicle commander hands her a pair of headphones and shows her how to stand in the hatch. Her guards file into the interior. The camera crews keep Aiah in their sights as the *Golden Lady* jerks, belches fumes, and lurches for the exit on its six solid-steel wheels. Enjoying this, Aiah breaks into a grin, and forgets to adopt for the cameras the stern expression of the Golden Lady painted onto the side of her vehicle.

Outside the rain has ended, though water still pours from drain spouts and fills the gutters. Shieldlight is breaking through dark cloud, and the stormlights are flickering off. The vehicle lurches into a higher gear and Aiah lowers herself behind the armored hatch combing to cut the chilling wind.

The convoy picks up speed once it gets on the Sealine Highway and rolls across the Caraqui border at 06:10, receiving waves and salutes from puzzled soldiers guarding the customs stations. Columns begin to split from the main body, aiming for different objectives. Well before 06:30, Ceison reports to Aiah that the first objectives have been seized, and that complete surprise has been achieved.

In brilliant Shieldlight, at 06:45, Aiah's column rolls to a halt in front of the district militia headquarters, and soldiers and camera teams spill out. Aiah's guards tug at her trouser legs to bring her down out of the hatch and behind the vehicle's armor, but she insists on remaining in plain view, where the cameras and population can see her.

There is no resistance, no bullets, no plasm blasts, and the soldiers occupy the building without so much as a protest from its puzzled sleep-shift occupants.

And, when the militia members begin turning up for work at 08:00, they are quietly arrested and disarmed. Seized militia records provide names and addresses of those not present, and army combat teams move to their apartments to confiscate any weaponry they may possess.

But by that point Aiah has shifted to a local plasm station, where her PED identification gains entrance and where she can commandeer an antenna, dive into the well, and provide magical support for her soldiers. Since, commanding a station, she has practically unlimited plasm at her disposal, she crafts a blazing golden anima to fly above the steets and soar to her soldiers' aid.

At 08:00, while the Golden Lady cruises above the city, Constantine appears on radio and video to announce that he and the president-triumvir, Faltheg, have ordered the army to suppress disorder and to disarm and disperse the Dalavan Militia. The sumptuary laws are summarily repealed. The reconstituted police forces, now ready under Randay, the Minister of Public Security, will assume all responsibility for public order.

When she hears the news some hours later, Aiah reflects that she had almost forgotten about Randay and the restructured civilian police. She has her doubts about how much better the new police will prove than the old, but concludes they could hardly do worse than the militia.

Within another hour, the camera teams are delivering their raw video to broadcast stations, where the Golden Lady's identity is revealed for the first time.

There is remarkably little violence. The Dalavan Militia is used to pushing around helpless civilians, is short of competent magical support, and has received very little training. Its few members who attempt resistance prove hopelessly naive about the amount of firepower that can be generated by a well-trained, well-equipped combat team, and are either immediately blown from existence or so intimidated by the formidable response that they immediately surrender.

By 12:00, the situation is well in hand, and Aiah leaves the plasm station and returns to the Aerial Palace. She will dismiss Togthan, fire every person he appointed, rehire the twisted people he had forced her to send away.

When she arrives, she discovers she is famous. Her image has been playing on the video for hours. Togthan accepts his dismissal stonily, and many of his hires have either left already or not bothered to report to work, saving her the bother of firing them.

Parq, from his refuge in the Grand Temple, issues bulletins denouncing the other two triumvirs, and then—when the other two insist that he leave the Grand Temple for a meeting—sends his resignation instead.

Adaveth is recalled to the government—not to the cabinet, but to take Parq's place as triumvir. Sweet irony, Aiah thinks, that Parq should be replaced by one of the polluted flesh.

Ethemark returns to the department late in the day. She cannot read the expression in his face, but she hears the anger still in his voice.

"You knew," he says. "You knew this would happen."

"I didn't know," Aiah says, and then adds a comforting falsehood. "I only hoped."

He nods, reserving his judgment, and passes on.

In the days to come Aiah discovers that video is intermetropolitan in nature and does not stop at borders. Her image finds its way around the world. Aldemar, calling a few days later, is the fifth person offering to buy the exclusive rights to base a chromoplay on her story. Many more calls come from journalists.

She hires an agent in Chemra to deal with it all.

She has to decide what she wants from fame before she can decide how to handle it.

TWENTY-THREE

~~~~~~~~~

"You should have trusted me, Triumvir," Aiah says.

Constantine's dreamy eyes contemplate columns of brilliant bubbles rising in golden liquid. He holds the crystal glass to the light that streams in the windows of his limousine, observing the way the crystal casts rainbows on the vehicle's interior, and when he speaks his voice seems to drift into the car from far away.

"Do you remember, that time we spent together in Achanos, I spoke of my grandfather?"

"Yes, I remember."

The facets of the crystal dapple Constantine's face with little rainbows. A thoughtful frown touches his lips, and he touches a button that causes a slab of bulletproof glass to rise between the passenger compartment and the driver and bodyguard in the front seat.

"Do you remember when I spoke of my grandfather's abdication? How he put his enemies in power, and arranged for them to fail, and then came back with everyone's blessing to resume his place as Metropolitan—do you remember that?"

The memory floats to the surface of Aiah's mind. He *had* told her, she thinks, exactly what he would do, and furthermore he had, when he first warned her of Parq's rise, bade her to remember Achanos. She had thought, instead, he was trying to manipulate her through the memories of a moment of love.

"Yes," she says. "I remember."

Constantine's eyes drift from the glass to Aiah. "I told you then what I planned, near as I dared."

"But that was when the war was still in progress," Aiah says. "You had made plans for Parq even then?"

"Of course. I had *always* intended, from the first, even before war came upon us, to deal with Parq exactly as I have."

Knowledge of these deep-laid plans darkens the complexion of Aiah's thought. What, she wonders, is his plan for *her?*

The limousine, part of a convoy with guards fore and aft and mages floating overhead on invisible tethers, turns to cross a canal. Shieldlight winks off the spiderweb supports of the suspension bridge; below the canal glitters greenly. The hum of the contra-rotating flywheels set between the driver's and passengers' compartments grows louder.

"But why?" Aiah asks. "Why put Parq in power in the first place? He was treacherous even during the revolution, and no credit to the government afterward."

Constantine sips his wine and lets it hang on his palate for a long moment, savoring it, a reward of success.

"Because," he says finally, "following the fall of the Keremaths, there were always a number of alternatives that presented themselves, and one of them was the concept of *theocracy.* The Dalavans are potentially a great power here, two out of every five people, and if they united behind Parq's alternative, behind a theocratic concept, they could overpower any opposition. Theocracies, when they are not corrupt, are always vicious, always trying to impose their moral absolutes on an imperfect humanity. But they always *sound* attractive—their language seduces, like ecclesiastical architecture, music. . . . Why *not* form a government of godly, disinterested people? Why not let them direct society in harmony with divine inspiration? Why not make people good? And so, on this promising moral premise, we find the coercive powers of the state united with the coercive powers of faith—people must be *made* good, the *state* must make them so when religion cannot; and if one is *not* good, one is not merely disobeying a custom or a law made by mortals, one is defying the universal truths behind the operation of the universe, one is opposing *all that is true, all that is divine,* and so the penalties must be savage for such willful perversity, such obstinacy in the face of revealed truth. . . ."

He sips his wine again. "It is a powerful notion, and it was necessary that such a notion be discredited. And so Parq was given what he wished—power over the state, power to persecute and confiscate—and everyone in Caraqui got a taste of what it is like to live in a theocracy . . . and now, as a result, the concept of theocracy is discredited beyond saving. As long as there is a living memory of Parq's abuses, the notion of rule by the godly will not raise its head in Caraqui, not for three generations at least, and by then I hope other institutions will be so firmly in place that theocracy will never be chosen but by a discontented few."

"All the chaos was necessary?" Aiah asks. "The violence, the terror?"

Constantine gives her an indulgent look. "It got the matter over with in ten days. If theocracy had gained lodgment by another means—coming to power through an election, say, or by coup against a regime deemed insufficiently devout—there would have been *years* of terror."

"*If,* you say, they had come to power. It might never have happened."

Constantine frowns, sips at his wine. "*If,*" he repeats. "I thought we could not take the chance, Parq being Parq, and Caraqui being Caraqui."

"And elections," Aiah observes, "being within a few weeks."

Constantine smiles to himself. "Even so." He chuckles deep in his throat. "I can predict Parq's next move. He will begin to intrigue with the Provisionals, and that will be the end of him. Because—count on it—I will monitor this conspiracy, and document it well, and then under threat of exposing it will make Parq my instrument forever."

"Still," Aiah says, "you should have trusted me, and made

my part plain. I was forced to improvise, and I put myself in a dangerous situation."

Constantine permits a look of irritation to cross his face. "I trusted no one. I told no one at all, not directly, not till the last moment, when I had to give the army its orders. It was not a thing to be spread about—and though I could trust you with a secret, I could not trust your reactions. I *wanted* you to be outraged about Togthan's moves in your department, I wanted that emotion to be genuine. I didn't want you turning smug and implying that you knew something Parq and Togthan didn't."

"I would not have done such a thing, Triumvir," Aiah says.

"It was not a necessary thing for you to know," Constantine insists. "I only do that which is necessary."

Aiah is not willing, for her part, to let the matter go.

"You should also have consulted me about the movement of Karlo's Brigade," she says.

Grudgingly he looks at her sidelong. "Perhaps," he allows.

Aiah presses in. "I think, in order to avoid these difficult situations in the future, the informal arrangement we have reached concerning the Barkazil Division should be put on a more formal basis. I suggest I become an employee of the War Ministry. I will not require a salary, but I want a place in the hierarchy. Vice-Minister for Barkazil Affairs. Something like that, but you may choose the exact wording."

"It is not necessary."

"Do you recall, a few days ago, when you said you would grant me anything in your power?"

Constantine puffs out a breath. "It is absurd for you to hold positions in two different ministries."

"Surely it is not beyond the combined powers of the War Minister, the Resources Minister, and a triumvir to grant me an exception."

Constantine gazes stolidly forward for a moment, then tilts his head back and laughs, the sound booming in the car. Wine dances in his glass.

"Very well," he says. "If the Ministerial Assistant for Barkazil Liaison will cease to plague me about matters long past and done with, I believe I may satisfy her on this matter."

Aiah smiles sweetly. "Thank you, Triumvir."

Constantine booms another laugh. "You're welcome, Miss Aiah." He leans forward, snatches a grape from a waiting basket of fruit, pops it in his mouth, and chews with pleasure.

Beyond the windows a desert looms. The vehicle convoy is approaching the Martyr's Canal, where a great battle had been fought, not in the war with the Provisionals, but in the original coup that had brought Constantine to Caraqui. The Burning Man had appeared here, in the midst of a quiet residential neighborhood, and set the entire district alight, a whirlwind of fiery horror that had killed at least twenty thousand people. Now the buildings are rubble or roofless shells, some mere steel skeletons, some with traces of fine stonework, graceful plaster accents, noble arches, fluted pillars that now support . . . nothing. Occasionally a forlorn Dalavan hermit is seen, hanging in a sack from a scorched wall, and election graffiti is splashed over anything left standing. The clouds float undisturbed overhead: no advertising flashes in the sky here, because there is no one to buy.

Many of the destroyed buildings were torn down to make way for new construction, but the Provisionals' countercoup interrupted the work, and dozens of the dangerous, roofless ruins still stand open to the weather. The promised new contruction hasn't materialized, either, funds dried up by the war, and the entire district stands bereft of life except for the campsites of refugees with nowhere else to go.

A perfect workshop, Constantine considers it; a laboratory for experimentation.

Rohder is planning to perform a miracle here within the next hour.

Constantine's convoy pulls off the road into an area bulldozed free of rubble. The song of the car's flywheels decreases in volume. Constantine's guards pour out of their vehicles and set up a watchful perimeter. A tugboat's whistle shrieks on the nearby canal.

Constantine remains in the vehicle. After what happened at Rohder's last outdoor demonstration, Constantine has decided to play it safe.

Rohder, already on the site with some of his assistants and a battery of complex instruments, approaches the car. He is wearing a red hard hat and heavy work boots.

Constantine presses a button and electric motors sing the window into the car's armor. Aiah sees the guards grow more alert at the sign of this chink in their defenses. Rohder peers into the car, removes the inevitable cigaret from his lips, and says, "We are making some last-minute preparations. It's very complex, and—"

"Take all the time you need, Mr. Rohder."

Rohder nods and rejoins his assistants. Constantine smiles, sends the window up, settles back into the soft leather seat just as the telephone, set on the built-up area behind the driver, gives an urgent buzz. Constantine makes a face and moves forward into the seat opposite Aiah, picks up the headset, answers. A lengthy conversation follows, which from its diplomatic context Aiah concludes is with Belckon, the Minister of State. Constantine gives detailed instructions concerning something he calls "compensated demobilization," then returns the headset to its cradle.

"Lanbola," he sighs. "We will surrender it, now that Parq is gone and we have clear policy, but the details are complex. We do not want the Popular Democrats back, and we want some compensation for the expenses of the war, but our neighbors want us out—they do not like the precedent we have set."

"Their protests have not been very loud," Aiah says. "I was surprised."

"They take note of the size of our army," Constantine says, "and how swiftly Lanbola fell. It occurs to the wise among them not to protest too loudly, and it occurs especially to Nesca and Charna, who supported the Provisionals from the beginning . . . and it has occurred to some to hire mercenaries, and look to their own defense, but on hearing of their inquiries in Sayven, we told them these hires would *not* be considered friendly, and they have again chosen to act with caution. So even Adabil, which does not have a border in common with us, will not offer sanctuary to the surviving Provisionals or to Lanbola's Popular Democrats, and Kerehorn and Great-Uncle Rathmen and their cohorts have been forced to Garshab, which is content to play host to the refugees so long as they bring their money with them."

"'Compensated demobilization'?" Aiah asks.

Constantine makes an amused sound deep in his throat. "Our vast army is destabilizing to the region, and very expensive. Armies are expensive even to demobilize, and there are secondary effects, such as the economic consequences of releasing so many soldiers into the civilian economy at once. So we hope to acquire Polar League funds, both to rebuild our damaged homes and industry and to demobilize the army." Merriment glitters in his eyes. "Our neighbors will pay us not to threaten them anymore. It will be cheaper for them than to raise armies of their own, and less dangerous. . . . It is a fine sort of blackmail, one for which we need do nothing—not even threaten, for the mere presence of our army is enough—and I think I can bring it off." He glances out the window, sees Rohder still talking to his staff, and then turns back to Aiah.

"Adabil, considering itself safe on account of our not having a border in common, will be against giving us aid, but unfortunately when we took Lanbola we discovered a store of documents detailing just who among them created the Provisionals, and why, and for how much. Does Adabil's parliament know, I wonder, that its government drew twenty-two billions from the Secret Fund to support Kerehorn and his soldiers? Twenty-two billions!" He smiles grimly. "I will bring down their government with this, I think. It is just a matter of timing, and deciding how, and to whom, the discoveries will be leaked."

Leaks, Aiah thinks; maneuverings, blinds, diplomacy, concessions, extortion. Behind it all, the threat of raw military power. All things that she must learn if the Ministerial Assistant for Barkazil Liaison is ever to prosper.

"We may thank the war for rationalizing much of the state," Constantine muses. "Under pressure of the emergency, the tax laws were reformed at a single stroke. The government cut loose the various enterprises that were hampering its real work. Government departments could be relieved of their excess personnel, with the army to absorb the unemployed. Whole classes of criminals were swept away by the PED and the militia, and now the militia are swept away. Theocracy reduced, the Keremaths discredited beyond redemption, and our neighbors anxious to be our friends. Good laws, good armies—the foundation of a strong state. Such did the blood of our martyrs buy us."

The phone buzzes again. Constantine gives an impatient look, answers, then hands the headset to Aiah. "For you," he says.

It is Alfeg. "The interviewer from *Third Shift* wanted to change his appointment to 14:00 tomorrow. I checked with Anstine and your schedule is clear; shall I say yes?"

"I suppose. Why not?"

The Golden Lady was very much in demand these days.

"And the *Wire* called again."

Aiah sighs. The news service was doing a long piece on Aiah—she had been getting calls from her relatives about reporters turning up—and it seems it was doing some serious digging into Aiah's life. Aiah dreaded a thorough investigation into the plasm she'd stolen in Jaspeer, dreaded what Charduq the Hermit might say in an interview, dreaded what her mother might be persuaded to say.

Dreaded, perhaps more than anything, a reporter talking to her former lover Gil.

And the results available over the *Wire,* in Jaspeer and half the world.

She sighs again. "We'll use the *Third Shift* interview as a rehearsal," she says. "Schedule the *Wire* for three or four days—that will give me time to prepare."

"Very good. I'll call Anstine and check your appointment schedule for a time, then call back and clear it with you."

"Do that."

She returns the headset to its box. Constantine gives her a skeptical look.

"You are discovering the perils of celebrity."

"I am. Yes."

"*Use* it, Miss Aiah. It is not always up to you whether or not you are famous, but the use you make of it is yours."

"Yes," she says. "I'll try to do that."

There is a shadow at the window, a knock. It is one of

Rohder's assistants. Constantine lowers the window by a few inches.

"Mr. Rohder says we may begin now."

"Tell him to proceed," Constantine says, and reaches for another grape.

Constantine and Aiah shift to seats on the port side of the limousine, nearer Rohder's group. Rohder himself stands stiffly, his head thrown back—for Rohder this is an unusual posture, and Aiah concludes it is because he is in contact with one of his mages.

A broken wall stands before them, once part of a block of middle-class flats that had occupied the surface of this huge pontoon. The wall is broken now, cracked, fire-blackened, ragged-edged, its original peak gone. Tenuous plant life is taking root in its various niches. It is barely a wall at all.

There is a pause. Constantine fidgets as he looks out the window. And then a strange effect begins to take place around the wall, light shifted into a different spectrum, or a shade raised between the wall and the Shield. Constantine narrows his eyes, absorbed in the magework. The wall shimmers in the light and seems to expand, as if it has grown liquid and is filling an invisible mold. An apex forms, ready to support a roof, and the wall sheds its blackened color, shaking the soot from its skin.

Atmospheric generation. From out of nothing, something.

Difficult, or it would be more common. Hermetic plasm transformations are most often used in making or alloying metal, creating chemicals and materials for plastics, and sometimes for generating food substances. . . . All that is relatively simple, one reaction at a time. But creating matter, and doing it in the open air, outside a factory or other controlled environment, is exacting, exhausting, and potentially dangerous.

The effects fade, and there is a wall there, intact, solid, real. Rohder's crew grin, chatter, make excited gestures. Rohder scans the instruments on the table, nods, gropes in the pocket of his jacket for a cigaret. Puffing, he approaches the vehicle.

"Congratulations, Mr. Rohder," Constantine says. "And congratulations as well to your mages."

An uncharacteristic pleasure glows in Rohder's blue eyes. "The transformation was very well controlled," Rohder says. "So little radiation that my instruments barely detected it, and we kept heat within limits. The wall should be a bit warm to the touch, but the heat will dissipate. And our engineers will examine the wall in the next few minutes—take measurings and core samples and so on—and we shall see if it is structurally sound."

"I have no doubt that the experiment was a complete success," Constantine says. "I hope you will accelerate the project."

Rohder gives him a judicious look. "It is difficult to train people to this work," he says. "Even if things go better than expected, our progress will be slow."

"Amplify your sense of scale, Mr. Rohder," Constantine says. "Caraqui needs housing, and needs it cheaply, and soon. You may call upon every government resource."

"We'll take the samples," Rohder says, "and see."

Rohder's caution does not dampen Constantine's enthusiasm— all the way back to the Palace he speaks of hermetics, of the creation of living space for the city's tens of thousands of refugees, for those now confined to the half-worlds. "And now that Rohder's FIT theory is demonstrated, we can make use of that in construction—make certain that building skeletons are placed in the proper ratios, or even, through freestanding transformation, create *retroactively* a new structure within the old. Multiply plasm generation, and then use the new plasm to generate even more . . ."

Aiah watches him, smiling at his enthusiasm—this is a glimpse into a younger Constantine, one just formulating his ideas, a man subsequently eclipsed by disappointment, tragedy, his own cold irony. Constantine pauses, and gives her a sudden, sharp look.

"I have been meaning to ask," he says, "and it has slipped my mind—I am addressing a New City Party election rally at Alaphen Plaza tomorrow. May I hope that my new ministerial assistant will persuade the Golden Lady to appear?" He smiles. "I think it will give greater impact to my harangue, and may guarantee a wider coverage on the video reports."

Aiah considers this and finds herself surprised. "You expect that *I* will be able to secure *you* greater coverage on video?" she says. "Is this something new? Is this the Constantine I know?"

His look turns haughty, but there is self-mockery there as well. "I did not achieve my present station," he says, "by overlooking a chance to secure myself a place on video screens."

"No," Aiah agrees. "I'm sure you have not."

ELECTION ENTERS FINAL DAYS

NEW CITY LEADS IN POLLS

The Golden Lady appears on cue at the rally, flying over the heads of the assembled crowd while Constantine, in a large bulletproof enclosure shielded from mage attack, watches as the crowd goes wild, chanting Aiah's name over and over again. It is exhilarating, swooping over this endless expanse of waving arms and upturned faces, a human sea teeming with life.

Not bad, Aiah thinks, for a ministerial assistant.

And then she swoops over the speakers' platform and sees Constantine, a little sullen twist on his lips, a considered calculation in his eyes. His own reception from the crowd had been somewhat less rapturous than this.

Perhaps, she thinks, he is beginning to view the Golden Lady as a rival.

The *Third Shift* interview goes well. The *Wire* interview is tougher—they have built an interesting, though circumstantial, plasm theft case against her. But she denies everything, and they have no evidence.

Her heart gives a little lurch as Gil's name comes up. Apparently they have interviewed him, but he declined to say much, and wisely did not mention the ten thousand dalders she had wired him.

The elections are held with a certain amount of confusion, but with no violence, no suggestion of large-scale tampering.

The New City Party wins 40 percent of the popular vote. Parq's Spiritual Renewal Party comes in second with 12 percent, and Adaveth's Altered People's Party takes slightly under 10 percent.

The Liberal Coalition, the party to which President Faltheg has lately attached himself, takes less than 8 percent of the vote, and a host of smaller parties split the rest.

Faltheg, presumably concluding from the totals that he had failed to kindle the enthusiasm of the electorate, resigns his post as president of the triumvirate—to his relief, Aiah suspects—though he remains one of the triumvirs, and also continues as Minister for Economic Development, a post for which he has genuine ability.

Constantine becomes president of the triumvirate, first among the three alleged equals. With his own party, Faltheg's, Adaveth's, and as many of the smaller parties as he can tempt to his side with promises of rewards and offices, he reforms the cabinet and government. He promises on taking office that martial law will be relaxed in stages and the normal processes of justice and government resumed.

On the day following the Caraqui elections, the government of Adabil falls as its parliament discovers a gap in the budget twenty-two billions wide. The new government is much less hostile to Caraqui, and much less friendly to the Provisionals.

Other neighbors, Aiah trusts, are taking note.

Negotiations with the Polar League continue, and Lanbola and compensated demobilization is much discussed. The envoy Licinias returns and is cordially received. When he meets Aiah, he bows in his courtly way and expresses his pleasure at meeting the Golden Lady.

"I am very pleased to see you here," she says. "I hope you negotiate for us a hundred-year peace."

He looks doubtful. "I will do my best," he says. "Certainly things seem to be falling President Constantine's way—I am pleased I was wrong in my predictions of a stalemated war. But Constantine's swift passage to power may have left turbulence in his wake—dangerous whirlpools, I fear—and these may yet prove troubling to his state."

Aiah can only hope that Licinias remains a poor prophet.

HANDMAN FOUND DEAD
IN LOUNGE BAR

FRIENDS ALLEGE
"PARTY SICKNESS"

"Oh, no. I'm not disappointed."

Aldemar is a sufficiently good actress that Aiah can't really figure out whether she is telling the truth or not.

"It's a shame," Aiah says. "I wouldn't mind having the world thinking I look as good as you on screen."

Aldemar, acting as her own producer, has lost the bidding war for a chromoplay based on the story of the Golden Lady. Aiah, delicate golden headset pressed to her ears, is calling from her apartment to express condolences.

"They would have made it a sequel to the chromo I just finished," Aldemar says, "and it would have been as dreadful as the first."

"It's not very good?" Aiah is dismayed. Aldemar has sent her tickets to the premiere, which is taking place in Chemra. A visit to Chemra would also give her a chance to visit her agent, a man she's never met.

"It had promise, but they wrecked it in the editing." There is resignation in Aldemar's voice. "Don't worry—if you come for a premiere, I won't make you watch the whole thing. You can slip out early and go to the party."

"If you can watch it," Aiah says bravely, "I can."

"You'll be luckier with your production," Aldemar assures her. "You've got more money behind it, and Olli is a first-rate producer. He always does a high-class production."

There is a moment's pause. "You'll get quite a bit of money, you know."

Aiah will, in fact, receive a sum that, as a girl in Old Shorings, she would have thought beyond her wildest imagination. If she is not quite able to consider herself rich, she can certainly consider herself very, very lucky.

"With some competent management," Aldemar says,

"the money should keep you comfortable for the rest of your life."

"I'll keep myself in less comfort," says Aiah, "because I'm going to give half the money to charities for refugees here in Caraqui."

"That's admirable."

"They did all the suffering, and I got all the glory. It's their story, too, and they deserve some of the profits."

"In that case," Aldemar says, "it's more important that the money you keep be handled well. I can introduce you to some good money managers—they've made me a lot over the years."

"Thank you, yes," Aiah says. "It's not a world I know much about."

Her world, she thinks, is beginning to overlap with others in interesting ways. Requests for interviews, people who want her as a speaker at various functions, the continuing demands of her job . . . She needs a manager for everything, she thinks, not just her money.

Perhaps she can talk Constantine into allowing her an assistant.

THE GOLDEN LADY

A SPECIAL DOCUMENTARY—THIRD SHIFT ON CHANNEL 51!

"There is someone to see you." Aiah's receptionist Anstine, unusually pale, slides into Aiah's office and quietly closes the door behind him.

"Yes?" Aiah says, looking up from a desk overflowing with documents relating to her department's budgetary health. It's an unusual visitor who actually prompts Anstine to enter her office, when he can just call her on the intercom from his desk.

Anstine bites his lip. "He—I *think* it's a he—he says he knows you. He gives his name as Doctor Romus."

The talons of the Adrenaline Monster dig into her back and Aiah starts upright, all at the sudden thought of

Aground, of sudden death and terror. She looks into
Anstine's eyes and sees a look of concern cross his face at her
reaction.

"Oh. Well," she says. "Send him in."

Anstine looks dubious, but leaves without comment. Aiah
looks down at the documents covering her desk—all that
postponed wartime paperwork catching up—and takes a
long breath to calm her trip-hammer heart.

The war is over. Why does the Adrenaline Monster still
lurk in her tissues, ready to rake her nerves with his chemical
claws?

The door opens and Romus glides in, feathery tentacles
fluttering around his little brown face. "Miss Aiah," he says
in his reedy voice, "I am honored to make the acquaintance
of the Golden Lady."

Aiah rises and tries to look at the unearthly figure without
flinching. She represses an urge to shake hands: Romus has
no hand to shake. She wonders if she should offer him a
chair.

"I'm relieved you survived," she says. "Ethemark has been
trying to find people from Aground, but there are so many
refugees, so many transit centers. . . ."

Romus coils his lower body before Aiah's desk and
rears his head to her level. "I think most are dead," he
says. "The mercenaries killed everyone they could find,
whether they were armed or not. Most of the able-bodied
died trying to protect their families, and none had my gift
of hiding."

Sorrow floats through Aiah's mind even as her body jitters to the Adrenaline Monster. *Your fault,* a voice whispers.
She resumes her seat, and Romus curls his upper body into a
fishhook to keep his face level with hers. "I wish," she says,
"things were different."

No trace of sentiment glimmers in Romus's yellow eyes.
"Sergeant Lamarath knew the risk he was taking," he says.
"He agreed willingly."

Aiah looks at him. "And what did he agree *to,* exactly?"

"He asked for money, medicine, and weapons, and he got
them. He—*we,* for I advised him—felt it was a gamble worth
taking."

"And the other people who died? Did they think the gamble was worth taking?"

"For us," Romus says, "all life is a gamble. The war could have killed us all without anyone ever knowing. The militia could have got us afterward. It could even have been an inhabitant of Aground who betrayed your mission—we tried to keep it a secret, but in a place like that it was impossible."

Aiah does not find this reply entirely satisfactory, but finds no reason to dispute it. Romus, too, must live with his memories.

"I'm glad you are here, in any case," Aiah says. "I wanted to thank you for helping me when the Provisionals attacked."

Romus tilts his head. "You are welcome." He licks his lips. "I would be very pleased should it prove possible for your gratitude to take a more material form."

Aiah feels a more calculating, warier self sliding efficiently into place behind her politician's face. She is not prepared, she thinks, to be taken for a *passu* by a giant snake.

"Yes?" she prompts.

"Quite frankly," Romus says, "I could use a job. I have no home, no place, and no prospects."

"What sort of job did you have in mind?"

A morbid smile crosses his lips. "I would hope that, in my case at least, genetics does not equal destiny. Mages created my kind for the purpose of inspecting pipes from the inside, or conducting repairs in tight places. The truth is that I find such duty about as fulfilling as you might, if you were forced into such work."

"You hope for a job as a mage? Are you actually a doctor of some sort?"

Romus bobs his upper body in a kind of nervous apology. "Titles in the half-worlds are strictly honorary. The boss is called sergeant, and his assistant is called doctor. Though I took the title as seriously as I could, and did what was possible to look after the health of Aground's population, I am strictly self-taught."

"I'm afraid we don't really need medicos, self-taught or otherwise," she says.

"I have other experience with plasm. I have done quite a

bit of surveillance, and"—he licks his lips, and bobs his upper body again—"and a certain degree of bodyguard and enforcement work. The half-worlds are dubious places, and sometimes such things are necessary."

Aiah finds herself in no position to criticize. She folds her hands on the desk, frowns, gives the matter her consideration. Romus very possibly saved her life, and she will employ him if she can.

"It's a mixture of talents that we can use," Aiah says. She leans forward and looks into Romus's eyes. The strength of her position gives her the power to look into the eerie face without flinching. "But I want to explain that our entrance exams are very stringent—we're going to do a brain scan that *will* uncover any past criminal activity and any present notions of treachery. If you're working for someone else, we'll find it. If you're planning on selling any information you find here, we'll find *that*. So if there's anything you're not comfortable revealing to government interrogators, you might consider applying for a job in another department. I will give you a high recommendation."

Romus considers for a long moment. His yellow eyes turn uneasily away. "I will admit to you now that I have stolen plasm in the past," he says. "I will also state that I have no intention of stealing any in the future."

"If that is true, the plasm scans will reveal it. And, I should add, all hiring and firing in this department ultimately rests with me. I am not interested in prosecuting any minor criminality that may have taken place in the past, under a different regime. But if there is any danger of future misbehavior, then my hand is forced. The PED is the only clean agency of law enforcement in the government, and it will remain so."

Romus's tentacles flutter uneasily. "I will take the test," he decides.

"Very good. I will have Anstine give you the application forms and schedule the scan."

Aiah watches Romus leave, then returns to the piles of paper spread before her.

She decides she needs a bigger desk.

THE GOLDEN LADY—FREEDOM FIGHTER
OR PLASM THIEF

TOMORROW ON THE *WIRE*

Aiah looks stonily at the jerky video as another arrested suspect explodes. Fortunately the soldier carrying the camera faints almost immediately, and the video is short.

"Did you see the room?" Kelban says. "Bottles everywhere. Pills. Take-out food. And a girl had just left, a pro—surveillance saw her exit."

Nictitating membranes half-lid Ethemark's eyes. "The Party Sickness," he says.

"Two people with Party Sickness symptoms, and they both blow up when arrested," Kelban says. "This is *not* a coincidence."

"But the first fellow to explode," Ethemark remarks, "did so in front of his family. No Party Sickness there."

Kelban frowns. "Maybe he was in the early stages."

Maybe he was starting the party with the wife, Aiah thinks. She ventures a cautious shrug. "What can we do?" she says. "I've never heard of an illness that acts this way, and we're not the Health Ministry in any case."

Ethemark tilts his head back, considers. "We are not empowered to act on matters of public health, true. But if this is the result of a Slaver Mage, say, or an ice man, then this is definitely a case of misused plasm, and therefore falls within our purview."

"I'd like an opinion from counsel in that regard," Aiah says.

"Still," says Kelban, "if this is a case of some kind of supernatural possession, then its only victims are Handmen. This mage, or whatever it is, is doing us favors."

"We don't know that its only victims are Handmen," Ethemark points out. He turns to Aiah. "I'd like authorization to open a file on this, perhaps commit some of our investigators."

"It looks like a dead end to me," Aiah says. "We have no evidence, nothing but some bodies."

"We don't have any evidence *yet*. We haven't looked—I want to thoroughly investigate the movements of the victims, who they saw, when and if they began to act strangely."

That seems harmless enough, Aiah thinks. Certainly digging through the victims' files and backgrounds is not going to lead anyone to Constantine.

"All right," Aiah says. "Submit a proposal, then, and I'll approve it, providing it doesn't take too many personnel from their regular duties."

Ethemark looks at her. "Very good. I don't think we'll need more than one mage, and maybe one good investigator on the ground."

"Not full-time, I trust."

"Probably not."

"Well. Submit your proposal, and we'll see."

Aiah wonders if Ethemark has heard the same rumor that Khorsa had, that Constantine interviews prisoners, orders them released, and that they subsequently die of the Party Sickness. If this is an attempt by Ethemark, or Ethemark and Adaveth together, to discover something they can use against Constantine, or to hold over him.

Aiah remembers Constantine in the limousine just a few days ago, smiling as he gazed into his wineglass, firmly in command of Caraqui and himself, confident in his ability to manage any crisis. Taikoen was an element of his confidence, his power, but a dangerous element.

She wonders if it is possible to kill a hanged man, and how.

JABZI ATTACKS "GOLDEN LADY"

AIAH "COMMON CRIMINAL,"
SAYS INFORMATION MINISTER

"The hearings in the Timocracy came to nothing," Colonel Galagas is pleased to report. He touches his mustache, smiles. "No evidence was ever developed, and none of the Escaliers were ever required to testify."

"I'm pleased for you."

Aiah has little actual interest in the findings, but they allow Galagas and the Escaliers to keep their standing within their profession. Invitations to the other mercenaries' regimental dinners will continue.

Aiah leans forward across her desk and asks the question that truly interests her.

"Have the hearings revealed who betrayed us?"

Galagas shakes his head. Plasm displays, reflected from the window behind Aiah, glow gold and red in his eyes.

"I regret to say that they did not. The order to attack the Escaliers came from the headquarters of a Provisional general named Escart, but he was killed in the fighting, and we don't know where he got his information."

"Who could have told him?"

"Quite a few people, unfortunately. The information could have come from above, which would have meant army group or Provisional headquarters in Lanbola. Or below, possibly his own intelligence section."

"Is there a way to find out?"

He gives a thin smile. "The Escaliers, too, have an intelligence section. They're working on it—there is little else for them to do, really—and we'll let you know if we find anything. Provisional headquarters no longer exists, and a number of their employees are now hard up for funds."

Aiah returns Galagas's smile. "The PED has a small budget for informers," she says.

"Ah." Galagas's look brightens. "That is good to know." He touches his mustache again. "When I was in the Tim-ocracy," he says, "I looked at the *Wire's* piece on you."

Aiah finds herself making a face. "And?" she says.

"They made no effort to understand Barkazils, but otherwise I thought it was fair enough. And you?"

Aiah tries to banish the tension she feels in her shoulders. The *Wire's* investigation had been extremely thorough, though fortunately it was reasonably objective—it gave her credit for investigating plasm thefts in Jaspeer and for her work against the Silver Hand and the militia, even as it raised suspicions about other activities.

Her heart had lurched when she'd seen her ex-lover quoted, but to her surprise, Gil had spoken nothing but praise, and defended her against any suggestion of criminality, something that relieved and gratified her. She should send him a wire of thanks, she thinks.

"I hate to see those old charges raked over," Aiah says. "But at least they admitted they couldn't find evidence."

"The Cunning People leave no trace," Galagas says. There is a confiding little gleam in his eye.

Aiah can only hope that, as far as the Escaliers and her own activities in Jaspeer are concerned, Galagas is speaking the truth.

MARTIAL LAW TO BE EASED

TERRORISTS, SILVER HAND STILL SUBJECT TO EMERGENCY POWERS

Rohder's computer gives a rumble, shudders slightly, and at length offers up its data, first in a tentative flickering upon the screen, and then with firmer, shining confidence.

"The trend's continuing," Rohder says.

Aiah glances over his shoulder at the columns of figures. "Good."

"More for the Strategic Plasm Reserve." Rohder frowns, looks at the data. "If only I knew why. The figures shouldn't be this good."

"An element you haven't accounted for in your theory?"

"Oh, of course." Dismissively. "There must be." Rohder's blue eyes brood upon the figures. "Our original experiments were necessarily on a small scale; but here we see a leap in plasm production beginning . . ." He traces a line of figures across the computer display with a horny thumbnail. "*Here.* Almost four months ago. A few weeks after the war started. And with the war destroying so many plasm-generating structures, there should have been less plasm, not more. . . . But still the dip in generation is not as great as it should have been, and now, even though so much of the city has been wrecked, our overall plasm generation is better than before the war started."

He rubs his chin. "I am straining my mind to find a theory that will accurately account for this rise. And I can think of none."

"I can't think of this plasm increase as anything but a blessing." Aiah shifts an overflowing ashtray on Rohder's glass-topped desk, then perches on the desk's corner, crossing her ankles and lazily swinging her feet.

"And your other work?" she asks.

"The atmospheric generation teams continue to report success, and the minister continues to press us to actually erect a building. We are on the verge of achieving a degree of expertise that may permit that, but I will not do such a thing until I'm ready." He shakes his head, reaches absently into his shirt pocket for a packet of cigarets, and produces only an empty one. Crumpled, it joins other empty packets in the vicinity of his wastebasket. He looks at it with a drift of sadness in his eyes.

"You are going to get a formal report on this tomorrow," he says, "but I may as well tell you now about the results from our Havilak's team. You recall we were going to perform some freestanding transformations on an office building owned by the Ministry of Works—retroactively alter the internal structure to bring it in line with FIT—and they found the most extraordinary thing: *it had already been done.*" Rohder's watery blue eyes gaze up at Aiah in bemusement. "Some unknown mage, or maybe a group of mages, had already gone into the building and done the job on it!"

Aiah looks at him. She has been in charge of a government department long enough to know that the cause probably lies within the bureaucracy.

"Our people didn't get the work order mixed up? The job wasn't done accidentally by another of your teams?"

"That's the first thing we checked, and the answer's no. None of our teams had ever done a job that large—we'd only been experimenting with empty, war-damaged buildings until we could be certain we could do the job safely." He shakes his head. "Besides, the job was done differently

from the way we'd planned it. We chose that particular
building because it was new, only a hundred and eighty
years old, and we had the plans on file—our engineers had
planned every change we were going to make ahead of
time. And when we discovered the changes already made,
we discovered that they were different, though still made in
perfect accord with fractionate interval theory. . . ." He
shakes his head. "Who would have done such a thing? And
why?"

"Fraud, perhaps?" Aiah ventures. "Trying to raise the
amount of plasm generated by the structure, and siphoning
it off for their own use?" She reaches for a pad and paper.
"I'll have the ministry send a team to inspect the meters—"

"I already have," Rohder says. "And I checked the building's records—they *show* the increase. No one stole it. The
excess went into the public mains, just as it ought."

Aiah looks at him. "So who, then? And why?"

Rohder considers. "The *who* is most interesting. Who in
Caraqui knows enough of fractionate interval theory to make
such concrete application?"

"FIT isn't a secret."

"No." Rohder's voice turns rueful. "Not a secret, but I
doubt that more than a handful of people have ever read
Proceedings. So far as I know, our own teams are the only
people ever to try to apply the theory in practice."

"Perhaps someone on our transformation team is working
on his own? Maybe the office building was just practice, and
he intends to strike out on his own?"

"But why pick a building that he *knew* we were going to
alter?"

Aiah looks out the window. Plasm displays shimmer on
the near horizon. She bites her lip at the relentless conclusions that fall into place in her mind.

"Altering that building was illegal," she says. "The plasm
used to make the alterations might have been stolen." She
looks at him uneasily. "I regret to say that one part of my
department may have to start an investigation of another
part."

Rohder leans back in his chair, looks at the data. "I can
narrow the investigation for you. I can safely say that there

are only a dozen or so people in my section that could have pulled this off."

A falcon dives past the window, talons arched for prey. Aiah turns to Rohder again. "Very good. If you would send me the names . . . ?"

Rohder gives a reluctant sigh, his eyes never leaving the screen. "I suppose I must."

Regret sighs through Aiah's mind. She herself, working for Rohder, had deceived him; it is possible, therefore, that someone else had.

Rohder's division hadn't undergone the stringent security checks required of the more paramilitary PED; Rohder had just hired as much young talent as he could find.

And it is necessary that an investigation be performed. In order to clear Rohder and Aiah themselves, at least.

An investigation might eventually mean brain scans for some of Rohder's most skilled, valuable mages. Aiah wouldn't be surprised if some of them quit rather than submit.

And in the end the mages involved might prove to be another group entirely.

Aiah bites her lip, then brings up the matter that has brought her to Rohder's office in the first place.

"On another subject entirely," she says, "what do you know about hanged men?"

Surprise lights Rohder's eyes. He rears back in his seat and cranes his neck to look at her, the discomfort of his position a reflection of the discomfort visible in his face.

"Ice men, you mean?" he asks. "The damned?"

"Yes."

Rohder frowns. "*If* they exist—and I am not entirely convinced that they do—then hanged men are very rare and highly dangerous. Toxic. If you ever encounter one, I would run as fast as possible and pray to Vida the Merciful while I ran."

"How do you kill them?"

"It's far harder than the chromoplays would suggest." His frown deepens. "Why are you asking?"

Aiah leans closer. "I trust this will go no farther?"

He shrugs. "Who would I tell?"

Were Rohder a Barkazil, his returning a question in this

manner would tell Aiah that he was planning on telling everyone in the world; but Rohder is not a Barkazil, and Aiah reckons she can trust him with the falsehood she has carefully prepared.

Even lies, she knows, require a degree of trust. She retrieves her story from the mental closet where she has stored it. "I've found . . . *something* . . . out there in the plasm well. The thing scares me—it's cold and it's strong, and it's lurking around the Aerial Palace. I'm afraid it might be scouting for an attack."

Rohder's look turns inward, calculating. He gropes in his pocket for a cigaret, remembers he's run out, and instead gnaws a nicotine-stained thumbnail.

"If it *is* a hanged man," he says carefully, "and not some kind of plasm construction, I don't know anything that can stop it should it decide to attack."

"If it isn't a hanged man," Aiah says, "it's something else that can live and move in a plasm well, so we might as well *call* it a hanged man."

Rohder's absorbed, thoughtful expression shows no sign that he's heard. "If it is a hanged man," he says slowly, "and it's moving through the Palace plasm well, then it may be an ally of someone already *in* the Palace. Someone very powerful."

A series of barking curses chase each other through Aiah's mind. Rohder wasn't supposed to work this out, at least not yet.

Vexed with herself for not anticipating this, she reminds herself that he is over three hundred years old. He may not be very worldly, but he's done very little but deal with bureaucracy for all his professional life, and he understands the architecture of power.

Aiah needs to remember that next time she tries to use him as her *passu.*

"If this thing is a pet of someone in the building," Aiah says, "that makes it worse. I don't think anyone should have such a creature at his beck and call."

The fierce conviction in her words surprises her, and she sees Rohder's eyes widen a bit at her evident fire.

He sighs heavily, then turns to his computer display. "I

will find out what I can," he says. "There are some people I can contact at Margai University."

Aiah leans toward him, puts a hand on his shoulder. "Thank you, Mr. Rohder. This could be important."

Rueful humor settles onto his face. "I don't promise results," he says. His hands automatically search his empty pockets for cigarets.

Aiah leans back, takes a pack of Amber Milds from behind the computer, and hands it to him with a smile as she heads for the door.

It's nice, she concludes, for once in her life to leave Rohder's office without the stench of tobacco on her clothes.

TIMETABLE FOR LANBOLA WITHDRAWAL
TO BE NEGOTIATED

POLAR LEAGUE AID TO BE RESUMED

PRINCIPLE OF COMPENSATED
DEMOBILIZATION ACCEPTED

"Thank you for seeing me, Miss Aiah." Dr. Romus sways into Aiah's office, moving by throwing a thick loop of his body ahead of him, then pulling the rest after.

Aiah wants to turn away from the sinuous, unnatural movement, but she compels a grave smile to appear on her face and rises to greet him.

"You said it was important?" she says.

The reedy voice echoes oddly from her office walls. "I can't think it can be anything *but* important," Romus says. Aiah sits, and Romus lowers his upper body to keep his head on a level with hers, his usual act of courtesy.

Aiah had difficulty justifying his hiring, particularly in light of his plasm scan, which revealed a long life—he is over a hundred—rich with various crimes, major and minor. But none of the crimes were vicious—most concerned theft of state property, like plasm, electricity, or fresh water—and any violence seemed to be in the interests of defending himself or protecting his half-world.

The plasm scan also revealed he had no intention of using his position in the PED for any illegal advantage. His criminality, he seemed to suggest, was in part justified by his desperate position in the world; once in a better position, there would no longer be a need for such activity.

It was not a justification that sits easily with Aiah's judgment. But it was one she used herself—it had brought her here, to her position in Caraqui—and so she'd decided to take a calculated risk.

So far it seems to have paid off. Romus has been working for the PED for two weeks now, and reports from his superiors have been positive. He's clever, they say, and he minimizes use of plasm. He's very good at surveillance, very patient, and his reports are models of clarity.

"What's the problem?" Aiah asks.

Shieldlight glitters in Romus's yellow eyes. "I saw something first shift yesterday," he says. "In the lobby of the secure room."

A warning cry sounds in Aiah's nerves. "What were you doing there? You're not authorized for the secure room."

"I was not *in* the secure room. I was in the lobby, resting. Sleeping, actually." The cilia surrounding Romus's face writhe uneasily. "I have no place to live, you see. I eat in the Palace restaurants using my meal ticket, and my other needs are few. So when I have no work, and if there is someone working in the office I share, I usually find a quiet place and sleep. The secure room lobby is quiet—the clerk on duty usually has very little business during sleep shift—and . . ." A little tongue licks his thin brown lips. "Because I am not *shaped* as the average human, my sleeping places tend to be where others might not expect to find a person. . . . I am often overlooked. You have overlooked me yourself."

"Yes," Aiah says. Dread settles cold into her bones; she knows what is coming. "Go on," she says.

"The triumvir came in around 02:30," Romus says. "He came in with the giant guard, Martinus. He asked the clerk to leave and wait outside, then went into the secure room.

He was there for twenty minutes or so. I could hear him opening drawers and looking through files. And then . . ." There is a look of fear in the yellow eyes. "And then something came. It didn't come through the door, it just . . . it was just *there*."

"What sort of thing was it?" Aiah asks.

"Unnatural. A presence . . . a creature of some sort." His head bobs, turns away from Aiah's glance. "I would have to invoke myth to describe it. A demon, an evil angel. A *force*. It was terror without form. My only instinct was to flee." A trace of anger enters his voice. "I don't understand how it got there. The secure room is fully shielded! It was—" Words fail him for a moment, and when they return, they grow increasingly dogmatic. "An impossibility. It should not have happened at all. It violates every law of—"

"Tell me what happened," Aiah interrupts.

Romus's head sways in agitation. "The thing spoke to the triumvir. It made demands of some sort. . . . I could not quite understand what it wanted. The triumvir said that he was doing his best, that he was—I believe the word he used was *searching*. The demon was arrogant, threatening. It said that the triumvir was *late*. I began to understand that it was demanding . . . *people*. As if the triumvir was to sacrifice to it, as to an evil god. And then the triumvir said, Very well, these will do, but you must come to my suite, I can't do it here. And then the creature left . . . just faded away.

"When the triumvir left a few moments later, he called the clerk back and checked out a file. After a few hours, Martinus returned the file, and it was checked in." Romus rapidly licks his lips.

"I do not know if these things are usual. I do not know if I am permitted to speak of them. I come to you more for advice and—" He looks away again. "I wish to know if I am in danger for seeing this thing."

Aiah clasps her hands to keep them from trembling. Too many people know, she thinks. . . . It only requires them to start talking to each other for the secret to be revealed. And once word gets out, Constantine will be ruined. . . .

Consorting with a demon. What would Parq and the Dalavans make of that?

"Have you told anyone else?" Aiah asks.

"No. I couldn't make up my mind what to do. In the end I just came to you."

His head sways toward her on the end of his long neck. Aiah starts back, then catches herself. She presses her hands to the cool top of the desk.

"Firstly," Aiah says, "you must tell no one else. That *will* put you in danger."

Romus's head bobs. "I understand."

"Secondly," taking a breath, "please believe I am aware of the existence of this thing, and that I know it is very dangerous. The problem is capable of resolution, and steps are being taken. I can't reveal what steps exactly, but I implore you to understand that this will take time. The nature of this creature is such that we cannot afford any mistake—if the strike against him misses, there will be no chance for another."

A grimace passes across Romus's homunculus face. "I have had the strangest notions since I saw this thing. Now I wonder how many of these creatures exist in the world, if they *all* attach themselves to powerful men, and how much of the evil in the world might be explained this way. . . ."

For a moment Aiah considers this notion, the thought of a secret evil behind the veils of the world, Taikoen and his kin feeding forever on the weakness of the great.

Romus continues, the reedy voice thoughtful. "I concluded, however, that there cannot be very many of these things, because otherwise they would not hide, they would move openly and prey on whomever they wished."

"There is only one that I know of," Aiah says. She tries to put confidence in her voice. "And this one will be destroyed. But in the meantime . . ."

"Silence." Romus's head bows. "I understand."

She has made Romus her *passu*, Aiah thinks. She has given him a version of the truth that may serve to keep him silent, at least for now, and perhaps given him a confidence that all this may be dealt with, that Aiah will see Taikoen destroyed.

Perhaps, Aiah thinks, she has made a *passu* of herself,

convinced herself that there is a solution to this problem, and that it is within her grasp.

Taikoen, she thinks bleakly, might have made a *passu* out of everyone, from Constantine on down.

GOLDEN LADY CHROMOPLAY ANNOUNCED

PRODUCER OF *METRO FLIGHT* ACQUIRES RIGHTS

OLLI PLANS CHROMO OF "EPIC SCOPE"

And now, to Aiah's strange, heterogeneous Caraqui family comes her *real* family—some of them anyway: her sister Henley and her cousins Esmon and Spano—riding the pneuma to Caraqui for Esmon's marriage to Khorsa.

Khorsa's sister Dhival performs the rites, linking the couple to the Three Horses and spreading the Yellow Paper Umbrella, with its vermilion symbols, above their heads. As they share the marriage cup, drums roll, the audience breaks out in shouts of joy and congratulation, and a rolling barrage of firecrackers fills the room with its pungent scent.

The Barkazil Division provides musicians for the reception, and the eerie sound of the vertical Barkazil fiddle floats above the throng. General Ceison takes his turn dancing with the bride. Rohder watches from the corner with an expression of amiable bemusement.

Constantine stands tall amid the crowd, splendid in his black velvet jacket, brilliant white lace, and a glittering diamond stickpin in the shape of the fabled sea horse. He moves as easily amid the Barkazil throng as he does anywhere else.

Aiah holds his arm, pleased that on a private occasion such as this there is no necessity of maintaining in public the formal relationship of the minister and his subordinate: they can be together as conspicuously as they like.

"Esmon looks splendid." Constantine nods toward Aiah's cousin, who stands in a jacket of glittering jet beadwork that contrasts with both his billowing lace and the foolish grin on his face.

Aiah smiles. "He's always had a highly distinctive style sense."

Especially since he's been seeing Khorsa, who almost certainly bought this coat and any other fine clothes Esmon may have brought with him.

"He will take up residence here in Caraqui?"

"He already has."

"Does he have a job yet?"

Aiah cocks an eyebrow at him. "Do you have a vacancy?"

"I don't have one in *mind,* no. I don't know what your cousin can do," amusement invading his face, "unless it's to model new uniforms for the military."

"I'm sure he'd do that very well," Aiah says. "But until that opportunity arises, I'm sending him around to various government departments, along with my letter of recommendation."

"I'm sure that will obtain him a position."

The fact is, Aiah knows, that though Esmon is one of her favorite relatives, and a perfectly charming man, he isn't suited to do anything in particular; his last job, before he was laid off almost a year ago, was as a janitor in a home for the elderly.

Aiah waits for a few seconds to see if Constantine will make a point of offering Esmon a job, but he doesn't; and she long ago promised herself not to ask Constantine for special favors for friends or relatives.

Alfeg approaches and asks her to dance, and she steps onto the floor with him. He is technically a fine dancer, but the spirit is not quite there; he thinks about it too much. At one point she catches the look he gives her—awed, worshipful—and it makes her cheeks flame.

He really believes, she realizes, what Charduq the Hermit has been saying. He truly believes she is an incarnation of Karlo or some other immortal, one of the Old Oelphil guardians of her people. It isn't just a game; it isn't just a notion he's been playing with—Alfeg really believes it.

No wonder the dance doesn't feel quite right. He's almost afraid to touch her.

At the end of the dance, Alfeg returns Aiah to Constantine, who she finds chatting with her sister Henley. Henley is gesturing with her hands—lovely hands, long and graceful,

once crippled by an Operation street lieutenant and then
made even worse by arthritis, hands which Aiah, over the
last months, arranged to have repaired.

Henley catches Aiah looking at her hands. She flushes,
smiles, breathes the words, "Thank you."

Aiah takes one of Henley's hands and presses it. "I'm
happy I was able to help," she says.

Constantine watches this with a benign smile.

"Excuse me, sir," Alfeg says.

Constantine gazes down at him. "Yes?"

"I thought I'd mention that we seem to be having no trou-
ble at all recruiting replacements for the Barkazil Division.
We've got swarms of applicants—more than we can use.
We'll have our pick of some very good men."

"Splendid," said Constantine. "Carry on."

"But I feel I should mention—" Alfeg searches for words,
then decides simply to say it. "If the government should ever
decide to raise *another* Barkazil Division, or to expand the
current division to a full three brigades, I would have no
trouble finding recruits."

Constantine's eyes narrow as he considers this. "The military budget is due for reduction, not expansion," he says.
"But if the need should arise, I will bear this news in mind."

Alfeg makes an effort to conceal his disappointment.
"Yes," he says. "Thank you, sir."

"One other thing."

"Sir?"

Constantine speaks quietly, a little abstractedly, like a
teacher giving a well-worn lecture to his students. "You
should consider that a number of your recruits will almost
certainly be spies, most likely from Jabzi, who will be
inserted into the Barkazil Division with the intention of discovering whether our recruits will be used to subvert the
arrangement whereby the Barkazi Sectors are partitioned. Or
perhaps these spies will even be there to subvert *us*."

Aiah sees Alfeg's astonished stare and knows it probably
mirrors her own. "You know this?" he says. "Do you have
any—anything concrete?"

"I note simply that Jabzi, which had formerly maintained
only an honorary consul just over our border in Charna—a

local fellow who operated more as a tourist agent than a diplomatic representative—is now upgrading their presence to that of a full embassy, with a staff of over sixty people. Why should they do that in a metropolis half a world away, with which they do so very little trade? I assume that the entire purpose of this establishment is to keep an eye on what Miss Aiah and the Barkazil Division are doing here in Caraqui."

A kind of resigned amusement dwells in Constantine's eyes, as if he could not expect anything better from his fellow creatures.

"And though *I* know that the threat you pose to Jabzi is small," he says, "perhaps nil, I also assume that by the time this new embassy finishes its reports, you are going to be a full-blown menace to the security not just of Jabzi, but of the world. The jobs of those sixty people depend on your being a menace, and as far as they are concerned, you *will* be a menace."

"When," Aiah wonders thoughtfully, "did you discover this?"

"Yesterday."

"Is there anything we can do about it?"

"I will have Belckon send someone to Jabzi to have what are usually described as 'full and frank discussions,' but I suspect their government has already made up its mind and is unlikely to alter its position anytime soon." He scowls and allows an edge of anger into his voice. "I would hate for the Provisionals to get a new sponsor at this point, just as they're losing their old ones."

Alfeg still seems taken aback by this intelligence, but Aiah is already considering the consequences. Jabzi's previous official reaction to events in Caraqui—their banning the *Mystery of Aiah* video—had backfired, increasing both Aiah's celebrity and demand for the video. Perhaps Jabzi's new action could be turned to similar account.

Aiah probably couldn't make much of any espionage in the Barkazil Division, but if it were ever discovered that Jabzi had gone so far as to support the Caraqui Provisionals . . .

They fear Barkazil freedom so much, Aiah thinks, *that they try to suppress it half a world away.*

A useful slogan to keep in reserve.

Amusement tugs at Constantine's lips as he observes Aiah's reflections. He puts a hand on her shoulder. "Politics tomorrow, Miss Aiah," he reminds. "Celebration today."

Aiah laughs. "You're right." She cocks an ear to the music, then grins at Constantine. "Do you dance the koola?"

Constantine answers gravely. "I have not had that pleasure."

"If you're going to go to Barkazil parties, you should know the dances."

He holds out his arms. "I am willing to be instructed."

Constantine learns the dance quickly, even the strange, unpredictable rhythmic elision, a kind of sideways musical hiccup, that Barkazils call "the slip." A tigerish smile settles onto his face as he gains confidence, and he settles powerfully into the movements, as if he were projecting himself into the dance, making it an instrument of his will, a proud extension of himself into the world.

"You've been practicing in secret," Aiah says.

"I have not practiced. But I have *observed.* This isn't the first koola danced at this reception."

"I congratulate you on your observational powers, then."

"Thank you—"

There is a moment of suspense during "the slip"—the dance hangs suspended for an instant, then begins in another place. Aiah and Constantine gracefully manage the transition.

"Thank you very much," he finishes. A secret smile crosses his face. "I hope I will be able to sharpen my observational powers, as—in your company, I hope—I will have a unique chance for observation beyond the ordinary."

"Yes?"

His smile broadens. "Second quarterbreak, second shift today—a hundred twenty days to the minute after you discovered the first flaw in the Shield—our rooftop detectors revealed that a small eyelet, less than two paces across, opened overhead, remained open for seventy-five seconds, and then closed. In ninety days' time, I hope you will join me for an excursion through the eyelet I expect will open at that time."

The music, and the world with it, gives a sideways lurch.

Aiah missteps. The universe spins in her head, and her knees go rubbery. Constantine catches her before she falls.

He braces her shoulders within the span of one powerful arm and walks her off the dance floor. "Perhaps I should have mentioned this at another time," he says.

"It happened, then," Aiah says. A strange little laugh froths up in her like bubbles in champagne. "It happened and I didn't make it up and it wasn't a hallucination and nobody planted it in my mind." Relief sings through her, and she feels the flight of her soul, as if it is soaring telepresent over the world.

"It actually happened," she repeats, drunk with sudden joy and wonder.

"And it will happen again," Constantine says. He touches her cheek, turns her head toward him, kisses her for a long, warm moment. "We will share that—we will be the first in millennia to bear a message outward." He straightens, and Aiah sees anger smouldering in half-lidded eyes. "The worlds you have seen beyond the Shield are our right, and we will tell them so."

"Did you hurt yourself?" Esmon has rushed up, a look of concern on his face. "Did you twist an ankle?"

"I'm fine." She gives the groom a hug, presses herself to the beaded jacket, and gives him a kiss on the cheek. "Just a little mishap, that's all."

"Careful now." Esmon grins. "It's bad luck if people get hurt at my wedding."

Aiah shifts weight onto her legs, finds they will hold her. Constantine keeps a protective hand on her elbow. Aiah glances up at him.

"Don't worry," she says. "I think our luck may have changed."

LIVE FOREVER?

WHY NOT???

NEW LOW RATES

In his suite afterward, Constantine is full of plans and speculations about the Shield and the path that Aiah has found through it. He wonders whether to do something spectacular—a plasm display, perhaps—that will call immediate attention to their presence, or to spend the first several missions simply reconnoitering. He considers the possibility of putting some manner of detector through the gap—"in orbit," as he puts it—and then bringing it down on the next trip.

A touch of resentment enters Aiah's mind at this energetic speculation. It was *her* vision, she thinks, it is one of the things that made *her* special, and here is Constantine, usurping her place with all his plans.

Not that she had ever been able to develop any plans of her own, she admits.

She wonders whether to raise the subject of Taikoen, to tell Constantine that he and the ice man have been seen, and she decides against it. It would be too dangerous for Romus, she thinks. Let more time go by, she concludes, so that it won't be so certain that this last visit of Taikoen's was the one that was observed.

A few hours later, after bed, Aiah snaps upright in the grip of the Adrenaline Monster. She sits gasping on the bed, pulse thudding in her ears, an invisible claw around her throat. Ears strain for the rain of artillery. Hot tears spill down her face.

She jumps as she feels Constantine's warm hand on her back.

"Are you all right?"

"Yes." She swabs with a hand at the sweat that limns her throat. "Sometimes I wake up like this."

She senses him sitting up. His hand strokes her bare back. "How often?" he asks.

"I don't know, I—" She gulps air and decides to stop being brave. "Often," she says. "Every sleep shift, usually more than once. I haven't had a decent sleep in . . . in months. It's the plasm that keeps me going."

She can sense his calm scrutiny, draws strength from it, calms her flailing heart.

"I've known soldiers to develop this condition," he says. "Restful sleep isn't a survival trait for people in combat, so their adrenal glands compel them to remain alert with an occasional burst of adrenaline or norepinephrine."

"Is there a cure?" she asks.

His deep voice returns after a thoughtful silence. "Deep magic. Someone very talented will have to adjust your adrenal gland in a very subtle way. But that sort of thing is closer to an art than a science—it can easily go wrong. Still, if you wish, I will try to find a specialist."

"I don't know," she says, and rubs her face. "I've been hoping it will go away by itself."

"It may not."

She lets her head droop between her knees. "Let's talk about it later."

"Can you sleep now?"

Terror still trembles in her limbs. Aiah doubts it will permit her any rest. "I can try," she says.

Constantine seems to fall asleep almost at once. Sheltering in the curve of one of his arms, Aiah rests her head on his shoulder and tries to sleep.

With little success. She is still perfectly awake when Constantine's steward wakes them at the beginning of the new shift.

FALCONS OF FREEDOM

ALDEMAR'S EXCITING NEW CHROMOPLAY

OPENING SOON!!!

Aiah floats through the reception in Chemra, nodding graciously to one world-famous person after another, as if she were Meldurnë playing host to high society in one of her chromoplays. Wrapped in a sheath of gold moiré silk, Aiah plays the Golden Lady, knowing what will attract the attention of these people and what will not. The gold silk contrasts favorably with the room's decor, which leans to polished brass rails and pale green glass and is dominated by man-sized standing lamps with green glass petals that unfold like tulips.

The background buzz of conversation brightens with applause as Aldemar enters. The reception celebrates the premiere of *Falcons of Freedom,* her new chromoplay, which Aiah and the others have just seen. It isn't precisely an inspired piece of work, Aiah judges, but neither was it as bad as Aldemar had made out. She has overheard the conversation of some relieved distribution executives who seem to think it will make a decent profit.

Aldemar passes through the room with a glittering professional smile on her face. Aiah busses her on both cheeks as she passes, hears the actress's low voice say, "Let's talk later," and nods in answer as Aldemar passes on to chat with the distributors Aiah had overheard earlier.

"You're the Golden Lady, aren't you?"

Metallic silver irises glitter strangely at Aiah in the green-tinged light. It's Phaesa, who'd had her irises altered for a chromoplay decades ago, and who subsequently made them her trademark.

Aiah's mother was a huge Phaesa fan. She will be thrilled to hear of this encounter.

Aiah takes the extended hand. "Aiah," she says.

"Of course." The silver irises flicker over the room. "Are you without an escort?"

"I'm with Olli, but he needed to speak with someone—a banker, I believe."

"How discourteous of him. But that's Olli for you—obsessed with the business." Phaesa's hands close firmly about Aiah's arm. "And I'm sure you don't know anyone here. Do you need that drink freshened?"

Aiah allows herself to be towed into Phaesa's wake. Another green tulip glass of white wine is pressed into Aiah's hands. She sips, sees her reflection in the intent, glittering irises.

"Everyone in our business is talking about the Golden Lady," Phaesa says. "It's a part every actress is salivating over."

Olli, her producer, had told Aiah there would be moments like this, and had provided her with ammunition in the form of the appropriate response, which Aiah promptly chambers and fires.

"Unfortunately," she says, "I have no power over who gets the part."

"I'm sure Olli would consider your wishes."

"I will mention your name, if you like."

A smile touches Phaesa's lips. "Yes. Thank you."

Aiah gazes into the unearthly silver eyes and finds herself wondering out loud, "I wonder if the Golden Lady can have silver eyes?"

"I can change them," Phaesa says.

I can change them, Aiah thinks.

Of course.

It is one of those moments in which Chemra, and perhaps the whole world, seems to snap into perfect focus.

I can change them, Aiah's mind chatters. *I can be younger. I can be thinner. I can be smarter. . . .*

"I wonder," Phaesa continues, "if we might have luncheon at some point."

"I'm not in Chemra for long, unfortunately." Aiah says. "I have a whole government department to run, and it's more than a full-time job."

"But still—"

"Miss Aiah?" One of the waiters rescues her. "A call for you, from Caraqui. A gentleman named Ethemark, who says it is urgent."

Aiah looks sidelong at Phaesa. "My apologies. I'd better take this."

Phaesa puts a hand on her arm. "I'll talk to you later, then."

"Certainly."

Aiah follows the waiter to a phone booth with sides of stained-glass green shoots and yellow flowers. "We've switched the call here," he says, and bows as he hands her the headset of brass wire and green ceramic.

"Thank you." Aiah shuts the door and carefully puts the headset on over her ringlets.

"Yes? This is Aiah."

Ethemark's deep voice rumbles in her ears. "Miss Aiah? We have a situation here. I thought you should be informed."

"Yes?" The connection is bad, with an electric snarl fading in and out, and the conversation outside is loud. Aiah cups her hands over the earpieces to smother the sounds of the reception.

"There has been a coup in Charna," Ethemark says, "one group of soldiers overthrowing another. The new government has declared its allegiance to the New City, and everyone seems to think it's our fault. Koroneia and Barchab are making threats, and Nesca's parliament has gone into executive session. The chairman of the Polar League has called the Emergency Committee into session."

"Great Senko." Aiah closes her eyes while a long throb of sorrow rolls through her. Everything was finally going well—an architecture for peace being hammered into place, the new regime safely established at last, principles for demobilization created. And now the whole fragile structure was in danger of being kicked over.

Ethemark continues. "I've been ordered to present a report on our plasm reserves to the triumvirate in just a few hours—23:30."

Aiah rubs her forehead and looks at her watch. Almost 22:00. "I'll try to get there," she says, "though I don't think I'll make it by 23:30. Can you have someone on duty charter an aerocar here, and leave a message at my hotel concerning how to meet it?"

"What's your hotel? Does it have a landing pad?"

"The Plum. And I don't know."

"I will find out and leave a message there."

Aiah peers through the stained glass, sees the crowd outside through shifting pastel colors. Her bodyguards and driver are outside the banquet room, and she's going to need to say good-bye to Olli and Aldemar on her way out. Perhaps from the hotel she can call Constantine and find out what really happened, and who was behind the coup.

But Aiah suspects she already knows.

TWENTY-FOUR

~~~~~~~~~

"Well, honestly," Sorya says, "what was I to *do?*" She shrugs her slim shoulders inside her uniform jacket. "Charna supported the Provisionals against us, and so, logically enough, we contacted people inside Charna who were opposed to the government—idealistic officers, as it happens, disgusted with their leaders' corruption—and we encouraged them to, ah, do their utmost to alter the policy of their superiors. We provided them with a certain amount of cash and logistical support—they already had guns, being soldiers—but their plans took longer than anticipated to mature. *Our* war was over by the time they were ready."

She takes a breath, folds her manicured hands in her lap. "They'd risked their lives for us, and we encouraged them. Could I tell them, 'Stop, we don't need you anymore'? Or even worse, betray the people who trusted us, sell their names to their government?" She shrugs again. "So we limited our contacts and tried to keep informed. Any assistance we gave to them is deniable, and we now have a friendly government on our northern border. I can't do other than consider this a positive development."

Faltheg gives Constantine a cynical look. "The fact that their junta is proclaiming the birth of a New City regime tends

to cast something of a shadow on our claims of deniability,"
says the late candidate of the Liberal Coalition.

Aiah, still in her gold gown, kicks off her high-heeled
pumps and flexes her toes in the soft carpet of the lounge.
Despite crossing half the world in the fastest aerocar she
could hire, she arrived too late for the cabinet meeting; but
she was in time for an informal meeting afterward, a kind of
postmortem on the Charna situation, in one of the private
lounges in the Swan Wing.

A curved bar, all dark exotic wood banded with brushed
aluminum, sits in the corner beneath mirror and ranked crystal; plush burnt-orange furniture is grouped around a low
glass-topped table. The Swan Wing's solid-gold ashtrays wait
on tables. The air is scented by the coffee that has been set
brewing behind the bar, a fragrance that does not quite elim-
inate the sour sweat of men who have been awake too long.

The aged Minister of State adjusts his spectacles and
looks at notes he'd made during the earlier meeting. "This
has damaged us badly," Belckon says. "Our neighbors know
how to count. The Keremaths overthrown, Lanbola invaded
and occupied, the government of Adabil fallen, however con-
stitutionally, and now a violent coup in Charna. They can't
help but wonder who will be next."

Sorya sips mineral water from her crystal goblet. "Of the
four chief supporters of the Provisionals," she says, "three
have been replaced by regimes hostile to the Provisionals and
favorable to us. We have firmly established that other governments interfere with us at their peril. It will not hurt us in
the long run to have our neighbors wary of us." She gives her
lilting laugh. "I wonder what Nesca's premier is thinking
right now."

Constantine gives Sorya a heavy-lidded glance. "What
should Nesca's premier be thinking?" he asks. "Are we
engaged in anything deniable over there?"

Disdain curls Sorya's lip. "Nesca's military, such as it is,
remains loyal to its government. But both Nesca and its military are negligible and in matters involving real power may
be discounted."

Belckon runs his hands through his hair, stifles a sleep-
shift yawn. "I am disturbed," he says, "that this convulsion

should occur in a neighboring metropolis—apparently with our help, however deniable—and the triumvirate simply not know of it until it happens." He glances across the table at Constantine and Adaveth. "Unless I am wrong in this assumption, and I was not informed while others were?"

Translucent membranes slide over Adaveth's goggle eyes. "It came as a surprise to me," he says.

"And to me," Constantine echoes.

A delicate smile touches Sorya's lips. "I apologize, truly," she says. "The fact is, contact with the Charni officers had been curtailed after war's end, a single case officer was assigned, here in Caraqui because there was surveillance on our embassy, and he had other work. . . . If I'd had detailed information or a definite date, I would have passed it on. It was a failure, I admit, but insofar as the result was favorable to us, hardly a catastrophic one."

There is a moment of silence. Sorya reaches for a cigaret, lights it with her diamond-and-platinum lighter, languorously breathes in smoke.

"It would seem," Faltheg says finally, "that however this happened, we must decide how to react. Denial is possible, so we must deny."

Sorya tosses her head, exhales smoke over her shoulder, picks a bit of tobacco off her lip. "Others may try to dislodge our friends in Charna, as they tried to dislodge us," she points out. "We must make it clear that the new government has our support."

"I would phrase it more diplomatically," Belckon says. "To the effect, perhaps, that we support the right of any metropolis to change its government unhindered."

"That should make our point well enough," Sorya says, and gives her lilting laugh. "That," she adds, "and all the guns in all the hands of all our soldiers."

Later, Aiah walks barefoot down the silent, carpeted hall of the Swan Wing, her shoes dangling by their straps in one hand, the other hand in Constantine's.

"I can tell you what will happen," Aiah says. "Once Sorya has got us to announce support for the new government in Charna, she will stage-manage a confrontation—or perhaps she's confident it will occur without her intervention. A countercoup, a threat of invasion from another metropolis, a wave of terror and assassination . . . some threat to Charna that will force us to respond. And once we respond, the confrontations will escalate, and those fine soldiers and all their fine guns, as Sorya calls them, will get used again, all for her purposes and not our own."

Constantine looks down at her. "You know this?"

"I know Sorya's style." She answers his look with one of her own. "And so should you."

His brooding eyes look inward. "Yes. Her pattern is there."

They approach one of the bronze-and-glass compartment doors, and it slides open on silent ball bearings. They pass the door and it rolls shut: Aiah finds herself glancing behind, making sure they are secure from any snooping trail of plasm.

"The last time she had her way," she says, "she started a war." She holds his hand more tightly, looks up at him. "You said, once it began, that you needed her to help us win it."

"Yes." He nods. "And her service was invaluable, brilliant."

"The war is won," Aiah reminds. "She is a danger as long as she remains with the Force of the Interior. You know that."

His chin lifts a little, and there is a glimmer in his eyes, as if reacting to a challenge. "She is dangerous, yes. But then," pensively, "I admire Sorya most when she is dangerous. She is at her best then, superb. And . . ." He tilts his head, as if to consider the problem from another angle. "Removing her from her position would not necessarily make her less dangerous," he says. "She knows much about me, about the war . . . a dangerous amount. She might be more dangerous on her own, given what she knows."

"Don't fire her, then," Aiah says. "Pin a medal on her and promote her. A bigger department, a bigger budget, a bigger salary. Let's see how dangerous she can be once she's Minister of Education."

Mock alarm enters his eyes. "You aren't terrified by the idea of letting Sorya educate the next generation?"

"Post and Communications, then. Or Waterways."

A mischievous smile touches Constantine's lips. "Or let her exercise her humanitarian instincts as chairman of the Refugee Resettlement Commission."

"As you like."

Constantine gives a contemplative look. "I will give the matter more serious thought. All these proposals are amusing, but they would not make suitable use of Sorya's talents, and she would see through the scheme at once. No, I must give her a promotion that would flatter her into accepting it."

He gives an offhand wave to the invisible security man behind the elaborately framed mirror at the end of the hall, thumbs numbers on the gold twelve-key pad on the door to his suite, and presses the wing-shaped door handle.

Aiah steps into the silence of Constantine's suite, listening to the whisper of the circulating air, and then Constantine's voice comes low to her ear.

"That's a very attractive gown. It suits you well."

"Thank you. Aldcmar recommended the designer. Hairdresser, too."

His hand sweeps the hair back from Aiah's ear, sifts through it as if assaying its worth.

"I would not have had you cut short your trip to Chemra. This crisis didn't require your presence."

She turns to him. "Well. I'm here now."

He looks at her, reflective. "I think we may have an hour or two before the next crisis calls me away. But you must be tired."

"I'm used to being tired." She puts her arms around Constantine, presses herself to him, his lace fluttering against her cheek. "Since I have known you, I have never been anything but tired."

His hand speculatively strokes her back. "Officially," he says, "you are still on leave for a few days. There is nothing in your office that immediately requires your presence. Why don't you stay away from the PED for that time? I will endeavor"—amusement touches his lips—"to spend as much time as possible with you, except when crises call me away."

She lifts her face to his, kisses him. "I accept," she says, and he smiles.

But if she's right about Sorya and her intentions, she muses, the next crisis will be soon.

COUNCIL OF COLONELS CONTROLS CHARNA

FORMER GOVERNMENT FLEES TO NESCA

"I have done as you requested," Rohder says. Though he sits at the dining table in her apartment, he speaks in a low voice, as if afraid he might be overheard. He opens the green plastic file cover on the table, glances down at the files.

"I discovered that there is a rather lively scientific literature in regard to hanged men, one that till the present had escaped my notice," he says. "There is a great deal of arcana and speculation, very little of it reliable, but I have combed through it for articles written by people who might actually be qualified to discuss such matters, and . . ."

He looks down at his notes, shakes his head. "There was a hanged man operating in Injido about a century and a half ago, killing people at random, it seems, and I read the report from the head of the team that hunted it down and killed it— or thought they'd killed it; at any rate it did not reappear." His faded blue eyes drift up from the page. "A number of bystanders were killed in the course of suppressing the creature. Several of the team were hospitalized after telepresent contact with the thing. Shock, mental disorders of a type associated with trauma. One remained institutionalized for the rest of her life.

"Another case," looking down at the notes again, "concerned a kind of extortion ring in Qanibar about two centuries ago. A gang of criminals were working in league with a hanged man, somehow aiding the creature to possess the bodies of living people, wealthy victims. It would turn over the victims' wealth to its human allies in exchange for a few days in a human body, after which the contact with the hanged man somehow caused the body to fail. But so many people died in this way that the authorities became suspicious, and managed to trace the money to the criminals' bank accounts. One of the extortionists cracked under interrogation, and the police were able to ambush the hanged man when it turned up for a meeting."

"How did they . . . dispose of it?"

Rohder turns away, fumbles awkwardly for a cigaret, pats his pocket for a lighter. "Each team developed its own method," Rohder said. "I do not find either of them entirely satisfactory from an operational point of view—both are based on theories that are in essence unproven, and the only way to prove either was to risk life and sanity."

"Tell me."

Rohder sighs, looks unhappy. "Both teams operated on the assumption that hanged men are a kind of living being that exists in the plasm well, a kind of modulation in plasm itself. They assumed that these creatures will die if deprived of plasm, or forced to live outside of the plasm well without a human host.

"In Injido the team managed to locate the hanged man within an office building—it had killed someone there—and then shut off the plasm supply to that building. They then attacked the creature with plasm drawn from outside—they tried to nullify the creature, overwhelm it with masses of destructive plasm. The mages were told to configure plasm using the focus of the Great Bull, which is supposed to aid offensive action. They also intended to compel it to use up all available plasm in the building in repelling their attacks, in effect to use up its life force in its own defense. Wear it out."

He shrugs. "It was messy. The building was not empty—full of workers—and the hanged man rampaged through it. It killed over a dozen people. You don't want to see the chromographs of that, and I didn't bring them. The Great Bull aside, none of the mages really knew how to configure plasm so as to kill a hanged man, and it kept slipping away while they improvised their attacks. Reading the reports, I have the impression that there was a great deal of chaos within the mage team, perhaps some panic. Finally the target creature tried to merge with the plasm that was attacking it . . . tried to *become* the plasm, to seize control of it from the minds of the mages who were using it. The mages fought off the thing's attacks, but several were so traumatized by mind-to-mind contact that they required hospital care, two for extended stays, and one, as I said, for good. Eventually they killed it, or so the team believed. In any case, if it got away, it did not return to Injido."

A dozen people killed, several mages hospitalized. Hardly a satisfactory solution.

"And the Qanibar group?" Aiah asks.

"They had an advantage—the extortionist who cooperated with the authorities. He informed them of the body the creature was occupying, and agreed to lure the creature to a place where it was vulnerable. All plasm in the area was used before the creature turned up, and then the host body was attacked and destroyed. The creature was contained and then killed as it tried to escape to the nearest plasm source."

"Were there any casualties?" Aiah asks.

"No. But the Qanibar police had advantages given them by good intelligence—knowing where the hanged man was going to be—and also by the fact that Qanibar was at the time a totalitarian state. They opened the action by killing the hanged man's host, something the authorities certainly cannot do in any society that values the rights of humans beings and of victims." He looks troubled. "Nor am I certain that the creature was, properly speaking, a hanged man or ice man. Perhaps it was a Slaver Mage who had convinced the extortionists he was a hanged man, or maybe it was a . . . vampire. . . ." His face twists uncomfortably at having to deal with yet another creature out of superstition. "Perhaps something that has not been categorized," he continues, "or a delusion. I will continue searching for information, if you like."

"I wish you would."

"I also found this . . . curiosity." He takes out a sheaf of plastic flimsies, pushes it across the table to Aiah. "It is mostly speculation, but I thought you might want to read it, for reasons of historical and personal interest."

The plastic flimsies smell of developing fluid. "Toward a Psychology of the Ice Man," Aiah reads, by Constantine of Cheloki.

Aiah's mouth goes dry. "How old is this?" she asks.

"It was published thirty-seven years ago, in a journal of

philosophy." An analytical smile touches Rohder's lips. "There is very little science in it."

Constantine must have met Taikoen by then, Aiah thinks.

She tries for a moment to read the blue eyes, the ruddy skin, the network of fine lines in the old mage's face, and wonders what it is he knows. She gives up, looks down at the article, then drops her hand over it.

"I'll look at it later. Can I see the other reports?"

Rohder closes the folder and pushes it across the polished table surface. The soft plastic cover and the flimsies inside flutter in the brief breeze. Aiah picks up the article by Constantine and slips it into the folder. She feels the throb of her heart, its acceleration to a higher state of alertness, a touch of the Adrenaline Monster upon her nerves. . . . It is as if she is responding to the notion that the file itself is a threat, and she wonders if she will ever have the courage to make use of this information, to somehow put an end to Taikoen, or even to read the article, of historic and personal interest, that Rohder has given her.

She looks up at Rohder, forces a polite smile onto her lips. "Would you like some coffee?" she asks.

Talk turns to other matters, particularly to Rohder's teams, who are busy increasing Caraqui's plasm supply, and then the old man takes his leave. Aiah turns up the ventilation to clear the cloud of cigaret smoke and looks at the closed folder waiting for her on the table.

Her nerves hum louder than the ventilation fans.

She opens the green folder, slips out Constantine's article, and composes herself to read it: sitting straight in the straight chair, feet flat on the floor, hands framing the pages on the table. As if she were a schoolgirl at her desk.

Constantine's style, she notices, is informed but not quite at ease. She can tell he's been to college: he uses words like *noetic* and *mensuration*. The later Constantine, with less need to impress, would adopt a less specialized vocabulary, and a more accessible style.

He discusses at some length the legendary attributes of the ice man and discusses theories of how such creatures may be created. The tone is speculative—he endeavors to make it seem that he knows less about this matter than, in fact, he does. And then he addresses the primary contradiction of the ice man legends.

Why would the ice man, he asks, *who exists in the core of creation, in the plasm itself, the great transformational substance, the heart of contingent reality that underlies our whole postmetropolitan world, wish to inhabit the body of a human being?*

Constantine finds the answer in the hanged man's lost body itself.

The attractions of plasm are many, but the most intense are those based on sensation. It is these appeals to the sensual, to enhanced and extended sight and hearing, to the stimulus of nerves and groin, that most often impel those who habituate themselves to plasm as an addict to morphia; and this sensual attraction, in subtler form, is a factor in the attraction of plasm to many of its other users, who experience sense gratification alongside plasm's other enjoyments. . . .

For the ice man there are no longer nerves to stimulate, no sensory organs to enhance, no sexual impulse to satisfy. The vital element of sensory feedback is missing: no longer is the sensual body able to bring pleasure to its now detached, and oddly diminished, mind.

But, Aiah thinks, a protest half-formed in her mind; but Constantine answers her objection before she can properly form it.

It is true that when mages project themselves through telepresence they use plasm to build a sensorium, an array of ectomorphic sense-artifacts used to bring sense-stimulation to the receptive centers of the mind. But the sensorium, however enhanced it may be, is built in imitation of the body's own natural sense organs, and furthermore upon a series of sense-memories contained within the mind. Without a material body and its sense-organs to apprehend the world, and without a sensual memory, reinforced at every moment by a thousand natural stimuli, how is a detached, immaterial mentality to apprehend the world?

. . . The ice man must apprehend the world only through a created sensorium. For a human mage, a sensorium will be based on the mage's own sense-organs and on sense-

*experience and memory. For an ice man, a sensorium will
be based on organs that no longer exist and memories that
grow ever more distant. Without an anchor planted in the
body's own sensual experience and memory, the ice man's
perceptions will become ever more distorted.*

Aiah knits her brows and contemplates Constantine's
argument. It *must* be true, she thinks; Constantine *knew*
Taikoen when he wrote this, and must have based all this on
observation.

The hanged man lives in a world of erratic, distorted
sense impressions. And Taikoen, the real man, died *centuries*
ago. How, Aiah wonders, does he see the world now?

*Presumably it takes the ice man a period of time to realize
that the old pleasures are no longer there. The ice man at
first may be gratified at being rid of the irritations and
demands of the body. He can create an artificial sensorium
and stimulate it as he wishes. The distortion of perception
may not be at first apparent.*

*But when the realization comes, it must be devastating.
The body, the center of perception, no longer exists.
Perceptions are growing distorted, even deranged. Even self-
stimulation may prove futile, as the ice man, lost in the
transphysical plasm well, begins to forget even the nature of
pleasure. The ice man may well grow desperate.*

Constantine goes on to discuss the phenomenon of possession in some detail, explaining it, after numerous schol-
arly digressions, as a desperate attempt by the ice man to
regain the sense perceptions that had once made him human.

Aiah turns the page, reads Constantine's conclusion. A
metallic taste tingles along her tongue.

*What are we, then, to say of the psyche of the ice man, a
murderous creature of deranged perception, forever isolated
from the humanity that nurtured him, so desperate for a
return to a world of sensible appearances and pleasures that
it will accept temporary humanity at the cost of a human life?*

*We now know which taxonomy is appropriate for this
phenomenon. This creature that is at once powerful and
diminished, ubiquitous and isolated, desperate and raging,
deadly but impotent, possessed of being but not truly alive.
Hanged man is not the appropriate name, nor ice man. The*

only appropriate name for this creature is our third choice—
the damned.

*The conditions in which the ice man exists are, in almost
literal terms, hellish. Uncertain as to its own perceptions, its
spirit isolated, all pleasures artificial and fading, its only
companions either victims or exploiters, the situation of the
ice man is a compound of desperation and exile. Although
its victims deserve our sorrow, the creature itself—damned—
deserves more than a share of our compassion. Given the
horrifying conditions under which the ice man must exist, an
end to its existence must be looked on not as a death, not
even as justice, but as a release, an act of mercy.*

Aiah looks down at the last plastic flimsy, at the bottom
crowded with endnotes in tiny print, at the slight smear on
one corner caused by an error in copying. Her nerves sing
with the document's strangeness.

Why, she wonders, did Constantine write this thing?
Even though it is in a speculative style, it still betrays too
much knowledge. Anyone who had ever had dealings with an
actual ice man would look at this and know without doubt
that Constantine was a secret brother. . . .

Perhaps when Constantine wrote this he simply didn't
care—his first encounter with Taikoen had not come at an
edifying point of his life—but Aiah senses there's something
else at work here. She looks again over the last paragraph.

*. . . the creature itself deserves more than a share of our
compassion.*

She wonders if Constantine is trying to make her feel sympathy for the ice man—*pity my friend, he only kills because
he's a lonely perceptual cripple!* But it doesn't work, Aiah
has actually *met* the thing. And then she wonders if Constantine wants the reader to feel sorry for Constantine himself, for the person who, out of compassion and at the risk of
his life and soul, associates with the damned, with something
that others would view as a demon. . . .

That, Aiah considers, seems more plausible. It isn't as if
Constantine has not been known to turn his life into drama.

She scans the words again. . . . *an end to its existence
must be looked on not as a death, not even as justice, but as
a release, an act of mercy.*

A crystal comprehension forms in Aiah's mind, and suddenly she knows.

Constantine was trying to justify an attempt to end Taikoen's existence. To kill it.

But he didn't. He never tried. He couldn't bring himself to do it, or he found a reason to keep Taikoen alive.

The columns of print swim before Aiah's eyes. She takes a deep breath, tips her head back, and lets what she knows of Constantine's biography enter her mind. Constantine would have encountered Taikoen in his early twenties, before he met Aldemar and went into the School of Radritha. Constantine had been a member of a kind of cult, and then his cousin and all the other cult members were killed, and Constantine wrote his article and went to university for an advanced degree, and from there, and from Aldemar, to the monkish order of the School of Radritha, where he was taught an extreme self-discipline, a philosophy based on the denial of the world and of passion, a retreat from action and power.

He was fleeing, Aiah realizes. Running from Taikoen, from what with this essay he had promised to do . . . But the university had not been far enough, nor had Aldemar's arms; he needed something more radical, like Radritha, a school which maintained that nothing mattered outside the perfectly balanced, passionless mind. If nothing outside the mind mattered, it didn't signify whether Taikoen existed or not.

Aiah glances out the window, sees splashes of brightness in the sky where disembodied clothing dances in ecstasy over Colorsafe Soap. A cold hand brushes her spine. The thought of Constantine *afraid* is in itself frightening: he has never seemed afraid of anything.

Of course, she thinks immediately, he was young. Later he left the school and returned to Cheloki to begin his New City campaign, and there were no hesitations there.

But when he reestablished contact with Taikoen, it was an alliance that Constantine offered, a bargain. Two lives per month, two bodies, and then, when he needed Taikoen again, more lives, more bodies.

Color bleeds across the sky. Aiah closes her eyes and

510   WALTER JON WILLIAMS

wonders if she will have the courage to face the thing that
Constantine did not.

GARGELIUS ENCHUK WEARS GULMAN SHOES

WHY DON'T YOU?

Aiah strolls into the antechamber to the secure room,
and smiles at the clerk, a huge stoneface who could probably keep the files safe simply through her intimidating
presence.

"Hello," the clerk says. "I thought you were on vacation."

"Officially. But there was something I need to look at. I
need to check the logs and see which files I had out last
week."

The clerk obligingly turns the logbook around to face
Aiah, who pages back through the book until she finds
Constantine's signature. Only four days ago. Her nerves hum
as she jots the file numbers down—no names are used in the
logs, nothing that might reveal their contents to an outsider—and then she turns the book around again and thanks
the clerk. "Let me just look one of those up," she says, and
heads for the secure room's barred gate.

Refiq, Tollan, Brandrag. The names attached to the files
that Constantine had read. Cousins—not Handmen, but bad
enough for all that. One of these, Aiah assumes, will be
Taikoen's next victim.

She checks the files out just long enough to copy the
pages and the cousins' chromographs, and then returns them
to the strong room.

And wonders about the next step.

COLONELS' COUNCIL DEMANDS EXTRADITION
OF FORMER OFFICIALS

NESCA DECLINES TO REVOKE ASYLUM

"Did you have a good time?" Aiah asks.

Khorsa nods. "Very fine, yes. Lost a few too many dinars in the casinos, though."

"And the airship?"

Khorsa smiles. "The *Dharku* was lovely. The smoothest, most comfortable trip imaginable. And the views! We spent half our time in the observation lounge."

"I'm glad. Would you like some coffee before you sit down?"

Khorsa, just back from her honeymoon, helps herself to some. Alfeg is already present, his notebook ready.

"By the way," he says, "you have a request from the *Sector Gazette* for an interview."

Sector was a euphemism for Barkazi, as the latter did not, officially, exist. The evasion permitted the magazine's distribution in Jabzi, where the word *Barkazi* did not officially exist either.

"When?" Aiah asks. She is sick of interviews.

"Deadline's in three days." Alfeg offers a modest smile. "They must have noticed how much that profile in *Corona* boosted circulation."

"I'll think about it. Next time they should give more warning."

Khorsa stirs sugar in her coffee and drops into a chair. Aiah pushes files toward them.

Refiq, Tollan, Brandrag.

"I need the two of you to set up a rotating surveillance on these three," she says. "This surveillance involves the highest possible security. Only the three of us know about this assignment. I want the surveillance to be run with extreme caution, from a distance. Configure your sensorium so that you can perceive plasm. Assume that the subjects are wired to plasm at all times, and are aware they might be surveilled. No one else must be permitted to know what the two of you are up to."

Alfeg picks up a file, looks through it, then glances up at Aiah.

"This is a copy of the original file," he says.

Aiah nods. "Yes."

"These files aren't supposed to be copied."

Aiah looks coldly into Alfeg's eyes. "Yes," she says.

Alfeg glances nervously down at the file. "Ah," he says.

Khorsa pages through another file. "I don't see anything unusual about this Mr. Brandrag," she says. "A typical cousin, so far as I can see. Why does the surveillance have to be so secret?"

Aiah looks at them both. "Because," she says, "one of these three men is scheduled to come down with the Party Sickness."

COLONELS' COUNCIL DEMANDS EXTRADITION, MOBILIZES FORCES

NESCA "WILL NOT BOW TO INTIMIDATION"

Aiah arrives breathless in Constantine's anteroom, briefcase full of the latest plasm figures, and finds others waiting outside the office door: the other triumvirs clustered with Belckon, Sorya smoking a cigaret in the corner, Geymard and Arviro, both in undress uniform, and Personal Secretary Drusus pretending to look busy behind his desk. . . .

Martinus, the bodyguard, stands quietly in front of Constantine's door, his callused hands folded quietly. His attitude is polite, but clearly nothing is getting past him right now.

Aiah pauses at the door, catches her breath. The message had said, *Come at once.*

Come yesterday is what its tone had implied.

And now Constantine is keeping even the other triumvirs waiting outside his door. Aiah can tell from their expressions that they aren't happy about it.

Aiah walks up to the guard, lifts her brows in a silent query, receives in return a minute shake of Martinus's armored head. She turns back toward the room and drifts toward Drusus's desk.

"Mr. Drusus? Is the president—?"

"The triumvir is on the phone," softly. "It's urgent."

Aiah glances down at Drusus's communications array and

sees that no lights shine to mark that any of the phone lines are being used. She bends down and whispers into his ear.

"If the triumvir were on the phone," she says, "there would be something lit, ne?"

A look of horror crosses Drusus's face. He picks up a headset from the cradle and presses buttons. Lights begin to flash. Aiah straightens, moves away from the desk, and wonders if anyone else has observed this discrepancy.

Plasm buzzes in her nerves. Before the panic started, she'd given herself a dose to clear her head and burn off the fatigue toxins. Now she finds plasm-energy twitching at her, making her want to do anything rather than sit in a waiting room.

"I fear this will end any funds for compensated demobilization," Belckon says in a low voice to the two triumvirs. "And we may lose other Polar League funds as well, for rebuilding and refugee work."

"These military upstarts are jeopardizing everything," Faltheg murmurs. "They don't have the slightest idea how to behave."

"Or to run a country," says Adaveth. "If our policy is shackled to them, they'll bring us down."

"But they're New City. Constantine can't disavow them, and . . ."

Faltheg falls silent, then gives a sharp look over his shoulder at Aiah. Aiah feels herself flush—she had not meant to overhear—she gives him an apologetic smile and backs away, toward Martinus and the door.

Without warning ice water floods Aiah's spine, and she manages to bottle up her cry of terror at the last instant. Blood hammers at her ears.

Now she knows why Constantine is keeping his own administration locked out.

Taikoen is inside. Making demands, refusing to be sent away, forcing Constantine to deal with him *now*. Aiah's plasm-charged nerves are just sensitive enough to detect his presence.

Aiah whirls, gives an alarmed look to Martinus. The man's face is expressionless, but Aiah sees a knowing look in his deep-set eyes.

And then it occurs to Aiah that if she can detect Taikoen, Taikoen might be able to detect *her*. The thought sends a pulse of terror through her heart. She wills herself not to flee and, hoping she is not too conspicuous in her haste, backs away from the door.

Aiah gives a start as Sorya's voice comes low in her ear. "I have received some intriguing news. A religious leader in Charna—a wandering priestess I believe, has just proclaimed that I am an emanation of a god." A lazy, amused tone enters her voice. "I hope I may have your congratulations, one celestial sister to another."

Aiah clenches her teeth, tries to control her flailing nerves. The presence of Taikoen doesn't seem so strong here, and perhaps wouldn't be detectable at all if Aiah didn't already know he was just beyond the door.

"Congratulations," she tells Sorya. "I remember when you predicted the appearance of this, ah, priestess."

Sorya's laugh tinkles out. "Superhuman prescience, of course." A touch of ice enters her tone. "I wish my foreknowledge extended to the point of predicting a fat chromoplay contract like yours."

Aiah turns to face her. "You don't need the money."

"No, not really, though money of course is always useful." Sorya tilts her head, considers. "But I could use the publicity. That's the problem with being in the secret service—no one ever knows how splendidly you do your job." She shows her delicate, pearly teeth in a smile. "Constantine restarted his career with *Lords of the New City*. You may do well with your *Golden Lady* chromo—you may even ascend in Barkazi, who can tell?"

"Who can tell?" Aiah echoes.

Sorya touches her tongue to her teeth in languid amusement, and then gives a meaningful look in the direction of Constantine's door. "And with both of us being goddesses—well, practically goddesses—I wonder what that makes our mutual lover."

"He was a god before we were, according to some."

"But did he make use of those people?" Scorn narrows her green eyes. "They were a resource—admittedly a mind-impoverished one—and he threw them away. Something could have been made of them, with proper direction. In contrast," nodding as if awarding Aiah a point, "you've done very well with your moldy old hermit."

"I work with the material I'm given," Aiah says, deadpan.

Sorya seems immune to Aiah's irony. "*My* prophet has the advantage of mobility—she can travel about, make converts, acquire donations. I expect the faith to be in the black within two or three years."

"Well done." One goddess to another.

Sorya glances across the room at Adaveth, Belkon, and Faltheg, and scorn glitters in her green eyes. "I do not understand why Constantine allows himself to be fettered to those . . . people." Some residual caution has clearly replaced one description with another. "I would sweep away the lot," she says, "and both I and the metropolis would be the better. But rather than taking control, Constantine prefers to let events narrow his choices and impel him in the direction he would have taken all along. He rules with one eye toward the history books, and concerns himself with what they will say when he is dead. He wants them to credit him with good intentions." She shrugs.

"Ah well, that way his hand is not seen in events, though it makes for more confusion than one would desire. . . ." She smiles, pinches out her cigaret with finger and thumb. "He will go where he wishes, but he lets others choose the time. He sacrifices initiative for deniability. I prefer to shape things directly, and will take the responsibility for success and failure both."

She turns to find an ashtray for her cigaret, and Aiah wonders how much to trust Sorya's judgment in this: that Constantine has somehow desired the constant crises since his arrival in Caraqui, and has preferred to let others create them . . . and, Aiah now adds, has put others in a position to solve these crises for him. Taikoen has solved certain problems, it occurs to her, and now—a shiver goes up her spine— perhaps she is to solve the problem of Taikoen.

And take the blame if anything goes wrong.

Sorya drops her cigaret into the ashtray and turns back to Aiah, a delicate smile on her lips. Aiah's mind is still cautiously palpating this new vision of Constantine. She doesn't wish to accept Sorya's views of Constantine, but on the other hand she knows it is a logical enough view and that it fits with the facts, if also with Sorya's prejudices. . . .

But the proof will be before her today. If Constantine supports Sorya's provocations in Charna, it will demonstrate he has desired such a thing all along.

Suddenly the door opens and Constantine appears, all smiles and apologies. "I am truly sorry," he says. "There was a matter of some urgency having to do with . . ." He waves a hand. "But what does it matter? We must deal with Charna."

As the others file into Constantine's office, Aiah wonders if only she notices the t-grip sitting plainly on a side table, its cable still plugged into the socket—the t-grip that Constantine had undoubtedly used to project himself to Taikoen's next victim and to put the hanged man in control.

But perhaps Aiah is the only one who notices, because the others are concerned solely with Charna. Sitting around Constantine's spacious ebony desk, the other triumvirs insist that they have no reason to support Charna's new government, let alone back a demented invasion threat. Belckon also speaks out strongly on the intermetropolitan repercussions of being associated with Charna's junta and its reckless behavior.

Despite the tension and disagreement, Constantine seems perfectly at ease, almost lounging in his chair, a contrast to the others, who have to edge their chairs up to his desk to make their points. Despite the air of informality, Constantine is clearly controlling the meeting, indicating with a glance or a word who should speak next. Aiah can see Sorya's face harden as one person after another speaks against her policy.

"I beg to disagree," Sorya says when Constantine finally allows her to speak. "These people, however inept, are among our few friends in the region. They must be supported—yes, and guided. A communiqué must be issued promising action on our part if Charna is attacked. As for this foolish invasion threat—well, the invasion will not happen. President Constantine can see to that with a single phone call."

Adaveth's nictitating membranes slide partway over his eyes. "I beg to disagree with Madam Sorya's premise. Charna is not *our* friend. Perhaps this Council of Colonels is the ideological ally of certain members of our government, but not all of us, and not our metropolis." He leans forward, jabs the desk with a delicate hand. "I will utterly oppose any statement of support for Charna."

"And I," says Faltheg. "These people are out of control."

Sorya's lips press into a thin, white line. "What matters," she says, "is power, and who has it, and who is willing to use it. If we do not support our friends, it will not matter how large our army may be, our word and our counsels will be ignored by everyone, and we will be seen as ripe for overthrow. For I remind everyone here," tossing her head, "that we took power through force, and maintained ourselves through force, and if we do not show our willingness to use force to support our friends, compel neutrals, and punish our enemies, we will be seen as vulnerable by every pathetic little interventionist in the region; that *this* misapprehension is far more dangerous for us than any impression that we are *dangerous,* as our recent history has proved."

In the quiet chill that follows, Adaveth and Faltheg gaze at Sorya with the same cold expression on their dissimilar faces. Belckon polishes his spectacles. Constantine breaks the silence.

"I will make the phone call that Madam Sorya proposes," he says. "The best support we can give for anyone in our region is to help them extricate themselves from their difficulties. If Charna backs down, the crisis is over. And we will avoid making any official statements until the phone call is made."

"*Never* back down," Sorya murmurs, scorn on her face, but she turns away, backing down herself.

There is another long silence. Aiah looks at Geymard and Arviro, who are holding sheafs of documents about readiness levels and ammunition and fuel availability, and then down at the briefcase in her lap, with its latest statistics on the availability of plasm in case of military conflict . . . and feels a wave of thankfulness that the statistics will probably not be required.

Constantine steeples his fingers, gazes frowningly over them at the members of his government. "I have also considered ways in which we may suppress the reckless behavior of our Charni friends—or *my* Charni friends, if you will it so. They are clearly unfamiliar with the proper mechanisms and conventions of government, and I would help them if I can—make them *our* friends, then, and responsible friends, too. So perhaps a delegation from our government to their government, a diplomatic and economic mission—clearly *not* military—to help Charna's new government control their metropolis."

Adaveth suspiciously unveils a single eye. "A New City mission?" he asks.

"I would rather it represented *all* our metropolis," Constantine says. He smiles pleasantly over his fingertips, then looks at Sorya. "I thought Madam Sorya would serve as its head, remaining of course under Minister Belckon's direction." Alarm flashes into the others' eyes, and Constantine speaks quickly. "This will unfortunately require her resignation from the Force of the Interior, where she has done such excellent work . . . but I know she desires a more public role, and head of this special mission would, of course, be a promotion."

Aiah can see the others working out the implications of this offer—and so is Sorya herself, who toys with the silver cuff buttons of her uniform jacket as she weighs this offer. On the one hand, she would be removed from her dangerous position as head of the secret service; on the other, she would serve as the principal advisor to a group of military officers already proven dangerously precipitate and headstrong. . . . Sorya looks up.

"May I consider this offer before accepting, Triumvir?"

"Yes. Of course." He looks at the others. "Perhaps I should make that phone call now, yes? Would you all like to listen?"

Constantine is affability itself on the phone, but when coming to the point he is firm. "My government wishes you to know that we cannot support any threats of military action on your part. If you do this, you do it alone, and we will be unable to assist you in any fashion. Our country is too weary and too damaged by war to risk our hard-won peace in another conflict."

Which seems to bring the Charni to their senses swiftly

enough. The rest of the conversation considers face-saving methods by which the Charni can back down from their threat.

Constantine removes his headset. "And that is that," he says. "May I offer you all some refreshment?"

"You're giving Sorya her own metropolis?" Aiah asks later, after the others have gone.

Constantine looks at her levelly. "I am giving her a mission to Charna. She will be surrounded by a large delegation, few of whom will be *her* choice—most will be mine, and judging by the interest of Adaveth and Faltheg in the matter, they will want their own people there as well." Amusement glitters in Constantine's eyes. "Sorya will be in another metropolis, surrounded by spies hostile to her interests, and separated from her power base in the secret service, which itself will now receive a new head, my choice." He laughs. "If Sorya makes herself the principal power in Charna, she will deserve her reward."

"I wouldn't put it past her," Aiah says.

He gives Aiah a wry look. "I would give her a challenge. This last attempt—this maladroit attempt to start a war—it was clumsy. Transparent." He sniffs. "Beneath her, really."

Aiah doesn't see how to respond to this save to return to her theme.

"Sorya is dangerous."

"Danger is what I value in her." His eyes soften, and he raises a hand to touch Aiah's cheek. "And loyalty, dear Aiah, is what I most treasure in you."

Aiah looks up at him and wonders whether he would say that if he could read behind her eyes, if he knew what she was planning.

And then she considers that if Sorya is right about Constantine's approach to governing, perhaps it *would* be loyalty to deal with Taikoen. Perhaps it is what Constantine has wanted from her all along, part of his long-range plan, the way he had planned Parq's fall months before it happened.

"Constantine," she says, "you must finish Taikoen."

The warmth in Constantine's eyes dies away. He takes his hand from her cheek.

"That is not possible," he says flatly, and turns away.

"It *is* possible," Aiah says, "and it must be done. Taikoen kept us all kicking our heels in the anteroom just now—and in a crisis—while you found him a new body. He's out of control."

Constantine frowns out the window, feigning fascination with a plasm display for next shift's episode of *Durq's Room*.

"Not now," he says.

"He's been seen in the Palace. With you."

Constantine stiffens in surprise, gives Aiah a look over his shoulder. She shivers under his compelling eagle stare.

"*What* has been seen?" he demands.

"You have been seen, in this building, in . . . *conference* . . . with Taikoen. *Constantine trafficking with a demon for a human soul.* That's what was seen. And it's not far wrong."

Calculation stirs in Constantine's eyes. "Who saw this?"

Aiah's mouth goes dry. She will not give up Dr. Romus; she does not want to be responsible for what might happen to the twisted mage if his name were mentioned.

"It doesn't matter," she says, defying Constantine's look, which declares, clear as the Shield, that it matters very much. "I managed to contain it for now. But the pieces are already there, for anyone intelligent enough to put them together. Three times, Taikoen was in the bodies of Handmen who were arrested, and whom he killed when he escaped. . . ."

Distaste curls Constantine's lip. "I know. He demanded new bodies to replace the ones arrested."

"And there are rumors among the Handmen, rumors that you visit the prisons and interview people who are later released and die of the Party Sickness. All that is necessary for anyone to discover the truth is to put that rumor together with a few other facts, and . . ."

He turns to face the window again, waves a hand. "Not now," he says. "There is a crisis, and Taikoen may be needed."

"*Do* you visit the prisons, Constantine?"

Constantine gazes at the window with narrowed, defiant eyes. "I don't anymore. I did, at one point. . . . It seemed best to distract Taikoen with a succession of bodies, keep him occupied. Pay ahead, as it were, on his contract."

"If this brings you down," Aiah says, her voice turning

hard, "you will have lost everything you have worked for, and you will still be in bondage to Taikoen."

He looks at her over his shoulder again, plasm displays glittering in his eyes. "Contain it. There is no proof. It is deniable. I need Taikoen now, as I need you."

"It is not as containable as you think. Even a rumor can wreck you."

"Enough!" Fury storms in his voice. *"I will not hear any more of this!"*

Constantine roars from the room, the door crashing shut behind him. Aiah stares after him. Frustration claws at her nerves. And then she looks about in surprise.

I have driven him out of his own office, she thinks. She drifts toward the side table with the t-grip sitting atop it, brushes the grip with her fingertips. No charge tingles through her nerves; Constantine has switched the plasm off. Her reflection gazes back at her from the polished ebony table.

Taikoen has also driven Constantine away, she thinks, not just from a room, but from the life that he had led. Constantine had tried to work himself up to killing Taikoen, and he'd failed and run, and is still running. Perhaps it is the one great failure of his life, Aiah muses. A failure that he still cannot face.

Aiah takes in a breath, lets it out. Someone, she thinks, is going to have to face Taikoen on Constantine's behalf.

Startled, she gazes out the window at her own face. It is her image carved in plasm, ten stories tall, looming over the city . . . and then it fades, replaced by the image of a burning building, of windows shattering as rockets explode nearby . . . and then Aiah's image is back, gazing with intensity into the eyeless sockets of a skull wreathed with strawberry leaves.

It is one of the Dreaming Sisters' plasm displays . . . but this one is *huge,* covering half the sky. The sober, evolving images are all of carnage and destruction: buildings in flames, staring corpses, armored vehicles poised over stacks of burning bodies. It's like all the horrors of the late war condensed into a few seconds, with Aiah somehow woven into it, as if she were somehow key to all the terror . . . and it's *sad,* not simply in the way that images of war are sad, but in the way a composition can be sad, or a chromoplay; it inspires sorrow not as a polemic about war, but as a work of art. Tears sting Aiah's eyes, and she feels an ache deep in her throat.

The rolling images fade, leaving behind only a lingering representation of Aiah's face, gazing out over the city with a stricken look that Aiah knows is mirrored on her own, real face, a portrait of her staring at her portrait, half in fear and half in wonder.

ARMIES STAND DOWN

CHARNI SPOKESMAN CLAIMS "MISUNDERSTANDING"

"I got your message," Aiah tells the woman called Whore.

Whore raises eyelids heavy with dreaming, and with a languid hand she takes the copper plasm contact from her lips. "We sent you no message," she says, "but we are pleased to see you here. If you will follow me, I will take you to Order of Eternity."

Aiah tells her guards to wait in the lobby while she follows Whore into the sisters' stone maze. As she passes through the first doorway she finds a pair of carved images gazing at her in the glow of the hanging lamps, dim light and trompe l'oeil artistry giving the faces a disturbing air of life. She knows the faces, Sorya and herself, *The Shadow* and *The Apprentice,* confronting each other across the corridor, one with a knife and the other looking up a recipe.

A metaphor, she admits, sufficient to describe their relationship.

She approaches an alcove where a dreaming sister lies, and Aiah's nerves sing in surprise as the woman's eyes open and turn to face the visitor. It is as startling an effect as if one of the imagoes' eyes had opened. As Aiah continues through the corridor, the sister puts her plasm contact down, rises from her couch, and with a soft slap of bare feet on cool stones begins to follow Aiah along the winding path.

Another imago appears, *The Architect,* with Constantine's stern face and powerful body superimposed on the image of the man holding the protractor and a pair of dividers, and with a shiver Aiah remembers that *The Architect*'s meaning is *failure*—noble aspirations gone wrong, crumbled into dust.

In the next alcove two sisters lie dreaming. As Aiah passes their eyes open, one set dark and one light, they turn to Aiah with an identical incurious gaze, and after she walks past they rise and follow.

Here is *The Shadow* again, Sorya's predator eyes, her ambiguous smile. Another dreaming sister opens her eyes, watches Aiah go by, and then follows. Here is an imago called *The Mage,* and it has Rohder's face, lined and youthful at once, lacking only his ruddy complexion. Aiah appears as *The Apprentice* again, and Constantine as *The Architect.* Two more dreaming sisters, one of them the genetically altered Avian Aiah had seen earlier, rise from their couch and follow. Aiah, following Whore, feels her neck prickle under the gaze of intent raptor eyes.

More dreaming sisters rise from their couches and follow Aiah, feet slapping on stone, faces impassive as sleep-walkers'.

Death. Aiah's mind whirls, and she stops dead before the imago. It is Taikoen, a bodiless form, vaguely humanoid, somehow inscribed onto stone, its indistinct outlines fading into the dimly lit scene. As Aiah looks at the image, its contours actually seem to *blur* and *shift,* as if the plasm-creature was moving uneasily within its portrait. Terror throbs in Aiah's throat. She looks wildly after Whore and sees her guide walking calmly away. Aiah almost runs after her.

Rohder, Sorya, Constantine, Aiah, and, stalking them all, Taikoen, *Death.* The forms repeat themselves again and again. More sisters rise from their alcoves to join the silent, dreamy throng that follow Aiah through the maze. Aiah doesn't see a single *Mage* that isn't Rohder, no *Apprentice* that isn't Aiah. And then finally she sees a new face, the dreaming sister Order of Eternity, who waits for her calmly, seated on the mattress in one of the alcoves, legs dangling over the side, crossed at her delicate ankles.

"There is joy in the plasm now," Order of Eternity says, the words coming in her girlish voice. "We have felt it. There is a change beginning, a change that moves through the heart of reality."

"I thought you told me that nothing changes," Aiah says.

"I said that no change is permanent. The change we feel may not last. But it is unlike anything any of us have experienced." Her pale face lights with joy. "It is as if the plasm were singing to us. Singing of its pleasure."

"I've been using plasm every day," Aiah says. "I haven't felt anything different."

"Perhaps you are not listening."

"I may not have listened, but I've *seen*," Aiah says. "You put my face all over the sky, in one of the biggest plasm displays I've ever witnessed. Me and war and death. What was that about?"

The dreaming sister hesitates. She looks away, face sober beneath her pale cap of hair. "We have seen you in our meditations. The plasm displays are nothing we *do*, nothing we create consciously. . . . They are reflections of our meditations, of what we feel in the plasm. And though we feel the plasm's pleasure, we also sense, through our contemplation of the imagoes, that their present interaction is likely to lead to violence."

"The plasm is pleased by the idea of war?"

The dreaming sister seems shocked. "No. Of course not. The plasm's joy is in the present, and the war, if our visions are true, will be in the future. The war is not a dream, it is a nightmare, and it haunts us."

"My face was all over the sky, and it's all over this building. And other faces are repeating themselves, Sorya and Constantine and . . ."

"Yes." Order of Eternity rises from her couch and takes a few thoughtful steps. "We are seeing the faces on the imagoes repeating one another. Every *Apprentice* is you, every *Architect* is the same man, the one with the braided hair. You are all important to the plasm, somehow. It has to do with the change that we sense, the plasm that sings to us, in us. This has not happened before, not in the memory of any-one here, and we suspect not in the history of our order."

"*Death,*" Aiah says.

The sister's eyes turn hard. "Yes. We have felt that one, too, creeping about the plasm mains. An unholy thing, half-unreal, a perversion of plasm itself."

"Help me kill it," Aiah says.

Order of Eternity looks up at her, surprise on her face. "You can't kill Death," she says.

"*This* Death can be killed," Aiah says. "And if it is per-verting the plasm that is giving you such joy, you'll want it destroyed."

"We do not *act,*" insistently. "We *contemplate.* We observe the things that are, the things that are fundamental. We do nothing in the world. We do not kill, we do not undo, not even the things that are better undone."

Aiah narrows her eyes as she looks at the smaller woman. Put it, she thinks, in their terms.

"Death," Aiah says, "*this* Death, this particular Death, will bring down the Architect. The Architect, the Apprentice, and the Mage are changing the world, building something new, and the plasm is singing to you—the plasm itself is telling you that it approves of what the Architect is doing. If Death and the Shadow have their way, the war will come—the vision of war that haunts your dreams, the vision that you spread across the sky yesterday so the whole metropolis could share in your nightmare."

Order of Eternity spreads her hands, gives Aiah a helpless look. "We do not *do,*" she says.

The sisters' insistence grates on Aiah's nerves. She, Aiah, has been on the front lines of one battle or another for months, and she has no patience left for those who can't choose sides.

"Then you will be right, by your own lights," she says. "You will do nothing, and you will be right, and Death and the war will come. People who do nothing are *always* right, they always retain their moral superiority over the rest of us," sarcasm touching her voice, "but that's not because it's right to do nothing, it's because if you act, you take a chance that your action might be wrong, and you're not the sort to take chances, are you? You've never had your ideas tested, and if you have anything to say about it, they never *will* be tested. . . ."

Order of Eternity merely looks at her. Aiah stares back, anger a dull ache at the back of her skull. She is willing to continue the argument until the sisters give in from sheer weariness, but she knows there must be a better way, a key that Cunning Aiah can find, then turn to unlock the situation. She looks around to view her audience, the group of sisters who stare back at her, expressionless, as if she were but a figure in a dream. Behind them, framed on the wall, is a relief of *The Apprentice,* Aiah's own frowning face gazing at the book of recipes.

Ah, Aiah thinks. She has forgotten, lost in this maze, that her image possesses power, that she is, to these people, a splinter of their own dreaming. . . .

She turns back to Order of Eternity, straightens her spine, looks down at the smaller woman. "I am an imago," she says. "An imago stands before you to tell you these things, and the plasm that forms these imagoes would not lie to you. I tell you this: *The Death must die! The Architect must be saved! The war must not come to pass!* I come from your own dreams to tell you this!"

Order of Eternity stares at her, eyes wide, a touch of fear crossing her young, freckled face. She sighs, turns away, takes Aiah's arm, leads her to the alcove.

"Come sit in my place," she says. "And explain these things to us. We do not know you, not really, and we don't know these other people whose images lie in our dreams, and—for the first time, perhaps, in ages—we would hear of the world outside."

"First," Aiah says, "tell me about The Mage."

"The Mage is a powerful imago," says Order of Eternity. "The Mage is he who reorders nature in accordance with his will, who demands obedience from reality itself. But he is heedless as to consequence—his actions proceed from his own will alone, without regard for what follows. His actions can lead to tragedy as well as glory. His force of will makes him nearly invincible, but he is a dangerous figure to know, and often fatal to those around him."

Rohder? she thinks. Dangerous? The world-bending will
sounds much more like Constantine than the mild-mannered
Rohder.

Well, she thinks, the imagoes can't be right all the time.

Aiah sits in the alcove and gazes out at her audience, two
dozen or so women in gray shifts, all looking at her with
solemn, youthful faces, the one exception the twisted Avian
with the fierce eyes and the brown, barred wings tented over
her shoulders. "Please sit down," she tells them, and as they do
Aiah smiles at this reflection of the classroom, with herself the
teacher and these ageless, youthful-seeming women in their
gray uniforms the students. She remembers herself, seated
before a speaker on Career Day, drowsing through a lecture
on the joys of being a marketing executive for Colorsafe Soap.

The Dreaming Sisters know nothing of the world outside,
and Aiah has to explain who the players are. A few of the
younger sisters have heard of Constantine; none have heard
of Sorya or Rohder or the PED. She finds it easier, in the
end, to speak of the Architect, the Shadow, and the Mage.

She is aware, as she speaks, that the interpretation she is
feeding them may not be true—it may not be Rohder's techniques that are making the plasm sing in the sisters' minds; it
may not be Taikoen that is threatening the peace of their
dreaming—every word she speaks might be a lie, a piece of
pure manipulation.

But so might the sisters be manipulating her: stealing
plasm to create the huge displays that lured her here, divert-
ing her from an investigation by putting her face on the imagoes, all for some subterranean purpose of their own.

Users and the used: who is the *passu,* who the *pascol?* It
doesn't matter.

She needs their cooperation, and she must do what she
can to get it.

In the end, the Dreaming Sisters agree to do as she asks.

Death will die.

TWENTY-FIVE

~~~~~~

Aiah returns from her visit to the Dreaming Sisters and finds Alfeg waiting in the corridor near her apartment, standing uneasily beneath a carving of apricots and carnations. He holds a file in his hand, and his eyes are grave.

Aiah signs him not to speak until she opens her door and leaves the surveillance zone outside her apartment. The scent of massed flowers strikes her as she presses the light switch and she sees the surprising floral blaze, flowers everywhere, on every table, chair, or horizontal surface, their combined aromas heavy in the room.

Alfeg gives a tight smile. "It would seem that someone loves you," he says.

Aiah wanders to a towering spray of gladiolas, yellow and azure with splashes of red, and touches the attached note, inscribed in Constantine's bold hand.

"Possibly," she concedes. She does not want to cope with Constantine right now, and turns to Alfeg. "Something happened last shift, didn't it?"

He nods. "It's Refiq." He hesitates, then adds, "What *was* that thing? What happened to him? It was terrifying."

Aiah looks at him. "Tell me what you saw." She had never seen Taikoen in the act of capturing a human.

Alfeg hesitates. "I was telepresent, had my sensorium across the canal from Refiq's apartment, trying to be as inconspicuous as possible. I had configured my sensorium with farvision, to bring his apartment up close. I couldn't have got into his apartment anyway, because he'd screened it very thoroughly, but I could peek through the windows. At 14:42 precisely I saw a plasm tether descend from the sky and pause outside the apartment as if it contained a sensorium that was doing some surveilling of its own. Whoever it was, he wasn't trying to be subtle—I had the impression of haste, if anything."

That would be Constantine, Aiah thinks, trying to locate Taikoen's next victim while his government waited outside his office.

"And then *something* moved behind the kitchen window, something . . ." Alfeg swallows. "Something very disturbing. I only caught a glimpse of it, but it was menacing, as if someone had constructed an anima for a fright party. And then the window just blew out into the street, like an explosion, and the plasm tether shot in." He licks his lips. "I wondered what to do. If I should try to break the plasm tether, or follow it to its point of origin, but in the end I decided just to keep watching."

Taikoen, who could pass through plasm screens, had entered the apartment and opened the screen for Constantine to enter. Then, presumably, Constantine had subdued Refiq and performed whatever unholy midwifery was necessary.

"The plasm tether remained in the apartment for twenty minutes or so, and then it dissolved, as if the mage on the other end had simply broken the connection. A few minutes after that, I saw the subject, Refiq, examining the broken window from the inside. He was disheveled, like he had fallen, or maybe was drunk. He didn't seem to be walking or moving very well. He brushed some broken glass off the windowsill, then went back into his apartment."

"Where is he now?" Aiah asked.

"He put on some clothes—lace, studs; you know the way the cousins dress—and then he went to his bank. Withdrew some dinars, I guess, because next he went to a bar and ordered drinks for everybody. I turned over surveillance to Khorsa, and so far as I know, he's still at the bar—he's got himself quite an entourage by now, so I don't think he'll leave anytime soon."

"Good."

A haunted look comes into Alfeg's face. "Aiah," he whispers. "What *was* that?"

Aiah hesitates. "I'll go into more detail later," she says. "But what you should know is that Refiq is dead now—he no longer exists. The creature has him. And the creature will take others until we put a stop to it."

Aiah can see a little muscle jumping in Alfeg's cheek.

"Tell no one," Aiah reminds. "I'll talk to you and Khorsa later."

After Alfeg leaves, Aiah calls Aratha, the mage-major of Karlo's Brigade, and sets an appointment for 06:00 next day. Then she heads for the offices of the PED, looks into Dr. Romus's office, and sees only the man who shares his office.

"Is Doctor Romus in?" she asks. "Do you know if he's in the Palace?"

"I'm here," says Romus. His upper body snakes out from behind his desk, gliding with a lithe purposefulness toward Aiah's ankles, and Aiah takes an involuntary step backward.

"I was sleeping," Romus says. His body flows into the center of the room, and his face lifts level with hers. "I'm not on duty till second shift tomorrow."

Aiah tries to calm her startled heart. "Will you join me in my office, please?" she asks.

"Certainly."

Aiah leads him to her office, trying not to hear the slithering sounds of his body sawing to and fro on the carpet as he follows. She enters the office, holds the door until Romus joins her, and then closes it behind him. She takes her seat, then a breath.

"It is time," she says, "to move against the creature you saw that first shift in the secure room."

Romus's eyes go wide in what looks like fear. His little tongue licks his lips. "I see," he says.

"We know where it is," Aiah says, "and we know it's vulnerable now, for the next few days. I intend to establish a task force—a very secret one—to destroy the creature. My question is, Will you join it?"

Romus hesitates, his head swinging left and right on his long neck. "I have no experience in this," he says.

"None of us do."

"Is the triumvir a part of this scheme?"

Aiah hesitates. "He has given me to understand," she says, "that this action will meet with his approval."

Romus's cilia give an uneasy, boneless shiver. "That is, forgive me, an evasive answer."

It's also a lie, of course. Aiah reminds herself that she should be more sparing with them.

"The triumvir does not know of this action," Aiah says finally. "No one does. You do not, and I do not, and the creature does not exist."

Romus is patient. "That is not quite an answer, either."

Aiah runs her hands through her ringlets, throws her hair over her shoulders. "If you join this group," she says finally, "it will be as a favor to me, and at some risk to yourself, and you will be doing immeasurable good to the community. If you choose not to join . . ." She sighs, shrugs. "Nothing more will be said. I only implore you to keep this a complete secret, both for your sake and mine."

Romus sways back and forth while the silence builds. Aiah turns away, her nerves crawling with the unnatural motion. Finally, in Romus's reedy tones, the answer comes.

"I have lived a long while," he says, "and I am now, long after my first century is past, inclined to wonder for what. I spent years in the half-worlds, hardly ever seeing the Shield, scheming to advance my security, aiding people who have now all been murdered. Even my title of doctor is less than honorary, more a nickname than a real title. Now I have a job, and half an office, and a meal ticket . . . more than I've ever had, I suppose, but it hardly seems worth a century of effort." Something uncertain flickers in his dark eyes. "If that thing, that demon, kills me now, what will I have lost? Half an office . . . so why does this half an office seem so precious?"

Having nothing to offer him, no more words of persuasion or consolation, Aiah waits. Eventually Romus pauses in his swaying, looks down at her.

"Very well," he says. "I will join."

"Thank you, Doctor," Aiah says.

NEGOTIATIONS COLLAPSE

FUND WITHDRAWAL IMMINENT

"COMPENSATED DEMOBILIZATION" CALLED
"DEAD ISSUE"

Rohder blinks at Aiah with his pale blue eyes. "No," he says. She looks at him in surprise. Of all those she'd hoped to talk into destroying Taikoen, Rohder was the one she'd felt most sure of.

He lays his cigaret on the edge of the ashtray carefully, as if he were laying an artillery tube on an enemy objective, and gives a meditative frown.

"I have a number of objections," he says. "What you propose is illegal, even under our current martial law. It is well outside our department's authorization, and it violates the procedural and security standards which you yourself have established. And this action is highly dangerous for a group of untrained, inexperienced mages. . . . What are you going to do if there are casualties? That creature—if it exists—could burn away the minds of half your people, and you *still* might not catch it."

"If we work together," Aiah says. "If we all know what we are doing . . ."

"You will *not* know what you are doing." Rohder brushes cigaret ash from his shirtfront. "And I am far too old for this sort of thing," he adds. "The last time I coped with a plasm emergency—the Bursary Street flamer, you remember, back in Jaspeer—I ended up in the hospital. I cannot expose my neurons to plasm of that strength, not any longer."

"Well. I understand. If it's a matter of your health . . ."

"No, it's *not,*" says Rohder sharply. "Haven't you been listening? It is not simply unhealthy—it is dangerous, it's illegal, and . . ." He leans forward, a kind of cold anger in his blue eyes. "And this creature has a measure of political protection, does he not?"

Aiah finds herself paralyzed for a moment beneath the certainty of those watery eyes, beneath the intelligence that had just unraveled the secret she had been trying so desperately to preserve with lies she had thought so cunning.

"Yes," she finally says. "But it's unwilling protection. The person doesn't want—"

Rohder nods thoughtfully to himself. "I knew when I read Constantine's article: It was too outside his usual sphere . . . far too assured." He nods as if confirming something to himself. "He found a use for the thing, then. I'd wondered how so many of the Keremaths had died, in the first minutes of the coup, in such a well-shielded building."

"It's *haunting* him," Aiah says. "It can destroy everything he's built. We've got to get rid of it."

Rohder takes a meditative draw on his cigaret. "Then why is Constantine not leading the charge?" he says. "Why isn't *he* putting a group of mages together—he can find more suitable ones than you can, I'm sure. Why isn't Constantine solving his own problem?"

"He can't. He's too caught up in it. And—" There is an ache in her throat, because she doesn't want to admit this of him, not this kind of weakness. It's not, after all, a flaw of greatness; not a crime of excess, like those she's got used to, a desire for women, or an uncontrollable appetite for conspiracy. A baffling subtlety of policy.

"Constantine is afraid of the thing," she admits. "He's known it for years, and—"

"If he's afraid of it," reasonably, "then perhaps it is with good reason. Perhaps you should be as afraid as he."

"The secret is very near to being revealed," Aiah insists. "There is no one who can follow Constantine, no one capable of continuing his work. If he is linked with this creature, he falls, and all our work, yours and mine, goes for nothing. I haven't given my life to Caraqui to have it wrecked by something like this."

Rohder leans back and considers. A spasm, amusement perhaps, crosses his features. "You want to keep your job," he says. "That is a reason I can respect."

"That is not what I mean!" Frustration and anger fire her words into the air like bullets. "It's not just *me,* it's the tens of thousands who died, all the people who lost their homes. . . . All they've got left is hope, and I can't let them lose that, too, not when I could have helped. . . ." Her nails bite the metal of the chair arm, leave silver scars in the gray paint.

Rohder regards the matter, nods. "I will offer what advice I can, though I will not confront this thing directly, nor will I play a part in your actual operation."

Aiah feels her frustration abate somewhat. "Thank you," she says.

"And in regard to our jobs, our *official* jobs," reaching for a file, "I have another report from the Havilak's Transformation team. They have found another altered office building, the Communications and Telephony Center down on Orange Canal."

"Altered." The shift in subject matter bewilders her for a moment. "Oh—you mean—"

"Another building, which we'd scheduled for internal reshaping along the lines of fractionate interval theory, was found to have been altered before we could get there. A complete job this time, not half-finished like the first."

The Dreaming Sisters, Aiah thinks, a burst of revelation. It's the sisters who are altering these buildings, giving themselves the plasm for those huge displays. They must have discovered FIT long ago, kept it to themselves, along with their theories of life extension and plasm use. . . .

"As before," Rohder continues, "the meters have shown the increase, which occurred gradually about a month ago, and there is no evidence that any plasm was stolen."

They only used the plasm for a brief display, Aiah thinks. Afterward they let it flow into the public supply.

Perhaps she will confront them with this knowledge at some time, or through this matter of Taikoen earn their trust so that they will share their secrets with her.

"If there was no plasm stolen," Aiah says, "then it's not the business of our department."

"I find it difficult to believe," Rohder says, "in these omnibenevolent mages who creep about in secret to improve the structure of our public buildings. I would like to know what they're after."

"Maybe you'll meet them someday."

He narrows his eyes, suspicious of her sudden gaiety.

"Maybe," he says.

CONSTANTINE PROMISES
"HOUSING OUT OF THIN AIR"

PLANS NEAR COMPLETION

Alfeg's office is filled with Barkazil memorabilia: old Holy League recruiting posters, a frame chromo of the Coffee Factory before the war, pictures of long-dead politicians, and, in a wetsilver frame, the same cheap portrait of Karlo that hangs in Aiah's flat.

The metal door is locked from the inside. Aiah sits on the desk, Khorsa and Alfeg are in chairs, and Dr. Romus is coiled on the floor. Refiq is back in his apartment, with booze, pills, and a girl he picked up, and will probably be there for a while.

"Destroying the hanged man," Aiah tells them, "will mean destroying Refiq's body along with it. Refiq is already dead, but we can't prove it, and it won't look that way to an observer. It will look like a violation of the victim's rights. Even under martial law we've had to obtain warrants for our arrests, we've presented evidence to military judges, and the sentences passed have been legal under martial-law decree. If we destroy the hanged man, we will be acting in violation of law."

She looks at the solemn faces of Khorsa, Alfeg, and Dr. Romus. "That's why I've spoken only to you three. Whatever we do here, I want absolute secrecy in this matter, and I want you to understand that this mission will not take place officially, that there will be no files, no casework, no commendations. It's a job that needs to be done in complete secrecy, so complete that no one else can ever be told."

Khorsa sits below a framed blowup of the cover of *Corona*, Aiah smiling from the balcony of the Falcon Tower, her skin tones subtly tinged with gold. Khorsa tilts her head in thought. "This is where the Party Sickness comes from, isn't it?" she says.

"Yes. It's the hanged man trying to get the most out of his stolen body before it dies. The Party Sickness is always fatal, remember."

"Ethemark is forming a task group on the Party Sickness. Does he know about this?"

Aiah looks at her. "No. Ethemark is a talented mage and administrator, but he is a political appointee with his own agenda. I do not wish to bring him into this, because there are political implications which I do not wish to see any party in Caraqui attempt to exploit."

Alfeg seems surprised. "How is this a political issue?"

Aiah looks at him and unloads the half-truth she has ready. Risky, because she knows that Romus already knows more than she plans to tell the rest of the team.

"I have detected the hanged man in the Palace," she says. Alfeg and Khorsa stare up at her with horror in their eyes.

"I don't believe anyone in the Palace has suffered from the Party Sickness," Aiah continues, "but everyone here is vulnerable not only to having our bodies possessed by this creature, but to physical attack as well."

Alfeg stammers out a question. "Shouldn't you tell—I don't know—the army? The president? *Someone?*"

Aiah looks at him. "How do I know this isn't the army's creature? Or the ally of someone in the Palace? Or maybe spying on behalf of one of our own government departments?" She looks at them each in turn.

"Force of the Interior," Khorsa murmurs.

Aiah gives Khorsa a look as if to say *yes.* Aiah has no objection to their all believing the hanged man is something of Sorya's.

"We keep the existence of this thing entirely in this room," Aiah emphasizes, "and we tell no one."

"Not even—?" Khorsa ventures to suggest.

"*No one,*" Aiah says. Khorsa looks uncertain. "Who is the creature likely to be spying on, if it's here to spy?" Aiah asks. "Exactly the person you're thinking of, most likely. And we don't know for certain how many of these creatures there are." She shakes her head. "The matter stays here. And we handle it ourselves, and with the help of some others we can trust."

Change the subject now, she thinks, before they have a chance to work up objections. She turns to Alfeg. "We're going to try to lure Refiq to a place we can control, and then finish him off."

"Just the four of us?" Khorsa asks.

"No." A demonic little grin tweaks the corners of Aiah's mouth. "No. We are going to be assisted by two hundred and fifty-six other mages."

POLAR LEAGUE FREEZES FUNDS, DEMANDS DEMOBILIZATION

"Hanged man, eh?" Aratha says. She puts down her coffee mug. "I may have material on how to fight creatures of the sort—mind if I check something?"

Aiah looks at her in wonder. "Please do."

Mage-Major Aratha is a solid woman, broad-shouldered and powerful, with deep cinnamon skin and surprising green eyes. Aiah had flown to Lanbola to meet her in her small apartment, before normal work hours, and found her in the middle of breakfast.

Aiah, who has not eaten for the last twenty-four hours, is finding the look and scent of Aratha's toasted muffin very inviting.

Aratha steps into the living alcove, unstraps a military-looking trunk of battered gray metal, and opens the lid. She pulls out a series of plastic-bound volumes, finds the one she is looking for, and returns the others to the trunk. *"Phantasm and Plasm Emanation Manual,"* she says as she returns to the table. Aiah's mouth quietly waters as Aratha bites into her muffin while leafing through the index.

"Does the military encounter hanged men often?" Aiah asks.

Aratha chews with gusto, shakes her head in answer, then swallows. "I don't know anyone who ever has," she says, "but since we encounter a lot of odd things in the course of our duty, we're supposed to be prepared for anything. There's usually a procedure for encountering anything you can imagine. *See also vampires,*" reading, narrowing her eyes. "I haven't reviewed this since my academy days, so please forgive my poor memory."

She flips pages and reads quietly while eating. When she is done, she puts down the book and looks up at Aiah. "You've got yourself a problem, all right. You couldn't pick anything simple, like a flamer or an incarnate demon sword or anything, it had to be a hanged man."

"The hanged man," Aiah says, "picked Caraqui."

"The biggest problem is going to be *finding* it—configuring your sensorium to detect not just plasm, but a modulation in plasm, which is what this thing *is,* according to what I read here. And if you can't see it, you can't confine it. Fortunately the manual has some ideas."

"We're going to lure it into an isolated plasm well, then use up the plasm. The creature will die when the plasm runs out."

"The manual says that's possible, but you want to know it's *in* the plasm well."

"I'd like to see the manual, if I may."

Aratha shoves it across the table to her. Aiah looks with dismay at columns of fine print, a bewildering amount of jargon, and a large dose of acronyms. *Configuration of the PMDS should be completed before arrival at the ASoO,* she reads.

"You're going to do this today?" Aratha says. "I'll get a team together—two of my mages, people who survived the war, which means they're both good and used to practically everything. And myself, of course."

Aiah looks at her in surprise. She had not yet asked Aratha for anything. Aratha sees her look, misunderstands it.

"You won't be wanting us?" she says.

"I will. I'm relieved that you're so willing."

"Oh." Aratha shrugs. "You're our Ministerial Assistant for Barkazil Liaison, after all. We're under your orders."

"This whole operation may be illegal. I can't give you an order for it."

Another shrug. "Verbal order will do. Then you class the

whole operation as secret and no one will think about it ever again." She gives Aiah a reassuring look. "Don't worry. You have no idea how often this sort of thing comes up in wartime. I'll pick trustworthy people."

Aratha's war, Aiah thinks, was probably very bad, all madness and terror and reflex. Practically all a military mage did involved the deliberate murder of the enemy, or alternatively, frantic attempts to keep her own people or herself from being killed. But Aratha had survived it, and survival had given her a kind of serene, uncomplicated confidence—she felt she could view anything, deal with anything, engage with any kind of enemy, and on short notice.

Aiah's war, probably less perilous, had left her feeling isolated, with only the Adrenaline Monster for company. But then Aratha had all the other officers to support her, the entire military culture. Aiah had little support in her life, only crushing responsibilities that did not permit her any weakness.

"Thank you," Aiah says simply.

"It will do us good," Aratha judges, "to get away from routine for a while."

NECESSITY IS THE WATCHWORD OF THE GODS.

A THOUGHT-MESSAGE FROM HIS PERFECTION,
THE PROPHET OF AJAS

"Refiq?" Alfeg says. "This is Dulat. I wanted to remind you about the party. Third shift today, 21:00."

He holds the heavy plastic headset to his ears as he listens, looks up at Aiah, mouths the words, "He's drunk."

"Everything's laid on," Alfeg says, when he gets a chance to speak. "The best liquor, the best pills, entertainment, and more girls than you can imagine. Do you have the address?"

Alfeg waits again, presumably for Refiq to find something to write with, then says, "100 Cold Canal. It's a really strange building, all carved stone, off the Seahorse Waterway. Do you need directions, or will you just take a water taxi?"

Sweat is gleaming on his forehead by the time Alfeg

finishes the call. "He believed me, I think." He looks up at Aiah. "He—it—doesn't have Refiq's memories, right? He doesn't know that Dulat is just someone we made up?"

"Refiq's *gone,*" Aiah assures him. "There's only that thing in there."

Alfeg wipes his forehead with the back of his hand. "I was terrified," he says, "just knowing what was on the other end of the line."

"If he was drunk," Khorsa says, "do you think he'll remember about the party?"

"We'll have someone call later and remind him," Aiah says. "Melko."

She looks up at Melko, one of the two mages that Aratha has brought with her from Lanbola. He is tall, gangly, and wears black plastic-rimmed glasses tied around his ears with loops of elastic. He looks far too young to be the captain his collar tabs proclaim him to be.

Aratha's other mage looks too young to be anywhere but in school. A silent, spotty girl, painfully thin, Kari sits atop a file cabinet with her legs drawn up and plays nervously with the dangling geomantic charms on her bracelet.

Combat mages tend to be young, Aiah has discovered. The young have a sense of invulnerability that is useful in that line of work.

"In the meantime," Aiah says, "Khorsa needs to continue our surveillance to make sure Refiq doesn't get away. I have reserved the small Operations Room for all third shift today and first shift tomorrow. And—"

There's a knock on the door. Aiah goes to the door, unlocks it, cracks it open, and sees her receptionist, Anstine.

"The president's on the phone for you," he says. "I told him I'd see if you're available."

"I suppose I must be," Aiah decides.

She walks to her office, where she picks up the delicate headset and places it over her ears.

"Yes?" she says.

Constantine's deep voice rumbles in her ears. "Did you get the flowers?"

Aiah is suddenly weary. She folds into her chair. "You know I did."

"And did you read the note?"

"No. I haven't had the time."

There is a moment's awkward silence, then, "What's so urgent? I thought you were taking these days off?"

"An investigation coming to a head. I won't bore you with detail." She's too weary to make them up anyway.

"The note," Constantine says, "contained, I thought, a very well-phrased apology, eloquent yet humble, a model of its kind."

"I'll read it," Aiah says, "when I have the time to appreciate such a piece of art."

"I hope you will take its sentiments to heart."

"I hope," Aiah says, "that I may be able to."

There is another moment's pause, and then Constantine says, "Sorya is going to Charna. Tomorrow. I am dining with her late third shift to say good-bye. These things must be done properly—farewells gracefully said, closures correctly made."

Aiah pictures the ransacking of files that must be going on in Sorya's department now, information plundered to be carried off to Charna, or destroyed to keep from the hands of her successor. And then, she thinks, the gracious dinner in Constantine's apartment while minions stuff secret after secret into Sorya's trunks.

"Tomorrow, and after," Constantine says, "I am available to you. I hope to see you as soon as you can find the time."

Tomorrow, Aiah thinks, if this all goes wrong, she may be dead or hiding from Taikoen. If she is hiding, Constantine will have to decide between Aiah and Taikoen, could not keep them both, might decide that he loved her and turn against his monster.

For a wild, irrational minute she hopes that the attempt will fail, that this affirmation will come to pass.

The moment fades. She knows what Constantine is, what truly moves his heart. . . . It is not tender affections that are important to him, but his dreams, realizing in stone and steel the glorious phantasm city that, all his life, he has constructed in his mind.

"I hope I will see you as well," she says. If she is still alive.

"Remember," Constantine says, voice kind and confident

now, certain that he has won her, "remember that in less than four months' time we have an appointment beyond the Shield. We will change the world together."

"I hope so," Aiah says.

"I know we will." Smoothly. Anger flares darkly in Aiah, anger at the cream in Constantine's voice, at his confidence, his assumptions that she will remain his instrument forever.

She will show him otherwise, she thinks. He has made her a power, but she will not be the Apprentice for all time; the Golden Lady lives by other rules, she must have new arrangements, a new disposition.

"I have to go," she says. "I'll talk to you when I can."

"I hope it will be soon," Constantine says.

Soon, Aiah thinks. *Soon I will have solved your greatest problem for you.*

And then, as she returns the headset to its hook, she thinks, *I wonder if you will be grateful.*

"GOLDEN LADY SOCIETY" BANNED IN JABZI

"SUBVERSIVE THOUGHT" CONDEMNED BY SECURITY CHIEF

The sanctuary of the Dreaming Sisters stands gray beneath its gleaming copper dome, a maze within a maze. Aiah waits telepresent across Cold Canal, her PMDS, which turns out to be the plasm-modulation detecting sensorium, prepared to venture into the ASoO, the assumed site of operations. Aratha had called plasm into the small PED operations room, had a ball of bright reality dancing on her fingertips; she pulsed modulations through it, complex and shimmering patterns, and let the others tune their perceptions to it, distinguish it from a ball of undifferentiated plasm she was holding on the palm of her other hand.

Thus they hope to detect Taikoen once he is free of his mortal mask. If, of course, Taikoen is not some other modulation altogether, if he is not something entirely other than what they have been led to believe.

Ministry workers have cut the plasm mains around the sisters' building, and once their little plasm accumulator is empty, there will be nothing more. It is hoped that Taikoen, battered by his pursuers, will be trapped in the plasm well as it drains, and die.

"The aerial tram is coming into Seahorse Station." Alfeg's voice, echoing through Aiah's mind from the operations center. Alfeg has been following Refiq all day. Refiq had picked the fastest mode of transportation available for crossing the city, the swift-flying trams.

Aiah's sensorium can see the swaying tram car sliding into its bay atop the silver tower, sees through windows the tiny figures crowding the exits.

Soon.

Aiah shifts her weight in her chair, t-grip held lightly in a damp palm. The song of plasm in her veins is louder than the snarl of the Adrenaline Monster, than her own doubts. She is the Golden Lady again, invincible, a perfect warrior, all reality at her call.

"Refiq's taking a water taxi from the station," Alfeg reports.

"Who's *that?*" Khorsa's voice, a little excited. "Over the temple—look!"

Aiah looks with ectomorphic eyes configured to see plasm, and beneath a sky flaming with adverts sees someone's anima just hanging above the sisters' copper dome. As if someone telepresent is gazing down at the neighborhood, or perhaps trying to work out the nature of the complex carvings on the Dreaming Sisters' refuge.

"Is that one of ours?" Aiah asks, and receives only negatives from the people around her.

"Khorsa," she orders, "backtrack the sourceline. See if it's local."

Khorsa flies off from her perch over Cold Canal, a silver track across the sky. "Not from the district," she reports. "The sourceline tracks a good many radii to the southeast. Do you want me to follow it all the way to its origin?"

"No." Aiah considers. She doesn't want a bystander

hovering nearby, no matter who he might be. Taikoen might well attack him, thinking him an enemy or simply not caring, and then the stranger could end up in some padded room, mind scorched to madness by the encounter.

"No," she repeats, "I want you to wait where you are and cut the stranger's sourceline as soon as the operation commences. Then return to the operations site and join the rest of us, ne?"

"Da."

"Taxi turning into Cold Canal," reports Alfeg.

Aiah can see it, a dingy white motorboat with a cracked windscreen.

"Stand by," she says.

The taxi motors to the sisters' rusting pier. Refiq, Aiah thinks, looks like hell: he leans heavily on the gunwale, one hand swaying over the bright green water. His powerful body rolls listlessly with the waves, and the face beneath the shock of black hair is pale and slack, eyes wide and staring at nothing. For a moment Aiah wonders if he is already dead.

The little gray embryo cabman hops over Refiq's outstretched legs to tie up the cab, and then Refiq rises slowly to his feet, takes several shuffling steps toward the cabman, pays him, and accepts the little fellow's help getting to the pier.

Taikoen has nearly worn this body out. Refiq crosses the pier with quick tottering steps, like a man recovering from a stroke, and then takes his time climbing the metal stair to the paved area in front of the Dreaming Sisters' retreat.

The cabman casts off and motors away. He moves fast, not bothering to look for customers in this battered neighborhood.

Refiq reaches the top of the stair and takes a few steps into the plaza. Once there he pauses and looks with a strange resignation at the mass of carved stone.

And then Aiah's heart leaps into her throat as the stranger, the telepresent stranger hovering over the copper dome, descends on his plasm tether toward Refiq.

"What's he *doing*?" Alfeg's startled voice.

Refiq raises his ravaged face, as if he senses the approach of the stranger, and then the telepresent stranger touches him, coming into contact as if for communication.

Constantine, Aiah realizes. He is here to help Refiq leave this wrecked body and claim another one.

No time to lose.

"Clever Karlo!" Aiah shouts, the signal agreed upon.

And Aratha, from her hiding place across the canal, fires a silver arrow of plasm-energy straight through Refiq's heart. It's the kind of work she is used to. Aiah wanted to do it herself, wanted to take the responsibility of killing Refiq's empty shell, but she was afraid that she'd hesitate, or do it wrong, and finally gave in to Aratha's calm insistence.

Refiq gives a cry and flings out his arms, shot in the back by a blast of pure reality. Other shots are already on their way, propelled by the readier reflexes of the military mages. Aiah forms and flings her own bolt, blasting a body already dead, the force of her angry fire lifting the corpse from the stone pathway where it had crumpled. But something is already rising from Refiq's shattered shell, a kind of buzzing silver madness, insubstantial but infused with dire purpose, like a swarm of scintillating bees, and the next bolt, fired by one of Aratha's military mages, hits it dead on, spraying bits of silver chaff, Taikoen's strange essence, through the air. . . . Another bolt strikes, fired from another quarter. Some bits of the hanged man spark off into nowhere, and others, still under his command, loop back to rejoin his form.

But Constantine is reacting, moving with his usual uncommon swiftness and readiness. His anima grows, forms a great amorphous shield that flies across the canal toward the attackers, trying to scoop up the plasm bolts. . . . Aiah ducks around the shield, preparing another attack, but the shield suddenly extends itself in her direction and she contacts it, striking it with a kind of mental concussion that, back in the Palace, sends her bolt upright in her padded opsroom chair. In a brief instant of mental contact she can feel Constantine's recognition of her, his profound surprise. . . .

And then he's gone, vanished completely—Khorsa has cut his sourceline.

Aiah looks to the hanged man, finds him unmoved, launches her bolt of fire. Taikoen is either stunned or is having difficulty disentangling his essence from Refiq's remains.

Hit him! Hit him! Hit him! Aiah can't tell whether she's shouting the words out loud or not.

It is safer to attack this way, Aratha's manual suggests. Blast Taikoen from a distance, fire discrete bolts and not a steady stream of plasm that he could turn against its user.

A half-dozen bolts blaze into Taikoen. His scintillating body scatters, loops, reforms. Once free of Refiq he will not be able to survive for long without plasm. He floats away from Refiq, lets the blasts drive him toward the sisters' building, and then, with a sinuous, purposeful little twist of his form, Taikoen slides through the image on the huge door, Enters the Gateway, enters the maze that waits for him. . . .

Aiah pursues, spreading phantom arms wide as she flies across Cold Canal at the speed of thought, fast as one of her plasm bullets. There is a strange high-pitched drone humming somewhere in her senses, and she realizes it's Dr. Romus, a kind of buzzing battle-cry he's uttering unconsciously as he flies to the attack. Aiah dives through the doorway—the sisters' building is transparent to plasm, completely unshielded—and there is one of the Dreaming Sisters on her couch, not Whore but someone Aiah doesn't know, lying with eyes closed and plasm contact in her mouth, and the sister has lifted a hand to point down the rightmost of the two corridors. . . . Aiah flies in that direction, catches bits of Taikoen's form speeding along the floor, as if he is in the process of diving into a plasm main just below the surface of the flags. Aiah gives a yelp of triumph and fires a bolt, sees bits of Taikoen flare up and scatter like sparks. Another of Aiah's team fires a bolt—and Taikoen submerges completely, like a dolphin diving beneath the surface of the sea.

There are Dreaming Sisters in all the alcoves, and with a shiver at their strange knowing Aiah sees that each has raised a languid arm, fingers pointing down the corridor, directing Aiah and the others to their prey. The corridor loops right and down and then branches, but Aiah follows the sisters' drowsing fingers, all lazily pointing at one spot in the wall, a carved trompe l'oeil of Rohder.

Aiah gathers herself and punches through the image, briefly feeling the chill of the stone around her—and then there is Taikoen, a figure hunched over one of the Dreaming

Sisters, the violence already over, a spray of blood dripping down the alcove wall and the sister's eyes a staring witness to her final terror. In her last instant, torn from her unearthly dreaming and her inhuman serenity, she had become human again, pain and raw emotion plain on her face.

But more eerie than this are the sisters in the other alcoves, all lying in repose, eyes closed in dream, minds far removed from the grisly scene save for the uplifted arms, the fingers pointing in silent, certain accusation, toward the guilty thief who has stolen their sister's life.

Taikoen has taken the copper contact from the sister's slack mouth; he is trying to take plasm. Aiah gathers energy, as if filling her lungs with air, and then flings the power at the hanged man, a ball of destruction. The hanged man shudders—the fury of the bolt splatters stone along the corridor, sets afire the dead sister's mattress. Other animas fly into the corridor, surround Taikoen with a storm of fire. But he's using the dead sister's plasm now, creating a bubble shield that surrounds him. The bolts ricochet off the shield, strike sparks and splinter shards from the stone walls.

"Khorsa!" Aiah barks. "Alfeg! Protect the sisters! The rest of you—*keep hitting him!*"

The more plasm they fire at the hanged man, Aiah assumes, the faster he'll use up his available supply. She wonders why he's making a stand here, why he doesn't simply dive into the nearest plasm main and run.

Maybe, she thinks, the sisters are making the plasm mains uncomfortable for him.

She fires bolt after bolt. The bubble shield spins, lurches, blazes with strange color. And then frost shivers up her veins at the sound of Taikoen's insinuating voice.

"*You,* is it, girl-mage? Do you desire death so absolutely? I will oblige, young one. . . ."

He recognizes me, she thinks in sudden terror; *if this doesn't work I'm dead.* But the burning plasm in her veins provides an answer, draws Aiah's lips back in a snarl. "Your death is overdue, creature. And it is the Golden Lady who brings it."

She doesn't know whether he hears her or not, whether

she is projecting the words to him or just speaking them aloud in the Operations Room, but he acts as if he hears. Taikoen and the plasm-shield make a lunge, straight for Aiah's anima, and she feels a sudden shock of contact, the touch of the thing's cold, immortal mind, its dread intention, and knows its goal is to conquer her, nullify her, drive her mind into mad byways and seize her plasm for his own.

And as his mind presses upon hers she catches a glimpse of the way he *sees* things, the world bent and distorted, plasm the focus of the whole world, all other reality *twisted* toward it, *leaning inward,* strangely curved and warped, the colors shimmering in odd spectra, some strangely alive, imbued with a strange *purpose* . . . and what purpose could a *color* have . . . ?

It is fear that saves her, a pure reflex that sends the plasm blasting from her into Taikoen, driving the ice from her in a spray of burning plasm fire. Molten metal sings in her veins. There is a roar of thwarted anger, a kind of snarl, and then the hanged man's body twists again, a strange little Möbius shiver, and vanishes into the wall, into the building's plasm conduits.

Aiah pauses—in the Operations Room she is aware of sweat pouring down her neck, of her heart hammering her ribs—and she turns her focus to the Dreaming Sisters, to the outstretched, pointing arms that seem to bridge the world of dreaming and not-dreaming. . . .

The arms sway like compass needles, pointing up and right, and Aiah flies, penetrating the arched ceiling to the story above; and here the sisters' arms are level, all pointing deeper into the building, and Aiah follows them, flying through walls and ceilings, through alcoves and images, penetrating as if entering a mirror her own image in *The Apprentice,* Sorya's scornful gaze in *The Shadow,* Rohder's thoughtful *Mage.* Contact with Taikoen's mind seems to have deranged her perception in some way: the corridors and images seem warped, twisted, looming toward her as if threatening. She tries to ignore the effect, the distorted and ominous images, and concentrate only on her blazing pursuit.

She realizes as she flies that she is wearing the Golden

Lady anima, the featureless icon of blazing gold. . . . She can't remember willing this, and wonders how long she has borne this form, whether she automatically slipped into it when she began to fly or perhaps took it on when she invoked the Golden Lady's name, when she shouted at Taikoen in her plasm-pride.

She passes through a wall and finds herself in the dome room, sees Shieldlight passing through the slits in the dome to illuminate the gleaming plasm accumulator, copper and black ceramic behind its carved screen. A dreaming sister lies dead atop a control panel, blood spattering the dials and switches, the sight all the more horrible in Aiah's distorted perceptions. Taikoen shimmers toward the accumulator, disappears into it before Aiah can launch a plasm blast. Other animas fly into the room, hover about the accumulator like a swarm of angry insects.

It is Taikoen's last refuge. Plasm was flowing in the mains, and flowing only in one direction, from the accumulator to the sisters' contacts. Taikoen fled upstream, as it were, to the source of the plasm. Perhaps he'd expected to find a plasm main that would carry him away, allow him to merge with Caraqui's vast plasm well and vanish; but instead he'd found only a dead end, trapped himself here. He can still run, but if he does he will have to flee into a plasm conduit with less plasm than he has access to now, and he will find himself weaker and still lost, still caught in the sisters' maze.

The dreaming sister Order of Eternity lies on a couch on the other side of the circular room. She sits upright, opens her eyes.

"Hit him from all sides," Aiah says. "Destroy the accumulator and he has nowhere to run. Ready . . . on my command."

"No." Order of Eternity raises a hand. Her words are slurred by the plasm contact still in her mouth. "It is our turn. We will end it."

Aiah hesitates. And then the dome room, the Sisters' stony refuge, the world itself, seems to undergo a *shift*, a transformation. Aiah sees everything as through a pulsing wave, and she feels herself uplifted, as if buoyed up by a surge of the sea. There is a moment in which all seems to hang suspended. . . . Aiah thinks wildly of the "slip" in the Barkazil dance, a hesitation between beats.

The world falls into place again, somehow more intense than before, more real. Aiah gazes at the dead sister, and recognizes the woman she knows as Inaction. The dead woman stares at her, a horrified expression that says, *I was not expecting this.*

The world shivers again to another pulse of . . . of what? Reality is *changing,* Aiah thinks, the pace of her thoughts fervid, they are *changing the world.*

"What is going on?" Khorsa wonders aloud in the breathless moment that follows, like a pause before the clapper strikes the bell.

Another pulse, another endless moment in which the world changes. Aiah feels herself buoyed up by a wave of gentle power. A cry of wonder parts her lips. The figures on the screen seem to move, shift, engage with one another in a solemn dance, the world-dance that Aiah has seen beyond the Shield, the dance of eternity, the dance of the Woman who is the Moon.

The timeless moment ends, and reality falls into place again, stone by slow stone.

"Wahhh," Alfeg breathes in awe.

Order of Eternity stands, removes the contact from her mouth, and walks around the screen to where Aiah, the Golden Lady, waits. She seems to move with unnatural lithe movements, and her face is distorted, all eyes and forehead, the mouth and chin tiny. Taikoen's perceptions have left their imprint on Aiah's mind.

"The creature is dead," says the sister. "We have abolished it."

"How?" The question spills from Aiah's mind.

"It existed as a modulation in plasm. Once the creature ceased its movement and was contained in one place, and we had the leisure to do so, we modulated the same plasm in a way as to reduce the creature's modulation to zero—we canceled the creature out, like one wave precisely canceling another and leaving the sea smooth."

"Ask her if she's *sure.*" Aratha's skeptical voice sounds in Aiah's ear. "I don't want to have to go through this again."

"I didn't know such a thing could be done," Aiah tells the sister.

Order of Eternity walks on bare feet to the control panel, reaches out to touch, in a familiar gesture of tenderness, Inaction's short black hair. "To understand plasm is to control reality," she says. "Through our understanding, we made the thing unreal."

And then Aiah feels fingers on her throat and she is torn from the dome room, from the calm gaze of the dreaming sister, and finds herself in the Operations Room, with one of Constantine's huge hands about her neck. He pulls her from her chair, the t-grip flying from her hand as it reaches the end of its cable. His face is distorted, all anger and teeth. Behind him Aiah sees his guards, Martinus included, yanking t-grip cables from their sockets, disarming Aiah's team.

"What are you doing?" Constantine cries. *"What is this treason?"* He bends her backward over the desk, claw on her windpipe. Aiah seizes his thick wrist in both hands, tries to tear him off her, finds him immovable as iron. Tears come to her eyes as she tries to drag air into her lungs. *"Have you gone mad?"* Constantine roars.

Then plasm sizzles the air and Constantine flies backward with a grunt, as if he's been hit in the stomach. He tangles with Aiah's chair and goes down. The world seems to lean in, as if about to crush them all. Aiah clutches her throat. Heat flashes on Aiah's skin. The bodyguards, with their portable plasm packs, are dueling with the mages they haven't yet disarmed.

"Stop this!" Aiah shouts. Constantine rises from the floor, murder in his eyes, and lunges for Aiah again. She gets her feet between them, drives at him with her legs, keeps him off. Out of the corner of her eye Aiah sees a guard with a gun, and her cry of warning occurs simultaneously with the gun's exploding at the touch of plasm, all its ammunition detonating. The guard, face blackened, hand mangled, gives a cry and falls. Constantine lunges again, throws aside Aiah's legs, and dives atop her. He seizes her hair, beats her head against the desk. *"What is the matter with you?"* he demands. *"What is this spirit of treachery?"* Red explosions fill Aiah's head as he pounds her against the desk.

And then Constantine is torn off her again, and she hears him give a cry of rage, a cry abruptly choked off. Aiah sits up, clutching her throat, blinking furiously as she tries to bring her vision back. The room is filled with an ominous silence.

The red splashes fade, from Aiah's sight but waves of distortion flood her vision. Dr. Romus has wrapped his thick body about Constantine, has pinned his arms and brought him down, a loop around his throat. Martinus has been thrown against the wall, his arms held there, obviously by plasm. Another guard is unconscious, and the guard whose gun exploded rolls on the floor, clutching his maimed hand. The military mages—Aratha, Kari, and Melko—stand erect in their uniforms, transference grips in their hands, shields buzzing before them. In command. The room seems to bend toward them as if in homage.

Alfeg touches a split lip, a black eye. Khorsa, businesslike, plugs in her t-grip and arms herself.

Alarmed faces—PED employees—blink at the scene from the doorway.

Constantine gives Aiah a stricken look. "What are you doing?" he whispers, using the little air Romus has left him. "What is this madness?"

Aiah massages her throat. "It's finished," she says. "The thing is dead."

A convulsion crosses Constantine's face. "You had no right!" he says. "He had more than a measure of greatness! My oldest"—he blinks—"oldest friend. Greatest advisor. The one to whom I owe . . ." His voice fails.

Friend, Constantine had called the monster. *Advisor.* New words for such a thing.

Aiah carefully puts her feet on the floor, lets her weight rest on them, looks down at Constantine.

"I had every right," she says. "I finished the job you couldn't, thirty-odd years ago. The job you ran from."

An ardent look comes to Constantine's face. "He was *useful.* He was *necessary.* My plans—"

His voice chokes off again as Dr. Romus shifts his coils, shuts his wind. Romus's reedy voice buzzes in the sudden silence.

"So *this* is the creature's protector," he says. His irony sizzles in the air. "This . . . *great man* . . . permitted so many to die. And he would have handed one of the Dreaming Sisters to such a thing."

"Gangsters," Constantine whispers. "I thought they were gangsters."

Romus's coils shift again, tightening on chest and throat, and Aiah can see fear enter Constantine's eyes. Aiah sees death settle onto his face, a smiling skull behind the purpling flesh. Romus turns his little face to Aiah.

"Shall I kill him, miss?" Romus asks. "It would be easy. . . . His usefulness to the world is over."

A great weariness falls on Aiah. She shakes her head.

"He may try to kill us all," Romus reminds.

"He can't," Aiah says. She looks at her people standing in the doorway, the people she has hired personally, made loyal to *her,* her PED, intended as an instrument of Constantine's will, now her own. And through the small crowd hurry members of Aiah's own guard—she normally does not use guards unless she leaves the building, but here they are now, summoned by calls from people in her division.

She looks down at Constantine. "It's gone too far," she says. "Too many people know now, or could put it together if they wished. Enough to destroy you if you press this. PED, Barkazils, the army." She passes a hand across her forehead, looks at her own guards taking up position in the room. "Your only hope," Aiah tells Con-stantine, "is if those who know remain silent—no, wrong," shaking her head. "You are safe *only if we deny certain things ever happened at all.* And for that, we will need to feel *safe.*"

Constantine mouths words that cannot be heard. Aiah looks up at Martinus, pinned by plasm against the wall. "You understand this, don't you?"

In Martinus's eyes she reads understanding. He gives a little nod, as much as the plasm bonds will let him. Aiah looks at Romus.

"Let him go," she says.

A touch of petulance enters the reedy voice. "I do not think," Romus says, "he will feel grateful for his life."

"That's up to him," Aiah says.

Dr. Romus loosens his coils. Constantine gasps for air, blinking dumbly at the world. His hand tugs at the lace at his throat.

"I want your resignation," he says. "I want it tomorrow."

"As the triumvir wishes," Aiah says, too tired to care.

Aiah and her team leave the room before Constantine, her guards a wall between her and his party. The crowd, the couple of dozen people working third shift, parts in silence. Aiah's deranged perception sees them as stick figures with huge, staring eyes. Aiah sees that Rohder is among them, cigaret dangling from his lips, his blue eyes observing with keen interest.

"Kari and I will return directly to the division by aerocar," Aratha says. "Melko will take a different route. We're going to stay shielded until we hear from you."

Aiah nods. "Of course. But we'll be safe enough, once Constantine has time to think."

"His right thoughts are best assured by our thorough preparation," Aratha says.

"Exactly," Khorsa adds. "I'm going to lock myself in the secure room and write up a full report."

"And so will I," Aratha says.

"Make sure you know where those reports are," Aiah says. "If the wrong people get ahold of them . . ."

"Not that I particularly give a damn," Khorsa says, "but if all works out as planned, no one will see my report at all." Her face turns hard. "The bastard," she adds.

Alfeg holds a handkerchief to his bleeding lip. "Miss Aiah," he says, "let me stay with you till tomorrow."

Aiah shakes her head. "Staying with *me* won't make *you* safer."

"That wasn't my point."

An exhausted smile touches Aiah's lips. "Yes. I know." She takes him in her arms, kisses his cheek. "Go to the infirmary. That eye looks nasty. And you might be concussed."

"So might you."

Aiah fingers the tender place at the back of her head, winces. "Possibly," she admits.

In the end it is agreed that Dr. Romus and her guards will accompany Aiah to her apartment.

Which they find filled with Constantine's flowers, hundreds of them, and a written apology, a model of its kind, still unread on the table.

TWENTY-SIX

~~~~~~

Romus and one of the guards enter the plasm well and stand sentry, ready to repel an attack.

It's a nice gesture, but Aiah knows it's futile. If Constantine wanted to attack her here, he would first shut off her plasm with a call to the control room deep in the bowels of the Palace, and then do whatever he wanted.

Rohder arrives an hour later, and the guards, after asking Aiah's permission, allow him in. Aiah and Rohder sit, Barkazil style, at the kitchen table, sip tea and munch biscuits Aiah has found in a cupboard. Aiah holds her aching head in her hands. The apartment is oppressive, the walls looming like angry giants in her deranged perception. Rohder lights a cigaret.

"It's been settled," he says. "Your resignation, if you've written it, will not be accepted."

"I did not think you were going to involve yourself in this," Aiah says.

He looks at her levelly. "As a loyal civil servant," he says, "I felt obliged to bring certain things to the triumvir's attention. That the PED is his idea, his brainchild, and that disaffection in its ranks would not help him. That disaffection in the military would not work to his benefit, either. That if my entire transformation team, as an example, found itself unhappy with the current administration, we could all resign and sell our valuable services elsewhere, and his much-publicized attempts to build housing out of nothing would be set back by months. That if any stories concerning hanged men or the Party Sickness reached the ears of our now uncensored press, his reputation would be severely compromised, perhaps damaged irrevocably. I pointed out that evidence *already exists,* evidence which he can neither suppress nor deny. I suggested to his imagination what might happen if a polemical genius like Hilthi obtained the evidence in question." He taps ash from the cigaret into a saucer. "I believe the triumvir saw reason."

Aiah looks at him, winces at the effort it costs her to keep him in focus. "Thank you," she says. Then, thinking aloud, "*Should* I be thanking you?"

"I don't know." Rohder sips tobacco smoke. "I did it entirely for my own benefit. I want an ally sitting between me and the administration."

Aiah looks at Rohder and thinks, He really *is The Mage.* . . . *He who reorders nature according to his will* . . . He is the only one of all of them who has got exactly what he wants. His transformation teams, his theory put into practice, his autonomy, and his presence indispensable to everyone concerned.

After Rohder leaves, Aiah sends her guards home—she embarrasses them by giving them baskets of flowers, all they can carry—and then turns to Dr. Romus.

"I want to thank you," she says. "Things could have gone badly there."

There is a fierce glint in Romus's yellow eyes. "Where I come from," he says, "we fight for our friends."

And that is all I was doing, Aiah thinks. *Fighting for Constantine.*

If only Constantine knew it.

She kisses Romus's wrinkled cheek—it is dry, like ancient bone—and lets him out.

And is alone with her apartment, her flowers, and her weariness.

YOUR LAST CHANCE TO SEE
LORDS OF THE NEW CITY

She wakes with the Adrenaline Monster pounding in her chest and the knowledge that she will die, that Constantine or Sorya lurk outside the door, waiting to finish her off, or that Taikoen—not dead after all—dwells next to her in the plasm main, ready to tear the life from her. . . . The walls loom in, threaten her with their silent solidity, with the knowledge that her very sight is contaminated by Taikoen's perceptions.

The terror fades. The heavy scent of Constantine's flowers fills her chest, makes it hard to breathe. She looks at the clock: 04:11.

She calls up a pair of her guards, apologizes for the hour, and asks them to meet her in the boat pool. Then she dresses, goes to the PED offices, and leaves a note on Khorsa's desk telling her where she plans to go. People stare at her as she goes about her errand. They are a different lot than were on duty last shift, but they've obviously heard what happened, and doubtless the story has not got any smaller in the interval.

At the water gate, Aiah meets her guards, signs out a motorboat, and leaves the Palace. Bright cloudless Shieldlight beats down on her aching head. The surrounding buildings threaten her like a hedge of spears. She wishes she had thought to bring shieldglasses.

She is still, officially, on vacation. No reason not to take advantage of it.

The gray stone home of the Dreaming Sisters squats beneath its gleaming copper dome like an intricately carved puzzle, its outward complexity—the carved, entangled faces and vines— only an intimation of the subtle convolutions within. On the doorstep she sends her guards back to the Palace.

"You'll be safe here?" one of them asks. "Are you sure, miss?"

"If I'm not safe here," Aiah tells him, "I won't be safe any-where."

The cool twilight of the sanctuary is a glorious relief after the unrelieved brightness of the Shield. The sister on duty— Aiah does not recognize her—takes her without a word to Order of Eternity, who greets her with her usual dreamy com-posure.

"I'm sorry," Aiah says, "for the deaths."

"We know the risks," calmly, "when imagoes war with one another. We put ourselves in the center of the battle willingly." Sadness crosses her features. "Though now that it is over, and two of our order lie dead, I cannot help but feel in my heart that our action was wrong."

"It was the right thing," Aiah says. "It was perhaps the only right thing done in all this affair."

The dreaming sister looks up at Aiah, weariness in her eyes. "I hope you are right," she says. "Time will tell." She reaches out a gentle hand, touches Aiah's throat. "You are bruised."

"There was violence afterward. I am all right."

"You don't *look* all right."

"I haven't slept. Not in months."

Order of Eternity tilts her head, speaks in her girlish voice. "Do you wish to sleep here?"

"Yes." Weariness falls on Aiah like a shower of cooling rain. "Yes, I'd like to sleep here."

A smile ghosts across the sister's face. "I think we can promise you good dreams."

Order of Eternity takes her arm, draws her down the corridor.

"It's supposed to be organic," Aiah says. "Something about the adrenal gland."

"We will repair it," says the dreaming sister, "and anything else we may find."

If anyone else had said this, Aiah would have fled at the very idea of this kind of plasm intrusion into her body. But if anyone had earned the right to float through Aiah's mind, the Dreaming Sisters had.

Besides, Aiah is too weary to resist. A hammer batters her skull with every beat of her heart.

They pass a carving of *Death,* and there is Taikoen, still with that eerie shimmer. Aiah gives a shudder and shrinks from the image.

"It's still there," she says. "Shouldn't it have changed by now?"

"These things come in time."

"I was afraid that it was still alive."

"No." On this point the sister is firm. "That configuration of being no longer exists."

"I feel him in my head, in the way I see things. I keep thinking he's alive."

"We will correct that as well."

She finds Aiah an empty alcove, helps Aiah lie down. The plasm contact is already there, and Order of Eternity uncoils it and hands the curved copper tip to Aiah.

"What do I do?" Aiah asks.

"Take the contact into your mouth," the sister says. "Close your eyes. Breathe deep. You need do nothing else—our meditations will find their way to *you*."

Aiah takes the cool metal into her mouth and feels at once the touch of plasm—not plasm fire, not the raging primal essence, but a soft tingling warmth, a glow. She had expected the copper to taste bitter, but it seems to have no taste at all. She closes her eyes.

"Thank you," she mumbles around the contact.

Order of Eternity does not answer, and instead Aiah hears the slap of the sister's feet on the flags as she withdraws.

The tingling warmth of plasm seems to steal into Aiah's frame. Like sleep, she thinks, but more than that, a kind of strange awareness of something *other* . . .

Images seem to pulse on the backs of Aiah's eyelids, mere phosphor glow at first, then things more concrete, images of airships and dolphins, children and trees, sky-topping buildings and birds in flight, all processing through her thoughts, dissolving one into the other . . . like the sisters' aerial displays, but far more stately, each image lingering, impressing itself on Aiah's mind, like figures in an eternal dance. And with them there is a sound, like a primal wind keening across the sharp corners of the world.

Ah, she thinks, *it's true! The plasm* does *sing*.

And then she topples into dream.

THE DISPOSSESSED
by Ursula K. Le Guin

This Science Fiction classic from bestselling and award-winning author Ursula K. Le Guin now has a stunning new package. A brilliant physicist must give up his family, and possibly his life, as he attempts to tear down the walls of hatred that have isolated his planet of anarchists.

A FISHERMAN OF THE INLAND SEA
by Ursula K. Le Guin

The National Book Award, Hugo, Nebula, and World Fantasy Award-winning author's first new collection in thirteen years—an astonishing assemblage of diversity and power from a major writer and mature artist at the height of her powers.

HarperPrism